WAR ON SOUND

A Novel

CHRISTOPHER HARRIS

ASPHALT
HOUSE

The author is grateful for permission to reprint brief excerpts from pp. 85, 188 from "I Dreamed Was A Very Clean Tramp" by Richard Hell (copyright © 2013 by Richard Meyers, reprinted by permission of HarperCollins Publishers) and
"Pale Fire" by Vladimir Nabokov (copyright © Vintage Press).

First Asphalt House paperback edition September 2016

Cover photography by Dawson Smith: dpdawsonproductions.com

ISBN: 0692685995
ISBN-13: 9780692685990

PRAISE FOR *WAR ON SOUND*

"*War on Sound* is a Homeric undertaking, a transcontinental story about four musicians trying to navigate a ruthless industry. Harris knows his subject and the novel crackles with realism. It's filled with sex, drugs and rock and roll, of course, but also dwells in youthful ideals, heartbreak and the uncommon joy of small victories. It will resonate with anyone who's ever tried to make a living doing something they love."
Chris Collingwood, Fountains of Wayne and Look Park

"Having spent most of my twenties in a touring rock band, I know a thing or two about the perils and pleasures of the rock and roll lifestyle. Harris lovingly captures the pathos and exhilaration of life on the road, allowing you to ride shotgun in a Ford Econoline."
Ross Flournoy, The Broken West and Apex Manor

"*War On Sound* reminds me of ambition, and the craziness of applying ambition to the mixed-up world of rock and roll specifically, and music more generally."
John Munson, Semisonic and The Twilight Hours

"We've been through the various rungs of the indie rock scene, and Harris gets it right on so many levels. His book is flashback-inducing and accurately portrays what it's like to be a struggling band in the indie scene."
Tommy Blank, Quiet Company

"*War On Sound* beautifully and vividly captures the crazy, heartbreaking, thrilling, monomaniacal dream of being in a rock band."
Marty Beller, drummer for They Might Be Giants

"*War On Sound* depicts an accurate and very evocative representation of life in the music business. An entertaining and thought-provoking novel."
Mark Reznicek, Toadies

To my family

ACKNOWLEDGMENTS

Codey Allen, Bik Aulakh, Marty Beller, Katie Bixby, Tommy Blank, Tony Catania, Bill Childs, Carl Clermont, Markeysha Davis, Gareth Dobson, Jim Fay, Ross Flournoy, Collin Hagood, Fredi Harris, George Harris, Rashonda Hosendove, Dillon McGaughey, Andrew Sanni, Dawson Smith, Mark Summa, Zep van Zeen, Chris Walsh and Gibson Guitars

PROLOGUE

There's an urge, on the biggest night of their four young lives, to glam it up. But they resist. Jeans and t-shirts have sufficed for three months' worth of shows. If they walk onto that stage wearing sequined leather or designer suits or, hell, monogrammed DJ beanies? Well, then what's it all been for? The plan is to make it as an actual rock band. So, quaint as it might seem, they'll dress like an actual rock band.

The low California sun is replicated in dented chrome and scratched sunglasses. It's a thirty-mile drive down out of the Valley and they give themselves plenty of time. The 101 moves like a dream. They play Spoon's *Transference*, a pre-show tradition that started to feel academic long around Wisconsin but today is mandatory. For most of the drive it seems like they'll arrive before the album finishes.

But when they turn onto the 110, ominous signs appear. Road closures. Seek alternate routes. It's dark when they get off the highway; all avenues into downtown are blocked. There's an honest-to-God nighttime marathon—thousands of runners, cops twirling flashlights like at a rave...plus sawhorse barricades and drink stations and a million crushed paper cups—between them and the Mayan. The showcase is one night only, with an audience full of people who have the power to grant wishes. They ask an officer the best way around and he points to the Staples Center. But traffic is absolutely stuck. *Transference* ends and they idle in panicked silence.

What can they say? Each of them has approximately the same nightmare scenario playing out in his or her head: their slot comes up, their name is announced, the very few people who've seen them at a bar or a sidewalk festival or a high school clap politely, the stage lights flicker. And eventually they're declared a no-show, everyone laughs, and their Big Break goes unbroken. They arrive late, accompanied by various backstage sighs and eye-rolls. Plus, they're a rock act. Not exactly on the bleeding edge. Showcase time is probably better spent discovering the next EDM act. Anyway, nobody goes on late. Maybe next year.

The weeks of planning, schmoozing, dreaming...vaporized by a traffic jam. They phone and text the promoter and the promoter's son, and get no answer. How close are they to the Mayan? Could one of them hop out and run? This is the way the world ends.

At a dead stop, they look at one another. Each thinks: *These are the people I've bound myself to? These are the people I'll live or die with?* Because of course that's what it feels like. There'll be no starting from scratch with a different band. They don't have that kind of resistance in them anymore. A phase of their lives is coming to an end tonight, one way or another. They love and hate each other. They annoy one another in inexplicable ways. They're a family without blood, plagued by all the unspoken inquisitions and outrages, all the befuddlements. *How did we get here?*

How stupid. How stupid that a few songs can make a family.

A cement truck halted in front of them reads: "UNITED."

They crawl around the Staples Center, are stopped again. This time it seems even more permanent. Horns contain futile notes. They look longingly at the 110, but even traffic up there is dragging now. A woman with four children pulls up alongside their van, talking on a cell, rubbing her forehead, explaining something in painful detail. She jabs the steering wheel with her forefinger.

It's really only left to shout, to honk, to pull out hair, to pray. *Just let us play our stupid songs. At least give us a chance. To miss our spot sitting in a thousand tons of steel. To have a marathon end our marathon.*

It's more than an hour since they got down off the highway. The mute unforgiving clockworks around them crank on—the world trying to get in—and they're left to contemplate the past year....

PART I

WELL, I MEAN LISTEN

Thrillsville is a skinny Ninth Avenue café that serves martinis at night and houses a bellows organ no bigger than a stand-up piano. Scott comes here late weekday afternoons when the coffee crowd is over but Happy Hour hasn't begun. While business is quiet, the bartending baristas don't mind if he slides a paint-drizzled canvas off the organ and sits blocking the men's room.

He plays Paul & the Patients and the Dodos, singing along at a coolly low decibel at first but usually losing his head by the bridge. He plays Foreign Born and Free Energy *("...you said there's nothing to wait for, there's nothing to know...")*, but all those numbers are very three years ago and when any woman comes alone into Thrillsville, he switches to the new Shins single, pumping the foot pedals, slapping the single row of keys, and thinking how quirky and attractive and retro he must look.

Today he watches an unfamiliar dark-haired woman step in out of the cold. Yes, for her he plays "Simple Song," and tries to make himself feel electricity coming up through the *D-A-D-A-G-A-G-A*, but he messes up the B-minor leaking into the chorus and it's no good, he's honking like a seagull. He hates himself and stops, and sees the woman sit alone at the bar; she's broad and tall in a dark pea-coat, and announces that she's returning from her grandmother's funeral.

Mark, the hairy bartender, says, "Oh, geez. Sorry, Gabby."

"I just got off the train from Bellmore. And it so happens I also just saw my birth certificate for the very first time."

"Wow," Mark says, working a dishrag inside a highball glass. Scott can't help standing up and walking over. Gabby unfastens her coat, hoists a big velveteen purse—embroidered with *Some Like It Juicy*—onto the bar, and scoops her thumbs under curtains of hair.

"Yup," she says, "apparently I'm adopted."

"Holy crap," says Scott.

She looks at him, but carries on. "My mother died when I was five. What I thought was my mother."

"You're in shock," says Mark. "Let me get you a drink."

"There's something else," she says. "Something." She starts to sob.

Mark pours Campari into soda and Gabby draws down half the glass. Scott sees a song in these proceedings: the overcast winter light fuzzing the edges in here, the young woman scrabbling through her bag, the bartender and his liquid comfort.

"On my birth certificate. There's no father's name, but there's a mother. Here it is. 'M.L. Ciccone.' I looked it up on my phone."

"No shit," Scott says. "No *shit*. What year were you born?"

Mark's eyebrows rise.

Gabby empties her drink. Scott finds her features vaguely Asian, maybe Latina. She's not beautiful, but she's cool, underwhelmed even as she's overwhelmed. She grins, her eyes are sad and wet, she sighs or burps into the back of her hand.

"I don't get it," says Mark.

Everybody looks at everybody with a secret in the air. The fact that nobody speaks seems orchestrated. Scott finds many moments like this in New York: pauses where young people seem about to express a well-worn truth by way of comfort and recognition—a secret code, a speakeasy password, the name of God—but veer away with averted eyes and dumb hushes, missing one another.

But Gabby is apparently desperate, because she puts the lie to Scott's calculations. With full throat, she says, "I think my biological mother might be Madonna."

Somebody outside honks a car horn, which triggers five or six other honks, then a jackhammer, then a siren, and as that finally abates Scott hears the kick drum in his chest.

"The *fuck*?" Mark says.

Gabby almost laughs. "How insane would that be?" she says. "I mean. Wow."

"You have money problems?" says Scott. "Of course you do, everyone in the city has money problems. Poof. There they go, bye-bye." Then he thinks the financial aspects of this situation are obviously beside the point, and bringing them up has painted him crass. He tries to smile with complicated irony.

"My grandmother raised me, and now she's gone. But instead of just being sad, this is what I get. Why do it to me now? Today the lawyer comes up and hands me an envelope with a birth certificate in it." She looks at Scott. "Do we know each other?"

"What's this like?" says Mark. "A Disney story. Born into poverty."

"You know we weren't poor," she says. "My grandfather owned that boiler plant."

"The princess and the something. You want a freshener?"

Gabby drops her head onto her folded arms and weeps. She shouts formless vowels, stuttering as she refills her lungs. Mark touches her shoulder. Scott is impressed by the volume of her contralto vibrating his skin.

Jane, a bartender early for the evening shift, enters the café and makes horrified eyes at the drama. But for some reason Scott is deep in this: maybe he's drowsy from last night at the Grand Mal or maybe his head is still somewhere in the music, where characters in songs don't let stories like this pass by. Anyway, he squints right back at Jane. When Gabby finally looks up again she's a study in grief no cynic could forsake.

So they surround her, and one-by-one give her hugs. When his turn comes, Scott feels his libido kick in. He coughs and steps away.

"Show me the envelope, darling," says Mark. "We're gonna fix this for you."

He calls Gabby darling—it comes out *dwallin'* in his Long Island patois—because it turns out they used to date, which comes clearer to Scott when she tries to kiss Mark's bearded cheek and he pulls away, pretending he hasn't seen.

Gabby agrees to go home and sleep, and after she's gone Jane says, "When was she born? My sister used to be, like, obsessed with Madonna. I saw *Truth or Dare* a hundred times when I was little. She put that DVD on after church and I used to think God must look like Warren Beatty."

"Born May 2, 1991," reads Mark. "St. Luke's-Roosevelt, five

blocks from here. Mother's address on Central Park West. Baby's weight: seven pounds. That's it."

Jane preps herself a coffee drink, raises her eyebrows at Scott to see if he wants anything. It's unclear whether she's offering for free, so he declines. "This should be easy," she says. "Aren't there, like, Madonna timelines?"

"I need a gasper," Mark says, removing his apron, gesturing to Scott that he should follow him outside. In the cold they're both already breathing smoke; Mark lights up and offers the pack, but Scott is paranoid about doing something to his voice. "We don't want that one involved," pointing through the window at Jane: her button-down sweater and horn rims. "Trust me."

"Involved."

"Sorry, man. The way you looked at Gabby, I figured you were interested in her."

Scott's thoughts go to his songs. It's a shame-calculus: first he experiences the shadow of what his life is supposed to be at 25—established career, serious relationship with a smart and beautiful admirer of his work—and in self-defense he leaps to what he considers the best part of him, the *reason* for his loneliness and posing, the thing for which he sacrifices. He tried playing a new song provisionally called "Garlic Whiskers" at the Grand Mal open mic last night. It sounded all right for a minute, then needed drums or something.

"You're a smart dude," says Mark. "What do you think? Check out the hospital? Try and call Madonna's record company or her agent or something?"

"Well, I mean," feeling a minor endorphin buzz for having been called smart. "I guess I wonder what's the point."

"The point is find out the truth for Gabby, let her decide. Everyone's dead, but the grandmother gives her one last shot at family. From beyond the grave!"

"And if that family happens to take the form of a millionaire superstar."

Mark tries to draw a dollar sign on Thrillsville's window glass, but the steam is on the inside.

Scott says, "I've seen you carrying around a drum machine sometimes?"

"Yeah, hey you should come to one of our shows, dude. Standing gig every Wednesday night at Simplex up on East 83rd.

Fun shit."

Scott does calculations. Simplex is yet another new place where kids gobble ecstasy and hop around to EDM as loud as aircraft engines, so it's easy for Scott to look down his nose. He says, "Well, all right. Cool, man."

"Come on, help me figure this out," says Mark. "I'm off work. What's the first step, the hospital? I'm betting Gabby'd really appreciate it."

Scott pretends to sigh. "I just have so much on my plate. I mean, all those episodes of 'Judge Judy'? Plus my email won't refresh itself a thousand times before dinner."

"Ha."

"The address on Central Park West. I guess that's where I'd go first, see if it's Madonna's place."

So they walk north in slush and steam, first past mostly empty bars and restaurants, then up to Lincoln Center. The Philharmonic's concrete bunker is bright with electricity, doing its best not to seem stodgy. The orchestra is away touring Europe; pennants portraying ductile ballerinas droop from light posts. 64th Street is a suffocated trench: double-parked trucks on each side, construction canopies shielding the sidewalks, metal tubing keeping pedestrians in line, so many impediments of such breathtaking variety that the idea of making eye contact with anyone is priceless. Scott and Mark are single-file. They catch momentary views of the lovely brownstones here, the scratching bare trees and wrought-iron window guards, but in New York beauty lays low behind its gates.

They find the right building, which has a courtyard sign that reads "All Visitors Must Be Announced" and a rent-a-cop in a booth. They tell him they're looking for Madonna and show him the birth certificate; for some reason the guy holds it up to the light. Then, instead of shooing them away, he reluctantly phones upstairs. Mark elbows Scott's ribs.

A giant black man in sunglasses comes down. Mark brandishes the certificate, and the man takes it.

"This is some shit," he says.

"Go ahead and keep it," says Mark. "I'm sure the hospital can make more copies."

"Not if I burn the fucker down."

"She's really up there?" Scott says.

The bodyguard is noncommittal.

"How old were you in '91?" Mark says. "I was six. How about you, Scotty? Anyway, I'm guessing maybe you didn't guard Madonna's body way back then. So maybe you don't have what they call first-hand knowledge of the situation."

"Have a good day, sir."

"That's it?" says Mark. "Your next visitor could be some reporters asking about how come she won't admit her love child."

The bodyguard folds his arms.

An idea occurs to Scott. He says, "What kind of singer is she, really?"

"..."

"I mean, you're around her. There's a bunch of production there, obviously, maybe some Auto-Tune. But maybe she sings in the limo. Maybe you catch her doing Adele in the elevator, right? You're blown away?"

"Man, I ain't talking to you."

"Right, why would you? Unless she's amazing, then I guess you'd probably defend her. If you didn't say anything, that would kind of be an answer in itself."

From behind his sunglasses: "Most talented person I ever met, dog. It's ridiculous."

"We'll wait here," says Mark. "C'mon, man. Just show her the paper."

The bodyguard frowns and inhales. "Y'all dudes don't get it. You know the shit she gets hit with every damn *day*? Y'all ain't even the first to camp out here today."

"But they didn't come with documentation," Scott says, thinly, he thinks, in the underdog's voice that's his by choice, the pose that fends off achievement.

"And gosh," Mark says, "are we ever harmless. Look at us. No cameras."

"You boys have a good one," says the bodyguard, and he keeps the certificate and nods at the rent-a-cop in his booth, he's gone, Scott looks around and Manhattan is huge again, the park over there, the cars, the noise. One side of his personality is maybe something of a mercenary. But it's attached to the sad suckling at his core, happy to obey, sycophantic nodder, brow furrower, inventor of fake texts (so ladies at the Grand Mal—who are almost assuredly *not* eying Scott—might feel jealous about his profligate

life), the one who finds an excuse to take late-night strolls up from
42nd to the Penthouse Club but never inside, instead maundering
past the glass-enclosed lean-to out front and making innocent eye
contact with the cigarette-smoking strippers, *you can do better, look
how easy it is to walk on by, can't you see how the clean life of showing those
magnificent breasts only to me would simplify things, we could wander together
past the Intrepid and forget everything.*

But what does Scott have to forget? He's under glass himself.
Life hasn't quite begun.

"What do we do?" says Mark.

"There's lights on all up and down the building. Let's wait a
few minutes. Maybe he's showing it to her." They cross 64th and sit
on some short office stairs, out of the rent-a-cop's sightline. Mark
fidgets with his phone.

"What's your band's name?" says Scott.

"For a while we were The Failure. Now we're Beta Synth,
mostly because our DJ calls himself 'Beta X.'"

"Axis of influences."

"Hm…Daft Punk? Swedish House Mafia? A little Zedd
mixed in? I mean, hopefully we've got our own thing. I used to
have a guitar band: we covered Decembrists, Old 97's, Blue
Mountain, but playing for ten kids on somebody's deck, y'know?"

"And the plan for Beta Synth is?"

"It's three of us, we started out as a joke. Now we have this
regular gig? X thinks we'll get a tour, really start earning. But he's
kind of a dick, and if you want my secret opinion we're not ready.
But anyway, what about you? You got chops on the keyboard,
man."

"Me? No. Thanks, but no. I'm okay with a six-string. It's
actually stupid how many instruments I used to have. French horn.
Wheatstone concertina, bass clarinet. Never got a good-enough-
sounding keyboard, like, the organ in the coffee shop pretty much
rules."

"Wow," says Mark.

"Yeah. I'm *so great.*"

"Naw, dude. You played on anything I've heard?"

Scott is flying now. "Shit, no. I'm not ready either, man,"
knees jouncing, fingers playing chords on these cement stairs. Oh,
he's ready.

"Sounds like you live it, though. I go through periods where I try. Leave work, go straight home, make everyone get together and practice. But X's girlfriend is having a baby, and my weakness is that I really, really like to get high." Mark is bushy-haired, thick-bearded, muscled, streetlights now reflecting off his tinted glasses. He licks his lips and looks plaintive, jailed by his own social adequacy. "You play a lot, right? How do you eat, man?"

"You know those new apartment buildings on 42nd between 11th and 12th? I live in one, my brother's got an extra bedroom. They give it to him as part of his pay, he superintends. I just intend."

"Grow up in the city?"

"Boston 'burbs. Came here after college."

"All day, nothing but music? I'm jealous, man."

It's been nearly two years. Scott's parents and his brother are mostly patient, because they've seen dozens of musician biopics that reveal how rough the business is. Scott has worked his current rung on the ladder to a fine polish. He listens to old rock songs and writes lyrics and melodies and walks to Thrillsville and puts in time at the Grand Mal when basically nobody's watching. He picks up a few dollars every month tutoring rich kids for their SATs. At holidays his parents offer patronizing smiles and occasionally his brother comes upstairs with torn fingernails shouting at him to get a job, and he imagines the judgment of former classmates and girlfriends, compares his stasis to his dreams.

"Then again," Mark says, "if I had all day to play guitar, I'd probably wind up hooked on crack just for something else to do. I'm a fucking great one for *not* fucking playing guitar."

"Hey," says Scott, because there's still enough light across 64th to see that the bodyguard has reemerged, and is looking around for them.

"Yo!" Mark says.

The bodyguard's sunglasses are off, and he looks beleaguered. He says, "Baby, it's your lucky day."

"She wants to see us."

"No. Y'all motherfuckers are about to look a gift horse in the mouth. Get it out of your head, you ain't goin' upstairs." He hands back the copy of Gabby's birth certificate. "It was one of her dancers."

"…"

"She paid the bills, and put her name on there so the lady's family wouldn't know. She takes care of her own, man."

Mark says, "Weren't all her dancers gay dudes?"

"What's the mother's real name?" says Scott.

The bodyguard shakes his head, looks at the sky. "Well, I best be gettin' back."

"What, you want money for the name? Jesus, who the hell has money?"

"Son," the bodyguard says, "I think what you learned today is you boys ain't got any idea how *any* of this here shit works." And he waddles back into one of the city's most recherché addresses.

Mark gets in a cab and asks if Scott wants to come party out in Brooklyn. Scott knows he should. He's lonely, wakes up some nights weeping over the long-departed family dog, gets his sleep schedule screwed up and then for twenty-four hours fails to see another human being in a city of nine million. But tonight he goes home and sniffs around the Internet. It takes half an hour to find the names of Madonna's four female dancers circa late 1990.

One is a reality-show judge in Los Angeles. Two have Broadway careers. The last died in 2005. Scott finds the Twitter account of the reality judge, follows her, and sends: "@brillsheila - mission of mercy. trying to track down madonna backup dancer who gave secret birth in 1991 NYC. is it you?" and then he goes to bed. His brother Frank is either out wringing cocktails and female accomplices from the Meatpacking District, or else is fixing someone's garbage disposal. Scott closes his eyes and counts backwards from a hundred, restarting whenever his cadence bobbles. It's only 9:30. The high-quality windows in this luxury tower baffle highway noise, and blackout curtains cover those windows.

But his bedroom's nighttime ceiling displays the songs he'll never write. He panics, just lying there. Things are supposed to be better by now. He's not supposed to be scrambling for open-mic time, competing against teens with laptops. He's supposed to be *efficient*. Why can't he write a song a day? What the hell else is he doing? These thoughts terrorize him and yet the experience is also tiresome, because he does this to himself *every* night, by reflex, as though to see how badly he can scare himself.

He finally falls asleep, then at 3 a.m. he wakes and the reality judge has written back with a direct message: "@scotttungsten - if this is for real, and I have my doubts, DM me a number where I can call you."

Over in the corner, Scott has an exhaustive bootleg and soundboard CD collection of Spoon shows, probably the world's foremost assemblage acquired via week after week of horse-trading and downloading. Leaning against the wall is his attempt at creating an Infinite Guitar—there are supposedly only three actual Infinite Guitars in the world, though Kramer and Fernandes both produced knockoffs—for which Scott spent a month learning about circuits and coils and soldering. On a table is his sculpture of Clearwell Castle, the gothic English mansion where Led Zeppelin recorded, made of hundreds of guitar picks painstakingly fused together by a hot-melt glue gun. And so it's not a stretch to say that Scott recognizes his obsessive nature, though he excuses it as part of his artistic temperament. Tonight there's a comfortable click in his skull, because a new quest lies before him. He types his phone number into Twitter and sends it across the continent.

She calls him at nine. She says, "If you're recording this."

"I'm not."

"Well, if you are, for the record. It wasn't me."

Scott pictures her in a stainless-steel kitchen, looking out over the Pacific and drinking a kale smoothie.

"Hello?" she says. For a moment something is weird with the connection, and her voice sounds like a bee in a jar.

"I'm here."

"I promise, I'm not your mother."

"Oh, I'm not the baby," says Scott. "It's a friend of mine. Not really a friend, I just met her. We all saw the name on the birth certificate and started fantasizing about a reunion. And massive extortion plans, maybe."

"Hwell. That's honest. But y'know Madonna's *got* kids. Anyway, I was there that whole entire tour. Multiple tours. What's your name?"

"Scott."

"As long we're being honest, Scott, when I got your tweet I was pretty sure you were TMZ. I dated one of our contestants and it got out of hand, well, I mean listen, they follow me around. But hearing your voice."

"…"

"How old are you? You don't sound like someone doing a money grab."

"That's because I'm not."

"So this girl just wants to know who her mommy is."

Scott paces his bedroom. "I don't really know," he says. "I don't know her at all. She doesn't even know I'm calling around like this."

"So you want to…get with her?"

"I guess."

"Well that's convincing. What, you're gay?"

"No-ho."

"I'm fascinated," she says. "You're fascinating me at six in the a.m., Scott."

"I'm circling in on Madonna. I mean: *on Madonna*. I have this need to be near celebrities. I mean, I *need* it. Like, I dumpster-dive just hoping to see their used tissues."

"Come on. I can tell you're kidding."

"What kind of singer is she?" says Scott. "You're standing ten feet away, and she just knocks you over with the power and perfect pitch?"

"Yeah," she says, "I mean, it's been a long time. But sure: Madonna's the real deal. She's genuinely amazing. I'm having a hard time figuring out what exactly you want here, Scott. You said it was a mission of mercy. Mercy to who, if the girl doesn't even know?"

"Just: none of the other dancers were pregnant either?"

"Not that I knew of. I remember one tour we lost a girl, but I can't remember when that was. We're talking twenty years ago. This is just curiosity with you?"

"Well," he says, "I'm a musician."

"Ah. Now I get it. Looking for a foot in the door. Looking for an audience. You don't really believe there was a secret pregnancy. You're manipulating this poor girl into a career move. I apologize, Scott, I misjudged your game."

"…"

"Well, you can cross me off the list kiddo. What, the plan is catch the all-powerful Madonna in a lie, and that means the baby has to be hers? Then you spring into action and go, 'Ah-hah! You owe me a recording contract!' It's funny, because I just went for a walk with my puppy this morning and we saw this toad on the street that had been flattened by a bunch of cars, and its arms and legs were all spread out like a cartoon character run over by a steamroller, and I was about to say that's just what your voice sounds like. But now I know better."

The weekend goes by. Scott tries not to pursue his line of inquiry any further. On Monday evening he gathers up his blue Ovation acoustic and walks past the 11th Avenue construction craters to the poor old Grand Mal on 46th. It's a sunken brick room with a deep stage and a good p.a., which excuses the short barstools and the cinnamon/antiseptic bouquet. Stephanie is the owner's girlfriend and the keeper of the open-mic list, and she sees Scott coming.

"Sorry you're here," she says.

"I know."

"You've conquered us. There are better planks you could walk."

"I know."

Stephanie shrugs and scrawls his name.

The crowd is mostly other musicians, and it's a kind fraternity. Nobody has made the mistake of being successful, so it's easy for everyone to be generous. Just sitting here, Scott feels the others watching him. He's been coming in longer than anyone and rather than producing comfort, this embarrasses him.

He's seen the Hold Steady and Fountains of Wayne half-fill this place, and in crowds for such older bands he feels young. But not tonight. Everyone else in here now is just starting out; their faces don't seem fully formed. Scott knows they're probably scared, and aren't judging him. He gets onstage and plays his crowd-pleasingest number, "Sliding Around In Socks," to get everyone on his side. It's a wimp move.

When it's over a couple kids shake his hand and slap his back.

"Man," says one, "that was a fucked-up level of awesome."

"Thanks," Scott says. "Thank you."

"They should let you do a whole set. God, some of this shit is just painful."

Scott smiles. He wants and wants.

"What's your day job?" says a different child.

"Oh, just this."

"That's awesome. Are you in a band? You want to play with us sometime?"

"Well," Scott says, "Thanks. You boys headed up next?"

"We got a drummer tonight," the first kid says. "They're

finding an old kit to set up."

Scott sits with these two moppets and drinks their beer; up on the stage a kid is plugging in his computer. The Grand Mal is an old-fashioned rock dive: one speaker cabinet is on top of a piano, another is perched on a larger, non-functioning amp and squeezed under an asbestos-looking duct, the place has old guitars affixed to its walls, plus an "In Utero" handbill from the Roseland (July 23, 1993: Scott was seven) and an outsized Jimi Hendrix silk-screen poster. But these days the Grand Mal is teetering toward bankruptcy, and only makes its rent when it can lure famous DJs Scott has never heard. The open mic isn't all rock-and-folk anymore; onstage now, the kid drops a loud beat and dons giant headphones. He swirls in a Kelly Clarkson song, speeding it up to match his own rhythm. Scott sees several faces in the audience light up, sees many arms pump the air. The boys here at this table make gagging expressions.

"Congratulations!" one of them says. "You can click a mouse!"

But there's still a way to do it playing actual instruments, isn't there? Get discovered, get signed, get huge? Looking around the room, it's an easy sharks-and-jets comparison: the players versus the samplers. But surely the pie is still big enough for everyone! Playing guitar is still a path to fortune and love! Yes, in here, Scott sees enough people bored by this DJ wannabe that he can imagine himself part of a majority…though he's read dozens of veteran rockers complain that concert sales and contracts are drying up. *You just have to be that much better*, Scott thinks, *that much more organized, that much more ruthless. It's still possible.*

The Kelly Clarkson remix ends, and the two young guys and their drummer jump onto the stage and plug in. They plink and plunk, tuning for several minutes, until the drummer—a full-figured woman with a pixie hairdo—gets impatient and taps out a rhythm on her rims, reaches around to grab a mic, and sings an off-key impromptu version of "Somebody That I Used To Know" which these days is on the radio every seven seconds. People sing along and it's a little bit thrilling. Scott looks over at Stephanie, and she winks and makes a kissy face. The room is now inviting and magical, a home; tension leaves Scott's ribcage. Onstage the trio finally plays and it's terrible, the guitars can't keep up with the drums, they miss notes and fumble over chords, but Scott sees the

Grand Mal through happy eyes he wishes he carried around all the time.

When the night ends, he rides the chilly way back down. He politely declines an invite to drink at a warehouse club next door, packing up the battered old roundback Ovation like someone who has somewhere to be. He'll eat something and work on a song.

But cold air shows him the truth: there's an itch in his head he can't scratch, and he exhales through gritted teeth as his phone sends him to the Wikipedia pages of Madonna's other two surviving female dancers.

He meets the first on Tuesday morning. She's a wiry lady in her forties he lures to a Times Square Starbucks by claiming to be the reality judge's son. When he tells the truth she gathers up her giant handbag.

"I've never had a child," she says. "It's one of the compromises we make. The idea someone would go to these lengths just to get halfway close to a famous person, it's pathetic. Do you kids really need to get close to fame that bad? Here's a news flash: your every whistle and fart isn't worthy of YouTube. You don't wake up in the morning and deserve to be famous." As she delivers this speech, she touches Scott's arm. The contact makes him improbably lightheaded.

Late in the afternoon, he puts in his earbuds and stands outside a ballet school between Broadway and West End Avenue. The final dancer is a part-time teacher therein. Scott has no guarantee she's here, but waits anyway. He listens to Spoon:

I know it could be worse
I'm not standing here
I'm not standing here

He doesn't know what he wants. Well, he does. He wants out of this stupid maze he's built. He has these routines and when he breaks them, as now, it's some wild signifier. The only part of him that doesn't want to keep waiting here is the part that's still reluctant to start a conversation with a stranger. Britt Daniel sings, "Some people are so easily shuffled and dealt." Little girls stream out of the ballet school.

Here come two female teachers down the stairs, enjoying some lively debate. Scott steps forward and says, "Sophie Vickers?"

They tell him she's inside.

He finds her alone writing something at a desk. She's curly-haired with a cleft chin and well-defined bare shoulders. He tells her everything he knows.

"I haven't seen Madonna for ten years," Sophie says. "What a ridiculous time I had. I've never worked harder. It sounds like you already know what I'm going to say. I mean, I've never been pregnant. You're on a wild goose chase."

"There was one dancer who died," says Scott.

"Yes. Miriam. Much later."

"But I'm starting to think you're all just a cover. I'm starting to think it really was the great lady herself. Who had the baby."

"I'm sorry, I didn't spend enough time around her when we weren't touring. I wouldn't have known for sure if she was pregnant."

He sits. This room is dust-moted, creaking like a wooden ship. Sophie wears a wedding ring and a sympathetic white smile. He puts his foot up on a table support, his elbow on his knee, his hand over his eyes. His fingertips are long since callused over from the guitar.

"You're not recording me," she says, "not writing anything down. You're not a reporter."

"..."

"But you're chasing leads like a detective who wasn't hired. You can see that's a little troublesome?"

"I mean, don't talk to me like I'm crazy."

"No," she says. "No, you're not crazy. You're in pain. But what do you have to be in pain about? You barely know this girl?"

"Yes. Right."

"So what's the difference who her mother is?"

"I think it's really Madonna."

"So what?" says Sophie. "So what if it is? You want to meet her?"

"No," he says. "I don't care about that."

"Then tell me. Why are you in pain?"

Because the closed system of hard work is self-eating. Because to be judged is a knife in the side. Because when he's clear-headed and honest, he's not exactly sure what his dreams even *are*, whether he wants fame, whether he cares. Because he actually does try hard to be liked, and often isn't. Because reaching out doesn't work.

Because he needs an excuse to try.

"I'm not," he says.

"Well. Good luck with your case."

He looks at her collarbone, which is symmetrical and deeply indented. He feels desire for her, that sinking hopelessness. He imagines the brownstone to which she'll return, the well-hung husband, the clean kitchen and plentiful closet space. Meanwhile he knows exactly what will constitute his night, down to the smallest detail, now that there isn't time to get to Thrillsville before Happy Hour.

"Is she a great singer?" Scott says.

"Who, Madonna? Yes. Of course."

"…"

"What a strange thing to ask."

"…"

"What's really going on here?" She stands and crosses the room. She grabs the back of his chair and shakes it. "Should I be calling her up and warning her? Should she be on alert?"

He's enough of a puzzle to himself that he envisions some parallel track, where he reaches up and kisses her. As it is, he looks away, to her painted toenails. Her finger is in his face.

"Seriously! If you hurt anybody!"

"Okay. Okay!" He snaps his neck around, trying to get away from the finger.

Sophie shoves his chair. "*I'm* sorry. You're not here right now. I'll leave a message at the beep."

"…"

"It means get out."

He rises, feels heaviness in his chest. "I just thought if she's really Madonna's kid."

"Then what? You'd marry her and be rich?"

"No." He steps to the door. "Jesus. No."

"…"

"I thought…. I thought we could be in a band together."

Sophie squinches her eyes, places her hands on her hips, thumbs forward. "Why couldn't you be in a band with her anyway?" she says.

His heart is breaking for some reason. He feels like crying. For the millionth time he promises himself he'll change. Now is his big chance.

CONVERGENCE

Kate Grush is on her fourteenth mile of the morning, crossing over the Chenango in the rain, when gunfire erupts. It's unmistakable in its repetition. She's running south on Front Street, and squad cars blaze past. There are the beginnings of a barricade before she can get to Main, and police are stalking a nondescript building marked "American Civic Association." Kate stops, sweating unladylike, and stands for hours alongside other shocked people. As they wheel out bodies in bags, sometimes leaving bloody tracks, she gasps. Family members arrive wearing headscarves or religious-looking tunics. They wail and attempt to run inside. Kate tries to keep it together, to overhear what happened inside that nothing little one-story building with the white columns.

A man walked in with several guns and shot a receptionist in the head. Then he stepped into an ESL classroom and opened fire, hitting every single student. At least a dozen are dead. Nobody knows why. The gunman may have killed himself, too. Kate feels like she hasn't blinked in an hour. She's wearing her torn-up red jogging shirt and spandex workout pants, which she thinks make her look fat. She keeps touching her forehead.

Later she finds herself in a small diner behind a church. People eat sandwiches in silence and stare at the TV. Kate doesn't remember walking here. A commercial comes on and a waitress changes the channel. All the national networks have broken in to cover the story: Binghamton has the country's eye. Kate is in a booth, feeling her face. There's something in her hand, but she can't look at it.

"Do you mind if I sit down?" says a white-haired woman as she slides into the opposite seat.

Kate tries to smile because it's what they taught her. It occurs to her that the reason she keeps touching her face is that it's not responding. All she can do is imagine those poor people, their last petrified moments. There's water on the table, is how she knows she's crying.

"The world is going to hell," says the woman across from her. "There's more evidence every day. You wake up one day and go to school and somebody shoots you."

Kate looks around the diner. Baseball caps and stubble, lipstick and pearls. The TV is mounted high above the coffeepots so everyone's neck cranes up. A dessert case rotates; occasionally a fork scrapes a plate. It's well past lunch and there are twenty people in here. Everyone's face is floodlit from above, as a thunderstorm has darkened the outside world. Kate sees one person apart from the rest, a young Asian woman standing near the register with her arms folded. The woman flicks her eyes around the room, then calmly snags a few items from a shelf and slides them into her pocket.

"People used to take care of each other," says the white-haired woman.

There's something big in Kate's stomach. It trembles upward to her chest, shakes backward into her shoulders, up into her head. It's the strangest thing: like going up in a slow elevator. It's the feeling of height. The Asian woman opens the diner door and steps out into the rain.

The woman across from Kate leans across and whispers, "I'll tell you, it's gotten bad since we elected that n-word."

Kate finally looks into her own hand. She's holding a bullet.

She runs from the diner, sees the Asian woman on the next corner of this unfamiliar street. She has nothing to say, so she follows in the rain. This neighborhood wears the same pallor as the rest of the city. A hair salon, a DMV office, a rehab supply warehouse: they're all provisional and beside the point. In their fullness they are hopeful outposts in the ruins. Kate gives the Asian woman some distance, but not enough: she stops and turns, grinning.

"You're following me," says the woman. "Do you want to kiss me?"

"…"

"Do you want to do *more* than kiss me?"

"No," Kate says. A car sluices by.

"Do you want to come with me?"

"I don't know where you're going."

"Back to my friends. The van leaves in ten minutes."

"I saw something today," says Kate. "It was horrible. It was the most terrible thing I've ever seen. But you know what it did? It made me so sad and furious, it let me believe that before I saw it, I was happy. Like, I could pretend that when I got on the road this morning, I was happy. But I wasn't. I so wasn't."

"We're getting wet."

"How old are you?"

"I'm 19," says the Asian woman. "How old are you?"

"I'm 20."

"It feels old, doesn't it?"

Kate thinks about this. "Yes."

"You picked me out," the other woman says. "I saw you in the diner."

"What did you steal?"

"Nothing much." She puts her palms together, one up one down, and Kate is close enough to see her lovely uncolored nails and her perfect teeth. "I can only tell you what happened to me, and why I'm so happy," she says. "I got so tired of the meaninglessness."

"You don't seem like a hardened criminal."

Rain streams down their faces.

"Will your friends. Will they do anything to me?"

"…"

"Will they…hurt me?"

"Oh," says the Asian woman. "Oh, no."

They walk and Kate gets in the van. There are many faces squeezed into the rows of seats, all female. As the cityscape recedes, they sing "My Bonnie Lies over the Ocean." Deep into the dark, they belt out "He's Got the Whole World in His Hands" and "John Jacob Jingleheimer Schmidt." Everyone seems young except the driver, Maizie, who has a red dye-job and blows cigarette smoke out the window. They stop in Erie and get a bag of burgers from a drive-thru, then rent a room at the DeLuxe Motel. There are about ten women, and they all have sleeping bags; everyone finds floor-space and stretches out. Maizie gets one of the beds and, presumably because she's new and doesn't have a bedroll, Kate gets the other.

They drive for three months. It's a circuitous route, past the Great Lakes, as far west as Iowa, then into the Deep South. It's so wonderful. Kate listens to them talk about God and about their Church leader, James Randolph. The life is about structure and discipline. They sleep four hours a night, cover three or four towns while eating one meal a day. They sell soap and flowers, crucifixes when they have them, in the name of the Holy Church of Convergence.

It's miraculously easy to break down any modern cynicism they encounter. Yes, if the entire group approaches a hardware clerk or a security guard, they get nowhere, but when one of them breaks away and draws near by herself smiling sweetly, giving the hardware clerk or security guard individual attention…he always melts. Every time. Kate can't believe how foolproof it is and wonders if the public at large knows about it, how kind it turns out people actually are. They don't always buy, but they always melt.

Kate's jogging outfit is long since gone. They share clothing, everything goes into the wash every few days, and you get what you get.

"We're behind last month's pace, ladies," Maizie will say on the road. "The application of will is God's measuring stick. We can apply ourselves harder. We can show Him. Your will can never get too strong."

The women repeat mottoes to each other the way Kate's former friends recycled movie quotes:

"God views life as an opportunity to become perfect."

"Humans act as if they're here to wreck the planet."

"God gave us brains, so use them."

"Greed never fills a need."

"In heaven nobody cares how your toenails look."

"You have free will to decide everything about your life."

"Love is the thumping sound of your heart."

Kate becomes cheery about deprivation. There is always less one can eat and sleep. They push each other to greater heights:

"Father James can see you dawdling!" "Father James says leave the worrying to God!" The weather heats up and they're grubby, mostly sleeping on the ground outside the van. Maizie buys soap and flowers in bulk and stacks them in back. Kate knows they can beat last month's dollar figure. She hugs any stranger who'll let her.

Her favorite fellow traveler is a tall woman nicknamed Inch. They call her Inch because when the ladies are tired in the van, when their concentration is flagging, she always rallies the troops by saying, "If you give the devil an inch, he'll take a mile!" It's one of countless reminders they give each other every day—because they're human, because they lose focus and forget—that every moment spent breathing should be a step toward perfection. Kate knows some former version of herself would've chuckled at the corniness of their aphorisms. But she doesn't care, because now she believes something and it's more dangerous to believe, it's scarier to have skin in the game. Their trite expressions are a shorthand way to touch exalted feelings. She bypasses her old scoffing, cowardly rejection of such maxims, and feels the goodness of their source.

Inch says, "Take half my hamburger, Kate. I want you to have it."

"No," says Kate. "You take half of mine."

"I don't need it. We should tell Maizie to buy less food."

"She should save the money. It would count toward the month's total."

"We sleep too much," says Inch.

"Yes."

"Sometimes I wake up and look at the stars. Maybe I'm supposed to be thinking about God and infinite space, but all I want to do is stand up and start shouting. So everyone will get up, and we can get driving!"

"I'm awake, too," Kate says. "Maybe everyone's awake, thinking the same thing."

They're in Brookhaven, Mississippi, standing in a parking lot between a Piggly Wiggly and a Pump and Save. Housewives don't make good targets, so Kate and Inch wait for deliverymen in the shade of a single tree, standing out here on the blacktop.

"It's not a contest," says Inch. "I'm not trying to say I'm better than you."

"Yes but of course it *is* a contest," Kate says. "We're trying to defeat former monthly versions of ourselves."

Inch has met James Randolph, at the famous farmhouse in Winchester, Virginia. She doesn't brag about it, but it hangs in the air and this makes sense: Father James is the light. But Inch says when she met Father James, she clutched his arm and whispered, "You're the resurrection," and he nodded sagely and patted her arm and said, "And you are, too." Kate tries to keep track of how close they are to Virginia. Sometimes she has bad dreams about her mother's bathroom scale, and is grateful when she wakes up.

"Excuse me, sir," Inch says to a man in a pinstriped uniform. "Would you like to buy a flower?" She's so pretty: blonde with a long chin, a perfect nose, bare brown arms. He stops with his jaw cocked, scratching the side of his head.

"A flower and what else?" he says.

"Nothing else, sir."

"It's for your girl-scout troop?" says the man.

"No, sir. My friend and I are on the road."

"Huh. I know from personal experience that's not a friendly place to be." He reaches for his wallet. "Y'all look in need of several square meals."

"Oh, we're fine, sir."

"Maybe a shower, maybe some indoor plumbing. Here you go, darling. Keep the flowers."

"Thank you, sir. If you like, I could tell you what's made me so happy."

"I'm almost afraid to ask."

"It started in 1979, when Jesus appeared to James Randolph and asked him to continue His work. To bring together all Christian peoples with love and tolerance."

"I see," says the man.

"Father James tells us we're only truly together when we drop the ego of our personality. That's when God can see us shining."

Not unkindly, the man says, "I had a cousin like you. Y'all are brainwashed."

"My friend and I love you," says Inch. "We love you with or without your money."

"It's true," Kate says.

"I don't want you to take this wrong way," says the man, "but it's peculiar to be loved that way, girls. I gave up wanting to be loved unconditionally when I turned 10. People want to be loved for who they are."

"Unfortunately, you can't stop us," says Inch. "We just love you."

The uniformed man walks into the Piggly Wiggly. Kate looks at Inch and feels herself glowing from the inside.

"Peace be with you," Inch says. "I should've said peace be with you."

Kate reads Father James' literature, including his foundational text, *Divine Love*. The names of things: "The Pure Family." "Soul Restoration." "The Kiss of Peace." Kate recognizes the faith she used to put in things like money and language, and now sees how elegantly the Church pivots those unhealthy behaviors, makes money a conduit for introduction to beloved strangers, gives evocative new labels for the true sweet goals of a new life. She runs her fingers over printed text wishing she could feel the ink raised and legible like braille, then knows in fact she can.

There's Hannah who sings in her sleep; Sun whom Kate first followed into the van; Tanya who laughs like a horse; Lizzy who always asks if there are peanuts in the food Maizie buys, because she's allergic. Kate loves them. At first she was shy, but this core group is so committed, so sleepily single-minded, Kate must regularly hug and squeeze and pinch these women. Others around the margins come and go, usually in a hail of tears or a volley of recriminations. Some weeks the group numbers only seven or eight, and pressure is greater to move inventory; they might only sleep an hour each night—Kate welcomes this, fully believes in halving supposed necessities as frequently as possible—and crisscross entire states in a single day. Those times, Kate stands alone in an industrial parking lot or on an urban lawn, waiting for a shift to let out or passers-by to materialize, and reads *Divine Love*, often falling into the softest sleep imaginable and dreaming passages. *Walk the difficult path that puts one in connection with God and Jesus, learn your place in the order of things, hold hands with the angels above and below you.*

In a town outside Tallahassee, she watches a shirtless man berate a woman who's sitting at a picnic table. It's the kind of public scene that makes them invisible: people avert eyes and give a wide berth. But Kate strides right toward them. The man's wild, twangy words grow more distinct, and she hears, "...leave me all by myself at the hospital! You think I wanna be all by myself?"

Kate locks in a kind smile. She looks at this soft-chested sunburned guy and forces love into her heart by imagining him as a baby, then as Jesus.

"Hello!" she says.

"And who the fuck is this?" says the man. "Another one of your bitch friends?"

The seated woman looks up, revealing mascara streaked across her face.

"I heard you talking," Kate says, "and I wanted to let you know I agree. Feeling alone is the worst thing there is."

"Stay the fuck out of my business!"

But Kate moves closer. "Your sadness is right." She's inches away from this young man, who looms above her. His face is pocked, his nipples are dark smudges. "There's nothing worse than waking up alone."

"Who is this?" says the man. "Bitch, you're dirty and you smell foul."

"I can tell you how it changed for me," Kate says. "Would you like to know what's made me so happ—" but the man puts his hand on her throat, his thumb across her windpipe, and he slams her into a tree.

"Dax," says the blonde woman at the table. "Don't."

"You stepping to me?" Dax says.

Kate can only discharge strangling noises.

"You little cunt, mind your own fucking business."

Kate claws at his wrist, tries to pry away his fingers. She's malnourished and weak.

"I got a fucking tumor on my fucking *ball*," he says. "Don't tell me you know what it's like! You don't know what it's like, unless you got a package I don't know about!"

Kate looks down at the woman, who hasn't moved. She's staring at her own pale hands and square fingernails.

"What do you think, Charlene? Hey, shit-for-brains! You think this bitch got a dick-and-balls?" With his free hand, he reaches down under Kate's plain beige jumper then lifts high, pressing and digging hard against her vulva. "Nope, no package here, so don't go telling me that. Don't tell me you know what it's like." Kate feels him push harder. She feels him begin to peel away her underpants, which aren't actually hers. She brings up a knee, swift and square, directly into Dax's crotch.

His hands flutter away.

She steps from the tree, sees him fold forward. She tries to say something but all she can do is cough. Then she's reeling toward the acorn-covered ground, only realizing mid-fall that she's been punched in the face. Her head strikes the dirt. Dax is sputtering, standing over her. He kicks her in the ribcage. She curls tight, inhaling the dust of a Florida panhandle summer.

"*Dax!*" This is the seated woman, Charlene, shrieking. Kate can see her crossed feet. Then the man above Kate is gone, she hears a fleshy thump, and Charlene slides backwards off the picnic bench and settles onto the shaded ground, sobbing and covering her face.

"Ohh," Dax says. "Ohh, kick me in my fucking tumor."

Soon Kate feels people touching her shoulders. They pull her upright. Strangers blink and frown and fuss and she loves them. Charlene stands aside, one eye dark and swollen half-closed.

Later Charlene follows her into a park restroom. They examine their wounds in the mirrors. Kate hasn't focused on her own reflection in months, and is as surprised by her thorny unplucked eyebrows as much as the fist-sized welt across her cheek or the bruise beneath her left breast. Charlene's damaged eye is already unrealistically dark violet, like a makeup effect. Kate knows they're both plain women in a rotten-smelling bathroom but her mind glows with the beauty of right now, and this is the Church's blessed inversion.

"You can come with me," she tells Charlene, noticing an empty tampon dispenser in an open stall, and realizing she hasn't menstruated in recent memory.

"I got a job," Charlene says. "Come where?"

"Virginia. To Father James' house."

This is now the road's strongest allure. Nobody asks Maizie where they're headed next and she offers no clues, but Kate finds herself making calculations based on what she remembers of southeastern geography, and of the sun's position in the sky. She's not supposed to think about tomorrow, she's best served focusing only on right now, but the idea of Winchester, Virginia, hourly shoehorns its way into her thoughts. Charlene always sits on Kate's left as they drive (Inch is usually on the right), and sometimes she whispers, "How soon 'til Father James?" and Kate smiles sagely.

It takes weeks to advance up the Atlantic coast and then

inland to Charlotte. They lose Tanya in Greenville, South Carolina; they plead with Maizie to wait a few extra hours, disbelieving that sanguine, chortling Tanya could abandon the cause. But she never returns. There are three new women in the van's back row and Kate understands they're all junkies going through withdrawal. They return from an afternoon's selling with their inventories still nearly full, sometimes with their crucifixes covered in vomit. They put their foreheads against the van windows and look at the sun. They don't ever sing.

Maizie finds a lightly policed park in Charlotte and hides the van beneath a railroad trestle; they spread out under magnolias, sleeping atop their bedrolls. July nights here are short and Kate wakes before sunrise to pray. The sky is an expectant dark blue and the city's hum rises around her. The world begs us to understand it as part of us, but instead we shape it and fight it, drain near-infinite reservoirs to build megalopolises in deserts, burn and cut and kill, and all the world does is continue to speak in moments like this: *You are here, feel me chill your skin, you are part of me.* She feels around for the copy of *Divine Love* she often brings to bed but can't find it. It's not underneath her sleeping bag. She walks to the locked van and can't see the book on or behind any of the seats. Something jabs her foot, and Kate realizes she's standing on a piece of broken glass. She carefully lifts her leg to see if she's been cut.

"Looking for this?"

Kate spasms in surprise. It's Maizie, who flicks a plastic lighter to reveal the thick, battered copy of *Divine Love*.

"Yes," Kate says. "I was."

But Maizie doesn't hand it over. Instead, she pulls open the back cover to reveal that someone has carved a hole through the final hundred or so pages, like they do in prison break movies. It's a hidden compartment but Kate can't see what's inside.

"What would you like to tell me?" says Maizie.

"..."

"Now is the time to speak, before I kick you to the curb, young lady."

It comes to Kate how dizzy with hunger she is, how bad her teeth feel, how disoriented she is from lack of sleep. She wants to mount a defense against whatever this is, but her reservoir of self-respect is dry. Maizie re-flicks the lighter and pulls out three small connected packets with the word "Trojan" emblazoned across each. Beneath those are several used condoms whose openings have been tied into knots, trapping the fluid therein.

"What is the meaning?" Maizie says.

Kate has always prided herself on levelheadedness, on tears as an absolute last resort. But she bawls. It's almost dawn, and many of the others straggle over rubbing their eyes.

"I'm sure I don't have to remind any of you," says Maizie, "how wrong this kind of behavior is. Working for the Holy Church of Convergence is a privilege, and this young lady has abused it. Such sickening behavior. While the rest of you have been selling so hard, Kate has been making this...crude collection."

Kate falls weeping into Inch's arms.

"The book isn't only hers," says Charlene. "Just because she reads it most."

"Other people read it, too," Sun says. "I read it sometimes."

"It was someone," says Maizie. "It was one of you."

Kate sobs into Inch's breast, wishing Maizie would vanish, finding herself wishing God would strike Maizie down. One of the detoxing junkies steps forward, looks at the book's grotesquerie, and says in descending tones, "Mm, mm, mm."

Inch puts an arm across Kate's shoulders and leads her away from the group. They walk to a dry gulley and sit with their feet over the edge. Across a field and over a line of pin oaks, they can see tall buildings coming forward one by one out of the morning gloom, gradually enveloped less by night and more by fog. For a moment they could be in Binghamton, but then the taller buildings bloom orange with sunrise, resuming individuality, making cutout shapes against the sky. Kate hasn't had sex in more than a year.

"Here," says Inch, and she hands over several candy bars.

"Where'd you get these?" Kate says.

Inch makes one dimple. "Come on. It's all right."

Kate examines a cylindrical pack of Rolos.

"Eat it. You'll feel better."

Kate chews, and it's ambrosia.

"So, now you *are* the one who carries that book around most," Inch says. "I just have to ask."

"They're not mine. It's not me. Gosh!"

"All right. Okay. We'll figure it out. It's a mystery, and we'll follow the clues. Relax, sweetie."

But there are no clues. Every woman denies knowing anything

about the condoms. Maizie fumes for an hour, scandalizing each lady with nasty accusations, but nobody confesses. When Kate's turn comes she leans against the van, feeling hollowed out. Normally in such moments she turns to *Divine Love*.

"I want you to ask yourself how likely it is," says Maizie, "that you could walk around carrying that book and not know there's a hole in the back. That you wouldn't feel things jiggling around in there. All your sisters have denied it, Kate. Are you really calling one of them a liar?"

"..."

"This isn't a court of law, young lady. I don't need reasonable doubt. This is sinful and it won't be stood for."

"..."

"You have one last chance to tell me the truth, or I'm going to leave you by the side of the road."

Kate knows the others are close by and listening. She tries to imagine what it means, that someone has gathered different men's semen and saved it. It's a defiance of propriety that won't give her entry. It's borne of a sickness she can make herself love, but she wonders if she should. Every day presents reasons for shaken faith, but not like this.

While the others roll up their sleeping bags and pile in the van, she sits staring at the ground. She can't remember where she is, and she's exhausted. She tries to remember passages from *Divine Love*, but in her mind they're incomplete. The doors all close, the ignition fires. Her eyes never move. The engine thunders and Kate thinks how many miles they've traveled these months, and how amazing it is the van has never broken down once, except for a few flat tires. Dazed, she imagines their plaintive faces against the glass, and a part of her finds their sadness delicious.

The van clicks into gear. Kate doesn't watch.

Then there's a rolling noise, arms are around her, Kate is standing. Inch tells her, "Maizie says you can come if you promise never again."

They drive the rigid backbone of I-81. They sell flowers and soap in Blacksburg and Roanoke, Eagle Rock and Buena Vista. They're traveling north. Maizie acquires several cartons of liturgical calendars and they're popular with nearly everyone, so Kate wishes they had more. But mostly she's consumed by how close they must be getting to Winchester. Inch retells stories about Father James, and they all gather close. These are the times Kate still feels sewn into the same fabric as her sisters. Otherwise she feels herself lifting away, so she asks Inch for more details, more unexamined crannies of her visit to the farmhouse.

"There was bread," Inch says. "They had just baked many loaves of bread and the entire place smelled like it. I was in line with all the others, waiting for him to receive me and I was eating bread. It didn't seem like my turn would ever come, because he spent so much time with each person. He's old but not frail and he has wonderful perfect teeth."

"Tell us about the music," somebody says.

"There was music playing in the farmhouse. I kept trying to figure out what song it was, but it was beautiful piano music. It was everywhere. I remember I couldn't see any speakers or anything, and I don't think they had a live piano there, but it was still, like, everywhere you went. It makes you feel like the sounds are part of the place, like they're coming from.... Anyway, I can't imagine being there without that music. You girls are going to *love* it."

Kate and Charlene take armfuls of ox-eye daisies and flowering sage to an outdoor shopping mall. They're expert assessors now, can find the lonely men who like being talked to and giving up cash. It's more effective if they don't come on too heavy for the Church; Kate smiles and speaks quietly, listens when others talk, maybe emphasizes her thinness and sunken eyes, and soon the flowers are all gone. Today they're holding two hundred dollars, waiting in front of a Baby Gap for the van to return.

"That's a lot of money," says Charlene.

"I know!" Kate says.

"We could keep some and tell Maizie we had to lower our prices." But Charlene says this sweetly, without malice or intent. Kate grins into the sun. "Katie, did you ever wonder what Father James does with all the dough we send him?"

"…"

"Because I remember my grandmamma sending money to Creflo Dollar. And then on the Internet I saw pictures of him driving around in a Rolls Royce."

"No, I never think about it."

"…"

"I know you don't mean anything bad," Kate says, "but you have to train yourself not think that way. In life we have to decide to trust someone."

"But not everyone," says Charlene. "I mean, there's a girl in the van who put condoms inside that book and wouldn't fess."

"..."

"Everyone knows, Katie. Everyone knows it was Inch."

"..."

"She's the pretty one. She just throws away her flowers and fucks guys. That's where she gets her money. So how do you know who to trust?"

Kate's face roasts. She watches traffic out on the mall feeder and a long time passes. An old lady with a comical southern accent asks them to fetch her a shopping cart, and Kate does. It can't be true about Inch. It really can't.

"We'll be there soon," Kate finally says. Charlene's eyes flicker. "We're finally just a couple days away and we'll meet Father James in person, and I know he wouldn't mind the question. The one about trust. He'll laugh a little and show us all the good we're doing. Charlene, our lives really mean something."

"You can pick your friends," says Charlene, "and you can pick your nose. But you can't pick your—"

Then nothing. Because darkness falls across Kate's eyes and for half-an-instant she believes Jesus or Father James has called her home. But someone has tackled her around the chest, and she tries to move her legs but someone has grabbed those, too. She's off the ground. There's a muffled female shout that might be Charlene. Car tires yip, she bounces against something soft, a man says, "Go! Go! Go!" and the people holding her won't let her thrash. She feels momentum in her organs, the acceleration of a getaway ride.

"It's all right, Katherine," a voice above her says, and because she's half-sitting on this man, she can feel the voice vibrate against her, and she also maybe feels his hard-on against her hip. "We're friends. We're friends. Your parents will be very relieved."

"No!" she hears herself say. "Noooooooooooooooooooooooo!"

They sit her on a bed in an upscale hotel room and offer her a slice of pizza. She won't touch it. She's thinking about martyrs mentioned in *Divine Love*. St. Stephen sitting in a courtroom seeing God with Christ on his right hand. John Ball in the archbishop's prison with Kentish rebels about to free him. Simone Weil and Joan of Arc. Faith against all odds. Only faith makes the connection so. Let the charlatans around her dance.

"You've been gone a long time," the older man says. He has a gray mustache and an earring. "You can't imagine how much your mom and dad want to see you. They're flying down here."

They're about to tell me I'm deluded. They'll tell me I'm brainwashed.

"We've got pictures to show you," says the younger one. "Your high school graduation, see? Your Sweet Sixteen. Tell us what you remember."

If nobody had believed James Randolph, if everyone thought he was delusional, the Church could never have existed. So it also takes courage to be the second one in. Every impulse comes from God. Follow them all.

"You worked at a CVS in Binghamton, New York. You went to SUNY Binghamton for three semesters. You have friends. You live with your parents. You like running and you like oysters. You're a drummer, Katherine. Do you remember playing the drums in your parents' basement?"

God has sent me to this hotel as a test.

"Your therapist is Jean Dubront."

Kate closes her eyes.

"Do you remember me?" the younger one says. "We went to school together. K through 12. I'm Zack Jones. This is what I do now."

"With your parents' permission," says the older one, "Dr. Dubront told us some troubling things about your past. That perhaps there was abuse, which there often is in these cases. Do you remember what I'm talking about, Katherine?"

"I'm probationary. Butch only let me come along because I know you."

"Do you remember the abuse I'm talking about, Katherine?"

Only faith makes the connection so.

"Why don't you eat something, Kate? You look like you're starving. Do you remember eating wings at South Side Yanni's? I saw you there a few times. Remember all the fat dudes in Hawaiian shirts?"

"Mr. and Mrs. Grush are on a plane. I'm hoping we can get you cleaned up before then, Katherine, so they don't have to see you like this."

"We were in Mr. Palumbo's chemistry class together."

"You don't want to hurt your parents any more, do you, Katherine?"

If it's God's will to put me through this questioning, I can't hate these men, who are His implements. But she squinches her eyes and hates the men.

They talk to her for hours. They tell her that the Holy Church of Convergence is a scam, that James Randolph is a con artist. They show her photos of an older man in an expensive suit, boarding a private jet, and photos of women who've been beaten. She goes to the bathroom and tries to jimmy open the window, discovering that she's ten stories above the street. They show her photocopied newspaper articles about the Church's legal troubles. But it's nothing that couldn't be faked.

These are the tactics the devil would use. In his acrid smoke and crimson suit the devil isn't unconvincing. What did Maizie say? They were on the highway at the end of a long day, heads jiggling in the dark van, and one of Kate's sisters fretted aloud that they must almost be out of gas, she'd been counting mile markers and she knew the tank must be all but empty. And Maizie said, "Logic is the enemy of faith." Yes. The devil would be patient and have documentation.

Zack gets frustrated and lies down on the other bed. Butch just keeps going in his low voice, telling her things about herself. The only time she speaks, she asks to look out the suite's main window. Butch slides open the curtains and Kate can't tell if it's sunrise or sunset, but it's beautiful. The land is low around this tall hotel: cars with headlights line up everywhere, but she can see this age pass in a geological eye blink, these thousands of souls below her rise up faithlessly but are redeemed nonetheless. She's naked in this old beige jumper, more naked than if she disrobed, and she feels these thousands rustle against the openness of her heart and she doesn't know how to make it not hurt, she doesn't know how to laugh off all the pain. Her hands are on this vent, her forehead is against the window, she tries to see Inch and Sun and Maizie waiting. Would Charlene have told them of the abduction? Or would they think she abandoned them? She tries to feel her sisters but then the great sponge of loneliness is crushed and another drop falls into her mouth.

She makes a break for the door. Butch catches her easily and sets her gently back down on the bed. Zack plugs in his phone, turns up the volume and plays "I Predict a Riot" by Kaiser Chiefs, and "Walking with a Ghost" by Tegan and Sara, and "Lazy Eye" by Silversun Pickups, and "Seven Nation Army" by the White Stripes.

Her parents arrive and fret, weeping in her lap. They transport her by airplane to some kind of deprogramming facility where she spends what could be weeks. She attends group therapy, has one-on-one sessions, meets defrocked members of Father James' Church who tell her the real story. The nurses in this place have a dog and they let Kate take care of it. They let her feed it breakfast and dinner, and eventually they let her take it for walks. Her parents are staying somewhere nearby and visit daily. She doesn't get angry. She eats and sleeps.

Sometimes she thinks: *They never came back for me.*

She doesn't think about hurting herself. But she does wonder about ending her life.

The therapist in this place keeps calling her depressed, and Kate nods but hates it, because "depressed" makes it sound like she's just blue, like all she needs is a bowl of ice cream and everything will pick up.

No, what Kate feels is *awful.* It's what she felt before she left Binghamton, and it's what she feels now. The intervening months were a refuge, and no matter how corrupt the Holy Church of Convergence might be, she thanks it. Now she's back to assuming the rug will be pulled out from under her at any moment, that she's three heartbeats away from something terrible happening. The feeling comes in the morning: she can wake up in her institutional bed and see the sun coming through the windows and think about walking Sparks the dog, but then she feels the very edge of the bad feeling and she dreads it so intensely she actually brings it on, it's like an attack she can trigger simply by thinking about a possible attack. She used to have this feeling every day working at CVS, and every night watching television. The feeling is this: the moment she does something wrong, something unbelievably horrible will happen, but she doesn't know what the unbelievably horrible thing is, and she doesn't know what "correct" things she can do to prevent it. It's nameless and black, and she feels dumb trying to explain it.

The badness of this feeling only used to abate when she ran very long distances and when she played drums behind goofball friends holding guitars. But neither of those outlets is available to her now. Day after day, this familiar dark feeling is who she is. She knows she has to get out of this place.

So she gathers herself and playacts, and they start telling her she's making progress. By winter, she's sleeping in her bedroom in

Binghamton, though they don't make her return to the pharmacy. She goes to shows put on by guys who used to be in Kamikaze Hearts. A year goes by and she moves to New York.

She finds a roommate on Craig's List, a gorgeous and quiet "fashion accountant"—whatever that means—but the roommate has her own friends and is gone most of the time. Kate's parents pay her rent. She's on 121st Street just north of the university and has a distant view of the Riverside Church tower, a paraffin concoction against the gray Manhattan sky.

She gets a pixie haircut and starts running again. She feels like a Weeble, having gained back a ton of weight. One afternoon she's jogging on the West Side Highway heading north, passing the aircraft carrier that's parked on the Hudson alongside 46th Street, and she's focused on Brendan Canty's incredible drumming on "Glue Man," thinking here's a wonderful moment right here where that *feeling*—the "depression" that makes her feel like a ghost who's been thwacked out of its body to dangle like an exhaled lungful of sour smoke—can't get her.

She glances across the street at the Hustler Club and its giant photograph of a brassiere-clad woman, and when she looks back a bike accident has just happened: a helmetless woman has crashed hard to the sandy asphalt. Kate removes her earbuds and two laughing old construction workers leaning on a lamppost say, "Seen it happen at this intersection a million times! Haw! Fuckin' look out below!" Everyone else is standing around, or else continuing along pretending not to notice. Kate crouches to help the woman, who's shocked, in tears, cradling her arm as if it's come detached.

"Let me just see," Kate says.

GOLD MEDAL HONEY

"Hey. Is it you?"

"Yes. I'm me."

"I mean: Amanda?"

She wrinkles her nose. BrettMets09 is handsome: blond swirlybird hairdo and three days' beard, a white sports coat over a black rodeo shirt. *(About BrettMets09: "I'm good at being unselfish when it's needed, but I also can express an opinion.")*

"I'm Brett," he says. "You look just like your pictures. Am I late?"

The Christmas lights at Malatesta are still up, and the waiters—who are also unusually handsome—seem harried. It's loud in here even for 6:30 dinner. In blouses and suits, table-by-table the patrons are together alone, cheer thick as steam. Theirs is a club one wishes to belong to: those to whom faces are always familiar, those who seem loved. Walking toward the West Village from the subway, Amanda struggled over sidewalks clogged with protesters, then she found open space and the angry voices subsided, the city became black and glossy. Now again it's filled with substance: by these restaurant strangers who know things, who wear the correct glasses and order the right wine. She came from California unaware of these codes but now her boots are adorable fringed Qupids and last week she found a cashmere coat for an impossible four hundred dollars. Assembling oneself fashionably is far from pure vanity; it removes unwanted variables.

Brett's getup indicates he understands: better to exceed a fashion threshold and breeze in without question. Those who decry this game play others.

The hostess recognizes her. Malatesta is her go-to suggestion for many of these Internet dates.

After they sit, he shows her a thousand white teeth and says, "So we should probably get this out of the way: 'Have you been out with many people from OKCupid?'"

"Oh no," says Amanda. "You're my first. New Year's resolution."

"You're, like, my third? I should warn you, ha-ha, the others didn't go so well."

He'll tell her the other women were shallow (unlike her), or imply they were ugly (ditto). He'll work in the phrase, "real connection," look around fresh-faced as though he can't believe his luck.

After bread arrives, he asks about her work.

"Fashion accounting," she says, knowing about half of them never ask for an explanation.

He nods prettily, looking for the waiter. "Yeah, you mentioned how bored you get."

"The people I work for are psychotic. It's a Palestinian family and they're convinced everyone's a Jew who's out to get them. Today my big task was they sent me to 7-11 to fetch a banana."

"I like your laugh," Brett says.

"It's really what I did all afternoon. I took three hours to get a banana. And when I came back and the banana was half-frozen because I was carrying it around Midtown while I shopped for pantyhose and macaroons, the boss didn't comment. 'Put it on the desk over there.'"

"I guess his craving passed him by."

"It's a she, but yeah."

"Sounds pretty meaningless. Why don't you quit?"

Amanda tears a piece of ciabatta. "One of the designers and I have a plan to start our own thing. I'm making a dress now, it would knock your socks off. I mean, it's ridiculous."

"Hm. You make clothes? That's probably a pretty tough business." They order. "Hey, so your profile said…. Why don't you want kids?"

"Well, why *should* I want them? Why should that be the

default?"

"..."

"Like, wouldn't the world be better off if the default answer was no kids, and then only people who'd be terrific parents actually went the extra mile and had them?"

"I guess the biological imperative is why?"

"We overcome other imperatives. There are vegetarians."

He sips wine. "You don't like kids, I guess."

"I like them fine, and they love me. It never fails, whenever I meet someone's kids they just glom onto me. I like spending time around them. But why does that mean I should want my own?"

"But it's logical, you enjoy one of these major things in life, why wouldn't you want more of it?"

She smiles broadly, then semi-consciously covers her teeth with her lips, consuming the smile. "I guess this is really important to you?"

"No, no," Brett says. "I mean, maybe. But that's not a reason to break up just yet, right? Ha-ha. Y'know, it's flattering when an attractive woman writes me back. The ratio is ridiculous. I maybe get a reply once every twenty times I send an email? I guess I shouldn't be admitting this."

"Well, my friend was doing a profile," Amanda says. "She was nervous so she made me do one, too. I never send out emails."

His face darkens a touch.

But he's game. He talks about his job, gives her lots of eye contact. Waves of diners come and go but Amanda and Brett linger, and all the waiter's offers of Italian dessert followed by the check are for naught. She can see herself with Brett, he's cute and probably smart enough.

"This was really," he says, and kisses her.

A couple nights later she's in the kitchen at Fedora with her friends Connie and Maria. The chef is a guy Maria knows and he's treating them, throwing down plates of oysters and sweetbreads and scallops and tongue, smiling as they vamp in their fizzy dresses. They promise each other that extra trips to the gym are forthcoming, though Amanda doesn't belong to one.

She's supposed to meet Cleve87 for a first date at a nearby wine bar.

"Look at us," says Maria. They've all got their elbows on a big steel table, heads close, stabbing various dishes and giggling like a commercial. "Baby, we're fabulous!"

"The owner of this restaurant took food down to Zuccotti when people were sleeping there," Connie says. "Did you know they arrested more people on New Year's? One guy stabbed a cop's hand with some scissors."

"Amanda," says Maria, "hit us up with some thoughts about the nature of protest and the 99 percent. You're the philosopher-queen here."

"I'm the what?"

"Connie told me you read like a madwoman. And only deep stuff, like, nothing published in the last century."

Amanda takes another bite, slides into a pain-delivering version of her voice. "Well, I believe it was Kierkegaard who said, 'Don't patronize your friends, bitch.'" They laugh.

"Worst thing to come out of all this?" Maria says. "The new bankruptcy of the word 'occupy.' Like how long 'til we get a restaurant called 'Occupy Chili Cheese Fries'?"

"*That's* the worst thing?" Connie says. "Not the economy tanking or people losing their houses or the government arresting hundreds of protestors and not a single fucking stockbroker?"

"Funny to use the word bankruptcy," says their chef friend, bringing another dish.

Maria waits until Connie has forked home a slab of maple-glazed salmon then says, "Good to see you really suffering for your peeps."

Amanda receives a text from Cleve87. She doesn't usually exchange numbers before the first date, but this guy insisted. He writes >I'm here..., and she's about to be annoyed except it turns out she's already ten minutes late. She writes:

>sry. dinr w bgf in crisis. 30 mins?

There's a piqued virtual pause then he says >Sure. Her friends are still rolling around in the news, covering themselves with the scent of it.

Amanda tells them, "Sorry: I better deal with this, it's work," and clicks to her overflowing OKCupid mailbox.

She can clear out fifty unacceptable applicants in an afternoon and receive fifty more by night, to say nothing of the repeat offenders wheedling and occasionally threatening her for failure to reply. She doesn't speak about online dating to anyone who's in her actual life, but she believes this volume must be typical for any New York woman with all her teeth. Here, it seems, is the milieu that an avalanche of single men has waited for, and they are unrepentantly persistent with their "hey babes" and their "ur hots." The shirtless bathroom-mirror self-portraits, the literal transcription of bank account balances, the references to colossal genitalia...a yoke has been lifted off these men, the yoke of civilized behavior. But Amanda weeds and finds the readers and the spellers.

"I just picture Obama," Connie is saying, "furiously scribbling pardons for the bankers, a half-eaten apple browning on the desk."

"Of course I agree with the protesters' message," Maria says. "Of course the inequality is terrible. Just about everyone I know agrees. But I can't dedicate my life to being outraged, girl. When sitting around getting dirty and freezing is the only option they've got for me? I can't be frustrated every second of the day. I just can't think about it."

"That's what they want," Connie says. "That's why the system is built this way. Alienation through frustration."

"So what are you supposed to do?" says Maria.

"Well. This sounds dumb, but I was thinking of making a really big poster."

"..."

"It's something, right? I mean, better emotional support for protestors than nothing at all?"

"You're right. That sounds dumb."

"But this is really happening, right now. This is history swooshing all around us. I want to shout: 'Engage History!' Maybe that's what my poster should say."

Maria licks banana pudding off her finger. She says, "Ha, well, my engagement to Brad is history, anyway," and Connie gives her a high-five.

There's a message in Amanda's OKCupid inbox from a new guy named ReplacementsLuv. It reads: "Every new song you like, you first heard on a TV commercial." That's it. And his profile has a single picture: a close-up of a bright blue eyeball.

They ask Amanda what book she's reading now and she says, "*Fathers and Sons.* I love the really old Russians."

She skitters to the wine bar, trying not to crash to the icy sidewalk. Cleve87 sits foot-across-knee in the picture window, frowning at his phone. *(About Cleve87: "I feel life intensely, I like to express myself, and I hope to find someone similarly expressive and hopeful and hopeless and on and on.")* He's in love with his mood—New Yorkers luxuriate in their emotional weather—but when her eyes won't leave his and recognition snaps in, his face is happily surprised.

"I'm Tyler," he says. "I'd get you a glass of wine, but I don't recognize any of the kinds." He gestures helplessly at the chalkboard divided by "Bianchi" and "Rossi" and written in Italian.

"What do you like?" says Amanda. "I'll translate. I like the Tocai Friulano."

He orders two and they cluster at the bar's end. He looks at her in a way people don't look at one another in southern California—not exactly covetous, more like a false transaction: *this is what it looks like when people are connecting*—and he says, "I'm guessing you don't have to go online to find dates."

"Well, thanks."

"So…what are you?"

"…"

"I mean, are you Asian…?"

"My mom's black and my dad's white."

"All right. You don't have to look at me cross-eyed."

"I wasn't. I'm mulatto *and* blind."

He laughs. "You're gorgeous, is what you are."

She makes wet circles on the bar. He's decent-looking and confident, mildly a jackass, but he can write and talk. She doesn't need to get away yet.

"Tell me what you're thinking," he says.

"Where I live up on 121st there's a liquor store and on the door there's a saying from Benjamin Franklin: 'Beer is proof that God wants us to be happy.' And I realized that there are Franklin quotes about booze all over the city, and I started writing them down." She clicks open her phone's notepad. "'Alcohol does not drown sorrows, but waters them and helps them grow.' 'There can't be good living where there is not good drinking.' 'In wine there is wisdom, in beer there is freedom, in water there is bacteria.' 'I fear the man who drinks water and so remembers this morning what the rest of us said last night.' Seriously, I've seen every one of these."

"This is what you're thinking," says Tyler.

"You asked."

"I think I know you. You're one of those pretty girls who's secretly batshit crazy."

"So anyway," Amanda says, "I've decided I need to pick a really specific area and get super-quotable in it. Ben Franklin has alcohol, what do I have?"

"But Ben Franklin is quoted on an incredibly wide range of things. 'A stitch in time,' and all that."

"That's a good point."

"You're better off being quotable on an incredibly wide range of things."

"Well, I couldn't be gladder that I came here. I feel like my life's just gotten some real direction."

Tyler says, "How's your friend? The one in crisis?"

"Oh, I made that up," says Amanda. "Always keep 'em waiting."

"Like I said. Batshit crazy." He touches her hand. "Tell me about your job."

"It's awful and I hate it. Tell me about yours."

He does. He's an investment banker forced by the cultural climate into a defensive posture: "I won't feed you the line about wealth creation. I won't tout the perfection of the market. I admit I work in a parallel financial world that's speculative, the shadow economy that controls everything else. I admit it. But people who think money hasn't been finding other money from time immemorial…. I mean, it has. And we make the margins because we take the risks. Shit. I'm a friggin' Democrat."

She has another glass of wine and listens to him talk about his parents' boat. She says, "I'm thinking of writing an exposé about online dating."

"Oh, yeah? Been on a lot of these?"

"No. Of course not. This is the beginning of the exposé. You're my first."

"Would it be too cheesy," says Tyler, "to hope I'm your last?"

Her phone buzzes in her purse. It's an update from ReplacementsLuv. He's posted a new picture: the same blue eyeball, but now photographed from a slightly greater distance, so a dark eyebrow and shadow of a nose are visible. The accompanying message reads, "You and I are meaningless without someone watching us."

"You think I'm just some Wall Street type," Tyler says, and it's true, she does.

At home, having promised Tyler a second date, she logs into The Pirates' Lagoon. Its URL is ever-changing, but for twenty bucks a month hackers forward it via an encryption program she doesn't understand. Inside the Lagoon she can find almost any movie or song for immediate download. She spends nearly every late night in bed, watching on her laptop; the living room she shares with Kate has no TV or couch or table or chairs, and friends usually wonder aloud about such an antisocial setup, but the roommates have no need. They huddle in their respective bedrooms and are regularly jolted from half-consciousness on trips to the bathroom by a headless dressmaker's mannequin.

"Fuck The Corporate Purveyors Of Pap," reads the Lagoon's banner.

Tonight Amanda chooses *Memento*. At first it's a pleasure to be unstuck in time, recoiling from color to black-and-white. But the film's shape fades, its system of inquiries folds on itself, all is sublimated to Leonard Shelby's mental illness. Trauma has altered his brain; he can't make new memories. Amanda resists, forces herself to think about screen composition and Guy Pearce's curious mouth, but she's not disciplined enough and even if it takes the long way, her mind drifts to her mother. She curses her subconscious for selecting this film.

She dials her mother's cell. It's 11:30 p.m. in L.A. and Gloria answers right away.

"Did you go to the neurologist, mom?"

"Hi to you, too, baby. Mittens is making a speech. You hear him?"

"Don't be a crazy cat lady."

"She prides herself on her frankness," says Gloria. "None of those niceties for young Pish. She believes in cutting through cliché."

"Let me guess, you forgot the appointment."

"You're cruel to your mother, Pish. It's next Tuesday."

"You told me *this* Tuesday." Amanda blindly riffles some bedside papers. "I wrote it down."

"It expresses the depth of her feeling, dispensing with etiquette," Gloria says. "It shows how concerned."

"Lacey gives me reports, mother. I hear about the bills you

don't pay and the conversations you don't remember. I heard you forgot you already went to the supermarket. You came home with a carload of groceries two straight nights."

"Tch-tch-tch. I don't know what to tell you, Pish. The appointment is next Tuesday."

"I don't think you understand how upsetting the prospect is," Amanda says.

"Well, yes. Because in the end it's all about whether you-all are upset."

"What if I just call the doctor tomorrow?"

"..."

"Okay," Amanda says. "How's work?" Gloria works at a hospice, tending to three floors' worth of terminally ill patients.

"Been there for seven years. I'll let you know when it changes."

"Don't be annoyed with me, mom. Your daughters are worried about you. Don't be a martyr."

"This is the part in the argument where Lacey usually says it's why daddy left. She brings out the big guns."

"..."

"Tell me about you, Pish. Tell me what you do with yourself all day. You're so pretty."

And you're good, mother. You smile at brittle lady-wisps who choke on oxygen and you clean incontinent old men hours from the end.

"Your name in lights someday," says her mother.

She leaves her Wednesday lunch date with TooDrew early. *(About TooDrew: "I'm looking for something serious. Darcy and Elizabeth. Benedick and Beatrice. Westley and Buttercup. Commitment doesn't scare me.")* He's transparently sorting through his homosexuality, maybe the third such guy she's met on OKC. On the way back to work, her phone chirps and it's an email from BrettMets09; she clicks it away without reading. It's 12:30, five hours until The Brick.

In the office, she phones three retailers and walks them through their givebacks. They all love her, and don't stress when she brings discrepancies to light; it's her job to cultivate false friendships with these people, so they don't mind that she's squeezing every nickel from them in an industry that's legendarily fast-and-loose with financial details. But a design house like the one where Amanda works is always teetering on the edge of insolvency, so they need someone to keep spreadsheets and be a glorified collections agent. Today Amanda's calls are done in an hour, but the afternoon drops anchor before her. There are only so many times one can refresh Twitter or look at Craigslist for employment ideas. She clicks open a blank Word document and types:

He asked if it was me, and the experience of meeting strangers you already know is so disorienting, I didn't know what to say.

But this thought goes nowhere, so she plays Words With Friends. A graphics monkey starts humming a Beyoncé song, and crazy Ameena vaults to the outer office and rages at everyone to be quiet. She has a tyrant's tremble, a lipstick crumble on her chin. She returns hoarse to a conference call with her brothers, in which they loudly exchange accusations of profit skimming.

"Ah-*mahn*-da," she says later. "Travel agent has a package. Go get, and soy latte."

Amanda takes a cab. The sun launches muffled reflections off Fifth Avenue's distant moiré windows. Amanda finds it lovely; the driver squints. ReplacementsLuv now has posted a photo of two eyes. She can't know if it's really even him. The caption reads: "Prove your worth by killing something you love." She fetches the travel agent's packet then wears out the afternoon in the Public Library reading Turgenev and listening to a sneeze symphony.

Happy Hour finally comes and The Brick fills with rosy-cheeked aspirants who hand slips of paper to a kid behind a machine, then one-by-one step up and grab the mic. Amanda riffles the book and tells the kid to plunk down his finger, she'll sing whatever it lands on. She waits her turn, surrounded by clapping professional types whose smiles betray angst. She listens to a couple secretaries sing "We Found Love." Nobody here knows her name; when the kid queues up her song, he calls out, "Let's welcome Roxy! Roxy to the stage! Roxy please!"

She does the Janis Joplin version of "Ball and Chain," a song her dad played over and over way back when. The karaoke rendition of the screaming intro guitar is tame and foreshortened, the snare is synth, but the first time Amanda moans, "Oh-oh-woh-oh," she sees heads turn. Sweat trickles into the small of her back. She says, "Tell me why does every single little tiny thing I hold onto have to go wrong?" and makes a face, that squished face of painful love. She hits the highest part of the song without straining, the synth-drums go *bomp...bomp...bomp...* and she goes "Whoa!" between each of them, and now the crowd has dropped everything and their eyes are on her.

She brings herself up tall, nailing every inflection, grunt and groan. She howls and the guitar wails through the bridge—the solo is mostly three descending notes triggered in a weird syncopation—and then Amanda is back singing to every man in the room, and a guy close to the stage groans. The music gets quiet and she can barely hear the soundtrack because of the appreciative ruckus in here, people banging on tables and whistling and going "Yeah!" and "Whoo!" Their smiles are huge and vexed.

She presses on: doing a vibrato beyond the reach of most mortals. Mouths are agape. She feels this weird anxiety: trying to make it through the song without a mistake, while also never wanting it to end. Finally, she inhales hard and removes the governor from her voice, she could do this from six years old, just push air as hard as it can go up through her chest and somehow her voice never breaks. She looks at the Exit sign and says, *"Someone tell me why love is just like a ball and chain!"* The eight-bar blues thump to their conclusion and the applause gets thick, but Amanda sustains the final note.

Then it's over and the karaoke kid goes, "Roxy, everybody! Put your hands together for Roxy!"

She's a little dizzy, but she grins and does a mock-curtsy getting down off the tiny stage. A couple people touch her shoulders. Someone says, "My face just melted off. She just *melted my face off.*" Amanda feels the wet thicket of her hair and slips through the crowd, toward the front door. The further she goes, these well-dressed office types are less aware that she's the killer who just sang. She finds her coat and steps out into the freezing, then walks partway into an alley and everything is too big, she just weeps and weeps.

Manhattan's zeitgeist through the rest of January switches over to Occupy nostalgia. On almost every first date, the guy either asks if she's a protest hippie—in a peasant skirt and little makeup she absolutely can look the part—or, more commonly, he admits he regularly passes by Zuccotti Park and regrets seeing it barricaded. For her part, Amanda rarely ventures below SoHo, but it's difficult not to have an opinion. There seems to be a groundswell, a hypothesis even among cynics that it's possible many New Yorkers won't let go of their outrage. Yes, her more conservative suitors revel in the left's fractured causes, but even they sniff the air and fret that inertia may no longer be on their side. Weirdly, this is more present in January than it was in the fall. It sticks around for days and weeks, people wondering, "Why doesn't somebody *do* something about the injustice? Throw the assholes in jail! They fucked the economy!" When the Zuccotti barricades do come down, hundreds of protesters try and camp anew but are arrested in droves. Everybody knows someone who's been arrested. A Hispanic kid who looked great in his OKC pictures but has a big belly tells Amanda, "What would they do if we choked off their supply of expensive shoes and sports coats? Would they be able to look at themselves in the mirror? I'm waiting for something big to happen."

ReplacementsLuv's photos have stopped just above the mouth. If it's really him, he's young with a premature widow's peak and a straight nose, and by any measure would be considered gorgeous. His aphorisms come every few days, though she's never once written back; she imagines he's carpet-bombing every female in the 18 to 24 demographic, looking for takers. He says, "I'm alone in life because most of the time I can't find my phone" and "Love is a rear-screen projection theater" and "I should write a song that takes 24 hours to perform about what it feels like to be alienated all day" and "You're supposed to care about other people, but do you?" Every morning in the shower she squeezes out a caterpillar of apricot facial scrub, but there's still a lot left. Cool, she thinks, I don't have to get more for a while. *These* aren't the days that count. *This* isn't quite yet my life. There's lots of facial scrub left.

She's under her comforter watching Bresson's *A Man Escaped* and it's probably 3 a.m. in the deadest, darkest pit of winter, with the apartment's heat coming at a trickle. There's a sound outside her bedroom door, nothing, just a little creak. But it extends. It becomes a *creeeeeeeeeak*. It slips lightly into murderer territory: possibly one of the Internet boys she's blown off, ready to produce a reckoning. Violence lurks at the edges of every such date, the blind trust and the excitement at savage possibilities. She's in the process of dismissing her paranoia when the bedroom door actually clearly slowly begins to open.

"Get away!" Amanda says. "Get out! Get out! Get away!"

"Ah! Jesus!" It's Kate. "Sorry! I was sure you weren't here! You're never here! Sorry!"

"What do you mean?" says Amanda. "I'm always here."

"Sorry, your phone was ringing on the stove. I looked and it's your sister. I figured you forgot it, wherever you go."

"I'm here. I think I'm usually here."

Chubby Kate is wearing a Jack's Oyster House t-shirt over thermal underwear, and she extends the phone as though it's made of ice. Each woman teeters on the faltering annoyance of strangers in close quarters.

"Hi, Lacey," Amanda says into the phone. "I'm sorry," she tells Kate. "I didn't mean to yell like that."

"No, I'm sorry," and Kate is backing out, "I scared you. I just...."

"It's mom," says Lacey. "She lost her car."

The ceiling in Amanda's room drops several inches. She's entirely alone. "Where?"

"She doesn't black out," says her sister. "She doesn't lose time. She says it's like a window shade, Pish. The thing that happened is just through the window but she can't see."

"Did you find the car?"

Lacey is crying. "You went first," she says. "You disappeared first. Now here goes mom."

"Come on," says Amanda. "Don't exaggerate. I'm here. I'm still here." But the truth is that Amanda really *is* in the process of erasing California from her life. She's not sure she wants this to happen, but it is, as she skates above New York. If she's honest, maybe she doesn't want to hear these updates about her mother.

"What else can they take away?" says Lacey. "What else do I have that they want?"

"We don't know anything for sure," Amanda says. "The brain scans didn't show anything, right?"

"But that's not necessarily good, Pish. They diagnose Alzheimer's early based on ruling other stuff out."

"But her doctors aren't sure of anything. That's what you said, remember? They want to do a spinal tap? And there are a couple other specialists? That's what you said."

"I know she's afraid. She's worried she'll be locked in there alone, inside her own head."

Amanda's laptop goes dark, taking the bedroom with it. "You're the good daughter," she says. "You're there, and you gave her a grandson. She recognizes Max, right?"

"She recognizes everyone, is what I'm trying to say. You don't know what it's like. I'm not describing it very well. Dad was the asshole and she's always been the rock. How can she forget an entire phone call, Pish? Or whether she opened a letter?"

"..."

"First him, then you, now her," Lacey says.

"You have your own family now."

"You say that mean. You say that like it's a weapon against me."

"Of course not," says Amanda. "God, who wouldn't want what you have? Great husband, beautiful kid."

"You wouldn't."

"That's crazy. Don't throw all your self-doubt shit onto me, Lace."

"I'm trapped, too!" says her sister. "Oh, my God. I'm trapped, too." This could all disappear. Amanda wants to write it all down and have a million people read it. Then it wouldn't really be happening.

"Calm," she says. "A little distance. A little remove. Just the next thing, the thing right in front of your face."

Lacey blows her nose. "Jesus Christ, Pish. That's what the Nazis said."

A few days later she goes out with ConsciousChoice. *(About ConsciousChoice: "Living as though you're not connected to others is the ultimate trap of the 21st century. It's seductive to imagine it's just you, but it doesn't get you anywhere.")* It's a Sunday afternoon date and he suggests they meet at Thunder Jackson's on Bleecker which paints him as a sports-loving doof, but Amanda can go with the flow. She foregoes her cashmere coat for a cheap parka, ties her hair back and for half-an-hour stands in a crowd on the southbound A. In tunnels she watches her swaying reflection and bites her lips; in stations her fingers remain interlaced around the overhead bar as others play musical chairs.

"Man, you look really young," he tells her when she steps into the crowded bar. It's an exposed-brick place overwhelmed by wall knickknacks, with many flatscreens and a big sign recommending that real men order "Das Boot": ninety-six ounces of beer in a boot-shaped flagon. Her date has dark hair and eyes, an asymmetric smile and big shoulders. He's not fully handsome, but has a skittish cuteness that probably slays the ladies. Their online flirtation was brief—Amanda has mostly lost patience for long email exchanges—but she can tell he's smart. He's a PolySci grad student at NYU, and cultivates the sloppy flannel grace that accrues living from financial aid check to financial aid check.

"Thanks," she says, putting her jacket on a chairback and placing her long fingers on the table between them. She realizes she can't remember his real name.

"Wow, and you're really pretty. How many online dates have you gone on?"

"You're my first."

His forehead wrinkles. "I just ordered a beer. Sorry it's crowded: big game, Bulls-Heat. You probably remember I'm from Chicago."

"I like the Warriors."

"C'mon, I thought you were an L.A. girl," he says.

"My dad lives in the Bay Area."

He says, "Wow, you're more into sports than I am." Something happens in the game, and the bar raves. Dopes slap five all around them. "Yeah," he says, "I'm kind of a Bulls fan, but I don't really care. I like the wings here."

"I'm really not that into it, either," says Amanda. "I do sometimes watch Sharks games on the computer late at night, but usually to fall asleep. I was just fluffing up my street cred. You caught me."

He laughs, too much and a little unhinged, also trying to impress.

"You go to grad school right around here," she says.

"Yeah, like, pfft, three blocks that way."

"I didn't finish college. I might go back."

"Whatever," he says, "that's cool. It's overrated."

"I started at UCLA. But I had to get out. My best friend moved to New York. She went back home within a year, and I stayed."

He nods and looks around the room, and she wants him to say *don't worry about it, you're obviously smart and it sounds like you've got a good job in a terrible economy, it's clear you've done really well for yourself even without a degree.* The game heats up around them again, the crowd makes talking impossible, Amanda feels lost in here but then looks at ConsciousChoice (what *is* his name?) and knows she could kiss him unexpectedly if she wanted to and he'd respond, she can see it in his desperate edge, and this makes her feel warm and connected.

"Your profile was refreshing," he says. "It's nice not to have a woman write about *Twilight*, reality TV and *Fifty Shades of Grey*."

And this serves as enough praise, she's sufficiently differentiated from the pack, and she orders wings and laughs at this guy's jokes and thinks about what art film she'll watch in bed tonight.

But after they've eaten and the game is over, ConsciousChoice says, "Let's go up to the park. You must've heard about what happened in Oakland?"

"..."

"Protesters were trying to convert an abandoned building into a community center, totally peaceful, and the police came and fired tear gas and rubber bullets at them. Arrested four hundred. It's bullshit." For the first time tonight, he's dropped the hambone act aimed at getting into Amanda's pants. "A bunch of Occupy folks here are getting together in the park."

This news hasn't filtered through her baroque and compartmented life. Her father does live with his second wife in the Maxwell Park section of Oakland. But last summer Amanda woke up and realized how badly he'd treated Gloria those years ago, and how much it must hurt that Amanda continued to have a relationship with him after he ran out. The cheating that finally ended the marriage, the missed alimony and child support, the lies he still routinely told: all at once it felt disloyal to talk to him on the phone or go up for visits. Gloria didn't say a word, but Amanda hasn't spoken to him in months.

She follows ConsciousChoice up Sullivan Street.

Inside Washington Square Park a guy is waving a huge American flag, a drum circle has settled near the arch, and dozens of people are wandering around taking pictures and videos. Chants cycle into one another like a campfire game: "Bloomberg! Beware! Zuccotti Park is everywhere!" and "Whose park? Our park! Whose park? Our park!" and "New York is Oakland! Oakland is New York!" and to the growing population of police: "You're sexy! You're cute! Take off your riot suit!" Amanda puts on her wool hat, pushes her hands deep in her pockets, and shadows

ConsciousChoice through the crowd. He hugs several protesters hello, shouts encouragement. His apartment must be somewhere nearby and in the flashing discord and freezing cold she finds herself amenable to following him there. If he suggests it, she'll go. She smiles at the thought (it would be that easy) and looks at him in profile, then consumes the smile with her lips, wondering if he feels her acquiesce.

Someone in a letterman's jacket stands on a barrel and yells, and now they're all walking north on Fifth Avenue: probably three hundred protesters and half as many shepherding cops. Some chanting persists and there's lots of irritated chatter, but by far the loudest noises are police sirens screaming at contradictory frequencies as in Amanda's nightmare of a terrorist attack.

In front of a Food Emporium police surround a woman and shove her to the sidewalk as other protesters yell and curse and whoop. This causes ten policemen to start screaming "Get back!" and Amanda sees a leather glove as it approaches her chest, it's on her left breast and she's staring at it, and then it's gone and she's part of a retreating faction, pushed by these cops with their angry faces flashing red and blue. ConsciousChoice is here, too, yelling, "Who do you serve! Who do you serve!" and he looks demented, enraged, he's swinging a bottle and it comes out of his hand and clocks an officer across the face, the officer goes down and his brethren go wild. A nightstick is in the air above them, and it lands on Amanda's shoulder. Somehow she keeps moving, running away, hands still in her pockets. She thinks she's lost ConsciousChoice, he must be down on the pavement getting cuffed, but no, here he is, swearing, pointing, spitting. The cops have focused their ire on someone else, are punching and kicking an innocent man inside a tight circle while Amanda and ConsciousChoice cross to the west side of Fifth Avenue and blend with a different wave of protesters. Amanda's left shoulder throbs. She watches ConsciousChoice's wild eyes. The people around them take a right on 13th, so they do, too.

Every block or so, the sidewalk becomes impassable when a new beef starts: police reach into the crowd and remove someone, the milling ski-hatted hundreds go "Whoop! Whoop! Whoop!" and epithets fly again. ConsciousChoice tries to force his way forward; Amanda keeps by his side. Her left arm is numb. When she's shoved, she shoves back. The police are rough. But she feels pretty good and doesn't know why. She wants to be a faceless part of this angry mob and also wants to be plucked out and polished.

"No more police brutality!" they chant, yet so many of them are doing everything they can to provoke it. The cops funnel them south, down Second Avenue, they've been walking for what seems like more than an hour but are just blocks from where they began. Amanda sees two non-cops beating the hell out of one another, as one of them screams, "Snitch! Snitch! He's taping this for the cops!" and the other says through bloody teeth, "Are you being serious? I'm not a snitch!" A baby-faced cop sneers into Amanda's face and says, "Get a job," and someone behind her says, "There are no jobs! That's what this is about!" There's a loud pop-pop-popping sound that makes everyone duck their heads, but it's apparently far-off firecrackers. A girl screams and Amanda sees her being dragged away backwards by her hair.

They reach Tompkins Square, where somebody is strumming a mandolin among the shrieks and rage. There's a plywood fence blocking a condemned building and a guy in a black parka decides to scale it, which again sets the cops scrambling into the crowd to yank him down as he says, "Fuck the police! Fuck the police!" A low-flying helicopter shines a spotlight on them all. The guy in the black parka falls into the middle of the street and has twenty people taking his picture while ten policemen punch him. Amanda wants to run out there and jump on someone's back, start clawing.

"Why do you do it?" says ConsciousChoice.

She looks around. A fat bearded guy walks past, gawking at her, but she confirms that it's actually ConsciousChoice talking.

He says, "Why are you lying?"

"What?"

"This obviously isn't the first online date you've been on." They're inside Tompkins Square Park and it's past 10 o'clock and the protesters are spread out in this larger space. Without her realizing, he's walked her into a dark corner. "Why are you a tease? You just like to fuck with guys' heads?"

"Wait, what are you saying to me?"

ConsciousChoice wears a glassy venomous expression. "I've met girls like you."

Amanda is tall and strong. Law enforcement is everywhere. But her eyes excavate, desperate to discover he's kidding. "This was great," she says. "Quite an adventure."

"I'm serious, why do you do it?" he says. "I know I'll never see you again. I knew it the first five minutes I met you. You were nice to me, but you weren't really there."

"..."

"I mean, why go to the trouble? Just to have random guys tell you how pretty you are?"

"I think you should get away from me," Amanda says.

He wedges a hand into the pocket of his tight jeans and comes out with a knife. He opens the blade.

"Who knows you're here?" he says.

Many people are still in the park, and dozens of cops still loiter outside it, but nobody is close enough. If she calls for help and he's intent on cutting her, he'll have time.

"Your girlfriends are all waiting by their phones," says ConsciousChoice, "waiting to hear about the loser you made a fool of. Do you set up a conference call with them, or do you like telling the story over and over? 'Omigosh, so, he was *so* poor. You should see how he dresses! And his breath was terrible and he thought he was *so funny!*'"

Amanda won't say anything else. She looks at his hand. The blade is matte gray, not shiny, and that makes it seem more dangerous. He isn't shaking.

"'And get this, girls! He took me to a *rally*! I mean who the fuck *rallies* anymore, that's like *so* six months ago! It was pathetic, him and his buddies think they can *change* things.'"

She makes several backward steps but he follows, getting closer. He's three feet away and moving. The knife is right here. Her shoulder aches.

"Tell me how many guys.... No, that can wait. You can tell me later. Let's go someplace less crowded."

She doesn't know anything about violence. Houses get burgled where she grew up in West Hills, and there were gangs around during high school, but Amanda never saw a gun. A friend of Lacey's boyfriend got stabbed, but that was over in North Hollywood. But of course all the little California sun bunnies were programmed by formative years of rape whistles and Jennifer Lopez movies, and knew the larger world hid brutality. Standing here gives her a sense of cultural déjà vu. She's padded by her parka. Would one slash get through to her skin?

"Now. Let's go."

Amanda puts up her arms. She thinks she can smell him. She walks a few steps, getting a few extra feet away from him, then sprints. A few hundred feet away stand three grim cops and she runs for them. She was a hurdler at good old El Camino Real and she still runs around the reservoir a couple times a week and terror is a powerful motivator, the asphalt and brick are slippery and she thinks if she'd worn boots instead of sneakers she might already be dead. The pain in her shoulder tricks her into believing a knife has struck. It's a very young fear, a very familiar fear, knowing someone is gaining on you. That fucking mandolin is still playing.

She sees the cops seeing her, one of them puts his hand on his gun. She looks behind and nobody is there. ConsciousChoice isn't chasing, isn't even standing in that dark corner anymore. Her arms and legs go loose and she slows herself like a sprinter. One of the cops says, "Gold medal, honey," and she grins, then eats the grin. It seems impossible there was a knife at all. It seems impossible ConsciousChoice exists. Her breath comes fast; she wants to laugh but finds herself scowling.

Monday morning drops like a bank safe. She's at work, in the same chair, with the same drones pretending to design clothes seated all around her. Jennifer, her best friend in the office, has left for India to be with her husband's dying father, but the truth is Amanda probably wouldn't tell Jennifer anyway. And she hasn't contacted the police.

She opens the Word document and types:

This is probably where online dating was always going for me. What am I but a Jane Doe waiting for a name? But I ran, didn't I? I saw the knife and I ran. That's better. That's more like it. It's not just the "vulgarly mediocre" that repels me.

She saves the document and hides it in a folder among some work spreadsheets.

Ameena calls her into the big office and says, "Ah-*mahn*-da. Last Friday when you drive Jemal to school, does he tell you about his new girlfriend?"

"No. He didn't say anything."

"I see him with a little kike girl. When I pick him up, I see him."

"He's in fifth grade, Ameena. He's ten years old."

"They fuck too young now. If he fucks this little kike girl, I cut his throat."

Amanda shifts weight to one hip and folds her arms. The unreality of the street far below, its ping and whistle, makes her cold. The rally last night never happened, the knife never happened (but her shoulder is killing her, she wears a purple mark across her back like an ink blot), and the double-parked UPS truck down there and the jaywalkers streaming around it...are they real? Something bangs in her brain: Amanda misses something that hasn't come into her life yet. If she didn't have that, she'd have nothing.

Back at her desk, an email from ReplacementsLuv awaits her. She clicks his screen name and for the first time sees his entire face. He's maybe even younger than she expected, but he's amazing: brown hair high in the front, blue eyes, dark stubble, full lips in a half-sneer. She aches for him. But she doesn't read his message.

She blinks her eyes and is home. There's a note from Kate on the counter: "Going to play at the Grand Mal. You should come."

She blinks again and is shivering naked under a comforter. She's humming something but can't tell what song it is. She tries to let herself follow the melody but her awareness dissolves it. She puts her cold hands on her stomach.

The phone rings. It's Lacey.

"Pish? Hello? Pish?"

"I'm here."

"It's the best news! Mom just came from another specialist and she doesn't have Alzheimer's. He doesn't think so, anyway. He's seen it before, Pish: a person who has so much pain at work, who has to block it out in order to function. At the hospice mom sees a dozen people die in a week, and she has to be there for them and hold their hands, and to not go crazy she turns off a piece of her brain. To, like, keep the grief from swallowing her up. And sometimes people who have jobs like that get a side effect, which is you start forgetting other things, too. It carries over into the rest of your life. You start forgetting little things, big things, and remember how her brain doesn't really show any signs of disease, right? They got the spinal tap back and that's clean, too. This explains it. I'm making her quit. I'm making her move in with us.

She'll be fine!"

Amanda knows the song she was humming: Elvis doing "You'll Never Walk Alone."

"Are you supposed to get snow there tomorrow? We were just sitting here watching the Weather Channel."

Amanda exhales hard, filling the connection with white sound.

THREE DAYS OF ZINC

Sebastian never sleeps past six. His apartment always fills early with sunlight, and living on the last northerly polyp of Kingston Avenue—pressed between Fulton and Atlantic—means a morning thrash-metal serenade of dumpster hoists and hydraulic brakes. But it isn't the noise or light that wakes him. It's ambition. It's fear of a limited lifetime.

As he drinks coffee, he hears Randall Davies ascend the four flights. He looks through the hole in his front door where an eyepiece must once have been: Davies surveys the landing with a rictal twitch, the gesture of a man who's climbed at least a few rungs above Sebastian's, but remembers. He opens the door, shakes Davies' hand.

"Thanks for doing this so early," Davies says.

Sebastian leads them to the kitchenette table, avoiding a moldering spot in the floor through which he may one day plummet. His parents would pay for a better apartment, but Sebastian refuses. Davies places his phone between them, presses record.

"I want to talk to you about backlash," he says.

"Ha-ha, okay," says Sebastian.

"Let me play you a song." Davies pops a MacBook from his messenger bag. There's a driving syncopated drum pattern and a thick wall of synth, then a familiar man sings:

Look at that chin
Solo rocker kid
He'll get you a tab
Enough to lay you low
We're out here for years
Solo rocker kid
Whose chord did you take
Whose chord did you blow?

"What do you think?" says Davies.

"So I recognize Evan's voice," Sebastian says over more of the song. "That's what he's doing with Disapproving Dog? Writing songs about me?"

"The younger man doesn't react. Equanimity is his game." The song continues:

Comb my white hair
Like the waves blown back
The solo rocker kid
The chord is a snack

Sebastian says, "If Evan Seitz wants to write about me, I guess that's flattering. It sounds like a great record."

"Were you groomed for public relations?" says Davies. "How old are you really?"

"Ha-ha, I'm 22," Sebastian says, but this is a lie. He's 19.

"C'mon, give me something. The guy is calling you out. I'm writing about a feud, it doesn't make great copy if one of the sides won't play."

Sebastian bares his teeth. "You're writing about a feud?"

"Hey, it's what people like reading. How many stories can someone do about a wunderkind? 'I took the C to Bed-Stuy and got a tour of the Great Young Man's apartment. Wow, he has lots of musical instruments!' Yawn, Sebastian. Just: yawn."

"Um, okay. You want me to say something bad about Disapproving Dog, but I really like them. They're awesome."

"Do you understand why Evan is pissed off at you?"

"I don't know the guy," says Sebastian. "I respect his band a lot. They make great music."

Davies inhales. His website is important; most anything with an electronic edge that comes out of Brooklyn breaks with Davies. He wrinkles his nose. "All right, you leave me no choice. The proverbial big guns." He stops recording, shuffles for a sound file, and puts his phone close to Sebastian.

It's an interview with Evan Seitz: "I wrote it because little shits like Sebastian Torque don't pay their dues. Seriously, I don't want to play the old-guy card or whatever, like, I'm only 28. But it's about experience. There's a reason people pay their dues. It's so when success comes, they know what the fuck to do with it? So they know how to treat people, so they know how to write another good song, so they know where they should play. In some ways 'Chord' is a pretty good song, right? It's a sellout, but it's all right. But he doesn't know what to do with himself. He got his record deal. Awesome. But I don't fucking wanna hear that record. Because he just flashed outta nowhere, man, nobody really knows him. What other songs does he have? He's a pretty boy. He gets a deal without working hard, because of one sellout song and how he looks, and isn't that what's been wrong with music forever? It's not that big a deal, so I just…I wrote 'Solo Rocker Kid' about it."

Davies touches the phone again, and Seitz's voice stops.

"It's jealousy," Davies says. "He's being a little dick."

Sebastian knows his face has pinkened but his smile doesn't break. "I guess he's right, ha-ha. I guess I'm a fraud." He taps the table with the long fingernails of his right hand.

Davies sighs. "You thought I was coming here to talk with you about genre-busting and how you're making sounds with, like, spoons and chainsaws for your new record. Sorry, man. That won't cut it. I know what people want."

"I can't work up the hate," says Sebastian. "I can't help how another guy feels."

"Sebastian, this is the world you're in, my man. Who do you think High Lawn expects to buy your record when it comes out? Do they think you're Top 40?" He thinks about this. "Well, hell, maybe they do. But I know one thing: at the very least, they expect you to win over Seitz's audience, and my readership. If you can't, you're fucked. And that means you can't let Seitz paint you as an opportunistic pussy. It's what people will start thinking about you, I've seen it happen."

Sebastian laughs. "That was a great speech, man."

Davies packs up his laptop and phone, shaking his head.

Sebastian insists they have coffee together.

"Whoa," Davies says, "that's officially dark roast."

"Campo Alegre beans. A buddy of mine told me how amazing they are."

"You ever get up to Blue Bottle in Williamsburg?"

"Oh, yeah, God. It's awesome, right?"

A girl down on Kingston is shouting someone's name, like she's calling a lost dog. But there are no lost dogs around here and this girl is supposed to be in school. Last year a maintenance worker was raped cleaning the toilets in St. Andrew's Playground.

"All right, shoot," Davies says. "While I'm here you might as well tell me about the record. How's it going?"

"Who do you know at High Lawn?" Sebastian says.

"Oh, Butch and Jody, nobody down the line."

"Then it's going slow. Ha. In fact, I was pretty blocked until you came up here and suggested spoons and chainsaws. That's gonna be my big breakthrough, I think."

"Play me something?"

Sebastian feels vindicated for not having dished about Evan Seitz. He gets up and toggles through a couple files on his four-track: he's absolutely not ready to let anyone hear this stuff, but doesn't he always feel that way? He says, "Every song is perfect until it goes in someone's ears."

"Is that the title?"

"No. A philosophy, I guess."

Sebastian clicks play, and cranks up the speakers. His instruments are scattered around him as in a blast radius.

The song is really just a bed, a landing spot for a second melody he hasn't constructed yet. It drives hard, and has a wild edge Sebastian loves. There are no lyrics. The drums are Styrofoam peanuts popping between fingers. His apartment floor tremors as a synth grumble lifts through two octaves. Let them try and call this a sellout.

"What is that!" Davies says.

"What's what!"

"That chirping sound at the edges! It's cool!"

Sebastian leans toward an immaculate bookshelf, comes back with a metal guitar pick that he's snipped with metal shears. It scrapes the strings twice, and with the distortion just right makes his battered Tele squeak. He switches the four-track off. "It goes on like that for a while."

"Good stuff, Sebastian."

"It's not really a song."

"It will be," Davies says. "And not some shit Top 40 dance thing, either. My teeth hurt listening to it. That's a good sign."

"Your teeth?"

"Oh, they're rarely wrong. I have a buddy whose hobby is, get this, collecting illustrations depicting all the great classical music riots."

"Okay."

"Stravinsky's *Rite of Spring* is the one I recall, it was so intense audience members started punching one another and throwing things at the orchestra. He has a Wagner and a Strauss. Some Belgians in the 1830s apparently got so riled up by an opera they poured out into the streets and overthrew the king."

"..."

"My point being: musical orthodoxy. Pthhhht. Anyway, Seitz is wrong, man, 'Chord' isn't a pretty good song. It's better than that."

"Well, thanks, Mr. Davies. Thank you. I do sometimes think that song's a little bit of a curse. Even though I know you wouldn't be up here without it. High Lawn wouldn't ever have heard my name."

"What I hope for you," Davies says, "is that you don't get lured into the pop side of things, like, latch onto the idea that because 'Chord' has that hooky part, it means you have to keep recreating that to go mainstream. I mean, there's no formula obviously. But hearing what you just played me is heartening. Nobody will mistake that for a pop song."

Sebastian smiles and nods.

"But I guess I should get going. Don't want to stand in the way of the whiz kid."

"Oh, it's fine," says Sebastian.

"Make noise, young man." This is the tagline of Davies' website, and Sebastian wonders whether he's supposed to think it's really classy that he'd quote it now. "When's the record due to High Lawn?"

"..."

"Ah. Then I really should get going. Unfortunately I have to run what Seitz says about you. It's just too good, and you didn't exactly defend yourself. But I don't want your feelings to get hurt when you read it, okay? I'm rooting for you."

"When will you be writing it up?" says Sebastian, as they drift to the front door.

"Probably not today. And my wife has this thing…. I guess not until Monday."

"Three days."

"Oh, Jesus, don't worry. High Lawn won't care."

"…"

"Smile, Sebastian. Evan Seitz knows you've got more talent in your little finger…."

Alone again, Sebastian looks at his Kross synth and hates it, then hates himself for hating it. The rest of Friday and the weekend sprawl before him and no matter what Davies says, Monday will be hard on him. He doesn't take criticism well. He'd like to murder Seitz. He suffers many moments like this, wishing he'd never thought up "Chord," wishing he'd tried in high school and gone to college, wishing he was home for winter break in Oradell with nothing more stressful on his mind than a Friday night trying to scrounge pot from garage mechanics. Instead he's got blood pressure like a day trader and a perpetually sour stomach.

He brushes his teeth, flosses, takes his Zoloft and Wellbutrin, then lines up a pill each from his vitamin bottles: Flaxseed Oil, C, D, B-complex and zinc. For the fifth or sixth day in a row he shakes the zinc bottle and notes that it's nearly empty; today he turns it over, counts three tablets in his palm. The Foodtown on Fulton doesn't have vitamins. He'll have to make a trip to GNC: a three-quarter-mile walk, which for some reason seems frivolous and anxiety-provoking. Three days of zinc until he has to make that walk. He swallows one of the pills.

He showers and blow-dries, spends a good while picking out an English Laundry dress button-down, then throws on a tie and vest. He's humming something and wondering whether lyrics are coming to him; dressing well is kind of an Aspergian twitch, a well-worn groove that seems to pull music from him. There's a blurry overlap between thinking about clothes and thinking about songs. He hums more, trying to get lost mulling over the day's pair of sweet Naigai socks.

He fires up an amp and his battered little TASCAM that someone sold him for twenty bucks when he was 16 and plugs in the Tele. Lyrics come from mood, but mood comes from chords. He might figure progressions on the Kross' keyboard or this guitar, a necessary and somewhat mathematical first step. Many of his compositions wind up with a wall-of-sound sheen and no recognizable chord progressions, but Sebastian takes pride that they all begin this way. He doesn't use headphones. He just blasts away, and lets the neighbors complain.

Today he cranks it up and loses himself for an hour in fuzzed-out treble. Then he takes the TASCAM recorder into bed and listens back. When he finds a bit he likes, he bounces it to a new track, might loop it or slow it down, looking for something cool. He has dozens and dozens of such fragments and ideas, which will presumably come together and comprise his first record. Tony from High Lawn wants to hear something soon, but the label only gave Sebastian a thousand dollars up front, so it's not like they're holding an axe over his head. But it's been since the beginning of December. Six weeks. Sebastian doesn't have a single finished song.

In a silent space between recorded guitar noodles, he hears pounding on his apartment door. He checks his phone, sees several missed texts from Jack Dooley, the last of which indicates he's coming over.

"Yup!" Sebastian says. "Hold on!"

Here's Jack, chubby with a wood crucifix around his neck, wiping steam from his granny glasses with the tail of his black t-shirt, rosy-cheeked and full of pep. His rockabilly hair is a couple inches shorter than Sebastian's. He blinks like a myopic mouse and hums something, then he says, "No, no, don't bother answering your phone."

"Working. You should look into it."

Jack changes to whistling, pacing around the apartment like he's doing an inspection.

"Jesus," Sebastian says, "what are you whistling?"

"'Love Today.' Mika."

"Ugh. C'mon man, I'm trying to write."

Jack says, "You know that song was in a commercial for an Indonesian energy drink? Ha. Are we eating? Waffles at the T-Cup?"

"Seriously. You're trying to give me brain cancer, coming up here with a song like that."

"It can't all be Velvet Underground or whatever, dude."

"You never listened to a Velvet Underground song in your life."

"That's because I'm not a hundred years old."

Sebastian steps to the keyboard and plays "La Campanella." It's really loud and he's screwing around, his right hand back and forth across intervals, but he's also showing off, he's a showoff, he can't stop himself and he hates the disingenuousness of it. Jack is looking at something down on Kingston, waiting. Sebastian stops the Liszt mid-chord and says, "What's on the agenda for tonight?"

"What's the difference, man? You won't come. Q Lounge. Joymill opening for Inappropriate Uncle."

"Isn't that place a little stabby?"

"'A Little Stabby,'" says Jack. "Now, *that's* a song title alert. Joymill should be headlining. They use that phaser sound. I don't know how they do that. It sounds twisted and wrong, it's so great."

Sebastian hits a button on the Kross, pretending it's an accident. A snippet he saved last week bangs the room: pure techno, a wild synth hook over a dance beat. This is how he knows his desperation's depth, this solicitation for an opinion.

"Jesus," Jack says, "what the fuck are you, a Black Eyed Pea?"

He makes himself smile. "*You* are."

Jack prepares a white line on the kitchenette table and ducks his head. Sebastian knows he's here to share.

"Let me ask you this," says Jack. "Why the fuck do people still make music videos? I mean, someone sent me a link to a fucking Maroon 5 video and I didn't know what it was, and I clicked on it. Talk about brain cancer."

Sebastian looks at the little bag of speed, wavering. Knowing it's no use. "You answered your own question," he says. "They make videos for the links. They make videos so people can look them up on YouTube." He comes to the table, ducks his own head, and bumps. "By the way, what a snob you are."

"Top 10 bands that give people brain cancer," says Jack. "Go."

"Naw, I don't want to play."

"What a saint! What a saint! Mumble-mumble. You got the anxiety, Mr. Torque. It's written all over that vein in your forehead. It's February and you still ain't got no songs. I'll play for both of us: Nicki Minaj. Sugababes. LMFAO. Design the Skyline. *Maroon*

Fucking 5!"

Sebastian feels the kick. His mouth is drier than the heart of a haystack. Jack is an idiot. He needs to be alone so he can focus. There's something deep and good in the clip he played Davies this morning, and this upbeat dance riff might blend in well, but they're really both beds for melodies, maybe a snippet of the Liszt étude?, but no that's stupid. A guitar bit he just recorded on the TASCAM, maybe a simple D-G-A progression with a few flourishes…he's sure other musicians don't work this way, everyone else is more natural than he is, they don't have to turn themselves inside out like this. Jack is a bass player and probably doesn't have these self-eating torture sessions. He just plays. Sebastian envies him, understands it's this lack of hesitation that leads to Jack's glibness, which in turn endears him to an incredible number of club owners, promoters, bouncers, bartenders and sound guys, as well as Sebastian himself. Jack's not an idiot at all. He just doesn't have such a hard time metabolizing the world.

"I'm working on this idea for a song," Sebastian says. For an hour, Jack tries to get him to come for waffles, then leaves.

Late Friday night Sebastian is hunched over the MacBook his parents gave him when they heard "Chord" on NPR. He's trying to make GarageBand purr. He scratches back and forth over a seven-second clip more than a hundred times until he can't hear it any longer, and its components become industrial: a jigsaw through steel, a sheet-metal punch, some spark-throwing lathe. He's beholden! The excitement of having crafted a vaguely popular song is done. It's choking him now, and the only escape is making High Lawn happy. He needed the money. He doesn't work in clubs to pay rent on this awful apartment. Death never feels so close as in these wee hours with ambition roiling around him like a sarin cloud.

Now he doesn't even see the screen, all his thoughts find the same axis: hatred.

He records keyboard chords over the Tele shredding. He tries integrating the Liszt étude but gives up on it.

He types. For a moment he believes lyrics are coming out of him, but no. Instead he writes: "Kill what you love, love what you kill."

He opens a web browser and pastes this sentence into dozens of OKCupid pages, broadcasting to dozens of single women he finds attractive. Then he takes another picture of himself, revealing a bit more of his face, and posts it. He never checks to see if they've written him back.

He falls asleep and dreams a song and it comes so easy. He's on a beach lounger in his parents' backyard and birds splay into the wind and neither gain nor lose ground. With a similar wobbly grace the song descends into his ears, the whole thing right there effortless. Sebastian is weepingly happy. But then night creates day. When the Bed-Stuy morning symphony begins anew and he sits up at 6 a.m. Saturday, the song is gone, a ghostly taunt delivered by the world's real geniuses.

Tina calls at eight. "Can you come visit this weekend?" she says.

"We'll see, mom."

"I know what that means."

"I have a radio thing this morning."

"What station? What time can we listen?"

"They're just recording it," he says, "I don't know when it airs. But it doesn't matter, it's a podcast, too."

"We could come into the city," says his mother. "I can convince dad."

"I can't. I'm working on something."

"You know what you sound like," she says. "You sound like the boy with something to hide from the people who love him."

"Come on, I like hanging out with you. I want to finish this song by Monday. I at least want one song to give them. It's turning into a whole thing."

"What is?"

"I mean, there's this guy who's writing a story and I'm in it, and I don't think it'll be very flattering. And if High Lawn sees this story and I still haven't given them anything...."

"Not very flattering. I can't believe that."

"That's because you're a great mother, and you're not supposed to see my flaws."

"Uh-oh," she says. "When you start in with the praise is a big warning sign."

"Anyway, think of it like a deadline."

"Except it's not."

"Everything's really good," says Sebastian. "What could be wrong?"

His mother waits a long time, and says, "Are you still taking your meds?"

And pow, it's like there's a sun in place of his water-stained ceiling. Everything dies in the unfairness of its heat. It's nearly two years since he's had a single problem, two years since he couldn't get out of bed and couldn't play music and wouldn't answer his phone and wouldn't catch the bus for school. "I am. I'm taking them. You don't have to worry about me."

The phone rings again at ten and it's an NPR producer asking if he's ready to go. He gets patched through to a studio, and two breathy hosts tell him good morning.

"Thanks for doing this," says one of them.

"Sure. Of course. No problem."

"So we're calling you a guest contributor," says the other one. "The segment is we're telling about bands we've just seen live, how cool they are, then we play one of their songs. We already did ours, so now we'll bring you in."

"Oh, okay. Great. Okay."

"All right, here we go in three, two, one. And now for a third song, we asked our buddy Sebastian Torque to join in. What's going on Sebastian?"

"Hey guys, thanks for having me."

These middle-aged hosts sound unimpressed but also totally unironic. When one of them says, "Man, your song 'Chord' gets me so jazzed every time I hear it," it's just bizarre: the guy seems to mean it, but he also sounds utterly bored.

"Thanks," says Sebastian. "I don't think anyone would've heard it if it hadn't been for your show. So thank you."

"I don't know about all that. My son's about your age, and he's gotten lots of encouragement from me but it's not like he's made a hit record. So anyway, this is interesting, we started talking earlier in the show about millennials, and you're in that demo. What do you think, do you see a lot of entitlement in your generation?"

"Hm," Sebastian says. "I kind of don't know, because on the one hand, if I go blindly defending people my age, it sounds like I'm, whatever, being defensive."

"Yeah, we're not looking to generalize. In the music business, though, I get so many kids telling me how frustrated they are, how they're already better than everything they hear on the radio, and if

I'd just come listen to one of their shows I'd see how they deserve to be headlining at the Music Hall."

"From my end," says Sebastian, "it seems to me everybody I know works really hard. Maybe there's just more hustle going on. I mean take Evan Seitz. The kind of hustle that guy puts on is obvious, the way he really engages. With the world, I mean."

"Yeah, I guess we do talk a lot about the democratization of music, with Pro Tools and all that. Okay, so let's hear from you, Sebastian, what's a show you've been to recently that really knocked you out?"

"Well, I just mentioned Evan, and I'm going with Disapproving Dog. If people haven't seen them play out, I mean, they're amazing."

"Great pick, great pick. All right, let's hear a little bit of the Dog, this is my favorite from them: 'Atoms Are Not a Metaphor.' Sebastian Torque, thanks for doing this."

"Thanks so much for having me guys."

After a pause, never breaking his whispery character, one of them says, "That was great, Sebastian. You got chops, buddy. Someday we'll all be working for you."

Sebastian says, "God, thank *you* guys. It's really an honor. I've been listening to the show so long, and the day I found out you were playing my song, I just—" but they've long since hung up.

He brushes his teeth and takes his pills. He eats the second-to-last zinc.

The day outside is a deep snoring blue and Sebastian circles his empty room. Something enormous is ever out of reach. There's so much he wants to say. He was a prodigy at eight, winning piano competitions, learning a different five-minute Debussy piece every month. On #11, he could make his parents' baby grand sound like a harp; #6 was a cat chasing a mouse. A decade ago he was on his way toward Juilliard and a life of classical stardom and then someone played him "Come With Us" by the Chemical Brothers and his blood turned to battery acid. He stayed with classical lessons and recitals deep into high school, but listened to FaltyDL and Black Moth Super Rainbow, dreamed of music without paradigm. Right now is his biggest freakout, because now every song he tries to write sounds like it belongs to a category. And maybe "Chord" was his only successful leap above orthodoxy to date, but maybe it's quickly become its own damn paradigm.

And so authenticity. Well. Whenever he hears most people discuss what's musically authentic, he usually thinks they're really describing talent. There are way more people who *want* to be musicians than who *should* be musicians, and in the noise and shuffle it's easy to hear the rare transcendent performer and ascribe purity. But Sebastian also does see a distinction between skill and authenticity, and wants to be authentically himself because he contains indefinable qualities. *If I can write and play entirely without a filter,* goes the thought, *the music will reflect what it's like to be me.* And it pisses him off when he finds himself slumming, when he's crafting *just* a dance beat, *just* an ambient effect. When he wrote "Chord," Sebastian had amphetamines making reflective silver tracks in his veins and wasn't thinking anything.

He writes, "Your heart is a tapeworm; your tapeworm is a heart," and sends it to thirty-odd OKCupid ladies.

One song, just one finished song by Monday. He piles his hair high with Murray's Superior, trims his stubble, chooses the black-patterned gray cardigan his parents got him for Christmas and leaves his necktie loose. He sends a drum pattern from GarageBand up through the Kross and cranks it fast and loud. He's trying to thrill himself. He clicks buttons on the TASCAM, sending guitar figures into the room. He bounces like a child on a trampoline and plays "La Campanella" again—the little bell—and marvels at the quickness of his right pinkie, how his hands are still in great shape, are in fact the best part of him and maybe not completely under his control: they're his *younger* self, still classically inclined and virginal, whereas the rest of him is clunky and lazy. He looks at his hands playing the Liszt. He wants to switch off all the other sounds and just hear his hands impersonating skylarks, but he doesn't want to stop them playing. He sweats. It smells like failure.

What if he's merely possessed by the *idea* of creation, what if he simply wants *to have made* something, but actually has nothing to say?

Suddenly it's dark outside and Jack Dooley is at his door with a dozen friends and three cases of Pabst Blue Ribbon.

"If the boy genius won't come to the mountain..." Jack says.

A few faces are familiar, including a pretty dark-haired girl named Clementine with a spiderweb tattoo leaking out from under her tanktop, which if the drawing is inked to completion must also necessarily cover her left breast. One guy has a saxophone under his arm, and everyone wears a wallet chain. Sebastian shakes hands and hugs and high-fives, clicks off his amp and fires up a Hot Chip song that asks, "Remember when the world was round?" over and over.

"I know someone over at Domino," Sebastian tells Clementine. "This record doesn't officially come out 'til June."

"I guess it's good," says Clementine. "I can't tell anymore."

"When he says he knows someone at Domino," Jack says, "he means he shares files with them. How do I know they've never met in person? Because Sebastian never leaves this fucking apartment."

People get drunk and wrestle to control the songs on his laptop. He follows Clementine around as she listens to Jack tell stories. Her teeth are small and very dear. A guy who calls himself Diesel shoves his girlfriend into the front closet and says, "Don't call my music Emo! I'll never talk to you again!"

"That's what's wrong with club culture!" Jack tells everyone. "Auto-Tune is killing the buzz! Whenever you don't have any more ideas for a song, just plug in Auto-Tune and go to town! Nobody puts up a fight anymore!"

"Have you seen Madame Furie?" This is a tiny red-haired guy holding a quarter-filled bottle of Jack Daniels. "They play at Duckbomb sometimes." He lets Sebastian have a swig.

"I don't know them," Sebastian says, looking sadly at Clementine.

"Oh, man, you gotta. They're like Architecture in Helsinki getting fucked by Bowie…and then like, cut down by a schoolbus in the prime of life."

"Wow. It sounds really great, man."

"I can give you a demo if you're interested. I'll be honest, I'm the lead singer."

"Yeah, yeah, I would love that!" He watches Clementine laugh at someone's joke. In the recombinant way of loud parties, he looks away and the tiny redhead is gone, and an older woman is talking to him.

"I like this neighborhood. It's Bed-Stuy, right? A lot of Senegalese around here. I walked down Fulton this afternoon and had a lot of bald old guys going, 'Damn, sweetie, look at that ass' in a Senegalese accent."

"I guess that's right," Sebastian says.

"Not so many farm-to-table restaurants, not so many artsy

couples pushing babies in strollers. I live in North Williamsburg now, it's like an anorexic fashion show over there."

" . . ."

"If someone tries to sell you a cappuccino but they don't have a nose-ring in, you get your money back. This is your place? Jesus, how the fuck old are you?"

He tries to focus on her more completely and can't, is how he discovers he's drunk. She wears a black leotard and barrettes and is probably around thirty. Her name is Patricia.

"Who do you know?" he says.

"I came with the asshole in the fez." She aims a finger-pistol at a guy named Marcus or Marvin, a rock drummer Jack used to play with. "He was after me for weeks. I mean, came into the studio in his scuzzoid boots just hanging around waiting for me. I fucked him a few times and now he won't look at me."

"Ha-ha," says Sebastian. "Studio?"

"Yoga studio. Oh, look at that frown of disappointment. So you're a musician, too."

"No, I mean. Yeah. Yes. Musician."

Patricia watches Marcus or Marvin as he stands on a guitar case and shouts poetry: "God, don't cry / About the Earth / About what you're worth / The orbits you spin were set when you were small / The half-moons under your nails / The sad songs under the ridge / The desiccated bridge / The orbits you spin were set when you were small." And Sebastian thinks these lines are pretty good, at least better than anything from his own head, and he claps and smiles and tosses Marcus or Marvin a beer.

"He's a shit," Patricia says.

A few college girls are in a circle, shimmying and grinding against each other. Beta X and his huge Afro have just strolled in, and Jack howls and tackles the big DJ. Kids in the kitchenette are flicking lighted cigarettes at one another. Around the apartment's circumference, people ignore each other and text. Sebastian finds the Jack Daniels.

"This is what happens." Patricia's shoulder is against his, she's facing away but her lips touch his ear. "I don't know how you guys do it. I bet you don't know most of these people but you don't mind. I was never that spontaneous, even when I was your age. One afternoon I just say yes to the handsome drummer. But right away I'm mapping it out, what time I have to be done, what time my kid gets home from school, whether I've got a rubber in my bag. So I can't even be spontaneous, I have to see seven steps ahead. Yesterday the handsome drummer was getting another tattoo and wanted me to get one, and I'm thinking, 'Jesus, how saggy would that kittycat look in ten years?' But you just don't give a fuck, do you? I meditate to turn off my brain, I meditate to feel connected, and it turns out the only time I'm happy is getting passed around like a drunken prom date."

"What are we doing?" Beta X asks Sebastian later. They're splayed on the landing outside the apartment, heads touching. "Everything in Brooklyn is quirky and harmless now, man. How the fuck is anything going to change when all anyone gives a shit about is small-batch pickle making?"

"Is it Sunday or is it Monday?" says Sebastian. "Jesus, is it Monday already? I need one song. I love you on the turntable. You're so…. Hey, you know Disapproving Dog, right? They're so *good.*"

"Handlebar mustaches and…fucking…unicycles, man."

"I'd go put on some Disapproving Dog right now, but if I move I'll throw up."

"Man," says X. "You're all right."

"For an idiot."

X pushes aside his Afro and searches Sebastian's face. A lady's foot thuds between them and drunk kids are roaring in the stairwell: down, down, escaping the hermetic seal. Beta X's face turns mirthful and he says, "Naw, you're the only dude anybody even knows! You're convinced of your own centrality, man! These cats all want to be you!"

Sebastian sings tunelessly at the hall ceiling: "These cats all want to be you! These cats all want to be you! These cats all want to be you!" His designer sweater is smeared with grease and someone hands him another beer.

Then he's on his bed and discovers he's still singing something. He wonders if it's any good. The ceiling is moving and his feet are tied together. He wants to learn the song he's singing. It goes: "Oh! Jesus! Oh!" The ceiling is jerking back and forth. His feet aren't tied together; these are his pants around his ankles. Someone is on top of him. His cock is buried in someone.

He reaches up for her breasts and she responds favorably, gasping and pressing his hands harder. But he only wants to look, craning his neck, trying to see. Is there a spiderweb on the left one? She adjusts her angle, plants her feet crouching over him, grinds in circles.

"You're fucking gigantic," she tells him from way up in the shadows.

He stops singing and comes, hard, holding that left breast, still prodding its skin hoping the tattoo is there. She collapses and kisses him, he rolls her away and sees: no spider-web. It's Patricia.

"Where's your guitar?" she says.

She fetches the Tele and his amp, hooks them up to a small triangular speaker she evidently carries around with her. She plugs in and grins—she's older than thirty, might be closer to forty—and hands him the guitar.

"It'll sound like shit," he says.

Patricia's lids go heavy. She leans against the wall, puts the speaker between her breasts then slides it slowly, down her stomach, over her pelvic bone, and presses it hard against her vulva. Sebastian sits up and strikes a G chord. It sounds muffled and weird and she looks at him. *Not loud enough.* He steps to the amp and cranks it, his balls resting against the Tele's cold body. He twangs again and the noise is blown-out and actually pretty massive. Patricia's free hand thumps the wall.

He plays and she presses, squirming, gasping against the little speaker's vibrations. He crunches chords, seeing it's four in the morning, knowing someone could call the police. A wire connects them, Patricia feels her face, she writhes. He taps out a metal solo, does some rockabilly scales, but keeps coming back to thick chords which threaten to send her over the edge. She has the speaker halfway up in there and she trembles. He's grinning, laughing, thinking it would be even better if he knew any popular radio songs so he could play them and sing along, though he wouldn't be able to hear his own voice anyway. He goes Cm-F#m-D-E over and over, until he sees her toes curl.

At 8 a.m. she kisses his forehead and leaves. He sleeps deep into the afternoon.

Throughout his childhood, how he wanted to be Liszt: the prodigy never lacking a benefactor, composing gracefully, flitting from beautiful woman to beautiful woman before giving up the hedonistic life and contemplating infinity. But how like Debussy he's turned out: tortured, disordered. And even that comparison is a joke, because by 19 Debussy had published lovely chamber music, solo piano pieces, a symphony for four hands and many songs.

He texts Randall Davies asking for Evan Seitz's number, but doesn't hear back.

He showers, brushes, flosses and swallows the last zinc pill. The anxiety this causes is immense.

It's Sunday night. He needs to start making decisions. High Lawn *cannot* read Davies' piece without a great Sebastian Torque song in their hot little hands.

He tries for hours, grows furious and deletes everything, regrets it. He plays the Liszt and Debussy's 11th étude, switching between them; the Liszt's difficulty comes from its speed but conceptually it makes repetitive sense, while the slower Debussy swirls all over the place as his hands cross one another madly, unexpectedly. He's slumped rasping, watching his fingers.

His phone rings and he's glad. It's an unknown caller.

"I snuck a peek at your number before I left."

"..."

"Don't worry. I'm not looking for another boyfriend. I bet my son isn't even five years younger than you."

"Patricia."

"I was drunk. I'm really embarrassed."

Sebastian says, "Me, too," then thinks he sounds cruel. "I mean, it's a weird weekend."

"Anyway, I won't take up any more of your time."

"No no no."

"Maybe I just like musicians," she says. "My ex-husband is a clarinet player. He always looked down on electronic music; I think I must be acting out. But you're really just a baby."

"..."

"..."

"Don't worry about it," says Sebastian.

"But I'm the oldest girl you ever slept with. By a big margin, I bet. I guess I was just calling to make sure you're all right."

He looks at the hair on his right knuckles. "Yeah, of course!"

"I didn't, um, scar you permanently?"

"Come on, not a chance! I had fun. Didn't you have fun?"

But she's sobbing.

He listens for a minute. They sound like real tears, and not the unhinged kind. This woman is somebody's lonely mother. "There's nothing to be…. Nobody can judge what you do, right? Nobody walks in your shoes, Patricia."

She hangs up. He tries dialing her back but there's no answer. He can't fathom her, and like everything else, this seems like a taunt. *You think you can do this, but you can't. You can't tell stories. You don't understand anyone.* At the same time, his groin feels thick and heavy, and he knows this is an encounter that will recede into his personal history, and this is pleasurable. He deletes Patricia's number.

He's calm, yes. But hate still feels like something.

He writes deep into the night. He slows down the first eight measures of "La Campanella," records them as piano and overlays the same notes on guitar. He blends this over a bed of distortion made with the clipped metal guitar pick that Davies liked so much. For rhythm he samples the rusted metal chain that's been out in the hallway as long as he's lived here, quadruples it and adds bass. In sum it's electronic-sounding, disturbingly alien but also slow, funky, slick and menacing. It's no sellout. At 4 a.m. he prepares to record his voice. He can't sing well, but will wildly distort himself so it doesn't much matter. He brushes his teeth and looks at the upside-down zinc bottle on his sink. But he doesn't touch it. Now that he thinks about it, he's sure he can find a pharmacy that delivers.

He lays down the vocals:

There's a singer everybody knows
He got everybody dead to rights
He don't mean to act all bellicose
But he can't help it when he sees the (Seitz)

People makin' money over here
Man you know it burns him up inside
He say music should be so austere
Offer cash and he go run and hide

I saw him in this club
Watching the band
Writing shit down
Stealing their brand…and he says:

"I'm…a Dog who just don't know
How…to come up with my own dough
So I…guess I'll just go to bed
And take…this old bandfucker instead"

There's a singer everybody knows
You see him sometimes beggin' for some change
On guitar he beats up all the pros
Ain't no pop star that can top his range

Late at night you know the time is wrong
But his girls he knows they'll take a sip
They don't care that he can't sell his song
Just wanna suck his upper lip

I saw him on the street
Selling his ax
Giving up the game
Facing the facts…and he says:

"I'm…a Dog who just don't know
How…to come up with my own dough
So I…guess I'll just go to bed
And break…this old bandfucker instead"

PART II

TIGHTEN UP

"I'm trying so hard not to be a dick here," says Scott.

Nobody else says anything.

"But seriously. Can't we hate shit sold to us *purely* because it's quirky? We see a Wal-Mart commercial with an American flag and a wounded soldier hugging his daughter, and we barf because it's cynical and manipulative. Something that's quirky for its own sake, how is that not just as cynical and manipulative?"

Tires on the Pennsylvania Turnpike sound like an endless gutter-ball.

Scott shakes his head. "And you're telling me you love Wes Anderson movies."

"I like them," says Sebastian from the passenger's seat. "Definitely."

"All his characters are smug, self-infatuated navel gazers. Little kids walking around in bowties reading Wittgenstein, dancing badly to an ironic soundtrack. Precocious teens who can't stand girls their own age. Who the hell decided twee was cool? Why was I not at that meeting?"

"…"

"Tell me what's at stake in a Wes Anderson movie. Tell me you don't expect everything to work out just fine in the end. The purpose of all the precious clothing and harpsichord music and wacky overhead shots is to deny connection. If all the actors are busy with their dopey fidgets, nobody has to feel anything real.

Instead we can all look at the vintage eyeglasses and knit caps and rotary telephones and squeal."

Sebastian grins.

"C'mon," Scott says. "Tell me where I'm wrong. Fight back."

"Leave him alone," says Kate from the back seat.

Amanda is next to Kate. She says, "What about *Royal Tenenbaums* when Luke Wilson slits his wrists? That's dark."

Scott barrels them deeper into the afternoon, one finger on the steering wheel. "That's the one everyone brings up. It's the exception that proves the rule."

"Don't attack people for what they like," Kate says. "It's not nice."

"Yeah," says Amanda, "I'll bet you *say* you like minimalist Korean biopics but if I checked out your Netflix queue it'd be all Adam Sandler."

"Yeah," says Kate.

"Yeah," says Amanda.

Scott looks at Sebastian.

"Maybe you make some good points," says Sebastian. "But I still like his films."

It's two hours to Pittsburgh. Scott dislikes himself for getting overheated, and clams up. Amanda reaches between the front seats and pulls back Sebastian's hand, folding his fingers into hers. Kate fixes herself to the oncoming tree-studded mountains through which the turnpike carves, and half-wishes the ride was even longer. Music is their junction, the thing worth fighting for. It sounds different to each of them but similar enough. It forgives trespasses, at least so far.

Later, downstairs at the Silver Elf, they eat gratis macaroni and cheese in silence. A flyer on the stairwell says they're middling for two local acts, The Wobble Queen and Honeystuck. Their gear is still outside in the van, but there's no rush: it's 6 p.m. They just chew this five-cheese macaroni. Kate's knee is hopping a mile a minute under the table and Sebastian tries to get her to stop by smiling. Amanda plays Angry Birds Space. Everyone checks the clock a dozen times, and Scott resolves to drive slower on the way to Cleveland. Half their hundred-and-fifty-dollar handle is contingent on the Silver Elf hitting a threshold in liquor sales. They've got a reservation at a Motel 6.

The Friday dinner crowd picks up and they have to relinquish their table. They clomp upstairs to the tiny showroom, where the stage is one foot tall and ten feet deep, with three big windows overlooking Penn Avenue behind the band. Scott steps into the closet that passes for a green room and shuts the door to make a phone call. Everyone else mills around.

"I can have them bring you up some beers," Amy, the comely booker, tells them. "But just so you know, you have to pay for them. If it's me, I'd wait 'til you start playing, when it starts counting against your nut."

Nobody answers. They falter around the empty room until Kate finally says, "Sorry. Road-coma plus food-coma. I think we're pacing ourselves beerwise. But thank you."

"I love your stuff," Amy says, and Kate is about to answer they don't really have any stuff yet, but it becomes clear the booker is specifically talking to Sebastian, who's crammed his left hand inside Amanda's right-rear jeans pocket. "I love 'Chord,' it's really cool. We have a good techno scene in town; I've been getting our owners to move in that direction. We used to only have crotch rock. Have you ever been to Firehouse?"

"Thanks," says Sebastian. "Thank you, that's really nice. No, I've never been there. I've never been to Pittsburgh."

Amanda says, "He never left the tri-state area before this tour."

"Not true. I went to Oregon once for a wedding."

Amy removes a piece of pretend-lint from her chest. "Any chance I can get you to play 'Chord' or 'Bandfucker' tonight? My friends would so love it."

"Well, we made a good decision not to let me sing," says Sebastian.

"Hm," Amy says, and parades back downstairs.

"She's hot," says Amanda. "I'd do her."

Kate steps up to where her kit will be, and looks out at the showroom's funky baroque wallpaper. She felt nauseated as they drove through upstate New York, drawing nearer to Binghamton, but when they crashed on by without stopping it made her buoyant; the subsequent show in Ithaca was her favorite yet. Belonging is underrated. She spent two years in Manhattan dipping her toes in musical reciprocity at the Grand Mal, but those open-mic dalliances were designed to expire. Now she lets herself imagine years as a snug-fitting puzzle piece. She says, "Should we try and finish Scott's song? I could go get the stuff."

Sebastian says, "Man, that's embarrassing. Sorry guys. I don't know what to say when someone mentions those old tunes."

"I have a headache," says Amanda.

"There's pain stuff in the car," Kate says.

"I did have a new idea," says Sebastian. "We could do a song about how great Wes Anderson is."

"What are the odds we fill this place?" Amanda says.

"It'll be called, 'All You Need Is Bill Murray.'"

"Omigod, stop talking."

Amanda finds a chair and sits, elbows-on-knees, covering her face. Sebastian walks back to the soundboard and twists a couple knobs. He thinks about the shithole apartment in Bed-Stuy, on which it seems he's now officially broken the lease. He painted those walls with despair but sees how amazing it was, now that the mechanics of rehearsing and traveling and indigestion from greaseball burgers turn the day into a thousand reasons not to create. He's never had to "be creative" on a schedule, and it seems his creativity requires long stretches of goof-off time: check Facebook! watch *Flight of the Conchords*! masturbate! He's 20 now. *That* certainly doesn't feel right.

And Kate is embarrassed her bandmates are ignoring her naïve songwriting offer. Is that not what musicians do in downtime? She steps to a window, feels its cold-candy flatness on her forehead. She says, "It's getting dark so early."

Meanwhile Scott has squawked about how he needs privacy to call more clubs and fill out the schedule, but instead dials Jane who answers: "Hang *on*."

"*Mais bien sûr*," he says, looking around the green room at a cracked mirror, some orange food residue, and several wires jabbing from behind a brick wall, their ends stripped and unraveling. When he nudges the wires, they sputter and spark, causing his sneaker toe to melt.

"They reopened the shop yesterday," Jane says. "I had to come in. Why didn't you call this morning?"

"Didn't get to sleep 'til four, and then had to block out sex sounds from the beautiful wing of the band as they pretended they weren't going at it."

"I can only talk for a minute."

"I figured a minute is better than nothing. How's the city?"

"Underwater. Tunnels all still closed. Subway's getting better but Mark still can't get into Manhattan, which means I'm on a double today. Did you hear about the crane on West 57th? They evacuated everybody around there and they can't go home, and it's been almost a week."

"I'm just glad you're still okay."

"And of course Roger won't keep the shop closed. People *must* have their coffee and booze, even though nobody's working, so the customers are all just people who live around here. It's so stupid we're even open. I'm the world's best martyr, by the way."

"You are a pretty tremendous martyr."

"I know, and some guy just came in ten minutes ago and showed everybody his dick."

"And?"

"I mean, obviously. He's picking me up later for drinks."

Scott laughs. "So Pittsburgh tonight, Cleveland tomorrow. Send out good vibes."

"Sent. How was last night?"

"We have our moments. It can be really fun, but there are times when we just lose it. Sebastian is amazing but I get the sense he's incredibly bored, sticking to the same songs in the same structure. Like, if he could turn every night into an impromptu space opera springing forth spontaneously from his brain, he'd do that."

"But you should hear yourself when you talk about him," says Jane. "You're fucking worshipful."

"I mean, obviously, he's ridiculous. You've seen him."

"He's showy. You're just as good."

"I appreciate the lie," Scott says.

"The crazy thing is I never lost power, even though the lights flickered a few times. I ate Halloween candy. The cable did go out, though. So obviously I *suffered*."

"Obviously."

"I saw a pack of people around a dumpster on the Lower East today," she says, "rummaging through spoiled food. And it wasn't like they were homeless. Ho hum, just a normal day walking down streets no normal person could even afford to live on, and there's twenty people dumpster diving. Meanwhile, they're still having the marathon this weekend, probably because their corporate overlords would shit a brick if they didn't. I mean, what the fuck?"

"..."

"Anyway, are you accumulating *beaucoup* fans? Panties thrown onstage and stalker chicks at the hotel? The great breadbasket of America is filled with luscious Trixies."

"Funny. No, the invisible groupies can't get close enough, with all the invisible record execs fighting over us."

"Theresa is waving at me frantically. The masses have to have their whiskey sours."

"*Je suis désolé.* I'm bored. You'll just have to talk to me for another hour."

"Telephonic neediness," says Jane. "Awesome. Get your gorgeous amazon lead singer to do the dance of the seven veils for you."

"Actually, she's not that tall and—okay, you hung up. Okay. Bye."

The Wobble Queen starts playing at nine for a friends-and-family crowd, and they're pretty terrible: two guys chanting over two clonewheel organs, going *huh-huh-huh-huh-huh* like the world's weirdest hockey rally song. Amanda can't take it, and goes downstairs to warm up. In the van she fake-yawns to stretch her jaw, trills her lips over ascending and descending notes, and hums scales. She repeats the word "ma" over the first five steps of two octaves, sings the word "bumblebee" over the major scale, hisses to stretch her diaphragm. And she tops it off with the killer: with one huge breath she sings "eeeeeeeeee," softly at first but gaining strength, finally so loud she wonders if it could break auto glass, then gradually softening back to silence. Blinking and light-headed, she watches Pennsylvanians saunter in streetlight and wills them into the Silver Elf.

The Wobble Queen finishes: house lights up, stage lights down. "Titanium" blasts over the p.a. Kate tests her kick drum while Scott and Sebastian carry up her toms. They're ghosts to an audience two feet away. Amanda removes her fleece jacket, revealing a skintight baby-tee that reads *Scientist!* A kid near a speaker takes her picture. Sebastian plugs in his Tele and Scott fumbles with his big black Spector bass. He likes to show he's not just another two-string dope by ripping through a lead solo for his warmup, but the Spector either isn't plugged in or there's a loose wire, so he just looks dumb flailing away noiselessly. Sebastian kneels and fiddles with a junction and tells Scott to try again, and the bass pounds through speakers.

"Nice," they hear a drunk guy say from the audience. "Reeeeeal professional."

"Sir," says Scott, "I don't come to your work and tell you how to flip burgers."

"Freebird!" the guy says. He's tall and bearded, wearing huge reflective sunglasses, a backwards trucker hat, and a tanktop that reads *Free Hugs*. "C'mon, play some Eagles! Play Barry Manilow!"

"Oh, awesome," says Amanda.

"Yeah!" the guy says. "Yeeeeeeeah! Fight me! Fight me!" His friends smilingly urge him to calm down. Someone hands him another beer.

"How about shut up!" Scott says.

"Come on, muthafucka!" the guy says. "Forget the music, let's dance!"

"Fortunately," Amanda says into her microphone, "I have one of these. So here we go."

Kate gives a couple nervous rolls, taps out a cadence on her crash cymbal, thumps the bass again. Amanda locks eyes with a couple folks up front, then the red-and-white stage lights come up. There are maybe thirty souls in the audience. The p.a. cuts out, and a couple kids go "woo!"

Amanda pulls her shoulders back and shakes her hair so it frizzes wide. Her stomach twists and she *becomes*. It's natural. No part of her hesitates, every part of her is open. She thinks about what she'll say, then stops thinking. It's worth it. Twenty-three hours of bullshit in exchange for this feeling. She has the crowd's attention. She can see them wondering what she'll sound like.

Scott says to Sebastian: "What's the difference between a vacuum cleaner and a bass player? The vacuum cleaner has to be plugged in to suck."

"Hi," Amanda says into the mic, biting her grin. "We're Kid Centrifuge."

Kate counts them in.

They start fast and loud: Sebastian crunches through a solo that turns into a riff, with Kate hard on the snare and high hat, and Scott following. Sebastian's tone is crystalline; within a few seconds a listener knows that as a guitarist, he's utterly himself. He plays this highly technical opening—bending notes and filling with amazing little flourishes—like it's nothing, and somehow every note is heard, there's nothing particularly wanky about it, it's in service of the song. Then he drops out and Scott drives, his heart in his mouth. He knows he's just not as good. But he tries to be there, it feels great and terrifying, and it's working. It's as good as they can be, and this knowledge elevates the proceedings. Scott repeatedly bangs his top two strings, opening the door for Amanda to sing:

Hey! Come on!
Turpentine jackets
And paint-thinner pants
Strip it off, slip it off
Sandpaper dresses
And icepick heels
Chip it off, rip it off
Babies don't care
What mommies wear
Don't want my guru
Messin' with his hair
It's one-percent problem
And the rest is a scare
Because...
Styles! Make! Fights!

And as she shouts that one-line chorus again and again, the showroom's energy lifts: Sebastian and Scott make triple-hops in unison, and the crowd joins them with fist-pumps and happy expressions, as a few more people climb up from the restaurant. Amanda plants her feet and just *belts*. Every time she says "Fights!" the word grows longer, and the intensity in here feels thicker. She tries to melt the exit sign. Then she gives way to Sebastian, who plays his devilish little solo again. Kate observes the three of them in front of her and all she can think is, *My God, when did we get so tight?*

Another verse, another chorus, and they end abruptly: a hard smash, Amanda's arms rocking down hard against her pelvis, a sudden quiet. They look at each other amazed. Each wants to be sure the others feel it. The room fills with approving shouts and the bandmates gasp for air. This is better than doing it by yourself.

Alas, the giddiness dissipates quickly. The set's second song,

"Nipple Rouge," is supposed to alternate every measure between 4/4 and 3/4, but Sebastian keeps losing his way, playing lead licks directly over the beat and making a dissonant mess. He feels terrible about it and keeps trying to catch up. Amanda sings, "Fake her out, don't take her out!" while she steps to stage right so she can observe the others and figure out what the hell is going on with the music. Sebastian is humiliated. He stops playing, then bobs his head with the rhythm and picks back up, does a bonus little fandangle at the end of his verse phrasing, and unbelievably fucks up the time signature again. There's nowhere to hide. Amanda decides she'll just sing to the bass, and goes, "She wants to know! Hey! Now! He'll tell it all somehow! What's wrong is you! Everything you do! Just not when you go down!"

The song ends and they get a nice hand, but now they can't look at one another. Scott studies his five strings. Kate finds the bicycle clip on her ankle fascinating. Sebastian feels hated. Kid Centrifuge sees a dark hole before them: from as good as it gets to as bad, in five minutes flat.

They play three more original songs and covers of "Tighten Up" by the Black Keys and "Changing" by Airbone Toxic Event, and they're up-and-down. But the Silver Elf seems pretty happy with them. By set's end, the showroom is maybe half-filled. Amanda waves and high-fives her admirers, knowing her bandmates are breaking down equipment behind her, feeling a responsibility to be the frontwoman but also believing it's her reward: these boys in sweaty t-shirts holding bottles, loving her.

Members of Honeystuck shuffle them offstage: a drummer, a keyboard player and a guy with a turntable. Scott does a double take: the guy setting up the turntable is that tall bearded heckler in the *Free Hugs* shirt. Now he's sober and focused, and Scott wants to confront him, but he gets tugged away in the scrum of instruments. Back by the green room, Amy the booker hugs Sebastian and says, "That was really nice! And we already hit the booze quota easy. Do you have any shirts or CDs you want to put out?"

"Sorry, you guys," Sebastian says.

"Hey, well," says Scott, still seething at the *Free Hugs* guy.

"We don't have anything like that yet," Kate tells the booker. "Next time through."

"We'll all be better tomorrow," says Amanda. She steps on Scott's foot, believing he's about to lay into Sebastian.

"Ow! Jesus!"

"I didn't see you there, sweetie."

"You're a clodhopper," Scott says. "Good fucking God."

Honeystuck launches kind of a synth preamble, with the drummer twirling his sticks and the bearded DJ shouting into his mic, and here comes the party beat. Many more bodies pile into the showroom, decked in Day-Glo and blacklight paint. Kids are now stacked right up close to the stage, and everyone looks ecstatic.

"Okay!" says Amy, patting Sebastian's stomach. "I'm so psyched to see these guys. I hope you didn't lose anything in the hurricane!" and then she scurries off.

Amanda slow-motion punches Scott in the jaw, and neither of them knows what it means.

They play a V.F.W. in Cleveland on Saturday and a mini-festival at Eastern Michigan University on Sunday, but don't have a gig scheduled for five days after that. They drive to Chicago, hoping maybe Scott can scrounge something up before Friday's show at a cabaret club. They get to see Andrew Jackson Jihad at Bottom Lounge. Then they walk around to bars of increasing seediness, listening to kids talk earnestly about tomorrow's election. Finally, they crash on the floor of an out-of-town bass player someone knows. As is regularly the case, this good deed stems from people being familiar with Sebastian's electronic stuff.

They go to bed: the room is completely dark below window height, and they're all drunk. Amanda lies on freezing hardwood and sings a Fiona Apple song. "Every single night's a fight with my brai-ai-ai-ai-ai-ai-ai-ai-ain."

And Scott follows up with, "I just wanna feel everything."

"Is this like *Almost Famous?*" says Kate from the sofa. "Are we all about to start singing together on a bus?"

"I like Fiona Apple," says Scott.

"You like *looking* at Fiona Apple," says Kate.

"What's *Almost Famous?*" Sebastian says.

Out on the street, men shout angrily. The band was warned Pilsen can be a wild neighborhood, but as New Yorkers they felt obligated to scoff. Car brakes screech and someone honks a horn for about a minute straight. Leather-lunged neighbors scream a torrent of curses. It takes several more minutes for the block to quiet and when it does, the possibility of violence lingers.

"I was talking to a girl tonight," Amanda says, "who has guys send her shoes. She puts on the shoes, takes a few pictures, and posts the pictures online. That's it. They pay her for this, *and* she gets to keep the shoes."

"Wait," says Sebastian. "Fiona Apple isn't too twee for you?"

"Fiona Apple is awesomely talented," Scott says. "She's the opposite of what I'm talking about. She bleeds on those records."

"She wins the Scott Tungsten Seal of Approval?" says Kate. "Pretty rare stuff."

"I'm just saying, some people think she's pretty twee."

"How many guys do you think would send me shoes?" Amanda says. "How much could I charge each of them? I'm doing the math."

Sebastian says, "I guess one man's twee is another man's...what."

"'One Man's Twee,'" Kate says. "Song title alert."

"Okay, but seriously, Torque," Scott says. "Were you kidding or do you not know what *Almost Famous* is?"

"I have to pee," says Amanda.

"Don't step on my head, clodhopper."

They turn on a light and spend ten fruitless minutes trying to remember the apartment's Wi-Fi password ("He said it had something to do with sports or marine biology or something"), then they pick up a neighbor's unsecured signal and Amanda downloads *Almost Famous*. It's 3:45 a.m., but the four of them huddle around the laptop. When William Miller writes, "Industry Of Cool" in his notebook, Amanda elbows Sebastian hard. And when the band in the film starts talking about "The Buzz"—the thing they get from playing together—all four members of Kid Centrifuge nod, maybe because they feel they have to.

"I am a golden god," Kate whispers.

Scott tells Sebastian, "We'll make a goddamn grownup out of you yet."

THE BACKBONE

Kate wakes to shower sounds: water running and a male voice. It's around noon. She's on a stranger's couch and the floor is empty of bedrolls. She looks at her hands in sunlight, imagining she's married and this is her home, imagining she's back on the road with seven other ladies, imagining she's in her parents' basement waiting to be called for dinner. A gray cat walks into the room squinting. Kate places her feet on the floor and pats her lap, but the cat just struts around autographing the air with its tail. Kate gives it a middle finger, and remembers today they're in Minneapolis.

The man in the shower can sing, is how she knows it's Scott. He's really going at it, lyrics she can't recognize. The cat jumps onto a chair and knocks something over; keys and coins crash. Kate retrieves everything and finds a loose-leaf notebook open to a page with drawings on it. She shouldn't look.

It's a page of logos. A dozen hand-drawn attempts at a logo for Kid Centrifuge. She smiles and flips through the notebook and finds many pages filled with logo concepts: different fonts, abbreviations, shapes, shadings. The high-school obsessiveness of it makes her feel sour, like they're merely dreamers. She thinks about putting the notebook away, then decides to let him catch her in the act.

He comes in with wet hair, and rummages his duffel for socks. He nods at Kate, makes a kissy sound, and the cat sprints

over and rubs hard against his bare ankle. It reminds him of his
parents' cats, most of which have grown old and died.

"Ahem," says Kate. "Nice artwork."

Scott turns red and says, "Oh, yeah, thanks."

"Sure are a lot of 'em. You have a favorite?"

He makes a manly production of grunting and straining to put
on his shoes. "Not really."

"You have any sketches of cover art you feel like sharing? Or
tour bus designs?"

"Ha ha. Well, I guess we need to be able to make it through
an entire song without fucking up before we put out our first
record, right?"

"..."

"Every band needs a Mussolini," he says.

Kate sits down holding the notebook. "This one's kind of
cool. It reminds me of the Strokes. I like the ones that look slick, I
mean, the name already sounds a little sci-fi."

"I'm not surprised you dig the Strokes, your taste is excellent."

"Sure," says Kate. "When I was in junior high I hung out with
older kids in leather jackets. They got me into *Is This It* and what
else, 'She Fucking Hates Me.' Remember that song?"

"Puddle of Mudd."

"I mean I pretty much wanted to marry Julian Casablancas
until I found out his dad was a millionaire who ran a modeling
agency and his mom was Miss Denmark. That's so *not* punk rock to
a thirteen-year-old."

"I didn't draw them for any actual reason," he says. "I mean,
it's not like I'd make that kind of decision without anyone weighing
in. Sometimes I just can't sleep."

"No. It's fine."

"Hell, you're the one who'd really have to approve. It goes on
the kick drum, right?"

"'Met a girl...thought she was grand. Fell in love...found out
firsthand.' Deep lyrics." She folds the pee-smelling quilt beneath
which she slept. "Sometimes I can't tell whether you want us to be
interested in the business side of stuff."

"..."

"I don't want you to feel like you have to do everything by
yourself. But when Sebastian asks, sometimes you get a little...."

"I know."

"You got us these dates. Personally, I'm very impressed. We all are."

Scott says, "I'm trading on Sebastian's name. If there's anyone to be impressed with."

"He's great, too," says Kate. "And I never would've thought Amanda had that voice. You don't understand, when I answered the ad on Craigslist and she opened the apartment door, I hated her. I lived my life knowing that at least chicks who look like her are drones who'll never have an interesting thought in their lives. And then…Jesus, I heard her sing. But without you it would grind to a halt. I know I'm not making those calls. One rejection and I'd be sucking my thumb crying."

"I'm a rock bureaucrat. You wanna see?" Scott fires up his laptop and shows Kate his Excel spreadsheet devoted to the band. He's embarrassed, but unburdening himself also feels good. "This summer I did a three-day marathon, putting in every single club I could find along with whatever contact info, and I also tried sorting them by size and genre. And in this tab, I've got every record label anyone I know has ever heard of, and I did a whole bunch of research and that column is the A&R people at each label, if they have them. So if anyone ever tries to tell you the bass player is hopeless, I mean, whatever, I guess this spreadsheet is the greatest act of hope I can manage."

"Who would ever say you're hopeless?"

"I play guitar," says Scott. "I don't even know how to play bass. Here's one for you: boy comes home from his first bass lesson. His dad asks him how it went, and the boy says, 'Today we learned the E string.' The boy comes home from his second lesson and his dad asks him how it went, and the boy says, 'Today we learned the A string.' The boy comes home from his third lesson and his dad asks, 'So did you learn the D string today?' And the boy says, 'No, today I had a gig.'"

"Come on. We rock. We're the backbone."

"I met an A&R dude last night at Magnetic Fields," Scott says, scrolling down his spreadsheet. "This guy. Tom Bacon. He thought I was just some guy. I mean, I *am* just some guy. But he didn't know anything about us. I asked him all about the business, like I didn't know anything. He tells me he's a dying breed, you really have to love it because nobody gets rich anymore, he personally never gets to sign rock bands but instead gets stuck schmoozing all these kids with laptops. But then he mentioned a showcase: January in L.A. Last of its kind. They used to have shows like this all over, but now it's practically down to one: everyone in the crowd will be A&R. So the idea is build to that point. We have to record again, better than anything we did over the summer. Get people to start writing about us online. Get an invite to the L.A. showcase. This is how we get signed."

"I really feel like everyone would react better," says Kate, "if you told us all this stuff up front."

"I'm telling you. I just met this Bacon guy last night."

"That way we could all pull in the same direction."

"This is me, telling you."

Kate showers, thinking how nasty it is to share a bar of soap with at least three other people in the same morning, and when she's done, Scott is gone. Neither is there any sign of Amanda or Sebastian or any of the apartment's actual tenants. In chilly sunshine, Kate walks a half-mile to the river to meet one of her idols.

Billie Turner played with Lou Reed, the Who, Jimi Hendrix, Miles Davis and Frank Zappa, none of whom are exactly in Kate's musical sweet spot. But as far back as her first drum lesson at age 11, people told Kate about Billie: a lady percussionist who could bang or brush with the best. She and Sheila E. were the only female drummers anyone in Binghamton seemed to have heard of, and for whatever reason Kate latched onto Billie, bought any MP3 on which Billie had boomed, learned what it meant to inject personality into technical mastery. And Billie's Wikipedia page says she retired to Minneapolis, so last week Kate sent an email asking if a meeting was possible. "What's possible comes from behind your own eyes," was Billie's reply. "I wander the west parkway every afternoon it doesn't rain or snow, and I end up in the ruins, if you want to come see me."

So Kate walks over a still-green field, across a busy street, to the west bank of the Mississippi. Mill Ruins Park ends in an amphitheater of crumbling brick walls, rusted-out girders and crushed industrial equipment in the shadow of an old stone bridge. It's meant to capture the Twin Cities' flour-milling past, but Kate can't help feeling she's in the modern world's remains. It's cold and there's nobody else down here, but she sits on a few stacked quarry slabs looking out over a spillway. She starts up a Zappa tune because Billie's on it, but she finds it unlistenable and switches over to Japandroids. The only other person she sees is someone up on the stone bridge walking a dog. By 3 p.m. the sun is low and she's freezing.

Then here comes a little old lady in a marshmallow-puff windbreaker, favoring one hip. Kate sees a wrinkled-up beige face that could be Billie Turner, and waves noncommittally. Perhaps the old lady nods, but her pace doesn't change. She seems concerned about stumbling into the river. Kate shuts off her music and hears traffic sounds and a dog barking.

"Well, I thought you might be here," says the lady. She has a slight European accent. "It is very good to see you again."

Kate says, "Miss Turner?"

Up close, she's not so desperately old: perhaps mid-sixties with perfect white teeth and a beauty mark on her cheek. "Oh, yes," she says. "That is right."

"I'm Kate Grush. I sent you an email. I'm a drummer."

"Yes, I know," says Billie.

"Thanks for letting me talk with you. I'm such a big fan."

"Yes, dear, I saw you last night. We can dispense with the pleasantries. We had this same conversation last night."

Kate's heart drops. "Last night?" she says.

"You played wonderfully."

"…"

"I am sorry to have you out here on such a cold day. It has been freezing the past couple days, but it was just lovely this weekend. After so many years in Los Angeles, I am back to the cold weather of my youth, but I do not like it."

"I don't want to…. It's amazing to talk to you, Ms. Turner. I just don't want to do it under…. My band didn't play last night." Then it dawns on Kate. "Were you at First Avenue? The Magnetic Fields have a woman drummer, too. Her name is Claudia."

"Oh! Oh, goodness, yes, I am so embarrassed. Yes."

"No no. It's fine."

"Yes, that is right. I am so sorry, dear."

"I was at the show, too. It's so nice you get to see great bands."

"Yes, yes. *Claudia.*"

"My band is called Kid Centrifuge," Kate says. "We're just starting out. I guess people probably tell you that all the time."

"No, people do not say much to me. They certainly do not talk to me about their bands. 'Walk faster! Get out of my way, *Grootmoeder.*' That is mostly what they talk to me about. I am still very connected to music. I listen to new songs all the time. Maybe I will go back to Los Angeles after all."

"Do you still drum?"

"Not often," says Billie. "My legs are bad. That is why I walk every day. I find it heartbreaking to play the drums now, because I am so much less than I was. But you are very young and starting a group. This is exciting. It is more exciting to start a group than to play on a tour. It is a regret of mine."

"You weren't in the Pecking Order from the beginning?"

"Oh, I was. But we were not so successful. Some who are political break through, but we did not. 'Why would a corporation pay you money to criticize them? Make music to make people happy.' We sang protest songs, and maybe not enough people cared about what we were protesting."

"There's so much I'd like to ask you," says Kate. "What it was like."

"No, *psh.* You are at the beginning of things. Remind *me.*"

"Well, I don't...really have any stories yet."

"I am not interested in stories," Billie says. "I am interested in the feeling. I look at you. You look like you have pain behind those eyes."

Kate smiles defensively and bites the inside of her cheek.

Billie takes a few steps toward the river, laughing. "No, do not look so worried. I say it to everyone. Because everyone does have pain behind their eyes. Well. Do you love it? Do you love building the rhythm for everyone else to ride?"

"..."

"I could never practice. I did not like it. I never liked to play alone. And now I am alone all the time." She looks at the mill corpse around them.

Down the walkway, a man and his dog are approaching, maybe the same ones from the bridge. Kate is cold and hasn't eaten anything, but finds she wants Billie's guidance.

"Tell me what you feel when you play," says Billie.

"When it's good.... I don't know. I love them, it's like loving them. Like you said, they follow me. I find it very.... It's flattering that they follow me. I worry I'll screw it up and they'll stop giving their trust. I've only been playing with them a few months. But I have to tell you. I don't mean to change the subject, but I'm really just so moved to know you played with all those incredible musicians, and paved the way."

"No," says Billie.

"You're a black woman. You must've been so frustrated sometimes with how they treated you. You were the only one."

"No!" says Billie, and she steps away. Kate looks up. The dog is trying to jump in the spillway with its owner attached, they're wrestling stiffly, yanking one another, the owner leaning backward like he's reeling in a big fish. The dog barks wildly. Kate runs past Billie to help. She strains to grab the leash. Together, she and this man fight the young black lab, keeping him away from the water.

"He will get swept away!" Billie says, waving her fists. "Get him! Do not fall in!"

Kate works her hands down this leather leash, grappling, and finally gets to the dog's collar. She yanks hard and the dog relents wheezing, Kate has its neck in her arms and the man falls exhausted across the walkway. He's young and big, and is bundled into a dark blue anorak with the hood pulled tight around his dirty face. Billie steps this way and touches his shoulders. He wears a tranquil expression, just sitting on this cold metal walkway. He smells like filth.

Kate says, "Are you all right?" She scratches the dog's neck.

"Can you get up?" Billie says. The man doesn't react. "Let me help you up."

The man's face doesn't change; his eyes are unfocused.

"Is he drunk?" says Kate.

"I do not think he can hear me." Billie taps the side of his head. "Hello?"

Kate sees the man's hands: they're scarred and burned, with several of the nails torn away. The dog is clean and healthy. Billie snaps her fingers in front of his face, and he blinks, still wearing his faraway half-smile.

"Do you need help?" says Kate. "Do you have a...condition?"

"He looks like an Indian," Billie says.

"That's not a condition."

"They drink too much."

"..."

"He smells like shit and piss. I do not smell alcohol, but it is hard to tell." She claps her hands behind the man's head and he doesn't react. "I do not know sign language."

"I don't, either."

"Get him up," says Billie. Kate does the work, planting her feet and dragging the man up by an armpit. As she steadies him, he opens his mouth to speak, revealing gums but no teeth. He doesn't form any words, and doesn't make the nasal sounds Kate associates with a deaf person's voice. Instead he produces one long vowel, unbridled, unsocial. He reaches for the dog's leash, but Kate doesn't give it over. "I think he is mentally retarded," Billie says.

"They don't call it that anymore."

"Do not be so bothered with what people call things, especially when a man has shit himself. Well. Let's walk with him up to the street. Maybe he can show us where he lives."

They climb the ramp and bend away from the river, ending up beneath the cantilevered arm of a dark blue building, in view of another that reads "Gold Medal Flour." The man walks at Billie's slow pace leaving Kate out front to fight the dog, who wants to run. Billie links arms with the man—he's at least a foot taller—in a lovers' pose. Kate thinks: *I could give up the band and become Billie's assistant, out here a thousand miles from anyone I know.* Rent must be cheap, they have dazzling clubs and people come out to watch actual rock shows. Kate's heart soars and she hopes she hasn't offended Billie, wonders how she could lay the groundwork. But of course the nonsense factor of this sudden prophecy is high, and Kate recognizes this, and she feels guilty and sad. She uses two hands to snap the leash, and the lab yelps a little and looks up dolefully, and Kate feels cruel but thinks she can impart some discipline.

"There is a homeless shelter four blocks away," Billie says.

"Do we know for sure that he's…a shelter person?"

They walk to South 3rd, but it turns out the shelter here is only for families. The security guard won't let them in, but he recommends checking with a Catholic charity house about a half-mile away. Or he offers to call the police.

"Absolutely not," says Billie. She grabs the deaf man by his anorak. "What is your name? Where do you live? Hey! What. Is. Your. Name." Kate watches the dog's tail wag inquisitively.

Kate's phone rings; it's an unknown number. She clicks the call away.

"It is getting dark," Billie says.

"No, it's all right," says Kate.

"It gets dark earlier now than it ever did."

"..."

"I want to see this poor man home. He obviously cannot help himself."

"Yes," Kate says.

"I am strong enough," says Billie. "The walk will do me good. We can use the time to talk about your band. You were wonderful last night."

Kate sighs and enters the charity house address in her phone, and they clomp west. She thinks about hailing a taxi, but doubts a dog would be allowed. Does Billie have a car? Does she live close by? Would a homeless man have such a clean dog? Kid Centrifuge has a show tomorrow night in a venue that doubles as a junior high, but they're off tonight and apparently not planning to hang out together.

"I came from Ostend," Billie says as they walk. "It is a beach town but tourists are always disappointed because it is so cold. The beach is lovely and freezing. There is a movie called *Ex Drummer* that takes place in Ostend and five years ago all my Belgian friends asked if it was about me. But I would never watch such filth. My parents were lovely people who wanted me to marry a banker. But we cannot help it, can we? The beat takes us away."

Kate has convinced the dog to walk calmly alongside her, as the man is placidly following Billie. Kate says, "When did you come to the States?"

"1966. Straight to Los Angeles at nineteen years old. I was a pretty young fool. I would not try to trick you: it took years before I made my own money. I was not willing to sacrifice good food and a soft bed. I was a very spoiled child: my mother bought me a new dress every week, and I was not prepared to be a starving musician. I was already a very good player but men would not listen. So I was a double agent working from inside. If you are going to ignore me, I will just accept your food and your house and I will wait. I was a curiosity. That is always the way: how could such a little girl make such big noise? Pff, well, I wanted L.A. and I got it. You marry a manager and he finds you work. Then you leave that husband and marry a producer and he puts you in the studio. Then you leave that husband and marry a tour promoter and he puts you into big shows. Eventually all the men get used to it."

"The beat takes us away," says Kate.

"Let me tell you how I met my third husband. I went to a party in 1973. My friends were having a conversation about Archibald Cox and this mustached man enters, a very handsome man. He talks to me but he seemed very stiff. My husband Thomas was off wooing someone else, because it was California and that was what you did. And here is this handsome mustached man who began talking to me about what it is like to be a twin. He was very...he is wearing a coat and tie and everyone else is in hippie clothes, you know, *groovy* clothes. We have this word: he is *gespannen*, like this," and Billie makes a clenched face. "But he is so handsome. And he says his twin brother is the black sheep of the family, and then he says, 'No offense,' which made me laugh. I liked him, but he was too stiff. So I made an excuse to get away, I had some drinks. And here he comes again, except he does not have the mustache anymore and he is wearing love beads and some hippie shirt. He shakes my hand and introduces himself, and tells me his brother called him up and said come to the party, there is a beautiful drummer girl he should meet. But I got close to his face, and he smelled like shaving cream! I had a Christian friend, Joan Mineola, and she used to say, 'I may be born-again, but I was not born-again yesterday!' So I told him I know he is not a twin, he just changed clothes and shaved off his mustache. But oh, he denies it! He is very injured, he came because what a fan of the drums he is, and his brother knows this, and it is outrageous to be accused like this.... All in a very nice way, of course. The handsome ones, they can tell you the sky is purple and if they do it nicely you believe them. But I am no fool. I believe what I *see*. So I apologize to this handsome man and say I believe him, and he sits with me and flatters me, he touches my leg and tells me about the tours he promotes. He asks if I want to meet Mick Jagger, John Lennon, Elton John. I was sweet with him, and I forgot about my husband. He asked me to leave the party with him and come for dinner. And I said, 'Yes, darling, I would love to. Let me just go find your brother to say goodbye.'"

Kate laughs.

"And do you know what he did? He went looking for his twin brother, too, and then came back in the suit and tie with a mustache drawn on his lip. Smeared on like Groucho Marx."

"And you married him," says Kate.

"Oh, I married lots of people," Billie says. "I never saw my parents again. They died in a car accident."

"That's awful."

She hisses. "Ringo once told me something. A wonderful player, I will never understand why people do not think so. He said, 'Communication is poor with the ones we know best, and best with the ones we know poorly.' Then he said, 'Fie-rumbly-bee,' or something and tried to look down my blouse."

They shuffle past anonymous buildings, all of which seem connected by second-story walkways. They pass office towers, a big hotel and a radio station, and occasionally Kate turns to check this big man's face for a sign of recognition. Liquid drips from his nose, and he doesn't wipe it. He's still faintly smiling, walking past a "Minnesotans for Romney" bumper sticker.

A nun at St. Olaf who doesn't recognize the man or the dog directs them to a narrow brick building behind the church. It's dark now and even colder.

"Should I stay outside with the pooch?" Kate says, but Billie waves her into this foyer. There's no security guard, only some mailboxes and a locked entrance. There are steel buttons on the wall, one for every apartment, and Kate wonders if Billie will start buzzing them all.

"Is this where you live?" Billie says to the man. "Is this place familiar?" He gurgles.

Kate looks at the dog, who seems noncommittal.

"There is a sign here. 'Case Management Hours: 9-to-5, Monday-through-Friday.' What time is it, dear?"

"It's after six," says Kate.

"There is a number."

Kate calls. She won't be the one who tells Billie they should give up. She'll go as far as Billie wants.

A small older lady with wine-stained teeth comes downstairs and lets them into the lobby proper. "No pets are allowed," she says.

"We are not coming inside," says Billie. "This is as far as we are coming."

"No," the lady says, "I mean this man couldn't live here if he has a pet. We don't allow them."

"And you do not know him."

"I'm afraid I don't. The thing to do is call Human Services. Does he have identification? If he does, we call Human Services. If he doesn't, we call the police."

"I do not like the sound of either," Billie says. "It sounds like he winds up in a cell someplace. You can look at the man and see he needs help. You can smell him."

"My advice is the police," says this lady. "I look at his dog, neatly groomed and well fed, and I think someone else has been taking care of it. He may live with family, and they may be worried sick. About both of them. It happens more than you might think. Call the police is my advice. You can't wander around the city with him all night."

They all look at him, and he pays no mind. He's breathing hard and smiling, going *hoo-hoo-hoo* through pursed lips. Maybe he's impersonating the dog's panting. He gives off the shameless suggestion of a very small child, his gums exposed and his eyes squeezed almost shut.

"No police," Billie says.

"It's admirable," says the woman. "Not many people would care so much. Don't think I'm some hardened public servant. I wish St. Olaf had a hundred more beds. There's a shelter a few blocks away that has free breakfast and lunch every day, and free showers. Maybe they know him. But the dog makes me think he's got a family. I understand your mistrust, ma'am, but if it's me, I call the police."

Billie seems perturbed and slighted, but Kate looks at this woman and thinks about her life in this drab apartment building supporting dozens of people trying to get their lives together, thinks about her sacrifice, and she loves the little lady. "Thank you," she says. "You do a wonderful thing taking care of people."

"Anyone doing this wishes they could do more, but the money's all gone."

"Still," Kate croaks. "Really."

The man-child leans over to put his face directly in the dog's face. He goes *hoo-hoo-hoo* and the lab's ears turn. It looks at the rest of them apologetically, then kisses the man.

They step back outside and the cold stings more. Billie leads them around the corner to a bakery. Kate waits outside holding the leash and watches through a window: it's bustling inside, and Billie stands on line, holding the big man's hand. As each customer orders and leaves, Billie steps ahead and gives a small tug, whereupon he paces forward, too, looking around smiling. Kate's jacket isn't heavy enough for this. She pats her arms and her mind trips and travels to Binghamton nights at a neighbor's, surprisingly painless memories of warmth and board games, though when they came home her parents usually brought out the scale. Then she thinks of Florida under the stars, being so sticky above her sleeping bag it felt like the air was wool. She wonders if the man in the anorak understands the concept of secrets.

She thinks, *I go along. They ask me to get in a van and with no thought in my head, I do. They ask me to join a band and with no thought in my head, I do.*

Billie comes outside bearing sticky buns and scones, and several pieces of fruit pie. Kate munches as Billie pours bottled water for the dog. The man doesn't try to chew, he just swallows globs of pie.

"There was a bakery in Manhattan Beach," Billie says. "It is the thing I miss most. Croissants so big and soft you could wear them like mittens." They start walking again.

"Have you done this before?" says Kate.

"Maybe I will go back. California is calling me."

"Have you, Ms. Turner? Found someone and helped them get home like this?"

Billie pats the man-child's arm. "I cannot smell him anymore," she says.

They arrive at a building marked "House of Charity" and the young woman behind the desk knows sign language. She tries a few times, but the big man just giggles foolishly, ducking his head. "He doesn't understand," says this new lady. "I don't recognize him, and I know just about everyone who comes here or to the kitchen. And I'm afraid I can't spend any more time, because we're on lockdown. My advice is you should call the police."

"Thank you," says Billie. "Come on, we will be going." She takes the dog's leash from Kate and tugs the big man's anorak.

"Why are you on lockdown?" Kate says.

"We get these calls once a month. Some crime gets done and the police don't know who it is, and they ask us to lock down so we know who was in and who was out. Some city councilman's fascist idea of being tough on crime. You know how many crimes the homeless commit? Practically none."

Kate's three companions are already outside, walking away down 8ᵗʰ Street. She says, "And what happened today?"

"Some jogger got himself beaten up bad over in St. Paul, got his dog stolen. Like I said, once a month. To my knowledge, it's never, ever been a homeless person."

Kate steps into a fully formed nighttime and her cheeks prickle. She makes a brief project of huffing to see her breath; there it is: the cloud that proves she's alive. She catches up to Billie, and hears her singing:

When you get in trouble,
It's no use to screamin' and cryin', hmm.

"Where are you taking him now?" says Kate.

"Never mind," Billie says.

"Did you hear what that woman said? Someone hurt a jogger. The police are looking."

"No, Claudia, I didn't hear."

Kate's head feels thick. She's a couple paces behind them, checking the man's face: he's placid, smiling open-mouthed. And he's walking alongside Billie voluntarily, without his hand being held. Kate feels the calluses on her forefingers, and her hands twitch as though she's drumming out power triplets. The thing to do now is bow out gracefully.

"Are you headed for another shelter?" she says.

Billie doesn't answer.

"The jogger who got mugged. He had a dog."

Billie looks behind them, as if they're being followed.

"There are people whose job it is to figure this stuff out," says Kate.

"And if you trust those people," Billie says, "you are on the wrong damn side."

The rebuke slows Kate's pace, and she realizes her feet are getting sore. But she keeps walking, now several steps behind. She tries to remember why she's here, what caused her to follow along. Billie seems a furious, deluded little package, and Kate considers maybe *she's* also on the loose, having escaped a negligent caregiver.

They keep going, heading back toward the river. They pass near a stadium, a silent glowing soufflé close enough to touch. Rush hour is long over and the sidewalks are empty. Kate is underwater, pretending that as the person with the most marbles in her head, she's ultimately in control here and can make sure everyone ends up all right.

Her phone rings again: another unknown caller. She doesn't answer.

Another quarter-mile and Billie finally needs to rest. She sits on a bench beside a small playground, whose empty Technicolor castles and slides are baselessly optimistic. The dog buckles next to her, and the man stands guard behind. Billie's posture summons Kate to the bench.

"Well, I do not suppose I know exactly what I am doing with him," Billie says.

"You're trying to help," says Kate, sitting down.

"I do not think it is working."

They are specks. Minneapolis huffs compressed air at them, a byproduct of its million frantic stories. It's all they can do not to blow away.

"I always did like adventure," says Billie. "The moment anything becomes too settled."

"It's admirable," Kate says. "But nobody seems to know him, and it's freezing out here. You have to take care of yourself, too."

"I am sorry your visit has turned out so strange. I have never made a habit of turning out to be what people expected. There were always people at the fringes. They would come into the room, shake the hand of your friend, and your friend would disappear for a few minutes. Or the ones who talk as if they already know you, using words you are supposed to recognize. I want to follow these people and find out what they know. I do not have very much respect for what I am supposed to do."

"But it's over now, Ms. Turner. I can take you home."

"I am not explaining myself well. I am not interested in the ones who keep to themselves. If I had kept to myself, where would I be? Dead in a car crash with my poor parents, maybe. I was not anything special, but at least I never kept to myself."

"Nothing special?" says Kate. "You played with some of the greatest musicians in the world. You're an inspiration. I seriously can't even believe I met you."

Billie smiles. "I wonder if you could tell me: what is your favorite song of mine?"

"'Cool Simba.' I listened to it a thousand times. I still know it by heart."

"I remember the reviews of that album," says Billie. "Nobody could understand why they put an instrumental like that on a record with so many sweet pop songs. I cried when I read this." Her knees start joggling, her feet in practical rubber boots start tapping disconnected rhythms, and her gloved hands drum the air for just a moment. She looks up at the giant behind them—he transfers his weight from leg to leg, grunting a little as he breathes—then back to Kate. She says, "You do not keep to yourself, either."

"Thanks, Billie."

"Now let me ask you again. What do you feel when you play?"

Kate opens her mouth, but her voice catches. Something rushes upon her, memories and feelings, abasements we all hold at bay through force of will. She recalls what it's like to feel hopeless, to believe that she's about to make a mistake that will ruin her life. This is the paralysis that characterized her teenage years, being afraid that something awful was about to happen but not having the first clue what might cause it. Yet isn't it something, that she hasn't felt this way very often lately? "I feel *better*," she tells Billie.

"..."

"..."

"Well, you are the first person who ever followed me when I did this," says Billie. She reaches a hand backward, and pulls the big man around to this side of the bench, tugs him down until he's sitting between Billie and Kate. "Look at him," Billie says.

Kate does. Wisps of black hair peek from beneath the anorak's hood, encroaching on his dirty face. In the streetlight, Kate can see his black eyes and dirty pores. And he sees Kate, gives her a smile of recognition. His size is ridiculous; his mouth is the shape of an infant's.

"He is not a concept," Billie says.

Kate thinks about tomorrow's show. Midweek in a school gym sounds like a recipe for no audience. Yet she wants to be teleported there right now, feeling butterflies despite a big empty room.

Billie gets up, and leans over to hug the man. Kate can see both their faces, as he realizes what's happening and hugs back. They close their eyes and grin, chastely entwined. Billie's hands pat his shoulders and the man says, "Nnnngggggggg."

Then he begins to squeeze harder. Billie's expression sags, and she says, "Oh." The anorak slides against her cheek as his arms pull her tight. He opens his mouth—the dark hole from which a terrible smell arises—and he coos as he clenches her. Kate stands and the dog does, too. Billie lets go and her arms flail, her back arches and her feet come off the ground. He mashes her against him, her hands slap against his shoulders. There's a clicking, maybe buttons unsnapping, maybe bones coming apart. Kate sees Billie's eyes balloon.

Then he lets go. Billie's feet touch back down again, and she laughs like a child who's survived an amusement ride.

LET IT BE

They have sex in the bathroom and she keeps trying to get further away from him. He advances, she retreats: a wordless exchange because Kate and Scott are still sleeping in the other room. Both the shower and the tap are running. He's got her around the hips, looking at her brown butt and thinking how perfect she is, and she's keeping her pelvis thrust forward, trying to deny him full access. He thunders in grunting anyway, and she wants to love it, but it hurts. She sees herself in the mirror looking like a baffled game-show contestant. And she sees him seeing her, recognizing the lack of pleasure in her expression. He pulls back, thrusts more shallowly. She wonders if it would feel better in the shower.

Amanda has had many suitors, but only three other sex partners. Sebastian makes her nervous because he's huge, but also because by definition possessing such equipment makes him seem a virtuoso. She walks around with her lower abdomen feeling perpetually bruised, assuming her need for foreplay is amateurish. He knows one speed setting—jackhammer—and doesn't have many gentle impulses, quite surprising for someone who has such grace as a musician. But she loves and accepts him. Besides, she likes him dominant sometimes. It's all right.

Sebastian has been told by a dozen women how good he is. He gets confused the times Amanda doesn't claw his back or writhe beneath him, and he thinks about initiating a conversation, but then the next time she'll come screaming and he assumes they've figured it out. Anyway, it's an embarrassing subject to broach; Amanda is three years older. She explains movies to him, encourages him to read her favorite books, just yesterday she told him the expression "rule of thumb" came from the 1800s when it was legal for men to beat their wives, as long as they used a stick no wider than their thumb. He also laments the fact that apparently so many women watch so much porn these days; Amanda regularly asks if he wants to finish on her face, which he decidedly doesn't.

They towel off breathing through their noses. She kisses him and puts on a bra that hasn't been washed in a week. He covers up as she leaves the bathroom. Her face is everywhere he looks, this impossibly lovely shape that's somehow his. He takes his pills and tries to remember where they are. Right. Magnetic Fields was last night. Minneapolis.

Amanda sneaks over to her bag looking for a clean shirt. Scott's eyes open. She's in jeans and a shiny black bra. He sits up and she lingers; her midsection is muscled and impossible to ignore. She says, "Day off," and he says, "Yup." She has a tattoo of an infinity symbol on her lower back.

Sebastian and Amanda walk into Elliot Park and find a tiny red-and-white diner that's empty in the late morning. They sit wearing cheap sunglasses deciding how to divvy eight dollars. She grins and hands over her earbuds, presses play. He's not sure what he's listening to: a shuffle rhythm, a jangly guitar switching between G, A7 and Em7, a singer asking, "How young are you? How old am I?" At first he thinks it might be one of Scott's demos, which irks him, but he raises his eyebrows and nods.

"It's the Replacements," Amanda says. "I downloaded them in your honor."

"…"

"Minneapolis. This is where they came from. The Replacements. Your OKCupid screen name."

"Oh, right. Yeah."

She takes a sip of water. "Did you not recognize it?"

"Well. It was a screen name. I was cultivating a persona."

She laughs. "You're a fraud."

He doesn't listen to the rest of the song. He drops the earbuds onto the table and slides her phone a few inches away. She covers his hands with hers, fighting annoyance. They order an omelet to share. He surfs to a live Sascha Funke track on YouTube and offers it. She hears a few seconds of electronic bloops and a driving synth beat, and makes an exaggerated grouchy face and drops the earbuds, slides the phone away. Sebastian laughs and they're friends again.

"Young love," he says.

"We're adorable."

Amanda reads his splendid features, and somehow with longer stubble and bags under his eyes he's even more delicious. She imagines his depths, the beautiful sounds percolating inside him. He makes music seem effortless; guitars practically leap into his hands urging him on. The first time she heard him play was in his old apartment: it took an hour of coaxing and even then his shyness was overpowering, and it wasn't an act (something else she likes after so many swaggering Manhattan boys). But when he finally picked up his Telecaster he did crank his amp loud, and played something slow and incredibly pellucid and sweet. When she asked what it was, he told her it was nothing, he was just noodling. And even if that was sort of a pickup line, it was a damn good one. Sebastian is almost always kind. In a way, he's a person Amanda wishes she could be. He doesn't blame people. He's really, really calm. When Amanda's mother came to New York over the summer and met Sebastian, she said, "Pish, he looks like a movie star and acts like the understudy."

"Where have you been all my life?" she says now, a little sarcastic, still slightly irked and knowing she's also in love with being in love.

Sebastian smiles and says, "Playing music you hate."

"Eesh. I didn't hate it, I was kidding. I like it, actually. And I love your stuff. You know how much I love your songs."

"..."

"Let's not be manipulative now, okay?"

"No, I.... I was just thinking how the three of you have this world in common. It's not you, I just feel like I need to go to rock school or whatever."

"That's crazy," she says. "You played 'Waiting For The Man' the other day. You taught it to Scott, and he loved it."

"Yeah, I know. My uncle had that record. If I've heard it I can usually play it, but I just haven't heard too many."

"'And that was the day she agreed to take charge of his pop-music education.' But seriously here's what you do: just borrow Kate's phone. She's got everything on there. One long drive and you'll be completely caught up."

Sebastian draws figure-eights on the table. "The thing is...."

"..."

"I feel like I should want to. You're right about that. But I kind of *don't*. I don't really want to listen to, whatever, Tame Impala and War On Drugs. I'm probably being spoiled. I'm not complaining about the way things are going and all. But when we talked about it at first, I didn't think the songs would be so...." He knows he sounds unctuous. The reality of playing these same tunes the same way every time out...is having access to Amanda's naked body sufficient compensation? This summer when they all came together, they spoke in generalities but in retrospect Sebastian should've known it would be like this. It turns out Scott, Kate and Amanda had the same outmoded picture in their heads of what music stardom looks like. You pick up a guitar, you bang a drum, you numbly jam...and Father Label descends from the heavens and pronounces you worthy, bestows His riches. But Sebastian is the one who's had legit success, and it happened inside the confines of one crappy apartment. It's already a testament to persistence that they've gigged halfway across the country, but *this* is how their dreams will come true, playing quarter-filled clubs where all anyone can ask Sebastian is how come he's with a rock band? He says, "You know what? This is unfair. I'm really putting you in an unfair position."

"I'm open," says Amanda. "I think we're all open. What songs do you want us to learn?"

But that's the point. He doesn't want them to learn his songs. This summer he had this idea that they'd all create on the fly together, that their talent could augment his, but now he doesn't even know what that would look like. He thinks about how many hours of material he's thrown away in the past, how many false starts, how much anguish, how many dead ends. *He* never knows what he wants things to sound like. How could he ever expect three other people to know? "No. It's stupid. I'm being.... Listen, I don't know *what* the hell I'm doing half the time. Forget this. Can we rewind the tape?"

"Let's write together," she says. "I'll do whatever you want me to. Let's make a song together."

"…"

"You get bored," she says. "I get it. It's the price of being a gene…. A gene…."

"Don't say it."

"Being a gene…. A gene…. A gene…."

"Seriously, I'll throw maple syrup on you."

"A *genius.*"

Sebastian covers his face with his hands. He hasn't written a Kid Centrifuge song from scratch, has only ornamented Scott's compositions. He resolves to write a rock song, dammit. Tonight. And he'll adorn it with a complicated riff and a shifting meter; there's no reason one of these dopey rock tunes shouldn't retain the complexity of electronica or even jazz. He'll write something that's simple but still a challenge to play, something that can maybe be a little different every time. This is a code he can crack. He can write catchy songs that break the musician's back.

They finish eating and walk in weak sunlight through this low-rise city, past churches and light industry, through the Metrodome's shadow and onto a bike trail that passes over a spaghetti highway interchange. Amanda holds Sebastian's hand and wants to believe in soulmates. They arrive in the West Bank, and see places that remind them of home: an Ethiopian market, a Mediterranean deli, a Halal grocer, and a small park hosting four or five homeless ladies of the shopping-cart variety. It's past noon and despite their lack of funds, they decide a drink sounds good. A little place called Palmer's Bar is open, and they step inside.

It's a long skinny room with dozens of framed pictures on the walls. They split up: Sebastian takes a spot near the door, while Amanda walks further in and flounces onto a padded stool one seat away from the only other customers in here, who are huddled at the end of the bar. She takes off her cashmere coat and makes a production of tossing it onto a seat, so the buttons clack. The men seem in the middle of a hilarious story, but one of them turns, sees Amanda, and taps the leg of a compatriot. She folds her hands and grins.

They invite her over and spring for a drink. She orders a Turkey Ball, downs it quickly, and acts exhilarated, so these four guys fall over themselves to get her another, and that's when Sebastian saunters over and gives her a hug.

"Who the hell's buying my lady booze?" he says, and these

guys look horrified, then Sebastian says, "*Two* drinks? Hell, *I'll* go down on you for two drinks," and everyone laughs. It turns out this quartet is about to embark upon the Cinnamon Challenge, of which Sebastian has never heard.

"Seriously?" says Amanda. "They have this new thing called the Internet. You should really check it out."

"It sounds easy," Sebastian says. They pour him a teaspoon of cinnamon.

"Sixty seconds to swallow it," says a bleach-blond kid. "No water." His friends make rapturous faces.

"Ten bucks he craps the bed," Amanda says, but nobody takes the bet.

So Sebastian puts the spoonful into his mouth, and he tries to swallow but his saliva is gone. A trickle of dust touches the topmost part of his throat and he coughs out an orange cloud. Cinnamon flies up into his nose and he breathes fire as they laugh at him. He chokes and heaves, steps away from his barstool, feels like he's about to retch. He can't see anything. His hands are on his knees and they all slap his back. It's torture for several minutes.

The bartender comes over and draws him a beer, and it's a seriously expensive way to get a free drink. He doesn't even need to show his fake ID.

Three of the other guys also try and fail, and then it's the bleach-blond kid's turn. He shoves the cinnamon into one cheek and shuts his mouth tight, breathing through his nose. He looks at his watch, making kissy faces to build up saliva, and with five seconds left he takes a big swing at swallowing and almost makes it, but he gags, and a small brown ball ejects through his nostril. They all slap the bar, unable to breathe for laughter.

Someone buys a pitcher and they give Amanda and Sebastian plastic cups. The bleach-blond guy is named Spooner and he's in a band. He shows off a biceps tattoo that reads, *The Wesley Stripes*. "Nothing but balls-out rock," he says. "One bourbon, one scotch and one beer, baby. I play lead."

"Gosh," says Sebastian.

The group downs a few pitchers, then disperses. Amanda is feeling no pain, and hugs everyone as they leave. Spooner says, "Hey, what are you guys doing now?"

"Nothing," she says.

He's flabby and has "FAITH" in blue ink across his knuckles.

"You two wanna come help me stake out Bruce Springsteen?"

"Well, duh!" Sebastian says.

The Boss apparently played St. Paul on Sunday night, and the rumor is he stuck around the Twin Cities for a few days, before his next gig tomorrow in Omaha. Spooner claims to know Springsteen's secret location. They pile in his truck and drive back downtown, wobbly as hell.

There's no crowd where they park on Hennepin Avenue, and while Spooner and Amanda focus on a boutique hotel across the street, Sebastian checks out the Orpheum right in front of them: its marquee is brilliantly old-school and advertises a show for Rollerkick Beats w/DJ Droid. Before he met Amanda, before her enthusiasm roped him into this transnational gambol, he didn't like playing live. But now he imagines the course his solo career might've taken, and the songs that would've followed "Chord" and "Bandfucker," whipping up enough celebrity to fill a two-thousand-seat venue in a random Midwestern burg.

"My mom loves Bruce," Amanda says. "I heard he walks around the boardwalk by his house and sits on a bench and eats ice cream and plays guitar, like, you can walk right up to him and listen."

"This chick Marilyn knows a guy who works in the hotel laundry," says Spooner. "And the housekeepers are all sure it's him. Checked in Saturday, checking out tomorrow morning. If I meet him, he's signing my Strat, don't care what I have to do."

"You have your Strat with you?" says Sebastian. "Can I see that bad boy?"

"In the hard case behind the seat back there."

Sebastian reaches behind them and opens the guitar case. There's a red Stratocaster, and when he lifts it he also sees a little bag of white powder. The sight makes him tingle from his toes to his nose. He says, "My buzz is officially on the wane. Spooner, you feel like coming with me to get a refresh?" He looks meaningfully at the guitar.

"Oh, absofuckinglutely," Spooner says.

"Do what you want," says Amanda, "I'm checking out that lobby. And if I see Bruce, I can't be held responsible for what happens next." She hops out of the truck, hears Sebastian say, "Ew."

But there are no guests or bodyguards milling around inside

the hotel, only a couple desk clerks and a concierge. Amanda sits in a comfortable lobby chair, crosses her legs and slides home her earbuds, intent on waiting for the Boss. She starts up "Let It Be" and hears that jangling guitar again. She has no idea what happened to the Replacements and this notion has always startled her, that performers can be famous and then utterly gone; Scott lent her Bob Dylan's autobiography and Amanda's main takeaway was a litany of pop-culture names from fifty years ago of whom she's never heard. Dozens of them! And in the midst of the Tom Paleys and Erik Darlings and Bobby Vees, Harry Belafonte got mentioned—one she recognized—and somehow this is even more depressing.

The music stops.

Dammit, she's forgotten to charge her phone.

She's lonely and tipsy, and thinks Kate might get a kick out of stalking Springsteen. She uses the house phone to call Kate's number, but there's no answer. The apple-cheeked concierge walks over, all efficient tweedy butt-twitches, and stands too close.

"Can I help you?"

"No thanks," says Amanda.

"Are you waiting for a particular guest?"

"…"

"What I mean is," and she makes a servile, elliptical hand wave, "I could show you a more comfortable waiting area."

Amanda defensively re-buttons the top loop on her cashmere coat. "Oh."

They stride past an elevator, down a first-floor hallway and through an unmarked door. It's a ritzy hotel living room without a bedroom or bathroom. A window looks onto a busy street and a pub across the way, but the concierge draws the linen drapes. Amanda perches on a couch.

"All right," says the concierge. "Just wait here."

Amanda opens her mouth, but doesn't speak. The concierge leaves.

Is this weirdness Springsteen-related? Who hasn't heard stories of road managers finding new supplicants for their superstar acts? The smell in here is undeniably good: floral and privileged. She has the sense of a world opening, and waits, imagining Gulfstream jets and stadium tours. Every moment goes by clapping for attention, but she stays put.

Lacey, you'll never guess where I am. I'm backstage at Madison Square Garden about to open for one of the rock gods of the 20th century! Wish you could be here, big sis, but we both know that diaper won't change itself.

Someone knocks, and Amanda doesn't say anything.

A modestly handsome guy with a short haircut and a nice suit steps in ducking his head. He briefly meets her eyes, and otherwise watches the carpeting. He's got broad shoulders and a trim waist, and his deference paints him an underling.

"Hi!" he says, too loud, then modulates: "Wow, you're really pretty." The door slams behind him in the airless way of hotels.

"..."

"Do you mind if I...?" and he sits in a nearby chair. "Did they offer you anything to drink, or...?"

"I'm fine."

"I guess this is like the demo suite or something," he says. "Like the really high-end guests send their secretaries to come check out the hotel, and this is the room they show."

"Fascinating."

"Okay. I mean, before we go upstairs. Why don't you take off your shades?"

She hadn't realized she was still wearing them, and feels a bit thrilled. She says, "I don't think I will."

"What's your name?"

"Amanda."

"Amanda, take off the shades and take off your coat. Stay a while."

"Is he really upstairs?" she says. "Is that what this is?"

The man crosses his legs and laces his fingers around a knee, and in this position he looks more like a venture capitalist or marketing vice president, an older version of someone with whom she might've had an online date. He says, "Yes. He is."

She tosses the sunglasses onto this coffee table. "And you're his...what?"

"..."

"Manservant? Butler?"

"Hm. Let's say personal assistant."

She undoes the coat. "I mean, I want to meet him. But this is pretty gross."

He scopes her out. She's wearing a crappy old UCLA sweatshirt. "Amanda," he says, "let's talk numbers."

"…"

"You know it's a conversation we have to have. So let's have it."

She hears these words, but can't make them congeal into anything she understands. Numbers? A diesel truck chugs outside. For a moment she can't remember what city she's in. "Wait." She puts up her palms and she's absolutely sober. "Are you saying Bruce Springsteen wants to pay me for sex?"

The man smiles emptily at her.

"Wait, are you saying someone who's *not* Bruce Springsteen wants to pay me for sex?"

He looks at the sweatshirt.

"Some lady tells me to wait in here. What the hell is going on?"

He stands and walks to the far wall. He puts his hands on the mantelpiece above a false fireplace and she hears him sigh. She can't see his face as he makes a throat-slashing gesture at the wall, and draws something small and black out of his suit pocket. She recoils.

"Shut it down," he says into a small radio.

"…"

"Amanda, at this point can I take it you're not a call girl?"

"…"

"I'm Detective Walton and I'm about to catch an absolute raft of shit, so how do you feel about getting the fuck out of here?"

"How do I…?

"Seriously," he says. "We should really get you out of here. Like now."

They go. He takes a right turn out of the suite, and opens a fire door that lets out onto 9th Street. Amanda sees her feet moving, and she says, "How do I know this isn't a scam?" and he reaches back and shows her a badge, which is dull and brassy in the late-afternoon overcast. She looks down the block, and Spooner's truck is still over there, empty.

"Bruce Springsteen, huh?" he says.

He walks her past the State Theater—whose marquee announces DJ KillCrusha playing tomorrow night—and into a steakhouse. Chairs are still stacked on tables this early, but a host shakes the cop's hand and seats them in a corner.

"Whatever you want," the cop says. "It's on me. I'm very

sorry."

"..."

"All right. Relax. That hotel's a popular spot for it. Three hundred bucks a night minimum, and the penthouse is over a grand. Out-of-towners who can afford that are apparently spending on other luxury items, too."

"Jesus."

"We busted three high-end girls there yesterday, but they're trained not to give up the escort service." He loosens his tie. "But we were barking up the wrong tree with you, weren't we, Amanda? You were hoping to give it to the Boss for free."

She blushes. "I'm in a *band*. I thought he could...."

"I'm sure you did."

"My boyfriend was literally sitting right outside."

He grins. "Understanding boyfriend."

"Yeah, because this is definitely the best I can do for a sexy outfit."

"Anyway, again, my apologies. Believe me, this is the calm before the storm. My partner is somewhere still busting a gut, and we had a couple uniforms there, too. You're doing me a favor delaying the abuse."

"You said you were...his personal assistant."

"I said. It's called improvisation, right? Believe me, some weird shit winds up getting said."

Amanda looks at his strong and hairless hands. "I was just talking with someone about improvisation," she says.

"Well, I'm all in favor." He waves, and the host comes back and takes his order. Amanda thinks about a steak, but feels guilty eating without Sebastian. "In fact, it seems like you're an improviser at heart, too, Amanda. Considering you're sitting here with me." He makes a production of removing something from his pants pocket, and putting it on his finger: a wedding ring.

"Don't flatter yourself," she says. "You're old enough to be my father."

"I'm 33."

"Well you don't look a day over 45."

"Harsh. I'll tell you why you're really still here with me right now. It's because you're good-looking, and you think why not. What bad thing has ever happened that you couldn't fix because you were pretty?"

"Oh, that's such bullshit," says Amanda.

"Then tell me. I practically just ran you in for solicitation, and now we're having a nice dinner."

"Maybe I *am* a hooker, and I was just onto your game early."

"Like that," he says. "That's too flirty. You should be more careful."

"..."

"Hm. So this band. Have I heard of you?"

It's a question that stabs. Deep inside, she feels that by now, someone should've discovered her. She shouldn't be staggering around the nation week after week in that stupid van. P.J. Harvey and Shirley Manson and Lauryn Hill...they were born into the sweet spot, when everyone cared. And she's too late. Sometimes Amanda thinks she should ditch everyone and just go full-on sexy pop star: fly to L.A., get a manager who tells her what to wear, where to stand, what to sing. To this detective, she says, "Not yet."

"Are you country? I mostly listen to country."

"..."

He settles further into the booth. "I like George Strait. George Jones. Kenny Chesney. But I'll listen to Sugarland, too."

"I literally have heard of none of those people," Amanda says.

"You couldn't get me to listen to a Taylor Swift song if she was singing it naked right in front of me. It's the overproduced bullshit that gives country a bad name. The good stuff, the old guys, you know they're feeling it in their balls. The same slide guitar sounds fake with the frauds, and breaks your heart behind the Possum."

"Well, I'm the singer." She purses her lips. "And you'd believe me."

"The young lady doesn't lack for confidence," says the detective. "What makes you so sure?"

She makes her eyes go swimmy. "Because *I* believe it."

He moves his jaw to one side, contemplating something. Then he unwraps his silverware from a napkin's embrace. "Honey," he says, "I'm really not going to fuck you, if that's what you're asking."

And she thinks, *You would if I wanted you to.*

She realizes she's hearing music. Someone's turned on Muzak in this restaurant—"Eleanor Rigby"—and it makes her irritated with Sebastian: because he probably wouldn't recognize it, because he'd hide behind pretense. *Let's see...Beatles...Beatles...maybe I've heard of them...did Paul Oakenfold remake one of their songs?* She thinks about this morning in the bathroom, and the way the guys at Palmer's Bar looked at her.

Maybe the truth, if she's honest about things, is she's sitting here because she really does love Sebastian and isn't sure how much he loves her back. Amanda considers herself a no-nonsense person. Her sister calls her cold, and Amanda kind of likes it. Sentimentality is a way to abdicate responsibility. She blazes her own path! But there it is: maybe her feelings for Sebastian overwhelm her. Maybe. "So," she says. "Good old-fashioned country music."

His steak arrives. "I don't care if the singer is telling me what he really thinks, or if his songs show who he really is. Shit, I don't care if he's even singing his own song. It's about.... My precinct captain is this guy named Jacobsen, right? He walks into a room, you notice him. End of story. He's not big, he's not handsome. But it doesn't matter what room. It could be a brain surgeons' convention. He just has this...authority. You know it when you hear it."

"Okay," Amanda says.

"If it was him in there with you today, he could've talked you all the way upstairs. You'd have been up there naked looking for Springsteen under the bed."

"So this is interesting."

"All right."

"No, I mean it. You're really saying it's the singer tricking himself into believing, whether he really actually believes or not. That's what you like."

"..."

"'I didn't get divorced. I didn't shoot my dog. But I can sing like I did.' Taylor Swift really did break up with a million guys, but it doesn't matter because she sounds like a liar."

"Yeah, you are totally way too chatty to be a hooker."

"'I don't like playing these chords over and over. These songs are too simple.' Yeah, well, if you trick yourself into liking it, you'll be...authentic."

The cop listens as he chews. "But I guess maybe in the end who really cares?"

"You do. You just said you like those George guys because of their balls."

"I didn't say authentic. That's a big word." He taps his nose. "I'm just talking about the bullshit detector. Mine's an all-timer."

Amanda has an impulse to ask Detective Walton if his wife is pretty. Instead she says, "You should come see us play tomorrow night. It's five bands at a junior high school, but it just might be the last time you'd get to hear us face-to-face. We're on the elevator up."

"A junior high."

"Ha. That's nothing. In Indiana we played a county fair in a pig barn. In Wisconsin we played an opening for an auto parts store."

He lifts his beer. "To success at all costs."

"How long have you been married?" Amanda says.

"You really are something," says the detective. "I can't tell if you're the most confident person I ever met, or the least."

"..."

"Ah, well. Here's what I say about marriage. Men who have pierced ears are better prepared for it. They've experienced pain and bought jewelry."

She smiles at him, the full-frontal, and sees his professional cool flake away. She feels fully herself.

He takes a big old breath. "Where should we go after this?" he says.

At the same time, Sebastian and Spooner are in the bathroom of a tiny Scottish pub, and Sebastian has just bumped from Spooner's stash. It's incredible stuff. Sebastian feels wired, but also mellow at an elevated peak. Spooner arranges himself in front of a mirror, looking puffy and older. Scrutinizing his own pores, he says, "I didn't realize I was in the presence of such famousness."

"You're not," says Sebastian.

"That's the first time in my many years of coming to this place that Laura the bartender even looked at a guy. She knows your song, man."

"I think she was yanking your chain."

"Naw, dude. Now I need to hear you play."

Sebastian grins. "Meh."

"And how'd you get your hair that high? It's like a foot taller than you are."

A couple guys with no necks come in and crowd the urinals, which feels like a cue. Sebastian follows Spooner back into the main room, another long-and-skinny Minneapolis special that's beginning to buzz with Happy Hour traffic. Sebastian likes these close spaces, likes it when a stage's ceiling is so low he bangs his rings on the occasional guitar windmill. Spooner knows everyone, keeps stopping to cuff guys on the shoulder. It sounds like he says "heptathlon" to a few of them, but he keeps walking. They sit at the bar. "Well, it's no wonder how you got Amanda," he says.

"I put out one record. If she's with me for my fame, she made a bad mistake."

"Yeah, but you *got* a record," says Spooner. "What kind of music? The key question: do you kick ass?"

"Put it this way. I don't think you'd think I kick ass."

"I got my band in a real studio one night. We fucking sucked. Everything that's good about us live and sloppy for a bunch of our drunk friends vaporized. We started playing *quiet*. It was embarrassing."

Sebastian smiles at Laura the bartender as she comes over to mix a drink. Again he feels the urge to create. It's a confidence in his powers to accept the details of right now—neon colors of beer signs, everyone rolling into or out of parkas, a melancholic rumble of lonely men, Laura's bulging black tanktop—and distill his exalted watching into sounds. And yet he also knows, of course, that his regular inability to perform exactly this distillation is what torments him.

"Oh, shit, you know what?" says Spooner. "I totally forgot about Springsteen." They laugh, and Sebastian realizes he's either lost his phone, or left it with the band's gear. He goes outside to leave a note on the truck's dashboard, letting Amanda know where they are.

"If I'm totally honest," Sebastian says, back inside, "I wouldn't want that kind of fame. A little bit, but not the Springsteen kind."

Spooner peels paper off his beer bottle. "I call bullshit. You should see your face when you say that."

"I'm serious. Never be able to go anywhere without getting hassled? Fans always wondering why your new stuff isn't like the songs they fell in love with? Becoming this *thing* outside yourself that millions of people rely on?"

"And I say: Bull. Shit. You'd take it in a heartbeat. I only say that because anyone would. It's easy for your motives to be pretty when you're invisible."

"I know what you're saying," says Sebastian. "Maybe there'd be a way to do it, and keep it meaningful. Yeah, there probably is a way."

"You know *American Idiot?* Green Day album?"

Sebastian knows *American Idiot* exists, but doesn't remember hearing anything from it. He says, "Oh, yeah. It's the best, right?"

"They got together, made a record, and the masters got stolen out of the studio. And instead of doing the songs all over again, they decided it wasn't all that great in the first place, and made *American Idiot* from scratch instead. And you can't be our age, and listen to it, and not just rock the fuck *out*. And if some douchebag hadn't stolen those masters...."

Sebastian does believe in his worthiness; he can picture women lining up for his autograph. But he also wants to be important. And there's a difference between getting inside a million ears, and this other thing. Significance. He looks at Spooner and thinks: *Our* age?

Later Spooner's friends gather around, and by this point Sebastian's adrenaline is going wild. He can't stop laughing. He shakes everyone's hands, slaps a couple guys on the back, loving them all. This city is filled with good people, smart people. Someone buys a round of tequila and they talk about music. Sebastian looks at all the hand gestures and body art. He nods at Spooner and points to the bathroom.

"Naw, we're good, man," says Spooner.

"I totally hear you," Sebastian says. "Except I do need another taste. Well, I want one, anyway."

"The thing is, nobody likes to feel used."

"Absolutely. I get it. Sorry, Spooner. I got carried away."

"No, it's okay. All right."

"No no," says Sebastian. "I feel like a total dick."

"..."

"Really. Let's just hang out. What song is playing?"

While Spooner launches into a diatribe against Macklemore, Sebastian beams but he's thinking about Amanda, his girlfriend, this beautiful girl with a powerhouse voice, why shouldn't *she* write songs, isn't it kind of condescending that Scott stuffs lyrics in her mouth that he thinks a woman would sing? Fashion and going on dates and looking for self-esteem in callous dudes? Amanda reads like crazy, she's smart as hell, why not let her say what she wants to say?

"Heptathlon!"

Now someone has definitely said this word. Sebastian blinks and looks around, and it's Spooner, he's reaching over the bar to ring a bell and maybe ten of his friends have clustered. Sebastian reads that word on his knuckles again—FAITH—and starts giggling.

"You, sir!" Spooner says, in a British accent. "Do you dare mock the solemn occasion that is Heptathlon?"

Sebastian laughs with his shoulders, indicating how entertained he is.

"You and I!" says Spooner. "We both have something the other man wants!"

"I don't even know what we're even talking about," Sebastian says.

The onlookers shout, also in British accents: "Heptathlon, sir! Heptathlon! Heptathlon, sir?"

"To my truck," Spooner says, "and we shall fetch the Envelope of Events!"

And they're into the cold, and Sebastian notices it's nighttime. He says, "Do what now?"

"Seven events, picked at random, engaged guerilla style!" Spooner holds the envelope aloft. "I have issued a challenge! I will represent our local realm, and I hereby challenge this noble knight from the East!" Huzzahs and harrumphs on this sidewalk. Passersby give them plenty of space. "Sir Sebastian, be so kind as to select the first event!"

"First event."

"Just reach in there."

He does, this manila envelope, a kind he's seen bike messenger friends carrying around. It's filled with crumpled-up slips of paper. With his hand still in mid-grab, he says, "I don't, uh, get it."

"We play for honor! We play for dignity! And also we play for the contents of a particular baggie I'm holding, which I believe interest you."

"Honor!" the onlookers say. "Honor, your honor!"

Sebastian blinks again. "The entire baggie?"

"Indeed!"

The entire baggie is probably three grams, so maybe four hundred dollars? But who knows what it goes for out here in the hinterlands. Sebastian still feels the sweet drip in the back of his throat. "And what am I putting up?"

Spooner smiles with half his face, and talks in his regular voice. "What do you *think* you have that I want? Pick an event."

Sebastian takes out one of the paper slips, but keeps it in his fist. "She's not exactly my property to just *give*," he says.

"One night, just a date," says Spooner. "Obviously."

Everyone kind of pauses, checking Sebastian's expression. One of Scott's lyrics comes to mind:

We are ice cubes
Dropped into the world
It takes a lot of us
But eventually we transfer our cool

He remembers the torture and security of being in his old apartment for days at a time. But he's out here now. He nods, they all cheer, and he uncrumples this scrap of paper and reads, handwritten: "Russian Roulette."

"The hell?" he says.

But no firearms are involved. A couple guys run up Hennepin and return with a sixer of Grain Belt. Sebastian and Spooner cover their eyes, and the beer cans are laid out on the hood of Spooner's truck. One is shaken and placed among the others.

"Who goes first?" says Spooner. "You choose."

Sebastian admires the cloud coming out of him. He steps forward and picks up the nearest can. He pops the top…and no liquid comes out. He takes a long drag—it tastes like water, with a soapy piss finish—and passes the rest to a spectator.

Spooner rubs his palms together and selects a can, pops it, and also remains dry. He pounds the entire beer. "Can't touch a can unless you're picking it," he says.

A cop car fizzes by, and they all look up at the Orpheum's illuminated signage, scratch their necks, stub out make-believe cigarettes. Sebastian puts his fingers on his temples like a mind reader. He picks the can that corresponds to the middle loop of a G-clef, and puts his face right up against the pull-tab. He pops it…and again nothing happens. He sips, then tosses the can high in the air, trying to catch it behind his back, but it clatters to the sidewalk and foam spills out.

"You clown," Spooner says, and he selects the middle can, opens it, and a shower of beer catches him flush in the face. His friends hoot, and a couple horns honk on Hennepin. Spooner shakes his wet bleach-blond hair then pours the offending beer's remainder over his face. He says, "Goddammit. Next event."

Sebastian picks from the envelope and reads, "Little Drummer Boy."

Everyone scatters. Spooner jumps in his truck and Sebastian follows. They drive a few blocks then turn toward an immense parking structure that's thick with cars arriving for a basketball game. Spooner pulls into an alley adorned with all kinds of No Parking admonitions and clicks on his hazards. Still beer-soaked and chilly, he whispers to Sebastian: "Heptathlon."

The group has reconvened at a two-story building across from the Salvation Army. Spooner has a key. The first floor is subdivided into practice rooms, and they pile into one that has a drum kit.

"Remember," Spooner says, "I'm a goddamn guitar player." He takes the throne and removes his baja shirt, revealing a doughy midsection and more tattoos. He makes a face like he's eaten hot lava and whacks away at the cymbals, "swatting flies" with ludicrous arm waves. He plays a loud simple pattern on the ride, still slamming the snare, and flipping-and-catching each off-handed stick on either side of the beat. But he's not keeping tremendous time, and when he's done with the aerial show he kind of unintentionally slows down trying to do something funky on the high-hat. He wraps it up with a bunch of marching-band figures— paradiddles and ratamacues—that get faster until he drops one of the sticks. He tosses the other one after it and says, "Fuck! Never had one lesson!"

Sebastian hasn't been behind a kit in maybe six years, and avoids getting near Kate's setup for fear of creating some weird tension, but he did go through a middle-school phase in Tommy Glaze's garage. As he recalls, Mr. Glaze had about ten toms for all kinds of ridiculous rock fills, and Sebastian's growth spurt was late; now that he sits at a standard four-piece kit he feels like a giant. His wrists snap out some funk, he plays slow but with conviction and it takes a minute to realize he's playing a *song*, what the heck song did

Tommy used to blast when they...? Led Zeppelin, "Fool in the Rain." He only gets out a few more measures and Spooner tosses his shirt over the snare in surrender.

"Two-zip," he says.

The next event comes up "Donny Almost Died," which they explain is a timed chugging contest. They hit up a convenience store and buy two liters of water. Sebastian takes about thirty seconds to drink his, but Spooner practically unhinges his jaw and does it in twenty.

Next is "Bobby Fischer's Liver." There's some debate over where the necessary equipment currently resides—Spooner says it's been more than a year since this event has been pulled—but after a few phone calls they cross the river into St. Paul and a bar called Big V's, where stashed in the back is a chessboard with 32 shot glasses, each embossed with a symbol: bishop, rook, pawn, etc. They've lost a few of their onlookers, but the remainder asks Sebastian to pitch in for booze and he says, "Sorry, boys, my wallet's with my wager." They quarter-fill the shot glasses with whiskey, gin, vodka and (for the queens) Rumple Minze.

Every time a piece is captured, its owner drinks. As soon as Sebastian's got a knight and a pawn out on the board, Spooner is all over him, sacrificing pieces like crazy. In ten moves they're each down four pieces, and though technically speaking Sebastian's ahead, he has to drink as much for a lost pawn as Spooner does for a downed bishop. Sebastian tries to keep his pieces straight, but Spooner goes into stall mode, giving each move more thought. It works. The board starts spinning. Sebastian tries to castle and shatters his king on the floor. They make him use a wine cork as a replacement. He sends his queen forward and she dies in a peppermint-flavored slaughter. The Heptathlon is tied.

Spooner draws the next event, which is "Weather Stripping." Sebastian assumes he'll have to take his clothing off in the elements, but in fact the moveable tournament parks in someone's driveway and a big guy comes outside holding an actual coil of vinyl weather-stripping. Each man gets a four-foot length. "I hit you in the legs," says Spooner, "and you hit me in the legs. Back and forth until someone gives."

"That's pretty viol—*ow!*" Sebastian feels a welt rising on his right buttcheek. "Are you kidding me with this?"

"Now you." Spooner's head is floating here in the semi-dark.

"Nothing above the waist, and no dick-shots." They're down to three or four witnesses, all of whom seem to be cheering for Sebastian, hoping to see maximum pain inflicted on their friend.

Sebastian is blotto. He thinks about giving up, conceding the Heptathlon, maybe puking in the bushes over there, but before he can say anything conciliatory he hears Spooner go, "Holy *fuck*!" and it appears that he's whipped the chubby guitar player in the thigh.

They whack one another in the street, back and forth, and the pops echo around this neighborhood. At first Spooner is dramatic, turning pirouettes before he strikes, but as they proceed Sebastian realizes his drunkenness governs his pain while Spooner needs more and more recovery time between strikes. "Tell you what," says Sebastian, "I'll give you two shots for every one of mine."

"Fuck off. Just hit me in the—*agh!* He's made of fucking…! *Fuck!* I give!"

Sebastian wings the weather-stripping away, and it bounds off a parked car. He blinks…and they're inside another bar and everything smells like sweat. Above them people are dancing on disco squares, Spooner's here twirling an unlit cigarette, saying, "He's a fucking *famous musician*! What the fuck chance do I…!" A couple of his buddies are talking across the table but Sebastian can't hear what they're saying. He sees two beer bottles and assumes he's got double vision, but then he reaches for one of them and his arm is stuck, something's in the crook of his arm, and it's Amanda. She's here. She's laughing and sweaty. He says, "Hey, where you been all night?" and she can think of only one way to distract him, so under the table she puts her hand on his cock.

"The next five songs!" says Spooner. "No matter what they are! Best three out of five, whoever says the title first! Here we go! First one!"

"Oh shit," Sebastian says.

The first has a guitar riff he doesn't recognize. Squeals alight from the dance floor and Spooner goes, "One Direction! 'Live While We're Young!' I'm *so* fucking sad I know that!"

Even worse, they have to listen to the whole syrupy pop mess through to the end. Amanda kisses his cheek and doesn't ask any questions.

"Number two! Here it goes!"

This one is familiar, it's a song Kate played for them during rehearsals this summer, up in that warehouse in Harlem that smelled like hemp and mildew. "'Die Young' by Ke$ha!" says Spooner, and he makes a peevish face at Amanda.

"You're pretty amazing at this!" Sebastian says. "I kind of suck!"

"No buttering me up this close to the end!" Spooner says.

An endless promenade of thick girls in leather miniskirts wiggles around their table. The back of Sebastian's head keeps getting bumped by hips and elbows, and he has the sense none of this is really happening, he's napping home in Jersey waiting to be woken for church.

"By the way," says Spooner.

"..."

"I asked Laura. She said your song is all computer noises, that kind of shit. Said she likes to dance to it."

Time is moving faster than Sebastian's sodden ability to account for it. He burps. The Ke$ha song ends, and the resulting silence consists of a hundred people yelling.

A new song: a guitar, a high-hat, a drum...Sebastian has no idea, and looks helplessly into Amanda's eyes. Before anyone even starts singing Spooner goes, "'Blow Me One Last Kiss!' Pink!" and they're all even, three events apiece.

Mercifully they step outside. Sebastian leans on Amanda. Spooner waves the Envelope of Events under their noses as they falter down a sidewalk.

"One more," he says. "This one's for all the marbles."

"What marbles?" says Amanda.

"Pick," Spooner says.

There's a glass-enclosed bus stop ahead and Sebastian collapses into it. But everywhere he looks is that fucking envelope, so he reaches in and hands over the final slip of paper while Amanda sits beside him, her arm across his shoulders.

"'Penalty Kicks,'" says Spooner. "We need a soccer ball." It's just the three of them now.

"Can you give us a minute?" Amanda says.

So as Spooner stands on a wood railing dropping spit blobs into dead grass, the bandmates slouch into one another and grin abashedly. Amanda touches Sebastian's face, their age difference weighing heavily. He's spinning, clutching her knee. How would he have survived if she hadn't appeared? How did she know where he was?

"You'll be okay," says Amanda.

"What am I doing here?" he says.

"Shh," she says.

"How the hell did I ever get out here?"

Amanda exhales hard. She wants to go back to this morning: the feeling she had as he slept beside her, as the other three all slept and she imagined this day of freedom in a fun new place. Those final few minutes of lonely anticipation were so perfect they nearly made her bust apart from the density of her joy. Then Sebastian woke up, they went into the bathroom, and.... Anyway, weirdly, sitting here on the bench, she gets a song idea. She's literally never written a song from scratch, but here it is…major-chord sweet with a peppy salsa timing, and it'll *be* this morning's feeling: sun, peace, joy.

Sebastian sighs, and it's almost a sob.

Spooner knocks on the glass and says, "You know what? I think it's time to go home. So let's change the final event. No soccer ball. I just ask you one question, Sea-Bass. And that decides it. Deal?"

Sebastian drunkenly remembers the baggie of speed, and he wants it. But he can tell it's no longer riding in the balance, and of course that makes sense now that Amanda's here. He says, "You've been so cool, Spooner, showing us around town tonight. Thanks, man."

"All right, so one question." He points at Amanda. "If you're so devoted, which of her parents is she closer to?"

Sebastian sits up straighter. "Easy. I met her mother, they talk every day. Her father's up in Oakland. He cheated on his wife and ran away when she was pretty young. She hasn't talked to him in forever. He's a total shitbag asshole." He touches her back, feels the hard knob of her bra clasp. "Right?"

Amanda's lips soften, and she bites them. She thinks about her new song, and about taking a shower the minute they get back to the borrowed apartment.

HOW DID IT END UP LIKE THIS?

The day of Scott's arrest, he wakes up on someone's hardwood floor and his brain goes *get gas Mankato Sunday mic the drums right money from Chicago gig tighter tomorrow new demos L.A. showcase spreadsheet A&R Thanksgiving smile more mixed set list Facebook buy strings phone calls rent space record which songs cooler clothes maybe smile less.* Then Amanda is half-naked above him, her ribcage and wild hair, and she says, "Day off," and he says, "Yup." In the shower he sings a new song that so far is mainly a melody, though words start coming and he tries singing them with conviction ("...lash marks are his sergeant stripes..." and "...boo-boos from sidewalk cellar doors...") and he's thinking of calling it "Ron Paul." When he steps out of the bathroom to make notes on his phone, Kate is skimming the spiral-bound notebook in which he doodles during insomniac nights, which is to say: every night.

Late morning he drives the van—manual transmission, mediocre cabin heating—to Nicollet Mall and parks in a garage, guilty for the expense but better to spend a little for security with the band's equipment in back. He pulls out his Ovation and walks to a busy restaurant. A waitress smiles and he orders coffee.

This is Scott's routine, no matter the town: he enters cafés and bars and tunes himself to the babble and cry. He eavesdrops on lovers, watches the red splotches on a waitress' heels, diagnoses unnecessarily hearty laughter as stupidity masking pain, judges character. Nominally, it's to help him write songs. But also he wants to be *spoken* to. He wants to be found fascinating. This morning he sits at this counter for two hours, accepting refills and declining food, especially scanning every young woman in this place and wishing one would talk to him. Yes, Jane is back in Manhattan waiting for him; hell, he doesn't want to cheat on her. He doesn't know what it is. He's aware of the clothing under their parkas, the condition of their fingernails, the thickness of their ankles, the kindness in their eyes. He's 26 and it feels ancient. If only he'd learned to talk to strangers when he was 21, when he was a better catch. Now his hair is thinning in back and he utterly lacks muscle tone. Fifteen minutes spent next to a perfectly average, nice-seeming office worker is operatic: move your head so she *thinks* you're looking at her, but make sure you're looking past, then catch her making eye contact and smile, but that's all, gauge her body position for openness, measure how doggedly she guards the open seat on the other side of her, quantify how genuinely engrossed she is in a paperback or text exchange, could she be faking it for me? By the time the poor woman departs, Scott is either enflamed or enraged, and either way her absence stings.

He's tired. They need days off, this is good. But he doesn't sleep enough. If every active thought is a worry about Kid Centrifuge—about getting discovered—he never has to think about what else is agitating inside him.

Saturated with the crowd's effortless banality (and especially his own!), he goes outside to write. He finds some vacant cement stairs facing away from the street, plugs in his earbuds and listens to "Dissident" by Pearl Jam, a song he remembers Frank playing when Scott was 9. He puts on fingerless gloves, unzips his blue guitar and figures the opening riff way up on the G, with one added flourish on the B. It's a pilferable shape; even as Pearl Jam rocks out Scott slows it down and changes the rhythm, fingering the melody he sang in the shower. It transforms easily into big, crunchy chords *et voilà*: the rudiments of a new song, standing on the shoulders of giants. Songs are the units of life. It would be exaggerating to say he finds them scattered around prefabricated; working himself into a songwriting state is unpleasant, but once he's there songs can come floating, incomplete cubes asking to be fit together. He sings:

Don't tread on me

My heart couldn't take it
Give me liberty
Our love's no mistake and...how much
Freedom can we tolerate
From you I don't want it
We'll privately create
This feeling and flaunt it...
Lash marks are your sergeant stripes
I feel you here from your great height
You just marched in
You can just march out
You just marched in
You can just march out

Eventually the cold nudges his reverie, or maybe it's the bullhorn.

Behind and above Scott, an assembly is forming and its leader is lovely. She wears a down vest and a ponytail, and she looks angry. Maybe a hundred people have gathered around her, and she says, "Hey hey, ho ho, your money goes to the CEO!" and "That's bullshit, get off it, the enemy is profit!" and "Disease and starvation will not be solved by corporations!" Scott packs up and follows as they walk down Nicollet.

The crowd is young—mostly younger than Scott—and wears t-shirts and badges that read "Americans For A Fair Economy" and "Minnesotans For Tax Fairness." The leader bullhorns: "From 2008 to 2011, Verizon posted $19.8 billion in profits and paid zero federal income taxes! Thanks to the Bush tax cuts the CEO of Macy's saved $1.9 million in personal taxes in 2011 alone! Where do you think the money for Head Start and child immunization is going?" Scott walks closer to this woman, hoping she heard him playing and sees his guitar. Near a Scientology center she finally grins back. They move slowly, blocking traffic on 9th Street and earning unsympathetic horn bleats, then a quiet police car with cherries flashing pulls up behind them. Mostly Scott is thinking: meet cute meet cute meet cute.

They keep going. There's a weird bronze statue of a woman catching something that looks like a conch shell, and one of the protestors whacks it hard with his umbrella. A block later they come upon an American flag and a Minnesota flag mixed in with one devoted to "Xcel Energy," and someone picks a full garbage bag off the street and flings its contents at the white corporate flag. Finally, in front of the city library, just as it looks to Scott like the pony-tailed lady rabble-rouser is about to speak directly to him and maybe finally open up his world, someone throws a rock that shatters a streetlight.

"Don't be destructive!" the bullhorn woman says. "There's no money to fix these things!" But she's too late, many more police make themselves known and converge and these nerdy protestors start apologizing. Now there are sirens. The police seem polite and the fringe marchers quickly disband, back down Nicollet into the Walgreen's and Office Depot they just passed. But someone grabs Scott from behind—a bald-headed cop in sunglasses—and Scott finds himself in the back of a squad car.

He's never been in legal trouble, not once. He's not handcuffed, and this makes him slightly optimistic. He hopes to see the bullhorn woman arguing for his release, but it's all blue uniforms out there standing around congratulating themselves. Scott can't see anyone else under arrest. He's cold, and the cruiser's cinnamon antiseptic smell is awful. Kid Centrifuge has a show tomorrow.

Two policemen finally climb into the car. He's too scared to talk, and prays they'll let him off with a warning. But they wearily tell him his Miranda rights, and this is the kind of mix-up that gets a movie hero thrown down justice's dark corridor, where he's killed before anyone gets his story straight. The ignition dings and Scott's heart capsizes.

The drive is short. For a few minutes they sit him in a hallway completely by himself, and he wonders why he shouldn't just get up and run out. They ask him questions and tell him to empty his pockets, and they take his picture with an old Polaroid. They also fingerprint him. He looks around for a sympathetic face. A lifetime of police dramas has taught him to say little, lest his words be used against him. Then he's alone in a cold concrete holding cell.

He lies on a bench and exhales. Instead of viewing this crazy episode as a source for more songs, he wants to go home to Newton, Massachusetts, and live in his parents' spare room. He wants *out*. He keeps thinking maybe more protestors will be booked soon. But he's alone for at least a half-hour until a double door bangs open, a lock is turned, and a very big black man gets led in by two officers. This new prisoner nods at Scott, and sits elbows-on-knees across the way.

"Graduate school," the other man says.

"..."

"Graduate school."

"Huh?" says Scott.

"You're too old for undergrad. I got you on a DUI after an all-nighter. Me? I shot a dude. You know how it goes: drug beef. Cops sitting around the hospital hoping the nigger dies and they can put me away forever."

"..."

"When this tank gets crowded, I've seen a dude punching this other dude in the face while at the same time he's also butt-fucking this third dude. I've seen a nigger hang himself from that light socket up there. You feel me? Yo. You hear what I'm saying? Shit, you can't talk to people. They ain't listening."

"..."

The man steps this way, where Scott is still face up on the bench. "Man, are you crying?"

Scott wipes hot tracks leading from his eyes down the sides of his skull.

"*Hhhhhhhh.*"

"..."

"It's all right, man. It'll be all right." He sits closer now. His shirt is seersucker and big as a sail. "I'm bullshitting you," he says. "I've never been in here before. I got arrested for child support. I'm a nurse." His laceless boots tap the floor.

"..."

"My ex lives with a guy but they won't get married. Anyway, they pinched me at work and trust me, man, I did my crying out in the car." He scratches his shaved scalp.

"..."

"I'm Lee."

"..."

"Would you believe I had a conversation with myself this very morning, sitting around the hospital, right out loud: 'You don't deserve your life. It's going down the drain and you're not trying to stop it.'"

"Not grad school," Scott says. "I'm a musician."

"Ah, man," says Lee, like that explains it all.

After a while, Scott says, "Nobody knows. I think nobody knows how to stop it."

Lee ponders that. There's rattling down a distant hallway and they listen to see if someone is approaching, but nobody comes. "Yeah. For a while I thought it was my kids that kept life filled up. I loved them when they were really little. I mean, I still love them. But when they're totally helpless, man. Everything I did had a purpose, but they got older and it changed."

Scott decides to sit up. He tenderly brings his legs around, and he gets a head-rush. Lee has an overweight man's friendliness to his face, lines that make him look happy, but he also could be a complete over-talkative bullshitter.

"I was trying to think," Lee says. "When do I still feel really good?"

"Yeah." They're quiet for a long time.

"With a woman, I guess. Right at the beginning when shit is gooey. And I don't just mean fucking."

"Sure. Sometimes that's lonely as hell."

Lee laughs. "Never mind saying some other girl's name while you're doing it. You ever get fucked up and confuse your girl's tits with a different girl's? Like, I'm pretty drunk and I went reaching and found 'em and I go, 'Babe, what happened? They got so tiny!'"

Scott smiles. Jane needs it to be dark in her apartment. If a breeze moves the blinds she freezes.

"I got this one girl," says Lee, "it takes a lot to loosen her up. But when I get her there, she squirts. And that's gold, man, that's my jam. I like proof, right? But she *freaks out*. I have to pretend she *didn't* squirt, just to keep going. Otherwise she runs into the bathroom and splashes her cooch in the tub."

They laugh; Lee fairly busts a gut, with a hand on his forehead. Scott pictures Jane's heart-shaped face, white and severe behind granny glasses, and feels sorry for being distant. He wonders what it'll be like between them when he gets back to New York, what novel she's reading, which barista at Thrillsville she currently has a grudge against. Now Lee is looking at him, humor and pain in his expression.

The holding cell clanks open, and an officer says, "Scott Kopp!"

"Yeah," Scott says.

"Who do you want us to call for you?"

Scott thinks about his parents, a thousand miles away and already dubious about his life choices. Should he call a bail bondsman? He says, "I don't know the number. You have my phone, right? Can you call Kate Grush? She's in my band."

"Kate Grush. Check." The door bangs closed.

Lee says, "For a minute, I thought he said you're a cop."

"I mostly go by Tungsten."

"Fuck, man. If I could play music, who knows how the fuck I'd feel?"

Scott looks at the calluses on his left hand. "The same," he says. "Believe me."

"Well, then, we're just two miserable motherfuckers."

Scott thinks about the hundreds of hours he's spent on the band since last winter. What if all that time doesn't amount to anything? What if they can't get noticed, what if the songs aren't good, or their playing isn't tight enough?

No, it's not that.

It's also: what if they *are*, what if it *is*?

This big room is cold. The light is insufficient. It's good, very good, that he's not alone.

Lee says, "Man, here's what it is. Roll around in it for just a little while, feel like shit. But just a little while."

"I guess."

"'Cuz if not, Tungsten? If not, I guess we should all just take a dirt nap. Right fucking now."

"..."

They hold him overnight, but let him go at 8 a.m. No explanation, no bail, no court date. They just tear up his arrest report and let him go. The garage wants sixteen dollars for overnight parking and he doesn't have it. The kid in the booth opens the wood gate and says, "Happy early Thanksgiving," and Scott gives him a fiver.

That night they're third on a bill of five bands, so they sit in the junior high hallway listening to the opener and making small talk with these punkish-looking guys called Neutral Cloud, who go on next. The gym is pretty packed, mostly here to see the headliners: Call and Response, who supposedly just did a deal with WaterTower Records. C&R's manager is chain-smoking back here, checking for blue M&Ms or whatever, just hassling anyone holding a clipboard.

Neutral Cloud gets on and plays way too loud for the p.a. They do have a guitar player whose frantic scrubbing creates nasty feedback, but they've got no singer. Instead, two guys are behind two laptops, flinging out crazily mismatched beats and samples. The end result is a few screeching wall-of-sound numbers indiscernible from one another. Then the guitarist randomly starts to play "Mr. Brightside" by the Killers but it's terrible, he can't keep up with actual samples from the song and abandons it partway through, angrily throwing his guitar offstage so a couple C&R band techs have to scramble away to keep from being struck. The audience is silent. The promoter scrambles over to Scott and says not only is Neutral Cloud about to fuck him with a truncated set, but the fourth band is a no-show. He offers double the dollars for double the stage time. Scott tries not to look like he has money-wheels cranking around in place of his eyeballs. But in a way he also feels love—he's splitting open and rose-colored light radiates from his chest—and foolish vulnerability.

Kid Centrifuge walks onstage and plugs in. Amanda steps to the mic and says, "It's never a bad thing when they ask you to save the day."

They start with an Alabama Shakes song called "Hold On." Kate clicks them into a mid-tempo swing, thinking how Billie Turner would play it. Scott plays two notes per measure as in a jug band. Sebastian comes in low, nothing fancy, just a simple lead on two strings, giving him a chance to look out and see Spooner making dual devil-signs in the front row. Amanda gets to sing this soul torch song where she starts soft:

Bless my heart, bless my soul
Didn't think I'd make it to twenty-two years old

and by the end she blows the doors off, opening her throat and erupting. Sebastian injects a solo, Amanda struts shaking her head, channeling Aretha and Dinah and Etta and Mavis. When she looks down the audience is here, right up against the stage; the song ends and they actually go a little crazy.

Confident, they launch into "Styles Make Fights." Kate only gets the occasional flash of a face, but everyone down in the crowd seems pretty happy. Scott sees an opening at the front of the stage and steps into it; the lights flicker brighter here and it's a little like having a seizure. Music is armor. Amanda comes over, rocking in time with his bass, straddling closer and shouting at him, he pulls his strings hard and mouths the lyrics. She stumbles a little and her crotch grinds his knee; she lets it happen once, then again, looking him dead in the face. They finish hard, on the downbeat, and the audience yells.

Scott sweats like a June bride, crouched over his bass and looking up at Amanda. She grins down at him in a post-song reverie. She says, "This one's called 'Intense, Like Camping.'"

It's Kate's favorite song. She drives it with fills of increasing complexity; the space between each verse line has a mathematical progression, and a big satisfying ride-cymbal release leads into the chorus. Kate thinks of herself as a slinky drummer, willing to sacrifice metronomic precision for the sake of the groove, but "Intense, Like Camping" makes her sit forward and smack. She's powerful: this gymnasium is getting warm and she can see her sweat fan out in the light. But really she's not thinking much of anything, she's locked in, Sebastian is obviously bored over there stage left infinitely repeating a catchy power-chord hook but Kate lays out the three-dimensional path for the Kids to embroider as they will. The second chorus comes and she goes crazy on both cymbals and Amanda sings:

You're too serious and you don't sleep
Lonely boy come to rescue me
Stalking 'round 'til you found this ledge
Tried to kill me but I'm not dead

and the others let loose and rock out through a long, improvised, crashing jam, and Amanda decides to scream, "Not dead! Not dead! Not dead! Not dead! Not dead! Not dead! Not dead! Not dead! Not dead! Not dead!"

Scott says, "Wow."

They do "Nipple Rouge," "Caribou Boyfriend" and "Umpire" and pull them off. Those are all the finished original songs they have, but the promoter is literally in the wings making *stretch* gestures with his hands. Amanda, Sebastian and Kate all look at Scott.

"Uh," he says into the mic. "Okay, so here's the deal. They're telling us to stop. But you guys are the best crowd we've had

anywhere. So how about we play you a few more songs before they
drag us off? Mr. Torque, can I borrow your guitar?" Sebastian
hands over his Telecaster and Scott plays a fuzzy electric version of
"Sliding Around In Socks," the dumbest and happiest ditty he ever
wrote. Kate accompanies, and it goes over well. "Okay. Who wants
to hear Sebastian play 'Chord'?"

They cheer again. Sebastian is flattered, takes back his guitar.
He steps over to Amanda and says, "You sing it. Please. I can't..."
and she gives him a pitying look and he feels dreadful. But he plays
the riff he's played a million times and a bunch of these kids
recognize it, Scott follows along on the Spector, Kate thumps
lazily, and suddenly his beloved weird electronic masterpiece is a
rock jingle. But it sounds good, which kind of sucks. He looks at
Scott, who makes a funny little face back at him.

It goes like this for another half-hour. Amanda sings
"Bandfucker" and they play more covers. It's by far the longest set
they've done. From the looks of things backstage, Call and
Response is ready to come out, so Amanda thanks the crowd and
they head off. But Sebastian runs back on and leans into the mic to
say, "You should probably hear someone play this right," and he
fires off the "Mr. Brightside" riff. It's the biggest cheer of the
night. Kate sprints back to the kit and taps the high-hat, Scott also
runs back onstage, but Amanda is cool, staying unseen, letting
them repeat the intro four, five, six times before sauntering back
into the light. She's not sure she knows the words, but gives it a
shot:

How did it end up like this?
It was only a kiss

After, offstage, Amanda says, "I didn't know you even knew
that song," and Sebastian says, "I didn't really.... I just heard that
poor guy in Neutral Cloud almost play it."

"I mean, shit," says Scott.

They glisten with a conquering sweat. Kate drinks ginger ale
and smiles, wondering what the hell just happened.

Call and Response's throbbing show-opener echoes around
them and oscillating fans blow around newsprint paintings taped to
the walls, as if it's the music rattling the sad outsider kiddie art. A
lightshow begins out in the main room, and C&R's manager sags

into the hallway, his wrangling over for the moment. He's densely bearded, wearing the requisite sportsjacket-and-jeans, and he assumes a cool-guy pose on a radiator across from Scott. He texts madly and his eyes never leave his phone as he says, "It's not your fault. We're incredibly pissed, but I don't blame you. I'm just.... Make-goods. There'll be some make-goods here or you can forget this entire market. This is a *Call and Response* show. I mean, nothing personal, but if my guys wanted an opener to play oldies, they'd hire one."

Scott doesn't see a Bluetooth thing in this guy's ear, so he says, "I can't tell who you're talking to."

"Whoever the fuck put together this lineup.... Anyway, it's the last go-round we're playing in this tax bracket. So I guess I'm talking myself out of getting too chafed. I'll admit it, you're good at what you do. It was a pretty *long* fucking set, but it was good. And this one," the manager gestures to Amanda without looking up from his phone, "I'm thinking maybe she's a star."

Scott surveys his silent bandmates. "Of course she's a star. We call her Meal Ticket."

"Good sound on a bad p.a., that's one kind of art, right? Doesn't mean you sound good on a good p.a., but it's better than the alternative. We've been out for seven months and I have to say it's nearly impossible for me to watch most girl singers. Every pixie girl I watch puts a half-gulped 'y' at the end of every vowel. There's a difference between singing and baby talk, is what I'm saying."

A band tech strides by carrying water jugs. He looks Amanda directly in the chest, moves on.

"You're in the right tax bracket for now," says the manager. "We've outgrown it, but we've lived here a while. It takes a firm hand to go any higher, but I wouldn't be talking to you if I didn't think there was potential. And now I'm not chafed at all. Now I'm magnanimous. I'm not gonna lie: there's a whole bunch of itty-bitty rock acts out there and not much scratch to go around," and he looks in Scott's eyes, "but I just sent an email to the mothership, and they might know someone." A business card glides from his pocket into Scott's fingers. "One simple reason, kids: we get deals."

The card reads: "HOMEFORK – MUSIC MANAGEMENT" and gives this guy's name as Robbie Fine.

Kid Centrifuge look at one another, pause a beat, then all pretend to faint—fanning themselves, eyelids flapping, knuckles against foreheads—and Robbie Fine smirks and says, "Jackholes."

"Thanks," Scott says. "Seriously."

"But twenty percent of nothing is nothing," says the manager. "That, you should remember."

I'M PUNCHING YOU IN THE FACE

"My family will shit their pants."

"All our families will shit their pants."

"Well, not Amanda's."

"Hey. We're not in L.A. yet, either. Trust me, my mom's pants will contain the proper amount of shit."

They don't have enough time to sleep. It's hard to know who the ghosts are: the overnight waitress sleeping with her chin in her hand, the fry cook mournfully watching CNN, or Kid Centrifuge in a deco leatherette booth. They've driven to Denver overnight, seven hours from an Omaha rain headlong into all sixteen of these Fahrenheit Colorado degrees, with the van windows like a slot machine turning over views of Rocky Mountain attractions. Outside it's the punishing dark of 4:30 a.m., and they're the kind of tired where slow feels fast, and fast feels slow. Gargoyles wink in their vision; this diner is otherwise empty, and so seems hoisted out of a horror film.

"Missing Thanksgiving was already the most major problem imaginable," says Sebastian. "I don't think my parents are, like, speaking to me."

"I'm just saying," Kate says to Amanda, "if we decide to stay west, it's a pretty short bus ride for you."

Scott knows they can't return back East for Christmas, plus knows they know it. For once in his life, he keeps his mouth shut.

"What's the absolute least time it would take to drive back to

New York?" Amanda says. "Thirty hours. Something like that. So why do we have to decide nine whole days before?"

"Because I need to get them ready," says Sebastian. "I can't just call up next Sunday and go, 'Oh, yeah, by the way, I'm not coming.' Like Kate says, you *want* to stay, it makes it easy for you."

"Jesus," says Amanda, "you think your mom won't come up with a plane ticket if you ask? You want me to call her right now?"

"Maybe we should just get through today," Kate says.

"Why don't you say what you mean?" says Sebastian. "Why don't I just ask my parents to give us all some money, so we don't—"

"Here we go," Amanda says.

"—so we don't have to live like hobos? They should just sponsor an entire tour. I mean, they're not *rich*, Amanda."

They've roused the waitress, who comes around with two pots of coffee, though none of them are drinking decaf. Her nametag says: "Penny" and they all scrutinize it. She tells them stay occupied, cheese fries are on the way.

"The best decision we can make," says Kate, "is if we knew who'll hear them. Like what if Homefork could *guarantee* the new demos got into that guy's hands."

"Gondal," Scott says. "Russell Gondal."

"You're just pissed off," Amanda says, "because now you're facing the same long trip *I* was facing when we were supposed to be back in New York. Poor you. Call your mom."

"We *live* in New York," says Sebastian. "How was it ever unexpected you'd have to go back cross country for Christmas?"

"Well things *changed*. Things changed and you don't like it."

"They didn't change yet. Nobody's decided anything yet."

"You go ahead," says Amanda. "You go ahead and drive all the way back to New York and then turn around after Christmas and drive all the way back. Be my guest."

"Who says I'd even come back," Sebastian says.

Everyone looks at Scott. They don't actually have management yet. Teddy at Homefork agreed the band has done pretty well on its own so far, and boots on the ground wouldn't add much at this point. But he's awaiting demos and if they're strong, he promised Scott he'll show them around. So they're in Denver where Scott's college roommate works for a jet-leasing company, and agreed to sneak them into a particular hangar he swears has otherworldly acoustics.

"We'll just sell all our equipment," says Scott. "Sell the van, all the instruments. That would buy us all plane fare. Should I start posting ads online?"

Amanda can't decide which of the boys she wants to punch more. "How is this even a conversation?" she says.

"After two months," Kate says, "and me giving everyone the flu, and Scott almost getting shipped to Guantanamo, you're right. We can't quit now."

Sebastian's stress about the songs—their impulse toward empty-headed repetition—has only worsened. He's told himself: *It'll be better when I start writing. It'll be better when we have a real manager and Scott has to back off. It'll be better after we sleep in our own beds.* Yet here he is again, with dim escape fantasies bleeding into his thoughts. It's alarming he can feel this way on an increased dose of brain meds. He's been holding onto the idea of dominating Scott with his superior knowledge of recording, but now that it's demo day he's also filled by dread. But he squints and chuckles, snapping a sugar packet, and he says, "I'm just tired, guys. Sorry. Let me get caffeinated and you're right, either way it'll work out."

Amanda makes her voice conciliatory. "Maybe you should've slept in the car."

But Sebastian is grinning blankly and thinking about his dad making serial-killer faces with an electric carving knife.

Two plates of fries arrive, chili on the side. Scott watches the others dig in, hoping they've got enough cash left after gassing the van in Nebraska.

"The best Christmas present I ever got," says Kate, "was a razor scooter. I can't believe my parents actually got it for me, because I basically almost broke my ankle the first five minutes I played with it. There's this statue in Rec Park that seemed creepy even when I was 10, this guy sitting with his hand around a little girl's back, but anyway I jumped the scooter off that thing and almost killed myself."

"I was so happy when I got a Furby," says Amanda. "I loved it at first. Oh, look, he's watching me. But then I spent the next three years being terrorized at night. Turns out that thing was freaky. He blinked."

"Scott?" Kate says.

"Hm. Dell Dimension with a Pentium II processor running

Windows 95. I was 11 and I really, really wanted to send email to Eddie Vedder."

Sebastian laughs with the rest of them, then gets up to go to the bathroom. He got a used Richard Lipp baby grand piano when he was 8, and doesn't want to share this factoid. He redirects outside, opens the van, and finds a cigarette carton in the cup-holder way in the back. He lights up and stands against a stone wall that's emblazoned with a "Tom's Diner" logo. Play the songs. Do it right. Go fast. Don't experiment. As excuses, ignorance or sloppiness won't suffice; they know he knows the material, and they know he never forgets. He's really starting to hate the guitar. On its own, it's just boring. If they were going to an actual studio, where he could mess around with effects and also, whatever, lay down synth harmonies, then the guitar would know its place as a smaller piece of a sonic landscape. But these guys love his playing too much. They want to *hear* it.

Kate comes outside, still chewing. She stands next to him, feeling groggy and underwater. She's heard Sebastian say a few sharp words to Amanda when he thought nobody was around, but she's never seen him argue like what just happened. She says, "Sorry I didn't back you up more. I guess I'm never psyched to go back to Binghamton for any reason."

"Oh, yeah, no, I'm the one who's..." says Sebastian. "I'm just being...."

"Yeah. I'm just trying to imagine me like three years ago, if I could tell myself I'd be standing right here."

"I know, right?"

"What I mean is, I was pretty self-destructive back then. Now I'm out of my own way, ha ha, except not really."

Sebastian says, "Did you...hurt yourself?

"Not directly. Not the way you're thinking."

"..."

"I wasn't suicidal or anything."

"I mean, I had some problems, too," says Sebastian. "I didn't.... Senior year I just stopped doing anything. I missed a million classes." He laughs mirthlessly. "It went on for like weeks."

"..."

"I just wanted you to know. You were saying this stuff about yourself, and I didn't want you to feel like you were a freak or whatever."

"What happened?" Kate says.

"Amanda doesn't know about any of this. Yeah, I just...."

"…"

"Nothing happened. There was no reason. My parents were pissed at me, then they tried ignoring it, and then they freaked. I barely graduated, I stopped doing music."

"…"

"Really. Nothing happened. I guess I used to be pretty...death-obsessed."

"Oh."

A car goes by singing a high embittered song. He sees apparitions: all the thousands of now-broken-up bands in places like this, freezing in parking lots, the overlapping laments. But of course all behavior is forgiven doing these unnatural things, in the service of a ring they maybe can't each even agree is brass. "I didn't go goth or whatever. The vampire kids, they were such poseurs. This was more like: I couldn't get it out of my mind. I'd be doing something, watching TV or something. And my mind would always go there. I couldn't stop it. If it was an old movie, all I could think was: every single one of these actors is dead. But not just that. It could be anything, and suddenly I'm panicking because I know nothing matters, there's nothing I can do to get out of it, at some point relatively soon there'll be no more me. I was the most panicked comatose person ever. Nothing seemed like it had any point if everyone just ends up dead."

Kate looks at her toes. "But it's not really death," she says.

Sebastian takes a short bracing inhale, and it feels like peppermint inside his chest. He says, "Right."

"It's the idea it could happen at any moment and you'd go out with nobody knowing a single thing about you."

"…"

She says, "Because you were too busy with bullshit to actually tell anyone."

They look at one another, and they mean to be tender. But really, they're surveying each other for damage. Sebastian feels dread that Kate will find some.

Instead, she says, "But I mean we're here, right? I'm standing here in the cold next to this dreamy axman."

"And I'm standing here talking to the baddest drummer ever born."

"So," says Kate, "I dunno. Thank you?"

Sebastian laughs nervously, hates himself for it. "Yeah. Yeah, thank *you*. I mean, c'mon. Today's exciting, right? It's a long way from that dumb warehouse. We'll mic it right. You'll get one on the kick, and one over each shoulder, is what I'm thinking. It'll sound...obviously."

"Yeah, but screw the demos. It's nice to have a *thing* right up ahead."

"You don't want a smoke, right?"

"No. I'm gonna start running again soon. Yeah, just one little signpost to concentrate on, that's what I like. A show tomorrow in Denver. One after that...where? I don't remember. Doesn't matter. Me and the dreamy axman."

"Small bites."

"Song title alert."

They drive to Centennial Airport and Scott's pal Trevor flags them down. He's in Arctic explorer regalia, and can't fit his arms around Scott for a proper hug. On the way inside he says, "How close are you guys to that school? Sandy Hook?"

"Yeah, an hour south," says Scott.

"Bonnie wants to pull Andrew out of kindergarten. What, we're supposed to home-school him now?"

"People are a disaster," Scott says. They all trudge down a gray hallway carrying gear.

They did drive all of Sebastian's recording equipment with them across the nation, but the setup is a question mark. Scott and Sebastian have gone back and forth about how many tracks they should record into; Sebastian is adamant that the reason it sucked the first time—this summer when it sounded like they were playing inside a paper bag—came from trying to capture a "live" feeling with just two mics. Anyway, they've got fourteen hours in the hangar. Trevor leaves.

The guys start civilized and supportive, asking Kate to slowly and endlessly bang away at each item in her kit while they pass headphones back and forth nitpicking vibration and phase. She obliges shivering in three layers of clothing while Amanda sleeps in the van. Soon Scott is freaking out, insisting they've got it, insisting 7 p.m. is their hard out from the hangar. Sebastian keeps nodding at Kate, keep going, and he inches the three drum mics left and right, pressing the cans against his ears and squeezing his eyes shut.

"These are *demos*," says Scott. "They don't have to be perfect. We need five songs. I promised five fucking songs."

"..."

"You have ten more minutes, and we're moving on. That's it."

"..."

Sebastian frets that they don't have a condenser mic for the vocals, that his monitors sound dead, that the room's tone isn't warm enough. Scott facepalms himself. He has to go outside, and Trevor calls to find out how they're doing.

"Not close," says Scott. "Nowhere close to starting because our shithead guitar player wouldn't dare record himself in anything but perfection. If we're playing by noon I'll be shocked."

"Did you talk to him? I'm fired if there's any trace of you at seven."

"I talked to him, I talked to him. You don't know this fucking kid."

"Did you talk to him exactly like that? Because if it's me, and you sound like that, I'm punching you in the face."

"I have to watch *my* tone? He's the one bending us over a fucking.... I've spent two months begging him to play what the rest of us expect. It happens every so often, probably by fucking accident, and the rest of the time, Jesus fuck. He's literally pissing away our last chance to play this showcase. *Fuck!* And I have to walk back in there and fucking plead with him in a fucking hushed...?"

"'You're not wrong, Donny, you're just an asshole.'"

For his part, Sebastian knows he's overdoing it, but is freaked out because now if anything goes wrong, he's the idiot. But Kate can't hack it anymore and tells him in her sweetest voice that she's done. So he moves on to setting up cables and pre-amps and gets his laptop ready. Amanda walks in hugging herself, and leans against him groggily.

"I was thinking you could come to Christmas at my house," she says.

They play "Styles Make Fights" once all the way through, but only recording the drums. Kate has a click-track in her ear and absolutely nails it, every beat, every smash, not a single moment out of place. She looks up from the kit, and the others seem kind of insultingly shocked. Anyway, she goes outside and starts up the van to get warm, while inside her handiwork plays back through headphones. Next the plan is to play all the way through again, this time recording guitar and bass, but Sebastian just can't get through the song. He stops playing and says "Sorry" again and again and again. Scott smiles and nods encouragingly; Amanda sips water. Sebastian is sure they think he's trying to sabotage the day, but he's not.

"Let's just get through it once," says Amanda. "It doesn't have to be perfect, just get to the end of the song no matter what."

They try, and he stops again. "Sorry," he says.

"Pretend it's a show," Amanda says. "There's an audience, they're really into it, you have to keep going."

They queue up Kate's drumming five more times, and can't make him finish the song. He's sweating, shaking, humiliated. Scott can't help muttering, "I'll fucking play it," which he knows Sebastian hears.

Amanda takes him out into the gray hallway, pushes him against a couple hollow-sounding file cabinets and puts her lips against his ear. "Whatever you have to do," she says. "Right now, today, nobody cares. Whatever you have to take. Seriously. Just go to the bathroom, do what you need to do, and come back out with your head right."

It hasn't occurred to him that this is what's wrong. Nor has it occurred to him that Amanda knows anything about his drugs. He picked up a gram from a gregarious fan in St. Louis, a girl with a droopy eye who endlessly hung around after a show. He walks back into the hangar, unzips a pocket in his guitar case, finds the little plastic bag, and disappears into the men's room.

And in the next take, they nail it. Scott has a panicked moment where he thinks he can hear Amanda faintly singing in his bass playback, but they convince him he's crazy. It's left to Amanda to let loose on a vocal track; "Styles" will require her biggest performance of today's songs, which is why they're doing it first. She's been singing at half-strength until now, and she goes outside, does her voice exercises in the cold, and remembers going to the gym with her father when she was tiny: he got himself warm by shadowboxing. So she jogs in place, uppercuts the air, bobs and weaves. It affects her. She feels anger building in her chest and water gathering in her eyes. She thinks about her father and Sebastian and the places in her heart that still feel untouched. She doesn't know how smart she really is; her blankness allows the world to imagine her shrewd and profound. But Robbie Fine said she's a star. This thought finally pushes her fully into tears.

She kills it. Turpentine jackets and paint-thinner pants are no match. Every tongue-twister conquered, every note perfect.

It's 1 p.m. They've finished one song.

They record "Nipple Rouge" the same piecemeal way and it goes faster, but it still takes two hours. Trevor brings pizzas and they scarf. They decide to record "Caribou Boyfriend" live to see how it sounds, and the third time through it's not bad. "Umpire" takes six tries before they get it. Finally they've got two hours left for "Intense, Like Camping," a song whose parts they'll need to do separately, and Kate wants to go *last*: she and Scott do a scratch track, everyone else does their thing including Amanda, and then Kate goes back and plays the drums for real, with everyone else in her ears. She knows exactly how she wants to sound. It's worked this way since her early teens; at first she was incapable of echoing instructors' exercises, but she had music in her head and so could always improvise more advanced patterns than her skill level inferred. Sebastian removes the scratch track and plays back everything else and Kate experiences it as weirdly intimate, playing with the ghostly residue of her bandmates. She feels them, and it's moving: Amanda and Scott and Sebastian speak to her in this sound, she belongs to them and there's no net. Her arms and legs snap, she's down to one layer of clothes and sweating. She messes up a couple times, asks Sebastian to restart. It's the kind of fun that has no name, a connection that explodes one's chest.

They finish with half-an-hour to spare.

So Amanda decides to speak up. She asks if they can also record her song.

They haven't played it during an actual show, but it's a simple enough number. During motel room mornings and in the back of the van, Scott helped her work it out on the guitar—in her initial conception it was a pure salsa that didn't quite come off—plus he suggested an altered bridge, but everything else is hers. When she floated ideas for different titles, he insisted she keep her very first one: "Density of Joy."

Today, as Scott and Kate agree to make use of these final thirty minutes, Sebastian can't stop himself from pulling an aggravated face, but he deftly transitions to a fake sneeze. He thinks "Density of Joy" is a true piece of shit.

Kate clicks out a few measures of homogenous perkiness, and asks Amanda if she's remembering it right. The bassline is literally three notes: A-D-E...A-D-E...A-D-E.... And the guitar: Sebastian has one simple hook to play over and over and over. Even during the bridge, he just keeps hitting the same wiggly boring riff. He notes that Amanda has neglected to mention the possibility of doing this song until these last minutes, so there'll be no time for improvisation.

"No harm in trying," Scott says. "Roll through it live once?"

Kate nods, thinking the song doesn't sound anything like what she understands Kid Centrifuge to be, but it would be a nice thing to do for Amanda. And the politician within Sebastian decides he can't pick this moment to grow a spine.

Amanda says, "One...two...three...four...."

They play it, and she sings:

I'm talky, and I'm talkin' aboutcha
I only point west as a rule
Where the girls drink tequila sunrise
And the boys just play it cool
Well baby you can come over
I'm flying and you're the one
I'm not the person I was last year
I'm really much more fun
My name is: Joy Joy Joy Joy Joy
I know that you love me
You're my: Boy Boy Boy Boy Boy
When we dance I get hungry
We jump for: Joy Joy Joy Joy Joy
Your body's close and you love me
You're my: Boy Boy Boy Boy Boy
Just give me: Joy Joy Joy Joy Joy
Our name is: Joy Joy Joy Joy Joy

She knows it's kind of a silly little number, and over these many weeks she's taken pride in rocking the hell out. Fans—if it can be said they truly have "fans" yet—have celebrated their ballsiness, yet she's making the Kids record her little Petula Clark wannabe song? Well, maybe she's a little selfish here, indulging pop-princess impulses while she has these three great musicians at her disposal.

They don't have enough cash to take Trevor out for a thank-you dinner, so Amanda and Kate harangue him until he agrees to let them cook a meal for his young family. Meanwhile, Sebastian absently sits on the drum-stool and bangs the chorus of "Nipple Rouge," and Scott happens to be standing near the vocal mic and starts singing ("What's wrong is you, everything you do, just not when you go down...") and Sebastian is kind of amazed. He runs to the laptop, tells Scott to listen in the headphones, and plays the tracks over which Amanda sang. Scott belts it out, hard and loud the way he did when he wrote it this summer, by himself in his brother's apartment. His voice isn't in great shape but he doesn't have to save anything and he discovers himself pouring frustration into the performance. Sebastian saves the file. Everyone starts to pack up.

"That was..." says Sebastian.

"Thanks man," Scott says, coiling cables.

The shows keep coming. They play two clubs in Denver: everyone listens to the band with their eyes glued to their phones, Kate makes friends with a bartender who looks nine-and-a-half months pregnant, Scott gets yelled at for spilling a beer on some guy's lucky vest, they bust a gut over a surprisingly fit hot mom dancing by herself at both shows. During the day, Sebastian mixes the songs. Scott wants them *now*, fretting the closer they get to the holiday the less likely anyone will give them a serious listen. But Sebastian is making them better. Amanda sounds incredible. She's a rock diva with nuance, powerful but never shrill, warm and round and deep. And Sebastian wants to say: who cares if they miss the L.A. showcase, didn't Homefork notice them, and won't others? But he knows better.

They all know Scott's in full Ahab mode. Now he asks every booker, singer, promoter and floor-sweeper if they know anything about Russell Gondal's showcase, if they know anyone who's going, if they know anyone who's been. He's gotten better at talking to band managers: it turns out playing the naïf doesn't work, he has to basically engage in a pissing contest over who knows more. One rep at Larimer Lounge says he knows Gondal's cousin and Scott tosses out every name he's met over the past months, just to intimidate this guy into giving him the cousin's email. He meets two dudes who used to work for the Elephant 6, and spends an hour geeking out over Apples in Stereo, Beulah and Elf Power; then he hits them up for info about the quasi-famous people in those bands. In a drunken conversation with one booker, he just starts making up names: "Oh, man, you *know* the Dowagers will be in L.A., I heard Universal and Sony are fighting over them. Also Locust Farm? We ran into them in Milwaukee. They're great!" And these Denver interactions aren't all bullshit: he wedges into a conversation with an honest-to-goodness A&R guy from Fueled by Ramen, who's busy complaining how many unsolicited demos his office in New York gets. So Scott steers clear of promising him a package, and instead comes right out and asks if he'll be in L.A. for the January show.

"Yeah, man, are you guys playing?"

"I hope so," Scott says. "Any words of advice on how to squeeze in?"

"I mean, that's Russell's thing all the way, and I think the bill is probably pretty set. But I saw you guys got a nice note on Stereogum. Give me your contact stuff and if your show goes well tonight I can drop him a note, if it would help."

In Santa Fe the Friday night before Christmas, Scott meets a writer for Pitchfork named Thad. He's there for the headliner, Seahorses of the Apocalypse, an honest-to-goodness power-rock band whose first record has just dropped. The Kids have played on two other bills with the Seahorses and they get along well, so with the bands intermingling late after the show—and their drummer Charlie flirting madly with Amanda—it's only natural for Scott to sidle over to Thad.

"Nice job," Thad says. "You guys were strong."

"Thanks," says Scott. "You live here?"

"Moved out from L.A. last year, just totally done with the traffic and the zombies and I can do my work mostly from anywhere."

"Uh-oh," Kate says from across the bar. "You said the magic word."

"What word?" says Thad.

"L.A. Big mistake."

Thad looks around. "Uh, why?"

Scott says, "Because I ask everyone about the Gondal showcase. They're mocking me."

"Sure, yeah, I know it."

"You ever go?"

"I have," Thad says. "And frankly that's not a good sign."

"..."

"Ten years ago, there's no way some dude writing for a website could get into a thing like that. Too many record company guys lining up to do blow off Courtney Love's ass. But in case you haven't noticed, not quite as many record company guys as there used to be. What do they say? Now one percent of the bands make seventy-five percent of the money? Anyway, I went once, maybe three years ago, just to see what it was about. Some of the music was crap, some of the music was terrific, but the crowd was walking dead, man."

"Bang Bang Bang supposedly got signed right after their set last year."

"True. But my guess is Warner was already on them, and did Gondal a favor making it seem like his show was the reason. It's hard times in the promotions racket. And that Bang Bang Bang record tanked hard."

"You know Gondal?" says Scott.

"I know his kid. Ali. He's an actual, legit sweetheart. Rare in L.A."

"I know you just met us, and I feel like a dick for asking...."

"No, it's no problem," says Thad. "I'm sending him a note right now."

"That's amazing. Thank you."

Typing on his phone, Thad says, "Five years ago, I think you guys would already be signed, probably to a pretty big label. You've got a good sound and," indicating Amanda, "you've got her."

And Scott thinks about his brain's pleasure centers, how fucked up they must be getting, so that the only time he ever feels happy these days is the thirty seconds after one of these "inside" people helps push Kid Centrifuge forward.

They sit around with the Seahorses into the wee hours. It's possible to believe they're loose in time, living a fantasy that's nourished America's youth for sixty-odd years: all you need is a guitar....

Saturday night in Albuquerque they drive past the hip-hoppy Sunshine Theater, past a nightclub that has all the trappings of EDM including a long line around the corner, then past a smoke shop and a Holocaust and Intolerance Museum that Scott says maybe they should check out tomorrow morning. Their destination is the El Rey, a theater where Ella Fitzgerald, Bo Diddley, Weezer, Son Volt, Arlo Guthrie and the Shins have played. The marquee is old-style, movie-house cool, and unlike the basement lounges and county fairs and 'kicker bars they've gigged, this starts feeling like a reasonable facsimile of the big time.

"Wow, how'd we get this again?" says Kate.

"How do we ever get anything?" Scott says. "'Sorry, no, we don't need openers. Wait, you'll play for *how* little?'" And so they park around back feeling psyched. They unload and bang on the door and the guy who answers looks at them like they're crazy, but lets them in.

"Theaters sound great," Sebastian says. "Maybe we should record the show."

"Do we need permission?" says Kate.

Scott gets a look at one of tonight's flyers. The headliner is a band called Supermoon; Kid Centrifuge is the only opener listed. That's pretty crazy for a place with this kind of cachet. He asks a big dude in a black t-shirt if any other acts canceled, gets a shrug in return. This is starting to feel like a break.

"Maybe we get to do, like, actual full songs for soundcheck," Amanda says.

"Maybe catering," says Kate.

"Or electrical that won't shock us to death," says Sebastian.

They move through a poorly lit corridor, and hear voices droning close by. Is the public already filing in? Or is that a crowd gathering outside the theater? A door says "STAGE" and they open it.

Well, it doesn't lead to the stage. They find themselves on a carpeted floor right out in the middle of the venue. No theater seating, extensive sound and light boards in back, and maybe all four of them could barely fit on the actual stage except there's an aluminum-truss DJ stand up there in front of a big projection screen.

"Uh," Scott says, "maybe they're planning on moving the DJ stand?"

They're not planning on moving the DJ stand. Eight guys have set up security posts around the room's perimeter, are shouting instructions and confirmations, preparing to open the front doors. The Kids stand there holding gear, not knowing what comes next. Scott searches on his phone and discovers there are two acts named Supermoon. He'd assumed they were opening for the ska band—which, now that he digs deeper and realizes they play mostly in New Hampshire, was always pretty unlikely. The other Supermoon is a Japanese DJ getting his first live exposure in the U.S.

They find the El Rey's booker. He shakes everybody's hand. "You said Sebastian Torque. Hey," he says to Sebastian, "love your shit, man."

"So," says Scott, "we're actually a four-piece. We play rock songs."

The booker laughs. "Not tonight, you don't."

The doors open, and a bunch of really young white kids in tanktops, trucker hats and flower crowns rush to stake out territory behind the steel barricade nearest the stage.

The booker says, "Normally we could get your drums up there no problem. But anyway, that's not this crowd."

"How can you tell?" says Kate. "They look like every crowd we ever played for."

The booker shrugs and walks away.

"What do we...?" Amanda says.

"This is humiliating," says Sebastian, so Scott can hear.

They remove themselves from a new torrent of phat-panted onrushers who wave around glowsticks, pacifiers and candy bracelets, and who start hugging strangers and passing out more candy. The bandmates reconvene beside the stage.

"Two options," Scott says. "Just leave. But then no gas money."

Amanda says, "Or what? Play 'Styles Make Fights' acoustic standing on top of each other?"

Scott turns to Sebastian, gives him a big empty smile.

"Me?" says Sebastian.

"..."

"You're saying.... I don't have stuff they can *dance* to, Scott. You're saying just go up there. Just go up there and, like, do something I never did before, something I literally never wanted to do."

"I'd do it," Scott says. "I really would. But you heard the douchebag booker."

"My old songs, they're not even something you can make into

a show. They're not even.... Amanda, they're not even *fast*."

"..."

"You know what a joke this is? You know how many people in Brooklyn would say how not qualified I am to be a DJ? Want their phone numbers?"

Kate tells Scott, "It's not fair. He doesn't want to."

"If we had any other choice," Scott says.

Sebastian touches the top of his hairdo. "We do! We have a choice! We don't play! It's a misunderstanding! I'm not kidding, there's no way!"

And Scott bows in acquiescence but also wordlessly urges Amanda to step in, because boy do they need the cash. She knows he's right, and also wonders whether he put them in this position on purpose to prove some kind of point.

She picks up Sebastian's guitar case and seizes his hand and takes him into the bowels of the El Rey, finds a bathroom, unzips his designer jeans. She pulls him out.

"Ah," he says. "Ah. No?"

She kisses his neck and tugs at him, then leaves him hanging, opens the case, finds his damn baggie again. She presents it to him, and continues with both hands.

And a short time later he's up there in the purple light behind Supermoon's Technic 1200 turntables, plugging in his MacBook, furiously downloading DJ freeware and sorting through old files he might play. Amanda steps to a mic at stage left. Kate and Scott are down front, on the VIP side of the barrier. The El Rey plays "Party Rock Anthem" over the p.a., then plays it again.

Sebastian decides he's as ready as he'll ever be. He doesn't say anything, he just starts playing a beat file from the Bed-Stuy days and it's really loud. The crowd cheers and jumps around, ready to have a blast.

And it's going pretty well! He loops the beat then speeds it up and slows it down, and the El Rey crew casts swirly light onto the screen. Amanda sings, "Ooh! Ooh yeah! Ooh! Ooh yeah!" But after a few minutes of this, it's clear the audience is looking for something else, some kind of sound progression, and Sebastian feels that familiar ecstatic burn in his cerebral cortex and has full faith he can do this. Of course, he's never used these menus, and all the prepackaged sounds have names like Old-Skool Mud and Chili Swarm. He picks one called Ecstasy Dub, and his beat is completely replaced by the tooth-rattling honk of a million synchronized geese. He looks up and sees most everyone in the crowd reach for his or her ears.

Scott and Kate can't hear anything Sebastian is saying, but can see him lip-synching the word "sorry" over and over.

He can't find the pause button, so he unplugs the MacBook and hears all these kids shouting in pain.

He plugs back in. It takes him a minute to call up a new beat, so Amanda becomes a hype girl saying, "Gimme yeah, what? Gimme yeah, what? Gimme yeah, what?" and the audience has several good sports who echo back. Sebastian tries to bring up a new riff in time with what his girlfriend is chanting—even as he's fumbling on his trackpad, he's also imagining perfect samples from songs the Kids have covered—but he accidentally clicks on an early demo of "Chord" which starts with *slow* piano. He can see the booker offstage left, turning green.

But Sebastian can save it! He howls as loud as his lungs will go and randomly shuffles through all these menus, clicking all the sounds. It makes the loudest, most awful audio mess imaginable. He clicks, he clicks, and he slams down on the laptop a little too hard, and the laptop flips sideways off the DJ stand like a coin, spinning in strobe light and thus becoming a dozen different computers locked in midair peril, finally knocking against one of Supermoon's colossal monitors and toppling it off the stage. Scott sees this happening and rushes forward, catches the monitor like a baby from a burning building.

The computer is still plugged in, still blurting out nonsense, a testament to calamity engineering. Sebastian crawls under the table to fetch it and lowers the volume. Amanda assumes he's so high he's about to bring the whole DJ stand crashing down on top of himself. The booker steps onstage, applauding and pretending to be very happy. The audience can't see Sebastian and focuses on Amanda, looking to her for an explanation. She claps her hands, and she sings:

But we
Are never ever ever ever
Getting back together

She's got their attention; unfortunately she doesn't know any more words. But anyway at least she's got the whole place clapping.

And while he's out of sight, sitting cross-legged beneath thousands of dollars' worth of highly technical equipment, Sebastian just opens a browser and finds a video clip from a random EDM festival called Beyond Wonderland. He shuts down the DJ program. He goes back to YouTube. He hits play.

And that does it. He brings the computer back up to the stand, and Amanda is relieved to stop singing. A generically frantic synthesized beat booms from the MacBook, through the soundboard, and out into this legendary room and these kids wave their arms and throw back their heads and basically celebrate like lottery winners. Sweaty Sebastian plays the part. He hops around, pointing to the crowd, pantomiming laughter and joy, dancing, always keeping one hand on the laptop keyboard as if he's actually manipulating files. The booker sees exactly what he's doing, but his customers are finally dancing and grooving none the wiser. Amanda finds herself gesticulating like a rodeo cowgirl, whirling an invisible lasso above her head.

The video clip nears its end after twenty minutes, so Sebastian steps down the volume. The audience cheers, Sebastian and Amanda get the hell off the stage, and the Kids get their gas money. They hightail it out of Albuquerque in silence.

Sebastian's parents call the next morning and announce they're flying to Las Vegas for Christmas, and the band should drive over and meet them. It means another six hours in the van but by now that's nothing. They have an obligatory debate about detouring to the Grand Canyon, but nobody's heart is in it. The Torques are paying for an extra room, and the idea of two nights in the Monte Carlo unites them as nothing has since summer. They hand the van's keys over to the valet and wave goodbye to their instruments. In the lobby a lady wearing a wide chartreuse pantsuit shouts hello and hugs Sebastian so hard one of her fingernail extensions pops off. The older gent behind her has a face like wet carrot, and he shakes Sebastian's hand and says, "Hey, how's it going, Haircut?"

The others go off to dinner with the Torques but Kate stays behind, claiming she needs sleep. But she walks the Strip, jostled by bros in tight mesh shirts, drunk sorority girls and little track-suited guys snapping escort brochures in their hands. In this simulacrum of the country she's just crossed, she thinks about her own parents back in cold, cold upstate New York. She stands beside a dancing fountain, looking across the street through palm trees at a half-scale replica of the Eiffel Tower. Neither of her parents has been west of Buffalo or south of NYC, except for the one time she forced them to fly to Charlotte and then Kansas City to watch her get deprogrammed. She knows they love her. From the intensifying gravitational field created by Kid Centrifuge, she can see that fact clearer. She calls home.

Her mother answers coughing.

"Guess where I am," Kate says.

"Your apartment in New York?"

"I told you we're not coming back until after New Year's."

"I know, I thought maybe you were surprising me with good news."

"Las Vegas," says Kate. "I'm taking pictures."

"I wouldn't like it there. I don't like to gamble."

"Yeah. I'll be careful not to lose my millions."

"Daniel! Daniel, it's Katherine, pick up the phone!"

Kate pauses and hears another extension click in, but her father doesn't say anything. "I just had a few minutes," she says. "I was thinking about all the years. All the Christmases. I wanted to thank you."

"That's fine," says her mother. "You're welcome."

"I was telling everybody about the razor scooter you guys got me. I wore that thing out, I even used it on the ice. I think I'm supposed to thank you."

"What does that mean?" her father says. "What does it mean you're supposed to thank us? That sounds like something a politician says when he doesn't actually intend to thank anybody." He's been drinking.

"I said thank you. I just said it. Thank you. Thank you, again."

"Are you feeling all right?" says her mother. "Have you had any spells?"

Kate can't tell if her mom intends the condescension. In family parlance all Kate's varying problems with depression have become "spells," as if all she ever needed was a fainting couch. She says, "I'm feeling all right. I don't have to be feeling bad to call."

"No, I can just tell from your voice."

"Well, your radar's off. I'm in fabulous Las Vegas watching a guy on stilts dressed up as Willy Wonka. It makes you wonder where he got pants that long."

"We'll miss you on Tuesday," says her mother. "It's the first Christmas we won't see our baby."

"That's sweet, mom. I'll miss you, too."

"I just want to apologize, Katherine. Whatever I did. I just want to apologize."

"..."

"It's Christmas, and that means it's never too late. I'm very sorry."

"I'm not sure what you're apologizing for, mom." Kate realizes she's squeezing her phone, grinding it to dust.

"I'm not sure, either," her mother says. "But I thought if you felt forgiveness in your heart, you'd come home."

"..."

Her father says, "You are killing my wife. You're killing her. Why are you doing this? Why aren't you spending Christmas with your family? What vengeful, spiteful reasons do you have? I'd really like to know what's so awful. Why do you shove your mother away like this, when all she does is reach out?"

The scene around her—frat guys slapping each other to check out the half-exposed bottom of a tanned woman, a drunk girl crying on the sidewalk while friends argue above her, an older kissing couple groping each other's butts—darkens and shrinks to a pinpoint. At once, she realizes two things. First, she's been living a fairly happy life the past few months. Second, that happiness has probably been a complete lie. Because here comes anxiety, *whumph!*, as though it's been waiting all this time. That she can feel like this so quickly (and that she should've seen it coming, that she blithely brought it on by making this call) is an invalidation of any progress she thought she'd made.

Quietly, she says, "I called to make contact. This is all the contact I can handle right now, maybe."

"That's not an explanation," says her father. "I want to know. In my opinion, nothing can justify hating your family."

Kate says, "I don't...."

"Things happen in life, and you deal with them. You just deal with what's right in front of you and don't let whatever happened ruin you. Your mother grew up without a father. Does she complain about it all day? We lost a baby. Did we stop living?"

"She's living," her mother says. "Daniel, she's living."

"I don't remember a damn thing from being ten years old, or however old. Not one damn thing."

"Daniel, enough. One of us has to hang up now. Either you or me."

The phone is sticky against Kate's face. The problem is that she *believes* them. She believes the implication that there's something wrong with her. For years, therapists or deprogrammers have been telling her to stop blaming herself for things. But how can she explain to someone outside her head? How can she tell them what it's like to sink this low? The connection in her ear clicks.

Her mother says, "It's just us now."

"This has set me back," Kate says. "This has been terrible."

"Don't say that. He doesn't mean to hurt you. Don't you know he's ashamed? We never say one word about it to you, but we know why you're not coming for Christmas."

"I would come home," says Kate. She digs fingernails into her stupid fat palm. "We just have some more shows."

Her mother is crying. "All right."

"Really, mom. It's just logistics."

"No, it's running," her mother sobs. "It's running away."

"I'll call you on Christmas if I can."

"I keep thinking it would be better if we didn't move you to New York."

Kate realizes she's been pacing; she looks up, and she's blocking several Asian boys from moving down the sidewalk. She smiles an apology and it's a victory, to be able. She says, "No, you did the right thing, mom. Thank you." And she thinks: *If I hadn't finally moved away, I'd be dead.* "Be happy for me. I'm playing music every night."

Her mother has another coughing fit. "I can't shake this cold," she says.

Kate crosses the Strip and strolls through the casino inside Paris. A thousand slot machines bloop and ca-ching, an aural mess that a brilliant musical mind like Sebastian's might untangle into experimental fusion. The waitresses are dressed like sexy gendarmes and everyone is smoking cigarettes. But Kate is enchanted by the room itself: the ceiling is painted robin's-egg blue and the lighting is indirect, giving the uncanny feeling one is outdoors in a perpetual dusk. She feels carpeting under her feet, knows she's in the belly of a monolithic capitalist enterprise, but the illusion of being outside under open skies is incredible. She walks around in here for a long time, breathing, relieved. Outdoors but safe indoors.

Finally she grows tired and walks the long way back to the Monte Carlo. It's past midnight, but when she arrives at the Torques' extra room, the "Do Not Disturb" sign she left on the handle is still in place, and she opens the door.

The television is on in the dark, is all that really registers. She hears the sound of actors talking excitedly, and thinks maybe the TV is hooked up to some kind of fancy timer, or maybe she accidentally stepped on the remote as she was leaving. So she walks further into the room and flips on a light, and a distant quadrant of her brain is telling her that even though the TV *is* on, the sound is coming from the bed, and it turns out the sound isn't excited talking. It's moaning. This all happens in half-a-second. Kate understands there are bodies in here, and they're still moving. Amanda hasn't reacted to the light yet. She's hands-and-knees on one of the beds, eyes closed, going "ooooooooooo." Well, maybe she thinks the room seeming to light up is related to sex. She's open wide, bobbing her head, thinking *faster faster faster.* The hairy man standing on the bed isn't Sebastian. Kate watches his penis pounding down into Amanda in profile. Now Amanda understands the lights have actually gone on, and she hopes against hope that this handsome stranger has unwittingly hit a switch.

YOU VAGABONDS

Teddy Tenbrook likes the demos. That's all the commitment Scott can get out of him.

"You have to understand," Teddy says the Friday before New Year's, "personal taste doesn't factor. It doesn't matter what I personally respond to, it matters what I can sell. Rock is a bunch of people scrambling to eat anything that fell off the table. Homefork's going into electronic management in a major way, even if personally I think it's warmed-over disco." Anyway, he agrees to show the songs to his staff, and put them in the ears of a few label folks.

But Teddy's equivocation doesn't matter, because Ali Gondal writes them back. He loves the songs. He'll talk to his dad and get them an open spot in the showcase. They should come to L.A.

They get crazy-drunk New Year's Eve with Amanda's high school friends. Scott gets a lecture about the unfairness of the Academy Awards from a cute woman wearing a gold-lamé halter ("why shouldn't Batman be nominated, it made the most money"), and he can't stop watching her boobs jiggle. Sebastian calls his mom then drinks a pitcher of sangria. Amanda and Kate play beer pong and vanquish all comers. The countdown to midnight is a blur, and Sebastian wakes on a porch floor with an old lady's toes inches from his face. He's doesn't want to move. He just stares at these overgrown toenails, which look like a pile of boomerangs. Voices above him say:

"Why don't you listen to me, Momma?"

"Mm hm."

"No, I'm asking you, can't you understand the words coming out of my mouth?"

"I can understand them. Can you understand them?"

"It doesn't matter what you say to people anymore. It literally doesn't matter. I'm sitting here trying to talk to you about your pills, and you're going to do what you're going to do. There's no point even trying to talk anymore."

"I'm not the one talking. I'm not the one."

"Momma, what are you even saying?"

"This white boy dead?"

"No, Momma, the white boy isn't dead."

Sebastian sits up. He's in Amanda's backyard, still wearing his overcoat and getting ogled by her mother and grandmother. His mouth tastes like spoiled melon.

"What's going on up there?" says the grandmother. "You got those Mickey Mouse ears on?" Sebastian touches his head; it's his hair, pomaded over to one side.

"Take a good look at us," Gloria says. Both women are smoking cigarettes in housecoats, and have curlers in their hair. "You're looking at your future, Sebastian."

"I don't remember coming back here after the party," he says.

"And yet here you are. The others are sleeping inside. Pish was up early and she's driving my car around somewhere. You're a good influence on that girl."

"That other white boy," the grandmother says. "Why's he always looking at the floor all the time?"

"Momma, my understanding is that white boy is from Boston, which means he hasn't been in too many black folks' houses."

"He's a fool. Not like this one. This one is pretty."

Sebastian crawls to an empty wicker chair and climbs in, brain heavy and stomach sour. His hands dig into his coat pockets. "Thank you very much for letting us stay," he says. "It's not too chilly for you ladies, is it? This is so nice back here. Ohh. You beautiful ladies may never get rid of me."

"Why couldn't Lacey marry a boy like this?" says the grandmother. "Why she have to marry that House N—"

"*Momma.*"

"I guess she ain't pretty enough. Lacey ain't pretty enough to marry a boy like this."

"They're babies," says Gloria. "They're not thinking about marriage. Are you, Sebastian?"

He tries to think of a savvy response. Nothing happens, but instead of embarrassment he feels relief at his lack of morning distress. The cure for worrying apparently being nausea.

"You're going to scare him off," says the grandmother.

"He knows I'm just having fun with him," Gloria says. "Sebastian, you should hear the way Pish talks about you. It's so flattering, you're a music mastermind. And I have to say she's calmer lately. A mother worries about her child moving so far, and then she calls at all hours of the night? Oof. I'm glad those calls have stopped."

"I really love her."

"I know you do. I know you do. You're a baby but it's easy to see it in your face. You don't have to say a thing."

He squints at the avocado tree back here, feels the weight of suburbia pushed in against a rotting fence and a dirt yard. "What about you?" he says to Gloria. "How do you like your new job?"

"Oh, it's fine. I'm glad to have a Tuesday off, but it's better than moving in with Lacey. I love her to pieces but...."

"But she's crazy," says the grandmother. "And the husband. He's a...sissy."

"I should get up and brush my teeth," Sebastian says. "But I'm scared what you'll say about me when I'm gone."

"Aren't we all," the grandmother says.

Scott can't find any midweek gigs in the Valley, so one evening they play a few songs in Gloria's driveway. Friends and neighbors come around in shorts and flipflops and Amanda hugs everyone. It's weird not to sing into a mic, but she's tickled by these folks she's always known (who look vibrant and the same!) and she claps in time with Kate brushing on her muted snare. Three people are recording her on their phones, a common enough occurrence, except it's home; everyone tells her she's never sung better.

Finally Saturday comes: the night of the showcase.

But on the drive down, they're stopped by an immense, marathon-induced traffic jam. A woman with four children pulls up alongside the van, talking on a cell, rubbing her forehead, explaining something in painful detail. She jabs the steering wheel with her forefinger.

"God," Amanda says. "I irrationally hate that fucking woman."

"We have to do something," says Kate.

It's more than an hour since they got down off the highway. The showcase is probably underway.

"It can't end like this," Sebastian says.

"It won't," says Scott.

And it doesn't. He maneuvers them onto Pico, which is just as clogged, but he eases two tires up onto the median and revs it. His driver's side mirror gets smashed off by an exit-ramp support, but he keeps going. The boulevard goes under a building and he rides halfway on the sidewalk, overwhelming the van's suspension, eliciting honks and yells from outraged Angelinos. The Kids white-knuckle silently. A cop is directing traffic at Figueroa, so Scott puts on his blinker and inches ahead casually until someone lets him in. The cop blows his whistle but lets them go. Now they're within ten blocks of the Mayan and there's a packed parking lot on the right. A guy with an orange flashlight waves them off.

"Game already started," he says. "We're full. We're full up."

"If you let me park here," Scott says, "you can have my guitar."

"What I want your guitar for?"

"What do you want then?"

"We're full, man."

Scott looks at Amanda. She gets out of the van.

"Honey," says the attendant, "you can't stay here. You're blocking everything. What if somebody wants to get out?"

"Where do *you* park?" she says. "Can't we please leave our van where you park? We have a show over at Club Mayan. If we don't make it, we won't get a record contract. Please." She grinds together her shoulder blades. "We don't have money, but there must be some way."

There is. She gives him her iPhone.

They carry their gear: down Pico, up Hill. At 11th the road is barricaded and marathon runners—including a whole bunch of teens—are taking their sweet time. Kid Centrifuge makes a break for it and nobody stops them. Out of breath, arms and legs screaming, they arrive at the Mayan's crazy façade. People out front wear happy undead expressions, and the Kids can tell: the music escaping into the street may be canned and digital, but it has the unbalanced, bass-heavy edge that can only mean it's live. They ask the guys on the door to fetch Ali Gondal.

"Jesus," Ali says in a posh British accent. "What happened to you?" He's movie-star handsome in a silk shirt and three days' stubble. "Come around back. That way. I'll meet you."

They pile around the corner, weave through parked cars, and wait at the stage door. It's a gratified exhaustion, trying to find stars in the sky. Their shoulders sag and they grin.

"Come on in, you vagabonds," says Ali.

They clomp up some stairs and dump their burdens. They can see nightclub-style seating out front: candles on white tablecloths, three or four dignitaries per table, and the public roped-off behind them. Across the way, onstage, a dub-step band is about to hit the drop. The singer jumps around and his fedora pops off; the drummer is slamming electronic pads; the bass player thwacks away; and in the middle of them all is a familiar-looking bearded guy in a backwards trucker hat, standing behind a turntable, a laptop and a sequencer. He shouts at the ceiling, presses a button, and from a momentary respite comes a synthetic wall of sound that clatters everything backstage. Talking becomes impossible. Sebastian puts his arm around Amanda. Kate blows a forelock out of her eyes.

Eventually, Scott says, "Holy shit. The DJ out there, isn't that the guy from Pittsburgh?"

"…"

"Remember? Tall asshole? Wanted us to play Barry Manilow?"

"Oh yeah," says Kate. "Maybe."

"I mean, what the—?"

Ali interrupts. "You guys are truly magic." He looks at a watch whose diamonds blink. "I'm so pleased to meet you in person. Unfortunately, I did want to let you know we're…having an issue or two with the schedule." He says it *shed-yule*.

Scott forgets the guy from Pittsburgh.

"I'm afraid we're having a difficult time squeezing everyone onto tonight's roster."

"Ali," says Scott. "Mr. Gondal. Please, you can't be serious."

"Here's the thing. You're light years ahead of these acts." He gestures to the stage.

"You told us to come out," Scott says. "You said come to L.A. You're saying we're not booked. You said come to L.A."

"This show is for acts who really *need* help. Honestly, I'm not worried about you in the slightest."

"..."

"I feel bad about the miscommunication, but I'd feel much worse if you weren't so marvelously talented. I've no doubt you'll be signed within the month, and we'll look foolish."

"..."

"I'm awfully sorry. Look, there are so many moving parts when it comes to a show like this. I'm afraid in the end my father gets the final word, and...." He gestures down a hallway, where two men in headphones have stopped to converse.

"We could talk to him," says Kate. "We came all this way."

"I'm afraid there's nothing to be done. The showcase has undergone a...change in philosophy."

"What does that mean?" Scott says. "What does that even mean?"

"Can't we please just talk to your father?" Amanda says.

"This is impossible," says Scott, looking at Sebastian, who glares. "Seriously, this is fucking impossible."

"I certainly didn't mean for it to happen. Will you please stay and be my guests? I'll happily introduce you around to anyone you care to meet. In the meantime, I'm sorry, I must get those gentlemen's attention."

"Wait," Scott says. But he's gone.

And here they are, at the very end.

The dub-steppers finish their set and rush offstage, this way, smiling and fist-bumping. The bearded DJ really is the same guy, and he doesn't pay Kid Centrifuge a single scrap of attention. Scott steps forward, intending to punch him in the face. But Kate gets in his way. The guy goes frolicking by.

PLEASE HOLD

Sebastian is partway asleep when he suffers a panic attack. His parents will die. Amanda will die. Everything he cares about, and (he has to admit) most importantly himself. His chest, of which he's proud. His eyes. Gone. Nothing. He's stricken. How is it possible? What kind of sense does it make? The unfairness digs into his stomach, his lungs, his groin. As he attempts to think his way out of the problem of mortality, he lands—as always—on music. The escape hatch. Unsatisfactory, but a last resort. The only thing is make something that outlives you. It's cold comfort; it's *some* comfort. He claws his eyes trying not to cry. He rolls over and remembers Amanda isn't there.

She's on her mom's living room couch, drinking wine and flipping through channels. Kate is here, too. They stop on a Real Housewives spinoff.

"Must melt brain," says Amanda.

"We'll be okay," Kate says.

"Yeah. Hey, did she just call that other girl a camel-toe? Can they say that?"

"..."

"We should get cable in our apartment," Amanda says. "I'm getting hammered. This is fun."

"We have to do something about our boys," says Kate.

"They're tense."

"They are."

"You and me," Amanda says. "We'll kick 'em out and stay in L.A. Suntans by day, gigs and schmoozing by night."

"Sold," says Kate. "Not really, though."

"Yeah, it's just one show. People like us. We'll talk to the boys. We'll tell 'em no more macho bullshit. In this band, it's time for girl power." She smiles, bites her lip. "They'll listen to us. Right?"

Kate wants to say, *It depends on whether you're still having sex with random dudes.*

They watch in silence. Someone is crying for reasons that elude them, and seeing it feels pretty good.

In bed, something is making a slight chirping noise and it drives Sebastian nuts. He's absolutely still, sweating beneath this comforter, listening. Is there an insect in the room? Is some distant smoke detector running out of juice? There are faint glow-in-the-dark stars on the ceiling left by Amanda or Lacey or some previous occupant. What is that sound? *Chirp. Chirp. Chirp.*

He has to start writing songs. He can't just be the hapless kid anymore. They don't know anything more than he does, not really. They're not so much more experienced. But every time someone makes a reference he doesn't know—a band, a TV show, a movie—he's so...cowed. That's what he is: bullied and embarrassed, all the time. But no more! No more waiting, no more drugs. *Chirp. Chirp. Chirp.*

He rolls over. The sound intensifies.

It's the bedframe! The chirping's source is the bed beneath him. But how has it been squeaking so steadily...unless?

It's his heartbeat.

It resumes. He tries not to listen.

A couple days later they're in the mall on Topanga, sluggish in the food court. Scott hasn't called around to find gigs. Everyone wants to eat bad food and take a nap.

They still have the demos, and they still have Homefork maybe interested in representing them. There are plenty of small L.A. clubs to play, plus fairs and carnivals and farmers markets or whatever. They're not exactly the first band in history to get fucked over by a promoter. It's 2013 and the Internet is packed with articles that say a traditional record deal is no longer necessary, bands are bootstrapping, digital distribution has broken the monopoly. Hell, they've even got a tiny following online. They should keep doing what they've been doing.

So why does it feel like they're about to break up?

Gloria slipped Amanda some money, so they're pigging out on pretzels and crepes, frozen yogurt and macaroons. Everyone seems on the verge of saying something dire, but nobody does. In fact, the quartet hangs here together, as though afraid to let anyone out of sight.

They feel like. Such. Suckers.

For a while they discuss fixing the van's broken mirror, then they see a flyspecked Halliburton recruiting poster on the food court wall—"Opportunities in Bakersfield!"—and Scott says, "I'm doing it. I'm gonna go work for Dr. Evil."

"What's Halliburton?" says Sebastian, knowing he shouldn't.

And it makes Scott angry, so angry. Sebastian's kind of willful ignorance seems related to all the shit they've put up with. All the stupid people in stupid bars. All the asses they've kissed to no purpose. All the slack-jawed bouncers, and shameless greedy bookers, and dickheads making raunchy comments, and night clerks annoyed to be woken up, and the guy in Cleveland telling him don't quit his day job, and the guy in Lincoln claiming they ripped off all their songs, and the car they followed in Missouri that kept veering to run over helpless wildlife, and Ali Fucking Gondal.

In his most withering voice he says, "Don't worry, Sebastian, they're just the secret reason we went to war and the secret reason for the Gulf oil spill and the secret reason bad people in Nigeria can pay to have people killed and the secret force that runs *everything*. Seriously, don't worry your pretty head about it." His face pulses.

They're all quiet, then Sebastian says, "Oh."

They blow their remaining dough on a matinee of *Texas Chainsaw 3D*.

That evening Kate goes for a run. It's her first time in months and she feels it; her legs are fine but her wind is dreadful. The neighborhood streets are unlit. She sticks to sidewalks and eyes an endless chain of modest ranch houses. She puts her phone on shuffle and hears Little Green Cars. *("It's easy to fall in love with you....")*

She's in the pocket, completely vacant, thoughtless and so unaware of being without thought that it isn't even pleasurable, it just is. But then she hears the music fade in favor of a ringtone.

She assumes it's her parents and decides not to answer. But it's an unknown California caller.

"Is this Kate Grush?"

"Yes."

"Please hold for Miss Turner."

Kate stops running in a terrifying spot. Highway traffic hisses behind a fence to her right; to her left is a huge vacant hill that essentially makes this dark street inescapable. She can go forward and she can go back, but if, for example, Leatherface happens to be stalking her in the dark? She's in a whole heap of trouble.

Her brain goes: *Miss Turner?*

"Hello?" says an accented voice. "Hello, are you there?"

"Billie?" Kate says.

"Yes yes, hello. It is good to talk to you, and how have you been?"

Kate's breath is returning. She remembers that night in Minneapolis; she hasn't spoken with Billie Turner since. "I've been fine. I…. You're calling me. I don't think I gave you my phone number."

"No, well. Just so. I hope I am not calling too late, though. You are in New York?"

"Actually no. We kept going west. I'm in L.A."

"I think that is wonderful," says Billie. "I enjoy…your band so much."

Kate smiles ruefully, feels sweaty, pinches the bridge of her nose. "That's just…. How are *you*, Billie?"

"I am great. Really great. This is a happy coincidence because I am in Los Angeles, too."

"…"

"They have been asking me for years and I could not see it, really. I do not watch television anymore, I stopped watching probably before you were born."

"Uh-huh."

"But I still have friends here and some are very persistent. I hate to relive the past, which is why I would not listen. Who wants to walk around an old place seeing ghosts? I think it was you, dear Kate. It was after talking to you I found the courage. They told me Los Angeles has changed. And…I decided to believe them."

"Billie that's great."

"And my friends have become quite important in their old

age! But how are you, dear girl? How are the drums?"

"The drums are fine. But that homeless man we met, did you—"

"I listen to many songs now," Billie says. "I do not know the first thing about computers, but all you do is click...."

"..."

"You see, they trust my judgment! Would you believe it? Some songs they choose do not have to be so famous yet. Some songs they want to discover, and help make it famous."

"Billie, I'm sorry, I don't know what you're talking about."

"And just today, I received a song by Kid Centrifuge!"

"You...?"

"Of course I remember my lovely friend Kate. And I love your song! The music director is Adam, the sweetest, nicest boy. Really, if he was not married.... Well, maybe he is a little too old for you, but maybe you remember my policy about that. Anyway, Adam agrees with me."

"..."

"We want to use your song, Kate. We want to put it on *Glee*."

PART III

SETUP ONE

Kate and Colleen eat amazing pork-belly tacos out of a food truck and lurch into Star Bar to drink beer. Austin is melt-your-face-off hot. Tuesday afternoon buzzes abandoned, Shiner Bock bottles flop-sweat in the air conditioning, "Blurred Lines" tinnily noodles from ceiling speakers. They stretch out their legs in a booth.

"Man," says Kate.

"I know, right?" Colleen says.

"At South-By I didn't know the good places. I ate plastic-wrapped PB&Js."

"That's a crime against humanity. Only reason I don't move here full-time is I like seeing my toes." Colleen has her hands on her flat tummy, eyes closed.

"Don't think you have anything to worry about."

"You're sweet. But you get on the wrong side of 30, it takes work to keep anything resembling a bod. I ran seven miles in the sauna out there this morning."

"God, I have to run. Wake me up tomorrow. Get my fat butt out there with you."

"No way. You're a drummer. Drummers need power thighs."

The bartender comes over carrying shot glasses. "Mescal," he says. "On the house."

Kate feels a grin harden across her cheeks. She doesn't get recognized, but might it happen soon? Might it be happening now?

Or is the bartender just hitting on the hot chick?

"Sticking with beer, thanks," says Colleen. "Too many bad adventures with hard alcohol."

"I'll forgive you," says the bartender. "But only if you tell me the lowlights."

Colleen sits up. "Drinking tequila in Rio, I blacked out and woke up on someone's boat. My wallet and phone and shoes were gone. My band was nowhere to be found. I'd been sold in my sleep."

"Sold," Kate says.

"I was a sex slave for about two hours. I whined so much and dropped so many names they turned around and put me ashore. I was too annoying to keep."

They laugh and Kate accepts both mescals. She says, "Clearly I have to catch up."

"Yeah, you're the least of my worries," says Colleen.

"Should I be flattered?"

"Not flattered or unflattered. It's just the truth. I know borderline personalities. Hell, I am a borderline personality."

Kate says, "Maybe I could surprise you."

"Sometimes clichés are true. Drummers really are easiest to get along with. Your lead singer has Wild Child written all over her, and the guys.... Holy shit, on the flight down I got stuck listening to them argue about authenticity."

"They like the sound of their own voices."

"One says it comes from instinct, don't think, just play whatever comes. The other says, what, first drafts are shit and you'll never get it without hammering away. I can't remember who was who, my ears were bleeding."

"I guess I get the angst," says Kate. "We all kind of have a lot invested in being badass."

"..."

"And this song...."

"..."

"*Isn't.*"

"Oh, shit," says Colleen. "Yeah, I mean, that's the kind of thinking I have to squeeze out of you guys. You don't know how rare this is. The kind of money they're about to put into promoting this song is like when I first started. No matter what Scott and Sebastian say, it's still a rock record, and labels don't put money like this behind rock records anymore. We should all be pinching ourselves."

"I am. I do."

"It's a great fucking song, and the planes are lined up on the runway. It's an absolute, guaranteed smash. Gonna make you famous. The boys worrying about whether a song is beneath them, that's first-world guilt through and through."

Kate uses an ingénue's pout and says, "I love your sleeve."

Colleen looks at her own bare arm, which is tattooed from shoulder to elbow all the way around: some kind of chalice with eagle talons around it, jungle leafs and fleurs-de-lis. "It's finally done, I was adding to it for years and the Homefork guys made me get the last part a few months ago. Have any tats?"

"I don't."

"Hey, we should do that. Let me be your shepherd into the ink world."

"I don't know. Yours looks awesome, but I don't…think I could commit."

"We should just stop by, they have some awesome shops here. Or what else could we do? You want to go swimming? There's this natural spring pool right downtown."

Kate knows that essentially Colleen is someone she pays to be on hand, but the other Kids pay her too, and Colleen doesn't seem as interested in spending afternoons with them. Which is to say: Kate's flattered. Hanging out with this smart, accomplished manager has consistently produced the most fun she's had since all this began. In Atlanta, they sang karaoke at a gay bar and laughed for hours. In Nashville after Bonnaroo, they shopped for vintage cowboy boots and met some German guys who decided they must be roller-derby stars. She says, "How long do we have?"

"Mm. Four hours. Sunset probably isn't until 8:30."

"A responsible musician would catch a nap."

"You woke up like an hour ago," says Colleen. "Executive decision, we're finding you a new outfit for tonight." She gets up and waves at the bartender. "Thank you, garçon!" Kate follows along noiselessly like a little sister.

While they drive out into the hills in search of fashion, Amanda is still in her hotel room at the Driskill, alternately scrutinizing her bathrobed self and texting with Lucius Hawk. She met Lucius in New York back in March; he's a sweet, gentle person, but it seems they both know the romantic phase of their relationship is over. He won't stoop to complaining about it, he just checks in with her daily. Is he actually being friendly, or is he playing the Friend Card, showing what a stand-up guy she's letting slip away? She looks for the answer in the darker skin beneath her eyes: still smooth but hammered thin by travel and chaos. They'll apply whatever makeup they want on her later tonight, so she'll be damned if she's wasting time on it now.

She puts in her earbuds and queues up "Density of Joy." She lip-synchs to her own voice.

And she plays it over and over, watching her mouth produce the words, testing different levels of intensity and coquettishness.

Her phone bloops another message from Lucius:

>Biggest video budget I ever had was $0. Must be nice.

They fitted her last month at Lord & Taylor—five blocks away from Ameena and the old design office—in a private room stocked with fruit, cheese and champagne. Racks of clothes rolled in and out as she joked with the stylist how she wanted to keep all the outfits: a sweater-dress with a swooping neckline, a Diane von Furstenberg jacket over a microskirt, a leather bodice and thigh-high boots, a Gucci lambswool turtleneck. They decided on a tie-neck blouse and skinny jeans and she promised to do some biceps work before the shoot. So her wardrobe is somewhere downstairs waiting for her, and there's no reason to contemplate it. She texts back:

>iwbni u r good 2 me im nrvs

She watches herself kiss the air and wonders what she means. Is she kissing Lucius? Herself? The camera? She wants to enjoy tonight, to take mental photographs.

>Are you actually nervous? Why am I skeptical?

Her nose is super-sensitive, and it tells her something foul is going on either in this bathroom or the hotel suite proper. It's a whiff of sewage or animal remains and she wonders why she's only picking it up now. She carries her phone around the rooms, sniffing, frightened of what she might find behind the bed, under an end table, inside the closet. She finished *Lady Macbeth of the Mtsensk District* this spring, and the idea of comparing sympathetic women to the erstwhile Queen of Scotland is kicking around in her head.

>nrvs nuff 2 hallucin8

Colleen told her she's about to become a star, to be ready for it. Be ready to hire her own publicist and a lawyer to handle personal endorsements. Be ready for photographers shouting her name. Be ready to handle a front-woman's dilemmas: becoming the face of the band, having creepy guys send her stuff, balancing resentments from bandmates, on and on. Amanda is delighted in the abstract by these thoughts. To this point in her life, has she been calculating? She needed New York, she needed to brush up against all those strangers. Is it really only a year since she hung around with Connie and Maria, those *Sex and the City* phonies? Plus none of her L.A. pals seem the same now. It's possible Kate is her longest-standing actual friend. Anyway maybe everything has been leading this way, and now she's in a swank hotel with dozens of people hoping she'll show up on time.

>You'll be great.

She's having second thoughts about the tie-neck blouse. Shouldn't she wear something she usually performs in? She got this super-cool Arcade Fire t-shirt in Atlanta and wouldn't that be something, nodding to a band like that? What if the blouse comes across pretentious?

She disrobes in the bathroom and stares at herself. Her boobs are good. Her arms are buff. She makes a bodybuilding pose, squints and puffs out her cheeks; maybe she should do sit-ups right before shooting starts. But then she looks away sighing. It would be mortifying for anyone to know she performs these inspections. She wants to be the star who understands Russian lit. She gets out a little eye cream and rubs away the smudges under her eyelids.

Downstairs in the bar, Sebastian sloshes through a half-dozen light beers, peeling off each label and carefully arranging a coat-of-arms on the marble slab separating him from a mustachioed bartender. Road boredom is its own perdition. It's an eternal sick day; what you do *doesn't matter.* People in jail take extension courses. People in comas presumably experience an intense present. Sebastian should write music, but finds it impossible. Lying in a hotel bed he has ideas, but the energy required to get out his guitar and the TASCAM recorder daunts him, and he can't find the strength to separate a song from its rind.

Sidelong Records—a former indie label now owned by a giant—is the accelerant for the band's current unrest. Homefork officially signed on to manage when *Glee* got interested in the "Density of Joy" demo. But all parties agreed the song needed production and an actual release before it would be suitable for broadcast. So with a wink-wink TV agreement in hand, Homefork got the Kids tacked onto festivals while negotiating with labels. In June, Sidelong finally signed them to a 360 deal, gave them a (very) small chunk of change, and shipped them off to Totem Party in Brooklyn, a real studio with a superstar producer to crank out a finished draft of "Density." Whatever other songs they could record in three days would make a nice head start on their first album.

Then things got hairy.

At least when they played festival mini-sets on ancillary stages, they could pretend the world cared about the full Kid Centrifuge *oeuvre.* But this Randy Pope, this dickhead producer, ignored their other songs. When he caught them playing "Caribou Boyfriend" by way of warmup, he said, "All right, shit, I'll go grab some lunch. Come get me when you're done jerking each other off. But clean the fucking windows first." And when they got down to recording "Density," Sebastian stood there by himself in his own little booth listening to Amanda waste her talent, and he played the riff over and over, no variation, no embellishment, no solo. The morning of the third day, Pope shook his head and suggested they just loop the riff, and Scott had to step in and say no looping. It was just awful. Sebastian's confidence drifted away.

And now that the execs have been bowled over by the luck of having signed a rock band that's secretly a bubblegum factory, they apparently want nine more songs just like "Density of Joy."

But the bandmates told Colleen there's no way they'll work with Randy Pope on the rest of their album. So everything is on hold while Sidelong untangles the producer's contract, and in the meantime they're down here doing a video for a song Sebastian hates.

Other than that, things are great.

Scott texts asking where he is, then walks in bearing a funky stone necklace for his girlfriend. He shows it to Sebastian, who can't judge what would look good on over-serious Jane. He hates it when she talks French.

"It's hot outside," Scott says. "It's hotter than the temperature at which it's no longer possible to come up with something witty to compare how hot it is to."

"Indeed," says Sebastian, and he even slurs that.

"It'll still be hot tonight. We'll be in suits. Yikes."

". . ."

"But I guess the heat's right for you. Which level of hell are you living in these days?"

"Ha-ha! I'm fine."

Scott asks for a glass of water. "Yeah. You seem great."

"Just getting interesting, right?"

Scott clicks together his incisors. "Okay. I get it. We held our nose and did it their way for one song.

". . ."

"But think about it. Soon they're gonna come to us, and they're gonna say, 'Time to go back in the studio.'"

". . ."

"But the money's spent. You know what a shoot like this costs? They're fucking committed. They won't be able to back out, even if we start recording songs *we* want. Man, they think we're too young to know what's up."

"We kind of are," Sebastian breathes.

"So let's hit the reset button, Sebastian. Let's make something you want to make."

Sebastian laughs and loses control of a spit bubble. "Well, I don't even know what that even is."

"Let's just throw shit against the wall, then, you and me. No songs. We'll just fuck around in a studio." Scott is making his voice compassionate, though he resents coming in here and finding his young guitarist in a puddle. But he and Kate have to share the load. "I'll do whatever you tell me. I'll play whatever you want, seriously. I'm excited to learn. It's happy accidents, right? Make a lot of noise until you hear something you like. Between the eyes, blam comes a thunderbolt."

"Song title alert."

"I admit it. I'm a scavenger, Sebastian. It comes fast because I appropriate. But I can try being more original."

Sebastian is so tired of this conversation. He's so tired of Scott coming at him with some new angle. Scott wants to talk and talk. Today it's mollifying, yesterday it was mockery. They played a new song the other day at the Grand Mal—tentatively titled "Roshambo," another one of Scott's—and Sebastian could see the fun in his bandmates' faces, the quasi-surprise when a tempo change clicked and their respective sounds folded perfectly into one another. He knows these three people well enough now, can see when they're thrilled. They speak to one another in a wordless argot, and maybe it's the thing they most cherish about the band, the wallop of shedding one's skin and rollicking as avatars. But less and less frequently does Sebastian follow along. His bones are filled with lead.

"Sounds good," he tells Scott.

"Firing that asshole Pope was the best thing we could do," Scott says. "Don't regret it for one minute. Jacob's in Austin. If he gives us any crap for it, I'll take the hit."

"God, yeah," says Sebastian.

"Just give me joy joy joy joy joy, buddy. And don't show up shitfaced tonight, okay?"

Sebastian salutes.

Later Colleen comes in. She pats Sebastian's shoulder and says, "How are we enjoying Austin?"

"It's great. I really like it. Yeah. Really."

"That's terrific," she says. "Room 214, please. Ten minutes."

He pays his tab and thinks about getting some food, but his legs take him upstairs. Colleen lets him in and undoes his pants.

"Hurry up," she says, and gets on her knees.

"No, come here," says Sebastian. He kisses her and she bites his lip. He pulls off her t-shirt and licks her nipples. As ever, her boob job is spectacular. He reaches into her pants and puts two fingers inside her and she grabs his arm, not to remove it but to urge him on. They grapple toward her bed. He's got her underwear partway off and positions himself to plunge in, but when she feels him knocking she says, "Oh, fuck no. Eat me out first."

He tries. He kind of just slobbers all over the place. She

guides the back of his head but her lack of arousal seems obvious. Someone once told him nibble the skin near the top; someone else said try licking the letters of the alphabet. He throws the kitchen sink at her, praying at some point she'll start wriggling: just via the law of averages he must be doing *something* that feels good. His sinuses fill up and his hard-on wanes. He tries the trick of kissing her thighs and then her belly, moving north, but she pushes his shoulders down.

"Just soft and wet," she says. "Use your fingers, too. Otherwise you'll kill me with that hog."

He's in a full sweat and his face is windburned by the time she finally taps his cheek. He climbs up and knees apart her thighs.

Colleen hisses in his ear: "*Slow*, goddammit."

Finally, finally he gains entrance and begins pumping, and she reaches down and grabs his balls. But not in a good way. She squeezes and he yowls.

"I don't think you understand," she says, "that while your cock is a beautiful object, it's abnormally *big* and when you ram it around like you're *storming the fucking Bastille*, it doesn't feel good. Get up. Just get up."

Involuntary tears stripe his face, but he flops backward on the bed and she climbs on top. She descends on him gently, puts him halfway in, rocks around. He suppresses the urge to pound up at her. And it goes like this, she dances like this, and Sebastian is afraid to move. He watches her in terror: her eyes are closed and she plays with those preternaturally round tits. She comes urgently, angrily, then walks to the bathroom.

Sebastian examines the clock on her nightstand, and it looks like a ticking bomb.

"I like your drummer, I really do," says Colleen, emerging with a lit cigarette. "But she's kind of a weird little girl."

"…"

She gets into bed with him. "Relax. I said I *like* her. Just…I don't know what her expectations are."

"…"

"Maybe she's too sweet. Or maybe that's all an act. But she just seems nervous or something. Jittery about the band." She drags fingernails up his arm while ashing into an empty water bottle. "Obviously she's a good friend of yours."

"Very good," Sebastian says.

"I don't know exactly what I'm saying. I'm saying everyone has to pull in the same direction. No exceptions. In my experience, that's the difference between bands who've made it and the ones who haven't. You get one malcontent...."

Sebastian knows if anyone's the malcontent, it's him. He says, "Kate's the last person you have to worry about. She might be the most genuinely nice person I've ever met. She's not a malcontent."

"She is nice. You're right. But there's a difference between nice and.... She thinks you guys will bail. She thinks when 'Density' goes big, you and Scott will hate the kind of attention. You'll feel like sellouts."

"..."

"I told her you're smarter than that. You have the chance to set yourself up for the rest of your lives, and a person just doesn't blow that. But no, Kate insisted. She's like, 'If I know Sebastian, he'll do one interview with E! and then bolt.' Maybe what I'm saying is it's not healthy when everyone doesn't understand the goals up front. From that very first day at Sons of Essex, what you guys told me is you want to make it. You want to earn a living from your music, sure, but you want more than that. You want to matter. And what's about to happen right now, that's the best way, the biggest way you'll ever get to matter."

Sebastian's head is clearer. He keeps his voice calm. "You're talking about me. You're giving me a message. This isn't about Kate at all."

"She just needs to have more confidence in you," says Colleen. She reaches under the sheet. "Like I do."

He groans. It's silent in this dark room; the windows glow orange behind thick curtains. If everything is out of control, then he is too. "Just...don't talk shit about her, all right?"

"I didn't mean to. I'm serious, I love hanging out with Kate. You're right: she's the best." She strokes him and kisses his neck. "You can't expect me to be lucid after this guy has had his way with me." Her hand accelerates. "I just want everyone to accept it. You're going to be the biggest band in the world."

A van leaves from the Driskill at nine, and they're all on it. Sebastian's hair is wet and he sits as far as possible from Colleen. Amanda wears the Arcade Fire shirt and reads *Dead Souls*. Scott and Kate talk excitedly, jittery as junebugs. They cross Congress and see the Texas capitol building.

Scott looks at Kate and says, "'There's blood in my mouth 'cuz I've been biting my tongue all week,'" and Kate replies, "'I keep talking trash but I never say anything.'"

And they all sing the rest of "Portions For Foxes," a Rilo Kiley song they've covered in shows, and this peppy nihilist song about everybody winding up dead cheers them. They arrive at Zilker Park marveling at all the lights. They get made-up and dressed one-by-one in a trailer—Amanda goes with the blouse, Kate wears the outfit she bought this afternoon to see if anyone notices—and crew members hand them their instruments. It's dark and still probably ninety degrees as they climb up onto a stage. There are *so many* people here doing such specific things. This woman with a light meter. This guy retouching makeup. Jacob Shear is chatting in an amiable semicircle, possibly with other people from Sidelong Records. Eventually Jacob comes up here, too, and handshakes the bandmates.

"Make some joy joy joy joy joy," he says to each of them.

It seems like they're about to start, someone comes over who seems like he'd be the director but isn't, then someone else and someone else. Everyone has suggestions, thoughts, instructions. They describe camera movements, with the caveat that everything could change. They give conflicting directions about whether to look into the lens. For an hour the Kids stay on their marks suffering like tensed cats. Finally someone behind a bank of monitors gets up and comes over: he's a gray little guy wearing sunglasses.

"Have fun. Make it seem like you're playing. Only more so."

They count Kate in and playback starts. Their pop song blasts out into what the band assumes is a really big park—none of them has seen it in daylight—and they slither around pretending. Kate actually strikes her drums, but of course the others aren't plugged in; Amanda sings without amplification. Sebastian has the one lick to fake-play over and over for three minutes. Scott jumps back-to-back with Amanda, repeatedly banging the Spector against his hips. It's a dumb, exhilarating feeling, like getting caught by your best friend singing into a hairbrush. Amanda flings away the mic and struts offstage as the song fades. They look into the lights to see if anyone is impressed. After a few minutes, the director sends over someone to talk to them.

"Okay," she says. "First thing is we're wondering if anyone's smile muscles have been destroyed in a fire or any kind of industrial accident."

They "play" the song a dozen times, grinning, with cameras whirling and then a Steadicam running among them. Lights strobe around the stage, synched to the song's beat. Sebastian trips on a wire during one take but his fingers keep playing the riff even as he's sprawled on the stage, and he hopes it winds up in the final cut. Finally, through a megaphone, someone tells them Setup One is finished, and everyone should move on to Setup Two.

But that, too, is an incredibly long wait. They stand around with crewmembers in half-darkness and someone produces a passel of weed. Sebastian usually likes substances to take him in the other direction, but tonight this will do. He rolls for everyone; Kate and Amanda spark up, Scott declines. He yawns cavernously, trying to imply he's too tired. A lad no older than Sebastian says, "You fucking wail on guitar, man." Sebastian nods thanks. "Some of that arpeggio shit you do. Not on this song. But you know, in general."

Amanda smiles thinking Sebastian can't take a compliment like a human being.

"Reminds me of that guy from Muse," the kid says.

An older mustached crew guy says, "You're crazy. Bellamy is all feel. He's a mess technically and his solos are simple, but it doesn't matter because he's so intense and balls-out. Different kind of awesome. Torque, you're obviously classically trained, yeah?"

"..."

"All right," says the kid, "best rock guitarists in the world right now. Go."

"I mean," the mustached guys says, "Auerbach from Black Keys. St. Vincent. Ira Kaplan. Mary from Wild Flag."

"What about Blake Mills," says the kid. "I did a few of his shows, he was really interesting."

"Oh, c'mon, that slide shit."

Kate says, "Is it lame to say Dave Grohl?"

Both of the crew guys say, "Yes!"

"I know this game," says Amanda. "Only the obscure survive."

"Besides which," Scott chimes in, "did you pick a single player who's ever broken a string?"

"Black Keys aren't exactly obscure," says the mustached guy.

"No Thurston Moore and Lee Ranaldo?" says Scott. "J Mascis

and Lou Barlow? Alex Turner? Albert Hammond? We're in Austin, nobody says Britt Daniel?"

"Sonic Youth," scoffs the younger one. "If you ever had to stand twenty feet from Sonic Youth, you'd change your opinion pretty quick."

The mustached one takes a super-long drag through his half-grin. "Really? Dinosaur Jr.? Next you'll be selling me fucking Oasis, man. I thought we were talking, you know, *relevant* players."

Scott says, "'Watch The Corners?' The chord changes on that thing are sick."

"I mean, how old are you? You one of those fetish kids with the oldies?"

"That song's last year!"

"I like the guy from Vampire Weekend," says Kate.

The mustached guy says, "Yeah, I bet you mostly like his argyle socks."

"Hey, pretentious assholes," says Amanda. "When you get finished pissing down each other's legs, we'll be over there having actual fun."

She walks away, defining for these music geeks what cool really is. Sebastian follows. Kate sticks around, wanting to defend Scott, but the hostility disperses with most of them sleepy and high. They, too, wander toward the next lighted setup, and the mustached guy goes, "I really should've said Kurt Cobain. Because he's alive and living in an ashram in India. They got a blond corpse from the morgue and shot it in the face."

"Kurt who?" Scott says. "Sorry, before my time."

"Hey, I don't mean anything by it. Don't give me weed after midnight. No offense, it's really cool you got this video. We mostly do hip-hop guys spraying chicks with champagne."

They stumble down a hill and find searchlights aimed at two gantry towers, which the crew has telescoped up into the night sky. Two elastic ropes stretch down from the towers to a sphere of tubular steel: it's a reverse-bungee machine leased from a carnival, designed to fling people upward at great velocity, two at a time. The premise of the video is this: Amanda will flirt with a buff handsome male model while singing to him, and to account for the resultant exhilaration when she finally kisses him, the video will cut to Amanda and the model soaring skyward side-by-side in the reverse-bungee. These images will be intercut with footage they just recorded of the band playing onstage, and then the video will also show the other band members soaring, presumably because playing this peppy tune sends them into a kind of ecstasy, too.

The others are up ahead, and Scott says, "You know why the song is called 'Density of Joy'?"

"Why?" says the mustached crew guy.

"I like to think it's about a girl named Joy, and we're exploring just exactly how fucking dense she is."

The model comes by wearing a velour vest over nothing, so every contour of his hunky tanned arms announces its awesomeness. He bro-hugs Scott and Sebastian and real-hugs Kate, then inspects Amanda head-to-toe and says, "Hey, I'm Colton. Damn." He smells musky to Amanda, an overdone chemical musk that makes her think of South Village bars stocked by Ed Hardy guys. He's a different kind of gorgeous from Sebastian—chiseled by the gods, radiating stupidity—but the prospect of teasing and hugging and kissing him in tomorrow night's overflow shoot is acceptable. She says, "Damn yourself."

"All right," says a stage manager, "I've got Grush and Torque going up first. Come on in, have fun."

Kate loves roller coasters and clambers into the sphere; Sebastian takes the great-circle route, inspecting the platform, the electromagnetic lock that holds down the sphere, the surrounding grass. He remembers signing a waiver a few days ago. The generators over here make enough noise to cover his hyperventilation.

"Yo, Sebastian," says Scott. "It's 2 a.m. C'mon."

Someone carrying a clipboard tells the band they've been testing the apparatus all afternoon and evening, and it's perfectly safe.

"Yeah but, ah, I *really* don't want to do this," Sebastian tells Scott. "Who cares if I'm not actually inside the cage of death? Who'll notice?"

Scott pretends he's holding a walkie-talkie and says into it: "Code orange. The Velvet Glove is moist. Repeat: the Velvet Glove is moist."

"I just don't like that feeling in my stomach. What I'm saying is it's biological."

"You want me to go up first?" Scott says. "I'm sure they'd rearrange the schedule."

"See, the thing is if you go up first and live, then I'll be pretty sure the first shot loosened all the bolts. I sometimes get a little...nervous?"

"Yeah, not a giant shock, Sebastian. We're all aware."

"Whoever wrote the script wasn't aware."

"Listen, if you don't want to do this, I'll back you."

"..."

"I'm not kidding," says Scott. "Let's go talk to the director."

"No, I mean, I don't want to be that guy. Just tell them.... Give me a couple more minutes. I'll try and...think about something else. I'm sorry. Okay. Distract me. Wait. I know: make me feel ashamed about some movie I never saw or some book I never read. Or make a face at me like I just fucked up an easy thing on the guitar. Seriously, I think I could get through this if you'd just make me feel really, really shitty on a really deep, personal level."

"..."

"..."

"..."

"Sorry," Sebastian says. "I'm an asshole. I'll do it. I'm over here! Hey, I'm coming!" He walks back around and straps in next to Kate. Scott follows, bumbling for a retort.

A guy wearing a helmet shakes the four-way harness-buckles at their waists, lowers padded bars over their shoulders, and gives a thumbs-up. A dozen cameras are mounted all around the sphere's frame, pointing inward. Two larger cameras down on the ground are rolling. Someone blasts an air horn and yells a countdown. Sebastian wants to hold Kate's hand, but it's not allowed.

"Final ready?" says the guy in the helmet.

"Yes!" Kate says.

"Totes McGotes," says Sebastian. His dread of time's advancement has never been more profound. Every moment is intolerable for its increasing proximity to his destruction.

"I wonder why," says Kate.

"What?"

"I wonder why he has a helmet, and we—"

They launch. Sebastian forgets to look at the view, and merely screams. Kate sees downtown Austin scroll across her line of vision as they flip over. The hill country is mostly dark. Sebastian literally wonders if he's dead.

"Woooo!" Kate says. "I can't tell if you're really scared!"

"Oh, no!" says Sebastian in falsetto. "Totally fine."

When they're lowered back to the ground, Amanda and the male model are preparing for their launch. Sebastian climbs out and Scott comes over and gives him an ultra-vigorous high-five. And feels something bad happen in his back.

THE SPACESUIT

He's woken by the worst pain of his life. Curiously, it's not in his back at all: it's his right ankle. His lumbar aches, his butt seizes and his thigh twitches, but the outside of his ankle screams and never stops. It honestly feels like he's been shot.

It's daylight but his bandmates are certainly still sleeping. He doesn't want to see Sebastian. He worries the others heard about their confrontation by the bungee. In his shame, he decides to be selfless and wait before alerting anyone, to see if the pain will go away.

The only position that doesn't make him shriek is recumbent on his stomach. When he gets up to piss, he has five seconds before the ankle reaches catastrophic pain levels; he yells and cries finishing up in front of the toilet, and limp-sprints dribbling back to bed. He's never had a back injury before; it's a malady for an old person. He convinces himself that if he can make it past noon, the agony will abate. He checks his phone every five minutes, drunk with pain.

Eventually Kate texts to ask about breakfast and he sobs his relief. Against his halfhearted protests, Sebastian muscles him downstairs and Colleen drives him to an emergency room. They prescribe Vicodin and muscle relaxers and he gets used to the terminology: L5 nerve root and superior peroneal retinacula. It's a back injury, even if it doesn't feel like it. By nightfall his brain gets thicker and his ankle grows vague. He calls Jane and tries to summarize, but ends up shouting at her for forgetting to buy them Phoenix tickets and then apologizing in a tiny voice he doesn't recognize. Overnight, Amanda returns to Zilker Park and shoots the teasing/kissing footage with Colton-the-model. Sebastian stares at the ceiling above Colleen's bed. Kate watches *Pitch Perfect* on cable and couldn't love it more. She aca-seriously dreams herself a member of the Bellas: ruthless and skinny.

They fly back to New York and disperse. Scott sleeps twenty straight hours in Jane's bed but wakes up exhausted. His right calf and foot are numb. He fumbles around the kitchenette, experiencing some primal instinct to eat despite a total lack of hunger. This medicated fog puts him beyond language, maybe beyond music. He's some proto-Scott, crushed by loss yet relieved of the burden of trying to communicate it. He keeps dreaming of writing songs, keeps fooling himself into believing he's come up with something wonderful that he *must* remember upon fully waking. Or he's running on a circular stairway made of eighth-notes, or his mouth is stitched shut and he must converse via semaphore flags. He pours baking soda on his cereal.

Jane comes and goes. He can't remember if she's home. He limps around looking for her in the long skinny apartment she shared with another barista, before Scott moved in. He recalls that Herman Melville Square is right outside and gets it in his head that he wants to read *Moby-Dick*. He asks Jane to fetch him a copy and she does, but he can't get through more than a paragraph without falling asleep. He panics in a dream, thinking he left his guitars in Austin. He wakes and finds unchewed food in his mouth. He doesn't like all this nothing. Being led by pharmaceuticals ever deeper within himself, a place in which words are bullshit, songs are bullshit, there's no point, it's not even worth trying.

"*...cette stupide fille, une brunette, elle m'a appelée Sally—est-ce que je ressemble à Sally?*" Jane won't let him get out of bed for dinner, so they're getting pizza crumbs in the sheets.

"No, you don't look like a Sally," says Scott.

"I'm sorry. Am I boring you?"

"Not at all. This is my tone now. This is all the tone I can muster."

Jane is quirky-pretty: a wide, flat face, dirty blonde hair with barrettes, and thick granny glasses concealing giant eyes that are maybe a little extra-far apart. She knows she's an acquired taste, and doesn't care. She says, "Funny, when you told me about Sebastian fucking your manager, you mustered a little more tone, didn't you?"

"Allegedly," Scott says. "We have no proof."

"Even still. These are the doings of my day. If you're looking for something more exotic, you probably have the wrong girl."

"You're exotic. You're fine. I'm medicated. I'm underwater."

"One more day of sulking. That's your allotment."

"It's not sulking," says Scott. "What do I have to sulk about?"

"*C'est une bonne question,*" Jane says.

He showers holding himself up against ancient mildewed tile, legs shaking. From inside the drug haze he can't tell if his back even hurts. He's scared to get in the elevator, let alone walk outside. He wonders if he primed his back for such unexpected havoc by hunching alone for years over art projects, download projects, music projects. Surely there's an epiphany to be had about the months and years he hid inside his brother's apartment.

He wonders what day it is. He hasn't heard from anyone. Presumably they're supposed to start recording again. There has to be a full Kid Centrifuge album associated with "Density of Joy." Doesn't there?

Music is playing in his head. He fumbles for his phone and presses "record," tries to hum the notes he's hearing. But it's dark in here. He's either humming into his phone or Jane's vibrator. He blinks and is waking up, it's light again and she's above him saying his name, he focuses on her face but strangely she's older and prettier.

"Mom?"

"Glad to see you straightened the place up for me."

"..."

"I can't get the story out of your ladyfriend. Are you in pain, or are you not in pain? Is it your back or is it your ankle?"

He's naked under a thin blanket and his mother is actually here, too close. He tucks himself in, lest she gets the urge to roust him out of bed. She opens the blinds and begins picking dead leaves from Jane's plants. Then she disappears and returns with a cup of water, pours precise amounts into each.

"You know how bad my back has always been," she says. "You must have gotten it from me. Mine has been killing me for a month."

"Yeah, wow, are you okay?" says Scott.

She smiles prettily. "I guess one of us is tough. We took the train down and it was really the most relaxing thing. I find it's good for my back, you should try it."

"I can't even sit up, and you.... Oh, crap, you came down. It's Frank's birthday."

His mother lifts clothing off the floor, folds it and stacks it on a bureau. "Yes, well, we all know how busy you are."

"I am. This is the first time I've been in the city for more than.... I mailed you guys a link to the new song. Did you listen?"

"I think Dad did. I never got it. Are you sure you sent it to me?"

"Yeah. Definitely."

"Well, I never got it, so don't get defensive. I listened to the CD you sent. I could really tell how hard you worked on it."

"Mom," he says, "do you ever hear yourself talking?"

"What? I said it was good."

"You didn't, actually."

"I literally just said I listened to it, and I like it. Don't go looking for trouble, please. You sent it months ago, am I supposed to quote back every word to you? You don't have to be so insecure when it comes to your family."

Scott wiggles his right foot. It's still dead.

"Are you using a heating pad?" says his mother. "Alternate ice and heat."

"Jesus, Mom! It's a little more serious than that. A little heat and ice isn't going to fix.... I mean, do you want the full diagnosis? They think I crushed a nerve. The doctor says it could be a year before my foot gets back to normal."

"Thank God you kept your health insurance."

"I don't have to thank God," he says, "I can thank you and Dad. So thank you. I mean it."

"..."

"I didn't even *do* anything. I high-fived a guy. I feel so old...." He looks at his mother, who's snapping a dirty wet towel into shape so she can fold it. "That CD I sent, those were demos. But we're doing a full album."

"That's great! We're proud of you. You know what? Maybe you're just stressed, maybe that's why your back hurts. I know when I've got a deadline, I can get really sore."

"It's not…. It's actual muscles and ligaments and discs. This isn't in my head. My big toe is completely dead. It has no strength. Here, push down on it."

"Maybe you should put on some clothes," says his mother. "I'll wait with your ladyfriend."

Scott thinks: *Omigod, Jane met you.*

On her way out of the bedroom, his mother says, "Don't be so quick to take offense. You know my heart is in the right place."

He gets out of bed and into Jane's robe, and finds himself wishing his back hurt more. It actually feels pretty good, and he hasn't taken the muscle relaxers this morning. He judges his lack of pain as a perverse victory for his mother. He washes and finds everyone in the living room: mother, father, brother, Jane. They're making each other laugh. Scott exaggerates his limp.

They eat lunch at the Petite Abeille on 20th. There's a wait and his family lingers placidly. Several parties who arrived after them are seated sooner, and Jane tells Scott to ask why; he can see his mother and father recoil. The Kopps are the world's friendliest patrons, instantly chummy with waiters, loath to send mistakes back to the kitchen, extravagant tippers. His father reads the specials and pretends not to know what croquettes are, tells Jane that the family used to play that game in the backyard. They're finally seated, and Frank also keeps things expertly airy, detailing a fistfight between two tenants over not wiping down his building's gym equipment.

"Did that hurt?" says Scott's mother, pointing at Jane's nose-ring.

"Mom," Scott says.

"Terribly," says Jane. "This is actually a nasal implant. My original nose fell off."

"Ha!"

"I don't know what they're telling you down here," his father says. "But Boston has the best doctors in the world. I'll call Anthony Sweet's son, he's the right guy to start with. What is he, Margaret?"

"Spinal surgeon."

"I went to a physiatrist," Scott says. "They've seen this a dozen times, they know exactly what it is. It's not like they're guessing."

"I'm just trying to help," says his father. "I know you're

frustrated."

"It's scary to him," his mother says. "He can't feel his foot. Of course he's frustrated."

"The sciatic nerve recovers three inches per week. I just have to wait it out."

"I think you should have a shot," his father says. "Did they tell you they give shots to people recovering from back injuries?"

"Of course they told him," says his mother.

"Your concern is heartwarming, really. I wish it extended to listening to the song that's going to make us famous."

"I listened to it," his father says.

"Why am I not convinced?"

"Joy joy joy. I listened to it."

Frank laughs. "It's about the hundredth-best song you ever wrote."

"He didn't write it," says Jane. "Amanda wrote it."

"When you play in Boston," his mother says. "I'll hear it then. Do you like animals, Jane?"

"I do," she says. "I must. I don't eat them."

" . . . "

"You mean as pets. Well, everyone in my family is allergic. But my college boyfriend had dogs. They were wonderful to play with, and to be honest, I liked them more than I liked my college boyfriend. The dogs were old even then, but we broke up after graduation and I never saw him again, so I'm left in the fortunate position of being able to imagine those dogs are still alive."

Scott is charmed by this. "We have cats," his mother says.

"What kind of music do you like, Mrs. Kopp?"

Frank says, "Nu-disco. It's all nu-disco in their house."

"We like oldies," says his father.

"But you also like Pink Floyd," Scott says. "My dad was the best music influence. Pink Floyd. Beatles. Beach Boys. Queen."

"Those *are* oldies," says Frank.

"I went through a country phase," his mother says. "I like soundtracks."

"That reminds me," says his father. "I opened up iTunes yesterday and you know the first thing I saw?"

"Oh, Jesus," Scott says.

"We used to have these neighbors," his father tells Jane. "The Drupes. And their youngest son John, he's very big in Christian music. He's sold millions. There was an article about him on the *front page* of iTunes."

"I get it," says Scott. "John Drupe is a success, Dad. A big one. Major."

"Well. I guess I really can't say anything around you, can I, Scott?"

"No, you can say lots of things. You can say a nearly infinite array of things. Just please don't keep bringing up the only person you know with a recording career I can never hope to match. That would be sublime."

"You know," Frank says, "when Scott signed his record deal, it was just about the end of the world."

"Well, who wouldn't be proud?" says his red-faced father.

"Proud is one thing. They made me FaceTime so they could see my expression when they told me the news. But I already knew, I knew before they did. Dad's going, 'How do we conference call on this thing, let's get Scotty on the line, too,' and Mom's in the background I'm pretty sure crying."

"I wasn't crying." Their mother chews the inside of her cheek to minimize a smile. "But it was very nice."

It's a story they haven't told Scott before. He feels dizzy, and gets up to go to the bathroom. He grunts and keeps his face stoic, to show how strong he's being.

When they're alone later, Jane says, "Did your parents take you aside and confide that they love me and think I'm a keeper?"

"Clearly you don't know my family. They're likelier to tell the hotel maid."

"Hm. Yeah. This afternoon really did explain a lot."

Scott is on the couch, and runs his finger over the top of his dead foot. He says, "How To Raise An Overachieving Kid. Chapter One. Throw around praise like manhole covers. Be totally inconsistent with affection. Let your own mood dictate how annoying you find the child to be. Overreact to the child's flare-ups, and escalate tension whenever possible. Communicate a general dissatisfaction with anything outside the norm. Imply there's a finish line somewhere out there in the distance, but until you reach it, nothing's good enough."

"Well. That's not exactly what I meant."

"..."

"I just mean it's obvious how much they wind you up."

"Did you hear her? She'll listen to the song when we play it for her live, not before then. Is that not a fucked-up thing for a mother to say? I'm so tired of people calling me oversensitive. I mean, seriously, my whole fucking life."

"Yeah, but I guess it's your choice. Your choice whether you care what they say."

"I care," Scott says. "I care, okay? I'm tuned to the room. That's what they did to me. I can sense the moment anyone has the slightest bad feeling about me. I'm programmed to try and fix it, and freak out if I can't."

"You didn't take your muscle relaxer today?"

"..."

"..."

"I'm just numb. It doesn't hurt anymore."

Jane sits beside him and wiggles his big toe. "Yeah. We both know *that's* not true." He puts his face against her neck. "Hey, I had lunch with Lucius yesterday. Did you know he used to be a masseuse?"

Scott knows life has to be bigger than all these tiny personal anarchies. He feels the world blow outward from this Flatiron apartment, into millions of lives beset by disease and disadvantage, but he only knows the details of his own game: a crushed nerve, an unknown band, slightly narcissistic parents. Part of the urge toward fame is that hackneyed old idea that goes *I'm gonna change the world!* Scott wonders if the other Kids feel that same itch, and if they have any better idea than he does…what would they change the world *to?* He feels his skull's contours and says, "I really want to get out of here."

Later he cabs to Lucius Hawk's place in Park Slope. It's a modest walkup three blocks from the park, and its only bedroom is now a recording studio; Lucius sleeps on a futon in the living room. The walls are thick with framed photos, and a big print of Basquiat's Fallen Angel rises above a bricked-over fireplace. This afternoon Lucius has moved aside his furniture and set up a professional massage table. He wrings his hands, cracks his knuckles, and says, "I wouldn't say masseuse. More like…therapeutic bodywork."

"Well, Jane appreciates it. And me, too."

"Yeah, that Jane. She's something else, man. Don't cross the smart ones." Lucius is over six feet with an athlete's shoulders, and his dreads are short. "But really. You know why I said I'd do this."

"..."

"Amanda. Looking for some recon."

"Ah."

"She's tough to pin down," says Lucius. "Not what you'd call loquacious. Well, she's still happy to text me and such, but she won't say yes to a sit-down. I'm thinking that's not a very good sign."

"Yeah," Scott says, "The band's pretty busy, though."

"It's honestly cool. You can tell me things for real, man. I'm pretty sure she's blowing me off. And I'm not a guy who does the chase real well. So if that's it, it's it."

"..."

"All right. Hey, but I don't want you to get me wrong. It's not like I just go crazy because she's a pretty girl or whatever. I do okay in that area. I do fine. Amanda's got something else going on, you know? She's tough to figure out. All I know, every time we were hanging out here and then she'd go home, I couldn't figure out if it was because she decided something about me, like, she gets this look, and it could mean she's decided I'm full of shit, or it could mean she's thinking about her clothes or something."

"Inscrutable," says Scott.

"So you can tell me, since it's not a big deal." Lucius busies himself in a storage trunk, sorting through massage accessories. "She's...uh, sleeping with somebody else?"

"I mean. Lucius. When Amanda and Sebastian broke up.... I don't have experience in a lot of bands, but I'm pretty sure this is...."

"..."

"Not that I know of."

"How old are you, Scott?"

"26."

"I got ten years on you, dude, but you're already wiser than I am." He laughs. "Now tell me what's going on with you."

"Me. I'm good. I'm really good. Trying to picture good things happening, trying not to picture getting cancer the minute someone says we've got a hit. You might've heard there was some drama. We're waiting to get back in the studio. The record guys want what they want."

Lucius spreads a clean sheet over the massage table. "No, I

meant what's going on with your back."

Scott gets naked with Lucius out of the room, and slides beneath the sheet. Lucius comes in and rubs him with hot rocks, and it feels great. His faced squashed by padding, he says, "So this is what you did before hip-hop."

"Hell, I did it while I was coming up. I had in-house jobs all over the Upper East. Take care of old white ladies by day, spit fire by night. *Scott*, man. Holy shit. How are you walking around like this?"

"Like what?"

"The technical term is: 'broke-down.' Every muscle from your ribs to your butt is twice original size. You were in a car wreck and didn't tell anybody?"

"It doesn't hurt that bad."

"I don't take pleasure in saying this. After I'm done with you, it will."

Lucius kills him. He excavates. His hands are like iron; he works them into the muscles beside Scott's spine and there's nothing pleasurable about it. Then he starts digging with his elbows. For a few minutes, Scott says nothing. Then he realizes Lucius is waiting for him to shout. He keeps elbowing harder and deeper into Scott's back, and finally Scott yells, "Motherfucker!" and Lucius backs off.

"Okay," he says. "We got our limit for today."

"Fuck," says Scott.

"The more it hurts in here, the less it hurts out there."

" . . . "

"*You're* not sleeping with Amanda, right?" He elbows him super-hard again. "I'm kidding, man. I'm just kidding."

"I'm gonna videotape this," Scott says. "Your fans will never stop laughing."

"Yeah, that's right," Lucius says, "antagonize the guy with his elbow crushing your deep tissue."

"S-s-s-song title alert."

Lucius is positioned as the thinking-man's rapper, an alternative to the shouters and haters. His poetics are a satirist's, and his rhymes tackle the record industry, urban renewal, the sweet fun of drugs, white kids talking like hood rats, and a million minute points of pop-culture life including references to food co-ops, Call of Duty, Pinterest, Trayvon Martin and the Black Avengers. ("Iron

Man's dad weren't no millionaire / so his suit's made outta sadness and underwear") He's biting and self-effacing and smart, which he says pretty much guarantees he'll never break big. He's on Awkward Meshpoint and they don't advance him much cash or make heavy demands; his shows are well-attended and mellow but always cramped. His ceiling makes him bitter, but his bitterness makes him funny.

"Holy shit," says Scott. "How often do I have to get this done?"

"Think about something else," Lucius says.

"I can't. Thinking about something else isn't my strong suit."

"Tell me about your other bands you've been in."

"I wasn't ever in bands," Scott says. "This is my first one."

"Okay, tell me about the new record. Tell me about the drama."

"We did one track, hated the producer. Sidelong is putting big money behind it. He was really a dick to us."

"I've heard the song," says Lucius. "Hooky as hell."

"But anyway now the clock is ticking. I just want to sit someplace and make it on our own. Do people still even need producers anymore?"

"They do if they want to avoid knife fights in the band."

"Fucking *God*, Lucius!"

"I know. Sorry, man. The album got a title?"

"..."

"You gonna cry?"

"No! Maybe!"

"Tell me the title."

"I'm thinking of: 'Sadistic Asshole.'"

"Here's what I'll do for you," Lucius says. "I'll list your five favorite bands of all time. You write the songs in Kid Centrifuge, yeah? That's all I need: it's a talent of mine. You ready?"

"Oh...*fuck!*"

"First of all, obviously: Spoon. Killers, heard you cover them. Fountains of Wayne."

"You know Fountains of Wayne?"

"'Do I know...?' Shit, dude. 'Radiation Vibe.' You were two years old when that song came out, man. I was a grown person. That was my goddamn jam."

"I mean, I was 10."

"Black Keys. And…I'll say New Pornographers."

"You know New Pornographers!"

"You realize," says Lucius, "the more racist you get, the more I hurt you."

"My number one teenage crush: Neko Case. I mean, seriously. Love isn't a strong enough word. If she told me to rob a bank, I still think I'd do it."

"But the later stuff, though," Lucius says. "'Myriad Harbour.' I first heard that weird little falsetto: 'I took a plane, I took a train.' And that guitar."

"Is that one AC Newman?"

"Naw, I think it's Bejar. You like his other band Destroyer?"

"I don't know them," says Scott.

Lucius interrupts the massage and steps into his studio, and Scott hears a shuffling mid-tempo Strat and echoed vocals singing about Snow White: "How can you win some? How can you win some?" It's weird and awesome. Scott has never gone this deep talking music with Lucius—probably he hasn't talked about *anything* with Lucius for this long—and the excitement makes him feel young: when it wasn't about out-obscuring someone else, when it was just fun to crawl inside another person's head and sample their musical tastes. It's the same kind of thrill he first got playing with Sebastian last year.

"This song is awesome," he says. "He's fucking fanta*aaaaaaaaaaaa*…. Oh *motherfucking shit*, Lucius!"

He comes the next three days, and Lucius pummels him and plays tunes. There's no p.r. talk, no studio talk, no tour talk. Though he still has the same numbness in his foot, Scott's back is looser, so the massages themselves are less agonizing. He suggests Arctic Monkeys and Our Lady Peace songs, while Lucius tries to ease him into a hip-hop education playing him the Roots, Reflection Eternal, the Coup, and also acts Scott's never heard of like Lifesavas and the Cool Kids.

Today, they get into a disquisition on Spoon's *Ga Ga Ga Ga Ga*.

"It's only ten songs," says Scott. "It's epic at, whatever, thirty-five minutes. 'You Got Yr. Cherry Bomb' is so perfect it almost makes me cry."

"You know what?" Lucius says. "I ripped them off bad. I did a mix-tape a few years ago, with this cut 'Broseph Stalin.' I thought about sampling 'Rhthm & Soul,' but for whatever reason I just wound up swiping the melody and singing it myself. It's my words, but their notes. Pure plagiarism. I wouldn't let them put it on the last CD. But man, it gets in your head, right?"

"A question," says Scott. "Inarguably great records are always more than just a collection of songs you like. But why?"

"All right."

"Sometimes it's a concept. I mean, the *Sgt. Pepper's* thing. But not always. I can't get the characters in *Ga Ga Ga Ga Ga* to line up in the same story."

"Okay. I get you. And it's not just a vibe. *Straight Outta Compton* has 'Fuck Tha Police,' but it's also got 'Express Yourself' with Dre being all sweet saying not to spark up."

"Plus when it *tries* to be all unified you can get some awful shit. My dad had *Kilroy Was Here*. The story of a jailed rock star impersonating a robot. Oy."

"Or maybe they capture a mood," says Lucius. "Like: these players, this space, this time. You can imagine yourself in the room while they're making it."

"..."

"Watching Outkast make *Speakerboxxx*."

"Watching Jack White make *Elephant*."

"*Illmatic*."

"*Hot Fuss*."

"..."

"..."

"..."

"Okay," Scott says. "How do I make one like *those*?"

Lucius puts on "Black Like Me," the final song from *Ga Ga Ga Ga Ga*. It's a hopelessly hopeful story about a man disconnected from a woman, a metaphorical joke conflating the man's soul and the soles of his boots, and a direct appeal for connection from the weird kids up front. It speaks for the album's several hopeful slackers—its self-exiled loners—and their faith that someone will take care of them tonight. Scott has heard the human body stores toxins that massage can release, and as they surge free can slap you hard. Or it's the song. He's face-down inside the headrest, eyes wet.

"I sound old," says Lucius. "And maybe I am. But I can't connect to the big hip-hop cuts now. Can't even fucking listen to them. I think back to '03, and I dogged guys like Puffy and the Fugees. But man, at least they had some actual joy in the songs. Their worst shit would be welcome on the radio now. You listen to 'What They Do' from the Roots or De La Soul doing 'Stakes Is High,' and they called it even way back in '96. I can't even tell you the last time I got obsessed with a hip-hop track. You remember when you were a kid, and you got a new CD and you loved it so much you couldn't listen to anything else? Man, anytime that happens to me now it's indie rock or electronic."

He sends Scott home with J. Dilla's album *Donuts*: thirty-one tracks and only one of them longer than two minutes. Maybe it's because he admires Lucius so much, or maybe the album is just that good, but Scott feels his musical ideals shift beneath him. He recognizes samples from James Brown, Stevie Wonder, Dionne Warwick, Kool & the Gang, Frank Zappa and Smokey Robinson, but there are many more he doesn't know. Dilla died of a blood disease three days after *Donuts* was released, and in fact recorded most of it in the hospital. The poignancy of the story wrings Scott out; he puts himself in that bed. *Donuts* doesn't seem like a fleshed-out collection of fully realized songs, but rather a mosaic of beats, a genius portfolio. It's such a different approach to the way Scott thinks about music, his head kind of caves in. It sends him back to a few of Sebastian's older songs, particularly "Bandfucker" where Sebastian is speak-singing with dozens of sounds beneath him. Scott really listens.

"Okay, what do you want your new record to be?" Lucius asks him. "What's the point of making it, right? I'm guessing you don't want to make it just to make it. You need a why. The label, they'll pay for it and they'll tell you how excited they are for you to make art. Something lasting, who knows what they'll say. The truth is they're striking while the iron is hot. They want singles, they want a tour, they want money. But those can't be your reasons, or it'll turn out shitty. It might sell, but it'll be shitty."

"A particular space and time," says Scott, between massage-grunts. "How do we do that?"

"Maybe you go out somewhere in the country, lock everybody in a room until you come out with a record."

"…"

"Well, anyway. I ever tell you about the time I was on a job at a really swanky place on Fifth Avenue? I noticed my massage oil was leaking so I put it in a Poland Springs bottle. And the lady is face down on the table, and she's talking to me and I'm listening and I get thirsty and forget and take a swig of oil. I'm like, oh shit. The woman's husband is in the bathroom, and the kitchen is blocked off for remodeling. I'm still massaging her, but I've got a mouthful of oil. There's nowhere to spit. At some point the lady falls asleep and I'm practically choking on the oil. Finally I just spit it back into the bottle. And of course, I still had to use it on her."

"No."

"Yeah, when I got finished, I was like, 'Uh, sometimes it's good to take a long hot shower afterwards....'"

Scott laughs into his cushion. "Man. I'm face-down and defenseless here. What aren't you telling *me*?"

"Yeah, some people are easy, man. Some people just have a way."

"You're easy, Lucius."

"Man, I can *play* easy."

Scott feels his ribs compress, and his back zings. Only one thing erases the feeling that other people—people who aren't him—are out there actually talking to one another, getting what they want. He thinks whatever's wrong with him as a human being works wonderfully for him as a musician. He says, "I want you to produce our record, Lucius."

"..."

"I told you we need somebody."

"Thanks. But your label will literally never approve."

"How do you know?"

"They'll make you use a name, man. They're a big fucking operation. Literally never."

Lucius finishes the massage, Scott gets dressed, and they order Thai food. A Mets game is on and a wildfire sunset slants through blinds.

"You still need to figure out why," Lucius says. "Why make this record."

Scott steps into the studio and clicks the laptop. He resists checking his inbox—which will no doubt contain a noxious chain of record-company missives—and plays *Rubberneck* by the Toadies. On hearing the staccato guitar intro to "Mexican Hairless," Lucius starts playing air guitar and Scott joins. Their heads bob in synch.

A little while later, Scott breathes deep and lets himself talk:

"Why. Because I'm a closed fist. Because I barely have friends. Because I'm tired of being like this. Instead of treating music like a spacesuit.... What if it can do something for me that I can't do for myself? I want to make a record that pulls me out of the spacesuit and never lets me back in."

Lucius seems about to respond, but the delivery guy knocks. They make a production of welcoming the kid and tipping lavishly.

A SYMBOL TO HERSELF

"We should go on *TRL*."

"We should get a song on *NOW That's What I Call Music!*"

"Ooh, let's go city to city and record radio bumpers. 'Hi, this is Amanda from Kid Centrifuge, and you're listening to Tulsa's Power 101.'"

"I had a Nickelodeon clock radio when I was little," Kate says. "I think it only played Nickelodeon acts. Is that possible?"

"Or MySpace. Do we have a MySpace page yet?"

They're in the 121st Street apartment. The living room is still unfurnished, and the floor is rimmed with dust-mice. First-draft radio promotion packages—laminated folders containing press releases, one-sheets, glossy band photos and cardboard sleeves where CDs will go—fan across the room. At first it was shocking to see the kind of money Sidelong Records is ready to spend on arcane marketing channels, trying to get program and music directors excited about "Density of Joy." But after meetings over the past few days they feel like veterans. There's also a box of buttons over here; Colleen has tasked Kate and Amanda with asking strangers around the city to pin them onto their clothing and pose for selfies—"Hello My Name Is: Joy Joy Joy Joy Joy"—that'll subsequently go on social media and the band's website. They're supposedly playing a private online concert for satellite radio subscribers next month, plus the song will be featured on a Chevy TV ad and in a forthcoming Saints Row video game. Jacob from

Sidelong accosted them at a meeting today, thrilled because someone printed up snazzy business cards which advertise a "Special Code To Get Free Kid Centrifuge Downloads!"

"What the hell is happening?" Kate says.

"Everything is," says Amanda. "We are."

Kate looks at her roommate sprawled like this, and knows a basic truth: nobody would be this interested in the band if Amanda didn't look like a model. It's such an unspoken bedrock fact that it's easy to forget; Kate wonders if Amanda walks around with this trump card in the front of her mind. It's hard not to notice Jacob speaking mostly to her while the other three of them sit around awkward. Label folks are a lot of things, but opaque isn't one of them. Yet Kate feels a sense among the bandmates that no matter the resentments they've mustered over the past year-plus, the closest they'll get to real support will come from each other. They're like indifferent basic training classmates thrust into combat.

For her part, Amanda has some Chekhov here with her, and she reads: "'To avoid everything petty, everything illusory, everything that prevents one from being free and happy, that is the whole meaning and purpose of our life. Forward! We march on irresistibly towards that bright star which burns far, far before us! Forward! Don't tarry, comrades!'"

"Exactly," says Kate.

They listen to the latest Flying Lotus record, a favorite of Sebastian's that's heavy on ambient beats and instrumentals. Someone knocks on the front door. Kate thinks it must be one of Amanda's suitors. Amanda thinks maybe it's Sebastian, and her heart bucks nonsensically. But it's Sebastian's bass-playing pal Jack Dooley.

"Hey, guys! Is Torque hanging out here?"

"Mm, no…" says Amanda. "You know he's living in Jersey."

"Oh. Because I got this documentary," he waves around a DVD case, "and I figured he'd probably really like it."

"What is it?" Kate says.

"If only," says Amanda, "there was some kind of personal handheld device you could use to locate him. You know, like send him messages made out of text or something."

Jack scans the living room. "You guys, ah, don't have a TV?"

"What's the movie?" says Kate.

"Beware of Mr. Baker. It's about this rock drummer. Like, I play with a couple old guys who say he's the greatest of all time." Jack uses a pompadour and glasses and ironic t-shirts to obscure a kind of burdensome decency. It slips out via his big belly and his husky grin.

"Sounds cool," says Kate. "I mean, we're really not doing anything. If you're trying to find Sebastian, I'll come along."

"Or, you know. If you have a computer."

They look at Amanda.

"I don't think I'd get it," she says.

"No no," says Kate.

"I'm just kidding, I'll watch with you guys. But listen. I literally did just get a bunch of emails, let me just.... Go ahead and get it started, and I'll jump in."

Kate fetches Amanda's laptop and sets it up on the living room floor. Jack retires to the bathroom.

"Should I try calling Sebastian?" says Kate.

"That would be a no," Amanda says. "He came looking for you."

"..."

"Come on. A drumming documentary? It's the most romantic thing I ever heard. I seriously might puke."

Kate breathes in, endorphins fizzing. She wonders: what should her face look like? What kind of half smile indicates sly complicity?

"I'm out," says Amanda, hoisting a jacket and her bag and leaving the apartment.

Kate and Jack sit on the floor with the laptop between them. Ginger Baker is this old cranky drummer who yells at the film crew, and tells them, "It's not how fast you play, it's what you say." He invokes names of drummers Kate doesn't know—Art Blakey and Elvin Jones, but no mention of Billie Turner—and then there's this archival footage of him absolutely *wailing*, keeping perfect and different time with four limbs. Right when Ginger says, "To have a good time, it depends on who you're playing with," Jack leans over and kisses Kate. She macked with a guy in L.A. and perpetrated some degree of drunken hookup with the bass player from Seahorses of the Apocalypse, but either way it's been a *long* damn time. She kisses back. Jack is warm and sweet.

And his hand is on her breast and she's doing calculus: he's a musician and presumably there's some threshold she has to let him cross, but virtue also has its requirements and she wants to be placed in "potential girlfriend" territory, plus she hasn't done much intimate grooming of late. *Of course I don't really know Jack and shouldn't I figure out whether I actually like him?* His hand fumbles up her t-shirt and he groans. *Should I be finding this so strange?*

She hears music and ascribes it to him. She wants him to be wonderful.

He lifts her shirt and kisses her nipples and his crotch is right there, she's deciding, he lifts his requesting hips. It's good to be attractive. Amanda is somewhere walking around alone.

He's breathing hard, whistling through his nose. She wants to cover up her flabby midsection, where his hands press in. But it feels *nice*, dammit. His breathing is *quite* loud, kind of a piping flying-saucer special effect.

Without deciding anything she says, "I think there's something wrong." Jack lifts his head. "I mean with the DVD." And indeed, the whistling wasn't Jack at all; the computer's screen has gone dark and the DVD is clattering around in there trying to get back on track. She's got Jack by the hair, and as he closes his eyes and tries to lower himself back onto her, she holds him away. "We should probably fix it," she says.

He sits up chewing his lip, riffling his hair. She ejects the movie and examines a fine series of scratches.

"It's not that big a deal," says Jack.

Kate lowers her shirt; her bra is still unhooked and loose around her back. Jack's eyes are low. She thinks they should laugh, hug, realize things were going too quickly. It would be easy. But they sit like ragdolls and refuse to let one another off the hook. On Amanda's desktop is a file marked "2001: A Space Odyssey" and Kate clicks it. They watch monkeys and a monolith, they watch a waltz of spaceships... and a computer who acts human, and humans who act like robots. Kate finds the film immeasurably sad: this doomed serenade of stilted, formal parents and children who build massive toys to cover up their aloneness. Jack smirks at her but stays, maybe feeling like he can't get out of it. She finds a bottle of butterscotch schnapps on top of the refrigerator and they pass it back and forth, tasting crusted sugar on the rim.

Meanwhile Amanda has Garvey Park on her mind, but gets about a block from home when her phone really does vibrate, and it's a text from Jacob Shear. Does she want to come watch a Beyoncé concert with him? She's dressed like a hobo and she's not busting back in on Kate, so she politely declines. A few seconds later Jacob phones.

"I insist," he says.

"I'm not so good with last minute," says Amanda, and wonders if it's true.

"Let me say thank you. It's the least."

"Seriously, you should see me. I'm really not in any condition."

"That's impossible," says Jacob. "And I'm in your neighborhood. Let me be a gentleman caller. Don't deny me the pleasure of throwing myself on your mercy."

She used to be thrilled by moments like this. Now she's divided: part careerist, part schoolmarm. If they want to keep giving her things, why shouldn't she take them? And also: nothing is free. Still, when a guy breaks through the typical dumb lines and rude eyes—when he lets a little self-mockery undercut the act—Amanda does respond. It's easy to tell herself saying yes will be good for the band.

Jacob picks her up in a chauffeured Town Car at the spot where Eighth Avenue becomes Frederick Douglass Boulevard. He's in a silk suit whose jacket is tossed over the passenger headrest. He looks at her brown tanktop and tartan skirt and says, "I'll change when we get there."

Saturday FDR traffic is bearable and they cross into Brooklyn. Amanda has a thought that they're only a couple miles from Sebastian's old apartment, and just then they veer onto a side street and stop in a twilit park. The driver clicks open the sunroof, pops the trunk and gets out. He brings them a tray of foie gras and cracked lobster. Jacob texts someone then converts his face into a leisure king's. He's probably 40, doesn't wear a ring, is thoroughly tanned and handsome in a forgettable way.

"I'm sorry things didn't work out with Pope," he says. "They tell me he can be a little gruff, but he's produced great stuff for us. I guess there were just too many strong personalities in the room."

"..."

"You didn't expect me to talk business. You thought it would be all about impressing you with delicious food and great tickets."

"I stand by Scott and Sebastian," says Amanda.

"This is just idle chat. We're having a snack, and we have to talk about something. Tell me what you'll say in interviews. A divine light struck you between the eyes. A sick child inspired you on a volunteer hospital trip. It's the first song you ever finished?"

"It is."

"Incredible. So many musicians we deal with, they've been looking for something as good as 'Density' all their careers. For them it comes hard, and they want to take you inside their torment. Well, we got one great song out of your collaboration with Pope. Even if it was painful...."

Amanda says, "I guess it wasn't really so bad."

"I can't write. I can't even relate to it, where it comes from. But I know a big one when I hear it. This one's an earwig."

"..."

Jacob reaches into a seat compartment and comes out with a wrapped present. He hands it to Amanda.

She says, "You were pretty sure I'd agree to come along." She unwraps, and it's a first edition of the 1912 translation of *The Brothers Karamazov.*

"I wasn't sure," he says. "But I had hopes. I'd have gotten you the Russian version, but my research says you don't read Russian yet."

"It's...really nice. Wow. I mean."

"I know you've probably read it many times.... I'm self-conscious giving you a book I've never read."

"It's my favorite. It's probably my favorite book in the world. This is really...." She removes the silverware between them and leans across the seat, and they hug. "Wow. It's amazingly thoughtful, Jacob."

"I want to read it," he says. "I mean, I really hear...good things. No, I do. Hey, I've heard of it! Heh. Well, I feel like I want to read it now that I know it's your favorite. I mean, that part was just lucky."

She eats more lobster and wonders where the driver went.

"I have a feeling," says Jacob, "that now this whole night is coming off a little stalkerish. I really just was thinking about you, and thought it would be nice to spend an evening."

"No, I think I'm taking it the right way."

"I'm a showoff. It's a character flaw. I get enthusiastic."

Amanda reads the book's back cover and says, "You have

kids?"

"..."

"I'm just curious."

"Well. There's a line from *The Godfather*: 'This is the business we've chosen.' Yeah, I mean. Listen, you don't want my heartbreak stories. No kids. Things have blown up work-wise and gotten so crazy. I'm flying all over.... The record industry hasn't been a relationship kind of lifestyle."

"I can sniff out lies," Amanda says. "Just so you know."

Jacob looks at her, unsmiling. "Nobody's looking for a trophy anything," he says.

She says, "It's objectively nice to be treated like this. I fully admit it. But you know: a person sits here and her mind naturally wanders. How many other girls have taken this same ride?"

"Ha. You're giving me too much credit."

Amanda simply taps her nose.

Jacob leans forward between the seats and honks the car horn. The driver returns and gathers up their dishes. They continue up into the traffic's blinking system of lights. Amanda thinks she's successfully fended him off, or warned him she's not just some cookie. She has the clarity and sense of well-being that usually comes after a hangover or the flu. They sneak past a sedan whose engine appears to have just caught fire, and Jacob takes a scored white pill from a tin he keeps in his pants pocket, and he swallows it. He doesn't seem to have any intention of changing clothes.

"How about this?" Jacob says. "I'll tell you something against my own interests. Firing a producer, that's not news. But I get the impression Scott thinks he's got Sidelong over a barrel. Like, he can just keep making demands and we have to give in, because we're committed to rolling out 'Density of Joy.' And listen, I want to see you guys make a big album, I want a bunch of big songs, and I'm inclined to give you some rope. Those pipes you've got, you're worth it. But if everything goes bad, and your band goes on strike or goes kablooey or something? I don't have the smallest problem in the world firing all of you and making numbers off a single with no album. Or how about this: it just so happens I'm a close personal friend of the writer and singer of that particular song, and if everything goes bad, I would probably explore whether she's interested in a solo career. Beginning with launching 'Density of Joy' as her first single."

They arrive at the Barclays Center, and the limo doors open. "Why is telling me that against your interests?" Amanda says. "It sounds like you're planning to screw us."

Jacob blushes at her choice of words. "Absolutely not. I'm planning on everything going great. I was planning on Pope working out. But it's against my interest because I just gave you a leg up in solo contract negotiations."

He gets out of the car; she thinks about this. She sees pulsing magenta lights, silent blue-and-white cop lights. She smells a river wind. Her toes are pointing inward, her loose fists are curled in her lap. The sound outside is hard to place, until she realizes it's people: an incredible distant susurrus like factory thunder or a high-tide ocean. Here in VIP parking, three little girls in ballet costumes run and shriek. Amanda remembers her mother taking her to a TLC concert at the hockey rink in Anaheim, the long walk in a freezing cold with Lacey complaining alongside, but then they were inside and the stage lit up, those ladies shimmied on giant screens and nobody went home disappointed. She steps out of the car and Jacob waits unobtrusively, holding a door for her.

The seats are amazing and Beyoncé nearly makes Amanda cry. She just seems so genuinely *sweet*. The lights and thumping begin, they play "Run The World" and Beyoncé is unbelievably charismatic, telling the screamers and the weepers in this huge crowd how she just hopes everyone will forget their cares for a little while and have a great time, how they can all make memories together. She's a couple hundred feet away, all hair and teeth, she casts many shadows from the trays of lights all over the place, she bends and pirouettes (in high heels!) and changes her wardrobe, and it's joyous as hell. Amanda has never really cared about Beyoncé's music but recognizes some of the songs; Jacob knows every word and sings along, clapping, smiling. He isn't faking; it's love. They get gratis champagne—or at least Amanda believes it's gratis, no cash changes hands—and she drains several flutes. Like a waking flower her own hair has spread out in the arena's humidity, and its curlicues keep brushing Jacob's face, so he keeps absently shooing them away. The cynic in Amanda's heart goes malnourished. It's fucking *great*. By the time they play "Crazy In Love" and "Single Ladies," she wonders if this is actually who she wants to be.

The house lights go up after two encores and Amanda finds

herself transformed, this is what a show can do: faces around you, your own hands, all the embossed wires dangling perfectly vertical from the ceiling in geometric harmony…it's your *eyes* that are new. She wonders if Jacob is about to get them backstage and realizes she doesn't really want it, the experience is fully formed and immersive and *over* without any phony-baloney flesh-pressing. Everyone is smiling. What other times in life do you ever see thousands of people around you all smiling?

She and Jacob don't speak. They take a private stairway that leads directly to the VIP lot. His necktie is loose and she can see he has a bit of a belly. She wonders if it's possible to want him independent of what he can do for her, independent of his money and influence, and she feels constrained by this perpetual equation: being wanted. That's the ground she walks on, it's not ego, it's the truth. Being wanted. That's the conversation. There are no other terms, and she knows she's supposed to fight against it, she's supposed to countermand whatever patriarchic bullshit she inspires in all these men by being smarter and more independent than they expect. But sometimes she just wants to say yes. She can't always be a symbol to herself.

Back in the limo, she says, "Thank you. It was amazing."

"Pretty good, right? Aren't you glad you said yes?"

"I'd already be in bed watching a movie." She doesn't want to think about her own face, but she is, helplessly. And she feels bad about it, knowing so much of her energy goes to expression maintenance. The limo inches them back toward the bridge and the stars above them gleam chemically. "Do you think you could raise the partition?" Amanda says.

"Oh," says Jacob. "Sure." And he does, a black polymer shield snicks into place. She feels like a marionette, manipulated by Jacob's careful scheming into feeling this way. But she does feel this way. He says, "You don't play tennis by any chance, do you?"

"…"

"I was thinking of heading up to Travers Island tomorrow. Or if you maybe just wanted to swim at the club?"

She leans into him across this leather bench and kisses his neck. His arm goes around her shoulder. She sees his pants grow taut at the crotch and tries to come up with something witty to say, this is the man who's given Kid Centrifuge a record deal, this is an awful, awful idea, and she wants to comment on the inappropriateness but she also wants to know him and control him, to wield power over power. Even if she's been manipulated by an evening of romance, she can win. She hears him wheeze, feels him tense, ultimately unprepared.

She unzips his fly and puts her mouth on his cock.

Jacob reacts as if zapped by a thousand volts. His hips jerk and he turns away, tossing Amanda back across the seat. He fumbles with his pants, redoing them, and he says, "Sorry, oh."

She smiles reflexively. "No no."

"I'm really sorry," says Jacob.

"It's all right! Of course!"

His shirttail is stuck in his zipper, he tugs, she wants to help. "Crap. I really.... I'm so sorry."

Amanda thinks, *I just ruined everything.*

"I want to," says Jacob. "Of course I do. I really, really like you. I feel so...."

"..."

"It's just fast," he says. "This is kind of embarrassing when you're supposed to have an image as this shark. But Amanda, I'm a Christian."

"..."

"It's not something I...."

"Oh," Amanda says. "Oh, I'm so sorry. I mean, not because you're...."

"It's one of those things," he says.

"Yeah, no."

"I'm divorced. It happened then. I went on this retreat, I really started reading.... I really just needed to find some.... Listen, it's okay. Seriously. I don't talk about it because it's the one thing you have to stay away from, like, just about anything else is fair game but the conversation goes to God and everybody's eyes roll."

Amanda feels something coming up from her stomach, and worries it's champagne and cracked lobster.

"My intentions.... I.... It's the kind of thing you can't just tell somebody."

Yes, something is coming up, and Amanda puts her hands across her chest. It's laughter. She can't help it—she howls.

COMPETENCE IS A VAMPIRE

1. Two-Person Job

Sebastian and Kate scuff into a coffee shop in the town center. Every patron seems miserable over a laptop or textbook. They wait on line behind an older guy who bears a huge half-red, half-blue flag tattoo on his forearm, and Kate sees a familiar young woman sitting at the bar. The woman kneads at a keyboard and mouths whatever song comes through her earbuds; her red lipstick matches the fat frames of her eyeglasses. Kate can't place her, which leads to the conclusion that she must be a Binghamton girl. And this causes Kate's face and hands to tingle unpleasantly.

"I need to find a pharmacy," says Sebastian. He's wearing a handloom madras shirt, German conductor pants and Tricker's brogues.

"They have them," Kate says. "We're not in Yakutsk."

"Song title alert. But do they not have pharmacies in Yakutsk? Where's Yakutsk?"

The flag-tattoo guy steps aside to wait on his order. Kate asks for chai and Sebastian dithers with the menu. The jazz in here is oppressive. Kate looks everywhere except that one far corner of the bar. She doesn't want to know.

Sebastian puts his folded nylon wallet on the counter, thinking nothing, and bodies are rumbling around him, someone is shoved, he thinks the baristas' system of placing and receiving orders is hugely inefficient if people are going to carom into each other like this, but then he looks down and his wallet is no longer on the counter. And a guy is sprinting out the side door. Sebastian thinks they had to come out to the Massachusetts woods to get robbed.

He chases.

They streak though an alley and come out on the main drag, cross onto a common. A lone protestor wearing an Uncle Sam top hat waves a sign that reads, "9/11 Was An Inside Job." Sebastian is close enough to see the pickpocket's long curly hair and slender shoulders beneath a poplin jacket: it's a teenage boy. But he's fast. They charge along a cement path, through traffic, onto what looks like a college campus. A gentle incline heads toward a library and the boy is up on his toes with no deference to the slope. Sebastian suffers. His phone is ringing. His wind is gone, his legs get heavy. It's been how many years since he did any physical activity, the kid pulls away, purple-clad students double-take out of academic lassitude and probably wonder if they should stop this bully's pursuit. Sebastian staggers gasping onto an academic quad. He can't see the kid.

He looks at his phone: it was Kate calling. This annoys him. Was he supposed to answer on the dead run? He dials her back.

"What happened?" she says. "Did you catch him?"

"Don't...know...yet," says Sebastian, looking at the students around him.

"You're crazy. What if he has a gun?"

"..."

"I know it's a pain in the butt, Sebastian. Getting a new driver's license or whatever. And maybe losing a little money. It's not worth getting hurt over."

"He's 13. He's a middle-school shit."

"Do they not make guns that middle-school shits can figure out? Do they not make knives?"

"I'm not...."

Kate says, "Come on. Where are you, we're late. This time the shit wins."

Sebastian walks beneath ancient boughs, in an autumnal paradise out of a marketing brochure. Tubby squirrels bellyache at one another, bounding by. Large wooden lounge chairs dot the quad. A few students are flat on the earth, knees bent and arms akimbo, either reveling in perfect weather or overmatched by their lives. Sebastian appraises a future that was never his. He thinks:

What does a dorm room look like?

"I wasn't kidding about needing a pharmacy," he says. "There's a prescription in the wallet. I'm out. I really need it."

Kate exhales.

"Not that. Not anything bad. It fixes my brain chemistry. You know: I'm crazy."

"You're not crazy," she says. "Believe me."

"You want the good me without worrying I'll O.D. or whatever, right?"

"Sebastian, come back. Where are you?"

He's at the quad's far end, beside a statue of an old guy with a book in his hands. Sebastian's neck and armpits prickle. He can tell Kate is surprised with him, she's surprised he needs meds and that he cares enough about anything to take off running. The band thinks of him as their pet sloth, when to himself he seems absolutely driven.

"There's no good you and bad you," she says.

"I'm the one who fucks up, and don't bother arguing. But you ordered three weeks of focus? Coming right up."

Kate says, "I want you to listen to me. Are you listening to me?"

"..."

"Listen up, Dumbo."

"*Okay.*"

"You are amazing, and I love you. I am fully and completely under your spell. You're sweet and you're kind and everybody you meet wants to talk to you and that doesn't just happen. People don't gravitate to just anyone. You give off a vibe that says...I don't know what it says, but you make friends out of thin air. It doesn't matter what you do. It sure doesn't matter what you say. It doesn't matter if you mangle a song—which you basically never do, by the way. If you need meds, we'll get you another prescription for meds. I mean. Come on."

"..."

Kate is a little carried away, standing on the sidewalk outside the coffee shop. "Relax. Like a brother. I love you like a brother."

Sebastian says, "Wow." He's walked back around to the library again. Groggy students in cutoffs and flipflops stagger around him, clutching pencils that bear huge erasers. "Thanks. Thank you. You're *so* great. I mean I'm just so glad to have you around. You're the greatest." He doesn't even hear himself talking, but can tell he's still going. "I'm way luckier to have you, Kate. Thanks for saying those things."

"..."

"Hello?"

Kate can tell when Sebastian has clicked over into Sunshine Mode, his big defense mechanism. There's no reaching him now. She says, "Come on back to the coffee shop. I'm waiting here."

Sebastian hangs up and stares at the library. A professor strolls by in a tweed blazer, a craggy handsome man with tufts of white hair sprouting from his collar, greeting a young student by name and shaking her hand. They walk away talking of no-doubt-magnificent things, and Sebastian feels elevated. For the thousandth time he thinks, and hates himself for thinking: *Kate really is wonderful and maybe if she lost a little weight....*

And then he sees the longhaired teenage boy coming back out of the library.

He takes the stairs up two-at-a-time and gives the boy no exit. The kid sags. Sebastian grabs him by his jacket.

"Don't! Ow!"

"..."

"I don't have the wallet. I don't, I swear. It's a two-person job. I just run to distract you. I'm the runner."

"Then who has it?"

He's a handsome brown-eyed boy with curly locks. He's not particularly afraid. He's kind of laughing at the whole thing.

"I will seriously pound the living shit out of you." Sebastian looks around, and a few undergrads are staring at him bug-eyed. "Walk," he says, and shoves the kid back down the stairs. When the boy tries to run, Sebastian holds him by his stylin' little mauve jacket.

"I always tell him choose old people," says the pickpocket. "He doesn't listen."

They march down the hill. "Who?" Sebastian says.

"Dougie. His dad's a cop."

"So Dougie has my wallet? Hey. Dougie has my wallet? Where do you little monsters meet up after your big heist?"

"..."

Sebastian shakes him, fist still hard against his back. "Where?"

The kid—deep-voiced and shallow-chested—starts crying.

"Ow!" he says. "Don't!"

They cross the street. A couple ancient hippies have joined Uncle Sam. They're all holding signs and yelling at cars.

"I'll show you where. Don't hurt me. Please don't hurt me."

Sebastian can't remember where the alley is, the one that leads back to the coffee shop. He yanks the kid like a dog on a leash. He almost asks Uncle Sam which way to go, but then looks into the guy's eyes: he's like the janitor at River Dell who according to legend lost himself dropping too much acid, and could often be seen in school hallways staring at fire extinguishers.

"I'll make Dougie give it back," says the boy. He struggles to speak through tears. "My dad will hit me. Please, I'm sorry. I don't know why I do things."

"Cross the street," Sebastian says. "Now."

"I'm going. Please. Help!" They reach a downtown sidewalk. Men and women are taking notice. "Please! Help! Somebody get this guy off me!"

Sebastian looks around. "Jesus. Just tell me where Dougie is."

"Pervert! Pervert!" the kid says. "He's gonna rape me! Help! Help!"

Oh, the decency of humanity. A few Samaritans stop and frown at Sebastian. He reads actual violence in their eyes. He lets go of the boy's jacket.

The kid gives a veteran's grin and reaches into his pocket. He comes out with the folded nylon wallet. "Man," he says. "You're the dumbest pussy I ever met. Yeah, definitely don't search me first. Fucking *stupid*." And he runs again, waving the wallet.

Sebastian doesn't chase. Misunderstood from all sides, he stands heedless of the rumpus around him.

He and Lucius stay late in the studio. Among the sound files Sebastian brought with him is a kind of buzzing ritornello, a grinding minute-long theme he constructed at his parents' house out of piano and wall-of-sound guitar set to shrieking reverb. He mixed the sounds over one another with great care and thought maybe the piece would be finished with Kate on the toms, but the moment Lucius hears it he jumps out of his chair to pull the tracks apart. He wants that distinctive guitar sound, the chirp Sebastian gets with his clipped metal picks, but he wants it slower, more distorted, fading in and out. So he records Sebastian fresh, asks him to strike and hold notes. Sebastian's temptation is to add harmonic taps, but Lucius keeps coming over the p.a. asking him to stop, just play the note and bend it, drag it out. He won't even let Sebastian hear the prerecorded piano part. Which means Sebastian is in a full pout when Lucius sits him down at 3 a.m. and plays him the reformulated bed, wherein the guitar and piano go in and out as if emerging from and fading behind clouds.

"Wow," Sebastian says. "Cool."

"I don't know what it is, man," Lucius says. "We just spent an all-nighter on something that's not really even a song. But it's *deep*."

"Let me do one thing. Play it all back for me in there?"

He steps to the vocals mic. The composition has transformed, now it's something soft and dark and alone.

Sebastian sings/says: "The shits win.... The shits win.... The shits win.... The shits win...."

2. Brown Study

Amanda wakes in the Webster Room with Kate snoring in the other bed. It's afternoon. There's a wire sculpture of an old-timey bicycle—giant front wheel, comically tiny back wheel—mounted on the wall. The intense lady at the front desk said Noah Webster wrote his dictionary's first chunk in this town, and now Amanda sees a thick weathered paperback on the nightstand. She thinks about someone actually writing it. Every word! An exacting, accountant's act, surely, but also one of audacious creativity. It appeals to her: this naming. This is what they're here to do. Name the world as they see it. Bright-sounding and loud, with the occasional gut-punch; and they'll do it in a different language, Mr. Webster, because Amanda's chest houses an instrument of terror. It doesn't much matter what she sings. It's the *sound*.

She leans over and realizes this isn't a dictionary at all. It's the blighted copy of *War and Peace* she found yesterday at a used-book store.

They walk through campus and sit outdoors at a bagel shop. Kate's sunglasses feel heavy on her face. She sees a line of impoverished-looking people standing at a bus stop in front of a post office. Amanda reads: *Here the conversation seemed interesting and he stood waiting for an opportunity to express his own views, as young people are fond of doing.*

Kate daubs the last sliver of butter onto her mid-afternoon breakfast. An older guy has a newspaper up to his face, but he keeps sneaking looks at Amanda, who doesn't notice. He's familiar: a gaunt fiftysomething exuding either beneficence or nastiness. Kate truly can't imagine being that old, and wonders if seeing vibrancy in an Amanda-shaped package simply makes such a man baleful. He rearranges his paper, and Kate notices the inside of his forearm, recognizes the large flag tattoo. But before she can decide whether to say something, Amanda stands and stretches, and they're walking to the studio.

Sebastian and Scott have been at it for six hours, Sebastian on his Tele, Scott on a collector's item the studio just had lying around: a contused Les Paul Goldtop. Sebastian isn't only a fast player; he's six steps ahead, ideas fly off him, he interrupts himself and rewrites *in medias res*, and after playing together more than a year it's still difficult for Scott to keep up. But he's the man with the groove, despite being unable to tap out time with his dead foot. He's got the Goldtop fed through an effects pedal and a Vox AC30 Heritage Handwired amp, so his sound is woolly. Lucius has his feet up on the board, and may not be listening. Pacman isn't around. Colleen is apparently sleeping on the futon. Sebastian grinds on a motif he brought with him, but Scott keeps trying to simplify it down into a riff. (Sebastian has long since stopped trying to explain to his bandmates the difference between a "motif" and a "riff.") They aren't talking much. Scott lets Sebastian wail away, just keeps trying to supply chords that go with the Torque panoply. He thinks he's being selfless.

They've got a song. Sebastian resists the knowledge that it's taken shape as a four-minute rocker. He sees the note-pattern he brought with him as a starting point, an opportunity for recombination. Scott heard those six notes and played power chords under them. But Sebastian wonders if there's another sequence/pace/temperament they might find beyond the pop iteration, and fears in their haste to declare something "finished," they'll miss its best self. This is why they don't speak much. Scott can tell what's going on with Sebastian by the fact that he keeps playing something different. Sebastian can tell what's going on with Scott by the fact that he keeps playing the exact same thing.

But Scott's going to win. Lucius jolts up, and while they can't see his hands, it's presumably because he's started recording something he likes. Scott plays bass on the Goldtop. Sebastian tries to resist, but finds his fingers succumbing to four-four time, imagining a backbeat.

Lucius' voice comes over the p.a.: "For fuck's sake, dudes, that's great. Sing something with that."

Scott does. Nonsense-word shapes come out of him.

Kate and Amanda arrive and stand behind the board. Everyone nods along. Then there's a thumping sound and someone is screaming.

A table falls over, a body is on the ground. Colleen is on hands-and-knees, shouting, slapping herself in the head.

"Something's on me! Something's on me!"

Amanda covers her mouth to laugh. Lucius strides across the room and puts a hand on Colleen's shoulder. Kate raps the glass, waving at Sebastian and Scott.

"Ahhhhhhh! What is it! Ahhhhhhh!"

"It's nothing, is what," Amanda says from way over here. "Calm down." She wants to say: *You were just dreaming of seven dicks slapping you in the face.*

Then there's a screeching that is decidedly nonhuman, and something really does fly up at Kate and Amanda. They duck. Something smacks the wall. Scott and Sebastian are here. Scott thinks the Goldtop's sustain does really ring forever, but Sebastian knows: it's a bat. They're all looking around and this is a bat, squeaking, thrashing itself against the drop ceiling. Kate and Lucius stand over Colleen who scrubs her face and moans, Amanda crouches and cracks up, and Scott says, "Does anyone have a tennis racket?"

"Don't kill it!" says Kate.

"Kill it!" Colleen says. "Kill that fucking thing! I'm bit! Am I bit?"

"I don't want to freak anyone out," says Amanda, "but I think she's growing fangs."

The bat slips through the playing-room door, Scott and Sebastian chase after. Sebastian clatters into Kate's drum kit. The bat scuds against the baffling in here, making sad little thumps like someone punching a mouse in the stomach.

"Where's Pacman?" says Scott. "Isn't he at least supposed to be looking after the place?"

"I need a net," Sebastian says. "We can only tell if it's rabid if we dissect the brain. It's on the move! It's moving!"

"It fucking attacked me!" says Colleen, standing up. "I was

sleeping." Kate sees a series of tiny perforations on Colleen's chin.

"Goddamn," Lucius says.

"Here it comes! It's coming back in here!"

It does, and Colleen hides her face against Kate's neck.

Amanda—who grew up squaring off against raccoons that stole the cat's food, who saw snakes and opossums just about every day of her idyllic Valley childhood—is annoyed, mostly because anything that originates with Colleen annoys her. Scott and Sebastian hover beneath the bat, arms out, like they're waiting for it to jump into a swimming pool. Kind of goofing, Amanda picks up the big chunky studio key that has a Post-It laminated across its face and on the Post-It is a hand-drawn quarter-note, she takes this key and fires it batward: she doesn't really mean anything, she's not really aiming. But the bat is struck and drops with the particular gravity of dead things. It lands on the polypropylene carpet, the key lodged in its body.

Everyone looks at Amanda.

"Ninja," Scott whispers.

Amanda says, "Little sonofabitch said I couldn't sing."

They pass around vending-machine peanuts and convene in the playing room to learn the new song. Kate kills it, Amanda scats comically in spots where it seems like lyrics should go. They break for sandwiches and Scott takes his into a frowzy little office. He writes a few couplets about the murdered bat, but realizes he's just being arch. What did he tell Lucius? It's not the pose, or about labeling things. They're coming together to *be* together. A song's mood isn't only its music, so what if this major-chord rocker is actually about its own absence? He remembers a phrase he read in a magazine: *Brown Study*. A moody daydream.

I dreamed about an island
The movies said it was wrong
Say anything
Make millions of friends
It's better than dying alone

I dreamed about an island
Snapped out of it by a quest
Found out her mom
Wasn't the bomb

Probably all for the best

So I hitched up as a singer
Met a hundred folks a day
Got fired
Rehired
Sold music from Seoul to L.A.

Just always wanted to be alone
I'm not supposed to
I shouldn't want to
But I dream about an island
I dream about an island
I dream about an island

Amanda loves the lyrics. When she sings them for real, as the music fades, she throws in a spoken line: "Hey! By the way! Follow me on Twitter!" For now, they keep it in.

3. Density of Joy

Their last night in town, bags finally packed, Kate dreams.

It's a welcome respite from arguing.

Tomorrow morning, they'll walk to the studio one more time, because out of spite and at the last minute Sebastian managed to rouse from his stupor and insist they redo everything on "Density of Joy." He hated Randy Pope so much, he doesn't want their first producer's name anywhere on the album. Pope is one of those music insiders dedicated to making anyone he hasn't known for thirty years feel like a come-lately piece of shit, a lordly old satyr secreting cigarette smells. Sebastian couldn't screw up the courage to fight Pope in the moment—he relied on Scott to do it for him—so now he'll erase Pope's presence *in absentia*.

Talia tried to veto. She held tonight's Indian food hostage and said, "If y'all are coming back in tomorrow, maybe we could try a different chorus on 'Tock.' Jacob thinks it could go faster, I really think he'd appreciate it if y'all tried."

Amanda walked out of the room and Sebastian laughed derisively. Kate said, "Maybe."

"Give him a win," Talia said.

Scott said, "Not gonna happen."

"You've been in a weird position," said Kate.

But if Talia has felt beaten down by these last ten days, she's kept it sealed away. "Let's just find a little extra time, y'all. It's the right thing to do. He's the boss." And she shuffled away from the food, marking a checkbox.

Maybe it's feeling like she's stuck in a lifeboat with her bandmates, maybe it's the idea of being crushed back together with them again on tour, maybe it's a subliminal wish to rewrite the past few weeks, but tonight Kate dreams she's adopted. And it's wonderful.

Her mother steps into the kitchen, where Kate is halfway through a jigsaw puzzle of Elvis Presley. It smells like yeast in here. Her mother's hands are wilted but she wears a gold wedding band brighter and more hopeful than anything her father ever actually purchased. Kate drags a piece around the puzzle architecture, looking for its home. Her mother says something. Kate adds to Elvis' rhinestone cufflink.

"Yes?" she says.

"What would you like to tell me?" says her mother.

Kate merely smiles.

"Now is the time to speak, before I kick you to the curb, young lady." There's a bathroom scale here on the floor.

An engine revs outside her childhood home. A jetliner also drones overhead and water drips in the sink, jangling a spoon. Kate knows her father is reading a newspaper someplace in the house, squinting through bifocals and chewing his lips. Kate stands and her mother flinches. But Kate kisses the older woman on the mouth and smiles the smile of the liberated.

"You're not my mother," she says. "He's not my father."

The old woman doesn't nod, but her eyes assent.

"I'm getting in the van out there to meet my real parents."

"..."

"I'll just grab a snack before I go." Kate takes several Otter Pops out of the freezer, and they instantly melt to liquid in her hands. She inspects them for leaks, then belly laughs. Out the kitchen door, she can see two silhouettes in the van. She's so happy. "Goodbye. Goodbye."

4. Tock

They arrive on a Tuesday, after a three-hour drive up through backwoods New England which for all its sun-dappled green armor also feels blank enough to invite revelation. Minuteman Studios is a huge converted farmhouse set back from the main road, with a willow weeping on its dirt driveway and the roof caved in on its furthest quadrant. Dilapidation adds to a fecund atmosphere—they could be on some crumbling Carolina plantation—and the Kids decide to revel in it.

Lucius bro-hugs Tom Washington, Minuteman's owner. On short notice this place was the best Lucius could do; he and Tom were freshman-year roommates at Bard and he's used Minuteman for some of his own more complicated mixing projects. Plus Scott and Lucius had tipsy blueprint sessions where getting out of the city seemed more and more essential. They unload and Lucius sets up shop in the control room at an old Quad Eight board, a real aircraft carrier that's retrofitted to a couple laptops. Amanda walks around recording video on her phone, narrating for future fans:

"There's Kate setting up the kit, we call her KitKate…and see there's a little window and in there is Lucius…hi, Lucius…over here I guess is some moldy kitchen, gross…wow, okay, I guess that's a lot of wires and stuff…out there you can see the well-dressed Sebastian Torque who apparently does *not* want to say anything, but that's all right, ladies, I know you only want to look at him…these are maybe just…offices…I don't know if you guys can see but this hallway is scary…the door's locked but we can…oh, look, a rehearsal room…all right…let's just go…this room has a bunch of pictures on the wall…hey, hi, what's your name?"

He's a haggard, chicken-boned guy with a front incisor missing. The camera pinions him to a wall. "I…ah…Pacman. I'm Pacman. I run the board, I'm the engineer."

"And why do they call you Pacman?" says Amanda.

"…"

"Let the record show that Pacman was without comment. Well, I'm excited, Pacman. We're excited to be here!"

Pacman lets slip a guffaw and looks like a delirious muppet.

By mid-afternoon they've pretty well set up. Tom has ideas about the main room's sweet spots, but Sebastian moves an amp around with the Tele slung over his shoulder, playing "Für Elise" and letting the walls and gobos speak to him. The quilt baffle over Minuteman's Kawai upright piano is lavender with dust. Scott stands in the corner playing "Purple Haze" and covertly checking to see if anyone is smiling with recognition. Colleen fetches pizza. Amanda does her exercises.

That ill-fated long weekend at Totem Party felt baggy, with nobody forcing the issue and the guys all arguing about tiny aural differences, and they've resolved to be professionals for twenty-two days. A week's rehearsal in New York means they have several songs ready to go. Lucius pipes in crowd noise to give them some juice, and they practice a rocked-up version of one of Scott's earliest songs called "Tock," a paean to his first guitar: an inherited Takamine. They've played "Tock" any number of times at live shows; it's fun and has wide-open spaces where Sebastian can stretch out and play whatever he likes. Four times through today, he does four wildly different solos, warming to the challenge. After the final time, as the last cymbal crashes, Amanda says into the mic: "We're ready, for real this time."

"Kate," says Lucius through the p.a. "You okay with that?"

Kate sees everyone turn to look at her, and the dynamic is familiar: she's a part of the furniture cruising along self-contained, feeling mildly addled, and suddenly people are staring at her, for an instant making her question her membership. *Oh, right, I'm a fraud.* But they only want to know if she's ready to make magic. She charms them, tightening the Velcro on her fingerless gloves, and everyone smiles at what an easy character she is. And while most of her brain loves them and can't wait to play the song again, a different little part goes: *crisis averted.*

They go. But they play too fast, and Lucius stops them. It's pure red-light fever, and they laugh.

"Nothing says we have to get it perfect today," says Scott.

"No, come on," Amanda says. "We got this."

"But seriously." Scott knocks both sets of knuckles on the Spector. "Let's just make sure we do the record we want. Fuck Sidelong. Fuck Jacob Shear. How much have they already sunk into 'Density'? They're committed."

Amanda leans on her mic stand.

The afternoon speeds by, and the song takes its shape. "Tock" is all major-chord fun but the words slip in a haymaker or two, because Scott was really writing about playing guitar as a kid instead of having actual friends. One verse goes:

Good times ahead

By yourself on the bed
Sideshow Scott on the ax
Plays for two doggies max
As the waterline keeps getting higher

That evening they check into a bed-and-breakfast that oozes ascetic grace. Kate is sweaty and exhausted, and eats a bag of Sugar Babies. She looks back on the day and admires it; walking into a studio and coming out hours later with a song is a kind of alchemy. But the stress is deadly and it wasn't what she'd call fun. In fact, at the moment she finds herself unhappy with the bitter residue of a thing won at a hard price. Twenty-one more days of this? Of blown takes, prolonged waits, crabby faces? The point of music is to chase a feeling: being out of control and totally *in* control, to be elevated beyond a single person's limits until you can't believe you're part of it. If this is no longer that, what's the point?

She says to Amanda, "So remind me again why we're working so hard?"

Amanda is in her bathrobe, having intended to take a shower but accidentally finding herself asleep on the bed. But her response doesn't miss a beat. "Fame. My God, fame."

5. Dancing With The Women

They return to the Steel Pier without fanfare, keeping their heads down while in line to show their IDs. It's the same bouncer but he shows no recognition until it's Sebastian's turn. Sebastian doesn't have a license, his wallet having been stolen, and he squints in the flashlight glare. He says, "You know me, man," and holds his breath. Does he really even want to get inside? Does he give a shit? He's last in line, and the others skulk to a far corner. A Drake song is playing. It's 10 p.m. on a Wednesday and the place is thoroughly dead.

"Yeah," says the bouncer.

"..."

"Just don't be an asshole again, all right?"

They sit at a picnic table and don't say much. Kate and Colleen nod hello to the lumberjack-Santa-Claus bartender—who also books this place—and buy two pitchers. Pacman disappears for a while, comes back sneezing. Sebastian burrows his fingernails into the tabletop, making his face mild and happy but burning a hole in the bouncer with his eyes.

He says, "*Everyone* who pisses me off is dying of cancer."

"Scott," says Lucius. "I don't think I ever asked why you changed your name to Tungsten."

Scott says, "It's not official or anything. It's a *nomme de*…something." He watches the others swig beer, but only trusts himself to sip. "I just like how it sounds. High school chemistry, it's this super-hard metal. I guess…heavy metal, right?" The truth is that Britt Daniel from Spoon used to perform under the name Drake Tungsten, but for some reason he doesn't want to admit the thievery.

"Ah," Lucius says. "Badassery and some shit."

Scott looks at Sebastian, who's now looking at Amanda.

"So Tom's got this friend up here in town," says Lucius. "Gave me an idea. Maybe help you with that bellybutton problem you got."

"…"

"Get you out of your head, is what I mean. This is a charity guy, music education for kids. Like, he said there's a music program, and all these kids whose families can barely afford to feed them, now some of these kids are prodigies, man. Think about having *that* kind of effect on the world."

"He wants money? People are coming to me for money?"

"Nobody's coming, I'm just talking. Been sitting at your elbow for however many days, reading lyrics of woe. Plus it's not so hard to believe, right? Get used to it. People are going to start looking at you and seeing hot-and-cold running cash."

"Lyrics of woe?"

"Anyway, he sold me. Most of what Sidelong's giving me up front for this gig is going to his charity."

"Really."

"Sure, what the hell. The fuck I know about producing anyway?" He winks.

Scott looks at Lucius to see if he's kidding. This Kid Centrifuge record they're riding keeps threatening to buck them off, especially with Sebastian grinding harder and harder, getting into fights, sleeping less and even then only in Minuteman's spoor-infested cot closet. He's lost weight and added dark pockets under his eyes, making him look even more like a genius Romantic consumptive. By now he can make the Quad Eight hum better than Pacman or Lucius, and he's got a colossal inventory of sounds to lay under Scott's compositions. But he still hasn't contributed a full traditional song himself, only the instrumental they envision as the opener, "Two-Person Job." Scott admits this whole enterprise could spiral away from them and never result in anything usable, especially given Jacob's speech the other day. They really might have to start over a third time.

"How much money are we talking?" he says. "How much do they need?"

"From what I understand, they need it all, man. But whatever you got. Or don't, and that's cool, too."

Colleen has sweet-talked the bartender into putting on Pearl Jam's new CD, a pre-release copy of which they've had going in the studio off and on this week. Scott notices "Infallible" is playing and he smiles mournfully, because it's sweet and sad and urgent and uplifting, the kind of big beautiful statement he considers beyond him:

Keep on locking your doors
Keep on building your floors
Keep on just as before

A few more weeknight revelers come in, and one of them points to the ceiling and says, "Jesus, these guys haven't made a good record in like a decade."

Pacman slaps down a handful of orange capsules with G-clefs printed on them. He says, "More presents from my uncle." These are hits of molly, and everyone but Scott swallows one.

They start rolling. For Amanda it's music assuming a physical form...by now a Ne-Yo song is on the p.a. and she hears it in colors. She walks away from her bandmates, steps to the bar feeling like a panther and walks up to some huge buff guy in a tanktop— he's so yoked he looks like a bag of walnuts—and she says, "I can't find the one."

He says, "What?"

"I'm a singer. I sing. But it's a real problem when you can't find the one. You know: the downbeat. One-two-three-four."

"You're looking for the one?"

"Exactly."

"Sorry," he says. "I don't think I'm him."

"No, you don't understand...." But his muscles are amazing. How often must a person lift weights to get definition like this? His biceps is a canned ham. Amanda's euphoria sends her keening into admiration for this guy's dedication. She says, "What are your favorite books?"

"..."

"Favorite art-house movies. Favorite concert clarinetists. Sorry, I'm being pretentious because I'm insecure. I never went to college."

"I went to college," he says. "And I don't know anybody who plays the clarinet."

"It's all right," says Amanda. "Actually I'm in a real anti-intellectual phase. Live a life of the body. Live a life of sensations. Do you have any books in your house? Like, one single book on your coffee table?"

"I guess you don't have to be nice to me," says the guy.

"If you tell me your favorite band, and it's my band, I'll love you forever."

He fully turns to face her. His pecs are so big they're probably a cup-size up from Amanda's. His head is a cube. But he's pitilessly handsome and she wants to put both hands around his arm, to see if her fingers touch. He says, "What if I don't want you to love me forever?"

"That's the spirit," says Amanda. "What the hell does forever mean when you're pumping iron, feeling your soul leak out your eyeballs?"

He smiles kindly. "I can't tell if you're messing with me or hitting on me."

The drug forces love into her heart and her jaw clenches hard. She only wants to feel the incredible body on which this guy worked so diligently. She thinks, *Everyone has their own kind of intelligence, and his is simply housed in pouches all around his skeleton.* She says, "Have you ever felt as alive as you do right now?" She wants to say: Does your cum have steroids in it?

"You're pretty crazy. What's your name?"

She hears herself say, "Perry," and that's how she knows she's going to sleep with him.

Later, Sebastian asks Lucius if he can borrow his car keys. "I just want to lie down in the backseat," he says.

"You promise you won't drive off and leave us here?"

"Aw, geez. Would I do that?"

Lucius takes a mellow sip of beer. "I don't get into hypotheticals, man. I'm saying *don't* do that. You got that look in your eye that says you'd rather be back in the studio. If that's so, come on, we'll go right now. I'll join you."

"I watched the news," Sebastian says. "More about Electric Zoo. Those two dead kids took what we just took. Makes me wonder if we're suicidal."

Pacman says, "I told you, spud: the shit those kids took was half bath salts. Can't get real molly in New York anymore, but my uncle's got a connection up here for the pure stuff. Keep it quiet, right? Last thing we need is more EDM fucks flooding the Happy Valley."

Sebastian is sweating hard and his jaw is nearly locked shut. He thinks, *Maybe I'm kind of an EDM fuck.* "Really," he says. "I just want to lie down and feel the breeze."

"Shit, take mine," says Pacman, and hands over a keychain made of interlocking steel Zs.

"Awesome, Pacman. Thanks. I really, really appreciate it."

"You got it, spud."

"Seriously, you're like a godsend, man. Lucius is right, he needs to make sure everybody gets home safe. But thanks, Pacman. Seriously. I'll just be lying in it."

"Yeah. Okay."

Sebastian goes outside, finds Pacman's Cutlass Supreme by the massive rust stain on its hood, and drives haltingly to Minuteman.

He just wants to be with the Quad Eight. He lines up dozens of files on the control laptop, cranks the board loud, then steps into the playing room and sits on the floor and watches all these sounds he's made drift out at him. It's beautiful and he starts laughing, the Richard Hell book at his side. Soon he falls asleep, and when he wakes the laptop has finished playing all his new snippets and landscapes, and has moved into older files, and Sebastian hears Scott's voice. It provokes love in his heart and gives him an idea.

Meantime Kate gets to stand behind the bar making drinks. She mixes gin and tonic in plastic cups, draws light beer into pint glasses. Massachusetts has the same smoking ban as New York, but the bartender is sitting over here on a low canvas chair, ashing into his hand. Kate makes a frozen-lemonade Tom Collins, and cackles when Colleen pulls a face and dunks in three extra spoonsful of sugar. *The Very Best of Bob Marley & The Wailers* is cranked to eleven. Kate hears Carly Barrett on drums, that Supraphonic snare and the single-head toms, and mostly that one-drop style: beats one and three are silent and the drummer is always behind but nonchalantly so, waving *ho* at the rest of the musicians. At this moment she desperately wants to back a reggae band.

Colleen has crept between two local ladies and started grooving with her arms in the air, thumping with her hips. It's impossible to resist. The ladies grind back, drinks held high. Kate takes a picture with her phone. Colleen is beautiful, almost not even sexual despite her incredible curves. It's charisma, the bright-eyed swallowing serpent: she smiles at you and the space-time continuum hiccups. And as a band manager, Colleen is a tidal wave. "Three Little Birds" is playing and a few more women emerge from the bathroom singing along. They join Colleen's group and everyone knows the words. Kate watches—they wrap arms around shoulders and belt it out like it's a Broadway finale—and she thinks about the blackness in the back of a van, the light smell of yeast and bubble gum. The Santa Claus bartender gets up and hugs Kate, and they do a little waltz before he leads her out into the main room, where the other women draw her in.

"Turn Your Lights Down Low" is next, and they all sway against one another. Several of these women are here together as couples and they kiss, and Colleen also kisses Kate on the cheek. The lyric goes:

Ooh
I want to give you some good, good loving

The junction between all of them is fire that doesn't scorch, Kate hugs and feels a hand in her hair and it feels so good. During shows she's seen Colleen wander away with gorgeous women, just as she's seen her make eyes at Sebastian. But there are no hang-ups about it, no dishonesty or drama but rather a kind of expanding outward; some would say Colleen spins webs and eats hearts, but Kate reads it as a musical openness. Feeling these bodies doing a mid-tempo grind against her, she realizes some of the ladies in Maizie's van *must* have been having sex with each other. Of course they were. And how could Kate have completely missed it? This should be a humiliating realization but for some reason right now, it isn't. Colleen bites her ear and says, "I want to taste you."

All Kate really knows is she doesn't want the hand massaging her scalp (whoever's it is) to ever stop. She says to Colleen, "Why?"

Another Marley tune has started—it's "One Love" and the women squeal—and Kate has limitless energy, she could run for miles. Colleen says, "Who cares why? It's what I want."

And soon they're in the Steel Pier's disgusting ladies' room, Kate's pants are down and Colleen is on hands-and-knees, lapping away. It feels good in a clinical way, like a poem about an orgasm. Kate wonders if she's hallucinating, then she wonders whether Colleen has also fucked Amanda and Scott. Maybe she should moan or touch the back of Colleen's head, but she just sees it happening, far away. To be honest, she'd like to be back out in the main room, swaying again. The Kids have been working on a driving song, with multi-tracked guitars descending a series of octaves and no traditional riff, with all kinds of strange digital sounds underneath. And now Kate knows what the song is about, and a few turns of phrase even materialize. She's not a songwriter, but it's too perfect. Later she's back at the B&B hearing the walls creak, and she writes lyrics, which Scott will later ornament:

My traveling companions and I
Roll into this one-horse town
Like a tornado of self-delusion
And vintage clothes

We get high and talk to people
But the words are ashes on our tongues
While our circus is dedicated
To selling flowers

But all these feelings go away
And I know I'm here to stay
Dancing with the women
The sight will save your soul

Folks look at us funny
Like we aren't all in pieces

Like the things we tell them
Don't come from anxiety and gloom

It's magic to be believed
Because weakness is far and wide
And strength is the thing you get
When others listen

But all these feelings go away
And I know I'm here to stay
Dancing with the women
The sight will save your soul

6. Dropfoot

Today's song starts with a tricky, arena-rock groove. Kate plays solid 16th-notes on the high-hat with her right hand, but halfway through each measure brings in the left hand to get 32nd-notes while at the same time filling with extra bass kicks. She got the pattern from listening to the Deftones and Wax Fang and also this English guy who gives YouTube drum tutorials. It's nasty, and she practiced it during the New York rehearsals and for an hour last night while everyone else was at the movies. But she's pretty much got it: a flam on the toms, ghost notes on the snare except for a hammer on beat three, and tangled cymbal work to make Steve Gadd proud. It's a drummer's point of pride not to be the reason a song's recording goes slowly.

But this song's recording goes slowly.

"It's cool," says Lucius' disembodied voice. "Calm down everybody. It wasn't all gonna be cake and ice cream." They're trying to fit together a few complicated guitar parts with Kate's high-tempo beat, and Scott wants his bass playing to be worthy of the others' technical mastery and flicks extra fractional notes but keeps getting himself off time. Sebastian huffs. Scott sweats and makes his voice gentle, asking for chances to try again.

"Just play it straight through once," Sebastian says. "Let's get the drums."

"No," says Scott.

Sebastian smiles. He's wearing a green knit cap, a wide-neck tanktop, Black Stretch 511 jeans and laced Oxfords. He says, "C'mon. Just play it."

"I don't want to settle," Scott says. "Kate knows: if I do the dumb version on bass, it'll change what *she* does."

Amanda has walked over to the window looking into the control room and breathes on the glass, drawing a skull-and-crossbones in the steam.

Kate is sopping wet. She says, "I'm fine. I can keep going."

"Here's one," Scott says. "How many bass players does it take to change a light bulb? None. The keyboard player does it with his left hand."

"Lucius, tell me you're recording these," says Sebastian. "Tell me we can follow up with a comedy record."

"Plus I don't think *you've* got it all the way down," Scott tells Sebastian. "Do we really want the pause coming back to verse two? It's this dense thing, and all of a sudden there's a pocket. It's...clichéd."

"Oh, *fuck* you," says Sebastian.

They look at him.

"Ha-ha," he says.

"That's a five," Lucius says through the p.a.

"Just *play* it," says Sebastian. "Or I'll play it, and it'll be better."

"Well, isn't that just the fucking height of irony," Scott says.

"Why the height of irony? Why the height of irony?"

"Says the guy who fucked up a hundred songs on the road. Says the guy who got us fucking kicked out of that place last night. Just shut the fuck up and worry about yourself."

"Guys," says Lucius, "you make me come in there, neither one of you goes to bed as pretty as when he woke up. Take a breath."

"Play it back," Scott says. "Play back the chorus into verse two. Tell me you don't think it sounds like fucking Nickelback."

Lucius shakes his head and plays it back. Sebastian thinks about throwing the Tele through a wall, thinks about driving back to the city, feels his skin around him like a force field. He's wrong, he knows he's wrong, but what can you do when everything hurts? The sockets on the wall are screaming. He remembers a couple years ago, sitting around high doing nothing with Jack Dooley. Everyone else in the world is having good times, and he's stuck in here. Colleen comes into the room and asks him to walk with her, and it's emasculating.

But he follows her into the hall. She blots his face with a pink washcloth and says, "What's that thing Lucius said about cancer?"

"Not now."

"You know how many times I've stood in a little room like that one and watched my bands fight? You know the difference between a fight and whatever this is?"

"It's not about the song."

"Right." The marks on her chin have almost healed.

"He's a controlling prick."

Colleen says, "Oh, this is news to you? You've made a big discovery about Scott Tungsten? Should I call a press conference and you can reveal your findings?"

"..."

"I mean, I like benz as much as the next girl."

But this isn't speed. Maybe it looks like speed, but he's not using. "I'm focused. I'm playing great. That part before the verse, it's a matter of opinion. I've never heard a Nickelback song in my life. Tell me I'm not playing great."

"You are. You're incredible. Listen, we could take the rest of the afternoon and you could fuck my brains out."

But Sebastian sees what Scott means. The pause is redundant. Tricks are unnecessary. He says, "Oh, shit."

"What is it, sweetie?"

"I think I'm so far up my own ass."

"Listen," she says. "It's not you versus him. You have two other people in that studio with you. Listen to *them*. Like, don't be such a boy."

"..."

"They're your friends. Even if they don't understand you, they're not judging you." She touches his face again. "You know, I have this book I want you to read...."

Meanwhile, Kate waits in the control room, and Lucius says, "Drama."

"..."

"Takes a lot more to faze you, though."

"Guess so."

"But what do you think of all this, Kate? You could tell them to knock it the hell off. Amanda not so much." Pacman, who's been hunched over the board, gets up for a smoke break.

"What about you?" she says to Lucius.

"Didn't I just try that? 'I'll turn this car around, you don't shut your mouths.' But all right, everybody's got their own style. The sphinxlike Kate. You're the leader and don't even know it."

"..."

"All right. Change of subject. Here's one for you: top five beats of all time, go."

"All time?" she says. "I haven't listened to enough."

"All right, all right. How about this, how about top five Kate Grush influencers."

"..."

"I mean I'll start," he says. "My favorites. 'Machine Gun' by Portishead. Killer beat, always loved it."

"Don't know it."

Lucius dials up the song; the drums are weird, maybe electronic or else heavily processed, or like captured sounds from a foundry.

"Okay," she says. "Play Kate Nash. 'Skeleton Song.' It's a pop tune, so it's not as cool...."

"Please. Who are you talking to? I'm the least cool brother since Urkel. All right. Yeah, yeah, I can feel this. You like your drums busy, as if I didn't know. Keep going."

"'Throw Away Your Television.' 'Scentless Apprentice.' Oh, I know. 'False Media.'"

"Don't patronize me, woman."

"No, really. Questlove. I mean, he's great."

Lucius puts his fingers on his temples and simulates an explosion: his mind being blown. "*Game Theory.* That record was...'06? I know what *I* was doing, I was rapping."

"Okay, why do people do that?" Kate says. "Who cares if I was in high school? Does that mean I like the Roots less, because I was young?"

Lucius has this soothing contemplative pause in his conversational repertoire, one that signals an actual willingness to listen. She also likes him as a producer because no idea is too dear. He says, "That's fair, Kate. I meant to put myself down, because the thought made me feel old. But it didn't come out that way."

"People putting their stuff onto other people," she says.

"You're absolutely right, Kate."

"Yeah, twenty takes in, I think I know what I'm talking about."

"Oh, I've seen worse," says Lucius, and she looks at him. "What you got in there is two dudes scared of their own shadow. They can play, and every so often they can listen. But we don't want to follow either one of 'em down the rabbit hole, right? I mean, I sit here going over a lyrics sheet with Scott, and it's like he hates every word he wrote until you try to change one. And Sebastian would record twenty-four hours of him changing strings and tuning. A band is a strange marriage of desires. Everybody's got their own trip, Kate, but you're the one everybody'll listen to."

She pulls a knob off the Quad Eight, and plays with the ribbed cylinder left behind. "But I never say anything."

"Yeah," Lucius says.

And Scott is prone on the studio floor, looking up at Amanda who has the Spector slung over her shoulder. She's thumping one note, listening to it reverb into infinity, then thumping another. Scott says, "I want these weeks and weeks of living with no feeling in my foot to be a…metaphor for something."

"For what?" she says. But she doesn't care. She's looking at the door.

"Yeah." Her feet are right here, her long legs. She's slapping notes, goofing around swaying. He says, "You know what? It turns out I really can't tell when I'm being a jerk."

The band hasn't argued much in these first two weeks and when they have, Amanda has skated above it. When things are good, she lets herself believe in their future; when they aren't, she daydreams. She wants to root for Scott because she recognizes his dismay that the world doesn't love him enough. She wants to tell him to stop trying so hard. But she knows: neither of them would've gotten this far heeding such advice.

"You know he's not in his right mind," she says. "Something's going on with him."

"I just assume he's high at all times."

"Don't do that," Amanda says. "I'm not going all intervention on anybody." She feels the top string. She grazes it and tries to hear a note coming out of the amps around her. What's the softest pressure she can apply that still registers?

Then her phone trills, and without checking she knows what it means.

Jacob Shear arrives with two assistants, one of whom is dressed like a porn director's conception of a businesswoman.

Jacob hands his phone and sunglasses to the male assistant and clambers up the front path, basically ten planks nailed together over a permanent mud puddle. Amanda holds open the door, arms folded, squinting out at him but also maybe winking. He gives her a thousand white teeth, but only shakes her hand.

"Salutations," he says walking into the control room, where Lucius is playing an old Schooly D song for Kate. They slam down the volume and shake up out of their chairs. "I'm sure there's some quote from an old general about surprise inspections." Amanda and Scott crowd in behind him. Jacob parks himself on the futon. The two assistants try and cram in, then Jacob points and they walk to the playing room and watch the meeting through glass.

"Nothing's mixed," Scott says. "Nothing's even close to mixed, is why we haven't sent any files down."

"Right," says Jacob. "Because I've only been in this business for two decades and can't tell if something's good unless it's mixed."

"Seriously. We've *got* songs. We're not wasting your money."

"I get it. I just happened to be in the neighborhood. Your guitar player is…somewhere?"

They look around. Amanda slips out to find Sebastian. She's shivering.

"I mean, I'm glad to sit here and chat. But everyone wants to know what I think, and however much time we spend dancing around that…."

"We're not even sure what we should play you," Scott says.

"Oh, just whatever," says Jacob.

Lucius looks at Kate, who inhales heavily. He clicks through subdirectories and finds the roughs over which they've toiled. He plays "Tock," "Brakes Are For Beginners," "Brown Study" and "Roshambo." Kate hasn't heard them in succession and she's proud. To Scott, it sounds like a meager amount of work, a feeling compounded when Jacob says, "And that's everything?"

"There's this chunk we were thinking about using as an overture," says Lucius. He clicks around, and plays "Two-Person Job."

Kate says, "What do you think, Jacob?"

"I think," he says. "I think you guys can really play."

"…"

"Why don't we wait until Amanda and Sebastian—"

"This is where we are," Scott says. Jacob and Kate and Lucius look at him. "It's what we are. You can't be surprised. This is what we've been playing on the road. This is what we do."

"I don't mean to burst your bubble human-psychology-wise," says Jacob. "But back me up on this one guys, you can't *tell* someone not to be surprised."

"You know what I mean. I don't think you should be. I don't want you to be. These are really good songs, nobody sounds like we do. I think Sidelong gets behind this record and people will just...really...."

Jacob is amused. Kate has always found him smugly handsome: even features cured by money, patrician posture, giant hairless hands. His picture should be on a bottle of yacht polish. "You have to relax, Scott. I'm not surprised. Lucius sent me the songs yesterday. All but that 'overture' bit, yeah?"

Lucius nods once, and shrugs at Scott.

"Don't be mad at him. Someone up here in your merry band has to be a grown-up."

Scott says, "Then why the show? Pretending like you were hearing them for the first time?"

"Maybe I wanted *you* to really listen. Or maybe I have a flair for the dramatic. Lucius, will you do me a favor and turn on the speakers in there so my associates can take notes? Thanks. I think you all know I've got A&R staff. Talia in there, she's a fresh A&R hire. But I've taken a personal interest in Kid Centrifuge, and don't think for one second that's a bad thing. Any meeting we have, when the subject of you guys comes up, everyone gives their best because they know it's important to me. Anyway, I want to ask you one question. Do you believe the songs we just heard would've gotten you signed?"

"Yes," says Scott. "Absolutely."

Jacob blinks several times and leans back against the futon. He snaps his fingers in what seems like an idle rhythm. "You may be right," he says. "But not by me."

Amanda comes back into the control room, alone. She gestures empty-handedly.

"That's all right," says Jacob. "I heard he had some troubles at a bar last night."

"He did," she says. "But it's okay, the other guy didn't want to press charges."

"That's grand."

"These are the kind of songs," Scott says, "that require multiple—"

"*Scott.*" This is Kate.

Jacob pats the futon and Amanda sits beside him, not too close. "The question I asked myself on the drive up here is the only important one. Do I believe in you or do I only believe in your song? 'Density of Joy' is how I fell in love with you. And the answer to this question, guys, I think it holds the key to our relationship. I admit that sometimes, with some of my artists, I don't always understand the direction but there's a trust. Usually they've built up an audience and they know that audience and they can get that audience to buy songs. But I wonder if anyone can tell me why, in your case, I should believe. In fact, maybe today I'm having a hard time finding a reason to believe. This was my conclusion this morning as I rode through the piney woods."

Scott looks at Kate, who shakes her head.

Amanda says, "We can't be costing you very much."

"But you can imagine," says Jacob, "the conversations I have with *my* bosses who, believe me if you think I'm insensitive to the plight of the true artist, you don't know the half. My bosses care about spreadsheets, and there's a big old minus sign next to you. And they're like, 'Yakub, vat iss zis Zentrifuge? Vy hef zey made uss no munny?' Which of course is totally an exaggeration because the Germans sold us to the Japanese, but when you're in some skyscraper, hat in hand, you're allowed some poetic license. Anyway, they don't have a sense of humor, and goddammit," his face darkens, "they don't *care* if you're a bunch of fucking geniuses."

The farmhouse ticks around them.

"You can see how honest I'm being. How much I'd *like* to believe. But what I want, kids. What I want is something we can sell."

Kate clears her throat, and it causes Scott to stifle the bubble of pain that wants to come up out of him. Amanda says, "We can appreciate that you have a better sense of that."

"I hear it in spots," Jacob says. "And I've got notes for you. I'll be leaving Talia behind for however long you're up here. She knows what I want. Okay, Talia, why don't you come on in."

She does, wearing a blouse and jacket several sizes too small, and a skirt so tight she can only waddle.

"A competitive landscape requires a collaborative effort," says Jacob. "I want you in the best possible position. If I wanted a brooding rock masterpiece, I'd hire some old guy who's already made five of them, and who sells records just by breathing. I want 'Density.' I want that energy, that fire. I want it to shine, I want it to shimmer, and I want kids to dance. You may not like to hear it, but that's why I'm paying you money. That's why I made you a video. That's how you're going to be huge. The songs you just played for me might've gone over big in, whatever, 2000. And hey," he smiles, "like I said, we're really only talking about tweaks. Just: know your audience. And your audience is *me*."

Now Scott is surprised he's able to say nothing. He looks at Talia.

Amanda says, "We can be flexible, right guys?"

"Of course we can," says Kate.

"One thing," Jacob says, "Mr. Hawk, I'm disappointed to hear you aren't finding a way to get some hip-hop in there. You know, in breaks or what have you. Let's see if we can't get a couple guest stars involved. A big 'featuring' name never hurt anything."

Lucius nods, but they see his eyes cloud.

Amanda shows Jacob around Minuteman—in the back office they walk in on Pacman who may or may not be pleasuring himself behind Tom Washington's computer—and she wonders if there's subtext between them, if Jacob is any closer to deciding Kid Centrifuge is an obsolete Amanda-delivery mechanism. But he just keeps stumbling into walls reading emails on his phone.

"I guess we'll talk soon," she tells him.

"Okay," he says.

Then they're back outside and Jacob is huddling with Talia, and then he's kissing her passionately with his hand on her butt. Amanda watches Talia wave as his limo kicks sand at her bare legs.

7. Roshambo

Pacman diverts their two-car caravan to the town center. They park nose-to-tail beside the unlit common, windows down, wind quickening. Some of them wonder why they've spent so much time together away from Minuteman. Some of them are nervous about playing new songs for an audience after a full day in the studio. They're quiet, not aggressively so; maybe it's comfort, maybe swaying traffic lights hypnotize. Nobody but Pacman seems to know why they're here, and he keeps whispering, *oh, spud spud spud spud.* A few cars crawl by, but the only other people they see are three old protestors holding signs nobody can read in the dark.

And but there's just this overall sense of okayness. Rather than feeling bored or claustrophobic, they are B&B residents who've adapted to this hamlet. They have a favorite pizza place and favorite takeout Chinese. They've made friends with baristas and bookshop clerks and have a favorite rock radio station to which both cars are now tuned, so when Seahorses of the Apocalypse start playing they all acquire the same dreamy, half-covetous smile. It's a song by guys they personally know! Their heads bob. Maybe each of them imagines a life lived here, though probably without the others.

After several more minutes of waiting, Pacman flicks his high-beams and one of the protestors breaks away from the others. His silhouette is gangly and impossibly tall, plus strangely squared-off at the head. But another car passes, and in the wake of headlights they see: it's an old guy dressed like Uncle Sam. He staggers over to Pacman's window and bends over like Frankenstein, until his top hat clacks against the car door. His eyes are still witless. Pacman clicks on the dome light so Sam can check everyone's face.

"Five hundred," Uncle Sam says, and Pacman hands over a money-shaped envelope, receiving a clear Ziploc of pills in return.

Pacman turns the ignition and gasses it out of there quick, and Lucius accelerates hard to keep pace; they make the main stoplight while it's still green but some idiot in a Lexus SUV decides to bang a left against the light and only Lucius being preternaturally quick at the steering wheel prevents a wreck. Everyone else in the car starts shouting and hooting at the fool in the Lexus, but Lucius keeps his cool. They ask him how, and he says, "I'll teach you a little trick. Whenever someone the next car over pisses you off driving like a jackass, imagine they just got off the phone with their doctor, who told them they're dying of cancer." Everyone likes this. They watch sub shops and apartment complexes go by, and ruminate.

The Steel Pier is way out on 116 and Pacman says it's hosted secret shows by acts recording at Minuteman for years. Amanda has her doubts. The Kids have played all manner of shack and shed, but it's hard to imagine established bands feeling great about pulling up to this tin-roofed, kudzu-covered hole in the ground.

The guys unload into a mold-smelling corridor, and Amanda peeks into the bar: it's a meandering, low-ceilinged place with ancient pinball machines, a karaoke stand, picnic tables and a parquet dance floor. The walls are overlaid with framed photos from Coney Island that are creepily devoid of people.

Her phone rings. She looks down and sees it's her father calling.

They haven't spoken in almost two years.

She once joked with Sebastian she wanted to start a side band and call it Daddy Issues. But she's *in control* of her life for God's sake, she doesn't need a man to crayon in some missing quadrant of herself. Every grown woman of divorced parents is *not* doomed to toil under the yoke of that One Big Thing.

And yet she feels young. She feels ten years old. *Just answer and see what Daddy wants.* This is the man who brought her chicken sandwiches on days she stayed home sick from school.

But still she watches his name.

If he *wasn't* her father, if he was just some asshole who mistreated their family, would she be obligated to listen to him spew bullshit? She's known for a while now that there's no way to talk to him. She spent high school making excuses for him, talking on the phone, visiting him against her mother's wishes, but it was always the same: enthusiasm at first, then he'd hand her a few dollars and disappear. And he's the one who cheated on Gloria, the one who bounced UCLA tuition checks, the one who ignored it when Lacey gave birth, the one who remarried a racist waitress, the one who never even tried to call last Christmas. *What a joke, why should I let him put me through anything?*

She lets him roll to voicemail.

And now she's older again. She'll be 25 in a few months. She's the woman, the force of nature, the voice. And she's changed. Hatred transitions quicker than ever to love. This ride has been so good for her.

She steps out into the New England breeze and phones her mother.

"Pish! Are you having fun, you beautiful creature? I was just telling Mrs. Scully about the new album. I can't wait to hear!"

And Amanda doesn't say a thing about the asshole.

There's an opening act: four longhaired kids who play trenchant, unironic death metal. From behind the screen of his bangs, the lead singer barks unintelligible Cookie-Monster denunciations, and the two guitarists' black-polished fingernails spider around like they're tickling infants. Three or four college-age girls up front are doing devil-horns with both hands, but pretty much everyone else in the bar covers his or her ears. Colleen still has a cotton bandage over her chin but is buoyant because the bat came back rabies-free; she shoots finger-pistols and does the twist, the swim and the watusi. She got them paid in booze, and they all partake.

When it's their turn, the house is half full and gives them a nice hand. There's no stage entrance—hell, there's no stage—so they push up through the crowd and over the dance floor. Amanda says, "We're Kid Centrifuge. I hope we can help you all forget your cares for a little while. This is a song we recorded today, it's called 'Roshambo.'"

It comes out messy, but loud and pretty fun. These kids don't know them, but are ready to rock and seem grateful nobody is assailing them with insane tremolo picking or blast beats. A few boys in the crowd do that pogo thing, hopping wildly in place and encouraging others to get up and dance. It feels good to play without a net again, and to see people actually taking pleasure from what they do. The Kids make eye contact with each other and these two weeks of hard work feel worth it. They get to the chorus and Amanda sings:

Rock...! Paper...! Scissors!
You're out!
Rock...! Paper...! Scissors!
You're out!

And when they get to the end, she twirls her finger at the band, *keep going*, so they repeat the final four measures again and again and Amanda walks into the crowd pointing at this guy and that girl, singing, "You're out! You're out!" then finally going double-time, telling everyone in her immediate radius, "You're out!" and then as Kate wraps it up with a roll, Amanda shouts, "I'm out!" and literally drops the mic. She's way at the center of the room and it's dark over here, and she looks over at her bandmates who are bright under the stage lights. She's a little drunk and they're beautiful, *beautiful*, and she wants to be back up there *now*.

Sebastian has fun. The new songs give him acres in which to spread out, provided he's willing to abandon the riff. The guitar feels great in his hands. He tosses away his plastic pick and brings out one of the clipped-steel ones, and it sounds funky and wrong. He doesn't look at Scott, who's no doubt furious. He jumps around, at one point accidentally kicking an older gentleman who's staring at Amanda and has a big rectangular tattoo on the inside of his forearm, and then "Brown Study" demands his attention. The show ends and several kids ask for his autograph.

"Wow, so fun!" says a girl with picket fence teeth, and she hugs Sebastian and poses for a picture. "Who are you guys! I'm in love!"

"You're so cute!" says a little redheaded gal in a tanktop and flipflops. She freezes in a kissy pose touching his cheek, snaps a selfie.

"Do you have a girlfriend?" says a tall woman, also waiting for a photo, and Sebastian thinks, *Sometimes...when she's horny.*

Later the Steel Pier converts to a dance club spinning R&B anthems and while the others join the fickle hoi polloi squealing at overproduced nonsense, Sebastian sneaks two beers out the front door.

He opens his contacts list and finds Randall Davies, lies back on Pacman's hood and holds up his phone so it partially obscures his view of a thousand stars in this provincial night sky. And his eyes focus back and forth: Call Contact. Infinite worlds. Send Message. Uncaring galaxies. FaceTime. Heat death.

He catches himself and thinks, *Holy shit, I was really about to call Randall Davies and ask him what I should do with my life.*

"There he is," someone says from across the parking lot. "He's over here." It's the death-metal lead singer, a tall kid whose elbow is bleeding. He ushers over a couple of his hardcore pals and Sebastian sits up. "I wanted to tell you to your face," says the singer. "You're everything that's wrong with music."

"..."

"Your band is corporate. Your singer is hot. Your sound is...peppy. I mean, fuck you and your cynical shit."

Sebastian puts his feet on the macadam lot. He conceals his thumbs in his hands and smells an animal kill somewhere out there in the dark. "Hey. I liked *your* guys' set, anyway."

The lead singer smirks. "These dudes aren't even in my

fucking band. See? He thinks everybody who's not in some poodle band looks the same." The other two guys don't react.

"I get it," Sebastian says. "Hey, you like Suicide Silence? They're tight." In fact, he's never heard a Suicide Silence song, but he remembers a conversation about them months ago, somebody said they were crazed relentless metal. "I know what you mean, though, it can be frustrating."

"Seriously, shut the fuck up." The singer steps closer. He's the wrong kind of sweaty, not the streaming sweat of exertion but the blotched, pulsing sweat of cocaine. His veins stretch his skin like wire hangers. He's scratching the forearm above his wristwatch, smiling but unhappy. "Look what you dress up in. For a rock show. Is there any time when you're primping yourself in front of a mirror for an hour before playing *a fucking rock show* when you feel like your priorities might be out of whack?"

"..."

The singer takes a big inhale through his nose, scraping his throat for excess liquid. One of his friends says, "Do it!" and then the singer hawks a sparkling wad of phlegm onto Sebastian's deconstructed wool herringbone trousers.

"..."

"Try something," the singer says. The three of them crowd him against Pacman's car; they're all taller than Sebastian, but doughy and big-hipped.

"You're too pretty to throw down," says one of them.

Sebastian thinks about Louie Gebara: his best friend in middle and high school, a kid who talked him through heartache and Pre-Calculus, this sweet guy whose awe for Sebastian's talent was manifest and who might actually have carried around a vaguely sexual crush if Sebastian had ever been self-aware enough to think about it. Louie was the best: good heart, sensitive but not maudlin, a dreamer and a daredevil. In tenth grade he broke into Colin Lovett's locker and held some nude Kim Kardashian magazine pictures hostage until Colin gave back Sebastian's Flip camera. But the reason Sebastian's mind rushes to Louie is that even quiet, wonderful Louie has been excised from his life. He doesn't want to know *anyone* from high school, from before his problems. He's off his meds for the first time since then and he's probably a little out of control and not himself. Or, rather, he's fully a self he's not sure he likes.

"Congratulations," Sebastian says. "You got picked on your whole entire lives, and this is some great revenge you're having. Three of you, one of me."

"Yeah, turn it around on us," says the singer. "What does it say about you, you want to sound exactly like everybody else?"

"They have these new things," says one of the other guys. "Minor chords. You should look into 'em."

Sebastian laughs with control.

"I'm fixing to get your singer alone," one of them says. "See what she sounds like with my dick shoved down her throat."

They laugh. "Yeah. First prize, you get to fuck the singer. Second prize, you *don't* have to fuck the fat-ass drummer."

Sebastian kicks the frontman in the balls. There's a horrible wheezing and Sebastian tackles the guy, taking him face-down into crushed stone. He feels the others grabbing his back, someone punches him softly. There's shouting around him. He's got the death-metal kid by the hair and he's elbowing, driving him with his knee, someone takes Sebastian around the throat and the lumpy guy beneath him squirms, but they can't stop him. What's the feeling? He's a creature let loose from the lab. And he makes the corresponding blobby vowel sounds, shredding his lungs, *aaaaooooooaaaaaauuuu*, and the metal kid stops offering much resistance but Sebastian doesn't stop. He punches down repeatedly, into a wet mess. Feet crunch this direction and someone yanks Sebastian off. It's a Steel Pier bouncer, wearing a mask of regret.

8. Competence Is A Vampire

With four days left in Massachusetts, Jane calls him. She says, "You're unbelievably talented and I know I'll look back one day and think, 'I could've been married to the biggest rock star in the world.' But man, you're a selfish prick sometimes, and you're obsessed with what other people think, people who aren't me. I talked to Frank and he said you can move back into his extra bedroom."

Scott tries to talk her out of it. "You're doing this over the phone? You're blaming me for not paying enough attention during the most important time in my life?"

"The biggest problem is I can barely tell the difference. You're here, you're not here."

He tries to manufacture as grievous a silence as possible.

"I'm sorry," she says. "You're right, I'm sorry to do it like this."

He hasn't thought about Jane in several days. And one part of him thinks, *that's because she's been my bedrock*, and another part thinks, *that's because I was waiting for the kind of fame that would give me access to a whole different class of woman*. He says, "If you do this, there's no going back. I'll never talk to you again."

"Wow," says Jane. "Emotional blackmail. All right, at least it's a start."

"Well which is it? Am I cold and emotionless, or am I a smothering narcissist? Jesus, make up your mind. At least give me the full story about why I'm not good enough."

She sighs. "*You're* not good enough. That's rich."

"Well, Jesus, Jane. You're good enough. Here I am, telling you you're good enough. You're the one dumping me."

"I'm not dumping you. I'm dumping the you-shaped hole in the bed next to me."

He doesn't tell his bandmates. They gather at Minuteman: Scott, Kate and Amanda in the studio, Lucius, Pacman and Colleen in the control room, and Sebastian presumably still sleeping out in the rehearsal space. Talia is also here, in another junior-miss secretary's skirt whose buttons must actually be nuclear-powered locks. For grins, Scott has gone back to his pre-Kids catalog and is teaching Amanda a few numbers. She sings:

The poets are blocked
When the sex is satisfactory
So he'll never
Go looking
Again

He also has an old song called "Go See The Trees" he thinks would make a pretty great ballad for Amanda, but in his own head he hears Sebastian grouse, "No rock ballads." Scott is happy. He looks at Amanda, who's scribbling something onto a lyrics sheet. They're not out of song candidates by any stretch—they're still considering whether to repurpose any of the Denver demos—but as long as Sebastian isn't in here, it's noodle time. Kate is at her kit, ostensibly checking drumheads and limbering up, but really she's looking into the control room at Colleen. Their bathroom tryst at the Steel Pier has gone unmentioned, but Kate still feels Colleen's heat on her. Had it been any more welcome than Jack Dooley's advances? What sort of signals is she giving off? In a way, the notion that people suddenly find her devastating is a kind of dream. But if she's undergone some kind of transmutation, shouldn't she know about it?

Scott rips out a scorcher of a blues solo on the Goldtop. When this non sequitur is over, Talia says, "I want to talk with y'all about 'Brakes.' Jacob's feedback is pretty clear. It needs to be shorter, it needs to be simpler, it needs to have more polish. And Amanda, could you sing the chorus faster?"

"We can't kick you out," says Scott. "But we're sure as hell not doing what you tell us."

"It's not me saying it. I'm just relating to y'all what Jacob wants. You heard him, Scott. He's got real concerns."

Scott strums a G. "That song is done."

"The middle part," says Talia. "It's just...weird. It doesn't sound right. It's messy and Jacob wants it taken out."

"It's called a bridge. Really technical term, I know. And we spent hours getting it *just* right. It's incredibly cool, and everyone we've played it for thinks so, except you and Jacob." He rubs his chin stubble.

Talia speaks to Kate and Amanda. "I just want to emphasize, we need to be flexible. I know Scott feels passionate, I can tell how much it all means to him, but...Jacob was pretty straightforward. Y'all heard him plain as day, standing right in there. And trust me, he toned it down. On the drive up here, he was a little more colorful about it. Listen, what if we just tried a few of his ideas to make things more...accessible in a couple of these songs? What if we just gave him some alternatives?"

Amanda feels no sympathy. Jacob is an asshole for doing this, for putting his ultra-green paramour in a terrible position. Talia sounds like a rookie stewardess. But Amanda is resigned to neutrality, which is her way of allowing the fates to decide whether the band will collapse under the weight of its so-called artistic integrity (whereupon she rises from its remains).

"Let's see, how would Sebastian say no?" says Scott. "'Yeah, I mean, I *totally* get where you're coming from, and *God*, like Jacob is just the *best* for trusting us so much. And we *really* appreciate how cool you're being with us, how patient. You're coming across loud and clear, really. Who'd have ever believed we'd even *get* so much studio time and all this *freedom*....' You know what? I take it back. Sebastian never says no."

Kate says, "There's no reason to be rude. Talia, let's bite off a small chunk. The bridge in 'Brakes,' like you said. Okay, so the guys worked hard on it, but you're right, it's complicated and it's probably a little..." she looks at Scott, "...backwards. I mean, let's listen to it right now, without the bridge."

Scott jabs his tongue into his cheek and examines the Goldtop's neck.

"Great," says Talia. "Okay. Excellent." It takes two minutes for Lucius to click around and then play it back. "Better. It's better. Amanda, what if we tried another version where you sound...a little more upbeat? Lucius, can we have playback?"

"I'm not really warmed up," Amanda says.

"Go ahead," says Kate. "Just to see if it works."

Scott says, "Fuck. Jesus. It's a song about crashing a limo through...oh, all right, you know what? Whatever." He unplugs the guitar and sets it down.

"It's y'all's song," says Talia. "We just want to punch it up a little bit."

So it goes. Half a day disappears with Amanda singing "sexier" on a few of the songs and directly on the beat, which Lucius changes from Kate to a synth drum. The bass thumps louder. Scott wouldn't say Lucius looks thrilled doing this hatchet work, but maybe it comes a little too quickly, maybe he's a little too comfortable putting on this particular kind of craptastic production sheen, the kind they fired Randy Pope over. At one point Talia says, "Guys, this is really great!" and Kate gives a thumbs-up she imagines perky people thrive on.

"Last one," she says to Talia.

"Oh, I get it!"

"Because we want to finish more songs."

"Yeah yeah yeah yeah yeah," says Talia, scrambling over this way on towering heels, thrilled someone has treated her as if she's visible. "It's great. I know how happy everyone at Sidelong will be, just having these as an option." As she bends, her stocking-tops and garters peek out and Scott gets an idea.

"Hey, Talia," he says, "will you come with me to the practice room, maybe help me wake up Sebastian or...something?" And his face is so red and so evidently lascivious, all three of the women in here synchronously go, "Ew."

But Sebastian is awake. He's crusty-eyed and still engrossed in the punk-autobiography Colleen gave him, *I Dreamed I Was A Very Clean Tramp*. For a few days, he's been sleeping on the parquet floor of the practice room, on a scrap of baffling with his feet beneath a folding chair. The room initially smelled like a mushroom-and-feta omelet, but now he finds it neutral. Spiders nest above dual exposed light bulbs, and the floor bears the residuum of last winter's salt. He wants to know Richard Hell in person. He's stuck on Hell's description of Robert Quine:

> I've played with a lot of exceptional guitarists, but the thing I've noticed about nearly all of them compared to Quine is the gap between skillful creative brilliance and genius. Quine was a genius guitar player. He assumed as fundamental the qualities that were the highest aspirations of most soloists, and he would then depart from that platform into previously unknown areas of emotion and musical inspiration. He was a complicated, volatile, sensitive, very smart person who humbly channeled everything he was and knew into his guitar playing.

Sebastian wants to be Quine. He wants to be held in this kind of esteem by a punk pioneer he'd never even heard of until a week ago, even as he knows it could never happen, because he's a fraud. Or, okay, not a *fraud*, but not instinctive enough. Not *something* enough. And this isn't low self-esteem talking, or it's not *only* low self-esteem talking. It's objective truth: he has to work too hard, transcendence is too hard-won, he doesn't trust himself enough. Yes. There it is. Don't blame the band, don't blame the music. Sebastian lacks a kind of commitment, the kind some would call "ballsiness." He believes things. (Doesn't he?) But he can see it: he hesitates through deference to possibility, which is just a layer of defense covering over...what? Dread of making mistakes? Who would care if Sebastian made a musical mistake? (And doesn't his indecision itself result in mistakes anyway?) No, decisiveness is a kind of...death. Cutting out every possibility but one, putting that decision into the inaccessible past. It's easier to dither, to lie, to charm.

They think he's been high this entire time in Massachusetts, but it's only been the past couple days, since the parking-lot fight. Pacman found him a baggie of ground-up Adderall. Why not? Sebastian thinks he may as well live up to every expectation they have for him. Maybe he should try more downers, but amphetamines have always been his thing; he's afraid to try something like heroin, afraid he'll like it too much. Anyway, he's conditioned to enjoy this smooth silver ride, heartbeat rattling his jowls. He feels good, he feels functional, his feet are shaking, but he doesn't want to go play with the others. He's able to see himself so clearly like this. Zoloft and Wellbutrin are muddlers. A man has to face what he is. Sebastian's stomach and thighs and fingers are warm with adrenaline and dread, his face is hot, his breathing is constricted by grief for things that haven't happened yet (but most assuredly will). *We live our lives pretending bad shit isn't about to happen. We trick ourselves.* But there's honor in trying to live truthfully, without psychotropics. He's glad for the chance.

He re-reads an account of Hell overdosing:

> For hours I lay in bed trying to remain still and limp. I'd keep my eyes closed until that would start to panic me too, and then I'd open them long enough to make sure I wasn't somewhere scarier than my room, and then because that was too bright and cold and dirty I'd close them again. I dispersed evenly. At my most solid I was a set of molecules coalesced in an illusion of more or less cooperative operation, but the true nature of the function of which was to ricochet and zoom around randomly in the void. I was permeable and undefined, space itself, meaningless cause and effect, like the rest of the universe, rather than a being of volition. Life was an extended car wreck.

I need a dark wizard like this in my life, Sebastian thinks.

By now the rest of them are eating Chinese food in the control room. Scott looks at a pile of meat dumplings and, thinking of Jane, decides he's a vegetarian now.

"What song are y'all doing after lunch?" says Talia.

"'Competence Is A Vampire,'" Kate says.

"Yeah, I don't get that. I don't get what that means."

Scott says, "It means being good at something can be like a prison. Being *merely* good. It'll suck the life out of you."

Talia chews ponderously. "Well, I guess I'm just not deep enough to get that!"

"You say that like you're proud of it," says Scott.

"…"

"I mean, like you take pride in your shallowness."

"Scott," Kate says.

"Like someone tells you how the meat that goes into your dumplings gets made, or about baby chicks getting their beaks ripped off so they can be raised in one tiny box without pecking each other to death, or Asian kids stitching your Old Navy clothes or whatever. But your eyes glaze over and you go, 'Oh, I don't like to think about that.'"

Talia twirls another forkful of noodles. "Oh, Scott. Y'all really know how to sweep a girl off her feet."

"…"

"I think she means you're flirting again," says Colleen.

"I know what she means. Jesus. I don't even know what...." He takes a sip of beer.

"A strong retort," Lucius says, and everybody laughs.

"It's a nice song," says Amanda. "It's an open-hearted song:"

Did you ever believe
You've felt every feeling
You're ever gonna feel
You know you should smile
Feel in touch with your life
It's all right
We're all scared
We all become heartache.

Scott bites his lips.

"Oh, yeah, I like it," Talia says. "I just don't get the title."

Colleen picks up an acoustic guitar and haltingly plays the three chords that comprise "La Bamba." They all sing with full mouths, despite not knowing the Spanish words. They just make dopey noises to approximate the lyrics of a long-dead poet.

"I can't believe sleep-away camp is almost over," says Kate. "I don't know what I'll do when I see my first tall building."

"First thing," Lucius says, "I'm at High Profile to work on this mess growing out of my head."

"I need macaroons," says Amanda. "And empanadas, maybe."

"You'll be back," Pacman says, vigorously rubbing the side of his dirty nose. "They always come back."

"Holy fuck, *real bagels*," says Colleen.

"Someone has to wake up Sebastian," Scott says.

"I do like this town," says Kate. "We could've done a lot worse."

"We should take pictures," Amanda says. "I don't feel like we've taken enough, and we could put a collage of them in the CD case. If they still have CD cases?"

Colleen leans over and grabs Pacman around his neck. "All I know is I want my picture taken with this fancy hot mess." Amanda brings out her phone and clicks them, as they make peace signs.

Scott gets up and leaves the control room. He's got to fetch Sebastian, they've got to record more songs. How many do they legitimately have? How much more meddling from Jacob will they have to tolerate? And what kind of messed-up state is their guitar player in?

As he stalks the hallway near Minuteman's front door, someone knocks. Scott answers.

It's a middle-aged guy wearing a white dress shirt over black pants, and Scott thinks he must be a salesman or deliveryman, but the guy goes, "Hi, thanks, how are you, hi, what's going on?" and steps inside.

"Hey," says Scott.

But this older guy looks around and shuffles down the hall, toward the control room.

"Can I help you?" Scott says. "Excuse me, can I help you?"

The man doesn't acknowledge. He pulls open the heavy control-room door, and Scott sees a rectangular tattoo on his forearm's underside.

The door opens and everyone thinks it's Scott returning. But it's this other guy, this older guy, and his eyes track immediately to Amanda. Kate has seen him around town, remembers watching him watch Amanda at breakfast one morning. The strangeness of this implies something hidden. She feels as though she's joined a conversation midstream, and is supposed to know who this man is. She watches Amanda for a reaction.

"Get out of here!"

But it isn't Amanda who's said this. She remains bright-eyed and curious.

Lucius gets up from the console and shakes the older guy's hand. "What are you doing here, Mr. Dalembert! Welcome, welcome."

"Mr. Hawk. I hope you don't mind. Tom said I could find you here today."

"People, this is Darly Dalembert, he's a friend of Tom Washington's. Scott, this is Mr. Dalembert, I told you about him. Runs music charities in Haiti."

Scott stands in the doorframe. "Oh, right."

"Well, I'm leaving for Port-au-Prince tomorrow morning," says Mr. Dalembert, "and Tom tells me you'll be gone by the time I'm back. I wanted to say hello, and say thank you one more time for your generosity. And perhaps also put in a good word to your young friends?" He steps over to Amanda's edge of the control-room futon. "You're just about the loveliest young woman I've ever seen. If coffee ice cream could take human form. Call me Darly."

"Hello."

"I'd kick myself if I didn't say hello to all of you, and leave some business cards with Mr. Hawk. We've had great success with our youth music programs. Getting equipment to some of those kids has been a true blessing. If there's any way you can help, anything you can give. What's your name, dear?"

"Amanda."

"I look at that beautiful young face and know you'll be a star. When it happens, I hope you won't forget your new friend Darly."

"..."

"Well, I flatter myself that a gorgeous creature such as yourself would ever look at me. In my mind, I'm still young and handsome and then unfortunately I look in the mirror."

"So," says Talia, "y'all buy instruments for little children?"

"We do, and we teach them, they learn songs. It's one branch of our charitable enterprises down there. Things haven't been the same since the quake, but we're getting people fed, we're getting them training. I don't have to tell you how learning music, feeling a degree of mastery, can make a child's entire prospects brighter, make him feel integrated."

"Amazing," Talia says. "It's God's work." Scott looks at her: the flesh of her thigh drawn taut by her ridiculous skirt, the clear outline of an underwire bra beneath her translucent blouse.

"I'll take one of those cards," he says.

9. Brakes Are For Beginners

Sebastian dresses in the bathroom but when he troops back to the bedroom, Scott isn't there. Instead, the B&B's male maid is hurriedly preparing his vacuum cleaner.

"Oh, sorry. Sorry. I didn't think anyone was here."

"No, it's fine," says Sebastian. "Stay. I'm about to leave."

"Okay, thanks. I knocked on one of the other doors this morning, and a lady came out and got really mad. She said I was too early and she was rude. I was really taken back."

"That's awful. I'm sorry that happened."

"Thanks. Yeah. I was just really taken back."

Sebastian wonders if the lady in question was associated with the Kids. He can't imagine Kate grousing to this guy, but Amanda? Colleen? "You want me to move those bags? They're kind of in the way. Sorry we kind of just left them sprawled out like that."

"No, it's fine."

"I hope you don't think we've trashed the place."

The maid looks around, working a rag over the picture windows that look down on the parking lot. "No," he says.

"I'm sleeping on the couch. It's two guys in here and we're not…. I don't know why I'm telling you this. I just feel bad somebody was so rude."

"It's okay. I was just taken back."

Sebastian smiles and nods, hands on hips, pleased for his own sensitivity. But is he really congratulating himself for being a man of the people? Really? Serene Lucius in the room directly below theirs, *he* can pull off populism. Sebastian just winds up a patronizing fool. He steps out of the Carhart Room, and doesn't say goodbye.

He can't wait to get to the studio. None of them can. It's been so damn *fun*. They play snippets of older songs, they teach each other covers, they show off and razz one another. Scott brought a notebook filled with ideas but seems more open to collaboration, and at times they've veered into areas Sebastian might actually call experimental. Amanda and Kate have written a few lyrics, amended others. They'll spend an hour on a chorus, five minutes on a riff, Scott and Lucius bean-counting and the rest of them trusting they're constructing songs out of all the scraps. This morning, after an hour of laughter, Sebastian realizes Scott is playing a familiar little tune. It's "Solo Rocker Kid," the Disapproving Dog song *about* Sebastian. He roars and plays along, delighted. And the ideas keep flying:

"What if we jump back to the chorus right there?"

"I love the way that sounds, and maybe you could even dirty it up a little."

"You remember that thing we heard Charlie playing that time? Where the hell were we?"

"You mean like this?"

"Right, so what I mean is, maybe I sing it before the thing you were just playing."

"It could be faster. I think we could go a lot faster."

"It's like...*bum*...*bum-bum-bum*...*bum-bum*...*bum-bum-bum*."

"Yeah, that's even better."

"Okay, I get what you're saying. There's that other part, what if we took that change, and put it right before?"

"You want me to come in close? You want a couple measures and let it breathe?"

"Yeah, and it's like...it builds to this big *thing*, it could be kind of emotional. Do we have lyrics?"

"I like a ton of ride there, like that really heavy sound you do, just *bomb-bomb-bomb*."

"When I hear you play it, it's like...it sounds slippery at first, and then *crash*."

"What if I play a wanky part right there, like...."

"Wow, this is really...."

"Right, then it goes *down*, the second time it goes down, because then we get back to E-minor, right...and I think the bridge goes E-minor, D-minor...C."

They look up and three hours have vanished.

"Crushing it in there, spud," Pacman says to Scott.

"Thanks. Yeah, not bad."

"Your drummer is fierce as shit."

Scott looks through the window at Kate, who's laughing at

something Sebastian just told her but is also thrashing around, ultra-coordinated striking all sorts of wild fractional notes, chewing gum. Scott reaches across the board and turns her up. Who's better than Kate? He remembers what a demure player she was eighteen months ago; now she's the envy of any band on the bill. He gets out his phone and video-records a minute of her goofing around, her smile that turns so easily into a wince at a stressful moment, but then changes right back to joy. Pacman is drumming two pens on the board, trying to keep up, and Lucius interlaces his fingers around the back of his own neck.

Scott realizes: as technical musicians, Kate is amazing, Sebastian is amazing, Amanda is amazing...and he's merely adequate. He's having a blast with them, but maybe that's only because they haven't caught on yet. He's proud for them. But he also curses his limitations. His pale fingers. Anyone can play rhythm guitar, anyone can play bass.

He disappears to write some lyrics. The others play a while longer, then wander into the control room. Their fingers and throats sting. They blink and wonder at the thing they're making. Lucius moves around files, overlaps a beat of Kate's onto a different jam, while giving Amanda a little elbow jab to the hip presumably to show what a good soldier he can be, how over her he is.

"We could try the one without a chorus," says Sebastian.

"Which one?" Kate says.

"I just assumed we'd find a chorus," says Amanda.

Lucius plays back some different stuff, until he finds the parts they mean. It's on the laid-back side, pop but not hackneyed, with room for a cool bridge and a nice, major-chord, mounting tension. It sounds like a Kid Centrifuge song.

"This is so great," says Kate.

Pacman shivers a giggle. "Tell 'em, spud."

"Naw," says Lucius. "We're just sitting here trying to come up with the foulest band names we can think of."

"The leader," Pacman says, "is Taint Pimple. 'Ladies and gentlemen! I introduce to you...the one...the only... *Taint Pimple!*'"

"Pretty gross," Amanda admits.

Sebastian thinks about it. "Diarrhea Soda."

"Oh! Nasty!"

They sit around laughing.

"Tumbling Vulva!"
"Placenta Omelet!"
"Speculum!"

Lucius plays the laid-back poppish tune again and Sebastian gets the idea of doing his solo backwards. He plays around with it in the studio, wondering whether it's better to record it frontwise and then reverse it, or if it might not be cooler to actually *play* it backwards, so the notes don't go from open-to-closed.

In a while, Scott returns. He sits at the Kawai upright and figures out this new song's chords on the keyboard. Once he's got it, he stands one of his scribbled-on notebooks on the rail and sings the lyrics he's just written:

A giant A.F. Clark sign
Way up above our eyes
Look at it from the side
You'll only see the lines

Driving a limo through the town
You turn into the crowd
You know I'm right beside
I'm along for the ride

The others in the back
Are Orpheus in tights
And his merry traveling wives
The curb goes flying by

Oh, whoa-whoa…whoa-whoa…whoa-whoa

The Kids in back are torn
They're all just waiting to be born

And in the back, the others fall asleep
The darkness comes, the hum of the machine
So we'll drive on 95
Crossing those state lines

The curb goes flying by
The Kids in back are torn

They're all just waiting to be born

Oh, whoa-whoa…whoa-whoa…whoa-whoa

"Wow," says Amanda.

"You guys like it?"

"That sign," Kate says. "That A.F. Clark sign is in the foyer of our hotel, over the mailboxes. What's the rest of it mean? What limo?"

"It's really good," Sebastian says. "And here, listen to this." He picks up Scott's Spector and thumbs out several measures—without any playback in his ear, without any obvious relation to whatever he's just been doing on the guitar—and then asks Lucius to lay this new baseline over the reversed solo he just played…and somehow they match perfectly, and everyone is amazed.

"This is awesome," says Scott. "Let's keep going."

10. *Nipple Rouge*

For as long as they've been up here, people have been telling them to cross the river and explore the next town over. Finally, with two days left, Scott, Lucius and Kate make the trip and walk through a large downtown filled with street musicians and shouting panhandlers, drag queens walking their dogs and sallow students getting caffeinated. There are music halls they can't believe they missed, restaurants whose fare they'll never taste. They watch folks bustling to work and exult in the formlessness of their days, sitting in sunglasses with a bag of croissants beside a frog statue.

"So here's the moment," says Lucius, "where I ask if you did the thing you wanted to do."

Scott chews.

"What's that supposed to mean?" Kate says. "What's the thing he wanted to do?"

"The music," says Lucius. "The record."

"Ah. It sounded sinister."

"Oh," Scott says, "he meant it sinister."

"Naw, man. I'm just asking." He rests a forearm on this recumbent bronze frog, whose pedestal reads: "Feed The Frog / Feed The Hungry." There's a donations slot at his base. Kate feels like she's in the middle of something that could get unpleasant, so she smiles.

"I don't know," says Scott. "Should I have tried to...write to a theme? Should I have put in lyrics that were more...? What I'm saying is it feels jumbled. It's like I can't look at it, I can't see it all at once, there's this nice little bit over here, a good piece there, but does it hang together?"

Lucius nods. "Remember I put out a few records of my own, man. And you just described the way I felt every single time."

"The producer's eye view," says Scott.

"Yup."

"Calmer than when he's the artist. Perspective coming out of his pores."

"Absolutely."

"It's good," says Kate. "It's really good. I just listened to everything last night."

"I agree," Lucius says. "It's really good."

"What I really want to know," Scott says, "is it *serious*. At the beginning, it's like we can be absolutely anything. And now? *This* is all we are? These songs?"

"It's enough," Kate says. "We're all in this together. We all pushed it."

"Don't get annoyed with me, Kate. I didn't say it right. I'm not saying it's *my* album. I'm saying I'm the least of us. If it doesn't work, if it's shallow and unchallenging and boring and commercial, it'll be my fault."

"Yeah, first of all," says Kate, "you take too much on your shoulders. We have to work on that. But second of all, think about it for a minute. What you're saying isn't fair to the rest of us. Hell, anyway, it isn't fair to me. I'm not some helpless little girl and—"

"I know you're—"

"And I'm not a bullet in your gun. I'm all over these songs, too, and I'm a piece of what they're doing." Her voice is calm. "I'm responsible, too."

Scott's good foot taps the sidewalk. "You're not getting what I mean. Argh. What I'm saying is.... We had a conversation, Lucius and I, when we first got the idea to work together. We wanted to make an album.... I don't know. We couldn't exactly put it into words."

Kate takes hold of his wrist. "And I'm saying no matter what you're talking about, it's not just you."

He sighs. "How can you tell a stage is perfectly level? Drool comes out of both sides of the bass player's mouth."

On the way back to Lucius' car, they detour to check out a music shop. Hanging from the ceiling is a phalanx of electric and acoustic guitars, a sight that makes Scott weak; he wants to play but hates jackasses who show off in music stores. They drag fingers over the spines and rivets of new gear, in ways they dimly realize could be construed as pornographic. Kate imagines a version of herself so wealthy and indulged that she's allowed to rampage: guitars smashed through sheetrock, saxophones clubbing keyboards, drumheads punctured by a rhinestone-encrusted violin. *Just bill my label.* She's about to show Scott a guitar strap that reads "Fuck Your Feelings" but backs into someone in the same aisle and nearly tumbles to the floor.

"I'm so sorry," she says, whereupon two levels of recognition rush across her mind. First, this is the woman she saw in a coffee shop one of their first days up here: red lipstick and thick red eyeglass frames. Second, the woman isn't familiar because Kate knew her in Binghamton, but rather....

"Omigod," says the woman.

"Charlene?"

"Holy shit. Kate. I can't believe this."

Kate feels they should hug and so they do, knocking over a stack of china cymbals. The gonging crash is ludicrous and entirely in proportion to Kate's panic. While Charlene and Scott gather the fallen cymbals, Kate peers through plate glass, scanning for Maizie and the Holy Church of Convergence van.

She makes vague introductions then tells Scott and Lucius to go on without her, she'll find a bus back across the river. Charlene leads her to a bakery that smells like a butter bomb just went off.

"I'm finally going back to school," Charlene says. "I got a scholarship. And you know what? I think about you all the time, Kate. How proud you'd be of me. You were the smartest one."

Kate looks up at the pressed-tin ceiling. "That's so great."

"The last time I saw you. Those men—"

"I know."

"I couldn't figure out who they were. It was so crazy. We were just talking and out of nowhere I see these guys in ski masks behind you and it's like, 'Well, they can't be coming this way,' but they put a bag over—"

"Yeah. Yup."

"I just.... I thought about trying to find you on the Internet. I don't know what I was scared of. Did you ever talk to any of the other girls?"

"No," Kate says.

"I email with Sun. She lives in Arizona and she had a baby. We left together, and it was just...."

Kate is the kind of shaky that makes her believe she could do anything. It's the opposite kind of wildness from losing herself behind the drums. Her mind takes her to Kansas City where she stayed in bed for a month, fighting and clawing when they dragged her out for group therapy. "I don't really even know how to talk about this," she says.

"It was a phase," says Charlene. "I look at it like: I needed somebody to tell me what to do for a while."

"It's my fault you were even there. I recruited you. You were my only recruit."

"Don't say that. Don't blame yourself for anything. Can you imagine if I stayed with Dax? I'd be dead. He was this thing I couldn't get away from. He would've killed me."

"They preyed on us," Kate says. "They found us in our weakest moments."

"It wasn't a moment. I really was that weak." Charlene sips her coffee. "You never wonder what happened to the rest of us? You don't think about all those days and nights? I think about it all the time. I can't help it, it's just so strange."

"I don't let myself. Little things remind me, but I stop myself. Mostly I'm just...embarrassed. If anyone ever found out."

"You shouldn't be embarrassed. We were doing selfless things."

"We were victims," Kate says. "We were treated like slaves so somebody we never met could get rich." She grinds a heel into her own ankle. "We were suckers."

"Here's what I think about that. Maybe the church really was a scam, I don't know."

"It *was*."

"Maybe. But even if it was, didn't I get something out of it? Didn't I feel like I belonged to something bigger than myself, didn't I feel genuine love for our sisters, didn't I learn how to quiet my mind that had gotten me in such trouble my whole life? You used to read *Divine Love* to me, Kate. I loved you so much. You can't tell me that wasn't real, or that it was worthless."

"It seems like it happened to somebody else."

"The girls listened to me. After you left, I sat in your seat and I read to everybody. I knew I was doing a bad imitation of you, and the others probably thought I was trying to *be* you. But we were in Tennessee and Hannah cut her leg, she got a ride with some lady who wanted to take her to the hospital but Hannah made her find Maizie instead and she gets out of the car, she's bleeding all over the place, and the first thing she does is rush over to me and hug me and cry on my shoulder. It started out with me looking up to Hannah and Lizzy and Sun, but suddenly they came to me. They wanted to know what I thought. When they had doubts, I was the one. I know so much was fucked up, Kate, and when I got out, I was petrified Father James would send someone after me. But I think about holding little Hannah and whispering in her ear and wiping her tears, and that's something I'll never forget. Nobody listens to anybody like that."

Kate can't put herself back in that van. But she can remember the day she joined: following Sun after the shootings. And what scares her is this: would she do it again? Is she any more stable, chasing Kid Centrifuge's hollow dream?

"What happened?" she says. "When did you wind up leaving?"

"Sun got really sick. It turns out she had Crohn's Disease, but all we knew is her stomach hurt so bad, she had bloody diarrhea, she had sores in her mouth. And Maizie just didn't care. Sun would be on the ground holding her stomach and Maizie would stand over her and scream, 'Get up! Get up you ingrate!' It was too much. I couldn't believe God wanted my sister to suffer like this, but Maizie had an answer, Maizie always had answers. Sun was pretending, playing the victim, whatever. She kept threatening to leave Sun behind, all these mornings in a row, and finally she did and I stayed with her. I had to get Sun to a doctor, but she's crying and pleading with me to stay, she knows Maizie will be back. Which probably was true, but I guess I had enough."

"Did you get to Winchester before that? Did you meet Father James at the farmhouse?"

"Kate, I don't think there even was a farmhouse."

She takes a sharp breath. "Inch went there. All those stories about the music and the bread and Father James in the receiving line."

"I tried to tell you this," Charlene says. "Inch was nuts. Maybe you could argue we all had something wrong. Probably we did. But Inch was a different kind of messed up. Like, I don't know what the hell she believed. Maybe she thought she'd really been to a farmhouse and met Father James, but after I left the church I went to Winchester and nobody knows anything about it. Maybe she didn't remember keeping jizz from all those guys, but she did it."

"..."

"She disappeared one day. She always went out alone. It was kind of a relief, even though I knew how much it would've hurt you. I know she was your friend."

"..."

"When I got out," says Charlene, "all I knew was I'm never going back to Florida. I'm never seeing Dax or my fucking parents. I can't hate the church, because it saved me from who I might've been. I'm close to my degree in social work, Kate, and I want a Master's. I went to Cairo for Arab Spring. White-trash Charlene Hambly cutting curfew with thousands of other people, with fighter jets passing low trying to scare us away. This sounds naïve, but it made me realize how sheltered I was, Kate. Hell, can you imagine a quarter-million Americans gathering for *any* reason, except maybe a Justin Bieber concert? But I was training to sleep on the bricks of Tahrir Square for months, wasn't I?"

"That's amazing," Kate says, then she thinks: *and I once followed a homeless guy around Minneapolis.*

But she doesn't want to tell Charlene. She won't say one word about music.

"Here," Charlene says. "Let me give you my phone number."

"That would be so great!" says Kate.

And while the former sisters grasp each other's hands in some dim pantomime of the way things used to be, Lucius and Scott drive back to the B&B understanding they may be about to waste their second-to-last day of studio time. Kate is across the river, Amanda is M.I.A. and it's anyone's guess what condition they'll find Sebastian in. Lucius gets a phone call and ducks into his room, leaving Scott to go upstairs and contemplate noontime alone. He opens a notebook and reads page after page of lyrics, some of which have made it into songs, many others of which are painfully sophomoric. A plant over there in the corner looks withered, though he can't tell if maybe it's a fake.

Somebody knocks.

It's Amanda, looking exhausted and still wearing the same dress as last night. She drops her shoes near the door and climbs onto the bed, spooning backwards against him. Scott tangles in silence.

He can't see if she's fallen asleep. Her hair is everyplace and her bare right leg is pressing against his dead foot. Scott can't tell if she's drunk or maybe even stoned, but in fact she's neither. She was out all night, first counting ceiling tiles above the bodybuilder's bed again and later walking to a charming little pond and skinny-dipping by starlight. Now she feels pretty good and doesn't want to sing.

Nothing is in Scott's way. Jane dumped him. Amanda came up here of her own volition. It's a terrible, terrible idea, but her arm is so defined, so perfect. He thinks she must be waiting for him to envelop her.

And the thought *has* occurred to her. Scott is talented and funny and he's wanted her from day one. He's not ugly; his features are even and his bald spot isn't overbearing. Plus what a ball of nervous energy, what would it be like to see him unburdened? Sebastian has charisma but for some reason he has to spend so much of his energy being cool, it consumes him and that makes him a fundamentally sad person masquerading as a dignified one, and Scott doesn't have those hang-ups. He lets his emotions fly. So while Sebastian has to work himself into this place where he's quietly the frittering center of everything, Scott gets to be everywhere else. Sebastian gets to pose and will always win, but Scott gets to be genuinely strong and honest. There's a familiar heat against her back and she hears him breathing.

He wonders if this is his fate: to brush up against his desires. He can't accept that she's just *here*; he has to figure out what it means, where a self-possessed man—Sebastian!—would simply take off her dress. He shifts, feigning innocence, so his hip is more directly against her butt.

Why is she doing this? It will screw up Kid Centrifuge. Plus he has a girlfriend, no-bullshit Jane, someone Amanda likes. Anyway, he's been available to her for months and months, so why now? She doesn't need to control him or, rather, feels like she already does. Young adulthood has been a process of awakening into herself: her ambitions, her needs, and yes, her libido. Controlling rather than being controlled. This isn't about men but rather their perception of her, their dismissal of her as a pretty face. She's not a man-eater. She's a human being with the gall to act on her motivations.

If he had to describe her without describing her physical person or her singing talent, what would he say? She likes to have a good time and goes with the flow. She has no overt religion, but has a kind of self-containedness he associates with religious people. She's often very quiet. Maybe she's quite stupid. But no, she's also funny in a biting way and she reads ravenously. Does he love her? Could he?

She thinks they're very much alike. Neither of them knows how to be happy yet.

God, he wants to fuck her.

She can see the merits either way.

He lets her fall asleep and inhales the oily-grape smell of her hair.

And eventually he gets up and walks to Minuteman. In the control room, he strolls in on Talia and Pacman kissing on the futon and this doesn't help matters. They stammer and straighten, but he just ducks out.

He paces down the hall, past the office, to Sebastian's practice room. He barges in, and Sebastian, wearing shorts and a dirty t-shirt and sitting on the floor, is snorting a white line off his knee.

"You fucking asshole!" Scott says. "You out-of-control fucking asshole!"

Sebastian can't remember how much he's slept, but he's still pretty sharp. He knows he looks like hell and he can't remember exactly what day it is, and when one of his bandmates finally came in here it was bound to be kind of a scene.

"Do you know what your problem is?" says Scott. "You've never been told no. You think your shit doesn't stink. People tiptoe around you because they're afraid of injuring your delicate sensibilities, but my God, you're a selfish fuck. Yeah, you're *so delicate*. The world hurts your gentle heart so much, we're supposed to look the other way when you get yourself so fucked up you can barely play, or when somebody dares look at you cross-eyed in a parking lot and you feel the need to beat the shit out of them. What the fuck ever really happened to you, Sebastian? What horrible thing has you on the brink? I met your parents. They're fucking *delightful.* Let's see, you had a hit record at 19, you've got hot women crawling all over themselves to be with you, and you play every instrument under the sun like a fucking angel. Yeah, right, I totally get why you're in pain. I totally get why you're fucked up all the time."

Sebastian wonders if he's rocking in place here on the floor. The Adderall is pumping through him. He feels like a sprinter at the starting line.

"I could try and be like you," Scott says. "I could try and imagine the world exists for me. But I can't do it. I think about how many damn people there are, how many billions, nobody can be at the center of a deity's attentions. But you. You believe it, don't you?"

"..."

"I'm fucking *done* with you. We are fucking *over.* Go make dance music. We both know it's what you really want. Why the fuck you're slumming with me is anybody's fucking guess."

Scott leaves and slams the door. Sebastian feels abased, and it's really good. At least Scott said it. And he's right. He has no reason to feel as he does. There's no justification, and there never was, even all the way back in high school. No explanation for his frailty, no trauma, no fountainhead. And that's humiliating. He sees now: his disdain for the type of songs Scott, Amanda and Kate prefer was never about the music. He just needed a reason to be distant. Probably all his onstage fucking up was subliminally the same thing. Keeping himself apart. Not fully giving himself over. For no reason.

Scott marches to the control room. Talia and Pacman are gone. He sits in Lucius' chair, fuming. As always, he hates himself for losing it. He had no right. He's not sure he can ever face Sebastian again.

He mouses furiously and sees a row of sound files on this laptop. One of them bears his name: "Nipple Rouge – Tungsten." He clicks it.

Sebastian has produced a mix of that early song, but with Scott singing. It's the vocal performance he gave in that hangar in Denver, as they were cleaning up and running out of time. Scott sounds exhausted, scratch-voiced, filled with loss. Sebastian has kept the drums and bass, but replaced his own year-old guitar work with a wild array of sounds not immediately identifiable as analog or digital. They don't overwhelm the song, but rather elevate it, rendering it unexpected and dangerous, but also warm with pain. Scott can't imagine where these weird noises came from, or how Sebastian could've composed them all during his solitary nights. The song has gone from tepid oppressed chick-rock to the kind of sad meditation Scott's been shooting for all month. Making it was an act of pure generosity. Scott plays it again, and listens to himself:

What's wrong is you
Everything you do

PART IV

HOW TO COOK

In advancement, life becomes a pinhole.

A notion becomes an act. A repertoire becomes a request. The world's generation of a new day is foreordained. Eyes closed, eyes open, Monday, Thursday, urgent, inattentive, appreciative, jaded...the gears grind heedless of all these. From the outside— from the perspective of their past selves—it looks glamorous. But it's one song. Over and over.

First they're in New York. Submerged again in the riptide of souls and skulls, they sleep in their respective beds and think about how the album they've just recorded, *Competence Is A Vampire*, hopefully makes them exempt from urban nonsense: shifty men smoking outside hardware stores, overindulged preteens braying into phones, clerks and cashiers and roving salespeople who look for reasons *not* to help or sell. But there isn't really even time to find out. They're playing it for Clear Channel execs. They're schlepping out to Bayside and then Brighton Beach to play it for podcasts. They're glad-handing Sidelong investors in a windowless Chrysler Building office. They're playing it in the tiniest TV studio ever for an online simulcast whose details are unknown to them. They're polishing faux-personal banter in two-minute chunks, especially for a midnight appearance on Z100 that results from Colleen being owed multiple favors by the nicotine-stained DJ. At every stop, it's "Density of Joy." Electric. Acoustic. Energetic. Comatose. Their biases for or against the song don't matter. There isn't enough time per sitting to cop attitudes. One song. Nobody asks them to do another. Hosts might smile or bob their heads slightly, but they aren't listening.

Sidelong flies them to L.A., and the cycle repeats in duplicate, then triplicate. Take touring, and remove every modicum of fun. It is waking up at annoying hours, it is logistics, it is convincing people who don't care to care. There are days off but those disappear via drinks and naps. Jacob calls on a Sunday and tells them to tune into a football game, and they do, in a shitty Inglewood motel, whereupon a quirky lady (so designated by her glasses) driving a Chevy Stag starts humming along to their song. Because they've got Stockholm Syndrome, they slap five and feel honored because in the parlance, this is a "win." The football game resumes and some poor guy with an immobilized neck is being carted off the field.

A few days later, the video premieres on MTV and Colleen buys them four mini-bottles of champagne. They know this airtime isn't any kind of actual endorsement of quality; the mechanics of how it happened are left intentionally vague, but there's a palpable cart-before-the-horse-ness in seeing themselves swaggering around in their Austin outfits *before* any kind of confirmation comes that they've got a hit song. Colleen tells them they don't understand: this is *why* they'll have a hit song. Anyway, to themselves they look puffy. The only one who looks great is Colton-the-model in his velour vest.

Congratulatory flowers keep turning up in their rooms. First from Jacob, then up the food chain from executives they've never met. There's talk of getting muscled into a guest shot on one of the late-night TV talk shows. There's talk of an awards ceremony slot. There's a *lot* of talk. They fly to Detroit and appear at a promotional event for the Stag where they have no idea what to say. Miscellaneous vice presidents pose for pictures and introduce them to subordinates who don't know who they are, either. Colleen stands beside them and explains everyone's job title, like one of those political aides paid to make senators look "in touch" with constituents. She charms everyone with lambent smiles and lingering handshakes. And then back at the hotel, she curses out Chevy for unprofessional scheduling, shoddy photography, an insufficient buffet. Either way, the Kids are pretty sure they're not getting free cars out of this.

As these promotions pile up, as the world is force-fed "Density of Joy" in tiny diabolical ways, there's a new twist. Colleen buys Amanda a Karen Millen bandage dress that rides so high she can't bend over, and takes her to several rapid-fire appearances without her bandmates. Pitchfork's lead R&B reviewer. "Sable Pop" on East Village Radio. A Complex freelancer and a guy from BET. The implication is clear, even if Colleen never says it: make it sexy. Three days seducing smart tastemakers in the same half-there outfit, also playing it a little more *urban* than usual, ignoring the three lily-white people who usually play behind her. And then a photo shoot in an Upper East loft: high ceilings, warehouse sunshine, lightboxes and reflective umbrellas and the bandage dress...then red lingerie in a fluffy bed, the photographer cooing and snapping and Amanda's clothes coming off almost of their own accord, until she's naked and concealing only her most private square inches. Assistants and interns discreetly rubberneck; only Colleen stands aside, checking her phone.

Their *Glee* episode finally airs. They gather at Frank's apartment like it's a Super Bowl party. Forty-five minutes in, two cute high schoolers portrayed by actors who are older than anyone in Kid Centrifuge decide to go to prom together, and celebrate by belting out the "Density of Joy" chorus. God, they look so happy singing it.

The Kids are booked to play a swank fashion party sponsored by Chevy, and they get by-now-familiar scrutiny when they unload a full drum kit and actual guitars. The black-clad party planner says he was sold the light and dancy "Density" and not some noisy rock band; fortunately, Colleen has worn a shirt so tight Scott jokes it's from the Talia Collection, and her boobs have the desired effect: the planner can't concentrate on his complaints, and they set up promising to keep it quiet. But the room is long and narrow, with one wall entirely made of windows that look out onto Madison. So the acoustics are insanely bad, and almost nothing they do will be quiet. Amanda prowls around worrying she'll see Ameena or one of the crazy brothers.

People in expensive clothing file in lauding each other, and descend on the free champagne like it's a tax break. Waiters distribute crab puffs. The party planner tells the Kids five minutes.

"And please," he says. "Some of these people are very old? I mean, we had Gloria Estefan last year?"

"Let me guess," says Scott. "We were cheaper."

"Times are tight?" the planner says. "So anyway unplugged would be nice? Or do you play any softer disco songs?"

There's no stage, just a partition to conceal the catering. They play "Density" and while Amanda sings at full volume, the others barely touch their instruments. It's as quiet as they can go while still actually plugged in. But the fashionistas immediately walk away creating a vacant semicircle around the band. Nobody dances. Nobody pays a lick of attention. They finish the song and Amanda says, "Thank you!" and nobody claps.

They start up "Dancing With The Women" and Sebastian is glad to play something fun; with a raised brow he asks Kate for eight more bars of intro and she gives them, and he backs away with the Tele, focused on his fingers until someone taps him on the shoulder.

It's a middle-aged lady with some kind of birdlike velvet contraption atop her head, and she points to the tuxedoed man next to her says, "This is very important. Could you stop until we finish this conversation?"

And that's the end of playing softly.

They wail for a few numbers, and it's left to Colleen to stand up front and dance by herself. A hunky male model joins her, and they make a charismatic couple: if this were a TV commercial, the stodgy old farts would find their defenses shattered by power-pop greatness and join in jitterbugging, until finally one old lady with opera glasses would stuffily stop the proceedings but then surprise everyone by moonwalking.

Instead, the party planner barges in at the end of "Brown Study," waving his arms, covering Amanda's mic. And *now* the skinny rich pricks applaud.

"You're done," the planner says. "You're gone. Get out."

"Oh, please," says Kate. "Won't you let us stay with this fabulous crowd all night? We promise we'll do more *unn-tss, unn-tss, unn-tss, unn-tss, unn-tss, unn-tss.*" And that's how they leave, lugging equipment through the upper crust, singing *unn-tss, unn-tss, unn-tss* in unison.

The promotions finally (finally!) trickle to a halt and "Density" has—in all industry senses—launched. Colleen tells the Kids to rest, because some manner of tour is upcoming; whether they're headlining will depend on how the single does.

But there's still the rest of *Vampire* to worry about. Lucius, Scott and Sebastian have finished mixing, but haven't heard a word from Sidelong. Colleen says she's in the dark, too; Scott doesn't believe her. When it comes to their manager—who practically arranges parades for a single word of praise in the *Casper Star-Tribune*—no news is bad news.

One October morning, Scott's fears snap to life in the form of an email from Jacob Shear, who instructs him to "listen to these files and come have a powwow with me this afternoon." There are links, and Scott clicks them. He downloads. He plays the first one, then the others. They're different mixes, new mixes of the *Vampire* songs.

He listens.

They're really bad.

He humps to Port Authority and misses his train, and so arrives late to the East Village. They let him rot in reception. In his earbuds, the Thrills urge: *So much for the city.*

Talia minces out and says, "Hi! Scott! Sorry, just a short spell longer," and disappears. Of course making him wait is some kind of executive jujitsu: Jacob establishing dominance. Scott feels himself getting pissed anyway, and then he's mostly pissed for being pissed.

When he's finally asked to enter Jacob's office, Talia isn't here. It's just the great man motionless before his insane view of Union Square, standing behind a desk and staring with his grin pre-locked-in.

"Well, that's not a happy face," Jacob says.

"You didn't expect a happy face," says Scott.

"I wanted to send the files to you first. Only you, so we could talk."

"Jacob, we poured ourselves into this record and you...."

"Yes?"

"..."

"Scott, I'm glad to see you. It's refreshing to have someone say what they mean, when day after day it's all politeness impersonating professionalism. So right down to the kernel. The bottom line is I can't sell what you delivered. 'Density' is great, and the rest is...muddled."

"..."

"I heard something in there. But it was too...well, it's

amateurish. And because I want to save this relationship I tried something proactive, and I'm sorry you don't approve. But I want you to swallow your pride and be objective, because I think if you really listen to them side-by-side, you won't hear that much difference between the two versions."

Scott says, "You can't seriously mean that."

"Pope barely touched the vocals. Did he cut out a few lines? He did. But what you were trying to say? It's all still there. The songs are just leaner now. That's the beginner's error: you think you can take your time. You have five seconds. That's the current research. Five seconds, and the listener is on to the next song. We play within the boundaries we're given. Hooks. A beat. Big shiny vocals. Everything 'Density' has."

"It's unrecognizable. Kate's barely on there. I'm barely on there. What's the point? If it's not our sound, why even bother?"

"Because it *is* your sound," says Jacob. "Because your sound can evolve for the better. I'll be honest: I'm very pleased with some of the new mixes. I know you have your differences with Randy Pope, but I think he worked wonders."

"..."

Jacob sits. "I'm not supposed to make this offer, Scott, but I can email you our testing. Pope's mix tests out so much stronger."

"I mean, first of all you can come up with a test to prove anything." Scott is trying to keep his voice out of a petulant octave. "But it's like…. Jacob. How could you ever think I'd be okay with this? We're not androids. You expect us to play the songs this way? Go on tour and do them like we're told?"

"Oh, absolutely! When you see yourselves headlining, when you see the reaction you get. This is crossover stuff. It's everything we saw in you this summer. A little rocker's edge. A little flamboyant diva. Catchy songs, a rebellious streak but not *too* rebellious, the sexy pop star, the brooding stud guitar player."

"You want us playing for tweens? I mean, don't you see how stupid that is? Tweens don't want us, they want—"

"Scott, who do you think goes to a Beyoncé show? Everyone, that's who. Katy Perry, Bruno Mars, Rihanna, Gaga. *Everyone.* That's who you want. You want to say, 'Welcome. Big tent here. Everybody's welcome.' I'm sorry, that's too big to mess with. From where I'm sitting the goal is people listening to your music. That's why you and I will continue to have a strong relationship, because we have the exact same incentive. People listening to your music."

"..."

"It *is* still your music. You wrote the words. You wrote the melodies. You think a great movie director doesn't have an editor?"

Scott thinks this is what the devil would sound like. He finally sits, in a chair whose seat is several inches lower than Jacob's.

"Okay," Jacob says. "The truth. The truth is that if you want to be the 15th-billed act on the Warped Tour or whatever, your mix is probably good enough. 'Who's that playing at noon on the fourth auxiliary stage? Oh, right, Kid Centrifuge.' The past few weeks, instead of getting you on Top 40 stations and podcasts that crush on iTunes, I could've had you doing College format. Except I'd never do that, because there's no money in it. What's the use trying to appeal to a market that isn't there anymore? Sure, a few years ago there were still people who got psyched about discovering a new rock act before their friends did. You know what they want now? They just want another Foo Fighters record. And maybe you find that frustrating, but we don't care, because there's only about thirty of those people anyway. We want *everyone*. That's the only reason to do this: because everyone will hear 'Density of Joy' and freak out and dance and love it and want to buy it, and then they'll want to do it again with our next song, and then again and again."

"You know what'll happen when you play these for Sebastian. He'll just walk out."

"Not if you talk to him. You know I'm right, so you'll talk to him." Jacob makes a tent of his fingers.

Scott has the sweaty shoulder blades that come when he's on the verge of saying something incendiary. "You don't like our version. But let's say we'll never, ever let you put our names on Pope's. Or even if you do, we'll never lift a finger to promote, or go on tour, nothing. Jacob, it sounds fucking *awful*. It sounds like a studio hack worked for about ten minutes to crank out an Amanda dance party. So now what? You're spending however much to turn our single into a hit. A *lot* of money, probably even more than I think. If we won't play along, then what? You're just pissing that money away? You won't do that. You won't shelve the thing we made you."

For weeks, this has been Scott's unplayed trump card. But a single look into Jacob's black-as-vinyl eyes undoes all his confidence.

Of course that's what Jacob will do.

Sidelong has hardly paid the Kids themselves anything, and the time at Minuteman was cheap. Whatever real money they've spent has gone for promotions. Jacob must think he'll make that back via iTunes. If that's true, everything else is gravy. If it's not, he wouldn't sell copies of the album anyway, no matter whose mixes get used. Which means the hammer Scott wanted to believe he was wielding all this time is actually hovering above him.

"But listen," Scott says. "Is that…is that really what you want? I mean, sure, okay, maybe you don't lose your shirt. But if Sidelong sits on the record, think of the wasted energy. There's such a thing as…emotional capital."

Jacob is ice cold. "I have to say, you're talking to me like you farted out *Highway 61 Revisited* or Mozart or something. It's a nice power-pop record that sounds like 2003. I just want to fast forward a decade, so we can sell a few."

This is what they mean. This is what they mean when they say beware of sharks. Scott pinches his kneecaps really hard. "What if…what if we can find another label to put out our version? Would you…ah. Would you let us go?"

"Scott, there's only so many ways I can say this. You've been waiting your whole life for someone to make this big an investment in you, and here I am. The groundwork is done. Let's reap the rewards together." And Jacob extends his hand.

That night Kate, Amanda and Scott go to Lucius' show at The Ostrich out in Williamsburg. God, it's so fun. Lucius is in a hip-hop collective called Molecular Drillbit and several members join him and his buddy Jules, who's spinning records. The room is tiny and everyone is seated, clapping, laughing. The air is about three-quarters cannabis.

Lucius raps:

Like every MC, I'm postmodern
Jump on in, I lead the slaughter
Line up your idols and I'll go full McLuhan
Ruin the beat, remind you Wayne ain't human
She's the prettiest girl at the parade
Soaking up praise, displayed in the rain
But the kids don't know her name

Just don't blame the Game or the champagne

Scott hasn't told anyone about the Pope mixes yet. It's horrible to withhold this information, but what does it really matter? Sometime soon enough, they'll listen together and make a decision. Probably he's just waiting to make up his own mind first.

Kate gets drunk and swears she does an amazing beatbox, whereupon Lucius drags her onstage and she's hilariously terrible because she can't stop laughing. There are so many moments across musical America when it seems possible that this kind of night should be for the masses again. Rooms, however small, that go apeshit. But maybe such ideals are, as Jacob claims, the debris of a fallen system. Or maybe they were secretly always bullshit.

They are waiting for the fame that will make it impossible to have integrity.

Sebastian is still staying with his parents out in Oradell. His mom—big Tina, potentate of the last sunken living room on Birchtree Lane—counters his exhaustion by being charming and funny. She hangs around all day making him sandwiches in a kind of last hurrah of close-up mothering. It's conceivable she keeps him nearby to blockade his using, except Sebastian doubts Tina considers him capable of polluting himself thusly. Anyway, if that's her goal, she's failing. He's still got a week's worth of Pacman's stuff left and enjoys lying in various spots around his childhood home, high and perfectly still, opening and closing his eyes like Richard Hell.

"I wish I knew where you came from," says Tina. "This isn't just mom talk. I listened to your new record again and it's beautiful, it just makes me want to cry."

Sebastian is underneath a crocheted blanket that's surely older than he is. He says, "Thanks."

"Dad was telling me about being a boy and saving up and buying some new rock music, and believe it or not he was very poetic. 'That was how I knew who to be. When I talked, I used the words I learned from Mick Jagger and John Lennon. When I picked out clothes, when I brushed my hair. And now our boy is doing that for other kids.'"

"…"

"But you know Dad. He can't sing a note. There's a pretty big distance from just wanting to. Anyway, I can tell you feel funny about the record. I know you've got a singer now, and you think maybe it takes less work to listen to it."

"..."

"And now, what, I'm supposed to believe you suddenly fell asleep? Anyway, I won't go on and on about the record, because I don't want you thinking it's some kind of sneaky way of saying I'm not proud of your old songs, just because they were, what? More of a challenge?"

"..."

"My pride is never in the balance," she says.

"I know it," says Sebastian.

"Sometimes I wonder if you do, honey."

"Oh, yeah." His eyes are still closed, and he's doing the sonar thing, calibrating where she is in the living room. "My shit doesn't stink. I know that." There's no response. "Sorry. My poop, I mean."

"All we care about is you're happy."

"Are you happy, Mom?" He hears his voice thicken. "Sorry."

"Sorry for what? I mean, I'm a middle-aged lady who avoids mirrors, so not every second of every day. But I wasn't promised every second of every day. I'm happy. Dad makes me laugh. We get pleasure telling stories about you. 'Remember the time he played street hockey in the driveway with Grandma Bertie?' 'Remember the time he memorized the lyrics to "Hotel California" and acted them out like it was a play?' You tickled us sometimes, I'll tell you that."

"What about the time I stopped playing music and cried for like a year?"

"..."

"It's just.... I'm assuming you don't tell funny stories about that."

When she answers, she's nearer to him and has stopped moving. "Because it wouldn't be fair," she says. "Because it's not...representative. Becoming an adult is hard. Some kids have a tough time, and you came out of it great."

It's his instinct to say, *Oh, I know, and you guys were so incredibly supportive and you got me the help I needed and I can never repay you.* He knows it makes him a narcissistic pissant, but he considers it progress that he stays silent.

A couple nights later, his parents host a crowd of neighbors for charades. "We need one more," his mother tells him. "Otherwise the teams won't be even."

"Subtle," Sebastian says.

The Torques make mojitos and there's much cackling. Sebastian gets to masquerade like he's the quiet kid in observational mode, refusing his share of responsibility for the evening's momentum. He's teamed with Mrs. Johnson and some bearded guy, and makes silly injured eye-rolls Mom-ward to show how aware he is that she's manipulating him.

When it's the bearded guy's turn to act out a clue, he flails around while Sebastian and Mrs. Johnson say:

"You're flying? You're falling?"

"Dance! High school dance! Senior prom!"

"It's an airplane. You're a stewardess."

"Wait, okay, it's music! You're playing a guitar!"

"Guitar hero."

"It's a movie, though!"

"Singer. Little. It's like...a little singer."

"Diving? You're swimming? Diving?"

"Jump? Playing a guitar and jumping."

"What's that movie!"

"You're strutting. You're onstage."

"The one that's not real! Making fun of heavy metal!"

"You're singing. You're playing guitar. You're waving. You're falling."

Sebastian's mother says, "Time's up! Good effort, show them their parting gifts."

The bearded guy is out of breath, and he smiles and scratches his scalp in frustration. "Sorry! Sorry!"

"What's that movie I was thinking of?" says Mrs. Johnson.

"You were thinking *Spinal Tap*," the guy says, "but that wasn't it. Crud, I was trying to do *Almost Famous*."

This catches Sebastian off guard and he laughs from his belly, a moment of stupid delight the likes of which he can't recall.

During a break, he follows his bearded teammate outside. The guy is having a smoke on the front lawn and flipping through stuff on his phone. He's early forties, potbellied and kind of desperately unhip. His shirt bears a Frosted Flakes logo.

"Hey," says Sebastian.

"Yeah, man."

"So I got roped into tonight by blood. How'd they get you?"

"..."

"Not that it's not fun."

"Wow," says the guy, "so I guess you're pretty high right now. What'd you take?"

"..."

"Don't worry. I'm just a really good detective." He further inspects Sebastian, whose skeleton has turned to magma. "I don't judge. In better days I'd be asking for a taste."

"Ha. I don't know what you're...."

"Please. Your secret's safe. Yeah, no, I don't, ah.... I live in Hoboken, just came up to dazzle with my miming skills. You want a cigarette?"

"..."

"..."

Sebastian says, "Why am I starting to smell a rat?"

"A rat."

"As in: I may have underestimated my mother."

The guy blows smoke. "Oh, I get it, you think this is an intervention. Incorrect. Tina did want us to meet, but for music reasons. I tried to tell her how uninteresting I am. I also tried to tell her you almost certainly never heard of *Spin*. You're, what, four years old?"

"I don't...."

"I'm her client. Your mom's. She comes to my apartment and teaches me how to cook."

Sebastian looks back up at the house.

"And you had no idea. Huh. Yeah, she's awesome. But so anyway, other than a rip-roaring game of charades, apparently that's why I'm here. She thinks you need industry advice, and I tried to tell her I don't really *know* the industry anymore, and I'm not sure there really even *is* an industry the way I used to understand it. But yeah, I guess in some vague way I'm still a rock writer."

"Oh, okay. Cool."

"And I have to say, the one thing I wasn't expecting was to show up and find a cokehead little motherfucker." The guy drops his cigarette onto a flagstone and puts away his phone. "But I mean, interesting is good. So you have a band. Tell me how I can help."

Sebastian thinks it should be Scott, the striver, who makes this connection; he'd drop names of old bands Sebastian doesn't know and form some kind of uneasy conversational rivalry with this guy—it's getting pretty embarrassing he doesn't know the guy's name—thereby earning a favor. Sebastian is pretty useless in this regard. All he can manage is, "My mom advertises cooking lessons on Craigslist?"

"And apparently set up this whole thing so we could talk."

"Wow," says Sebastian.

"Dude. How out of control is your habit? Don't be shy, I've been out on tour with some of the best drug abusers in history."

"I'm good. I'm great."

"You look like you just ran a marathon backwards. And I can't believe you're living with Tina and you're still that skinny." He holds out his cigarette carton again, and Sebastian now considers that taking or not taking a smoke is some kind of test. He doesn't take. "Jesus," the guy says, "relax."

"I don't live here," Sebastian says. "This is a pit stop."

"I like your mom a lot. But I promise I'm not telling her anything."

"..."

"..."

"I forgot your name," says Sebastian.

The guy whistles, and makes a long performance of shoving up his sleeves. "I'm Hoop," he says. In a sharp floodlight meant to terrorize prospective burglars, he shows Sebastian the insides of his elbows: shiny-white and hairless, and fully tracked with needle scars.

THE CHASE

Nobody would suppose Amanda expects failure. Surely the Kids view her as their buoyant center.

But in truth her confident bearing is indirectly proportional to her confidence. After all, she's the sole band member who had a day-job safety net, and she only indulged her music dreams via anonymous karaoke. Presumably she's also the only one who's already made escape plans in case the band fails.

Yes, the equation was always supposed to be: either the band reaches the top or hastily self-destructs. But now there's a gorilla sitting on her chest, and it keeps telling her Kid Centrifuge is doomed and her putative solo career will be contaminated in the wreckage.

Man, they really shouldn't have given her the Sidelong database URL.

She sits in the living room—she and Kate have furnished it with a couch and a table and a stained-glass pineapple lamp—and refreshes the metrics hourly. After the carpet-bombed TV ad, the *Glee* episode, the feted and arm-twisted promoters and program directors, the NYC and L.A. ground games, and all those appearances...shouldn't the numbers be better? Is there some formula that ensures a bump in downloads? She wants to ask Jacob, but worries that appearing panicked would be a rookie move.

What does actual failure look like? How can she decide

they've officially crossed over into failure territory?

The adult Amanda figures it's too soon. If the numbers were truly bad, she would've heard something; the label's institutional patience should be her model. Alas, the *rest* of Amanda thinks about rent. (Kate's parents spring for her half, and the guys are currently mooching off relatives.) But more than money, there's shame! She's apparently so ready to be shamed by this, to have her prize yanked away in a most humiliating fashion. And that leads her down the rabbit hole: could she have given more vocally on "Density," should she have been less aloof in the video, could she have groveled better to industry hotshots, should she have insisted in the back of Jacob's limo?

It's a punishing time. She counsels herself: *you can't control this, you're no expert, just wait another day, the numbers will spike.* She thinks about confiding in Kate, but it's impossible. Instead they natter about scary typhoons and practice British accents. She doesn't want to believe that the world owes her her fantasies. Nevertheless here she is, clinging to things she doesn't yet have.

Okay. It's okay. She goes for a walk. She inhales exhaust and strides past twenty-story brick projects, which always make her feel small and sheltered. In back of a skanky Met Foods, ski-hatted teens whip empty bottles against a dumpster and shout at each other about money borrowed, money owed. None of the college kids in the apartments around Amanda and Kate will come up here or ramble alone through Morningside Park, because they've heard apocryphal stories about the 3 Stacks and Manhattanville crews, and of course their aversion is enough to ensure Amanda *will* walk here flouting danger. And she basks in her equanimity with her nose in the air, and then remembers how freaked out she is about the single. And the carousel goes 'round.

The first sign her dread is justified comes on a Tuesday. She's included on an email that says Chevy is pulling the ad at the end of the week. Jacob has appended a note that reads: "This is standard! Much more about the state of the American car industry."

That afternoon she logs back into the database and since last night the download total has increased by exactly three, which seems like it must be a mistake. Only three!

Rejection! Baring its blood-soaked fangs!

Kate has "Gimme Shelter" blasting through the apartment—a favorite of Amanda's father—and this doesn't seem like a good sign at all.

Late that night, Amanda is in bed watching *Mulholland Dr.*, a movie that doesn't make tons of narrative sense but she sticks with it anyway. She's sure people would be pleasantly surprised to see her wrestling with this cool, weird film. Her phone delivers a text from Lacey:

>Pish, are you okay?

Amanda figures this is more passive-aggressive nonsense from her sister, a way to rope her into the latest familial melodrama. So she taps y? whereupon Lacey replies:

>www.pitchfork.com/digest

It's the third item down. First there's a note about "Get Lucky" winning an award. Then comes a snarky thing about Matchbox Twenty hosting a booze cruise in the Bahamas for fans. Then comes this:

> Nominee for Most Annoying of '13: That fucking joy-joy-joy song getting shoved down our throats-throats-throats every other commercial. Digging deep to channel their inner Selina Gomez, Kid Centrifuge can't even admit they're brainless *Glee*-sters, dressing up their garbage with the worst kind of barely-indie pretension, but with a sexy lead singer flaunting her goods to distract us from the sound. Please stop-stop-stop.

Lacey's presumably smug expression is scorched on her brain, but Amanda texts back:

>meh pfork = j/o's

Yes, that's the narrative: negativity equals jealousy. The Kids have skipped many rungs, which is the kind of upward mobility that a certain kind of miserable mid-lister will slag out of principle. They can rock, too. Amanda knows it; the world will know it. The bandmates are in this to be big. And if you're big, it doesn't matter what the fleas say.

She tears a hangnail down to her knuckle.

A few people have praised them on social media, but not nearly enough. Many more have tweeted things like, "wtf is this Chevy joy joy joy shit?" and "who's kid centrifuge, why do they suck?" and "my cock would give that singer joy joy joy" and "joy joy joy joy joy joy joy joy...<<blam!>>" Amanda can only find one other review—a Blip video where the guy spends five seconds on the song and a full minute on a slow-motion evaluation of her boobs—a silence that speaks louder than additional hatchet jobs ever could. It seems her fears weren't dire enough. Are the others doing these web searches, too? Are they undergoing their own private panics?

The next morning Kate knocks on her bedroom door, wearing an abstracted expression and carrying her laptop. Amanda thinks Kate has also discovered the bad review, and wants to commiserate. But in fact Kate wants to play her a song: the original dancier version of "Such Great Heights," the melancholy Iron & Wine version of which is one of their mutual all-time favorites. (And it was the theme song to an M&M's commercial!)

"The remake is so much better," says Kate. "It makes me think we should do a slow-mo version of 'Density.'"

"Kate, I have to ask. Have you been checking the numbers? I've been checking the numbers. I'm starting to get.... This is turning into a little bit of a...."

Kate leans on the bed. Amanda can be sneaky-tense despite all the effort she puts into being cool; Kate resolves that an honest admission of her own nerves would serve nobody. "Yeah, no. We should make a pact not to think about it."

"It's turning into a disaster."

"Nah," says Kate. "The pact is, any time someone starts freaking out we both have to do a whiskey shot."

"I'm realizing...if this song dies, the label will never forgive us."

"C'mon. Let's talk about something else."

"And it's my song," says Amanda. "It's my fault."

"Dude. Scott spins out enough for all of us. There's nothing we can do about it now, so let's—"

"They're focusing on the wrong thing. It's not about my outfit, or me being a...sex object or whatever."

Kate makes her voice colder. "Anyway, it's not going to be a disaster. Sidelong knows how to do this."

Amanda looks at her phone's dead face. "I'm starting to realize we shouldn't give Scott such a hard time. I don't think we should laugh at him anymore. It's really boring. He cares and it shows. He freaks out. So what? It's not even noon, but yeah, agreed. Go ahead. Get the whiskey." She realizes: at least she has one really, really good friend.

At the same time, Kate is wondering what exactly she gets out of this relationship. She fetches the bottle.

Later Colleen calls and they put her on speaker. "Okay," she says, "We just got dropped from Z100. I'm pretty pissed. My DJ buddy says they haven't heard from Sidelong in like two whole entire weeks, and he was really apologetic but he didn't have a choice. Clear Channel only lets DJs go out on a limb so far. I mean, if Sidelong can't get Tom Poleman on board by now.... He loved the song. I heard him say the words. 'I'm getting behind this song.' Something's going on. Something isn't right. Jacob's not calling me back."

Amanda makes terrified eyes at Kate, who says, "Colleen, there's something you should know. At this current moment we are...pretty drunk."

"I need you to call Jacob. I need *Amanda* to call Jacob."

"I'd say we're understanding, oh, about every third word."

"It's not too late to turn this around, girls. It's happened plenty of times. Poleman's a reasonable guy, he takes pride in the ground floor. I've got a call in. But at this point I think we need some help. Make a list. Everybody you met this summer, anyone big. Stars who'll vouch. We need people contacting Poleman, how he can't let you slip through. What else? CBS and Cox, I know people I can call. This is shit Jacob should be doing. Amanda, seriously, can you call Jacob for me?"

"What do I say?" asks Amanda. The apartment is chilly; her nose is running.

"You want to meet. I don't care what you have to promise. Then tell me where and when so I can ambush." Colleen hangs up.

Kate makes coffee, they giggle, cut the giggling, giggle more. Amanda pushes defeat deep into her abdomen. Kate blasts "Plays Pretty For Baby" by Zolof the Rock & Roll Destroyer. They don't call Scott or Sebastian.

Amanda presses Jacob's name, and hears it ring. They get his voicemail.

"Jacob, it's Amanda. I need to talk to you. Uhh. My life is so empty. I want to let God back into my heart, but I don't know how. Please, can you help?"

Kate says, "I can't tell if you were being sarcastic. Were you being sarcastic?"

What Amanda doesn't want is someone telling her she's in this for the wrong reasons, how she's supposed to be in it for the art, for the fun, for the camaraderie. Is it her fault people have been calling her a superstar-in-the-making her whole life? She's the furthest fucking thing from "entitled." She's as down-to-earth as they come. Maybe her sin has been believing bullshitters. The shock of this realization is more numbing than any alcohol.

"Let's go for a run," says Kate, but they stay put.

The next day, Sebastian comes into the city and Scott gathers him at Penn Station. Amanda and Kate meet them at Sidelong's building. If only the Minuteman sessions had seen them so singular of purpose. They get off the elevator and half-expect to find the Sidelong logo ripped from the wall and tumbleweeds rolling through the office. But things are calm in a dim powerful way. The receptionist doesn't seem upset to see them, but she rings Jacob's office and reports no answer. Ditto Talia. She offers to take a message.

"There must be somebody else," Scott says. "Somebody must know where Jacob is, or what the hell is going on with our record. I was just in here last week." The others look at him. "We have a right to know. Does this mean you're dropping us? That's insane. How can you drop us?"

"Wow," says the receptionist. "I'm sure we're not dropping you! Honestly, I think you're about ten steps ahead. I know Jacob will get back to you soon. He's really good about that."

"Our manager has been calling every half-hour. I don't think he's returning messages."

"Well, I just love your song," the receptionist says. "It's so fun."

Back downstairs they call Colleen and give an update. Scott is staring across the street at the Irving Plaza marquee, which advertises DJ Sliink, Finatticz, Lil Debbie and Riff Raff. Into his phone, he says, "What are we supposed to do now?"

"Find me Jacob," says Colleen. "I'll rip him a new one."

"None of us knows where he lives. Sidelong won't tell."

"All right. Teddy might know."

Scott sidles away from his bandmates. "Colleen, did you know about the new mixes?"

"..."

"He played me new versions of the Massachusetts songs. Mixed by Randy Pope. They were awful dance/pop shit, and I told him no way."

"..."

"He wanted me to convince the band. Said he did test marketing, people loved it. You knew about this?"

"No, Scott. I did not know about this. And call me old fashioned, but this seems like information you'd actually want to *tell* your manager."

"I didn't tell anyone," says Scott.

"And what the fuck were you waiting for?"

A double-parked FedEx truck receives the braying horns of five consecutive taxis. "I guess I was waiting for a sign. You think this has something to do with that?"

"I think…. I think I better shut up before I say something that makes you fire me."

Amanda comes over and asks for the phone. "Jacob has a club," she tells Colleen. "One with a swimming pool. And he also mentioned Travers Island?"

"That's the NYAC. Okay. I'll call over there and lie my ass off. Stay by the phone."

"Colleen?"

"Yeah."

"This song everyone promised is a guaranteed hit. We're pretty sure it's dead now?"

It's an unexpected kindness when Colleen says, "I'll call you back."

The perfect weather is a taunt. Normally, this kind of neighborhood is the worst of Manhattan—that particular blend of theme park and ghost town where your lawyer spends ninety dollars for a USB cable at Best Buy and expenses it to your account—but today the sky is glorious, perky people go in and out of a gym, a delightful old couple kisses against a light post, and imps run around with balloons tied to their wrists. The Kids wander dazed around a corner and the plaza here is from a musical comedy: syncopated pedestrians and lighthearted lunchers. But finally, in front of a medical complex that faces the square, they smell something dire descending onto the street from open windows, some mixture of rot and illness that everyone notices. People wince and wave the air a few inches in front of their faces. By unspoken agreement the bandmates stop walking and face one another in the stink.

"What does it mean?" says Amanda. "Is there any way this isn't terrible news?"

"Okay," Scott says. "Facts only. The numbers are disappointing so far. And we're having a hard time connecting with the label."

"Maybe those facts just *seem* related," says Kate, not believing it.

Sebastian is texting.

"We did everything they wanted," says Amanda. "Nobody could've been a better soldier. Nobody could've complained less." She looks at Scott.

"Worst case," he says, knowing he's not about to describe the worst case, "they don't want anything to do with us, and we get a different label to put *Vampire* out. We know it's a great record."

"'We're building a relationship,'" Kate says. "'It's not just about one song.' Was Jacob just full of…?"

Amanda glowers at Sebastian until she gets him to look up from his phone. "Anything to add?"

"Hm. I guess not. I guess things will work out."

"Comforting," says Scott.

"Zen-like," says Kate.

"Cut the shit," Amanda says. "Say a real thing."

Sebastian shrugs.

It's easy for Amanda to want to kill him. She ended their relationship, but God knows he's been paying her back since, with Colleen and his habit and everything else. Fury at Sebastian momentarily feels simpler and purer than this stupid fake nonsense byzantine industry would ever allow. She could just push him into traffic.

"Don't fight," says Kate. "Nobody twisted anybody's arm. Nobody would've turned down our deal. Nobody."

"You take your shot," Scott says.

"Exactly."

Scott's eyes say: *But it was false pretenses. The song isn't representative. We should've stuck with what we were doing.*

Amanda's eyes say: *I didn't want to catch forty winks in the goddamn van before a gig in Fresno anymore.*

"We stay together," says Kate. "We ride it out, whatever happens. And we don't freak out over bad news until it actually comes."

Sebastian keeps texting with Hoop Stringfellow.

The terrible hospital smell dissipates over the next fifteen minutes, and the air grows autumnal and lovely. Scott's phone rings and it's Colleen.

"255 West 11th. Go over there now, it's a fifteen-minute walk. Corner him but don't make him feel cornered. I'll get there inside an hour. Amanda's with you, right? Have Amanda keep him occupied. Seriously. Whatever she has to do."

They cross the square, which moans at the breeze riffling its oaks. For a couple long avenue blocks they seem unified. Strangers loom above, lounging on their micro-terraces and hissing cigarette smoke, heedless of the death march below. Sidewalk saplings quiver at the band's approach, or in the wind. The door of a white limo up ahead hinges open and they wonder who's about to step out. But by the time they get up to Seventh Avenue and gawk, nobody inside is visible.

"Our ride's here," says Scott. Nobody laughs.

They wait for the light, but when it changes Sebastian is still texting.

"I'm not going with you guys," he says.

"..."

"There's something I want to go see," and he points north.

"What?" says Scott. "What do you want to see?"

"C'mon, what are we gonna do?" Sebastian says. "Tackle Jacob? Hold him down until he promises to do whatever Colleen wants? I'm pretty sure there's nothing we can say. It's like Kate said, we did everything they asked. Don't you think at this point we're just embarrassing ourselves?"

"We might as well try," says Kate. "It's better than doing nothing."

"Tell me exactly what you plan on saying. 'Please give us more time. Please spend more money.'"

"Fuck," says Amanda. "Jacob's ignoring us. Colleen thinks there's more he can do, and he's fucking *ignoring* us."

"Oh, sure," Sebastian says. "How many hundreds of thousands has Jacob sunk into this...into this stupid song, and—"

"*Stupid* song."

"—and you guys think he hasn't turned over every rock? Come on."

Amanda laughs, but it sounds like a bark. "You always hated the song. He always hated the song."

"But the point is," says Kate, "let's go talk to Jacob and find out."

"..."

"You have to admit it's pretty awful not to return our calls."

"Come with us," Scott says. "It looks bad if we're not all there."

"Sorry," says Sebastian. "I'm going that way."

Scott spins and bolts across Seventh, his pique synched perfectly with the walk signal. He's cleansed by the specificity of his rage, and at the same time proud of himself for not cursing Sebastian out. Amanda jump-steps to catch up with him. Kate lets them go and says, "Don't be selfish, Sebastian."

This makes him laugh. He likes Kate; he doesn't want to make her feel bad, and tries to turn the laugh into a cough. But her feelings are hurt. Sebastian is the one she's always understood best: his gentleness is a struggle, he doesn't want to burden anyone but he's sensitive to cruelty, feels it intensely then buries it in manners and silence. Plus they've each got a medicated past. She squints at him with one eye, a disapproving expression she recognizes as her mother's. For a moment, neither of them wants to walk away, then they both do.

Sebastian isn't much of a Manhattan guy, and isn't positive he's pointed in the right direction until he sees the street numbers increasing. It's just sprawl here: luxury condos designed to make you feel like you could be anyplace, in any city, with the requisite drycleaners and Subways and Duane Reades shoehorned into first floors. Just over there, he now knows, stands the Chelsea Hotel: in one of his texts, Hoop used it as a landmark to help Sebastian find today's thing, and was aghast that the younger man hadn't heard of it, hadn't spent his youth worshipping the romance of Tom Waits and Iggy Pop getting wrecked at the Chelsea. Sebastian's destination is a Chase branch across from a Whole Foods, but when he arrives he doesn't see his bearded acquaintance. He clicks around on his phone and reconfirms the address.

Hoop has been sending him texts for a few days, but Sebastian wrote him back only after they didn't find Jacob at Sidelong. At that point he decided no more tracking Jacob down, no more groveling, no more abasement. He does care what the Kids have wrought, but he's tired of selling. To do this promotion, to travel around essentially with his hand out and then complain that Sidelong sent them to the wrong places or had them panhandle the wrong people...it's distasteful. It's a distasteful end to a distasteful song that deserves its fate. It may not be beneath the others to rend garments over this, but it's beneath him.

He's on the corner of Seventh and 24th, inspecting decades' worth of chewing gum pressed like soft coins into the sidewalk. He doesn't know what's supposed to happen here. Hoop just said it would be fun.

Bodies are behind him. It feels like one of those New York throngs that bottleneck at a construction site or a particularly offensive display of emotion or homelessness. But then it's more than that: Sebastian hears a clicking that turns out to be several people snapping their fingers. Something is happening behind him; he turns to face the bank branch.

An older guy with a swooping blond forelock has an acoustic guitar strapped against his chest. He's wearing a white suit over a black tunic, with a clerical collar clinching his neck. Several people surround him. They all wear papier-mâché bird heads. Sebastian stumbles backwards and he trips off the curb.

"Ladies and gentleman!" says the blond man. "I am Reverend Johnny! Can somebody give me a Hallelujah?"

The bird-headed people have joined hands and appear to be blockading the bank's front door. They shout, "Hallelujah!"

Reverend Johnny says, "Can I get a Changelujah?"

The birds say, "Changelujah!"

"Can I get an Earthelujah?"

"Earthelujah!"

Sebastian climbs back onto the sidewalk. Onlookers are gathering, wrinkling brows, smiling warily. There's an only-in-New-York vibe. Yes, a few people thread through the congregation spitting mad, but everyone else is assembling details for a story-to-be. People hold up their phones like Geiger counters.

"I'm going to need everybody to help us out," says Reverend Johnny. "I hope you'll *all* sing along, and not just the little birdies around me. Let me explain. J.P. Morgan Chase is the world's leading financier of climate change. Its holdings emit more methane and carbon monoxide into the air than any other investor on the planet. And Chase also invests in mountaintop removal and coal-fired plants, which is why my little birdies are here, because like many species, the red-shouldered hawk faces extinction."

The bird-headed people wave their linked hands and share an ecstatic "Scree!" Sebastian tries to identify a beard beneath one of the masks.

"I promise," says Reverend Johnny. "Ten minutes of your time, and we'll be gone. Here we go!" He strums simple chords, and sings:

If your money's inside this bank
You're a little bit responsible
Yes this is a silly prank
But you're a little bit responsible
So sing with me:
Life is wonderful!
Life is wonderful!
Life is wonderful!
Life is wonderful!

And the bird-heads around him dance and echo this call, and it's all good-spirited and Reverend Johnny is cleft-chinned and handsome and smiling and probably a little too old to be doing this, and soon many people including Sebastian are singing, "Life is wonderful!"

Reverend Johnny keeps plucking the guitar, and goes back to speaking: "I know it seems impossible. We're all just tiny little people with lives and jobs and families, and it's a *bummer* to think about what corporations are doing. But what else can we do? We have a responsibility to fix it, even just a little bit. We have to hold corporations accountable when they break the social contract." He faces the bird-heads and sings:

Chase counts on your frustration
Because change comes so slow

It's hard to face these headaches
But we've got to tell them no!
Now sing with me:
Nature's wonderful!
Nature's wonderful!
Nature's wonderful!
Nature's wonderful!

The guy can carry a tune, and the bird-heads have choreographed a bawdy little dance where they grab the hips of the next birdy and throw back their heads, shouting "ooh!" and then spin around and do the same to their other neighbor bird. New Yorkers are clapping in time; even folks trapped in the ATM alcove are chuckling and pointing.

It goes for a couple more verses. Sebastian sees police cruisers barreling south on Seventh; that they touch down at this corner without screech or siren is somehow more alarming than your traditional deafening raid. Reverend Johnny unstraps the guitar and gently leans it against the building, then puts up his hands in surrender. Several of the bird-heads do the same, though a few scatter back around the corner from whence they came. Onlookers boo the cops. It's a fantastic mixer: sculpted blue uniforms aware a dozen people are recording the arrests, weaving among the protestors and cuffing them delicately, allowing them to remain masked and freaky. Reverend Johnny makes no struggle; he has the aura of a much-jailed man. Passing close to Sebastian, he says, "This is the best thing for everybody, please tell your friends." One of the cops is thoughtful enough to stow the guitar in his cruiser.

Sebastian still can't identify which bird-head is his mother's cooking student. Neither does he understand why Hoop wanted him here. The ATM patrons exit and the smilers move on. A temporary Chase-logo banner hangs crookedly in the window, but Sebastian can't recall if it was already thus. Probably it was.

His phone rings. It's Colleen.

"I turned my cab around," she says. "I finally got through to the bigwigs. Jacob's fired."

"He's…?"

"Canned from the company he founded. Selling out means you get overlords. But nobody's crying for the little shit, he's still worth however many million."

"Wow. What happened?"

"You know what happened."

"It was us?"

"I mean, nobody's gonna give a straight answer," says Colleen. "I'm sure he made other wrong calls. But yeah. It was us."

"My God. I seriously can't believe it."

"He fucked it up so bad, Sebastian. It was so incompetent, how he spent that money. He'd have been better off just handing out free CDs. Or Jesus, free dollar bills. I guess I'd like to believe it was Talia, like he put trust in the wrong inexperienced person. But who the hell knows?"

Sebastian expects to feel liberated. In a flash he's out from under "Density" and everything else. Nobody would blame him if he left Kid Centrifuge and went back to his music. Is there any chance he could get the Kingston Avenue apartment back? But standing here alone his mind hustles to the rest of *Competence Is A Vampire*. It takes this insane news to reveal one final fact: he loves those songs.

"It was a miscalculation," Colleen says. "They tried to make a pop act out of a rock band. We probably should've been wary."

Sebastian remembers all the meetings with labels this summer, Colleen selling the band almost exclusively on the basis of *Glee* and their demo of "Density." But it's almost like she's not a hypocrite. It's almost like she absolutely believes what she's saying. "I have friends at High Lawn Music," he says. "I worked with them, I mean you know that. It's not their usual thing, but I bet they'd be interested."

"Yeah, no. Unfortunately the way this works is…. Sidelong owns the record, Sebastian. They paid for it. And given Jacob's head rolling around on the sidewalk, I'm guessing two things. One, it's going unreleased into somebody's desk drawer as what you might call a cautionary tale. Two, it would cost a pantload to get 'em to sell it to another label."

"Instead of taking whatever they can get? Or just putting it out, and seeing what happens? That's stupid."

"Hi," says Colleen. "Welcome to the record business."

He wonders if the others already know that the past six months never happened.

"I know everyone's feeling bruised. We'll get you guys together in the same room and figure out where you go from here.

I know I can get the Homefork guys to lend a conference room."

Sebastian sees a pretty Asian woman crossing the street in his direction. She's wearing a white knit cap, and she's rapping along obscurely with whatever's playing in her earbuds. She smiles at Sebastian. Behind her, in an alley across Seventh, a truck has hoisted a mammoth dumpster to empty its contents, and waves it around like it's nothing, like it's a bag of popcorn with a few kernels stuck to the bottom. He says, "Will I ever see you again?"

The connection gets hollow, maybe a horn honks.

TABLE SCRAPS

"I was on a plane with the singer taking turns going to the bathroom to shoot up. I'm not trying to say they were the biggest band in the world or anything, but you want to know why ska rhythm was a big thing in, like, '96, look no further. Anyway, I don't know who else was hooked on smack but everybody in the band was an alcoholic for sure. I hate to say it, but it was probably the luckiest break of my career. I traveled with them for a couple weeks, wrote the piece, and the day the edits were done, the singer OD'd. It got the cover and was one of the biggest things I ever did.

"But anyway, the point is, these guys were legitimately messed up. As in: didn't even know how they sounded sober. My last day with them, they got arrested for bringing a rented tiger into the gig, like, an actual tiger from the zoo, they were gonna ride it around onstage. Anyway, they got together for a reunion thing a few years ago, but otherwise nobody's really been heard from. I don't know what happened to the rest of them, but I stayed in touch with the bass player. He was in a few more bands in the 2000s and did all right, but then he got tired of sleeping on the floor or whatever. Nowadays he ghostwrites for country stars. Three top-ten singles, uses a fake name because he'd be embarrassed if the old fans knew. Dick Studs."

*

One of the packets from Scott's mass-mailing lands in a slush pile in Greenpoint. An intern named Dana—whose mood is daily corrupted by her commute from Flushing—attacks a week's worth of mail with virtuosic derision. Bad spellers are immediately trashed. Anyone declaring themselves the "next" anything gets ten seconds of the first song. Dana has been on the job for just a few weeks (and will only get course credit through the holidays), so she's unclear whether an unsolicited CD has ever led to a signing. Plowing through them is the worst kind of busywork. For some stupid reason, the company doesn't take email submissions.

She makes two piles: "Hell No" and "I Can't Tell, Have Barry Listen." She supposes there's a third stack, called "I Totally Dig This And Will Champion It In The Morning Meeting," but nothing has yet risen to that theoretical level.

Eventually, she gets to Kid Centrifuge. After a dozen submissions that split between terrible Justin Bieber and terrible Deadmau5, Dana doesn't mind hearing an actual guitar. And the guy can play. It has a little life. Alas, at this point she doesn't trust herself; veteran office drones have taken such pleasure in proving that every assumption she has about the business is backward, she expects that an experienced hand would consider anything she likes knee-jerk unmarketable. For a few moments she flirts with putting a couple of these tunes onto her phone, then the air behind her gets cold and she's annoyed how slow some people close the damn door. She puts Kid Centrifuge in Barry's pile. And by the time Barry gets back from his Jensen Beach vacation, the backlog is too much to handle, and he tosses the entire bunch into office recycling.

*

"I can't remember what they called themselves at first. Mishakiff, something like that. They changed the name, got the cover, won a Grammy in 2002. But that singer was just such a dick, he was so convinced of his genius. The only time I ever got him to answer a question, he'd pretend he was thinking so hard, then he'd say something like, 'The best rock-and-roll bands don't suck the audience's cock, they force the audience to suck theirs.' I'm not doing it justice. He had an Aussie accent, made me want to strangle him even more. The band kicked him out as soon as they could and he tried to die tragically, but couldn't manage it. And what does that momentarily famous asshole do for a living now? He writes sonic backgrounds for a video game series aimed at preteen girls, called *Princess Akira*."

*

At Colleen Just's request, the boys at Weekend Nihilism don't cold-dump Scott's email. This isn't altruism, nor is it borne of a desire to find a new band. Rather, Derek intends to give the appearance of a favor, because he wants to get into Colleen's pants.

The two partners recognize that their emphatic afternoon ritual of one-hitters and Ring Dings is a sad mid-twenties attempt to freeze the past in the present. But what's the alternative? Marry your girlfriend? Buy a co-op? Prospect Park is outside the conference room windows, just dangling there. Everyone at the label *expects* Tim and Derek to stuff towels under the door like this. What message of propriety and servility would *not* getting high every day send to their employees?

Anyway, they're thoroughly fucked up on Bruce Banner #3, and Derek thinks about Colleen's chest hovering beneath a t-shirt. Which leads him to rifling around until he finds Scott's email, and he clicks on the alphabetically first link, called "Brakes Are For Beginners." The song starts.

"Jesus," says Tim. "It's 2004. Everyone's wearing vintage clothes and Janet Jackson's nipple is poking America in the eye. And, what, I'm 17."

"This is that thing I flagged," Derek says. "Colleen's thing that shat the bed."

"I listened to it."

"I want to give her notes. What do we have?"

"Apparently we have a boner for Colleen," Tim says. "All right. Tight production, can't argue with the musicianship. Derivative isn't bad, but derivative of oldies? Strokes with a girl singer. Phantom Planet. Uh…Yeah Yeah Yeahs."

"I mean it's not right for us, I know."

"Find a retro shop. In it just for the love, not to move units."

Derek hears nostalgia in the sound and that's what he'll tell Colleen. *Sometimes if you're lucky nostalgia touches the right nerve and blows up*. But honestly, he can't tell if it's the music or the weed provoking this wistful feeling, which prowls around him these days waiting to be catalyzed.

"The band, I give an outside chance," says Tim. "You? With that dime-piece Colleen?" He frowns and delivers a cruel headshake.

*

"The Chili Peppers' guitar player said fuck it and quit rock-and-roll. Skrillex was the singer in a screamo band on Epitaph. Jesus, don't even talk to me about whatever the fuck Radiohead is now. But I mean, make an artistic choice, I might not agree but you've already got more money than God, do what you want.

"But how craven are the fucking bookers and promoters and managers and labels and producers who know the main reasons for EDM are drugs and cost-effectiveness? It's much cheaper not to create anything. 'We're music curators.' Fuck. No expenses to make any of that pesky actual music. I mean, best case, if you'd gone out with Kid Centrifuge and gotten huge, you're making, what, one-third of a given show's take? DJs don't have roadies. They don't have setup. They have a fucking thumb drive.

"And I'm telling you, three-quarters of any rock guys I brushed up against before 2009 are lining up to beg Tiësto for table scraps. Part of the reason I'm just a contributor now is I won't write about this garbage. Jake Hough, he was such a fucking legend—he wrote amazing stuff on Cobain and a Keith Richards book and a million other things. Now he makes his living doing these bemused pieces, like, 'Are These Geeks The New Rock Stars?' Hough knows he's a massive fraud, he emailed me the other day: 'How long 'til they vertically integrate, start taking a piece of the ecstasy concessions?'"

*

Scott's phone rings.

"Can I speak with Mr. Tungsten?"

"This is."

"Mr. Tungsten, I'm Evie Higginbottom with Fame Island Management, am I catching you at a good time?"

"Oh. Sure, yeah. I think I sent you some songs."

"Absolutely," says Evie, "I've got your submission right here. It's quite something. We don't usually receive such polished work."

"I'm flattered."

"We're interested, Mr. Tungsten, certainly. We're interested in being in business with Kid Centrifuge."

Scott blindly wallops the window with his hand and sees nothing but rescue. "So as I said in my.... Those specific songs are still under some legal dispute. But longer term, you know, we have plenty of others, and I hope that won't discourage you from—"

"Not at all," she says. "Not at all. It's obvious you're serious, and that goes a long way with Fame Island."

"We had prior management. It ended amicably, they just weren't.... I'm wondering. I don't mean to be rude, but can I ask if you're in the U.S.?"

"You mean my accent. You can take the girl out of London.... Yes, I'm in New York. I think that's where you're based as well?"

"Well. This is great. This really is great news."

"For me as well. Is there a mailing address where I can send you a contract?"

"Oh. Uh, sure. But listen, I mean go ahead and send it but obviously I have to check with.... There are three other people in the band. I think before we sign they'll be more comfortable if we meet and talk about the.... I think we all have thoughts about what direction we want to go?"

"Of course, of course—"

"No no."

"I realize it's quite quick," she says. "And obviously it's most important that you feel comfortable. Rest assured my primary motive here is simply to make you aware of how interested we are. I'm afraid sometimes I come on strong, but it's only because I'd hate to see you wind up somewhere else. And if I do say so, our terms are among the best in the industry."

"Terms."

"For a band with your obvious talent and experience, our retainer is quite reasonable."

Scott says, "Oh, uh-huh. Great."

"So I'll get these papers right out to you, Mr. Tungsten. What's the address?"

"Okay, but wait. When you say 'retainer....'"

"I'll let you read the details once you get a copy of the agreement."

"Right, but by retainer do you mean...?"

"It's really the gold standard in the industry," she says. "And we've had great success with acts of your type. I've no doubt at all: with the opportunities Fame Island secures, you'll make back the retainer almost immediately."

Scott's palm is still pressed on the window, presenting his worth to the world: Liminal Talent Under Glass. Lemon in his frown, he says, "How much?"

"It does depend on which plan you choose, Scott. For artists with as much promise as you and your friends, I'd recommend the Platinum Level, five thousand per month. Among many other benefits, that gets you unlimited calls with our team and a customized media plan."

"We, ah. We write you a check up front."

"And in exchange receive a dedicated management team with instructions to move you to the front of the queue in all matters. You can find testimonial letters on the Fame Island website. It's the package I'd choose, but again, you have freedom to select whatever works best for you."

Scott feels so lonely, his stubble hurts.

*

"2010 was the last time I bothered with South By Southwest. It got depressing, covering the same event every year, even with every badge known to man draped around me. Believe it or not, getting blowjobs from pretty girl singers because of the lanyard you're wearing eventually does get old. So that last year I loaded up on amyl nitrite poppers and wrote the feature as a quest narrative. I asked every single person I ran into to sum up the festival in one word, and I wasn't gonna stop until I got the right answer.

"Now, I'll be the first to admit this wasn't exactly a journalistically sound approach. Deciding the story before I ever got on the plane and all that. But man, I was on my way out. Anyway what do you think I got for answers? 'Exciting.' 'Possibilities.' 'Fame.' 'Deal.' Every so often a wiseass would go, 'Sawdust Vomit, but that's two words!' but they didn't really mean it. The kneejerk is to be cynical about getting noticed among a thousand bands and a hundred thousand hangers-on, but every goddamn act paid the money to get on the bill, waited 'til 1 a.m. and rocked hard at some forlorn barbecue joint. That's optimism. Because as steep as the mountain looked, there were examples, right? Newly minted indie gods. Black Keys, Vampire Weekend, Arcade Fire. 'Why can't that happen to *our* band?' But the dirty secret is: those bands only seem newly minted. They got in under the wire. Three years ago is too long. It doesn't count that Vampire Weekend still sells records. They're a legacy band from a different era. It's done. Name the last big act to get signed out of South-By. The Strokes and the Polyphonic Spree are old as shit. Why do you think Austin gets overrun with interactive and film bullshit? They're waiting for the jig to be up on the music any year now.

"And I never got the right one-word answer, buddy. I don't mean to ruin it, if you're planning on looking up the column later. But the right answer is: 'Delusional.'"

*

Scott gave extra attention to the package bound for Jack Marolo Management, because Marolo seems to be bucking the trend and doubling down on his rock acts. His name is regularly attached to cool, smaller shows people point to when they proclaim that a "boutique" philosophy can still make money. So Scott filled the cover letter with personalized details, how he admires what Marolo has done with Dog Foam and Tweaked Oblique—even though he has no idea whether these acts have made cash on any kind of significant level—and adheres a Post-It on which he handwrites: "It would really be an honor to meet with you guys."

But it's not an advantage with Marolo's people to have a big ol' bust on your résumé. Jack's assistant reads the letter and remembers "Density of Joy." She takes an added ounce of grim pleasure tossing it into the circular file.

*

"You want to know what I think about? Who makes the fantasies. That's where the power is, right? It's not the church anymore, it's not any government. I guess the cynic in me says it's corporations, and that's probably closer to reality than anything else, at least on some general level. And I'm not sure you can possibly have an appreciation for how much stupider things are than when I was your age, and my parents would say the same thing to me. It really is a downward spiral of stupidity sold to youth culture as freedom.

"Anyway, I wonder what changed. Or, really, *why* it changed. How intentional was it? Did someone in a boardroom somewhere literally think up this new dream of music stardom? I guess probably yes. Some marketing genius with a hundred reports open on his desk, poring through data. How do you get kids to want what you want them to want? Well for fuck's sake, you do it with the concept of *cool*. I guess I was an instrument of that architecture. For as long as I agreed the things I wrote about really were cool. But I mean what the hell difference should that have made? I was a junkie. Did I really think I was so much better than everyone else?

"I mean, I *was*. Obviously."

*

Of Scott's 114 email inquiries, 73 are deleted without ever being opened.

*

"If you don't mind touring for tiny audiences until the end of time. If you don't mind no savings and no health insurance. If you don't mind a million nattering opinions about how to make it big. If you're that self-contained. If you're that satisfied with your personal definition of cool."

*

One guy calls Scott at 3 a.m. and says, "Hey, I don't want you to take this personally. But I hate your music. Your band fucking sucks."

EMOTIONAL GRAMMAR

The first Saturday afternoon in December, Kate's mother is eating at Applebee's in a green sweater that half-conceals her bulk. She paws at the white silk scarf around her neck, says, "Oh, I need a reading," and drops face-first into her shrimp 'n parmesan sirloin. Kate's father can't revive her; she's suffered a stroke and by that night, she's dead.

Amanda insists on taking Kate to Binghamton. She borrows a car from her old office-mate Jennifer and barrels them over the George Washington Bridge through static-clung snowflakes the size of postage stamps. Three hours and they play no music. Kate wants to, but worries it would be inappropriate. She bothers herself with a mosaic of memories that never settles, never gets specific enough to steer her into hysterics. The Christopher Columbus Highway is accommodating, delivers the news: winter is here, the hills are sauced brown, the trees are gristle and bone. Amanda is lightly thrilled by the chance to prove her worth. She begins by speaking when spoken to, which means they're almost entirely silent.

They're past Scranton, are almost back into New York state, when Jennifer's car blows a rear tire. Amanda does yeoman's work avoiding a wreck; she feels a chattering wrongness beneath them and leans into the breakdown lane, skidding, feeling sand flood against the undercarriage. They are nowhere. A rock pile doubles as a guardrail and an ancient billboard advertises a fireworks superstore. They creep forward on the bad tire and see a blue "Rest Area" sign.

"Please tell me she's got a spare," Amanda says. Kate doesn't know how to respond.

There's one other car in this frigid little way station, an empty old Hyundai. Amanda pulls up beside it, sees a packet of neon-orange tickets under its wipers. Kate fiddles with her coat buttons and puts on her ski cap. She assumes Amanda has few practical skills.

But they both get out. It's a bright morning, below freezing and windy. Amanda opens the trunk and finds a donut and a miniaturized jack assembly. The jack goes between the wheels, and the crowbar fits together like…so? Amanda goes hands-and-knees and wants to tell Kate to get back in the car, she'll handle it, but…. Dammit, this isn't the kind her father taught her to use. There's a fist-sized nut on one end, it needs to be turned and Amanda can't figure out how. The crowbar segments clank on pavement.

Amanda is nothing if not persistent. Her hands freeze. Finally the jack is tight beneath the car but now she can't fake it, she won't be able to actually lift the car without properly decoding these scratched black crowbar pieces. Long ago, Kate took turns changing tires with Maizie and the sisters, and can see what Amanda is doing wrong. By momentarily withholding this knowledge, she isn't intentionally delaying their arrival in Binghamton, and she's not sparing Amanda's feelings. She's merely waiting to see how things turn out.

What good is action?

She thinks about the drums. She resolves: listen to *Vampire* all the way through and catalog her tendencies. What are her knee-jerk fills? Is her busyness itself a lazy pattern? Does she ever cross up her own vernacular? Was she secretly the reason for their failure? Then a part of her thinks: *What am I talking about? What does it matter?* Maybe she'll move in and take care of her father and never leave Binghamton. Its music scene, such as it is, will become hers. She'll rejoin her old musician pals, or find a high school friend who spends his days fabricating helicopters at Lockheed and his nights waiting for a karaoke slot at T. Mulligan's, and she'll hang around until it seems like the idea of starting a cover band together just materializes from thin air. And then she thinks: *Oh, no. I'm gonna have to introduce Binghamton people to Amanda.*

She says, "Here, let me try."

So Amanda steps back, knuckles scraped, and watches Kate finagle the jack together and twist it with economy, and the car seems to sigh, relieved of its load. It goes up. With a surgeon's twitch Kate's fingers ask for the lug wrench. Amanda obliges. Then she leans against the abandoned Hyundai and feels something beneath her foot. It's a black Coach wallet. There's no cash or ID inside, but plenty of credit cards in the name of "Constantina Ochagavia." Amanda slides the wallet into her waistband and says nothing.

They continue on. Kate directs them down off the interstate and directly into a neighborhood facing a cemetery. The street ends at Antique Row, and a store called "Yesteryear." Next they turn onto a peeling-paint underpass beneath a railroad bridge and up into a greener enclave where the cookie-box houses are in better repair. A couple blocks down Chapin Street Kate sees that the family manor persists despite all. It's yellow with green trim, skinny and deep, three steps up to the porch where Kate's mom performed mitten and umbrella inspections. Blue sacks of raked leaves lean against the house half-open, surrendering their contents to the wind. Kate's stomach is a loose bag of warm slop. She folds forward in the passenger seat.

"I just realized it's Sunday," she says. "He might be at church. I don't have a key."

"We'll try," says Amanda. "Let's go try."

There's a red sticker on the second-floor window; Kate gets out, and her eyes never leave it. Did her parents ever think of razoring it off? She knows it says "Exploding Hearts," the name of a Portland band she loved in 2003, when they perished in a van crash driving home from a gig. Did her parents remember how hard she took that news? Did they remember the black armband she fashioned from an old velvet jumper? It would've been more like her father to notice the destruction of a favored preteen outfit from Kate's skinnier days, and interpret it as surrender to girth. Yet the sticker's continued existence was the first thing she noticed coming home after deprogramming, and here it still is, peering out over Chapin like a punk mini-Cerberus.

The front door is unlocked. Kate's father is in his recliner in the back study, watching an old war movie. Any urge to weep decamps from her heart. They will be the stoic upstaters suffering no illusions about life's fairness.

"We're here, Dad."

"Yes, hello. The service is Tuesday. I wanted it sooner."

"I drove up with my roommate," she says. "I want to help."

"Hi," says Amanda, still standing in the 1950s kitchen. "I'm so sorry."

"Help by coming to church," says her father. "Help by praying your ass off. I'm heading back over there this afternoon. Sit if you're going to sit. Or stand. You can watch me pretend I'm Burt Lancaster. Who outlived his wife by two decades, I should mention."

Kate's mind goes to a poem Sebastian showed her up in Massachusetts: about the little things that lead to madness, a broken shoelace or a stopped-up sink. It isn't a little thing to stand in this room with her mother gone, but his eyeglasses with the hinge Scotch-taped and the ancient maroon plaster parrot by the fireplace with a filament of spiderweb spanning from beak to tail and the overlarge brass crucifix and the absence of any gift their only child ever made or bought for them...they are such little things.

Amanda says, "Actually, I think I read that Burt Lancaster got divorced twice and was survived by his third wife."

Daniel Grush doesn't find this charming. He runs his tongue over his front teeth and nods.

"Have you eaten anything?" Kate says. "What can I make you?"

He grumbles that he's not hungry.

"I'm sorry, Dad. I'm really sorry she left so quickly. I know it must be really hard."

He looks at her for the first time. "You should be sorry," he says.

He intends to be vicious, but it doesn't sting as badly as it could. She can see his blasted heart, its need for a scapegoat. She doesn't have to believe what he's implying. But the tragedy here is exactly this insight: if the things they say don't hurt so much anymore, why hasn't she been here to see them in nearly two years? Anyway, if Kate sees change in herself, it's that today she felt calamity lift scales from her eyes and she ran *toward* Binghamton.

Kate leads them upstairs and Amanda feels awkward, not having considered that happy, mellow Kate could be estranged from anyone. She hears herself say, "I'm sure he's just in shock."

The front bedroom—formerly Kate's—is now a lightly used craft station with a daybed, but she's still magnetized to take that left turn. A new satellite dish looms in the side window, blocking a view of the McCutcheons' gray house and its "sun room" which is literally just four pieces of weather-treated sheetrock tacked onto a hole in a second-floor hallway. Amanda observes a spread of tarot cards hanging on for dear life atop a slanted drafting table. She thinks of Kate's mother interpreting this sitting, perhaps just hours ago, and then she thinks of the poem in *Pale Fire*: "I'm reasonably sure that we survive / And that my darling somewhere is alive / As I am reasonably sure that I / Shall wake at six tomorrow," the gag being that the poet is killed that afternoon.

"So," says Kate, "I don't want you to feel obligated. To come along and listen to the fire and brimstone, I mean."

"Yeah, no, I don't mind." Amanda looks at the tarot. "You grew up pretty religious?"

"There weren't any gypsies around here in my time. Yeah, Methodists in a sea of Catholics. I stopped going when I was 10."

"They didn't force you. That's great."

"I learned to translate 'Jesus died for your sins' as 'God is dead and it's your fault.'"

"I'm not trying to pry," says Amanda. "Whatever you want to talk about, or not talk about. Anything you need."

"Thanks." Kate inspects the open closet, which used to be *her* closet. Peering out from the shadows: is that the old bathroom scale? "Today will be my first mass in, what, almost fifteen years."

"..."

"There was this one time I went on a church camping retreat, I shared a tent with Opal Muggs. No idea where we were, but it was near a river. Five or six little tents off to the side and it was spring but still cold and the only other campers were a family with a pickup truck. They were mountain people or hill people or whatever, and their little girl cried and whimpered all night. The church sisters made a campfire and lit up a hibachi and decided they'd cook all our meat at once, store it away for the rest of the weekend. The sisters seemed so old, but probably were our age now. They sat there talking with us, cutting cooked sausages and for some reason ripping meat from the casings until their fingers burned. They said little prayers each time it hurt: 'Father forgive me!' and 'Most heavenly angels!' Eventually they tucked us all in and Opal and I shivered in our sleeping bags. But then someone was unzipping our tent. It was the father of the mountain family. He must've been pretty drunk. The top half of his body came floating in and I couldn't get my flashlight to go on and he said, 'I'm guessing you girls don't have a lighter?' We said no. Like, he ogled us for a minute and then he left, zipping the zipper back up.

"I don't even know what I thought. Maybe I thought this was pretty normal, of *course* strange men busted into your tent and asked to borrow your lighter when you were 10. The little mountain child was sobbing in the dark and I guess it was pretty eerie, but I might not have even given it a second thought except Opal started trembling and praying: 'And the Lord shall deliver me from every evil work,' stuff like that. I got my flashlight working, and I was goofing around trying to calm her down. I started making shadow puppets, but that majorly backfired. Suddenly there are *animals* outside, we could hear them breathing. And when I put the flashlight up against the tent wall you could see this weird reverse-shadow from the outside, there was a nose and whiskers sniffing us. Opal was weeping and praying. We really thought we were about to get killed and eaten.

"I turned off the light and cried, we both cried, too afraid to call for help or run out of the tent. Maybe a bear was waiting out there for us, or maybe that mountain dad. Opal was so scared she peed in her sleeping bag. But an hour went by and nothing happened. I didn't hear any more animal breathing, and the mountain girl stopped sobbing, and Opal fell asleep. I started to think probably we weren't about to die. But I couldn't fall asleep. I wasn't scared anymore. I was mad. Because even if we were safe, some kids somewhere in the world really were getting killed. And how could that be God's plan?" She lifts the flowery blinds and touches the Exploding Hearts sticker thereunder. "I was *so* profound."

"What happened?" says Amanda. "What was it outside the tent?"

"So then I told my mom I didn't believe in God. No more church for me. They made me go a few more times, but I cried and complained and eventually they gave up." She could swear the sticker feels warmer than the glass around it. "I guess it was cooking all that meat. It attracted some wild beasts. Or maybe it was the hill family's dog? Opal swore it was a bear. Anyway, when we woke up there was nothing. The sisters didn't believe us."

Amanda still has the wallet in her waistband. Is she hiding it from Kate? "When we were little, my dad used to say, 'Religions are all wonderful. They're self-destructing traps.' Like, you get snared by one and it feels like you'll never get out and it teaches you everything it knows. But then it breaks and you get away until the next guru gets you. Gloria did not appreciate this metaphor."

"Funny," Kate says. "I really don't know a single person in New York who goes to church."

Amanda picks up a card from the pile: an old man holding a lantern and a staff, with the words "The Hermit" across the bottom. She says, "Maybe New York has other traps."

Kate looks around. This tiny former bedroom—its doll reenactments of *Titanic,* and the letters to Santa Claus she found in the kitchen trash, and her perpetual re-reading of *The Commitments* which is probably still the only novel she ever read of her own free will, and Sarah McCutcheon texting to tell Mitchell Hesley that Kate like-liked him—offers up mortality in a way her own mother's passing hasn't yet done. The only thing she can think to say is, *Sometimes I felt in control when I lived here.* People would never believe how worried she always was.

They drive her father to church downtown. The redbrick façade is still lovely, but it faces a boarded-up building that used to be a coffee shop beneath a shoe warehouse, on a street with several vacant storefronts and a two-story garage with a chain across its entrance. Amanda finds the church interior opulent, and tries to remove the hick filter Kate has prefixed to this town. But each time they see an old schoolmate's mother or the family of a dimly remembered coworker of her father's, Amanda can feel impatience coming off Kate like a sunburn. Condolences permit contact: sad hugs and awkward double-handshakes. Kate feels annoyed by chipped nail polish and grandmotherly jowls. Her father peacocks around the pews. The white-robed minister steps down to have a private word with him. She sympathizes with her former self's desire for escape.

Partway through a sermon about biblical suffering of the righteous, Amanda's phone rings. She smoothly clicks it silent from outside her pocket and bites her lips.

Kate can't get out of there soon enough. And Amanda admits

it's painful. They want to be solemn and perhaps a weakness of their generation is that solemnity is only tolerable in miniature. There are no ironic eyes around them. Kate sees her father watching her pray and she really puts her back into it, contorts her face. There used to be a tree a couple blocks away that she'd climb after services, while her parents socialized: a perch from which to survey what passed for downtown's grandeur. The haunted house hotel and the baseball stadium. The two-dimensional government ziggurat. The buses wheezing around adorned with that caveman on a stone unicycle. But even that tree's stump is long since gone, replaced by nothing.

They leave the car with her father and walk a few frosty blocks to Toad In The Hole, where some of Kate's old music friends still drink and dream around an Aughts-dominated jukebox. When they walk in, "Trouble Comes Running" is falling into the big empty space and they pull faces, thinking how many times this album guided them to a next gig on their endless greenhorn escapade around the nation. But Spoon stops playing, and a Dressy Bessy song comes on.

Kate leads the way, doesn't recognize the bartender and figures this is about to be one more stupid Binghamton letdown in her life. But several people are gathered in the back, and Kate knows them! They rise and pull her in. She's lightly kissed and spanked.

"You guys, here's Amanda," she says. "First singer I ever played with who doesn't turn herself up any chance she gets."

Everyone goes, "Ohh!" like this is a major diss, and one of the guys says, "Fuck you, I like to hear my golden voice at all times."

"This is David," says Kate. "Violet, Bill, Kenny and Tracy."

"Hi," Amanda says, wondering whether these friends know about the band, its carnage.

"Your mom…" says Violet, and Kate is able to quiet the sentiment with her eyes.

They are waiters and auto mechanics. Nobody wears eyeglasses and gravity hasn't had its way with them. They talk about summer trips down the Delaware, coolers tied to inner tubes. They take turns going to the bathroom to bump coke. Kenny says, "Welcome to the edge of the world," and Kate and Amanda can see the life that might've been Kate's, knitted into this scene. It's not a sad vision. These high school classmates understand the ridiculousness—that they still live here, that their parents still spend hours fretting how little they understand their children—and have built a province around it. They don't talk to their friends who became doctors. They don't dream of New York or L.A. They have fun and rock out.

"Did it hurt?" Bill asks Amanda.

"Did what hurt?"

"When you fell from heaven...and landed on a Chevy Stag?"

The group cracks up.

But they're hyper and kind. They show Kate pictures on their phones, recent gigs around the Finger Lakes, and those gigs' aftermaths. They finish each other's sentences, but gently. Tracy had a recent pregnancy scare and they're trying to find the best infant name of each gender. The current leaders are "Blip" if it's a ghost-girl, and "Fuzz" if it's a ghost-boy.

"Do you ever want to get out of here?" Kate says to Violet, a girl who also gained weight around the same time in their early teenage years but now is gaunt. "I don't say it to be mean."

"I'd go somewhere," Violet says, "if someone could prove to me that everywhere isn't exactly the same."

"It isn't. I don't think it is."

"This is the point in the conversation when you tell me about the Chinese food at four in the morning in New York. I know there are *more* people. I'm just not convinced they're any different."

This is patently ridiculous and Kate wants to say so, wants to talk about ethnicities and income brackets and sexual orientations, but of course she's barely friends with anyone not in her band. Amanda is telling Kenny and David about *Oblomov*.

A new guy comes in carrying a cardboard box and Bill freaks out.

"Oh, this is the thing!" says Tracy.

Over here by the dartboards, Bill and this new guy unpack the box, and the others hold their pint glasses and watch in a circle. Red plastic components are wrapped in clear bags. The new guy puts a thumb drive into a MacBook while Bill reads through instructions.

"This part goes over your face," he says. "Okay, and then just one of these on each hand, I guess. This is like eighty percent 3-D printed material. The guy just made it himself using CAD drawings or something."

"What is it?" says Amanda.

Nobody answers. Kate has known Bill since they were six; he's the drummer she replaced in David's band, and he in turn replaced her when she left for the city. He puts on gloves that have circular sensors for each finger and exposed circuitry and wiring along the wrists and forearms. They look like Iron Man's gauntlets. The third piece is a red ring that goes around his neck, and has a mouthpiece with more exposed wires. Bill turns everything on. The pieces light up green at his fingers and his mouth.

"Jesus," someone says.

Bill walks to the laptop. "All right. He already loaded a bunch of default sounds on here, so I guess let me fuck around."

He holds out his arms and starts clicking his finger-sensors. The laptop issues a techno beat, and Bill controls the pace and sounds by rotating his hands. He overlays new noises onto the beat, fingering more sensors which light up purple and then yellow. Then he blows into the mouthpiece and there's a cool high synthetic whine over the beat bed. When he swings his hands out, the whine loses its hard edge, and now the beat itself becomes a synth trumpet. He slows it down, dancing now, grinning and blowing. The new guy turns the laptop volume way up, and everyone dances with Bill.

It seems like he can do anything. His white-boy boogying *becomes* the beat. He clicks his fingers, changes the sounds by raising his arms, slows things by crouching and blowing into the tube, leaps back up again, points and clicks, makes the beat even louder and more electric by windmilling his arms. Kate and Amanda circle him and it feels like ring-dancing around some 24th-century musical android, as though the music literally comes from Bill's extremities.

"This is fucking incredible!" Kenny says, sidling behind Amanda, touching her hips. She eases herself away. "No more DJ standing behind the laptop!"

"Is this what you guys do!" says Kate.

"It is now!" Kenny says. They used to call him Special-K at least partly for his devotion to ketamine, but he's hyper now, bounding all over the place to Bill's one-man show.

So this is how the night passes, getting drunk and acting crazy: more people coming into Toad In The Hole and turning it into a rave, forms in the half-light streaming by mutely, gesturing vainly but delighted, Amanda with the bartender pulling levers and delivering beers, hypnotized by liquids gushing into glasses, the coy silver foam, Bill eventually gets exhausted and gives up his robotic gear, offers it to Kate, who almost does it, almost dons this crazy paraphernalia and becomes the future. But something pulls her back. Tracy—a wunderkind piano player from the first day Kate met her in the community center basement—slips on the gloves, grinning frightened and delighted, like a child at the zoo being allowed to touch her first elephant.

Soused later on the back-study couch, Amanda listens to a voicemail:

"Mandy, it's Evan Kenner's office calling. Evan would like to discuss *American Idol* and *The Price Is Right*. If you could call us back...."

She ponders the phone's brushed-steel exterior. While she's here to support her best friend at a terrible time, she's also here to ask permission. Maybe their rock dreams were never actually hers. Why should she join them beating their heads against that wall again? Yes, she feels like a turncoat opportunist, with headshots. But the goal isn't a particular *kind* of stardom, is it?

The TV's dead eye glows slightly, and spins. She opens a browser on her phone and looks up Constantina Ochagavia. An address in Susquehanna....

Kate wakes crooked on the daybed. Ancestral light crowds her old bedroom and she doesn't feel that bad. Dry mouth, empty stomach. She's still dressed in last night's clothes, which will require maintenance before the funeral tomorrow. Her suitcase contains sweatpants, too tight. She stands and walks into the hall, knowing she's supposed to expect her mother's voice from the back bedroom or down in the kitchen. She's prepared for that trauma. But she's numb. It's difficult to tell if the numbness is insulating her from pain, or if things actually don't hurt.

Lightly hypnotized by the octagonal window at the stairs' side landing, she's aware of a new runner beneath her feet, wonders when her father installed it. (Certainly he did it himself.) She lands on the first floor in a geometric sunlight pool, bathes in it. Maybe it's not surprising she feels like this is a new place, and not a schoolgirl prison. Somehow the world has taught her about grieving: it will feel unreal, you will see things differently.

The kitchen and living room are empty, so the last chance to find someone home is the study: site of begged permission, headshakes, outdated cultural references and so many TV guffaws. Kate waits in the kitchen and tries to torture herself by speculatively remembering things about her mother. The time she heard other girls teasing Kate because the daughter spilled chocolate milk on herself, so the mother poured it across her own blouse and laughed. The time her mom heard Derek Cooper telling Kate he didn't like her "that way," but pretended she hadn't, and took her to Little Venice where she told scandalous jokes about the Cooper family and they laughed all night. Even the way she wept over Kate's presumably lost soul. It wasn't merely a matter of a distant, disapproving mother with more faith in God than in her daughter. It was complicated: because her mother sensed something in Kate had broken. What would it have been like to watch herself grow up? The need to fit in, coupled with a readiness to abandon ship at the first sign she didn't. The bold, depthless assertions. (Has any child ever been easier to talk out of an opinion?) The discovery of the drums, practice on which seemed only to isolate her further. In her mother's mind, they'd laid down a bed of faith, something to protect and comfort Kate if only she'd abandon a contrariness permanently implanted by…something. And to top it off, Kate vanished into the Holy Church of Convergence, a mockery. The captured daughter screaming that she *does* believe in God, she *does* have faith…but the blasphemous kind. Brainwashed. Imagine how painful that was.

Kate understands what this day will be. She doesn't go into the study. She strides back upstairs, changes clothes, and discovers that her father's and Jennifer's cars are gone. But that's all right. It's not a long walk.

At the same time, Amanda is driving back into Pennsylvania. Finding a street address for Constantina Ochagavia was simple, but a cursory web search also turned up the woman's arrest record. She recently finished nine months in Muncy for child endangerment.

So why not just throw the wallet away, or hand it off to police?

Well, it's the details: a newspaper account said Constantina held her ex-husband at gunpoint, tearily demanding child support. Amanda wants to believe she isn't defined by her own broken home…yet she can't help imagining a woman—a family—who needs one good turn, and she's not sure she trusts the cops to actually deliver the wallet. So she's driving listening to whatever's on her phone, which at first is the Replacements but she shuts that down right quick. The wallet rides in the passenger's seat. *It's a pretty nice wallet. She's got a lot of credit cards. Was that her abandoned Hyundai?*

Yes, by any objective measure this is dumb, especially keeping up with highway traffic wearing a donut on her back wheel. But maybe getting away for a couple hours makes sense. She doesn't text Kate. Kate doesn't text her. She sings:

Susquehanna
Oh don't you cry for me
I come from California
With an agent stalking me

Constantina's address is far outside the cute town. The road slithers deep into the dying hills, then simply ends. Her phone has it wrong: there's no connector to LR 1007 here. Road dust eddies through her dead-end view of a lake blooming with algae. Of course, where others see signs to give up, Amanda doubles down. "To win Pish's heart," her mother has said, "all a boy has to do is get himself buried in a secret tomb in the Arctic Circle and mail her a sketchy map."

The maze leads her back north, then across a mushy path east. Her wheels wiggle. "For real?" she says, and imagines the donut bucking completely off. But she keeps going.

She should call Gloria. Later.

A trailer park comes up on her left; it's a snarl of interred mobile homes and rusted-out pickups. She gets out at the entrance, begging for a decipherable numbering system. None is evident. Maybe in summer this grove is green and charming, but the year's end isn't kind to it. A fat raindrop slaps Amanda on the forehead, and every trailer underside and overturned barrel seems it might conceal a wild dog, or worse. There are...three...four...five homes in here, all up on cinderblocks, no mailboxes, no office, no sign of life. She steps over slushy vegetation to knock on the first door; the loose metal clomp speaks to the place's abandonment. She's approaching the second door when she sees movement near the fourth.

Rain comes. The path between homes immediately turns to mud, and the horror-movie setup is basically complete. She leaps over the ground's softest spots, and approaches the fourth trailer. The door opens before she gets to it.

A woman Amanda's age wears a flower dress and taps a Band-Aid-covered knuckle against the doorframe.

Amanda says, "Are you Constantina?"

"No," says the woman. "I am Nadia." She does have a Slavic accent.

"Does Constantina live here? I have something for her."

Nadia gives an unintentionally comic look over her shoulder. Amanda can see into the kitchen: garbage on the floor, toys tipped, crayon drawings stuck to a refrigerator. Soft-chinned Nadia says, "No. Next house."

"It's not anything bad," says Amanda. "She'll be glad I came. I've got something that belongs to her." She shows the wallet. Nadia's eyes are magnetized by it.

"Mama!" she says, and steps back into the trailer. The place smells like cheap tobacco and shoe polish, and the raindrops-on-roof sound like someone throwing rocks through paper. Amanda can't help herself, and comes all the way inside.

Nadia waits in a little hallway, staring, decidedly not fetching her mother. "Is anything inside?" she says.

"Oh. Yeah. Credit cards, no money. I found it at a rest area up on the interstate."

"No money."

"Well," says Amanda. "It was empty. I didn't steal it."

"Yes," Nadia says. She's overweight and acne-scarred, but her curled hair is the result of professional attention, and her fingernails are newly painted. She doesn't smile, makes no effort to ingratiate, and Amanda doesn't know whether to chalk this up to cultural difference or rudeness.

"I looked her up on the Internet. Your mother."

"..."

"I wanted to...help."

"Thank you," says Nadia, drowsily holding out her hand. "I give to her."

"Why don't I...? I mean, I came all this way. Can I meet her?"

Nadia shrugs and walks to the living room. A muted TV is tuned to the kind of celebrity talk show on which until recently Amanda believed she'd soon appear. Nadia sits on a loveseat and slurps milk and porridge. No sounds come from the rest of the trailer.

"She's asleep?" Amanda says.

Nadia just eats.

"Are *you* Constantina?"

"No."

"There's nobody else in here, and I can see you have a child. If it's you.... I mean, I'm not judging or anything. I just don't want to leave this with someone it doesn't belong to. You can understand that."

"Mama!"

"It's just.... I know what it's like. I mean," she looks around, "I don't know everything, probably."

"What," says Nadia. "What do you know?"

"I know what it's like when the man exits the picture."

Nadia doesn't impress easily. She breathes into the back of her hand. "Leave the wallet. Do not leave it. But do not expect people to kiss you."

"Well," Amanda says. "I guess we're stuck. Because you want the wallet but claim you aren't the owner. And I'm only giving it to the owner."

Nadia guzzles the rest of her porridge.

"How old is your son or daughter?"

"I do not have one."

Amanda feels the kitchen wall indent against her weight. She makes her face read stubborn.

Nadia sighs. "She does not have a gun. Not anymore. There is no phone. So is difficult to call that man. Mr. Hopkins. Anyway she has no English. She plays durak with the ladies, and eats same soup for three days. She is simple. She still puts her kerchiefs over anthills."

"..."

"Search this place. See what you find." Nadia puts up her hands. "Mama!"

When did Amanda's radar get so ineffective? Is she listening to a social misfit or a madwoman referring to herself in the third person? "I'm not searching anything," Amanda says. "I mean, can't you see I've gone out of my way to do you a favor?"

Nadia watches the TV.

It only occurs now to Amanda that this is a scene from one of her Russian novels. Marmeladova and Chichikov, who in fact occasionally become more real to her than actual humans. Some archaic question of honor, some parable about being lost in plain sight. "Listen," she says, "I don't think you appreciate how strange this is. You're telling me…. I mean, look in your kitchen. There are toys all over your kitchen, and if you're saying you don't have a—"

"Oh, *fuck!*" Nadia says, and she's off the loveseat, hurtling in this direction. Amanda covers her face. But Nadia runs past her and now there are also sounds outside: a car engine coughing to life. The front door heaves open, Nadia is slopping out into the rain, Amanda follows. *"Mama!"* says Nadia.

Ahead of an oily cloud, one of the hoary pickups is swerving away in reverse. Amanda sees that the trailer has a side door, through which a middle-aged lady has for some reason escaped. Nadia waves her arms, calling, but the white-haired woman behind the wheel backs out of the trailer park, barely misses Jennifer's car, and slams the truck into drive.

"What's happening!" says Amanda.

"Oh, no," Nadia says. "Stupid woman. She hears us. She thinks you are…. Come!" She runs toward the road, slips in the rain.

Amanda chases after. "She thinks I'm what?"

Nadia reaches Jennifer's car and tries the locked door. "She does not have English. She thinks you are police."

"Why does she think that? What's she doing wrong?"

"Nothing. Nothing. Please. These ladies, they think it is Moscow. Please, help me."

Amanda reaches the car, doesn't unlock it. "Where's she going?"

"Maybe to the school to get Olie. She says, 'I will never go back to prison,' and I say, 'Call the parole officer Mr. Hopkins,' but the cellular does not work here and she does not call, so now she believes there is trouble. Please. Please, I borrow your car. She maybe will take Olie and run away."

"*You* thought I was police. *You* said search the place. Are you really her daughter?"

"She treats me like a daughter," says Nadia, stepping around the car, pulling at the passenger door. "So please."

Amanda thinks, *Jesus, whose fucking wallet is this?* But she clicks the car open and they're driving south on this half-paved road, and Nadia is saying, "Faster, faster."

"She really is Constantina?"

"Yes."

"Why didn't you just go get her for me?"

Nadia somehow manages to convey indifferent pique while also urging Amanda to speed.

They chase what they can't see. The wipers are on high, Amanda clicks the defogger and the A/C. The driving is crazy, and she thinks they're about to find overturned taillights in a ditch like in *Fargo*. Of course Amanda wants to stop, this is nonsense, these women say they haven't done anything wrong so there's nothing to run from. What if they're meth dealers? She imagines Gloria telling her to pull over, but she doesn't.

"Here!" says Nadia, pointing a manicured nail. "Left!"

They skid through a stop sign. How can the donut still be attached?

Now they're on a commercial street, albeit a thoroughly abandoned one. There's still nothing up ahead, no sign of the truck. Amanda finds herself pressing the accelerator hard. It's Monday noon, a funeral is tomorrow, and then there's a decision coming: to leave her friends in New York, to return to L.A. and trust more untrustworthy people.

"I don't want to do this anymore," she says, and Nadia says, "Please."

Amanda looks down and her right foot is flush against the car floor. They can barely see the street, let alone whether anything is coming at them in the rain. The engine's high whine is earsplitting. Even at rest, Nadia's mouth lands in a sneer.

"Olie's school," Nadia says, striking her window.

When one foot isn't enough, Amanda brakes with both. They skid. For a moment it feels like they'll flip. As they whip around in circles, Amanda looks at Nadia, whose lids are half-closed.

They're stopped. The wipers catch up with the rain. They were lucky to come at the school from its rear, in a massive, mostly vacant parking lot. Constantina's truck idles not far away, headlights on, driver's side door open.

"I really only just had her wallet," says Amanda.

Nadia gets out and lumbers toward the school. Amanda pursues. They bang through a fire exit and it's another maze: dim halls, classroom doors with rectangular portholes, an evacuation diagram displaying the floor plan. Amanda loses her bearings and just follows Nadia's flower dress, soaked, bereaved. Left, left, right, deep into the darkness, and for some reason Amanda thinks of Minuteman's layout, the practice rooms down here, the studio just over there. Failure isn't such a tragedy. The four of them haven't even consciously discussed taking a break, it's simply happened. She hasn't seen Sebastian since the day Jacob got fired and her tether has never had more slack. But she believed in what they played. It's incredible how crushed she actually is.

The old ex-con stands outside a classroom, gazing in, sobbing. Nadia approaches, and hugs her from behind. She whispers Russian words into Constantina's ear—if this really is Constantina—and the mother nods and sags forward under Nadia's weight, still watching the children on the glass' other side. Amanda has the wallet in both hands, and it feels like it's on fire.

Meantime, Kate is caught in the deluge. She's already most of the way down Chapin so there's no point turning back or running; she's soaked through. She could've grabbed her mother's slicker, imagines being lost in its musty bulk.

She crests the hill at Ayres, one that seemed unrelentingly steep atop a childhood bike. From here to the river is a descent, and the street is awash. She pauses, and feels the water pull at her sneakers. The Spieths lived in this red house with no yard, Miss Gosling used to have the first-floor apartment up there on the right, and further along Kate was once terrified of trick-or-treating at that brick house because Opal Muggs said she saw a girl get her dress pulled down near the bushes. And were the houses on Riverside always so jauntily colored? Half-red, half-orange; gray with a black front turret covered by yellow stars; shocking peach; electric purple. Has irony landed late in Binghamton after all?

Triangulated between a Catholic convent, a synagogue and a neoclassical Protestant church, Dr. Dubront's house emerges from behind its veil of rain. A hundred times Kate stood out here considering how stupid, paying a stranger to listen. But Jean was a good person. Without her, the end of high school and the years thereafter would've been even less tolerable. Kate can stack all the appointments atop one another: sitting in the back waiting room, Jean beckoning her in, removing her shoes, the same spot on the gold corduroy couch, the same two red pillows beneath her left elbow, handing over her parents' copay, waiting awkwardly while Jean fiddled with the calendar function on her PDA to schedule

Kate for next week. Seen one way, all those sessions came to nothing: she still vanished into Maizie's van. Seen another, these past couple years of fun maybe wouldn't have been possible.

There's still a little sign that says, "Please Ring The Doorbell, It Signals Your Arrival." Kate does, and steps inside. She sees a pair of men's shoes in front of Jean's closed office door. It still smells like potpourri in here.

The waiting room has the same old fish tank, the same old blue futon, the same old books: *Bygone Binghamton*, *LIFE: Our Century In Pictures*, *The Secret Language Of Birthdays*, *A New Earth*, *The Untethered Soul*, etc. Kate sees water on the battered wood floor, looks at the ceiling to discover what's leaking, then realizes it's her. She's a drowned rat, and she can't sit down like this. She also can't just stand here making puddles. Her breath comes fast. Is there anyplace to put her sodden coat? Should she turn on the space heater? *No, no: don't blame this place for your anxiety, fatty.*

She hasn't played the drums in…a month? More?

She does take off the coat, and carries it like a dead animal to the little-used back bathroom, which has a never-used claw-footed tub. She also takes off her shoes and socks and her sweater, and puts everything into the tub. Then she steps on all of it, back and forth in the tub, wringing it all out.

At which point there's a clattering in the hallway: the sounds of Jean coming out of her office. Kate stops squashing her clothes. She doesn't move. Footsteps creak this way.

It wasn't the bear sniffing at her tent that ruined Kate's faith.

"Hello?" It's Dr. Dubront's voice. "I'm not expecting another appointment for a half-hour."

Kate tries to say something, but discovers she's hiding. She looks at the bathroom door. It's cracked open.

"Frances, are you early?"

Kate sweeps her cold hair out of her face.

"I know someone's in here," Jean says. "You tracked rain all over the place."

If only this sudden storm would blow open a window or send a tree smashing into the house. Something to distract her former therapist, so Kate could escape.

The footsteps stop. Kate holds her breath. The bathroom door creaks open.

Jean's face is frightened, and she scans the room. Then she

becomes the woman Kate recalls: mildly curious, slightly exasperated. "Kate Grush? You're standing in my tub?"

She remembers me. I thought for sure she wouldn't.

"I was hoping," says Kate, "that you could see me."

"Huh," Jean says. "First tell me you're all right."

"Yes. I am. I just got really wet and I didn't want to drip—"

"I'm glad. Now, you know the way scheduling works, Kate. Showing up unannounced is inappropriate. You're welcome to stay as long as the rain lasts, but then I want you to go home and call us this afternoon, use the appropriate channels, and we'll schedule you."

Kate has a card she hadn't realized she was willing to play. She says, "My mom died. It was really sudden." She's shivering now, maybe surprised by her own treachery.

And she rediscovers the pleasure of momentarily stumping Jean Dubront.

"Oh, I.... Oh. I'm so sorry, Kate. That's...."

"I'm only in town for another day. Anyway, I was really hoping you could see me."

Jean looks warm in a heavy white turtleneck sweater. She looks like the embodiment of dry sanity. You do the next thing. You worry about what you can control. You don't bother with death until the time comes. The air between them is thick with the secrets Kate once shared.

They set up an appointment for three hours hence. Kate leaves her wet rags in the tub and sits beneath a blanket in the waiting room.

Other patients come at their assigned times. Kate smiles at them, but there's no desire for conversation. It's almost unthinkable: you arrive rehearsing what you'll say to the doctor, keeping your finger on the core of this week's emotional humiliations. Stuffed in this little room with another soul making similar calculations? The only possible interaction other than polite silence would be hysterical mocking laughter. One patient is an incredibly handsome Asian man, and Kate imagines wordlessly taking his shirt off, reading his tattoos. Then she realizes it's Corey Chin, younger brother of a snotty girl she knew in high school, and everything is awful.

During the last session before hers, she sleeps on the futon and dreams she's stuck on a highway: a snowstorm has caused an accident and traffic is stopped. She's forced to abandon her car and walk to a rest area, where she finds her mother trying to sell baked goods to a restaurant owner. The Grush women pretend not to know one another, and Kate takes a bite of one of her mother's pies and raves. It's a diabolical little scheme, but Kate has to play a gig a hundred miles away. She encourages the owner to purchase her mother's desserts and hitchhikes away in the freezing, realizing she won't meet anyone she knows ever again.

"Kate? I can see you now."

Jean's office furniture is completely changed: new couch, different desk, no pillows.

They endure twenty minutes of falseness, with Kate playing the despairing daughter updating her life's relatively happy recent events. Jean nods and smiles when appropriate, is never so engrossed that her eyes don't occasionally flicker to the clock behind the couch. In describing the rise and fall with Sidelong, Kate realizes she expected it: of course she found herself grist for another mill, of course they arrived too late on the scene, of course her belief was betrayed. Jean sketches a few notes.

Then she says, "I see two avenues for us this afternoon, Kate. I'd be glad to talk about how you're dealing with your mother's passing. But I hear something else going on."

"..."

"Do you want to talk about your music career?"

She doesn't. At the moment she could give two shits about the drums. She opens her mouth to answer, and she's nearly in tears. "Y'know, I was thinking.... I was thinking you could hypnotize me. I remember you offered a few times, and I was like, 'Uh, no.' But I think I need it."

"You need it bec—"

"I mean, you used to try to get me to talk about it, and being completely honest I wasn't really sure sometimes what we were even talking about and I know you thought I was playing dumb and maybe I was, but I was always afraid of, I dunno, being *defined* by something that happened a long time ago. Just...*listen* to me, Jean, even saying this I can't get out of my own way. I'm to the point where maybe I just...should know?"

Jean makes that stumped expression again, which is usually so gratifying. "Okay. First of all, while I think hypnotism can be a good tool, I devote an entire session to it, Kate, so I'm afraid we wouldn't have enough time left. And second of all...."

"Second of all you have no idea what I just said."

"No," says Jean. "I think I do. But I want to say: I'm hesitant. You're not a regular patient anymore, and you live far away. One session isn't...."

"..."

"..."

"If it happened, I want to know who," Kate says.

"..."

"Do you understand what I'm saying?"

"I think so," says Jean. "Your parents believed you were abused as a child, and you want to know whether it's true."

Kate holds her breath and touches her own face.

Jean gets up, crosses to a file cabinet, finds a thick folder and returns. Browsing the contents, she says, "This is complicated, Kate. It was always quite...complicated." For a few minutes, the doctor reads silently. Kate watches the second hand sweep around a portable clock whose numbers glow alien green. Rain still clobbers the windows, and her mother would probably say, *Thank God it isn't a few degrees colder.*

"I don't think you're aware," Jean says, "that I spoke with your parents many times. The first time, that's standard when I begin seeing a minor. But we talked extensively after that."

So. They were calculating behind her back, and not that long ago. Kate puts both hands on her own stomach.

"When you were nine or ten years old, you changed, it seemed like overnight to them. You said things. You didn't want to be touched. And when they tried to ask you about it, you retreated further. So when I talked with them, it was obviously many years later and some of the details had faded. At the time they didn't have the...I'll call it the emotional grammar."

"You never said this to me," says Kate. "You never came right out."

"I did suggest hypnotism, but no, you're right."

"You hinted. Coming here I always thought you were.... I was always ready for those *hints*. I was always ready to fight them off."

"It was such an awkward situation," Jean says. "I'm sure I could've handled it better."

"..."

"Obviously this is such a difficult.... Your mother being

gone."

"..."

"I wasn't sure if I believed them," Jean says. "I wasn't sure it happened. They thought it explained what they remembered: how you rebelled, refused church, gained weight. They believed it was the only possible explanation. They believed it explained everything, even when you...disappeared. They still came to me for sessions, to work through the guilt of what they allowed to happen."

The feeling of needing to cry evaporates. She sits forward and tries to hurt Dr. Dubront with her eyes.

"I never wanted to bring it up with you directly, Kate. I had severe doubts. In my observing, you didn't fit the pathology of someone who'd been molested as a younger child. But I worried if we talked about it out in the open, it might plant a suggestion, and set your anxiety back much further. But it's obvious I planted one anyway, it's obvious you were on to me. I was wrong. I'm sorry."

"Did it happen?" says Kate. "Or did they just make it up?"

The line of Jean's lips grows wider, a practiced gesture to convey neutrality.

"I mean are they just bad parents who couldn't deal with who I grew up into?"

"Your parents cared so much, they kept coming back. They wanted to investigate. We even got as far as assembling a list."

"..."

"You're right," Jean says. "In some ways, coming back to talk about you.... It was the closest they could come to examining themselves. But they expressed so much love. And I have to be honest: I can't disprove their conclusion, either. It's possible. So let me directly ask the questions I always shied away from. What memories do you have, Kate? Do you remember being...touched?"

Well, she doesn't.

Whatever might've happened to her is thoroughly wiped away. Is it possible the things she does remember have been sanitized? Failing to find a lighter, did the mountain father actually fully enter the tent and expose himself to Kate and Opal Muggs? Did her drum teacher lure her into a restroom? Did her Uncle Joe derive sick pleasure from horsey rides, the memories of which until now Kate has treasured?

"The feeling," she says. "That…feeling of disaster. I talked with you about it so many times. Does that mean something? Does it mean they were right?"

"Of course not. Of *course* not. And this was always my point. Rebellion comes in a million forms, for a million reasons. And really, how were you rebelling? Punk music? Too many sweets? You weren't in jail. You weren't promiscuous. You were such a good kid."

But it's possible. It *is* possible that there's an explanation for the anxiety that overfilled her teen years, and then sent her into Father James' clutches. She says, "Tell me about the list."

Jean squirms in her chair.

"You have it?"

The doctor hands over a sheet of yellow lined paper. There are maybe twenty names: her fourth-grade teacher, school staff, clergy, friends' parents.

The front doorbell rings. The next patient is here. Kate folds the list, puts it in her pocket. As they're saying goodbye, she notices the rain has stopped.

"Maybe you could come back tomorrow," Jean says as Kate puts her shoes back on.

"The funeral's tomorrow," says Kate.

Back home, she sees both cars parked in the driveway. She sits in the dining room, gazing at crystal wine glasses nobody ever uses. Amanda is on the phone upstairs and her father is presumably watching TV in the back. She unfolds the list.

It happened. It didn't happen.

She'll print out a map of Binghamton. She'll put a red 'X' on each former home of everyone on the list, and then research everyone's whereabouts fifteen years hence. She'll stay in town long enough to interview those who haven't fled. If anyone's died in the interim, she'll sweet-talk their relatives. Getting around the country to find the other suspects will be a challenge, but if she can cram herself into the back of an old van to ramble all over the place selling flowers or playing shows, surely she can borrow someone's car for targeted strikes.

She puts her head down on the table, this lacquered oak table where she once spread out college rejection letters, where Uncle Joe taught her how to play poker before he got locked up for kiting checks. Her eyes close.

What would it be like if she could talk to Inch again? The best friend she never had. Would Inch tell her to get going, tackle this problem head on, figure out the mystery of what happened to her—what *made* her sullen and hesitant—so she can get on with her life?

She stands before a puzzle.

It happened. It didn't happen.

She thinks for a long time.

She remembers all the gigs.

She calmly tears the yellow paper to bits.

Upstairs, Amanda hears Evan Kenner's assistant click back on the line. "Mandy? Are you still there? I don't have him. Can you hold?"

"It's fine," she says. "You can just have him phone me back."

"This other call shouldn't take long. Can you hold?"

Amanda stands over the tarot spread. Moving any of the cards seems like it would be disrespectful. She doesn't know the positions or what anything means…she reads "The World," "King of Wands," "Seven of Pentacles," "The Chariot," "Page of Cups," "Ace of Cups," "Queen of Swords," "Two of Pentacles," "The Hierophant" and "The Lovers." There's another click.

"Mandy?"

"Yes."

"I still don't have him."

"No problem."

"Can you hold? Let me check again."

The L.A. sun is no doubt burning outside this young guy's window. He can step out and see green, smell the jasmine and sugar and gasoline.

"Mandy?"

"Yes."

"I have Evan."

"Great."

The line clicks again.

"Mandy?"

"Yes."

"Hey, it's Evan. I was just on the phone with James Phelps at Fox. Let's just say he wouldn't discourage an *Idol* audition. It's not like you're advancing automatically to the finals, but on talent alone he's got no question, and obviously the conversation didn't actually happen on the record, and you couldn't have a formal relationship with us for however long you're on the show."

"I don't really watch it," says Amanda. "I mean, I've seen it."

"He was very complimentary. It's pretty rare to hear him get excited like that. He's usually a close-to-the-vest kind of guy."

"It kind of feels like a step back."

"A step back to take a hundred steps forward. The only comparable winner they've ever had on there is Carrie Underwood. I'm assuming you wouldn't sneeze at that kind of coin."

"Then there's the game show."

"Right," Evan says, as his voice changes to an irresolute version of itself. "Listen, your name is making the rounds. *Price Is Right* is looking for a pretty girl to turn over merchandise. Good money. But you want me to prove I'm not all about commission? I mean, you're a singer. The long game. We're all about the long game."

"So you're telling me to do what?"

"I can't tell you what to do, I mean, there'll be other offers. I don't do modeling personally but the agency does. Bobby can talk to you about reality TV if you want to head that way."

"Isn't *American Idol* reality TV?"

"You know what I mean. Go live in a house with a bunch of beautiful strangers. Go on a date, get a rose."

"And Kid Centrifuge?"

"Yeah. Okay. Remind me again?"

"Kid Centrifuge. My band."

"Oh, right. Again, not really my area. I did run the songs by those guys, but we're a big shop. The level of rock act we'd ever do a deal for, it's like, there's about five of them in the world and they've all got a dozen albums already. You as a solo, kind of a pop/dance thing? Listen. Maybe. We're full-service, there's a few producers I can call, okay? Think about it, Mandy, and I'll give you a shout later in the week."

"Does that mean you're hanging up?"

"It's great feedback. It lets me know where your head is at. I'm not worried. Don't worry, okay?"

She tumbles to the daybed, tightens her abs and glutes by habit, catches herself doing it. "Did *Price Is Right* make an offer? Evan? Hello?" But he's gone.

Back downstairs, Kate's cheekbone gets sore pressing against the dining room table, and she thinks by now her mother would've told her to stop smearing her oily skin all over the nice furniture.

Later, she's going upstairs to smash that fucking scale.

But now she gets up and walks to the kitchen, and realizes for two days she's been steadfastly *not* looking at anything: avoiding the chair where her mother drank coffee and did crosswords every morning, the pegs from which an unnecessary number of spare keys hang, the poetry magnets on the refrigerator that haven't moved in a decade ("God / Is / Hungry / For / Love"), the drawer beneath the silverware which conceals—perhaps only Kate knows this—a box containing the veil her mother wore at her first communion (she converted for Daniel) as well as a sonogram picture of the baby she lost. And the photographs. There are framed pictures on every wall and Kate hasn't examined a single one.

She finds herself in the back study. Her father is in his chair watching TV. She sits on the couch, her mother's spot. It was probably the last place she saw her mother alive. She places her hands on the fabric. Scott and Sebastian will be up tomorrow for the funeral, and then she'll leave, and maybe she's never coming back. She says, "Dad, I want to talk about what happens next," and her father makes a compassionate face and mutes the television.

"All right."

"I guess I'm wondering. Are you planning to go through her things?" But this isn't really what she's wondering.

"Yes," says her father. "I guess so."

"Because if you want. I can."

Her father's lips tighten, the way Jean Dubront's did.

What's been strange is how fine Kate has been, how at peace. But no more. The thoughts and acts of a woman who has a mother no longer apply. Her mom's gone. Not watching over. Not gently moving on. No matter how strained they became after the Church of Convergence, her mother cared more about Kate than any other person in the world. Felt tortured by the idea something might've happened to her daughter. Wished today's Kate would call more. Believed the future would bring them together. Died without answers. Kate tries to touch bottom, and recall the equanimity with which she's faced the past couple days. But it's gone. She's floating alone.

And she lets it out.

She is abject, and cries beyond the limits of her breath. It's a surrender, but no thoughts accompany it. It's all body. She bellows. Snot and tear-water everywhere. She shakes. It goes for several minutes, and she thinks she's got it under control and reaches to an end table for tissues. But no, it's here again, this visitation of pain. She cries more. It just keeps going.

At some point she looks at her father. He's watching her with cool empathy. And now she does think, she thinks: *Why doesn't he get up and hug me?* And this makes her weep harder, for the untouched infant she must have been, for the loneliness that's been her birthright. She tips into self-pity. The crying goes on much longer, and now she has to admit part of it is just to see if she can get him out of that fucking chair.

SURRENDER

He walks near the bodies. He's supposed to be impressed, but the names still don't mean anything to him. Bob Mould. Rick Nielsen. Billy Zoom. Someone named Gibby Haynes apparently demolished his, but still saw fit to sign it. Hoop gets offended when Sebastian isn't worshipful enough of these mounted guitars, so he pauses on entering, scratches his chin.

The living room is small and anarchic. Hoop already has his mahogany Taylor 324 across his lap, and he's playing along to an old-fashioned blues tune barking out of his seriously tall speakers. Sebastian clears away magazines, a dirty plate and a leaking tobacco pouch, so he can slide into the window seat. He's not an acoustic guy, but when Hoop suggested they play together some afternoons, he went to the Guitar Center in Paramus and bought a $129.99 Mitchell with his mother's credit card. It's got the world's tallest saddle and you could drive an 18-wheeler under the strings, but there's pride in making mediocre equipment sound good. Hoop's Top Grand cost somebody more than a grand—not Hoop, probably a musician friend—and it does have a ringing orchestral character. But Sebastian doesn't do guitar envy.

"Big Mama Thornton," says Hoop. "'Life Goes On.'"

"I'm not here for Music History 101," Sebastian says. "I'm here to play."

Hoop grins. "You little shit."

They click off the stereo. Hoop plays the beginning of "Wish You Were Here," and Sebastian fills in variants on blues licks that appear on the record. Hoop shakes his head, keeps going, sings the first verse. It's C-D-Am-G then D-C-Am-G and Sebastian is careful to watch Hoop's hands, and if the older man is struggling to get to the next chord, Sebastian pauses. A few days ago, Hoop introduced him to "Life By The Drop" by Stevie Ray Vaughn, so they do that one next: the lead-in is a pretty simple A-minor blues scale in the open position, but when Sebastian zips through it, Hoop goggles. The rest of the song is easy, and Hoop does a good job except on the F#m barre chord, on which they hear the telltale plink of a badly pressed string.

It's cool. These aren't lessons. On the surface it's just two pals messing around, and Sebastian doesn't get impatient. His bearded friend, the mischief-maker, has no designs on being a musician. Hoop makes a production over how Sebastian is slumming, coming in to Hoboken and putting up with his classic-rock mutilations. But of course each man knows what's really going on.

"You know 'Phantom Limb' by the Shins?" says Hoop. "Grab a capo."

"All right."

"Man, when I first started learning chords...I mean. I told you I was past thirty when I first really picked up a guitar, other than to move it so I could reach a needle. But anyway, when I first started learning, and I got the G and the D and the A. I was just so delighted how easy some of my favorite songs were to play. In the first week, I'm *almost* playing 'Bad Moon Rising.' A couple months of practicing, there were probably a dozen songs, two dozen, I could really play. That was cool. And then it got old. I mean, I started feeling disdain for these songs—some of my favorite songs in the world—because they were so rudimentary. As if I'd been fooled into thinking they were these works of art. I mean, they are. But they were so simple, it seemed like a cheat."

"Uh-huh."

"So in a way I get your complaints."

Sebastian looks at the street downstairs. There's a Century 21 sign in a flowerbed, a common sight on a block that was underwater a year ago thanks to Sandy. Hoop was trapped in this apartment for the better part of four days and, he says, probably would've used again out of distressed boredom, had any smack been close at hand. He's supposedly working on a book about Legs McNeil and *Punk* magazine, though Sebastian has never seen him write.

"But Jesus," Hoop says, "Stevie Ray. I mean, the way it makes you feel. He's *right there*, it's thrilling. You really think the electronic music zombies ever make anyone feel that way?"

These afternoons they talk a lot about music genres, and the terrible state of what's popular. When he's not genuflecting to the classics, Hoop has a roster of underappreciated acts—indie rockers mostly from five years ago—to which he regularly returns: Bishop Allen, Sun Kil Moon, Sondre Lerche, Wild Beasts, Pinback, the Donkeys, Blind Pilot, Shearwater, Minus the Bear, Ra Ra Riot, the Microphones.... Sebastian wishes his bandmates, who so delight in "educating" him, could hear this holy roster of obscurity and be shamed.

But today, Hoop's invocation of "electronic music" sounds like a taunt, and Sebastian feels a flare of anger, not least because he resisted a taste of Adderall before he drove over here. He says, "I hear you. But. Like, I would hate to think you're saying that I.... Scott and the rest of them, it's like they can't tell the difference between dance and electronica, right? You know the songs I used to record by myself."

"Sure. Of course."

"Based on that, you think I know a single thing that's popular in clubs right now?"

"I'm almost sure you don't," Hoop says.

"So I guess what I'm saying is what I don't need," he's cottonmouthed, "is another speech where somebody says *I'm* what's wrong, 'me and my type.'"

"Fair. That's fair, man."

"How many times have I heard it? 'If Sebastian had his way....' Or just looking at me funny, thinking I'm messing up a song on purpose because I want to play something else. The Sidelong remix? I think Scott expected me to hear it and be like, 'Hey, that's great!' Pope replaces the drums and speeds everything up, and because it's done on a computer I'm supposed to be like, 'Wow, finally, just what I always wanted.' But the point is," and now Sebastian is fully angry, "everybody's attitude is it's *my* world. What bullshit! I had a couple songs, one record nobody bought! Jesus, if it's my world, I sure wish somebody would've told me!"

Hoop scratches his biggish belly and inspects his guitar's neck. He says, "Randy Pope is a douchebag's douchebag." His lips are flat and chiseled-looking, expanding his meditative, warhorse look. "So, did you use today?"

Sebastian lets it go. He knows Hoop doesn't consider him part of the problem. He plays the chords to "Roshambo," double-time. In place of the lyrics, he sings, "No no no no no."

"Hey," says Hoop, "you want something to eat? I could order Chinese. Yeah, today's pop songs. Fuck. Even putting aside the music, the statements themselves are all just.... It's one of two choices. It's either 'I'm so different!' declarations, like you know that song 'Royals'? Ugh. Or else it's trash-talking self-aggrandizement. Either way, it ain't you. God, this bullshit we're living in. Pablum. And people think it's so revolutionary. There are writers out there who think rock deserves to be dead, and digital sounds are the only frontier worth exploring. 'Oh, it's a pop collage, how genius.' It's a fucking cul-de-sac, though. Nobody ever thinks they aren't living in revolutionary, tempestuous times. Take the most boring era ever. Eisenhower 1950s. You think people then weren't walking around believing they were at history's vortex, a swirling chaos previous generations couldn't possibly have identified with?"

"..."

They play several more songs Hoop knows, and none is ever so complex that Sebastian can't pick it up in moments. Hoop sings better than he plays, though key changes are pretty much out of his league. Sebastian has fun embellishing blindly, it's no magic trick— just listen to what the song is trying to do, dance around the root chords, flail up and down the fretboard a little—but his friend is awed, and occasionally tells Sebastian, "Solo!" whereupon the younger man, not having actually ever heard the recording, just makes stuff up. It pleases Hoop to no end.

"Okay, I want an answer," Hoop says. "No thinking. Quick. What are you most scared of?"

"Death. Dying."

Hoop plays the beginning to "Blister In The Sun" on his E-string. Then he reaches for something down by the clutter near his bare feet, and Sebastian figures it'll be an ashtray. But he comes up with a coin. "Do you want this? It's a 24-hour chip from N.A."

"I don't know," says Sebastian. "Do I?"

"It helps some people. Tangible representation of sobriety, all that." He tosses it over; it's an aluminum disc with a Masoniclooking triangular etching above the words "Hope Group."

"Thanks, I'm good." He places it on the window seat beside him.

"What scares you about death?"

Sebastian doesn't want to talk about it. He's refused Hoop's official offer of sponsorship, isn't interested in joining, listening, smiling, sharing. He knows how he sounds, but he's not entirely convinced he needs to kick. He's not an I.V. user, he's not in financial peril. His health is fine. Does every single drug user in the world *have* to quit? Is there not *one single person* who can manage his drug of choice recreationally? He has ups and downs. But he's back on his brain meds. He's managing. To Hoop, he says, "Yeah, no, what a freak I am for being afraid of dying."

"I mean what specifically about it? Being old? Being in pain?"

Sebastian looks at the wall over Hoop's couch and sees a framed poster for *Singin' In The Rain*: a woman and two men in raincoats, skipping beneath umbrellas. "No. Those don't sound great, but no. Getting...wiped away. Being gone."

"So you don't have religion," says Hoop.

"I'm not an atheist. I'm just not anything."

"And what's bad about being gone?"

Sebastian puts down his shitty guitar.

"Seriously."

"Right, because you're so serious most of the time." But something moves inside Sebastian, an internal nudge beneath his sternum going *hey, asshole, remember all those times you wished someone would try and understand?* He says, "Am I weird? Is this, like, a weird thing to you?"

"Not at all," says Hoop. "Fuck, man, I told you I almost did die. Scared me all the way sober."

"It's just.... I mean, what did it matter? What was the point? Why does anybody do anything? And don't say, 'Because you can work to make things better for future generations,' because future generations will just die anyway."

"So you panic over this."

"..."

"I'm saying I can relate. I've been there. Beating the shit out of myself for being so wound up about a deadline or catching a flight, knowing underneath all the frustration and rage literally nothing really matters because we don't actually understand life.

Like, we don't understand the first thing."

Sebastian says, "And that's why you stopped working at the magazine?"

"No, I told you, I got laid off. People didn't want to read what I wrote anymore." He looks at his fingernails.

"..."

"I'm really asking," says Hoop. "I really want to know what this does to you."

"What I think about," Sebastian says, "is ways to trick myself into *not* thinking about death every second of the day."

"Okay."

"I need strategies. Like, jerking off, that's a good one. Calling people on the phone. Uh, playing loud music. Yeah, getting high. If I could not put so much energy into distracting myself, I'd really be...so much more productive."

"Do you feel it now?"

"See?" says Sebastian. "Other people don't have this. You don't have this. You can barely even understand what I'm trying to say. It's like my brain's messed up and I don't even know why."

"Are you afraid right this very second?"

"No."

Hoop reaches to reclaim the 24-hour sobriety chip. He fusses with it, pretends he's studying it, wearing a pained expression or a mask of pain: there's always something self-tasting in his face. "Yeah, but connection doesn't solve everything. You worry about being by yourself again, knowing it'll creep right back up on you."

Sebastian nods.

"You're not a freak," Hoop says. "You're talking about the one thing we're most in denial about, the one thing that underpins all the other delusions in this country. We're built on individual identities, striving and building and carving out a homestead of your very own. Which of course is all illusion built on top of illusion. We're furious busybodies who believe that everything we see and the lives we construct and the ways we distinguish ourselves from the crowd, we believe it all has objective meaning, and if we can just *order* it and make it predictable, everything will be fine and death need not apply. But what the fuck's objective about life? There's no scorekeeper, unless you believe in a bearded man who lives on a cloud. There's no way of viewing the system *outside* the system. Not only will we eventually go extinct, not only will it all eventually disappear, but we don't even know what 'it' really is. What's a molecule? Oh, it's atoms. What's an atom? Oh, it's protons and electrons. What's an electron? Oh, it's just a name we gave to something that exists but we don't know how or why."

"Uh," Sebastian says.

"Sorry. But yeah, fear of dying, maybe you're on the right track."

Sebastian bends his toes downward inside his chukka boots, hard, until his joints crack. "I'm not on the right track, Hoop. I barely sleep."

"Maybe it just gets better as you get old. I know I used to think about it more."

Sebastian is near tears. He wants to say, *Help me.* Instead, he drains emotion from his voice and says, "It sucks."

Apparently lost in thought, Hoop taps his guitar with one hand and scratches his crotch with the other. "Do other kids your age think like this? Is this a new millennial curse, the result of too much childhood praise? I'm kidding. No, listen, I said it already, I think it's obsessing over order. We built this society where knowledge and, hell, the entire purpose of humanity comes down to predicting and ordering. And anything that doesn't help predict or order, it's either dumb superstition or just worthless. Your mind is so trained to make order out of things, then it's presented with the ultimate problem that has no solution, and it frics."

"I'm not the 'Order Guy,'" says Sebastian. "That's Scott."

Hoop makes a face like a crazy hermit. "Come on, buddy, don't try that with me. How many times you think I listened to 'Chord' and 'Bandfucker' over the past few weeks? It sometimes *sounds* like chaos, sure, but it's layers, and inside each layer it's practically mathematical most of the time. And listen, almost any musician, learning the notes and chords? Virtuosity is its own kind of order, yeah?"

"I don't know," Sebastian says. "All my life, all anybody tells me is how I'm so easygoing. Like it's a character flaw, like, why don't I stand up for myself?"

"Easygoing doesn't mean disordered, and anyway, don't confuse any of it for just being an accommodating wuss. If you're paralyzed by this particular fear? My opinion is it's because you're trying to solve an unsolvable question. Listen. They tell us we have two selves: the acting self and the subconscious self. Which is bullshit and a total invention. And that's where 'self-control' and 'self-consciousness' come from...because we try and control and dominate this supposed subconscious self with this supposed willful self. Hence anxiety! 'Am I controlling myself? Why did I do that? That's not the me I want to be!'"

"..."

"And then we try to cure the anxiety by learning all these techniques, reciting scripture, doing yoga, meditating, whatever. And we're American, dammit! We want results. But it's you! You *are* your own mind! There's only one self. So how can you get results when you're trying to define something indefinable using the very thing that is in itself indefinable? It's the arrow shooting itself. It's impossible. And it makes you crazy. And I know it all sounds like hippie nonsense, but the only way out of the impossible cycle is to *realize* it's impossible."

Sebastian knows one of his wiseass Brooklyn friends would say: *Jesus, in the time it took you to say all that, I probably really could've figured out the meaning of life.* But these visits to Hoboken—"Hobroken," Hoop calls it—have constructed an intimacy that make it possible for Sebastian to say real things, and to have real things said to him in return. The specifics sound nice, and maybe bounce off his noggin a little bit, but generally speaking a Hoop Stringfellow filibuster offers so much relief Sebastian can scarcely believe it.

Hoop leans over to click his laptop and the speakers play a song that goes:

Surrender
But don't give yourself away

Hoop says, "Teach me a Kid Centrifuge song."

"Which one?"

"'Styles Make Fights.' Only the classics."

"Right. Okay, I play rhythm and lead together, so let me figure out how to break it apart."

"You didn't overdub the lead? You play it that way in shows?"

Sebastian recalls by way of fiddling on his guitar, realizes there's a bunch of barre chords. "Don't blame me. I didn't write it." He walks Hoop through the progression and it's a slog. When Sebastian shows him the funky little strumming doodad that leads

into the chorus—a seventh-fret G, a ninth-fret A, a tenth-fret D—
Hoop thinks he's making it up on the spot just to torture him. So
they play the file, the Denver recording. Sebastian recalls that huge
hangar, the strife, all the aborted attempts. And hearing Amanda's
voice hurts. He remembers calling her inside from the cold to lay
down these vocals; she was warming up by hopping around, maybe
re-creating a childhood game of hopscotch. But he's right: they
listen to the recording, and there's the doodad.

"How?" Hoop says. "You're so…. It's basically a pretty little
throwaway, but so *fast*, dude. It's fucking insane."

They strum the song all the way through, with Sebastian
picking up whatever pieces Hoop can't handle. The older man
sings, badly, unselfconsciously.

"All right," he says, "my fingers are killing me. But I have one
actual concrete thought for you today. If you quit the guitar, I'll be
forced to kick your ass."

"Ha. Thanks."

"I'm serious. I fucking forbid it. You have to stay with rock,
Sebastian. I know you're great at other instruments. But the guitar
when people like you play it…I mean, it's sacred, man. And
touching the sacred—whether it's playing music or climbing a
mountain or fighting some big company injustice—that's what
elevates a person's life out of the quagmire. Do rock instead of
electronic because it's an actual conversation with, like, other
humans."

"Well, thanks. It's really flattering to hear you say that."

"I love those Kid Centrifuge songs," Hoop says. "It's pop,
but it's wild and different. It kicks ass. Well fuck me Jesus, I'll
fucking manage you. Ha. Let's get down to the business of not
making anybody money. Who do I talk to? Scott?"

Sebastian laughs. "Kate. When it comes to the Kids, Kate's
the one."

Later Hoop puts on a windbreaker bearing the worn-down
faces of Snap, Crackle and Pop, and walks up the street to fetch
takeout. And it's strange being here alone. Sebastian looks around
at all the Buddhist philosophy books and concert handbills and
pink-martini coasters and crumpled-up t-shirts, and the specificity
of this place is cleansing and suffocating. The apartment is *so*
Hoop. This guy over 40, this guy he met because Tina is a good
cook. Sebastian gets an idea. He steps around the Hoop detritus,

opens the drawers of a battered curio cabinet, checks the shelves above the fridge, wonders how easy it would be to unscrew and look inside the overhead light fixture. He checks the medicine cabinet, and the space beneath the bathroom sink, he checks the rollaway bedroom closet, the messy rows of sweaters, pockets of suit pants. He snaps his fingers and rummages through Hoop's guitar case, finding a dozen scribbled-on scraps of paper offering phone numbers or a few incoherent words ("Armpit Herpes," "Mustache Fart," "Fuckhorse"), as well as several plastic picks that have been obsessively chewed on. It's impossible, of course: Hoop won't be gone long enough for Sebastian to do a truly thorough search. But maybe this is enough. He's checked all the obvious hiding spots. Maybe he really can believe Hoop doesn't have a stash, isn't using, isn't completely full of shit.

On the kitchen counter there's a single sheet of paper, on which is printed a grinning black-and-white photo of Reverend Johnny, and these words: "You are not a solitary embodiment of logic and consciousness!"

RED FOOTPRINT

The day after Christmas, Lucius calls. Suburban Boston is muffled in cold and clouds. Scott is writing, ever writing. He plays ELO LPs on his father's hi-fi and finds a hundred great ideas: "Diary of Horace Wimp" with its scatting vocoder, the guitar in "Fire On High," and sweet Jesus all of *Secret Messages*, which is somehow poppy and baggy and expansive and genre-bending while also feeling like a series of intricate dioramas. The idea is put more and more songs between himself and *Vampire*. They'll get a new deal. They have to be ready.

Lucius says, "There's a problem."

What else is new? The single tanked. The album is in permanent limbo. Jane texts him hinting at sexual escapades. His brother has gout and can speak of nothing else. His mother casually left MBA catalogs on her coffee table. Still Scott writes. Maybe he walks into a Coolidge Corner sandwich shop and watches a beautiful couple—a blonde with thin ankles and paisley pants, a beefy mouth-breather walking around chewing gum in a long-sleeved Oxford shirt and shorts—and he can't stop telling their story. Maybe he wakes with the remembered smell of a St. Louis Super 8 bedeviling him. He's lonely again and it doesn't feel that bad, which is the thing that worries him.

"It's Darly Dalembert," says Lucius.

"Who?"

"Our man in Haiti. Dude disappeared."

Yes, in a spasm of altruism, high on achievement, Scott contributed one thousand dollars to Darly's charities. His understanding is that Lucius gave many times more. "What does 'disappeared' mean?"

"Gone. Under federal indictment and fled for parts unknown."

"Wow."

"First thing the FBI says is, 'Don't worry, you can still take the write-off.'"

"Oh, right, taxes. Yikes."

"Doesn't that piss you off?" Lucius says. "He was *specific* about it. Not we're buying food for kids. Not we're building houses. He knew we're musicians, so he plays that card."

"There were never any music-loving kids in the first place?"

"No there were, but they weren't the only ones he made promises to. He fucked over a whole bunch of folks. I did the background I should've done. Who the money was promised to. Who gets screwed as a result. I guess one's a private music school, they reach out to the community. And now can't pay teachers they just hired."

"That fully sucks."

"Obviously it's not my fault. It's not even my responsibility. But I feel involved, Scott. I'm serious about going down there myself. I want to see."

"Do they have any idea where he went? Maybe it's not too late, to get the money where it's supposed to go."

"Yeah, man, it wasn't like the dude was gonna tell me too much about the investigation. But I got the impression off-the-record, like, Darly's a damn *ghost*. A lot of people want to kick the hell out of him and he knows it."

"Asshole," Scott says, looking at a thirteen-year-old version of himself trapped in the confines of a hopelessly dated-looking family portrait.

"Anyway, I'm serious, man. I want to go down there. And I think you should come along."

"You...."

"Remember?" Lucius says. "That bellybutton problem of yours?"

"..."

"What I'm saying is, you need a break. I sure as hell need a break. It's getting cold, that's all I think about: 'I need a break.' No wife, no kid, what do I spend money on? Every five minutes I discover I'm checking plane fares to Hawaii. But what do I need a break from? What am I gonna do with my eyes closed on Waikiki Beach I'm not already doing? What am I gonna think, what lyrics am I gonna write? This is where I'm at, Scott: maybe I don't need to get away from things. Maybe I gotta get deeper into them."

"I need a break?"

"Four hours from JFK. Not even two hundred bucks."

"I'm not doing this," says Scott. "This is, y'know. Several steps beyond."

"You're probably right. Definitely don't check the email I just sent you, though. Pictures of smiling little babies, kids with guitars eight sizes too big, this one emaciated boy grinning ear-to-ear holding a medal he won playing piano at a competition in Miami."

"..."

"I include myself in this," Lucius says. "But did you ever think most every player you ever met was just pretending to dig deep?"

No. In fact, just the opposite. He looks at the fallen LPs around his feet. *Everyone is legit but me. I'm a goddamn magpie.*

Later he sees the email from Lucius and flips past it, because someone has tweeted him. One of his 74 followers: "Hey, @scotttungsten: Remember us?!? Good times on the road! Check it: http://bit.ly/1SYQBSp". He doesn't recognize the person's handle, assumes it's a twitbot, but his guard is down and he semi-consciously clicks the link.

It lands him on a web page for Honeystuck. And the song thereon is shit: a panderingly crunchy dance beat, various time changes and generic synth sequences and a lame sample of a sped-up Gwen Stefani saying "don't tell me 'cuz it hurts." And right there on the page is a photo of the tall guy Scott remembers from Pittsburgh and L.A., the heckling bearded Honeystuck douchebag in the *Free Hugs* t-shirt.

Sure enough, Scott checks Twitter and the link came from this same shithead's account. Robby Dover. He has 10,765 followers. Scott parses the original tweet for sarcasm. Is Robby rubbing actual success in his face? The only thing worse would be if he earnestly believes they're pals from the road. Apparently Honeystuck is on Black Sandwich Records and their stupid club song is nearing the upper echelon of the Hot 100.

The next day, his jealous frenzy has produced such obsessive self-loathing, he's incapable of not phoning Kate.

"Tell me none of this matters," he says.

"None of this matters. What are we talking about?" Kate happens to be standing on the broad concrete stairs leading up to the Met. She's never once been inside. Today's the day.

"The ice caps are melting. American politicians are...morally bankrupt. People shoot kids on the street in Florida and get away with it. And I'm getting worked up over singing songs. Not even singing songs, getting songs on the radio or whatever. Nobody's stopping me from singing songs. It doesn't matter, right? In the scheme of things?"

A guy wearing a fez grins at her. She makes a funny little wave as he goes by, one of those moments where it's easy to disbelieve the city's reputation for callousness. "It matters a little," she says. "It matters if it matters to you."

"I mean, who cares what the reasons were? Maybe we didn't put our best foot forward, maybe nobody was actually helping us make good decisions. But we got pretty far, right? And we have fun. Like, Sebastian getting dry-humped onstage by that crossdresser, and me freaking out because that girl's brother was gonna kick my ass and it turns out he's 14. But then I ask myself: is it really fun? Other people seem to be having fun. You seem to be having fun, Kate. And for me it's like this compulsion, this thing that gets in the way of everything else. I'm up here at my parents', and I haven't hung out with a single person from high school or college, I haven't talked to a single non-blood-related person. I'm locked away scheming."

"Sounds like you're spinning out. Don't do that."

"Yeah."

There's comfort knowing Scott's neurotic vibrations have been there to pilot the band. If only he could cut the existential crap. *I'm so lonely.* Who isn't lonely? "What if you stopped writing for a while?" she says. "Make yourself take a break."

"See, that's my point," he says. "A break is what I feel like I've been on. We haven't played in...what? When we get together I want to be ready."

"Amanda's in California."

"For Christmas, I know."

"I don't know when she's coming back," says Kate. "She's

still paying rent. But I don't think she has a return ticket."

He bites his lips, feels himself stretched further. "Okay."

"Did I ever mention how jealous I am of you, Scott? You have something you really believe in. I can see it, you believe there's a *right note*, a *perfect word*, and you'll run forever until you find it. I know it's hard on you, but don't minimize how rare that kind of clarity is."

"But it doesn't matter. The right note. Nobody cares."

"You care. The only relevant question is whether it's worth it to you."

He knows. He *knows*. There's no right way to live, there's no right thing to want. It's too hot in this house. He should take off this new sweater. His goals are wrong. What are his goals again? "I don't deal with things."

"You deal with things," she says. "You deal with things every day, every song. You deal with things more than almost any other person in the world. Can't you see that?"

He says, "How are you doing, Kate?"

"I think I'm okay," she says. "I'm okay. I'm about to head into the Met. I don't know anything about art. I mean: nothing."

"You're very good to talk to."

"Thanks. I'm going inside, to get warm and let culture take me away. I have a secret hope maybe if I learn enough stuff I can start figuring out what the hell our songs are about." He laughs gratefully. She's glad she wore comfortable shoes, thinks about what to have for lunch.

Scott spends a few days eating malaria pills, then he and Lucius fly to Port-au-Prince. They arrive at an airport gate, walk to an immigration hall where they show passports, then stand on a long line outdoors in the sun to get back to the main terminal. The year's second day is nearly ninety degrees. Their bags—including Scott's guitar—await them on a carousel, presumably having spun past dozens of times. Back outside Lucius looks for their contact but nobody has a sign bearing their names, and they're jostled by foot traffic that includes camo-wearing Brazilian soldiers. Scott feels himself panic, a different variety of panic. Many people around him speak Creole. Cab drivers look sleepy and dishonest. The sky is huge, the city low. He tells himself he can make a routine out of anything, just give it a few days.

A green Sentra pulls alongside them, a red ribbon hanging

from its front visor. The guy says, "To where?"

"Turgeau," says Lucius. "Rue Pacot."

The guy drives away.

"Just like New York," Scott says.

They consider several more compact cars with those same ribbons, and speak to the driver of a covered pickup painted like a psychedelic carnival, with religious icons everywhere and the words "Thank You Lord" emblazoned across the back window. The man wants fifty gourdes for the both of them, scarcely more than a dollar, but they see ten faces waiting patiently in the back of the truck and they hesitate. All day they've been joking about getting kidnapped and held for ransom, and while being with Lucius is a comfort—*he oozes cool, I'll stay close*—Scott thinks getting in the back of this tap-tap would be unwise. As they hesitate, he hears a squadron of slapping shoes behind him, and it's five or six little kids sprinting this way, ahead of a large grinning man walking with his arms out.

"Mr. Hawk!" he says. He wears a straw boater and a blue blazer with a crest over his heart. He's much darker than Lucius, has crooked yellow teeth and pink palms, and from within complicated sandals his toes appear strangely gray. This is Emmanuel from the New Rossini School. "I wanted to bring some students!" His accent is Creole. "But just try to get these devils organized!"

They all pile into an ancient van with that same crest crudely painted on its side. There's not enough room in back, so one of the little boys has to sit on Scott's lap. Emmanuel takes a left onto Route Nationale 1—a two-lane highway filled with twelve-wheel cargo trucks and battered sedans—and he talks with Lucius. But the van windows are open and the wind is loud, so Scott can't hear. The boy on his lap is fascinated by the hairs on Scott's forearm; he touches them with his palm, pinches and pulls them, lifts Scott's arm to hold them up in the light. Outside there is devastation: block after block of rubble or tin-roof shacks. Then a square filled with tents: strung-up bedsheets or squares of plastic. Then a series of former chemical tanks, which appear to have exploded. The one constant is crumbling rock: piled at the side of the road, tumbling out of dumpsters, crawling up the side of a ravaged monument. It's nearly four years since the earthquake and this place is still dismantled, still beset by the dust of the gods. Emmanuel points out Lucius' window and Scott hears the word "Soleil"; his guidebook says Cité Soleil is a gang-controlled slum that contains at least a quarter-million people in about eight square miles, and has been called the most dangerous place in the world. They drive past. Nearer in town the going is much slower, and most of the side roads are closed while people wander the streets, shading themselves with umbrellas. They get stuck behind a double-parked schoolbus loaded with cinderblocks, and Emmanuel holds down his horn. Scott sees a column of birds in the afternoon sky, a lovely coded waltz to the west, out over Port-au-Prince Bay.

"Yes-yes," Emmanuel says, "the people came to help, they came to rebuild. But mostly in Pétionville, where the foreign businessmen live. Very nice place, private security to shoot the boys who speak Creole. '*Ou pale kreyol? Wi?* Then bam!' Ha-ha. If you watch on TV, the foreign media go where the foreign businessmen are trapped. It was a very good TV show, digging them out! Ha-ha."

"Is your school rebuilt?" Lucius says. "We looked for pictures online."

"Ask the little devils. Little devils, do you go into the old school?"

In droning unison, the kids all say, "Nooooooo."

"It was a good place," says Emmanuel. "But the new shelter is a good place, too."

The boy in Scott's lap turns up his eyes and says, "*Mwen pral jwe gita.*"

"A woman named Ferdilia lived across from the old school. Her house fell on her and she died. She was a lovely person, the little devils always played for her. It is still impossible to clear the rubble from the old school, not until many other places are clear. But they got the crusher machines to Ferdilia's house. So for weeks, this is what we did: crank the crusher by hand, crush Ferdilia's rubble. And when it is clear, her sister says, 'You will use this place to make a New Rossini.'"

"*Gita*," says this urchin. "*Gita gita.*"

"Guitar," Emmanuel says. "English, please."

"Guitar," the boy says.

"What instruments do you have?" says Scott.

"The piano was lost, and many violins. In the old days, the children took violins home to practice but Croix-Deprez is too violent, too many were stolen or broken. We will never get a piano again until we move. Mr. Dalembert, I only met him once. He was supposed to give us more. But there are some instruments, yes."

"English!" the kids sing. "English English English English!"

They turn through a crowded square, dodging a makeshift market where umbrella-covered women sit behind tables and cry out. Pedestrians pay traffic no heed, just walk out into the street. They drive past a stadium, and Emmanuel tells them the homeless are no longer allowed to camp inside. There are tents everywhere else on this road, people reclining thereunder, staring out. Emmanuel says yesterday was Independence Day, but today is also a holiday: a day of reflection to spend with family. They cross over a dry canal and Scott sees a child squatting down there, relieving herself. Now there are more trees and a few more standing houses, but still they see an incredible number of bombed-out former residences, debris-filled lots, rectangular sand pits, makeshift shacks and decapitated houses of worship. There are no street signs. Emmanuel drives with his arm casually out the window, winding through quieter neighborhoods. The children are fidgety. Scott looks at Lucius' sweaty skull, lately shaven.

They stop on the apron of a tree-darkened lane. Emmanuel gets out, so Scott opens the back door and the kids clamber over him. Frogs and crickets whine and whir, hidden in palm, coconut and eucalyptus. Last night Scott craned his neck on the eighth floor to watch snow falling onto the Hudson.

The New Rossini is a group of canvas and plastic sheets strung against the surrounding skeletons of three decimated buildings. A few panels of propped-up corrugated steel demarcate three classrooms and Emmanuel's office, which is humming with flies. A pretty American woman is teaching multiplication tables to three kids. An older cornrowed woman, Emmanuel's wife Leila, smokes a cigarette and eats leftover *soup joumou* from yesterday. Nobody is playing music, and Scott can't see any instruments. He can't even see anyplace where instruments might conceivably be housed, or practiced.

"Even before the holiday," Emmanuel says. "some of the children did not come because there is no one to teach. We will send word, Monday they will all come back."

They walk down Rue Pacot and take a left. They pass a compound that looks like an oasis—palm fronds and a fountain and a spectacular cool breeze—but the house is simply gone, replaced by a two-foot-tall outline of its former self and piled high with white bags of foul-smelling garbage. Emmanuel tells them they're on Rue Bellevue. They enter a hostel. A man named Jean-Daniel guards the premises, shows them the shotgun he keeps beside his armchair. The place is clean and dark and filled with parrot sounds. There's a sunken common area with a double hotplate and an unplugged television, a carpeted hallway, and three bedrooms with five cots apiece. Jean-Daniel walks them into one of the bedrooms where they put down their bags. Scott reflexively checks his phone for service, and Jean-Daniel says, "Did you buy a Digicel at the airport? Emmanuel is very stupid. Get a Digicel and then buy phone cards on the street!"

"What about Internet?" says Lucius.

Jean-Daniel shrugs and nods.

In the evening, they unfold rusty lawn chairs in front of the school and drink Prestige beer as the sun goes down—Emmanuel, Leila, Scott, Lucius and two other teachers: Apolline is a smiling Haitian woman with short dreads and a wedding ring, and Jessica is the American they saw earlier. This is the entire New Rossini staff.

"How long will you stay?" Apolline says.

"I'm...not sure," says Scott.

"One day? Two days?"

"Well, hopefully a little longer than that." The others are chattering about world affairs.

Apolline indicates Jessica, says softly, "She came...two weeks ago? She is a banker's daughter from Texas. So we are her rebellious period. They tell me at night she cries for a manicure."

"Do the kids all speak English?"

"There is a summer camp in Croix-Deprez for the last four years. Most of our students have been to this camp, where they learned the basics of English. The girl who started this camp, *yon sen*, she is also American and still a college student.... Well, many of us aspire to the sweetness and selflessness of this girl. She will be here again this summer, and if you are still in Haiti that is the girl for you. Not this one," and again she gestures at Jessica.

"And they get music training at this camp, too?"

Apolline sips beer.

Scott says, "I mean, I'm not qualified to.... I barely made it through high school algebra."

"Many of them do sing well," says Apolline.

"There's an audition to get into the school?"

"My husband asked this question. I told him, 'The audition is they pay the tuition.'"

Scott wrinkles his forehead and tongues his front teeth. His is the last chair in a conversational row. There's a temptation to use every moment as fodder for songs but he resists the note-taking urge, he should *live it*, even from way over here where Emmanuel's oil-burning lamp barely brightens anything.

"A fleet of black Land Cruisers means kidnappers," says Apolline. "It means white boy, get out of wherever you are. And you will stay away from Croix-Deprez. All teachers stay away from there. It is not Cité Soleil, but it is not good."

He sees there are factions even in a faculty so small, and Apolline is claiming him. He scooches his chair a few inches to face the others and Apolline gets the message, momentarily stops dispensing wisdom.

"I am asking you to explain it to me," Emmanuel says. "I am giving you facts. Swine flu broke out in the Dominican, and the U.S. government was worried maybe it would spread to Haiti and ruin the American pork industry. So they killed 13 million Creole black pigs who weren't sick. The genocide of pigs! And these pigs were the poor Haitian man's bank account. The next year, school enrollment went down and stayed down."

"I don't know much about it," says Lucius. "I never heard of it."

"Your government eventually shipped some American pigs as compensation. But the American pigs needed more food, and they died in the heat. And when this happens, there is no more compensation. Oh well. Too bad. So there are only two possibilities, my American friends. Was it incompetence? Or was it another effort to help the Haitian government keep its people enslaved?"

"It sounds paranoid to me," Lucius says. Jessica is watching him. "I say whenever you have the chance to describe the U.S. as evil or stupid, just assume stupid."

"But the malice, Mr. Hawk. Miami rice also ruined our economy. American rice growers got so many subsidies from your government, and the Haitian tariffs were forced so low, a rice farmer in California could sell in Port-au-Prince at a cheaper price than a farmer in the Artibonite Valley just a hundred kilometers away. And those Haitian farmers still can't sell to Haitians, even after The Sinister. Their rice sits in a warehouse instead of feeding refugees. What is any of this, Mr. Hawk, but the patrimony of humanity?"

"'The Sinister?'" Scott says.

"It is what we call the earthquake," says Leila. "Also: *Goudou-Goudou.*"

He tries hard not to imagine writing a song called "The Sinister."

Scott and Lucius sleep a few feet from one another, sharing the room with two young Germans who come in comically soot-covered—as though they've been digging for treasure—and grunt hello before collapsing into their cots. Lucius turns on his book light and reads *Things Fall Apart*, as Scott pretends to doze. Then Lucius says, "Thanks for coming, Scott. I wouldn't have been brave enough by myself. Man, tomorrow is just tomorrow here, you know? That's all it is because that's all it can be."

On Monday, they give Scott twenty kids and seven composition books. In the blue glow of a plastic sheet that is their ceiling, he fakes his way through a lesson about parts of speech, then tells them to practice writing their names while he investigates the instrument situation. In Emmanuel and Leila's open-air office, the school servant—a tiny woman named Fanchon—directs him to a box containing many wood recorders, two tambourines and a fractured boula drum.

"The children do not share these," Fanchon says, indicating the recorders.

Leila also comes into the office and says, "Yes, each child should have his own because of the cholera."

"But these are all old," says Scott. "Which kid has used which recorder?"

"It is not ideal. Across the street, we had so many fine pieces. Violins, mandolins, ukuleles. And the beginnings of a marching band! I hope one day you can hear my Emmanuel play the piano. You would be very impressed someone so fat and simple could play like this."

"He's not fat and he's not simple," says Scott. "I heard him talking last night."

Leila professionally whacks a green-and-white pack of

cigarettes, some local brand with a 'C' across the front. She lights a match with one hand. Fanchon coughs and waves her arms; Leila scowls at her. She says, "We thought we had money coming."

"It's fine," says Scott. "I can make this work."

"Why are you here, Scott? You are guilty the other American tricked us? Guilt is one thing. But you will not save these children. There are too many. What matters is how you behave with them. Give them something to aspire to, and that is all. You are not their king, yes?"

"..."

"Your friend took the older boys out into Turgeau. Can you hear them singing? Yes, well, American students come here looking for an answer to questions Haitians can never understand. 'Why should I be forced to work in a beautiful air-conditioned office?' 'Why am I so addicted to the Internet?' Yes, very difficult, this addiction. But Haitians are stupid, too. If it were the other way around, if Americans needed Haitians to come help, would they go? They would form a committee, yes. They would definitely organize a march and take a nap."

"I guess I should get back."

"But you and your friend are not students," says Leila.

Scott says, "Then again, aren't we *all* students?" and is ironically solemn. She waves him away and speaks quickly in Creole to Fanchon, pointing to dirt that has blown onto the rugs in here.

Scott hands out recorders and tells the kids to write distinguishing marks on them, though it seems likely another class will use them, too. He thinks about cholera. What's cholera again? Is he putting these students at risk on his first day? He doesn't know any songs on the recorder, is how he justifies not putting his own lips on one. He works out "Mary Had A Little Lamb" by asking the little boy front and center—his name is Junior—to finger notes in sequence. Most of them have had some kind of music lesson, and pick the tune up quickly. They laugh away boredom.

"How old are you guys?" Scott says.

They all say different numbers. He hears some eights, some nines, some tens.

"Well, then this is baby stuff! I think you're old enough for something else." He removes his Ovation from its hard case. The kids hoot and slap the three folding tables around which they're clustered. He plays "Sloop John B," a Beach Boys song his grandfather used to boom out the windows of his orange VW Bug. The kids learn the chorus and sing, "I want to go home!" and chuckle at tales of the first mate getting drunk. One girl with a burgundy stain across her uniform stands up and dances for the class, an unselfconscious frolic that gets everyone slapping the tables in unison. Fanchon peeks around a steel panel.

"Again!" the kids say.

"Don't you want to hear a different one?"

"No! No, Mr. Gita! Again!"

It's possible to bask in their delight. He'll call Kate and Sebastian, ask them to round up as many old instruments as they can find: a shipment of guitars and accordions and rusty trumpets. He needs a system to learn their names. Will he get the same kids every day? How many are enrolled, how much do they pay? Most of them are so thin. Junior is a surpassingly beautiful child with charisma to burn; he stands and shakes one of the tambourines, encourages the others to clap along. He's small and beloved. After more Beach Boys renditions and many other songs, Leila comes in the room and tells the children lunch has arrived and most of Junior's classmates surround and tickle him until he collapses onto the dirt floor, breathless.

The kids all get up and glide outside, except one. He's a pudgy boy the size of a high schooler, but with a mushed-up baby face. His eyes hardly seem open and his graceless fat arms are squeezed over his knees.

"Don't you want to go run around?" says Scott.

"No, Mr. Gita."

"What's your name?"

"Stanley, Mr. Gita."

"And you don't want to eat?" The boy shakes his head. "I'm not hungry, either. But it's getting pretty hot under here."

"I am fat. I do not know how to say. *Fom fè rejim.*"

"How old are you, Stanley?"

"Eleven." He counts on his fingers. "*Onz an.*"

"Do you like music? Yes? What do you play?"

Stanley squirms and inspects the ground. In his husky bashfulness his cheeks go full Buddha. "*Senbal.*" He holds his hands apart, crashes the palms together. "But I do not like."

"What would you like to play?"

Again, Stanley can't conceal himself. He looks at the guitar with perfect lust.

Scott gives him a fifteen-minute lesson: neck-nut-frets-bridge-saddle, string names and major scale, finger position for the D, the G, the E-minor. Stanley has huge hands but weak fingers, can barely get an unplunked note. But he never speaks, doesn't smile, doesn't require childish encouragement. Concentration rids his face of timidity's self-importance. The sweat on Scott's stomach caused by the Ovation dries. He folds his arms and tells Stanley to try again.

That night the three Americans—Scott, Lucius and Jessica—borrow Emmanuel's van and drive to Pétionville, to drink at a nightclub inside a swank hotel. Jessica wears a strapless white dress and Scott imagines she'll look out of place, but they walk inside and it's an expat jubilee filled with trim lovely French, Germans, Brits and Americans. A glamorous singer belts tunes from the 1930s. Everything is white marble and brass and ferns and perfect teeth. Scott touches his wallet.

They drink rum punch and people-watch, then inevitably Lucius asks Jessica to dance and Scott sits alone, scanning for single-looking women on principle, knowing he won't leave his post. The same helpless nonsense as always runs through his mind: *grin wryly, puff out chest, stare at the empty chairs around you.* Eventually the others come back glistening. Jessica's thinness is a bit of a taunt.

"So what do you guys think of Emmanuel?" she says.

"He's…strident," says Scott.

"Don't get me wrong, I admire him. Big time. But he's always 'on.' My family supports the arts, so we were always going backstage at plays or getting introduced to actors at benefits or whatever. It's not like they were all phony, that's not it. Just they never let you see what was really going on."

"We know some people like that," Lucius says. "I used to date one in particular, who Scott knows pretty well."

"Maybe it's inevitable," she says. "When you're married to who he's married to, and when her best friend is Apolline. They grew up together, Leila and Apolline."

"What's inevitable?" says Scott. But she doesn't elaborate. "You have music training, Jessica?"

"Training. I mean, I played saxophone in the high school

band. I guess the school used to have more of a music focus. It's great you guys are here but my sense is, like, these kids are half-a-step from taking to the mountains, living in the jungle, whatever. The parents just want to get them out of the slum during the day, if they even have parents. Nobody's expecting anyone to come home a prodigy. I've been here a month, and I'm a big believer that things get better, like, glacially: they get exposed to modern thinking and a few molecules rub off, hopefully they carry that around with them, maybe their kids get it a little more, like that."

Lucius asks her if she knows anything about procuring weed in Port-au-Prince. Her posture becomes even more perfect. She really is lovely. "No, I.... I've heard Apolline talking about some brew her husband makes. I can't remember.... She was being sneaky, talking in Creole. I don't think they even know I know French."

On their way out, Jessica visits the ladies room, and Scott says, "The way she was talking about the students. Was I the only one getting uncomfortable?"

Lucius shrugs. Security guards walk by carrying Uzi pistols.

"You hear a lot about 'reaching kids,'" Jessica says, getting into the van. "Reaching, reaching. I don't know. They understand about a quarter of what we say."

"People can be reached," says Lucius. "If they want to be."

"Spoken like a hippie musician," Jessica says. Scott volunteers to sit in back, thinking life should be simpler here, distractions are nominally fewer, yet here's his tongue: tied.

A tropical week glides by. Lucius and Jessica move to the hostel's co-ed room. The generator goes out for a few nights and Scott tries to sleep early, ignoring the grunts of Jean-Daniel outside fiddling with wires and rotors, and other grunts from inside the house. It's impossible for him to sleep once the sun comes up, because of the parrots. Someone long ago decided it would be charming to keep a few parrots in the hostel; now a dozen live in the common area where seed is plentiful and predator birds are remote. The hostel windows are almost always open, yet the birds never leave. It's actually fine to sit at night and read—when there's electricity—and have a couple green *cotorras* walk on his shoulder, but Jean-Daniel is lamentably lax about scrubbing parrot shit from the cement floor.

At school, he ditches any semblance of a lesson plan and

holds daylong sing-alongs. He also fitfully learns his kids' names and circumstances. Chantale is a quiet girl who never smiles or sings, but always hugs Scott hard at day's end. Serge and Yann are roughhousing brothers who live with a revolving series of uncles. Paul One hasn't had his uniform laundered in recent memory, so Scott "sneaks" a bottle of water from the school's supply so they can scrub out stains. Paul Two makes his mother and Croix-Deprez neighbors crazy banging pots like drums. Wideline has yellow eyes from hepatitis but refuses when her friends offer extra water. Lovely has an angelic voice and wants Scott to write down the words for every song he plays, so she can take them home and practice. Junior is a scoundrel whose grin can rescue him from anything. Big Stanley's hands rarely leave his pockets—he watches his classmates run around as Scott imagines his underdog inner narrative—waiting for 4 p.m., when he and Scott steal away for a half-hour guitar lesson among the ruins next door.

One night Emmanuel and Leila host the teachers for dinner at their apartment on Rue Capois. Fanchon cooks and yells at Leila, and Leila yells back. They eat chicken with okra and *djon-djon*, but Scott is still vegetarian so he loads up on fritters made from black-eyed peas. Emmanuel says, "Lucius, I had no idea you were so famous!"

Lucius looks at Jessica, and says, "I'm not, man. Believe me."

"He has *five* CDs," says Jessica.

"My God!" Emmanuel says. "We will hold a concert! I love hip-hop music. The children do not get to hear it."

"You got the wrong guy. I'm glad to do it, but here's the guy you want, right here. Scott got his band signed to a huge deal, he made a TV commercial in the States. He's not a good songwriter. He's a great one." Scott blushes hard and makes squeamish faces of modesty, but loves it, just loves it, wants to hug Lucius for an hour.

"What!" says Emmanuel. He holds his hands wide. "How could we know! Two geniuses!"

"What was the commercial for?" says Apolline, a puncturing quality in her voice.

"A car," Scott admits.

"Don't let her embarrass you," Leila says. "A car is good."

Emmanuel claps. "We will put on your CDs now! Come, I have a player."

"Manny, they do not carry copies around with them."

Apolline hands Scott her beer. "Do not be so tight." She scrunches her lips. "I am judging you. Okay. What does it matter if I am judging you? I have just discovered you have enough dollars to buy me into slavery."

"Stop, Polly..." says Leila.

Apolline laughs. "A good lesson." Now she slurs a bit. "To discover the limits of control."

"Sweet Micky is our star," says Emmanuel. "Maybe you can play a *compas* concert with him, ha ha. But maybe he wants to finish rebuilding Haiti first, so you may have to wait for the year 3000."

After they eat, Scott and Lucius step outside to stretch their legs beneath a Fanmi Lavalas political poster.

"Apolline likes you, man."

"Hm," says Scott. "If true, a fact made less awesome by her being married and crazy."

"Just looking out for my little bro, right? Sorry I threw you under the bus. It's like: deflect attention by pointing to the bigger famous asshole. Then talk immediately goes to how great did your record sell, and I realize what I've done."

Out of the quiet and dark, a battered pickup scoots by with one headlight on. Six or seven workers are on the flatbed, drunk and singing. At first, Scott is sure they're belting out that fucking Honeystuck song, but that's impossible. He says, "I guess we never really did talk about *Vampire*."

"Yeah, shit," says Lucius. "What did I know and when did I know it? I could see it all sliding downhill."

"..."

"When the dude writing the checks tells you to do something...."

"Don't sweat it. You're right. There was nothing you could've done."

"Which doesn't mean I'm not guilty. You don't want to believe it's happening. You know it's...fraught, right? You know every bone in your body is telling you this music-industry dude is pure evil, like, a damn caricature. But maybe.... He's gotten pretty far. Maybe he's just putting up the shithead front, maybe deep down he's an exception. You want to believe it, so you believe it. And once you ignore the first alarm, how do you hear all the others? He puts some wet-behind-the-ears gal in charge, and you don't see it straight, maybe it can work, maybe she'll wind up on our side and fight for the songs. It's not like I wanted to believe what was happening."

"It's a lot of work for nothing," Scott says, wanting Lucius to protest that it wasn't for nothing.

"Ten years ago, we don't have a single problem. Thing gets released, reviews are good, everyone's happy. Believe that. But now the wind's blowing the other way."

"I can't decide whether that's bullshit, Lucius. I can't decide whether it's just self-pity when I tell myself I'm a victim of bad timing. You can put together a case: new rock bands don't get big deals, rock labels are dying, and I get that. But what if my songs just weren't good enough? What if that's the dirty secret nobody wants to whisper in my ear?"

In an uncertain distance, they hear firecrackers or pistol shots. This sprawling city is overstuffed with menace, and seems to extend into an unknowable forever. What grants a place coherence? Accents, rhythms, habits, systems? Decipherable avenues of commerce? Crime sequestered to undesirable peripheries? A checkerboard layout? P-a-P is webbed with sinister suggestions that Scott tries to dismiss. The limits of control, indeed.

"You want to know what I really think?" says Lucius.

"I do."

"Well, I don't know what's possible for a band like yours. It's not my—"

"Ours," Scott says. "A band like ours."

"It's not my area of expertise, right? But one thing seems pretty simple. That song."

"..."

"I mean, you know I have a soft spot for Amanda. And sure, I can see people dancing to that song. But it was never what you actually wanted to sound like."

"'A particular place and time,'" says Scott.

"Yeah, I'm all wise. But is it any better to sit around like yours truly, filled to the fucking brim with integrity?"

"It was a lot of aggravation. I never apologized for roping you into it."

Lucius reaches out and tweaks Scott's nose, and it's one of the kindest things ever.

He teaches his kids the Proclaimers song "500 Miles." He breaks it into several parts: melody and harmony on vocals and recorder, hands banging on desks, and a hilariously cute quasi-Scottish call and response on the "da da da da!" part. They sound great, and they're ecstatic. Junior is particularly hyper; he keeps doing a shimmy dance and goosing his eyebrows like a cartoon lothario. He loses his balance and clangs into a steel-panel wall, falls onto the hardpan floor and flops around giggling. Scott palm-mutes the Ovation on every chord change, sides aching. They want to do the song three times, then a fourth, at which point Scott sees Stanley wobble into the room. He's too big to miss, but he's trying to hide: smiling at his feet, shuffling kneeless. Nobody has told Scott that he's supposed to be monitoring attendance, let alone tardiness, so he just waves Stanley in. At lunchtime, per usual, most of the kids jump up shouting, anticipating the beans and rice—supplied by an NGO, occasionally accompanied by chicken or goat meat—that for most of them is their first meal of the day. And per usual Stanley waits, smiling like a blind man. But on his way outside, surrounded by friends, Junior detours and jump-steps toward Stanley, balls his fists, and takes a few mock swings at the bigger boy's face: jabs and uppercuts. Then he bounces away, laughing and taking refuge in his crew. Stanley looks ashamed for flinching.

Scott is angry. He wants to grab Junior and shake him. Before he can move, though, Stanley comes forward to ask for a quick turn with the guitar. Scott sees the boy's left eye is swollen and pink.

Could this be Junior's handiwork? He's half Stanley's size, but Stanley is a hunched and ungainly introvert. A familiar picture: a bullied boy fumbling for music's lifeline. He lifts the Ovation over his head and hands it to Stanley.

"What happened to your eye?"

"Eh...?"

"Your eye. Can you even see through it?"

"*Wi, Mesye Gita.*" He strums an A-minor. He's been squeezing rocks to make his hands stronger.

"Somebody hit you in the face, Stanley. It looks awful."

"No-no. I can learn 'Hold Your Hand'? Yes?" He pauses to think, unconsciously touches the tender eye, then like a Beatle says in falsetto: "'I can't hiiiiide.'"

"Tell me who did this," Scott says. "I'll fix it."

But Stanley isn't talking. Scott remembers the end of eighth grade, his homeroom torments. He complained vaguely to his parents, who went so far as to research private high schools. He discovered the guitar soon thereafter.

Scott takes hold of Stanley's shoulders. "Tell me. I really will fix it."

The boy doesn't sing as much as he whines: "'Oh yeah! I! Tell you some things!'"

Dammit if they don't feel like a pair. Things that make the kid laugh—like a tiny curly-tailed lizard sneaking up behind a stray cat and scaring the bejeezus out of it—tickle Scott when he thinks about them at night. Sometimes he dreams about Stanley famous, touring, beloved.

Later, after the class has reconvened, Scott asks Junior the square root of a hundred and pretends the boy's answer is disrespectful. He sends Junior to Emmanuel's office for discipline, and feels like an avenging angel.

Much of January passes in a haze of self-proclamation. *Here is how this experience is changing me. This is the kind of person I will be.* There's a memorial in front of the old Rossini to mark the earthquake's fourth anniversary. Leila and Apolline and Fanchon hug and many of the children cry. Scott uses fake-looking phone cards—one bears a panoramic view of a green valley with a squatting farmer in the foreground who may or may not be about to defecate, one bears a photo of a Digicel-sponsored soccer team—to call the States. His voice bounces up to a hollow orbiting sphere and down again to a first world that feels fictional; his mother indulges his many poetic invocations of P-a-P, only interrupting him occasionally to rephrase the question: "When are you getting the hell out of there?" One time he calls Kate, who seems confused that he feels a need to check in.

His life is cloistered in this pleasant neighborhood. He hasn't been back downtown even once, hasn't laid eyes again on Port-au-Prince Bay and certainly hasn't gone into any of the slums. He walks back and forth between the school and the hostel, occasionally gets driven to Pétionville to drink or shop, and when the kids filter north across Rue Sapotille it's as though they're materializing from nothing, so total is his ignorance of Croix-Deprez. Yes, a district of twenty thousand people begins not five hundred feet from the school, but Scott is warned every day (by Emmanuel, by Apolline, by Jean-Daniel) never to wander in alone. If he and Lucius want to see their students' living conditions, a tour can be arranged. For one reason or another, it never is.

But Scott does see poverty. It's in the face of the goatherd who shambles up Pacot to deliver milk to the school, in the wiry men who follow around the NGO consignment truck apparently hoping food will fall out into the dust. Occasionally a homeless family will be rousted, begging and pleading, from a neighborhood ruins in Turgeau. Scott missed hurricane season by a matter of weeks, and Jean-Daniel tells him how much worse conditions get from June to November, when the tent camps flood and sewage flows through the streets.

One Saturday morning he steps barefoot into the hostel's backyard, and finds it hard to breathe in the humidity of 7 a.m. Bands of light are coming out of clouds, and around the corner of Bellevue and Rue 6 he can see an incredibly fat man who has to turn sideways to navigate a flight of stairs. Scott realizes his right eye hurts. He tugs the lash, trying to extricate a foreign object. But he can't, and the thought comes: *What if something is really wrong and I have to see a doctor?* He knows it's probably just a cornea scratch; it'll go away in an hour or a day. But what if it doesn't? Would he ever trust a P-a-P doctor's diagnosis? Hell, would he ever trust the disinfection of a P-a-P doctor's office? Bad enough that his back gets creaky after six hours in a cot, and his fucking foot is still numb. In just a couple hours, he convinces himself this is early-onset blindness and imagines a cadre of well-meaning Haitian ophthalmologists gathered around him, helpless. He inspects himself in a hand mirror, convinced he can see a cancerous-looking shadow within the white of his eye.

By Sunday, the scratch on his eye is gone.

Stanley has fresh burn marks on his forearm, won't answer questions about them. Scott keeps the boy after school, for many hours, protecting him. Stanley sings: "Jojo leave his home in...Tussonarizonin...."

The evenings are lovely. The New Rossini teachers eat feasts prepared by Fanchon—now she also cooks meat alternatives for Scott—then align the lawn chairs in front of the school. Sometimes they graduate from beer to clairin, a cane-sugar moonshine that comes in small bottles which formerly contained Dominican rum.

Once drunk, Lucius and Jessica tease each other then bury the hatchet in a made-up language, as the others shake their heads over the stupidity of new love. One night Scott asks Emmanuel about a black van parked on the corner, and Emmanuel says, "It is the government. We should be flattered."

"It isn't really," Jessica says. "Is it?" Emmanuel half-smiles.

"There is much interest," says Leila, "in finding the educated Haitians who resist."

"Resist what?" Scott says.

"Oh. The sanitized culture. The steps we are supposed to follow to be considered 'modern' and earn America's blessings."

"Now I hope you know I'm not one to blindly rush to my country's defense," Lucius says. "But y'all sure do blame us for a lot of shit."

"…"

"I'm not smart enough to know if anything you say is wrong. But at some point, fix the problems, right? Do the reasons matter?"

"Yes," Emmanuel says. "If the U.S.-backed influences will not hold elections. If the government keeps arresting dissenters on made-up charges. If they reduce every need of the peasantry to more bottled water."

Lucius thinks about this, sipping on his cup of clairin. He's such a smart, reserved figure, such a listener. Scott is pleased that their Haitian friends also feel the need to impress him.

This tense moment passes, everyone settles back. Jessica hums "The Star-Spangled Banner" and they laugh. Scott is happy to let the others spar, to watch Leila and Apolline grin through false outrage and to bask in their occasional flirty attention. This is new, the intoxication that can come from other people's wives.

Without warning, Lucius is on his feet. Scott feels he's missed something but the others also seem confused. Lucius says, "Well, I guess let's go see what's up with these mutha*fuckas*," and strides toward the black van.

Emmanuel follows, going, "No no no no no no," and trying to grab Lucius' arm, but Lucius isn't having any of it.

"Hey!" he shouts at the van. "Hey! *My* man!"

Leila and Jessica join the chase.

Lucius says, "Let's just find out what the dude wants! Hey, in there! You see anything good? Come on out!" He walks around into the street, to the driver's side. Emmanuel holds one palm up, shaking his head and smiling apologetically. A dog barks nearby. The van's headlights click on.

"Lucius," says Leila. "Not safe. Really."

Scott sees the driver's window roll down. He's hasn't been drinking, which means he should be over there making peace. But he's still seated beside Apolline.

"No no no no no no," Emmanuel says.

A hand extends from the van window. The headlights illuminate Emmanuel and Leila and Jessica from the waist down. Lucius is so likable and winning, surely within minutes whoever's in that van will be his new best friend. Scott makes out a second figure inside the dark cab.

"I saw a newspaper article," Apolline tells him, "about something they call 'wax.'"

"..."

"Do you know this? It is vaporized hash oil, to give a stronger high than marijuana. Of course I have been to the States. But not since you began legalizing."

Emmanuel is laughing too loudly. Lucius is hunched, his fists balled. Someone else is talking. Leila shakes her head. What time is it? Can't everyone just go home and sleep?

Apolline says, "They will tell him they are here to protect the neighborhood, or stop a cocaine deal. They do speak English, but they will pretend they do not."

"Lucius!" says Jessica. "Let's go! I want to go!"

"He thinks they cannot shoot him," Apolline says. "He thinks he is in Boulder, Colorado."

Emmanuel starts speaking loudly in Creole, palms together now, grinning, nodding at the men in the van. Lucius jabs a finger at the driver. Scott can't tell what Lucius is saying. He hears his friend's baritone rising and receding, insisting. The van's engine turns over and roars to life.

"He thinks he is in Terre Haute, Indiana."

Jessica steps out of the headlights, but Leila stands her ground and waves her hands 'no.' Inside the van two silhouettes are gesturing and pointing and shouting, Emmanuel puts his arm over Lucius' shoulder and Lucius nearly loses his balance, staggers drunkenly but catches himself. It all takes a few seconds. There should be structure here, a way of understanding how serious everyone actually is. There should be obvious lines drawn, faces should match words, the bottom of things should be agreed upon. But nobody is listening. Everybody thinks they know best.

The van backfires. Scott flinches. Everybody looks around stunned.

The men drive away. Lucius howls like a wolf. The driver burns his tires, a last little fuck-you. In return, Lucius offers double-barreled middle fingers.

"Come with me," says Apolline.

"We should find out what happened," Scott says. "Are those guys in the van coming back? Are they bringing reinforcements?"

She rises and takes his hand. "You care about the children. But your spring," her wrist makes a key-turning motion. "Still too tight." She draws him away from the chairs and the school. He looks back: the others are shadowboxing in the street and don't see him go. Apolline pulls him north past a half-ravaged university and across Avenue Jean-Paul II, to a tiny freestanding house whose front wall is draped in kudzu vines. Floodlights from a nearby hospital brighten the scene; they hear a child crying and smell griot. Apolline dreamily steps up to the house and lets them in. On a short table near the door is an altar of rosaries and candles, several cloth dolls, and jars bearing images of Catholic saints. Apolline lights the candles, then turns her back to Scott and lifts off her Western blouse. He looks around the room for photographs, for a man's clothing, for a sign...and realizes his error.

"Your husband died," he says.

"Yes, in the *Goudou-Goudou*." She hesitates sliding on a white tunic, giving him a look at her bare breasts. "But I was very lucky. I found him, and we held the nine-night to set him free from his body." Perhaps Apolline is in her late thirties but now looks younger. She passes close, and Scott discovers he wants her. She touches a clay jar and says, "I cannot leave this *govi* in a temple. Some people now burn down our temples and the police do nothing. His soul is in here, and one day I will have the courage to break this *govi* and set him free."

"You're talking about vodou."

"Is it such a terrible word? It is the religion I grew up in, and also Leila. Well. It is a long time since Aristide. Now they destroy our temples and kill our priests and nobody blinks. Yes, a tourist can go to some vodou ceremonies, the Oloffson has vodou artifacts. But deep down Sweet Micky says we must be a Christian nation, Christian only."

"I don't know much," Scott says. "Spells and potions."

"And of course stabbing dolls. One for every child at New Rossini, so I can ruin their chances to get into heaven." She smiles sadly and hugs herself. The tunic implies her shape. "Oh yes, we are monsters."

A notion comes to Scott: this is his reward for ripping the spacesuit to shreds. Apolline is strange but sexy, weary but willing. He came all this way and it was leading to this, to fucking in a two-room house under threat of secret police busting down the door. He's so hard he can barely stand. Why was he ever resistant to the idea that Apolline liked him? Why did he ever hesitate? He says, "I'm sorry for your loss."

She fixes him with pretty black eyes. *"Poukisa ou pale kaka?* Ah. Well, you are…. It is not your fault." She comes forward and he slumps backward against a low wooden bench, and feels her chest press against him. She kisses his cheek, he turns his face and reaches for her slender waist. His hand finds her belly, her breath is in his ear, his arms extend to clutch her close…but she's not there. The linen tunic skims his hand and she's gone.

"…"

Apolline steps to her fireplace and strikes a match. She sets a black bowl onto the fire. "There is something I want you to see." She opens a battered cabinet and cuts lengths from two vines: both have green leaves, one also wears pink blossoms.

"What?"

She empties two bottles of water into the bowl. With a glistening knife, she strips the leaves. "That you can be happy without talking such *kaka*. That you can be happy without control, if you will finally pay attention."

He deflates onto the bench. She boils the leaves. Why hasn't he ever observed her subtly muscled arms and calves, her puffy lips and round rear end? The possibility still exists: she merely wants him to drink some love concoction before they screw.

"What is it?" he says.

"Ayahuasca."

"What does it do?"

She makes a tender expression. "Nothing you do not want it to."

The water froths. The night is loud here. P-a-P is a fallen

beehive, pummeled like a piñata.

Eventually she pours liquid into two plastic coffee cups. They steam. She says, "Just a few swallows. I am no shaman."

He stands and looks at the door.

She says, "You did not come all this way just to escape."

"We hardly know each other," he says.

"Enough to fuck me, but not enough to drink with me?" She sips.

"Should I go lie down on your bed?" He bites his cheek. She doesn't laugh, and he decides to swig the sour liquid.

For a long time nothing happens. Then Scott feels nauseated and sees Apolline on the floor, grinning with her eyes closed.

He thinks about what she really wants from him. She thinks he's so naïve.

Soon bright stars and triangles are floating his way and he hears music: nothing he's ever heard before, nothing he's written. He feels tricked. The dim room begins speaking to him and he tries to deny it. He observes the vodou items distributed around this place, and in turn they also observe him. It makes his stomach hurt. He's always been an expert in controlling how he's seen: knowing the facial contortions and music tastes and sense of humor that will allow him to pass. So to have everything in this room scrutinizing him at once is a nightmare. Probably a better-adjusted person would experience this as integration.

The judgment! Candles and icons and cabinets and ballpoint pens and folded bedsheets and dangling flypaper and dishtowels and shoetrees and miniature rubber plants and especially the little clay jar—the *govi*—all dissect him. Their many voices broadcast his inadequacy: his ugliness, his lack of talent and style, his gracelessness and unlovability.

The only solution is to shrink his bubble of consciousness closer and closer around himself, so the voices go muffled. Time disappears. He sweats cold.

Aloneness is the answer to survival? Shutting out everything that isn't me?

Amanda is here. She's beside him on the bench. Her beauty is inhumanly total.

She says, "When you discovered I was Kate's roommate, you couldn't believe your luck."

Yes.

"You didn't care what I sounded like. How I look is why you wanted me in the band."

Yes.

"You know why you listened to my music ideas."

Yes.

"It was always only because you wanted to be with me."

Yes.

"But it was my song that ruined us. So it was my fault."

He thinks about this. *No.*

"You thought about making me come. You believed it would validate your existence."

Yes.

"Do you still believe that?"

He thinks again. *Yes.*

"Because I'm pretty and unavailable."

Yes.

Suddenly he can hear the objects in this room shouting again. They're even louder and they're warning him, telling him to stop.

"What's it like, Scott?"

It doesn't matter.

"Seriously, I'd like to know."

Never mind.

"What's it like to be irrelevant?"

The objects are telling him not to listen.

"What's it like to try so hard and have it fall apart?"

Please.

"What's it like to know it doesn't matter how hard you try?"

The objects are screaming.

"What's it like to know the world doesn't care?"

It hurts.

Amanda covers her teeth with her lips. She looks at the room and gestures for its contents to quiet down. They do. She says, "It really does, doesn't it?"

But it's all right. It doesn't have to be true. He can still win.

Amanda vomits and it's like a bolt of beige flannel coming out of her. Except it turns out Amanda isn't really here, and Scott is the one vomiting. He belches liquid fire. Then he cleans himself and curls next to Apolline on the floor, kisses her short dreads, and falls asleep.

The next day Junior comes to school a bloody mess. He limps

into the classroom cradling his right hand. His knees are skinned and grisly, his front teeth are missing, his cheeks are high and shiny with a recent beating. The other children regard him at a distance; Junior woozily inspects the front-and-center seat that's usually his. For a second Scott thinks maybe the ayahuasca has kicked back in. But Junior collapses and it's real. Scott picks up the child and puts him on a table.

"Who did this?"

The kids won't look at him.

"Junior?" The boy's right hand is brutally fractured, the fingers all snapped. Scott can see bones. "I'm going to fix this. You'll be fine. Wideline, get Emmanuel and Leila. Go now. Okay, Junior. I'm right here. I'll make everything all right."

Junior finally begins to cry.

Scott looks around for Stanley and doesn't see him. The other children are silent but not terrified. Their lives unspool amid such havoc.

Leila clears the classroom and Emmanuel daubs Junior's wounds. The boy whimpers. "He does not have parents," Emmanuel says. "His tuition is paid by neighbors, but he does not live with them. We will fetch the doctor, and he can stay in our apartment."

Scott waits a long time while a bald old doctor treats Junior, wrapping the boy's hand in gauze without straightening the fingers. It's sweltering in here, and Junior seems to be asleep on the table. For a moment they're alone and Scott is running through scenarios. What story can he construct? It was a random attack, surely common in Croix Deprez. He'll say Stanley was off running an errand. Maybe he'll pay Jean-Daniel to testify that Stanley was at the hostel all morning. There's a way to do this. Stanley was always going to erupt one day; by good fortune, Scott is here to witness the eruption, and save him.

Scott whispers, "Did he finally stand up for himself? Did he finally fight back?"

Without opening his eyes, Junior says, *"Ki es?"*

"Stanley. He did this to you. He finally got fed up."

Tears flow down Junior's temples. "Stanley is very bad."

The adults return to take the boy away.

Paul Two and Serge sit on rocks along Rue Pacot, playing krik-krak with a few unfamiliar boys. One boy sings, *"Peti Pyè pati pou Pari pou peche pwason pou prezidan Petion.*" Scott stands over them, and they squint and shout, "Mr. Gita! Mr. Gita!"

"Kids, do you have any idea who did this to Junior?"

The boys don't say anything.

"Or maybe it could've been anyone. Maybe this just happens to people sometimes."

Serge looks at his friends and says, "It was Stanley."

"Maybe not," says Scott. "Maybe he was someplace else. Did you see it? Did you actually see Stanley do this?"

The other boys stand and walk away quietly. Serge nods. "Everybody see," he says.

"Everybody?"

Serge nods again.

Scott's fury builds. Of course this assault is unforgivable, of course Stanley will never be allowed back to New Rossini. In a single weak moment, Stanley has ruined his chances for escape. But is Scott supposed to ignore a sense that twisted justice was done? "How do I find him? Serge, will you take me to Stanley?"

Serge is shaken, hearing his teacher talk to him like this. But he searches Scott's face, and Scott softens his expression to make everything seem all right. These kids love him so much. It's what has tethered him to P-a-P as he floats above them all.

Serge agrees. They cross Pacot and Sapotille, and there's no signpost, no fence, they're simply in Croix-Deprez. The shanties begin in earnest, and there are women sitting at the side of the road selling goods: charcoal, fruit, soap, toothbrushes, cigarettes and mudpies. (Many of Scott's students bring these mudpies to school: salt and butter mixed with mud and baked in the sun.) There are no streets here, nothing wide enough to drive a car, only alleys between shacks. The stench of raw sewage is powerful. Scott feels hundreds of people looking at him as he follows Serge deeper into the district; they look up from their lives and see this sunburned fool keeping pace with a local boy. The alleys twist and narrow, they snake through a precinct of broken glass. And there are children, so many children: hunched over jacks, jumping rope, playing count-and-capture. Scott tries to figure the way they've come, scans to locate the sun. He sees a dead dog and has to step across a muddy trench filled with excrement. A toddler peeks out from a tent and cackles.

Serge's pace slows. They emerge from a final alley into

blinding light, where people mill around a concrete slab. Serge points.

On the foundation of what might've been a community center or a medical facility, a gang of young men holds court. They all wear green bandanas. They shout and jostle, they throw rocks at each other, a few of them sit on the same kind of folding chairs Emmanuel lines up outside the school.

Stanley is here, wearing a tight black t-shirt that squeezes against his bulk.

Serge taps Scott's hand and runs back the way they've come. His skinny uniformed shoulders disappear.

One of the young men sees Scott. He waves and speaks in Creole, and the others turn. Scott understands how bad a mistake this may turn out to be.

Stanley waddles over. He's smiling or squinting. He shows Scott a gun.

"Bang," he says. "Bang-bang."

"I want to know what happened," says Scott. "What did Junior say to you?"

"I do not know Junior."

"Didn't we have fun? Didn't you have fun learning how to play the guitar?"

Stanley looks at his feet. His bandana is made from a segment of nylon backpack, and his t-shirt reads "Britney Spears Onyx Hotel Tour 2004." He's perfectly dry in this heat.

"Tell me what he did," says Scott. "He pushed you too far. You couldn't take the teasing anymore. It even happens to grownups sometimes, people get pushed until they can't take it. Tell me what happened."

"I do not know you."

"Show me a G-chord, Stanley. How do you play a G-chord?"

The boy can't stop a grin. He holds his silver gun like a guitar, puts his fingers on the barrel.

"Right. A-minor? D? E-minor? Pretty good. Don't you want to come back to the school? I can help you. I know exactly what to do."

"…"

"You don't want all those lessons to be wasted, right?"

"Junior live in my *katye*. He does not pay? Tch."

Scott can't find an angle into this. How does Stanley want to be treated: like a boy or a man? "Why is he supposed to pay?"

Stanley fits his finger into the trigger and aims into the distance. "So I do not hurt him."

"That's crazy. Stanley, that's crazy. This isn't you. Junior's the one who picked on you. I saw him take a swing at you."

The boy's eyes shimmer. "In the school, he is brave."

Scott examines the other green bandanas. Eight men and boys, curious, staring at him. Taunting casually. Muscled, strapped-up. This is Stanley's other life, and it's impossible to know which piece is a pose. "I want to give you more lessons. I want to turn you into a rock star."

"*Wi!* I am the rock star!"

"Not if you don't practice, you're not. Not if you don't come to my lessons anymore."

"I come! Mr. Gita, tomorrow I come!"

"The children saw what you did to Junior," Scott says.

Stanley frowns. "No. Junior is very quiet. And the others. Very quiet."

"What do you want to be?" Scott says sharply. "Do you want to be one of them?" He looks again at the green bandanas.

"I am one," Stanley says.

"I don't understand. Why come to the school at all? If you're just going to mess up your life with those guys?"

The boy ponders the question with his tongue in his lower lip. Then he says, "I am very happy for a disaster. I am very happy for the *Goudou-Goudou*. Now I can live. The *Goudou-Goudou* makes me very strong."

"No," Scott says. He looks at the gun, wonders how the hell they have modern firearms amid this squalor. It's foolish to feel anger rising. But here he is getting pissed off, a white American probably—if he's honest—no more than a week from abandoning this Haitian dalliance and returning to his New York problems. "If you would just listen, Stanley."

"Yes."

"If you would just understand, I could help you. Listen to me and I'll tell you what to say. We'll figure something out, but you can't do things like this anymore. You have to be good. And you have to do exactly what I say."

"…"

"Otherwise this will be your life. This is it. Standing around in the slums. You'll never leave this exact spot! You'll terrorize little kids and then one day someone will shoot you and you'll be dead! If you would just do what I tell you, goddammit!"

Stanley stares at him. The other green bandanas gawp, too, and many people peer into this open space from several alleys. Scott's whiteness has mostly made him a popular object of fascination in P-a-P, but just now it wears like a bull's eye. He shakes with good intentions.

"Mr. Gita," says Stanley. He raises the gun, and traces Scott's path behind him, along the concrete slab's perimeter. There are strange wet spots along the ground, leading back the way Serge and Scott came.

"..."

It looks like blood.

Scott looks at the concrete behind him, and sees a red footprint. He says, "Serge?" but no. Serge is fine. He looks at his own feet. His right sneaker is covered in blood.

He walked through glass. And his foot is still numb, numb, fucking numb for months.

"Oh no."

He sits on the ground and removes the canvas shoe. His sock is drenched in blood. A nail has driven up through the sole and slashed all the way through his big toe. He doesn't feel anything.

That night he wakes with a fever, and his right leg swollen. Lucius takes him to the hospital near Apolline's house. His parents arrange for an airlift to Miami, where surgeons try their best but eventually have no choice: the infection is severe, and they amputate his big toe.

PART V

RECOGNIZE ME

Crimea falls. Boko Haram terrorizes Nigeria, and separatists stab hundreds of commuters at a train station in Kunming, China. Experts say a lost airliner was intentionally steered off course before it crashed into the Indian Ocean. The U.S. government is spying on *everybody*. This is the news, and it sucks, and they stop reading about it.

They wake at 4 p.m. with the blinds sealed shut. It's time to fill another gap in Sebastian's pop-culture awareness so they watch *This Is Spinal Tap*. The bread in Nigel's backstage catering is too small. The boys have mutual herpes. Derek gets caught in a space pod. "Sex Farm" goes to #5 in Japan. Tiny Stonehenge happens.

They throw open the blinds and there's Wilhelminastraat, all brick.

The first place they play is Winston Kingdom, down in what seems to be the oldest part of the city. It's a great little room that probably holds a hundred. Nobody knows who they are, but it's a pretty okay crowd. They wonder if they're opening for a bigger act, and the board guy says no.

Rock music is something they've carried with them to the hinterlands like a vestigial tail.

Scott and Kate step outside with the board guy and smoke Mexican Haze, standing in a bike-only lane. Sebastian fiddles with his P-155, looks at the fresh *Om* tattoo on the inside of his left wrist, and warms up with his old friends Liszt and Debussy.

They do "Bald-Spot Mohawk." It's Sebastian's composition, Scott's words. The piano part is wild and fun to play, especially because Kate is so adept keeping up. She starts out in a Purdie shuffle and watches Sebastian for cues as she might a bass player. Per Hoop's insistence, her drums are turned up high in the mix, higher than anything else. They also put the kit nearer to the front of the stage and give her a little light.

Scott plays chords and fills on Sebastian's old Telecaster. His instructions are pretty clear: listen to the others and don't drown them in fuzz.

The song launches to a blinding speed. Kate's swinging lope disappears in favor of hardcore, but instead of a blockade of sound, Sebastian's Yamaha drives part boogie-woogie and part rococo trills. No synth effects: just piano. Half as fast, it would be hard to play. Scott lays off, hopes some of their talent will wash onto him. Kate slams, loves it, waits for Sebastian's say-so. For these moments Winston Kingdom hovers a hundred feet above street level. The kids don't check their neighbors or their phones.

The beat slows again, and Scott sings:

The moon pays a toll with the tide
And smiling goes whistling by
Your toll is a bag on your head
Then a stranger tells you you're dead
You don't really want to know
What came between you
And the man you wanted to be

He's got the primary spotlight. He tries not to think about his face while the assembly contemplates him. Kate pumps faster again, Sebastian follows, Scott retreats. Sebastian dropped his electric toothbrush on the bathroom floor this afternoon and couldn't screw it back together, the pieces just wouldn't line up. It turned out there were magnets in there, two little magnets, and when the toothbrush struck the floor one of the magnets flipped half-an-inch on top of the other, which meant the toothbrush wouldn't twist closed. It was the highest kind of mystery until the exact moment it wasn't. Once he figured it out he wanted to tell the others, but stopped himself, knowing they could only pretend to care.

When the set is over, the booker gets on the p.a. and says, "*Dames en heren*, The Buggy Whips!"

They play another show at Winston Kingdom, then do a couple nights at Maloe Melo where they're six inches above the tiny pressed-together gathering. After, Kate watches the next act—Funka Din, whose kit she borrowed tonight—and thinks about wandering around the bars. A short blonde woman eases over and says, "I saw you running."

"..."

Her smile is elfin. "The Vondelpark. You know," and she pumps her arms like a jogger. "This afternoon. You were very intense."

"Oh. It must've been the music. I was listening to The Evens. You know them?" The woman is noncommittal. "It's old. I loved it in high school. I mean, I still love it."

"I do not remember very much music. It goes in the ear and...." This woman makes an escaping bird of her hands.

"Anyway, I'm, ah.... I'm in terrible shape. It's embarrassing. You run?"

"I do. I am Gertie."

"Kate."

Gertie points to several blond people standing beneath a disco ball. They're tall and thick and male: an advertisement for Dutch imperialism. "My friends did not believe me. *Ja! Zij was het!* The coincidence is too big for them to believe, to see you twice in one day. But you are a famous American, and yet," she has a mocking edge, "you run among us."

"Mm, yes. Yes, it's a gift I give to the people."

"I can buy you some beer?" says Gertie. "I cannot have it. I am in training."

Kate puts her sticks in a back pocket and gives Funka Din half her attention, clenching her jaw. "*Gosh*, Gertie, whatever are you in training *for*?"

"I train to be a triathlete. We do." Again, she indicates her friends. "How long have you been a Buggy Whip?"

"We've been playing together for...a couple years. More."

Gertie flails her fists. "*Ticka ticka ticka ticka ticka.* You play with anger. But I do not see so many shows, maybe they all play with anger." She's stout and pretty in the milkmaid way. Her socks are too high and her shoes look too new. "You will meet these boys who are my friends? They are so stupid you cannot believe."

She meets them. They are Joot and Marcel and Louis and Stef. None are drinkers. They tower shaggy and shy, talking too softly and from too high a distance to be heard over the music. Kate looks around for her bandmates and doesn't see them. Gertie shrieks at something funny, then invites Kate for a morning swim. She pictures trying to find a bathing suit, and then being *seen* in a bathing suit, and says no. So Gertie says, "What about a bike ride?" and she says she doesn't have a bike.

"You have been here how long? Well, I can borrow one for you. Just a friendly ride around the Ronde Hoep?"

Such an undersell is a bright red flag, but she agrees and the next day suffers through fifty kilometers in the countryside, chafing like a boss. These Dutch boys pretend to be very serious about their training but then shove each other off their bikes and spit on each other's wheels. Gertie wears wraparound sunglasses and eats protein goo out of small silver pouches. She slows down whenever Kate needs, and they watch Joot and Louis punching each other up ahead. Kate blasts Black Eyes and No Age through earbuds. Marcel takes a piss while still riding. Stef stops near a dead skunk and pokes it with a stick. They're all brown as berries and big-shouldered wearing sleeveless Lycra, and Kate laughs and thinks they must hail from the Binghamton of this country.

Her legs become noodles and she motions for Gertie to go on without her. Soon everyone is gone. She's *nowhere*. The air is cool and the grass is tall. The porcelain cows from her mother's lowboy are spread across this field. The borrowed bike's frame feels restorative against her thighs. No matter what she tries, she is the woman in wide-open spaces scanning her surroundings for meaning. Cram her into the darkest cranny of a rock club, and eventually she'll make her way out here: dwarfed. What is she supposed to want? She drinks water from a fuggy-smelling bottle and for a moment this is enough.

What did she think when they decided to make this trip? *Here I go again.*

She gets back in the saddle and proceeds at half-speed. Near a riverbend she sees a shaft of black smoke. She thinks it must be a barbecue or maybe some European method of garbage disposal, but the road winds toward a farmhouse that is clearly on fire. Kate takes out her earbuds and pedals over flat dirt. Her helmet strap strains at her chin. There are no sirens, but the smoke is everywhere: disgorging from second-floor windows, swallowing a barn, rolling out over these fields. A golden retriever is out front of the house barking wildly, spinning to bite its tail. Kate flings away the bike and runs up a front lawn that ends at the river, so much water so tantalizingly close.

She can see flames. Is the dog alarmed by smoke, or is it trying to say there are people inside? She stops at the front door and looks up: heat comes off the house in waves and the walls are hissing. She wants to touch the doorknob, fears it will burn her hand.

"Hello? Hello? Anybody in there?"

What does one do? What number does she dial for emergency in Amsterdam? How could she even describe the address? The dog follows Kate around the house. She keeps calling, the dog keeps barking. What if there are children inside? Through windows over here she can see a kitchen and it looks unburned. There's a glass door. It's crazy to think about going inside.

But what if someone's dying in there?

The drummer is always the foolish one.

She finds a metal rake in the side yard. Yes, the fire isn't so bad here. Break the glass, sprint inside. This is irresistibly possible.

Kate lifts the rake and wings it hard, like a javelin. It smashes through the door. The dog goes crazier.

"Hello! Hello!"

She thinks: *I will be okay.*

She covers her mouth and nose.

And as she steps up onto a single stair and lifts her leg to climb through, Kate is jolted from behind, and she knows she's dead. Something has happened: a gas line has exploded, a piece of the house has fallen on her. The rebellious shard in her is proud for having become a kind of seeker and there are faces overlaid around her—mother's eyes, father's mouth, Inch and Charlene, the cruel, the just—and she's terrified and it's familiar, maybe that fear is a thing music has let her experience every day. A dark face, a hot exhale. It has always been possible to explode, but better this than dread.

Kate feels herself fall.

But something catches her, and a hand is on her shoulder. She's falling, knocked off balance. Someone behind her on this side lawn has actually tackled Kate. She's not dead. Her helmet thumps turf.

It's an older man wearing overalls. The farmer. He pulls her arm. The dog is here touching Kate with its muddy paws, jumping around, yapping. The farmer's big hands encircle her biceps and he yanks her up off the ground. Her neck cracks. He's shaking his head and saying Dutch words. He brings her around to the backyard, where hills roll away and the fire roars and an entire family stands watching, mouths tiny, like a row of owls. Kate looks at her left side. She's scraped and muddy.

"Is there anybody in there? Are you sure everybody got out?"

They say more Dutch words. The dog leaps and crashes its forehead against Kate's knee. The roof breathes orange licks. She counts a father, a mother, a grandmother, three kids. Everyone holds artifacts: scrapbooks and picture frames, ancient-looking brass toys, sheaves of paper, shoes and sweaters. Their fingernails are ridged and square, like in old photos from less hygienic times. A wedding ring dances loose on a string around the mother's neck.

"Does anyone know English?" says Kate.

They look at her and she senses they understand. But they speak sharply to each other in Dutch, watching. The panting dog stands on Kate's foot. Someone comes around the house and she thinks it's going to be a fireman. But it's Gertie in her robot sunglasses, red-faced, her big Spandexed thighs jiggling. She storms over and says, "What are you doing?"

Kate points at the fire.

Gertie snaps at the farm family, the father answers. Gertie ignores the man and speaks Dutch into the mother's face, very close. The mother looks at the ground and responds. Kate hears a window's glass burst. She notices: the children aren't crying.

"We go," Gertie says, taking up the flab beneath Kate's armpit and pulling her away.

"Wait. Wait. At least wait for the fire department."

"Look at them. They do not want help."

Kate looks. The six family members are sloe-eyed beasts accepting slaughter. Only the dog seems to care. Gertie gets behind Kate and pushes her back toward the front of the disintegrating house. The old woman raises her hand as they leave.

"What's going on? Why don't they want...?"

"They do not say. Maybe they burn it themselves. Maybe

there is money for insurance. Take the bicycle and we go."

Kate sees the door she smashed. The kitchen behind it is now overrun with flames. Gertie hustles her away like she's a famous person who's done something wrong.

That same morning, earbuds blasting Bluetones, Scott walks deep into a park and steps across a ramp to a tiny island gazebo. Brilliant red flowers bloom in the grass below him. He has a joint in his pocket and feels scandalous about it. "Solomon Bites The Worm" fades momentarily and his phone bloops out a text from Amanda. He reads:

>y is la wf & vsf 2?

It's midnight in California and Scott imagines her partying, more *way fun* than *very sad face*. It annoys him. He wonders whether she contacts the others, or if she enjoys toying only with him. Helplessly, he types back:

>What happened?

He doesn't care. He'll get a response and whatever it is he'll put the phone away.

>8 a man 2day 8 a man & then just walked away but it wasn't ok

Is this how she flirts with him now? Old lyrics of '90s songs they used to sing in the van? She's probably drunk. He texts:

>Ha ha! Nice!

He takes off his sneakers and sits on the gazebo bench. He pulls out the joint and a plastic lighter and lines them up beside his phone. What is life but testing out personas? Should he let his hair and sideburns grow out? Should he find a secondhand jean jacket and a chain for his wallet? He's trying to be different. He sees a string of Scotts: high school with only a few friends, college as an r.a. strangling dorm fun, New York begging strangers to save him, shepherding Kid Centrifuge via tantrum and wheedle, blundering around Port-au-Prince with all the answers. Far down the gazebo path a couple roams holding hands and Scott can barely recall

Jane's face, Jane, the woman he drove away by being himself. But he can become warmer and cooler. He can smile more. Oh yes, sainthood is surely in the offing.

The four of them are staying in a two-bedroom apartment in Helmersbuurt. Hoop knows the guy who owns the building. Apparently Hoop knows an insane number of people everywhere. He jokes they should call him Colonel Tom Parker, but they pretend they don't get the reference. (Actually, Sebastian probably really doesn't get the reference.) Hoop occupies one of the bedrooms and Kate gets the couch, so Scott and Sebastian share a room. Whoever's home first gets the bed; last night after their lightly attended Maloe Melo gig, Scott slept atop three blankets on the cold wood floor.

Amanda texts again:

>wan2 ask u something
>r u da?

The phone stands on edge like a monolith. He wonders if its own sounds might knock it over. She doesn't wait for a response:

>f wtb vampire

All this was Hoop's idea.

He told them Amsterdam is a believer town. He said if there was one place he'd visited where rock would make its comeback, this was it. There are clubs where the guitar *qua* guitar is still worshipped, and kids are still interested in discovery. France and England have fallen to EDM, eastern Europe is all "Smoke on the Water," but you can roam these streets and hear strange, contemporary, multilingual rock: the Black Atlantic, Darlia, the Bohemes, Night Flowers, Royal Blood, Cloudmachine. The plan is: become Amsterdam's own. The plan has begun slowly. But nightly Hoop paints pictures about being associated with the right place at the right time: Seattle. Detroit. Portland. Amsterdam is long hair and tattoo spikes peeking up over collars and rooftop after-parties and everyone smoking cigarettes and walking around confidently like they've got someplace fun to be.

Lighter. Joint. Phone. He should use the former to set the latter two ablaze.

The phone startles him by ringing. He considers the expense and almost lets Amanda roll into voicemail. But no.

"Let me guess," he says. "High society. You're at a soiree with A-listers, cocktails on the beach."

"What are you talking about?" says Amanda. "I'm in bed."

"Ah. Watching what?"

"*Chinatown.* Am I crazy or is Faye Dunaway kind of creepy-looking?"

"Never saw the film."

"Yes you have. You're the one who told me about it." She hums one irked note. "How's everything with you guys?"

"Modest and good. Our reach is firmly within our grasp. How's TV?"

"It's really good. Silly. But I mean, it's just a few days a week."

"Someone wants to buy our record? What does that mean?"

"From Sidelong."

"Yeah," says Scott. "And do what with it?

"..."

"It's the album that sunk a label, does this person expect a bidding war?"

"It didn't sink the label. Jacob was spiraling down the drain, we were just his last big party."

"Whatever happened to old Jacob anyway? Let me guess: *he's* your mysterious friend. He wants to buy *Vampire* from the ashes of Sidelong and do it all over again."

"No," Amanda says, "come on. We both know Jacob is running as a Republican for governor of Virginia."

"Really?"

"No idea, but it seems right. Why are you being mean to me?"

"..."

"I get it. You're in the union now. You're pissed how hard it is to be the singer. I'm just saying what would our options be? Let's say we had the rights. I mean, could we just put it out ourselves?"

Scott wants to say: *We?*

"Or could we, like, find someone else to do it?"

"..."

"Or maybe we could even...?"

"..."

"I miss you guys," Amanda says. "I have some time off in a couple months. I was thinking of coming over there?"

She says this, and Scott floods with the relief of a relapse.

"I know I'm a flake," she says. "But I wouldn't horn in on the band, I just want to see you guys and hang out a little. And maybe we could talk about *Vampire*, which, y'know, we all still love."

"We're not hard to find. We're the ones wrecking Amsterdam."

"I don't know why you're mad at me, Scott."

"Who says I'm mad? Am I raising my voice? Am I swearing? I'm transformed. You wouldn't recognize me."

"Of course I would," she says, and they hang up.

It's hard for him to believe they're not fated to be together.

He runs the joint through his fingers and wonders if he should actually spark up here. Will the scent carry? He wishes he had a guitar with him, then halts mid-wish. No: how many times does the world have to tell him the old way is no good? Metabolizing his life via a rock song and expecting the universe to love it. Maybe if he were a rapper or a computer whiz there would still be a way to forge the disproportionate feedback loop of love. He flicks the lighter and inhales.

Another text arrives. It's a picture from Amanda: a close-up of one of her eyes. He snaps a picture of his own eye, and sends it back. Almost too quickly, she sends another one, this time her bellybutton. His heart vibrates. He takes one of his nipple. She fires back something indeterminate; when he asks, she writes "ass crack." This is nearing a point of no return and Scott veers away, leaning over the gazebo railing and getting super-close to one of the red flowers, its yellow filaments, and taking that picture. He sends it. She sends a close-up of her lampshade. They swap several more non-body-part pics and he's tickled, then he texts:

>This "friend" you're talking about is a new boyfriend?

She doesn't answer.

The following week, a guy helping them set up at the OCCII asks if Kate ever uses a click track, and Hoop says, "Fuck no! Fuck the fucking click track! Have you heard this woman play?"

"To be fair," says Kate, "I record with one."

"Not with me around you won't," says Hoop. "And I want that kick mixed higher than anything else, right?" The tech agrees. "Top five songs that changed the world. Go."

"Uhhh," Sebastian says. He's toggling around the tempo functions on his keyboard, clicking a button—*yes yes yes yes yes*—as everyone else scrambles.

"'Smells Like Teen Spirit,'" says Scott, ferrying the Tele cross-stage.

"Not changed the industry. Changed the *world.*"

"..."

"One of those benefit concerts," Kate says. "Bono something something?"

"Are you asking or telling?"

"Live Aid?"

"I'll allow it," Hoop says.

"That *Brokeback Mountain* Willie Nelson song?" says Scott.

"That's two."

Kate scooches behind tonight's borrowed kit, thumps to get her levels right. "I know the Spice Girls changed *my* world." This room has blue walls with silhouettes of trees and buildings painted black, maybe twenty-by-forty and half-filled with sleepwalking lipsticked goblins. A few more kids are up front at the bar.

Sebastian plays the riff to "Black Coffee In Bed," which Scott taught him once. He says, "I don't know songs."

"What's your point?" says Scott. "Music can't change the world?"

"No. Fuck. My point is it *can.*" Hoop steps off the stage and looks up at them. "My point is we're together every night and I've never once heard you geniuses mention the Beatles or Stones. Bob Dylan. 'My Generation.' 'London's Burning.' 'A Change Is Gonna Come.' 'Imagine.' 'Strange Fruit.' My point is just because the sheep say they want brainless music doesn't mean you have to give it to them. You think EDM will ever mean anything? My point is you can fucking *matter.* Aim high. Be perfect at everything. Kill."

The OCCII lights go down. They are fucking *ready.* And over here by the kit, Kate sees a bumper sticker that reads: "Rock is dead. Long live paper. Love live scissors."

They're great. "The Self-Denial of Skim" veers into punk. "Tiger Beats Bear" is syrupy with a calliope sound whirling out of Sebastian's fingers. "And Do What?" is a Spoon ripoff of Scott's that he loves too much to omit. The half-crowd goes "woo!" The headliner is a guy named Wouter Smit, and he's right there offstage cheering, encouraging them to do a couple more. Kate recalls the good feeling they'd occasionally get on the road in the States, and wonders if it was *this* good. They had fun in places like Ames and Colorado Springs, but maybe they're just better now? Maybe they're more genuine without a crutch named Amanda?

There's that thing where people watching your band start singing along even though they don't know the words, and have never heard of you. Maybe some nights, in the beginning, the presumptuous tickles you wrong. By now it's the shit. While singing, Scott has discovered himself interrogating a stranger's mouth, noting the parts where the stranger can predict the words well enough to match his own mouth-shapes. And without really knowing it, he thinks about the transference it would take to have his own mouth stop leading, start following: maybe now Scott is mumbling into the mic when this stranger doesn't know the words, only picking back up again in the chorus. He wouldn't exactly call singing any kind of burden, but there's special comfort merely in the idea of this transference: a kind of bliss.

A large woman with a thunderous laugh doesn't mean any harm, but here she is: right up front, unaware she's at a rock show and relating the funniest story in world history to her barren-faced friend. Scott considers accidentally toppling onto her.

Later, Sebastian follows Hoop out the back way, and they step onto Amstelveenseweg, a wide boulevard that could be from the East Village except for the tram tracks overhead. Kate is somewhere with her new friends, and Scott is across the way laughing with some biker-looking guys. Hoop lights a straight cigarette and says, "Hey, you go to a meeting today?"

"..."

"Humor me, man."

"Alano Club. Lunch session."

"Always welcome at the community center. I know it's kids. Just wanted to offer."

"..."

"Anyway, to me you're all kids."

Sebastian watches Scott on the corner across the street, framed in the window of an Italian restaurant, motionless except his drag arm. That's all of them over there: basically too cool to move.

"But for fuck's sake, Sebastian. The chicks that were staring at you in there tonight, dude."

"…"

"I'm just saying. I guess I'm the last to know you've got the makings of a pussy hound. A testament to my heterosexuality."

"Scott's over there blazing right now," says Sebastian.

"This is true. Then again who the hell are you to judge someone else using, and second of all, he's not in the program. I know he's uptight as hell but—"

"Actually, he's calmed down a lot."

Hoop does his spaced-out little Hoop smile, a kind of self-parody commenting on his age and life choices, what a fading dropout he is. In fact, of course, he pulls the strings. "I ever tell you about that Silver Jews song? 'Punks in the Beerlight?' It goes, 'You wanna smoke the gel off a fentanyl patch' and I didn't really even know what that was, but it sounded pretty good to me. So I went through this insane process of pretending I had an arthritic shoulder and eventually I got my hands on some and…you, like, carefully snip the corners off and squeeze out a blob of the gel and sizzle it on some aluminum foil and suck it up through a pen. When I think about it, Jesus."

"And…?"

"Does the trick. But colder than heroin. I wouldn't recommend it."

"…"

The story of Hoop's bottom is: he stole a gold record from his boss' office, pawned it right downstairs on Broadway, shot up in an alley and woke in a hospital handcuffed to a gurney, his wrists bandaged but still bleeding. He almost died. The doctors told him his wounds were self-inflicted. His boss didn't press charges. He was high when he got to his first NA meeting and got high again after.

He says, "Fuck, dude, how boring was your 21st? Everyone else gets a debauched story, and you played guitar with your sponsor, who in case you haven't noticed is just terrible at guitar."

Sebastian thinks he probably didn't really have a bottom. "I'm 21. Man."

"A baby. If only I'd gotten clean at your age. I'd probably be president."

Sebastian feels a swell of anger. Scott's taking a chance smoking out in the open like that. All they need is him getting deported.

"He's your big brother," says Hoop. "You should seriously see the two of you together."

"..."

"Top five brothers in the same band. One: The Allmans. Two: The Kinks. Three: The Replacements."

"The Replacements were brothers?"

"Four is the Stooges and five is Creedence. Yeah, two of them were: Bob and Tommy. Guitar and bass. Bob was an addict, didn't make it. Tommy was 12 when that band started, no shit. And they were all younger than you are now."

Sebastian looks at his tattoo. He notices a trio of blondes smiling at him, passing by.

"I missed the DIY times," Hoop says. "I was alienated as anyone in suburbia ever was, I was alienated as shit. But sorry, it was gonna take more to medicate me than a five-dollar punk show at the VFW. All right, boy wonder. What can I do to get you to snap out of it? You're not such great company tonight."

"Yeah."

Hoop scratches his beard and something like Parmesan particles tumble out. He comes out with his trickster expression. "I ever tell you I'm pals with Saul Bellow's last personal assistant? You know who Bellow is?"

"No."

"That's criminal, but anyway. A great writer. He was super-old, and among other things my friend would drive him around Boston. And he told me this story, one time they're out on Memorial Drive and it's a beautiful spring day and the students are everywhere, running and playing Frisbee and whipping around on bikes. And Bellow is in the passenger seat stopped at a red light and one kid pulls some crazy maneuver on his bike, almost gets sideswiped by a truck, and comes to rest right alongside Bellow's window. Bellow rolls the window down and looks at the kid, who almost surely doesn't even realize what danger he was just in, and Bellow looks at the kid and he says one word: 'Death.' And then he cackles like a crazy person and they drive away, this old dude looking like the Crypt Keeper howling with laughter."

"Is that my choice?" says Sebastian. "Be the biker or be the writer?"

"Both have their merits," Hoop says. "But no. Actually they're both right. The biker wasn't thinking about it. And the writer realized he couldn't do anything about it, so he had a belly laugh."

Sebastian likes the story, or likes the talking. "And now?"

"I'm reluctant to tell you," says Hoop. "Dead, unfortunately. Long dead."

Scott galumphs this way. Shaking his head, half across the street and mask half-dropped. The guys he just smoked with were critiquing the Buggy Whips, and Scott was spying. They didn't recognize him, and he piled on: called himself tone-deaf and smug, called his own guitar playing monochromatic and plagiarized. He looks down dizzy, assembling the pieces of himself and looking at the alphabet hidden in the many brick styles of the parallel parking lane, the sidewalk, the bike lane.

He says to Sebastian and Hoop, "I could not give less of a shit."

"Got that," says Hoop.

Scott rubs his forehead, agitated by the crowd's thinness and being told yet again by strangers that he'll never make it.

"*Illegitimi non carborundum*," Hoop says. "It was a great fucking show. What are we doing? Are we sucking our thumbs after a great show? Come on."

Sebastian thinks about death. Scott's pupils are snared in webs of red lines.

"So we're supposed to never let you guys off the stage? You're only happy up there?"

"I'm dazed," says Scott. "I'm merely dazed."

Hoop lights another American Spirit. "So it's on me to do another charming anecdote? All right. Hm." His cheeks divot, he dispenses smoke. "I followed around Alice In Chains and they wouldn't talk to anyone for three days after a show. Only would communicate with those...what are those flags you land seaplanes with? No, that's a lie...ah, but here's a true one: Billy Corgan once told me the only way he could come down after a gig is tell his manager what an incredible god he was, like, how much he appreciated everything he did, how they'd be totally lost without him. All right, he didn't say that. That one's a lie, too. I admit it."

"..."

"Guys, I'll talk to Jasper when it's time."

"When's that?" Scott says.

"Patience, grasshopper. The money isn't much different if you headline a place like this."

Scott tries his trick of scanning deep into a person's soul, but Hoop has deflector shields.

"Seriously," says Hoop. "Relax, it's cool."

"I'm just saying Jasper looked happy to me. We made him money tonight. In the States, we might even do something crazy like negotiate part of the door."

"Right right right, because I'm unfamiliar with the way the business works."

"..."

"What is it with you guys and your ruminations? Ceaseless ruminations."

"Song title alert," says Sebastian.

Well, he's tired of standing here. The truth behind *his* bewildered mood is: this is a time of evening that's perfect for the sweet trickle in the throat, the thing stretches the night. He doesn't say anything to them, and walks away down a skinny street, maybe looking for someone to give him something.

Scott watches him go, and says, "Collaborative. Is what you told us. No mysteries. No separation of church and state."

Hoop starts yet another cig. "It freaks me out none of you smoke these. I've been hanging out with musicians most of my life, and they *all* smoked. How'm I supposed to even relate to you healthy little shits?" He smiles. "What do you want to know, Scott? What do you think I'm keeping from you? There's no money yet. The money comes later. Play your ass off, that's your job. There's no barnstorming to raise funds anymore. There's pennies in the street, and that's it. Are you hungry? Are you cold at night? You're not chained to a radiator. If I didn't know better, I'd say this isn't really about what I'm telling you or not telling you."

"I've already seen the world," says Scott. "The world fucking sucks."

"You're trying to get something out of me. What piece of information do you think I'm withholding?"

"Maybe I want to know why you're even doing this, Hoop. Spending your own."

"Fun and adventure, man. It's only been a few weeks. I didn't think you'd be the one to crack."

Scott feels for the second joint in his pocket. He rolls back on his heels then forward again and his balance is pretty good. He can tell himself to live in the moment, but five seconds later he's thinking, *What if this doesn't work? What will I do then?*

Meanwhile Sebastian finds himself looking onto a canal gone shimmy with reflected light. Maybe it's better to feel bummed like this after a show. His hunger for drugs is worse when he's blissful after a gig, and then that bliss zips open to reveal his same old self. Lately (on Hoop's recommendation) he reads a lot of Watts and Ueshiba, Trungpa and Reps. Sometimes meditation is a way out of longing for amphetamines. He doesn't particularly believe in reincarnation but also knows it doesn't matter what he believes. Of course, the same things that offer relief one day are sometimes ineffectual the next. He knows the real way to feel good again: Adderall is insanely easy to find.

He stares at the canal's black water and that water's white edges.

Movement across the way catches his eye: outside a lighted commercial townhouse, several bodies dressed in black have gathered around a first-floor window.

Their shadows slouch and slink. Two of them pry at the window and shove it open, and a third lifts a leg and climbs inside. A tiny car passes on this side of the canal and Sebastian looks into the car then looks around, wondering if anyone else is seeing this. The first burglar lets in the others via a side door. Sebastian squints at an illuminated corporate logo, which appears to be one white word on a red field. He can't quite read it, but a quick search on his phone reveals the building's occupant: Halliburton.

A block north there's a bike bridge, and Sebastian runs across.

Scott once gave him a lecture about the evils of Halliburton, in his particular dilettantish Scott way: dismissive and resigned. The company (Sebastian inferred) represents the height of bad corporate citizenship, which means burglars confronting all that scary, infinitely-tendrilled immorality are probably good. He jets down Sloterkade imagining rebellion. Civil disobedience! Making mischief, like Hoop's crazy bird-headed friends in New York!

He slows and canvasses the building: four brick stories, probably once residential, converted to offices. There are three deserted bike racks out front and a circular sign that reads: *Inrit Vrijlaten.* He finds the pried-open window and looks inside: there's a shadowy hallway and someone is moving around just out of view. The night around him is dark and incautious.

He follows the initial burglar's lead and squeezes through the damaged window. For a moment he's stuck half-inside, has to balance himself on one hand and wedge his head around the jammed-open upper sash, scraping his big hairdo so it makes a frozen crispy sound in this quiet. But stealth isn't his goal. He wants to introduce himself to these people. He wants to know what they know. *Fill me with your outrage.*

This small office contains a desk and the doodads of a coconspirator: stress balls and Newton's cradles and plastic drinking birds and yo-yos. Sebastian hears voices. He thinks there must be safes to crack open, blueprints to scan, corporate defilements to verify. Of course, he has very little idea what Halliburton does, but these burglars must. Hoop was just his first step. He needs more guidance, another portal.

But he also needs a plan, because despite supposedly strict Dutch firearm laws, couldn't these guys easily be packing? Sneaking up on anyone would be unwise. He swallows hard, puts his hands up in a surrender pose, and steps out of this room.

A body is, in fact, standing out here. Someone has heard him. Oh, man, and now something is coming midair at Sebastian and he flinches, sober, horribly sober. He recognizes the ego in deciding to "allow" this burglary to happen. He's struck by something, in his shoulder. He's so stupid.

It clicks as it strikes. It hurts.

He looks down. It's a stapler.

The person runs away and Sebastian follows. There's a bullpen of half-height cubicles out here, and a receiving area with an expensive-looking glass Halliburton sign. Sebastian sees black-clad bodies slouching and receding: hiding from him. One guy is breathing loudly, cursing in Dutch. Another steps in from some distant office, carrying a flatscreen monitor. His mouth opens delicately and Sebastian sees the rotted yellow teeth of a tweaker.

"*Godverdomme*," someone says.

They all peek out at him and, not seeing a guard's uniform or a gun, emerge. Yes, they all wear dark clothing but not in some organized paramilitary way. They look homeless. One guy has on a torn Bart Simpson t-shirt; another wears shorts. The lone female has green hair.

"What are you guys doing?" says Sebastian.

"We go," one of them says. "No police." It's a ragtag gang of four and Sebastian can't stop himself from wondering which one of them is the Scott of the group, which is Kate, which is Amanda. He sits on an alarmingly comfortable rolling chair whose mesh conforms to his bottom.

The crackheads snuffle, ring-eyed, waiting to be rousted from the premises. One has a handful of Euro coins boosted from several desks. The girl scratches her arms and looks around for something good to steal when they make a break for it. Sebastian says, "I'm not here to stop you. This company sucks. Go at it."

They hesitate and examine each other.

Sebastian drums on the arms of his chair, thinking that getting clean isn't nearly enough. "I could not give less of a shit."

CAPITAL

The L.A.-to-Amsterdam red-eye is a thirteen-hour beast that connects through Minneapolis. Amanda ponders the last time she visited the Twin Cities, what, not quite two years ago? Staking out a hotel, looking for Bruce Springsteen? Her elbow is against the hot terminal window and she inspects shimmering airliner tailfins; the memory's stupidity is overpowering and she can't stifle a smile. She covers her mouth and covertly looks around to be sure nobody has taken her bitten grin as an invitation to become travel buddies.

She never gets recognized. The show's median audience is 64, and she doesn't hang out at Bingo or eat the Early Bird Special. The models sometimes kid with the producers that their viewership is surely dying out, and the producers ruin the joke by invoking actuarial stats. The older, poorer and fatter Americans get, the higher ad rates crank.

She has a two-year contract. She dislikes her job in the abstract, but trying on dresses and swimsuits and having her makeup fussed over is good fun, and the contestants…why does she love the contestants so much? Two shows a day, three days a week, three weeks a month, and Amanda never gets tired of the jumpy, shrieking knuckleheads who jostle to be called to Contestants Row. Maybe it's their lack of pretense. She's watched the producers interview three hundred hopefuls as they file into the studio—not more than twenty seconds of interview time apiece— and far from being annoyed by their antics, Amanda is tickled and not in a secretly-sickened way. Their exaggerated laughs and pleading faces are real and true. Finally, for once in their lives, they don't have to pretend. All the artifice that Amanda finds so unbearable is gone, and they are themselves: hungry animals.

One great pleasure of hiatus is letting her fingernails get grubby.

There are four other models (including one guy) and while their workdays are long, the job itself is predictably simple and unchallenging. It mostly boils down to appearing delighted by consumer products. Her cheeks and jaw are perpetually sore, and sometimes driving home she's surprised to find her face locked in an abstracted rictus. Audience members become flustered during meet-and-greets and snap selfies with their heads magnetized to hers, but it's obvious their love is situational: they're not interested in her name or story, and the models joke they're like Mickey and Minnie and Pluto over at Disneyland.

She lives with Caleb Flood, a 45-year-old movie producer with immune-system problems. He's tan and handsome and connected, and she *thinks* he's smart and funny, though his cleverness manifests almost entirely in relation to the film industry. When he's intuitive, it's about new sources of financing. When he's discerning, it's about lighting or special effects. When he's cutting, it's about a famous person he knows. Caleb admits at first he viewed Amanda as one more conquest to be swarmed under by his low-talking, understated charm and Bentley Flying Spur. But he became a true believer. They parasailed on Catalina Island, ate yellow-fin tuna, found karaoke at El Galleon, and fucked in a hotel suite, and Caleb was lost. He insisted on making room for Amanda in his huge Manhattan Beach house, has already implied that Gloria is welcome to move in, too.

He's also sick all the time. That first Catalina weekend may have been the healthiest Amanda has ever seen him. He's always stuffy and sore-throated, naps like an infant, and regularly sleeps in a guest room out of unspoken respect for Amanda's beauty rest (which of course is ridiculous because Amanda still only spends about three hours actually asleep per night). Caleb hints at a Chicago childhood of drafty bedrooms and meager blankets, but his real difficulty came after college out here in L.A. He tried doing standup and lived in a comics' house in Pico-Union whose landlord eventually wound up paying huge fines for all kinds of unsafe conditions; every resident of that particular house—all ages and genders—wound up with medical problems along the spectrum ranging from persistent sore throats to raging allergies to exotic cancers. Caleb has considered wearing a surgical mask when he leaves home, and the house itself has to be kept not only clean but bordering on sterile, to the point that he employs a specialty maid service run by biochemists. This adds to Amanda's sense that she lives in a mausoleum.

They have a lot of fun, though. It's a premiere every other weekend and fancy dinners in the hills and running on the beach. In some ways Caleb is younger than Amanda: he'll stay out drinking until she says it's time to go home, he DVRs soccer games and runs around the living room tearing out his hair, she goes with him to Chavez Ravine but refuses to do the Wave while he's up out of his seat encouraging little kids around them. The prospect of dating a millionaire producer sounded like a trapdoor into the offices of Clive Davis and David Geffen, or at least high-profile soundtrack work, but initially Caleb was clueless about music. He loved her voice—"a lot of people hit the notes; I hear your *anatomy*"—but had no taste: alone in his car he played Limp Bizkit and 50 Cent and Slipknot and Nelly.

But her agency dug up some names, and Caleb went to work on the phone. As a result she took meetings all over town and suffered mood swings indigenous to the Hollywood ingénue: stressing over clothing choices, rationalizing unreturned calls, decoding praise, puzzling out alliances, anticipating offers. In deference to Caleb, every exec or producer was suffocatingly positive at first; only the speed and intensity of their loss of interest distinguished them from each other. Advice was all over the place. Record a demo. Hire a consultant. Steal Iggy Azalea's producer, or Meghan Trainor's, or Ellie Goulding's. Leak a sex tape. When pressed, one Big Three label V.P. admitted—or pretended to admit—that he was flat-out prohibited from signing unknown acts. He told her: "Half-a-million Twitter followers is the ante." Amanda came home trembling from these meetings and Caleb massaged her feet.

A Thursday afternoon in Television City she was sucking in her tummy offstage while Melanie from wardrobe wrestled a too-small cocktail dress over Amanda's hips—sequins etching tooth marks on her ass—and Caleb phoned. She was topless, he was breathless. He'd made a breakthrough. She watched the skeletal brunette soap star wannabe waiting behind a curtain for her cue, and the Amazonian blonde Movie-of-the-Week veteran inspecting the state of her own makeup, the hung-over sometime country singer accepting Plinko instructions from a guy in headphones, even this Melanie with her hands pinching and tugging all over Amanda's body, exasperated, who once confided her dream of designing for Lindsay Lohan. Caleb said he'd finally been able to call in a favor and get her an in-studio audience with an impossible-to-attain producer. Amanda nodded amid the chaos, kept her poker face.

But it turned out the producer was Randy Pope. And he didn't remember her.

"First thing is I need to hear you," Pope said, flicking through a magazine on his iPad. "Go in that booth in there."

"Mr. Pope, you know me. We know each other. You produced some songs for a band I was in."

Pope looked up with sad expectancy. Amanda had gotten along with him fine last year but stood aside when Scott and Sebastian chose the nuclear option. To her, Pope was a tender figure: trying hard to be young with his dye job and his smeary wrist tattoos and his botoxed dead-fish eyes, playing at condescension to cover for pain. He'd been straight with her, had coached her with general tips he probably gave every singer ("chew your words...if you're not chewing the words, baby, you're just talking") but the tips were new to her, and she'd wanted Kid Centrifuge to work, and she'd chewed and chewed. It was the boys who'd butted heads with Pope, over production differences Amanda could barely hear.

"Right," Pope said now. "No record, got paid twice. Love jobs like that."

"I'm ready now," said Amanda. "I'm ready to work."

He sighed and looked at his watch, an expensive brand she was supposed to recognize. Every gesture meant to distance her actually made her hopeful, because he *didn't* piss her off, because she *could* stand his L.A. phoniness. It was such naked cover. "Baby, I don't remember. I really don't. Step in the booth?"

She did. This part was easy. The rest of living might be a mess but the thing in her chest could hold fraudulent walls at bay. She sang "Come Away With Me" with all that languid Norah Jones insistence and before Pope could say anything—she couldn't see him from in the booth—she thought it wise to illustrate the pop-tart angle and also did the Demi Lovato version of "Let It Go."

She came back out and he wasn't there.

His workstation beside the board featured strewn peanut shells, a stack of scribbled-to-death notebooks, a brass bust of Stalin, fruit flies buzzing around, a tub of Vaseline, and a framed photo of an unconscious, apparently vomit-streaked Little Richard. Amanda sat in his chair and waited. *People tell themselves stories about their own persistence,* she thought. *But they have no idea.*

What a break it was to have it be Pope. Anyone else, maybe she'd take the hint and go home. But she knew sticking it out would be rewarded. She swiveled in the chair and wondered which would be the best image: She is the *Price Is Right* beauty whose talent was right under everyone's nose! Or: She is the former rock frontwoman who found her calling in pop! Or: Where did *she* come from all of a sudden! This was a question for the new management Caleb would find her, of course, but if ever there was an appropriate moment to daydream. The world was but a funnel. Down and around, down and around, then surprising her with this chance meeting, everything leading directly to this moment.

He returned listening to assistants rattle off contract details. He offered a classic double-take that Amanda was still here, spinning in his chair no less. The assistants wore a dozen scarves and at least three rings on every finger. They retreated as though burned. Amanda saw in Pope's fish eyes that some test had been passed.

"Ho-kay," he said.

"I'm not sure if I was ever a person who knew what she really wanted," said Amanda. "I think I liked being the underdog, just following wherever the wind.... I mean, maybe I didn't impress you back then," knowing this couldn't be true, "but now it's just me and this is who I want to be."

He snapped his fingers. "Up."

"Sorry." They switched places.

"So I know what you think," Pope said. "You think nobody can resist those honey-thighs. You're hot, I grant you. If I was in a hornier mood I'd lock the door and make you a few promises. But you know someone who knows some serious people, baby, which means that's not a good career move for me. Anyway. When hot's enough? It's baby-girl hot. It's put a Catholic skirt on it. You're a little old for that, right?"

"..."

"So for you, it's about the voice."

"Okay."

"The voice isn't there, baby."

"..."

"Maybe nobody wants to tell you this because, well, look at you. It's not the notes. But it's just cold. Like, it's clinical, baby, I've seen it before. I'm not saying you're a lounge singer, you're better than that. But I don't believe you."

She kept grinning faintly. Air had combusted in her lungs, on her skin. She agreed. Dammit, she agreed. "I don't know what that means," she said.

"To you it's just words. And notes, too, yeah, but still. Here, listen. Once I had this French girl, big star over there. Somebody taught her American sounds and she made 'em perfect, like, nobody could tell she didn't speak the language. They gave her songs in English and she sang 'em and sang 'em, practiced for months until every little bit of her accent was gone. They played me her tapes, but didn't tell me about the French thing. And I said, 'This is what a zombie would sound like if it wanted to be a singer.'"

After the Kid Centrifuge ups and downs—the long nights and roadside peeing and rejection and teasing and frustration—Amanda had believed she'd hardened beyond tears. She searched Pope for mercy. But she could see this verdict *was* mercy.

She said, "You weren't even in the room. You weren't even listening. This is just something you say."

"Mid-twenties is old," he said. "My other advice is maybe go the fake-tit route."

That night she told Caleb that she never even got a chance to sing, because Randy Pope made a pass. She preemptively begged him not to seek retribution, and they went out to dinner, Caleb sneezing and snuffling and rubbing her neck.

The unfairness of Pope's judgment numbed her. She thought about his stupid words and disbelieved them, returned to them, spun them around, disbelieved them again. She had several incredibly happy days at work where her on-camera joy and spontaneity earned praise from the producers. Everyone could feel her warmth. Caleb asked if he should keep making phone calls and Amanda said she might be coming down with something, so maybe he should wait awhile. One Saturday he flew to Riyadh in search of financing and she sat on the second-floor porch overlooking the ocean's flat-toffee distance, the sun on her face, thinking this was exactly what everybody wanted, why was she struggling for something else?

It took a couple more days before she woke up and realized she could protect herself from further pronouncements by inducing Caleb to buy *Vampire* and getting the Kids back together. She ignored his suggestion that the songs should maybe be a little dancier.

On this trip she's reading Nabokov's translation of *A Hero of Our Time*: the "Princess Mary" section, in which the maddening Pechorin flirts scandalously with a princess while also falling back with his old lover Vera. Amanda hates Pechorin yet can't stop reading his story. He's arrogant and funny, nihilistic and punishing, he talks about the futility of life while tearing gloriously through it. He literally makes her heart race and she feels stupid about it, like a housewife caught reading mommy porn on the subway. If she's honest, some kernel inside her is engaged in measuring the men she knows against this Byronic ideal. Well, she doesn't *need* men, not that way. The older Dutch lady beside her reaches up to turn off the overhead light, *Amanda's* overhead light, and Amanda is forced to assert herself and explain that complete darkness isn't in the cards just now.

She calls Caleb when she lands in Amsterdam.

"Did you see any of them yet?"

"I'm getting a cab. I should take a shower first."

"Correct me if I'm wrong, but during your grubby beginnings you shared a van?"

"I don't know," she says. "You're right, it's just about unwinding."

"Have a great time. I miss you already."

"I'm psyched to see them play."

He says, "I must be a pretty secure guy sending you off to Europe to spend time with your ex."

"You really must be."

"…"

"I bought like seven bunches of kale," she says. "Make sure

you keep eating it, if you really think it's helping."

"I have a thing in Palm Springs. I'm told Jennifer Lawrence will be in attendance."

"Yes, Caleb, you're very handsome and many women want to be with you."

"Right," he says. "Just so we both keep that in mind."

His assistant made Amanda a reservation at an insanely expensive hotel overlooking the Keizersgracht, cuddled against 17th-century mansions. The lobby is wood-paneled Restoration; her room is a small recess-lighted box into which someone has squeezed a separate shower and tub, a step-up vanity, a chandelier, two wing chairs, an armoire, two double-bay windows and a poster bed fit for royalty. There's also a heavy ebony box she's afraid to open, having a terrible premonition that it's some kind of adorable long-distance engagement ring delivery mechanism. It turns out to be a selection of teas from around the globe.

Scott texts:

>Did you land okay?

She gets into the bed for just a moment—lights on, blinds open, still clothed—but falls asleep and dreams Kid Centrifuge is once again in Denver, recording demos. Long before Russell Gondal's showcase. Sebastian doesn't hate her yet. They're laying down those fun simple early songs. But in the dream she never gets up the nerve, she swallows her words, and they never record "Density of Joy." Instead they pack up their equipment early, look around the hangar with satisfaction. And it's lovely, everyone is smiling, nobody is betrayed. She has nothing to feel guilty about.

She's wakened by sounds of a shouting mob.

The windows are still pale gray, though a bedside clock indicates it's after 10 p.m. local time. Her phone reveals missed calls and more texts from Scott:

>Are you here?
>Are you still in L.A.?
>Hello?
>What's going on?
>In case you're in town, come see us at midnight: 115 Frederik Hendrikstraat.

Her mouth is pasty. Her hair is everyplace. She showers and averts her gaze getting dressed. She traveled light: just a few shirts, one skirt, one dress, a pair of jeans. This is the person she wants to be, no nonsense, unfettered. She notices there are four different wallpaper patterns in this room. Caleb's assistant has even bigger fake boobs than Colleen.

Downstairs it turns out everybody's watching soccer. She wanders over a canal bridge and sees a dozen open-air cafés where orange-clad fans are gathered around TVs, grunting and groaning with every kick. At really tense moments, thousands of louder roars echo around the Keizersgracht like competing philharmonics. Her phone says it's a fifteen-minute walk to Frederik Hendrikstraat and she crosses three canals; skiffs and houseboats are tied up all over the place, there are hundreds of bicycles left along the sidewalk, every window is open despite a chilly mist. A public park is set up with a big-screen TV and hundreds of fans clap and moan (and Amanda passes by a blue sculpture of an invisible man carrying a violin case). Finally she reaches the address and texts Scott.

He comes outside into the rainy roundabout. He's wearing a dark vest, a black shirt and a black tie. He's got copper scruff on his face and maybe he's thicker around the middle. Amanda thinks, *My God, he's dressing like Sebastian,* and rather than consider the ramifications she instinctively goes Full Reunion, waving her arms and scrunching up her face and screeching like he's a homecoming war vet. This ensures that when they hug, it means nothing.

To him, Amanda looks like Christmas morning. His knees won't bend.

They walk inside to the front room, which is a low circular bar behind which acoustic guitarists sometimes stand like blackjack dealers. Someone has rolled in a TV and the soccer fans look skittish. Scott leads Amanda downstairs to the Nieuwe Anita gig room, which is filling up. It's pretty big and no-frills to the extreme: concrete slab, hippie motif of bead curtains and rose-petal wallpaper, exposed wires wrapped around a PVC pipe, and little in the way of ventilation. To Amanda, it's the prototypical Euro-basement teetering between integrity and grime, but Scott is comfortable. He strides through the half-crowd and a couple people pat his back and shake his hand.

There's no stage, just a clearing amid bodies beneath a movie screen. Kate is here talking to a few Dutch cherubs; Sebastian isn't on the scene. Amanda taps Kate's shoulder and sees how different she looks: slimmer in the waist, broader across the shoulders, as if squeezed like a toothpaste tube. Kate also has a deep tan of serious outdoor pursuits, a brownness that grew from redness and seems to go an inch beneath the surface.

"My God," Amanda says. "You look so great." They hug, too. "Have you been working out? That's such a California thing to say."

"Believe it or not, I'm training for a triathlon." Gertie, Marcel, Joot and the others wish her luck and climb up to the balcony. Kate wears her fingerless gloves and fiddles with a stick. She wondered what her reaction would be, seeing Amanda. She feared a regression to envy, a shadow into which she would instinctively step. And her old roommate still is dazzling. But Kate has spent so much energy telling herself a story about the motherless girl who came to Europe three months ago to shed her old skin. It appears Amanda's light-devouring powers are no match for this tale, and that's how Kate knows they can still be friends.

"This is a great crowd," says Amanda.

"Yeah, it's okay. Thanks."

"Sometimes it's easy to think I made the wrong choice."

"Do you get to sing ever?"

"Just in the shower, ha ha. But I have time, I've just been lazy. I think coming out to see you guys will kick-start me to get back into it. So, I don't want to get all uncomfortable, but how's Sebastian doing?"

"Good, I think. He seems good."

"..."

"It's like, I'm not sure how much you...."

"No," Amanda says. "A lot of water under the whatever."

"I promise," says Kate, "it's not like we're some raging success. Tonight makes it look better than it is. We've only headlined a couple other times."

"..."

"Seriously. Hoop is still paying for everything. Who knows how long that lasts?"

Amanda picks up a whiff of pity coming from Kate, as though the drummer is downplaying something wonderful. She pulls back her shoulders and stretches to full height, far above her former roommate. "I hope we can hang out after?"

"Omigod," Kate says. "The decks are cleared. Definitely!"

Amanda climbs up to the balcony. More kids filter in downstairs, is how she knows the soccer game is over. Word spreads that the Netherlands lost to Argentina. Eventually a few of the pierced and tattooed people around her start a mini-chant: "Buggy...Buggy...Buggy...Buggy...."

There's no MC, they just come onstage and start. Sebastian looks gaunt and wears a jacket that's Scott's twin. Amanda actually sees the two of them exchange a fist bump as the audience whoops.

It's a little bit of a squeeze in here: a lot of orange jerseys but also some young women, a couple of whom tumble forward into Scott and lean over Sebastian's keyboard, seeking to hug both of them. There's no security. The guys just allow themselves to be pawed, wearing embarrassed grins. Sebastian's hair is amazingly shiny and high, like a wet seal. Kate counts them in.

It's a rocker. Kate bangs a pattern, Sebastian's hands swirl around his console, and Scott, guitarless, immediately brings his microphone into the crowd. He says, "Hi, everybody, we're the Buggy Whips." They cheer and he starts to sing:

Your birth certificate is an IOU
For the capital you'll one day pay
So let's undress in this mess while I confess
A strange address awaits your stay

There's a table against the far wall and Scott climbs up on it. The music is great. It's fast and big and sweet, and one of Sebastian's hands is playing ragtime piano while the other rocks out. Two or three fans grab at Scott's legs and feet and he stumbles on his four-toed foot, rights himself, and stands up, accidentally popping his head through the drop ceiling. He brings the mic up there with him and keeps singing, though the world can only see his bottom half:

Your bandage is a cover-up
And the capital is floodlit and dark
Wonder what we'll we do when we're free
The big three sing dirges in the park

Your asshole isn't yours anymore

It's a capital letter made of suede
They'll shake and take the break
That comes when the IOU goes unpaid

The show goes forty-five minutes and they play exactly zero Kid Centrifuge songs, and no covers. The houselights come back up blinding; the air is buzzy and hot with revelry. Amanda knows that in a couple minutes kids will be pecking at their phones again and memories of this show will fold atop others that have happened here, and others the kids have seen elsewhere. But in a way foreign to any other kind of gathering, and maybe any other kind of music, this rock show has been equal parts debauch and communion and for these final instants people still feel it in their ears and cheeks and guts (and sex organs). That this state has grown scarcer in the world seems to make it all the more precious, at least tonight.

Sebastian is sweaty and exultant, but he knows Amanda is here and he doesn't want to deal. He shakes Hoop's hand and confirms that Sanne and Arthur—two drug-addled computer programmers who apparently moonlight for Hoop, though considering how little money the bandmates have seen, Sebastian certainly hopes their part-time roadies aren't getting rich—will pack up and tend to the Yamaha. Sebastian slips upstairs and out into the strange July chill, and decides to walk back to the apartment on Wilhelminastraat.

Nightwalk out in the universe, undifferentiated from its fire and vultures.

A long time ago in Bed-Stuy, he'd start a hike late at night like this and feel pursued: killers around every corner, or criminal activities onto which he'd surely stumble and become embroiled. And it was ego: of *course* someone wanted to get him. Even a presumed victimhood puts the self at the center of events. Now he's older and understands his place on the periphery.

Across the street from the Nieuwe Anita he feels someone pull his elbow, and assumes it must be a mistake. But it's Kate.

"We both had the same idea," she says.

"Well, I know why it's awkward for me," he says.

Kate is still seeing the night in terms of what's laid out before her; when she's drumming from back of the room she certainly doesn't see everything, but it's a comfort knowing none of the madness can get behind her. "Oh, it's fine. She's fine. I'm glad she's visiting. Really, I'm just tired. You're heading home? Can I tag along?"

"Seeing Amanda super-makes me want to get high," he says.

"..."

"Yeah. Yes. Heading home."

They begin down Nassaukade and pass another club from which legit drums and a line of smokers issue, and they remember New York: brigades of sparkly-dressed women and beefy dudes angling to be deafened in dance clubs. The middling rock halls there were always reserved for once-titanic nostalgia acts.

"You coming home," says Kate. "Special occasion."

"Hey, I slept there Sunday. Ask Scott, he complained. There's more room for everyone if I'm not there."

"Oh, yeah," Kate says. "What a martyr you are."

"..."

"Sebastian, if I can't tease you a little.... The Dutch don't get sarcasm: they really believe I have to see a man about a dog. Every single time. 'Vat dog? Vy do you keep heffing to help zis man wiss his dog?'"

"Uh-huh."

"I like having you around, is all I'm saying. I'm being one hundred percent honest when I say: nights you stay somewhere else.... Well. Should we do something? What should we do?"

"..."

"..."

"Ah. Pass out, maybe?"

"Yeah," Kate says. "Y'know, one girl in there tonight was kind of sideways to me and she kept turning around, and she had on cutoff shorts and part of me was thinking, 'Boy, if she knew what her butt looks like in those shorts she'd be really embarrassed,' because it was kind of a total mess, but then part of me was thinking, 'Maybe she's totally aware how it looks and just doesn't care,' which would be kind of admirable. But I guess the larger point is: why am I thinking about this girl's butt instead of just playing, ha-ha."

"Well, you're bored?" says Sebastian.

She's not bored. Maybe she's just in much better physical condition and it takes less out of her to play. Maybe she's preoccupied by waking up at 6 a.m. to train: tomorrow the group will swim back-and-forth across the length of a lake down near the airport, something more than two miles. Or maybe she has a pair of eyes and a central nervous system and there's no accounting for what people think sometimes and she should just cut herself some slack.

"Lucius is getting married in Texas."

"Really?" Sebastian says.

"Amanda told Scott. Suspicion is: big wedding, everyone invited."

They pass another club where the combined chatter is almost a roar, but then it gets blown away by a super-loud Dobro. Sebastian stops to get a sense if the person can play: he or she is sliding, bending notes, but also plunking the occasional incorrect string. It's bluesy rock that also features a violin. Kate pretends not to notice Sebastian has hesitated. He hurries to catch up.

She says, "Do you really think she's just here for a visit?"

"Man," says Sebastian, "do we know who's playing in there? Don't we know everyone in the city by now?"

"..."

"I don't know. Suddenly I'm supposed to understand Amanda?"

Kate has two fingers on her wrist, and is counting her pulse rate. "She thinks we've got a good thing here and wants back in on it?"

Sebastian has stopped the Wellbutrin and Zoloft again. "The thought occurred."

They cross the street and turn onto Jacob van Lennepstraat, and see Lennep's unofficial monument: a giant naked woman painted along the full height of a four-story building, atop a Lennep poem written out in Dutch. The woman's vagina is pixelated out of the painting, and in front of her a small anonymous man is falling through space.

"Anyway, Amanda was interested in your romantic life. First thing she asked."

This thrills him a little, as it was intended to do. "Ack," he says.

"But you know where my loyalties are. I played it very cool."

Across this canal more music scuds into the sky, but it's impossible to figure whether it's live or recorded.

"I told you I saw a friend of yours?" says Kate. "After the

thing near the hostel the other day. Pretty gal."

"This is a big topic for you tonight."

"I don't see you much, dude. I give out information when I'm able. A brunette barmaid in a headscarf. Unbelievable cheekbones, gorgeous chin dimple. The message she asked me to deliver was mixed. On the one hand, 'Tell that asshole to go play in traffic.' On the other hand, 'Have him text me.' Hey, I'm flattered just to be recognized as the guy next to the guy."

"Come on," says Sebastian. He remembers the woman, doesn't remember her name: a tiny loft apartment with roommates near the IJ, this woman bent over a futon asking him to choke her as she also put a finger to her drawn-tight lips begging him to be silent.

"Maybe Hoop thinks we're stalling out? Called her to ramp the sex appeal back up?"

"Huh," he says.

"But he'd tell us first, right? He'd tell you."

Sebastian looks at his tattoo, which is slick with mist. "Maybe it isn't some evil thing. Maybe it's really just a visit."

These days Kate gets locked into watching her own feet, a habit she's reacquired from running so frequently. She thinks of Billie Turner. "I like Amanda. We went through a lot together."

Headlights make moving feathers against the dark brick building along this sidewalk. In room after room they can see TVs still tuned to postgame soccer reportage.

"Should we get food?" Sebastian says, and Kate makes a face. "It's weird, right? Never knowing what's going on with people you supposedly know pretty well? Not weird. Totally expected. But still pretty weird."

Music goes! It's on both their minds, and they both *know* it's on both their minds: sometimes the pauses between shows that constitute the rest of life, sometimes they pass so easily it's as if the songs are only on a break. Tonight, no. That Nieuwe Anita fun might well be a week ago, for the dearth of marks they feel on themselves now. And it was a big show! The triumph should last! That there isn't always an explanation for such things doesn't mean there isn't one tonight.

"So," says Kate. "Are we stalling out?"

" . . . "

" . . . "

"..."

She says, "In an apartment that would go for like 1,600 Euros a month and we personally haven't paid cent one?"

"..."

"..."

"Eventually we'll make another record," he says.

"..."

"You think she's here because she wants something, because you think that's how she is." They've entered the quiet neighborhood near home. They pass two sinister green metal boxes affixed to the bike lane. As always, they hum with electrical menace. "You think, be on high alert."

"Why do people call it that?" Kate says. "A 'record.' There hardly are actual records anymore. And they never say 'record.' It's 'reckerd.' 'I just got the latest Jack White reckerd.' Reckerd, reckerd, reckerd."

"I'll ask Hoop. He won't admit anything. He'll say she's pretty and then quote some book I never heard of."

"I'm trying not to feel like it's impossible," she says. "I'm trying not to feel like we're standing at the base of the same old giant wall trying to figure out ways to climb. It's just something we'll never get over, maybe. Too long, just waiting for the right person to say yes."

"We got far. We'll do it again."

"Definition of insanity," says Kate.

"The light," Sebastian says, pulling out the apartment key. "It just goes right to her, doesn't it?" He doesn't mean this as a compliment.

BAG OF WATER

Scott and Amanda sit in an after-hours club and get high on super-polm hash.

For a while they just look at each other and giggle. To Amanda, it's suddenly being here in Europe, smoking like this in public, seeing old friends, just basically being stupefied at the craziness. To Scott, it's seeing Amanda and the possibility of being seen by her in a new light. Except he also sees her laughing at him and fears she finds him ridiculous, so some of his giggling turns into self-mockery and trying to be seen as down-to-earth and cool and a worthy object of someone else's targeted giggling.

"So," Amanda says, "now you're a rabble-rouser."

"..."

"The songs. Stuff about, what, money and class? A baby with a briefcase? It's not 'Styles Make Fights,' anyway."

"When does your TV show start back up?"

"Couple weeks? What I mean is: you guys were great tonight. Seriously. It's not so different with the keyboard and no bass, the songs are.... I mean, it's really great. I can still hear what I always liked so much." She touches her face. "I am really feeling this."

"You want my last bass player joke? 'What's the difference between a bass and an onion? Nobody cries when you chop up a bass.'"

Amanda laughs, too hard. "Ohh," she says.

"I'm pretty blasted."

"How often do you smoke this stuff?"

"Yeah, I mean. Maybe once or twice a…. Not this stuff, this is a special occasion. But after shows sometimes. I told you," he says, "I loosened up."

"Song title alert."

This club is set up like a big living room in a light-industrial neighborhood, and they had to walk through an auto-body shop to get in. The pot and hash supposedly come from a coffeeshop right near where the band just played, though the prices are marked up pretty intensely, since the shops stop serving at 1 a.m. They're sitting close to some windows, and hear a few guys wolf-whistling after a group of women. Strangely, the women are in workout clothes at two in the morning. Amanda says, "I mean who doesn't look good in yoga pants?"

"…"

"That's enough for me. You finish." Her face drops and she's looking at her knees. She says, "It's like a movie about my life."

"What is?"

"You said that. You said that in the movie."

He fetches them cups of water. There's a fight on the street outside: angry soccer fans whose interpretive dance numbers keep crashing into one another. Blood marbles their jerseys. Amanda watches with the strongest *déjà vu* of her life. She doesn't feel conventionally drugged but rather as though the world has finally acquiesced and revealed itself in anti-paranoia. Nothing is connected, nobody is watching, but the movie is still being made.

"So about *Vampire*," she says.

"Who's selling?" says Scott. "Like, it's some bankruptcy court or something?"

"Well, I haven't gotten that far. This is mostly theoretical."

"…"

"Ha-ha, I'm kidding. It's the parent company. They already sold the computers and filing cabinets, it's a write-off. But *Vampire* was a sore spot…or at least, y'know. They pretended it was a sore spot."

Scott isn't actually all that high. "It seems like a hundred years ago."

"It took a month. The first guy I talked to, it was like ten minutes to register what I was asking about. Then I waited forever and eventually got his boss, who was…I guess, agitated? By the time I got the right woman, she was outraged." Amanda makes a series of wobbly escalating levels with the flat of her hand.

"Sidelong. Side. Long." He looks around. A couple tattooed guys enter through the swinging auto-body shop door. Armchairs leak stuffing, there's a hookah setup, and it's easy to imagine avatars hovering in a mist above each smoker in here, acting out some bleary fantasy grounded in self-annihilation.

Amanda says, "Music conglomerates go through this all the time. I'm sure. But the trick," she takes a big breath of just pure air, "is they always act like it's the first time."

"How much do they want for it?"

"'Well, I do declare, we here at Worldwide Amalgamated just get the *vapors* thinking about all the love and caring and other human feelings we put into that li'l ol' record. We simply can't *bear* to imagine parting with it.'"

"…"

"The amount is…agreed upon," says Amanda.

"Really? You got the record? Who bought it?"

She smiles, eats the smile. It seems like a long time goes by before she answers. "Caleb Flood? He's a movie producer who's…I guess breaking into music? He believes in the record."

"Holy."

Amanda laughs again, and doesn't know why. From five thousand miles away it was easy to imagine that Kid Centrifuge was merely on a break, but seeing tonight's show has put the lie to her optimism. They're a trio now, and this means she's here to change their minds. By instinct, even as she's experiencing all this in the third person, she begins to hatch tactics: every band member will demand their own strategy. Sebastian will require guilt, Kate will have to believe it's actually her own idea, and Scott…well, Scott is pretty obvious.

He says, "What are you asking? You want to…shop it around to labels who if they know anything about the Kids it's nothing good?"

She slaps the table and works to keep her chin upright. "It'll sell. We can sell it. It's great."

"…"

"What."

"This isn't….. I'm not the only one you need to convince. I know two other people who consider themselves Buggy Whips now."

"You're saying it's too late."

"I'm saying. I'm not saying anything." He feels for the necktie knot against his throat. "If this had happened right away, if this happened even six months ago...I mean, obviously. We would've jumped."

"So what's really changed? Are things that good here?"

"Who is this guy?" says Scott. "'Breaking into music?' Didn't we decide enough was enough with these guys? These ultra-rich guys who run everything and tell the world's sincerest lies."

Amanda considers grabbing his hands across the table, but doesn't. "We didn't get a real chance," she says. "Sidelong was totally wrong for us. It was my fault." She really needs to deliver these next lines. "I feel terrible about it, Scott. I already have one condition with Caleb, which is we use the original mixes and 'Density of Joy' is not on the album anymore."

He blinks and inspects the half-gone joint in his hand: the hash is rolled into a brown snake and peeks out from among tobacco flakes. It smells like incense and tastes like coffee and flowers. He has a moment of intense loneliness, the kind where everyone in the world is masked and unknowable and his best efforts at assimilation are doomed to fail. He masturbates so much whenever Sebastian stays somewhere else. Everywhere in the world is dark to him, but here's Amanda. "So this guy is getting into management?"

"..."

"*Caleb.* Who the hell has a name like that? Caleb."

"Yeah," she says.

They talk about nothing for a long time. The club settles way down into its midweek component parts, which include some very sleepy stoners. The counter guys are listening to *Yoshimi Battles the Pink Robots* and eating cheese sandwiches. Scott tries giving Amanda a hard time about *The Price Is Right*, but it's impossible because she keeps giving herself a much harder time.

"I'd like to write a song called 'Human Mannequin,'" she says, typing in the air, "except my fingers are too weighed down by borrowed jewelry."

"It's not any fun at all, making your face vacant and waving at dudes off camera?"

"Mm, it's *okay*, but what's better is listening to the other girls complain about doing three hours of yoga and Pilates and Stairmaster every day. And also it's super-fun blocking people on Twitter because they took time out of their busy day to send me pictures of their junk. Oh, yeah, this kind of fame—the kind where you're a pair of boobs and nobody knows your name—is the thing healthy little girls dream about."

At about 4 a.m. they look at the floor around them, as though jointly expecting to find many burdens to hoist and carry. But neither of them has anything, and they smile like jewel thieves making a clean getaway. As they're standing, the shop door heaves open again and two middle-aged guys come scuttling in. They're immensely fucked up. And one of them is Hoop.

"Oh, shit," says Scott.

"Hey!" Hoop says, lurching nautically over this way. "Yo, it's my lead shinger! Whatchoo doing here! Bazzy, come over, man. Come meet my lead shinger!"

Bazzy is a balding guy with a handsome brown face and a pencil mustache. He's so drunk he can't stand straight, and his eyes are one-third open. He hunches toward Scott and says, "Ah! Ah! Mister Tungsten, yes!" except he says it *tongue-stone*.

"Go shit down," Hoop says, overloud. He tries to reach in his pocket but misses, laughs a laugh that turns into a cough. "Bazzy. You shee that couch? I'm gonna...I'm gonna talk with my lead shinger a minute."

Bazzy stumbles away and says, "Tell the girl to stay." He bangs a knee against the octagonal wood cabinet that sits at the living room's center and houses the intricate hookah setup. They hear him say, "Oh, mommy," as he kicks vengefully at some pillows and rubs the knee. There are three or four other patrons left in here, but they're all asleep.

As Bazzy falls onto his couch, Hoop's smile disappears and he assumes a sober whisper. He says to Scott, "How the fuck do you know about this place?"

"Arthur and Sanne told me," says Scott. "This is Amanda, by the way. As in: you know, *Amanda*-Amanda."

"Hi, Amanda-Amanda. Glad to talk about the good old days, but you should get out of here." Hoop wrenches around again and drunkenly waves at Bazzy, who's sucking his teeth and massaging his knee, and Bazzy shouts, "That is why I love the rock music: beautiful girls!"

"Who is that guy?" Scott says.

Hoop takes a few uncertain steps toward the door, and he gestures for Scott and Amanda to join him outside. They do walk out; Hoop trips or pretends to trip against the doorjamb. They pass through bays of medieval car-torturing equipment, then step into the wet chill of night.

Hoop says, "Bazzy just so happens to be," and he ticks these things off on his fingers, "a wealthy and rock-loving individual, a relative of some seriously powerful oil money, the brother-in-law of the guy who books the Melkweg, *and* the cousin of the woman who basically runs Vechter Records, which for a while now I thought was actually 'Vector Records,' like, as in the direction. But it actually means 'fighter.'"

Scott and Amanda look at each other. Scott says, "Hoop, are you using?"

"Jesus, fuck." He wipes away crumbs or dust from the chest of his ancient t-shirt, whose pocket presumably once bore a consumer logo but is now adorned by a white blob. "Of course not."

" . . . "

"Bazzy is connected as anyone in the city."

Scott thinks maybe he hears Hoop slurring a little for real. He looks into the older man's eyes, and Hoop holds still to allow the inspection. It's true: the manager's expression is steady, but Scott does see one pupil more dilated than the other, and one of his irises is quivering.

"Go home," Hoop says. "Get rest." He shakes Amanda's hand. "It's good to meet you. Welcome to Amsterdam. Listen, we'll hang out later." He walks back into the garage singing something that gets lost in its own echoes.

"Am I crazy?" Scott says.

"No," says Amanda.

This neighborhood is car dealerships and gas stations and prefab two-story buildings, some of which reside behind serious security gates. Amanda can hear bells and barge-horns, though she can't actually see water. The moon is gibbous but fading.

"I'm going back in there," says Scott. "He used to be an addict."

"Then I'm going with you," Amanda says.

"Recovery is kind of his thing. Never shuts up about it."

She touches his shoulder. He gets a happy tickle down his sternum, stops himself from saying, *Wow I sure missed you.* She leads him in and Bazzy is still on the couch but now is suckling a hookah hose that isn't attached to anything. Hoop is ordering at the counter. Amanda topples onto the cushion beside Bazzy's. She says, "Hi, I'm Ginger! I like your suit!"

"Oh oh oh," says Bazzy. "Ginger. You have an eye for fine things. This is Brioni, the wool is from vicunas. I would invite you to join me but here you are."

"You boys have been drinking!" Amanda says.

Bazzy makes a *pshaw* gesture. "Americans worry too much about the habits of everybody else. What a lovely face you have. Who do you bring into my mind?"

"Oh, I'm not American, silly. I'm from the moon."

He tries to remove a cigarette from his pack without removing his eyes from her boobs. He says, "Ginger, Ginger, Ginger..." and somehow loses his balance while seated, capsizing backwards so she can see a nightcrawler scar that begins at one ear and wraps all the way down around his Adam's apple. She catches him and hauls him back up, smelling gin and butter and (there's no way around this) a hint of feces.

Scott stands with Hoop as he scans a laminated menu. The guys behind the counter are fresh and attentive; there are no clocks in this living room, perhaps so patrons never question the hour, like in a Vegas casino. Scott says, "What can you tell me about Caleb Flood?"

"Could I have the Orange Cream, please?" says Hoop. "See? I'll just tell him he's smoking hash. Who's Caleb Flood?"

"Yeah," Scott says.

"Be better if you left Bazzy to me. He's a fucking degenerate. But he came to the show tonight and clapped his hands a little. And I guess having your honey flirt with him is a pretty solid idea." Hoop hands over several Euros. "Thanks. Okay. Listen your concern is admirable, Scott. I'm not using." He pockets his change, but drops a couple twenty-cent coins that roll away. Hoop and Scott swap layered glances that could mean: *Who cares about a few cents?* or could mean: *My balance isn't good enough right now to go stooping all over the place.*

The four of them smoke the sweet tobacco in a circle. Bazzy puts his hand on Amanda's leg and blows rings. He also has a little ultraviolet bottle of something in his interior jacket pocket and keeps squeezing doses into his mouth. He holds the glass pipette dropper by its rubber bulb, seeking to feed Amanda like a baby bird, and she gives the appearance of accepting but lets the drops fall into the couch.

"Mm!" she says, and rubs her tummy.

"Shingle greatesht band in hishtory," Hoop says. "Who you got? Go."

"Trick question," says Scott. "Nobody could ever pick just one."

"I don't even *like* music!" says Amanda.

"Bazzy?"

"Mm? Yes. Of course I agree with Tongue-Stone. We are too many selves." He holds out both hands as though expecting a bounce-pass. "Whose arms are these? They belong to some old man."

Amanda places a finger on his wedding ring. "Oh, foo! Don't tell me you're married, Bazzy!" He frowns and practically twirls the tiny mustache. Amanda pretends to sulk.

"Now, now, Ginger."

"Wrong!" says Hoop. They look at him. He burps into his fist.

"You know my heart belongs to you," Bazzy tells Amanda.

"The ansher is the Pixiesh. The mosht perfect band of all time."

"..."

"The perfect dishtillation of everything that came before. The Roshetta Shtone for everything that came after." Scott thinks now Hoop has accidentally launched into a Sean Connery impression. "I can do you one better. The greatesht *shong* in hishtory!" He puffs obscenely at his hookah hose then sings in a high-pitched voice: "Ooh-ooh. Ooh-ooh."

Amanda-as-Ginger guffaws cruelly and says, "What's a Pixies? *You're so ooooold!* Don't worry, Bazzy, no matter how old you get you'll never be as old as him."

Hoop sings:

Where ish my mind?
Where ish my mind?
Wheeeeere ish my mind?

Scott is tired. Instead of feeling lonely now he's irritated with the segment of humanity known to him, and his Sisyphean lot in life: presented to a series of rich guys who stand with elbows folded safeguarding the stuff of his dreams. For a moment last year he thought he'd gotten behind the gates but it was a trick, a devil's bargain, wear this mask and we'll let you in. He says, "You know what? It isn't worth it. So we play tiny clubs the rest of our lives, or we just stop playing. We'll deal with it. Nobody ever promised anything."

"'Your head'll collapsh if theresh nothing in it,'" Hoop tells him.

He remembers Amanda that first summer when they rehearsed in Harlem, how she made them play songs over and over, how she barely smiled when the rest of them got excited about how good they sounded. She's the one who kept things on the rails up in Massachusetts, and made prescient little icy remarks aimed at Colleen. But maybe she's also Ginger. She abandoned them, and now she wants them back. He tries to read her now— kicking her legs out in delight, feeling Bazzy's biceps, fanning herself because the hookah smoke is *sooooo* strong—and her act is terrifying for its seamlessness.

The club closes at five. They find themselves under a perfectly bright sky though sunrise hasn't yet begun, and there's talk about heading to the *kamers* in De Wallen. But then it seems for some reason that Hoop has challenged Bazzy to a footrace.

"C'mon you old donkey," he says. "I'll run circles around you."

"What is this?" says Bazzy. "We are elegant men."

"Once around the block," Hoop says. "You win, you get this watch, which I stole from Bono's hotel suite. I win, you get your brother-in-law to book the Buggy Whips."

Bazzy scans all three of them, and for a moment is a mark recognizing the sting that has ensnared him. But instead of betraying disappointment, he paws at Amanda's backside and says, "I do not want the watch." He begins folding up his jacket in preparation.

"Wait a minute," Scott says.

"Ooh! Fun!" says Amanda.

Hoop starts doing deep knee-bends. "Left at the end of the block up there, then three more lefts. Scott, you're the referee."

"No," Bazzy says. "It is for Tongue-Stone's gain. He will not be fair. My lady Ginger, you will say the winner?"

Amanda agrees. She's shivery and sober, her hair sproings around her face. Hoop says Scott will follow them around the block to make sure Bazzy doesn't cheat.

"How will I cheat?" Bazzy says. "I will pull at your stupid beard?"

"Who's calling whose facial hair stupid?" says Hoop.

They toe an imaginary start/finish line. Hoop stoops over like a speed skater, and Bazzy also bends his knees trying to appear athletic for Amanda. She lets them wait, just like that. Hoop looks ready to pitch over. She makes a finger pistol and aims it at the Buggy Whips' manager.

"Bang!"

The older men take off, with Scott in pursuit. Hoop leads, but by the first turn he's winded. Bazzy's swank shoes skid around but he's in some semblance of physical shape, whereas Hoop is primarily powered by bacon. Scott sees how far back this block goes.

"Hey, ah," says Hoop, as Bazzy pulls even. "Did you know the Stones traded the rights to 'Paint It Black' for a lifetime supply of beer?"

"Mada?" Bazzy says.

"Tom Jones' chest hair is insured for seven million dollars."

Bazzy begins to laugh, which slows him down. "Are you telling me these things?"

"Termites chew wood two times faster when listening to rock music."

Bazzy turns his head to look at Hoop, and smacks face-first into a streetlight. Hoop runs away.

"Holy shit," says Scott, trailing. "Jesus! Hoop, come back! He's hurt!" Bazzy is on one knee, holding the left side of his face.

The manager's voice echoes: "No fucking way!"

Bazzy's cheek is bleeding. He breathes through his nose, furious, and touches his pants. "Ah-ah, my Brioni," he says. Scott helps him up and they look at the light post's graffiti: Anne Frank's face and the legend: "One Year As A Tiger." Scott says, "Song title alert."

Bazzy hightails it, a hole in one knee. Scott looks at this neighborhood—hardscrabble, anonymous, its silence roaring like a jetliner—and nothing seems worth it.

He runs ahead, fast enough to see Bazzy with his head down, arms swinging. They round the second corner and catch Hoop before the third, and he calls out, "Eric Clapton grew up thinking his mother was his sister!"

Bazzy is still pissed. He circles a thumb and forefinger and sticks the gesture in Hoop's face, then shows the Americans a V-sign with the back of his hand. He pulls to the lead and this is enough for Hoop, who stops, puts his hands against the body shop's exterior brick wall, and pukes a geyser of yellow syrup.

Gasping, forehead against the wall, he tells Scott, "All...part...of the plan."

Amanda sees Bazzy come around the final corner. She claps daffily, but then sees his face is bloody. He stops, leering and fighting the appearance of breathlessness, and she says, "Shoot, did you stab those other guys?"

Bazzy drives them for breakfast at a decaying diner. They eat omelets and tiny apple pancakes which Scott doesn't realize also contain ham until he's partway into his third. His self-pity is immense. Throughout the meal Amanda examines his pouty mouth and wants to smack him. She'll show all these men who's a prize.

Later Hoop climbs in a taxi. Scott holds the door open, but Amanda doesn't step from the sidewalk. She places a hand against Bazzy's provisionally bandaged cheek and says, "No, I have to go with him, silly!" Bazzy makes a closed-mouth 'o,' stifling laughter.

"We should really get home," Scott says. "You must be so tired."

"Ginger is from the moon," says Bazzy. "Do they get so tired on the moon?"

"See ya later, Scott," says Amanda. She smiles sweetly and bats her eyes.

"See you, Tongue-Stone."

"Enough," Scott says. "Amanda. Come on." He's never been so drained and it's easy to believe she never came to Amsterdam. This version, whoever this is...she ignores his plea. Gravity cranks tenfold, or perhaps it's only inside his heart.

As he steps into the taxi, he thinks he should say something cutting. But he doesn't. The cab pulls away and he watches her recede, and Hoop says, "Nirvana got kicked out of the *Nevermind* release party for starting a food fight."

Bazzy drives her to his apartment. They pull onto a narrow road abutting a canal and he says, "Private parking space!" as though it will make her wild with desire. He owns the third and fourth floors of a brownstone whose interior is so clean it might suit Caleb. She glides upstairs, fully Ginger.

He leaves her in a parlor before a full-length mirror. She looks fresh. This could be anywhere and any time and that's the point: burrow in heedless. Halfway around the world, why should she choose now to stand still? No suburban hell or trailer park, no bourgie striver or city cop, no marching orders but a song. *If I'm to be defined in opposition to so many other people and things, at least I'll present a moving target.* And she also thinks it's nice now that it doesn't much matter to her anymore what other people say.

Bazzy returns with wine, wearing a bathrobe. He's blissfully comfortable with being an ogre: it doesn't feel like a pose, like, there's no squishy Bazzy to break through a wicked shell. In a way, Amanda approves of the honesty. He hands her the wineglasses and executes a slow-motion R&B spin. A tidy square of fresh gauze is taped over his injured face. He lets the robe fall open and presents a penis that looks like a translucent bag of water.

Amanda finds a sideboard and puts down the glasses. She slinks over to Bazzy, locked on his eyes. His grin betrays a tremble. She looks down, feeling heat come off of him.

"Ohhhh," he says. "Ginger, please make me believe."

"Make you believe what?" says Amanda, not touching him.

"That you love me."

She takes out his black pupils, *pop-pop*, just by not blinking. "Hm," she says. "I'm afraid that'll have to wait. First I'll need you to get my friends' band booked."

His mustache is almost certainly drawn-on, a painstaking effort. He's focused on not showing weakness, an effort that's grotesquely weak. "No," he says. "This other thing—between you and me—must happen first."

"..."

"I do not book. It is my sister's husband."

"But the influence you must have." She's still very close to him. Now he smells like unwashed hair and ladies perfume.

"No of course not," he says. "How do I know you would do it? After?"

"But Bazzy, a favor like that. I would *want* to."

For a moment his face fights a gust only he can feel, then he clutches the robe and pulls back his pecker. "No. It is only this way, the way I say."

She nods and half-smiles. "Okay. If that's the only way. I'm sorry." She kisses his ear and strides to the front door.

It's one of those things she just sees: the old man closing his eyes, trying to reclaim the music she's just taken with her—the music of power, as reflected in all the eyes that have ever stared up at her, *fuck* Randy Pope—and, failing, looking over his shoulder evoking a thousand pathetic would-be cinematic lovers, the loser having lost.

"Please.... I accept."

So they drink wine and pretend Amanda hasn't won. He talks about the mosques of Medina, the pilgrims on whose backs his father made his initial money selling stolen copies of the Quran. Eventually she texts Scott for his address.

A groggy Hoop lets her in, inspects her stained mouth, and retreats to his bedroom. The living room is bright and empty. Amanda slips into the second bedroom. From the floor, Scott hears her but pretends to be asleep. They're back in the States, on the road, and she's poisoning him one morning at a time.

He hears her shoes thump off. He hears her sigh and leave the room. He hears the shower.

Sebastian would just fall asleep. That kid has it figured out. No woman is worth pain like this. Scott hasn't slept with anyone since Jane, though when the bandmates ask he implies occasional secret action. Sometimes on non-gig nights he stays out super-late by himself, drinking coffee and shuffling lyrics, and makes extra noise returning. Sometimes he checks out ladies that come to Buggy Whips shows, but they're interested in Sebastian. This morning he smiles and suffocates himself in his pillow.

She comes back wearing one of Sebastian's t-shirts. Scott hears bedsprings.

"Well?" he says.

"Did I really just get here yesterday? I can't believe it." She looks down. In dim light she can see his feet poking out from bedsheets, and his missing toe: a sorrel button of tissue that contrasts the milky-white rest of his foot. It's so real.

"..."

"He's gonna push his brother-in-law."

"You have a hotel room," says Scott. "What are you even doing here?"

"…"

"Did you, ah…."

"…"

"Did you?"

She lets the question breathe. It's mean; she feels bad how easy this is. She says, "Of course not. Go to sleep."

DESERVE IT

Sebastian and Amanda finally see each other late Friday morning. They meet in Dam Square, in front of the palace. Right when they come together the sky produces a hokey window of sun. His hair is low and he wears a white t-shirt and Bermuda shorts, a relative slovenliness Amanda can't interpret. But he's still crazy-gorgeous. Even hugging him hiplessly gives her a jolt.

"I didn't do anything yesterday," she says. "Where were you?"

He tries not to hear subtext. "Well, what do you want to see?"

They examine the snot-colored palace, its oxidized dome and various roof statues of green people doing athletic things. Across the way is a war memorial: a seventy-foot pillar bearing reliefs of white stone-people in various states of suffering. And just off the square is a 15th-century church with a three-story glass window bordered by museum lettering. They make funny faces at all the high culture. Madame Tussauds is the fourth point in this square.

It's €22 apiece, a total rip-off. They pay.

The creepiness of Tussauds is breathtaking. Cackling tourists sprint around snapping photos with wax ghosts. If asked, most would probably profess to being attracted by craftsmanship, and the models *are* uncanny. But of course, were they lifelike models of unfamous people, who would buy a ticket? So there's something about being granted proximity to facsimiles of inaccessible humans, but that's not quite it either. Death is in the air. It's not only that many of the models portray famous people no longer among the living, but also that they don't move. They are death masks with eyes open. Children in particular seem invigorated around these monuments to death-in-life; they squeal and twirl and run, delighted.

They pass a pajama'd Picasso, and Dali with a rooster on his shoulder, Einstein and Van Gogh and Mondrian, Steve Jobs on a staircase, and then come the musicians: Bono, Michael Jackson, Prince, George Michael, Bon Jovi and Lenny Kravitz in a circular stare-down, followed by a triumvirate of Elvis, David Bowie and Bob Marley. Sebastian lingers while Amanda filters into other areas, but she comes back frowning and says, "Horrendous. They have an Anne Frank writing at her desk."

"..."

"Not a lot of lady musicians, I notice. Poor murdered Jewish girls, hells-yes."

"He's got a great look," says Sebastian, admiring Elvis' black silk shirt and red satin jacket with sparkly black lapels. "But an acoustic? Agh."

"So," Amanda says, "you hate me now."

"Come on. Manipulative much?"

"You blew me off. You didn't want to see me."

"..."

"I was disloyal. You guys wanted to keep going, and I jumped ship. I know how much loyalty means to you, Sebastian."

"If this is what we're gonna talk about, you just figured out why I was avoiding you."

"I could give you a line about wanting to stay near my mom and my grandma. But you know being close to my family makes me crazy."

Sebastian wanders away. Freddie Mercury is singing into a mic, but his other arm is suspiciously in the *sieg heil* position. Then comes a bombshell standing by a window looking down on Dam: a blonde in a white halter who a placard says is "Doutzen Kroes," undoubtedly some Dutch beauty Sebastian should be embarrassed for not knowing about. Amanda is following him.

"Don't be a brat," she says.

He sees this scene—burbling white children racing around arms akimbo, an elderly couple mournfully observing an exhibit of a dead pope, his untouchable ex-girlfriend in almost the same posture as the white-haltered dummy and no less perfect—and thinks there's a sad song here. And the figurines themselves might be the least-sad part. The words don't come to him, but the feeling is there: something he can explain to Scott, who'll maybe chisel it down to actual lyrics.

"Sebastian."

"You want to tell me something?" he says. "I'm seriously chill and not mad at you. Go ahead and tell me something."

"I didn't think it was fair."

"…"

"We got a deal, we got all that promotion, and it happened fast and we had to ignore our past. Yours and mine. But once we didn't have to ignore it anymore…."

"Okay, I think you're about to put something on me that's pretty ridiculous."

"I figured you'd be happier if I wasn't around, so I stopped being ar—"

"Horseshit!" he says, is how he realizes he really is pissed off. A couple burbling children halt mid-scamper, as though expecting to be reprimanded. Sebastian does a *sorry* face, but isn't sorry. "Believe it or not, I have more going on in my life than worrying about who you're…" and he mouths the word *fucking*.

Amanda looks at Doutzen Kroes like she's only just noticed her. Two horndog teens in trucker hats await their turn; Tussauds lets you sidle up alongside the models and paw them and take pictures. Amanda's posture curves in. This next part is important. "Can we keep walking?"

They do.

It isn't news to Sebastian that he's been trying to wipe away his tactile memories of Amanda by touching a wide array of European women. He rarely sees any of them twice, but he's glad for the experience. It's easy to convince himself he's in a temporary "mistake-making" mode, egged on by a vicariously thrilled Hoop who talks about oats that need sowing. But walking here with Amanda—past Nelson Mandela and George W. Bush and JFK— forces recognition: he's been a child in a sandbox.

"So here's the thing," she says, spinning and cornering him in Mikhail Gorbachev's alcove. "You're right. Something happened that made me realize my reasoning was total bull."

"…"

"Okay, so I haven't told Scott or Kate or anyone…but I

haven't exactly had an easy time. It's like, I *took some meetings*, whatever. Sang for people. You know how phony L.A. is. But it's not any easier when you're just some girl who sings. I've been trying to get noticed. I've been trying a *lot*. I just haven't really been…getting anywhere."

He says, "Oh."

"Well Jesus, don't look so thrilled about it, Sebastian. At least the four of us had each other, now I'm the girl selling shit on a game show. But okay. In the process of trying to get people interested, I've also been playing them *Vampire*. And a little while ago someone was like, 'What about this record? Why don't we buy it back from Sidelong and put it out?' And that made me think."

"…"

"I was out west and you guys call me up and it's like we're going to Europe and *you need to decide right now*…. And I'm not afraid to say it, Sebastian. I know it got weird, I know we don't work as a couple. But I miss the band." Her voice hitches, and she's surprised to discover she's telling the truth. "I'm fucking lonely."

"Which is it?" he says. "You didn't come with us to spare my feelings, or because it was short notice?"

"You're mad. I deserve it."

He watches her. She's breathing hard, wet-eyed. It's easy to recall that time: she was beautiful and smart and funny, and she liked him, she loved his music. She would be the puzzle piece to complete his emergence and escape, out of Bed-Stuy into adulthood. He often couldn't believe his luck. But he hadn't tried to understand what she was, and what she was—what she is—was sometimes unpleasant. It was his mistake. "I don't know what I'm supposed to say to you, Amanda."

"Are things so great here? You're never coming back?"

"I don't know. How do I know?"

"…"

"Someone's buying *Vampire*?" he says. "Is it for sale?"

Bees are behind her eyes. She starts to cry, and it's real. She hates the unfairness beneath everything, and the guises it compels her to assume. There's also always been an undercurrent between them: Sebastian was the pure one, the sweet one, and however natural she tried to be with him it was never enough, she was a corrupting influence or at least the steward of corrupting influences. She sees herself weep, and is angry for being able to separate herself from the sadness, but it's real.

Sebastian looks at his own hands then realizes he has no choice, and hugs her. They crush against Gorbachev.

She snuffles and he says, "Hey, aren't you that lady from TV?" and this makes her laugh a little.

"I'm pathetic," says Amanda.

"No."

"I just don't want it to be too late."

"Maybe we should talk about something else," Sebastian says. "You want to get something to eat?"

"…"

"I assume you asked Scott first. What did he say?"

She breaks contact. Her sinuses are filled with cement. What's this feeling? A missed connection: a presence that should be in her life, but isn't. It's not Sebastian—this satisfied boy—but something else, something metaphysical or at least elusive. She knows people in this room are looking at her like she's an emotional maniac. "Scott wanted to know what *you* say."

But Sebastian doesn't know. He has a tiny copy of the *I Ching* in his pocket and a date with a German student tonight. Or Italian.

They leave the museum and wander. Strangers ask them to join in a soccer game. There's a protest over some racist character who annually appears during Dutch Christmas festivities, but it's ultra-polite and they hand out waffles. Amsterdam is comfortable in vaguely disconcerting ways: Sebastian has found that when they need a bank branch or a pharmacy, they turn a corner in the likeliest direction and there one is. And now, strolling just close enough to Amanda to avoid rudeness, he hears "Brill Bruisers" playing from a café patio: a New Pornographers song Scott anticipated for weeks that was released just yesterday. He thinks of telling Amanda about the wild coincidence—Scott played it on repeat all Thursday afternoon—but keeps the magic to himself…

…while at the same time, Scott actually happens to be listening to "Brill Bruisers" again through his earbuds, wondering whether the song's goosebump quotient has diminished yet. In college he once theorized a heroic act: when your favorite band releases a new record, play it like crazy except for one song. Save that song. Delete the file if you have to. Then, only when the rest of the record has lost its thrill, put the missing song in your bloodstream and get the goosebumps all over again.

He's disciplined, but he's not that disciplined. He's memorizing every second of "Brill Bruisers," deconstructing, theorizing production decisions, marveling. *Bo-ba-bo-ba-ba-bo.*

There's something eastern-European about the neighborhood through which he's walking: one-way lanes and cubic brick buildings with balcony railings like prison bars. He finds the community center address and the front door is locked; he knocks and puts his hands in the pouch of his hoodie. Kate lets him in. They step through dark hallways to a pea-soup-smelling cafeteria. They unstack folding chairs and put them in rows.

Hoop comes in and shows them a kitchen. There are three silver urns and they find steel wool beneath the sink and scour them. Copper-colored liquid drains out. They fill two of the urns with hot water, one with cold. They mix instant coffee into one of the hots, and carry the urns into the cafeteria. Hoop plugs in the hot urns and breaks open surplus packages of Oreos and Tuc bacon crackers and stacks Dutch-language pamphlets at the end of one of the tables. The hungry kids and families who use this place at lunch and dinner evidently grab as much food as they can and shovel it home with little regard for accuracy: the olive linoleum is crunchy with crumbs. Hoop shrugs and finds a mop.

The addicts are on time. They come in silently, manipulating their phones.

Kate and Scott blend backward into a wall of curled and aging photos stapled to corkboard. It feels awkward to be here and they avoid eye contact.

The back row fills first. The kids look exhausted by physical and psychic pain. They don't chat each other up, and nobody wears the chipper self-help expressions Kate remembers from Kansas City. Hoop shakes hands, touches shoulders, guides by elbows, says little. Kate and Scott watch the Styrofoam cup supply, ready to open a new bag. A shivering fifteen-year-old girl with spiked green hair and ruined fingernails pauses by the snack table, and Kate gives her a cookie and wordlessly encourages her to sit in a first-row corner seat. The girl is crying. Scott fetches her tea. Hoop told them the best thing is be present, don't overreact to emotional displays, don't make them feel odd for their helplessness.

A leather-jacketed guy hugs Hoop and shouts, "What is the only thing that is better than roses on your piano!" Hoop's soothing response is sub-audible. The chairs are almost all filled.

Hoop wears an Apple Jacks t-shirt to leave his needle tracks uncovered. This is a formerly defunct MWF Young Addicts NA meeting Hoop resuscitated after chatting with kids at Winston Kingdom. All these addicts are under 18; some look 12.

Hoop steps to the front. "Hello, everyone. My name is Willard, and I'm an addict."

Everyone says, "Hallo, Willard." Scott and Kate share huge eyes at the first name's revelation.

"You're all welcome here. We want you to feel safe, and anyone who wants to talk later should step right up. Nobody is here to judge you or cure you. We're all just people who know what you're going through." He scratches his beard. "And now for all you familiar faces, you know I can't get up here without talking about myself for a few minutes." The kids chuckle at this. "Actually I'm your commitment speaker for the day. I still think it would do us some good to bring in more speakers from other groups, to help us believe in the power of coming back, but I respect your wishes. Anyone who knows me knows I sure do love the sound of my own voice. Something you may remember about me is that I care about music and the people I hang out with are musicians and even though it was tempting, I feel proud that I didn't use last night and I didn't use this morning. And I'm in *Amsterdam* for fuck's sake."

The kids laugh again, louder, and Kate can see the little cult of personality springing up around Hoop's act. Hoop thinks Scott and Kate have volunteered today out of altruism. In fact, they're spying on their manager.

"Let me tell you about a time I was in Las Vegas. I was supposed to be hanging out with Van Halen, who none of you probably have ever heard of. Anyway, they're already pretty old by this point and they fired their lead singer, and they had this new singer and put out a new record. I'm in the MGM Grand lobby drunk out of my mind. There's another journalist also waiting for the band, some new kid, and I decided to fuck with him and I go, 'I'm Gary Cherone.' That was the new lead singer's name. So the kid starts interviewing me and even though I've got these big sunglasses on you'd think the kid would be a little suspicious, this big rock star just sitting down in the lobby to do an interview?

"So whatever, I'm talking out my ass. You know what cash-register honesty is? Like, 'I don't steal, I don't break the law, so how fucked-up can I really be?' So what if I'm lying about who I am, it's just for fun. I make up all this stuff about what it's like to be the new guy in Van Halen, and at some point a hotel employee comes over and says, 'Oh, are you Mr. Cherone?' Of course I say yes, and he takes me up in an elevator and let me tell you I'm wasted, but I guess the hotel guy is used to fucked-up rock stars. He takes me to this special floor, and it's like...how can I put it? It's super-high-roller, the swankiest thing you ever saw, gazelles roaming free with drink trays on their backs. And the high rollers come over and they're super-psyched to meet Van Halen's new lead singer, but none of them have any idea what the fuck Gary Cherone is supposed to look like, and this is before smartphones. I start making up stories, fun facts about the band, famous women I slept with. And then out comes the blow.

"We're talking mountains of coke. You can't even believe how much, like, you probably haven't seen *Scarface*, but it's piled in two-foot-high drifts on all these tables. This is just the best night of my life. I'm Gary Cherone! I covered musicians for my job most of my life and I always told people I didn't want that rock-and-roll lifestyle. But that was obviously a lie. Of course, it's all ego and you know what E.G.O. stands for? Edging God Out. Yeah, I don't really believe in the actual *God*-God either, we can have that conversation another time. But you have to turn yourself over to something outside yourself. It's the only way.

"And so I snorted so much I think I wrote an opera and incorporated four Internet start-ups in an hour, and now this really pretty woman comes up to me. Skinny, blonde, no makeup, star-struck. I'm in love. And she's like, 'Mr. Cherone, Mr. Cherone, can you follow me over here. We've got that meeting I talked to your manager about.' Well, you don't have to write it out longhand for me. I'm hip. That *meeting*? Sex was the thing that would make it a perfect night. And to think, I don't even like Van Halen! I didn't even want to come on this stupid trip. The woman leads me back to the elevator and my heart is going so hard...if you know what it's like on coke, your veins feel nuclear. We get on the elevator, just the two of us, and she's smiling at me, this smile that could melt platinum. Like, I could really see myself falling in love, even though I'd have to legally change my name.

"We reach our floor, I'm ready to make some moves on this lady, the doors open.... And there's a little stage and a room full of cancer kids. The ones who aren't publicly bald have chemo-scarves wrapped around their heads, and they have parents standing behind them who are just beaming. The woman shuffles me onto the little stage and she says to everyone, 'Boys and girls, moms and dads, this man is a rock star!' Everybody applauds. I mean, I was completely fucked up, but I swear they were shouting and banging their tables, who knows why a bunch of little kids would be such big fans of a band that was so old even then. The lady goes, 'Mr. Cherone, the children will be attending your show later. Would you say a few words to them?' I locked eyes with a little girl—I think she was a little girl, only based on the pink bathrobe, she had no feminine or masculine qualities, she was just drawn and hairless and jaundiced and grinning—and I saw an oxygen tank perched next to her, and I tried to smile back but I'd lost track of what my face was doing. The charity lady—because despite her hotness, it was now clear she was a charity lady—stepped aside also clapping and I took center stage....

"...and I couldn't say anything.

"I tried to make words. I tried to *lie*, because who cared if it was really Gary Cherone, as long as he said a few inspirational words about reaching for the moon and life being made better by love? I tried. But I couldn't say anything. I was completely blocked, like, a hundred competing sentences were so jumbled I couldn't say any of them. The kids thought it was funny at first, the girl in the pink robe clapped and I saw brass-colored studs too big for her earlobes. But my silence got much less charming pretty quick. The laughter stopped and the kids started wondering what was wrong, was this the world playing yet another trick on them?

"Yup, I was up there actively causing pain for some very sick children, and I wanted to talk but I couldn't say a word. Coke usually makes me a motor-mouth. My girl in the pink robe straight-up started crying. I felt like crying, too, but I couldn't even do that. *Just say something, Jesus, just get out of your own fucking shit and relate to these poor kids going through something you can't even imagine.* The charity lady made hand gestures like, come on asshole, and eventually—it must've been about three minutes but it felt like an hour—she lost patience and shuffled me off and it was humiliating. My skin was melting off. It's just...it's hard to talk about, actually. I haven't ever told this story. I saw myself wanting to cry. I want to cry now. Fathers started walking in my direction to have a word. But what could I say now? I ran to the elevator. I wanted to say...I wanted to say everything, I wanted to tell everybody it would be all right, but it was too late.

"I wish I could say I got sober after that, but it took much longer. Many years. Maybe you think I've learned some trick that you'll stumble into. Maybe there is such a thing, but I don't think so. Anyway I've never learned it. All I know how to do is come to that moment where it's a decision—use or don't use—and make a choice. It's so fucking hard. I know it's all clichés. 'I used to be like you.' But I did. I am. It still happens every day and it always will, and all we can do is talk about it and believe in each other and feel how helpless we are by ourselves. I'm trying. Thanks. Anyone who wants to, just come on up."

Nobody applauds, but Kate and Scott see a kind of funereal serenity on the kids' faces: appreciation for a well-earned finish line. Then the boys and girls start coming forward to speak, a few in English, most in Dutch. Though the bandmates don't understand the specifics, a word the Dutch-speakers all use near the beginning is *verslaafde*. Most of them have elaborate tattoos. Sometimes the stories go long, sometimes everyone chuckles simultaneously. Many have empathy for each other's sob-racked, humiliated admissions. Some seem not to be listening.

The green-haired girl vomits cookie. Kate urges her to stay seated; Scott covers her sick with paper towels. The meeting keeps going. Kate pats the girl's shoulder as she weeps.

There's a long break, then more speakers. Scott wants to be empathetic but has reached his limit. He watches Hoop: rapscallion and role model, whose unblinking eyes say, *Look at me listening with integrity!* Sebastian has certainly fallen for their manager's act. Scott goes back and forth.

Finally it's over and Hoop thanks Kate and Scott for helping. They step outside and it's warm, and the green-haired girl is smoking a cigarette scowling and heel-kicking a loose brick out of the front walkway. Hoop salutes them goodbye and walks toward Bilderdijkstraat with a few older kids.

Kate sees the green-haired girl looking at Scott. "What's your name?" she says. "Can we get you anything?"

"..."

Scott says, "You need a ride? We don't actually have a car, but I could give you a piggyback."

Despite herself, the green-haired girl smiles.

"They beat your brain in there," says Kate, "But you really should keep coming back. Do you promise to keep coming back?" The girl moves her head, not exactly an affirmation.

Scott watches Hoop recede. "Okay, what if he gets in a taxi?"

"Then we'll get in a taxi. Relax."

"Personally I'm not swimming in petty cash."

"All right," says Kate. "We're going." They start after Hoop. From behind, in buoyant, accented English, they hear, "Sofie! My name is Sofie!"

Kate walks backward for a few steps. She says, "Where do you live, Sofie?" and the green-haired girl puts out her palms meaning, *you're looking at it.* "She has a crush on you," Kate says to Scott.

"Awesome."

"It's flattering."

"Cool, finally some female attention."

Kate's eyes flick. "Women look at you at shows, dude. You're too dumb to notice." They see Hoop on a busy corner, still talking to NA kids.

They cloak themselves in a building's shadow. There goes Hoop, crossing against the light. He's walking east away from home, toward the city center, in a do-gooder's abstracted fog or maybe some flavor of withdrawal. They stay a block behind. This is palpably not America: a charming four-story sprawl dismembered by canals, freak flags flying at regular intervals—body-mod shop, lesbian chocolatier, ornate Dutch-language graffiti—but unable to overcome a certain brick-and-gable gentility. Hoop isn't just wandering. He has a destination in mind.

"Sebastian's pen pal at Universal got his hands on the new Spoon record," says Scott. "Sending it snail mail."

"You've mentioned," Kate says.

"Remember being young and counting down days to a record release? My brother supposedly camped outside a Tower Records a couple times."

"We're still young. Jesus."

"The fondest thought of my childhood was maybe someday I could be that exciting to someone."

The self-flogging act is not a shock to Kate. She says:

Young and bright
Now just a dim light...

Beneath a tarp-draped scaffold, they feel for a moment like it's New York (minus the urine smell) and look at each other with true eyes: expats clinging to something. Hoop reads the window of a suspicious-seeming massage parlor, reaches for the doorknob. They comically nudge elbows. But Hoop leaves the door and keeps walking. Pedestrians and bikes come thicker now. Country-flavored rock spins out of a beer garden, probably not live though it's difficult to say for sure. Scott makes a note to remember the address for a master list he no longer maintains. The road bends left, over the Prinsengracht, and gets even skinnier and more fashionable, then suddenly austere and abandoned and marked by antiquary bookshops. Dam Square is just north. Hoop keeps clomping; they get more suspicious the closer they get to the coffeeshops of De Wallen, watching Hoop's posture and inferring a hunger for poison.

"Long way to go for a beard grooming kit," says Kate.

"Long way to go for artisanal falafel," Scott says.

"Long way to go for condescension lessons."

"We're hilarious."

"We walked a mile in his shoes," Kate says. "What have we learned?"

"Good shape for an old guy."

"You're obsessed with age. Boring. Didn't anyone ever tell you it's just a number?"

Scott trips over an invisible dog. "I think I'm supposed to have a snappy response."

"Have we established what it would mean if he really is using?"

"You're telling me you didn't have plans? Like, 'By 25 I'll have a record out. By 30 I'll be on Letterman.'"

"You sound like Sebastian."

"Hey, he's slowing down." And Hoop has passed through a small neighborhood where the signs are written in both Dutch and Chinese, and now stands on a bridge, scanning for an upper floor across this ancient street. They hang back, south of yet another canal. A couple blocks from here are the *kamers*: rows of glass-doored rooms that display sex workers. This is the oldest part of Amsterdam and it's so aggressively charming that it seems to be overcompensating, dedicated to pretending mostly-naked ladies aren't *just over there*. It reminds Kate of her father subscribing to *Playboy* and leaving issues plainly visible around the house. The male faces they see wandering around this neighborhood have a serial-killer blankness that's probably all in her head.

Hoop steps forward across the canal and rings an apartment buzzer beside a sex shop. The door opens and he's gone.

"What would it mean?" says Scott. "Well, it would mean he's a liar."

"You're sure what you saw? Probably it's none of our business."

"Ask Amanda, seriously. We both looked in his eyes."

"You're right, though," Kate says. "If he's getting high, I'd want to know. I'm not sure why but I would."

A couple of shirtless teenagers with buzzcuts get off their bikes and sit on a bench across from where Scott and Kate stand. The building Hoop entered is redbrick, old and tall, with a Mayan pyramid for a front façade, a single window near the top, and then a skinny door even higher than that, with no balcony.

"Climb up to the attic and get your taste," says Scott. "But stay away from that door."

"The first step down's a doozy."

"If you smoke the magic bindle of crack, a little man comes out that door and rings a bell."

"Whole building looks like a cake." The buzzcuts are listening to them riff, and laugh. Tourists bustle all around.

Scott says, "It would mean we aren't all in it together. It would mean he's using us. We're just a way to…distract himself. Like: a way to look respectable, delaying his inevitable full-fledged relapse."

"Right. God forbid any of us act delusional."

"…"

"…"

"It would be bad," he says. "It would be…false pretenses."

"It would end the gravy train," says Kate. "Our sugar daddy's money would be going up his nose."

"So, what, you're saying it doesn't matter, since we're just delaying the inevitable, too?"

Kate squints. What if they've actually been making more money than Hoop has said? Scott's instincts are usually pretty dead-on. She says, "Hey, you fellas know what that building is?"

The buzzcuts seem embarrassed for eavesdropping, and point to their chests.

"Yeah, you guys. You hang around here a lot?"

"No," says one of them, looking at his belly. "No English."

"Yeah, *that's* not true," Kate says. "They were following right along."

"Agreed," says Scott. "They're counterintelligence. Willard sent 'em to track us tracking him."

"That one's got a nipple ring, probably has a radio transmitter in it."

"Radio. Ha. Old tech. Try GPS with a cyanide capsule. If the heat gets too bad, do not allow capture. Repeat: do not allow capture."

"Ha-ha," the thinner buzzcut says. "That building? No. No."

"My partner," says Kate, "can spot a liar a quarter-mile away. Show 'em what you do when suspects lie to us, Scott."

Scott pretend-chokes Kate and feels her impressive neck-muscle ropes, and she sticks out her tongue.

"I know yes," says the other kid. "This place, it is...mm...layer."

"Layer?"

"*Ja.* Upstairs is...is yoker."

"Yoker?" Scott says.

The kid guffaws and claps his hands. Scott and Kate consider that these buzzcuts might already be super-high themselves. The laughing teen slides across the bench and puts his face close to his friend's, clutches invisible lapels. His voice changes to a growl. "I'm Batman."

Scott says, "You're Batman?"

"I'm Batman."

"Wait," says Kate. "I get it. Yoker layer. Upstairs is a lair. It's the Joker's lair."

The buzzcuts fall apart laughing.

"But seriously," says Scott, "it's like a crack den or something?" The teens stand and shrug and pull down on their cargo shorts, grab their bikes and roll away. "See?" he says to Kate. "I'm old. So should we just go in and confront Hoop?"

Kate leans back against a railing over this canal, and closes her eyes in the sun. Things will work out and she'll run later. Or they won't, and she'll run later. Life's daily horrors seem less horrible than they used to. She doesn't know if this is capitulation. She says, "Know why I was never a jazz drummer?"

"You don't like jazz?"

"Good point. But no, mostly because it was intimidating. I had a drum teacher who played Buddy Rich and Tony Williams all the time and he'd tell us, 'This is what it's really all about, man. This is what's up.' But it just seemed way too hard for someone like me."

"You're my favorite drummer, Kate."

"Thanks. No, I'm not saying.... Now sometimes I think, 'I sure wish I'd had the guts to try back then. Unfortunately it's too late.' But that's the exact same intimidation. It's not too late. Why is it too late? So have I really changed at all?"

"Great," says Scott, "that's all you need. Jazz. Jump on a ship that's sinking even faster." He hears her sigh. "But I get your point. We spend a lot of time talking about things we don't get to do."

She opens her eyes and looks at him. That's it exactly.

A canal boat passing under them toots an air horn and they watch it go: four gray-haired senior citizens puttering cheerily, waving up at tourists taking their pictures. One of the gentlemen has a hand trailing in the water. A lady holds aloft a glass of wine. They drift away toward a canal intersection and hang a right, past an ancient moss-colored building that springs directly up out of the water and seems ready to crumble at any moment.

Kate has a Fruit Bats song in her head and realizes she's clicking its rhythm with her canines, a habit that will no doubt lead to future tooth problems. She hears a distant nautical clatter. A new assortment of pedestrians is passing by, and one is coming right this way, and Kate has a moment where she swears she recognizes him. Then she realizes it's Hoop. He sees them.

She slaps Scott's shoulder and points.

Hoop's phone is against his ear. He crosses the street and doesn't look angry.

"Quick what's our story?" says Scott.

"Jesus. Um."

"I know. I'm looking to supplement my income with sex work."

Kate cackles out of proportion to the joke, producing lots of noise so Hoop will think they're not snooping. Here he is, same Apple Jacks shirt, a stupid smile rollbrushed onto his beard's empty center.

"Hey!" Scott says. "Funny story."

Hoop holds up an index finger, focuses on his call.

Overhead a blimp malingers: hanging by puppet strings from a hand concealed in a cloud. The blimp wears an orange mohawk and appears to bear an advertisement for peaches.

"Okay," says Hoop. "Got it."

Scott wants Kate to see the relaxed face he's making. She's busy yawning into the backs of her battle-marred fingers.

"Yes. Great. Thank you very much." Hoop lowers his phone. His eyes flick between them. "So," he says. "What the fuck?"

"..."

"You two idiots are seriously terrible at stalking. At first I'm like, 'It has to be coincidence.' But there you still were, right behind me."

Scott tries to get a fix on Hoop's pupils. Kate says, "What's in that place? What were you doing up there?"

Hoop looks over at the Mayan pyramid. "Christ. I have to tell you? I'm a grown-ass man."

"Maybe we'll just take a stroll over there and see for ourselves," says Kate.

"Fuck. Please do."

"..."

"A friend of mine has an office in that building. He was just handing me off some files." From his pocket, Hoop produces a purple-camouflage thumb drive. "Nothing band-related. And for God's sake, nothing drug-related."

"Oh," Scott says.

"Huh," says Kate.

"I mean, when I fall off the wagon, I'm pretty sure my roommates will be the first to know and it'll be *obvious*. Put aside the fact that I'm over 40 and I even *have* roommates."

"Right. Okay."

"Now," Hoop says, "ask me why I'm smiling."

"What do I know?" says Kate. "I hit things with sticks."

"..."

"Okay, why are you smiling?"

"On the phone? That was Bazzy. I don't know how he did it. I don't know why he did it. But he got us on a bill at the Melkweg, as a fill-in. The motherfucking *Melkweg*. A week from tonight."

Kate claps and hugs Hoop. "Holy crap! Holy crap!"

Hoop hugs back, but has his eyes on Scott. "We'll middle for a couple Dutch bands. Pretty amazing, right?"

Scott feels sick as his dignity buckles. He accepts Hoop's high-five and barely feels it.

BUTTERFLIES TASTE WITH THEIR FEET

His dream is nothing. It is absence. Not even blackness because blackness is still something. It's a vacuum devoid of input, offering nothing that registers with his senses. His dream self is not a self. Selfhood is gone, taken away. It goes like this for an indeterminate while. He tries to name what it means—"Reversion to the Womb," "The Emptiness of Jacob Shear's Heart"—but can't change anything. His efforts mock him. There is no "him." It would even be fine if this was death, but it's not: it's entropy. It's what happens when he stops trying. Whatever this place is, there's definitely no music here.

A sound does yank a cord in his navel, hauls him up.

He wakes.

His phone. His phone is blowing up.

Text tones, voicemail beeps and bumblebee vibrations on the nightstand. He scrolls through messages from Hoop, Kate and Sebastian. Why is his first instinct to feel shame?

Hoop has unleashed the hounds. It's Monday morning, and music reporters want to interview him. Promoters he's met these past months want to congratulate him. The other Whips want him to get up. Yes, they're booked to play the Melkweg Old Hall, a legendary place that's ten times bigger than anywhere else they've gigged in Amsterdam. They did play tiny parts in mega-festivals last summer, but even in these disintegrating times the Melkweg has cache.

(Amanda has stayed at her hotel the past couple nights, and thankfully Sebastian has stayed here in the cramped Wilhelminastraat apartment. Obviously, Scott doesn't know where Bazzy has been sleeping.)

It's a story with some teeth: a transplanted American band springing up out of the Amsterdam scene. Over the weekend Hoop has called in every imaginable marker to generate buzz. Scott showers and walks downtown to drink coffee with a *Sp!ts* freelancer who goes, "Is there anyone to take on the Buggy Whips? Are you the new 'It Band' in Amsterdam?" which gives Scott a renewed appreciation for Hoop's ventriloquism skills. This nervous young writer wants to believe his city can be rock's new world headquarters. He doesn't really even need Scott to answer, so Scott doesn't. Instead he says, "Top five occupations going extinct. Go."

"..."

"Well, we're two. Rock musician and newspaper writer."

"Ha-ha. I see. Ah...DVD sales clerk?"

"Good one. Department store perfume squirter."

"I still see the...what is the English word?" He pantomimes a phone to his ear, and dials in the air between them.

"'Payphone!' Strong."

"Yes, payphone, right. Repair the payphone."

"Well-played, sir. Keep working the violin as the fire burns."

The writer scrunches up his nose and laughs, bewildered. "Shall I call you Wolfram?"

"..."

"In America you call it tungsten. In Europe, it is wolfram."

"Wolfram," Scott says. "I like it. A name for my inevitable side project."

"And...ah...you will record a Buggy Whips record soon?"

Scott thinks, *What you really mean is: we don't have so much as a song on iTunes, so how can we help fill a big prestigious venue on short notice?* But he's learned—they've all learned—showing false humility to reporters is bad policy. Doubt is for agnostics. He tries to sound bored and says, "Oh, definitely."

Sebastian records a TV hit on a Salto 1 music show hosted by two expat Americans. They lob him softballs—"We've both seen the Buggy Whips at smaller clubs and thought it was just a matter of time before you'd outgrow those places...did you feel that way, too?"—and Sebastian fires off immodest responses like: "During a show you're just playing. Before and after? Sure, we're a great rock band. Great rock bands get bigger."

"You'll be opening for Queen Mother Dilemma," they say. "Have you seen them play before?"

"We're not the opener," says Sebastian. "Sacred Kitten opens. No, I haven't seen them, but I've heard their songs."

"Yeah, they've been around for a long time, a pretty mellow groove. But do you worry about rocking out and getting everyone revved up, and upstaging a headliner?"

"We don't worry about it. It happens. It's up to the headliner to bring it."

"This is old hat for you, right Sebastian? Your last band had a song on a hit TV show in the States, and you put out a big single on a major label. No big deal?"

"It's a big deal. We want our fans to come out and give us love, and we think people who haven't seen us will have a blast. Bring earplugs. Can you bleep this out? We'll fuck your shit up."

Kate goes on 3FM and the host says, "So this has been the Summer of Rock in Amsterdam." She thinks some fulcrum has obviously been teetered over, because now the local media wants these grand pronouncements to be true. "Have you felt it?"

"It's a big place," Kate says. "We're proud to help start something huge."

"Is this the big break for your Buggy Whips?"

"Ha, let me say it slow and clear, so everyone will understand: You want to be there."

"Lovely to have you in studio. Friday night with QMD: I know, yes, I will be there. To say thank you, here is a song I think you know!" and the host plays 'Density of Joy.' Kate hears the riff Sebastian hates more than any piece of music in the world, and hopes he's not listening. Here comes her snare, smoothed by machines into hollow little shocks of electricity. And here's Amanda's voice. Kate finds it thinned where it once seemed piercing, further back in the mix than she remembers, as though having suffered digital erosion. She gives the host a weak thumbs-up.

She reaches Jack Dooley in New York and asks him to express her personal kit across the Atlantic, with the bill footed by Hoop's still-unextinguished resources. Then she picks up the mail and joins her triathlon group for a run. Six of them jog south along a river through a neighborhood with gems for names (Diamantstraat, Robijnstraat, Saffierstraat), down into a leafy suburb and onto a bike path occasionally menaced by scooters, under an elevated highway and into Amstel Park. The rhododendrons here smell like cinnamon root beer. Kate listens to a Clap Your Hands Say Yeah song followed by a Coldplay song. She's several minutes into oxygen deprivation—not a state that typically yields fruitful avenues of inquiry—but there's something about these tunes back to back, something lovely about the democracy of MP3s prowling up against one another. But it's sad, too: the beautiful CYHSY ditties most of the world will never share, and the overplayed Coldplay bombast she'd never admit is on her phone, but does love. It's all political if you let it be. And it's pretty much impossible not to let it be.

On the way back to the city center, in a pack of three-by-two, Gertie says, "Butterflies taste with their feet."

"What?"

"..."

"Butterflies? What's that supposed to mean?"

Gertie looks ahead at Joot, who's running alongside Louis and making comically big gestures as he holds court in Dutch. Gertie says, "The weight of all the ants in the world all added together is the same as the weight of all people in the world."

Kate says, "Animal facts?" Then she puts two and two together: for his day job, Joot works in a zoo. "Wait! You and Joot? No way! You said never. Never ever ever ever."

Gertie's nose is red, she's breathing hard, and she smiles so wide her doll's eyes flip closed.

"I thought Joot was asexual. Ha, sorry, no. I just can't imagine him being in a room without Louis for more than like five minutes."

"It is not so easy to be like a stone," says Gertie. "He is very nice."

"He really is," Kate says. "He's so tall and strong."

"It will be cold soon, and very dark: it is good for *praten*. He does not stop talking so I like to listen."

"He's been trying to get with you for a long time, right? He's lucky."

"Yes, he must be very happy!" says Gertie, and they laugh. "Now is your turn, Kate. Everybody needs sex!"

Kate is good at not blushing. "Ah, but who says you need another person to have it?"

"What!" Gertie slaps Kate's bouncing hands. "So I think maybe Sebastian is for you. He is very beautiful."

"I'll see if he can squeeze me in," says Kate.

"He will squeeze *you* in?"

"No, I mean.... He has girlfriends. Also we're like brother and sister."

"..."

"He's really sensitive, like, the amount of energy he puts into making sure nobody says anything mean about him." She feels nostalgic for the version of Sebastian that existed when they first hit the road in the States, and realizes she's really thinking about that off-course version of herself. "He's still really young."

"I am young," Gertie says. "I will squeeze him, ha-ha. Oh, but we are not fashion models, so who else? If I can say yes to big stupid Joot, who is yes for Kate?"

"..."

"Louis!"

Louis momentarily runs backward. *"Wat?"*

"You will go with Kate to a film?" Louis grunts and turns back around, blows a snot-blob out his nose.

"Perfection," says Kate.

"Marcel is homo I think," Gertie says. "Stef knows many waiters in Damrak. One of these, then."

"Okay, deal."

"I am serious."

"I know you are," Kate says. She puts a hand over Gertie's bulb-onion deltoid and shoves her off the path. Gertie nearly goes down in a muddy rosebush, regathers and hops to catch up, cackling and kicking Kate's thigh in retaliation, leaving a brown mud stain the shape of a Pearl Drums flame logo.

That evening, as a precursor to the Melkweg gig, the Buggy Whips play a Hoop-negotiated rooftop show in Indische Buurt. It's sponsored and will be captured on video by a popular Dutch culture website. The website's office is a crazy mishmash of Jonas Brothers posters, a homunculus-sized 3D Shrek, a life-size cutout of Daario from *Game of Thrones*, a cubicle carefully transformed into a World Cup soccer field (whose felt and posterboard have been smashed), magazine cutouts of Katy Perry doing unholy things to magazine cutouts of livestock, and a jungle of other cultural referents that make the Whips feel like the website's staff will be insufferable. But they're so nice and accommodating, they offer beer and set up chairs on the roof for the site's entire staff and workers in nearby buildings who might be curious about and/or annoyed by the noise.

Hoop is wearing an old-fashioned military helmet and is his usual pre-gig self, bustling around pretending like he's checking wires, chatting everyone up. Amanda sits as far away from the "stage" as possible.

"It's like 'Get Back,'" Hoop says. "It's like 'Where the Streets Have No Name.' Can I think of a top five?"

"Jefferson Airplane!" someone says.

The overcast above is lovely: striated without foretelling doom. It's windy up here and traffic on Javastraat is loud. This watchworks neighborhood, which is about as far east as they've been in Amsterdam, seems more diverse and less aggressively groovy than downtown. A man comes upstairs face-painted like a clown, and it turns out he's just a working guy who moonlights at kids' parties and he wanted to hear some music. He's also wearing a yarmulke.

There's a soundboard and three cameras on tripods, but no crew or director: they'll just hit record and edit later. The band does a quick soundcheck; the amp situation is basic, but they're plenty loud. Scott thinks about Zilker Park in Austin. He and Sebastian are wearing matching blue blazers and ultra-skinny ties, and all three of them don white-frame sunglasses.

"Everybody is ready?" says a French hostess. About forty folks are spread between Amanda and the band. A guy runs around and starts the cameras. "*Madames et monsieurs,*" the hostess says, "here is the Buggy Whips!"

They do "Capital" first. The groove gets going, and Sebastian's piano makes a rhythm to match Kate, and also plays a lead line that intertwines with Scott's guitar. When the song ends, Scott says, "Who-all is coming to see our big show Friday?" and he gets a cheer in response.

The French hostess, sitting stage right, bats Sebastian's knee, and he has a godlike view of her cleavage and smiles down.

Amanda has been hiding out at the hotel for a couple days, not answering texts and basically adding to the illusion that she's carrying on with poor Bazzy. Tonight she's deflected Scott's forlorn glances and is acting the part of a Buggy Whips groupie, but this is the difficult part: having to watch them play again. They're great as ever; the new songs are fun and idiosyncratic. And look at their faces! Scott in a bloom of distant roof lights, sweating like a coalminer. Kate thrashing, bobbing, eyes unfocused and hair in a crown of light. Sebastian beautiful and steady, cheeks puffing out then in, mouth appearing to say *wow* with regularity. If they're each governed by delusions, they also shrug them off when they play, finally conversing.

Next up is "And Do What?" It's scuffed-up and magniloquent, classically familiar as though hatched in an arena, but also temperamental. Scott opens his throat and exposes every crevice in his voice, so at his loudest some of the human aspects of the voice toggle over into a blown-out buzzing. He says:

Quick to marshal, slow to hear
They weave it when the camera's near
Lizards lick their eyes so they don't blink
Their mouths are moving side to side
A picture torn, a face denied
It's easy playing songs for the dumb…
…for the dumb…
…for the dumb can't find earmuffs

You can hear it in their creaky hips
Can hear it in the Japanese whiskey
Can hear it in the balloon ride
Can hear it…and do
And do
And do…

Baby comes, he's mute enough
His briefcase combo isn't tough
He can't sign his name on all the papers
Slow to listen, quick to talk
Pay ten percent for service stock
Keep everyone out while I play…
…while I play…
…while I play me a zombie

You can hear it in their creaky hips
Can hear it in the cigar guillotine
Can hear it in the mausoleums
Can hear it...and do
And do
And do...

They play "Tiger Beats Bear" and "Troll Culture" and "Bald-Spot Mohawk." They talked about doing a cover, but Hoop nixed the idea: given the chance, the website might ignore originals and promote a clickbait cover everyone knows. So the Whips look at each other deciding on a final tune; Scott feels courage and panic rising in equal measures, and he says into the mic, "A friend of ours is here. Maybe she'd like to sing one."

People look around. Amanda doesn't need convincing; she gets up and shakes her hair loose from a ponytail. She almost feels bad for him, but she also feels ebullient. Now everyone on this roof can be a convert. Sebastian looks at Kate.

Scott relinquishes center stage. Who's he kidding? He's feverish with jealousy over her, and how she got them the Melkweg gig. He keeps seeing that old man on top of her.... Amanda worries she hasn't warmed up but then stops worrying. Into the mic she says, "That was kind of a mysterious introduction, I bet you thought it was gonna be Lady Gaga or something." Someone hands her a bottle of water.

"What are we playing?" Sebastian says.

Amanda pulls in her stomach and pushes out her chest, and she says, "You guys wanna see some badass drumming?" The onlookers indicate they do. "How about 'Tents'?"

Kate snorts. She smacks out the pattern for "Intense, Like Camping," whose peppiness is almost mushy for the memories it provokes. The beat goes from simple to complex, with fills subdividing each measure into finer and finer units, and then Kate gets to hit her ride as hard as she can, which in the urban wind is like a high-dive into a tin swimming pool. The song's chords always bored Sebastian on guitar but here he gets to explore his higher octaves while Scott does the drudgery.

Amanda says, "Tried to kill me but...*I'm...not...dead!*" and utterly sells the repeat of those final two words. The once-improvised closing jam that grew stale is improvised anew: double-time and Amanda bouncing around losing her shit. It's obvious this is better. Look at the faces. Any moments of doubt—about coming here, about wooing them back to the States—are revealed as needless irresolution. They're a quartet. Of course they are. She looks over at Hoop, who's eating his upper lip.

"Ladies and gentlemen!" says Scott when it's over. "Amsterdamanda!"

There's a post-show gathering at the Flevopark and they drink "biological fruit gin," which someone from the website spends a long time explaining. (Sebastian and Hoop drink water.) Night comes incredibly late but it does come, and Kate follows Amanda out into a field that may be a cemetery annex. They lie down and watch big seabirds pinwheel in city light. They feel old. Bony fingers are beneath them, masquerading as sticks and twigs.

"Think we'll fill the place?" says Kate.

"Hell yes," Amanda says. "Definitely."

"Ha. You don't know. What do you know?"

"I'm bringing every single person in Amsterdam I know. So: just me."

"Whoooo. Have I mentioned it's easier to play the drums when you're not fat? I mean, I'm still fat."

"Ridiculous. You never were."

Kate feels sisterly. Like: protective. "You've been here how many days, and we've barely hung out. What happened this weekend?"

"I slept. I slept for like two days straight. Jetlag or that first night, I don't know if you remember but I *never* sleep like that."

"Do I remember, shoot, I remember movies playing from your bedroom at four in the morning. Yeah, I believe I'm familiar with Amanda the insomniac."

It's too dark to see each other. Amanda doesn't want to feel like she's bobbing and weaving, doesn't want to believe she's *just* picking the lock to Kate's loyalty. She says, "This is weird, right? Talking like we lived through some bygone era."

"Well, I dunno. It's pretty bygone."

"Don't say it like that."

Gin makes Kate sleepy. "You know the bands who've played this joint?" she says.

"..."

"Nirvana, U2, Pearl Jam, Beastie Boys, Snoop Dogg, uh…Strokes, Killers, Wilco, Sonic Youth, White Stripes…. Basically everyone we like."

Amanda downshifts into the forbearing version of her voice. "And once the show was done, of course they all stayed right here in Amsterdam and lived happily ever after…."

"Anyway so one of my roommates told me a juicy rumor about you, *dahhling*."

"Ah, which roommate would that be, *dearie?*"

"The one you used to kiss in the backseat when you thought we weren't looking."

"And what did he say, *precious?*"

Kate grins but of course Amanda can't see it. "I think you know what he said. He said you're buying back our record. You want to be Kid Centrifuge again."

"Well. I wanted to know what you think. What you want."

"…"

"But when I talked about that with Sebastian: it was before you got the Melkweg. Obviously now I just want to see you guys crush it."

"Do I believe you?" says Kate. "I'm not sure I believe you."

"Ouch."

Letting her head loll around on bare ground always does it to Kate: she's back in Mississippi or Florida using ambient light to dig deeper into *Divine Love*. She has to admit: sometimes she worries Amsterdam is another escape, another place she's run away to because things got unpleasant.

Learn your place in the order of things.

"I know this guy," Amanda says. "He told me a story how one day he was running on no sleep and he was exhausted, and he finally got to bed around noon. He woke up at twilight, but assumed he'd slept all the way through the night. The light looked like morning. So he starts his morning routine. Brushes his teeth, makes coffee, looks out his kitchen window at the beach. And there were more people out there than he'd ever *seen* at dawn, jogging and surfing and swimming. Totally freaked him out. He had a cold, too, so he had that fever thing of being really still and fascinated. He kept turning it over and over, like, what could the explanation be for hundreds of people flooding the beach at dawn, but not for some event, like, everyone was doing their own thing. It shook him up. Eventually he looked at a clock. But that unhinged feeling kind of stuck around for a while: the world just changed. Now this friend of mine, he's like, 'Can you live feeling that way all the time? That's my goal.'"

"Meaning?"

"Meaning, I don't know. Always try and look at things like they're new. Don't take things for granted. I should write greeting cards."

"You have *Vampire* free and clear?" Kate says. "Bring it over. Let Hoop sell it here."

"No, I admit it. Things are different from what I expected. I thought I'd find you struggling without me. I guess I have quite an ego."

"You only ever had an ego about not having an ego."

"…"

"Things aren't perfect," says Kate. "We don't have any money. Hoop is paying for everything and who knows how long that lasts? We're afraid to ask him."

"…"

"And Scott's worried we're Hoop's…midlife crisis, like, I dunno. Sometimes it's easy to think I'll go to the bathroom one morning and find him passed out with a needle in his arm."

"I guess there isn't any rush," Amanda says. "I'm not exactly setting L.A. on fire. You can see how it goes. I want you to come back. I want to sing with you again."

"You can start another band, Amanda. My God, I can't even imagine how many bands would want you."

"I'm afraid," she says.

"…"

"We know each other, and we're so good. I can't start over." Amanda hears her voice break. "I guess I'm hoping someday you'll rescue me."

"…"

"…"

"Aw," says Kate. She hears a hint of pleasure in her tone. "You don't need us like that."

"You. I need you."

They still hear birds, but no longer see them. Neither of them is drunk. Each wonders if the other is annoyed, but the truth is that they're calm in the way old buildings are calm. It used to be so natural to count differences between them.

"If I didn't come over here and at least tell you all this," Amanda says, "I wouldn't be able to live with myself. Please just think about it."

"I will."

They get up and walk back toward the party. Kate says, "Music is the cause and the solution to our problems."

"Ha," says Amanda, "I thought it was oxygen."

One group wants to go drinking and another wants food. Kate and Amanda decide they're hungry; they walk a few quiet blocks to a pizza place and sit outside with a couple website guys. Dutch flirting mainly consists of averted eyes and nonspecific laughter, as though these boys find something under the table hilarious. But Amanda and Kate are locked on each other anyway, relieved to live a few false moments together.

"Is L.A. any better now?" Kate says.

"Well. It was warm this winter. That's the best thing I can say."

"..."

"It's the west side, the highest-maintenance place in the known universe. Every tanned beach bum is a millionaire. Trophy wives and dog poop."

"It's tempting from the outside. People can't be more phony than New York."

"Different kind of phony," says Amanda. "When they backstab, you never see the knife."

"But you get to go out to cool restaurants and let guys buy you expensive dishes where you need a magnifying glass to see the food."

"Yeah. Uh, let's go over what it's like to date guys in L.A."

"Ha."

"Every guy wears distressed flannel and Red Wing boots and beanies that stand straight up on their own. Everybody's haircut is carefully sculpted to look like they haven't had a haircut in six months. Guys are so confident, like, the barista and the supermarket checkout guy and the random homeless dude carrying a dog in his backpack, they're all like, 'Hey, baby, you need to check out this student film I was an extra in a few years ago, here's a business card with the YouTube address.' Then they drive you an hour for artisanal quinoa at this special place, and *only* this place, because the monks who serve it have taken a special vow of silence that really brings out the flavor in the quinoa, and the guy never asks you more than one or two questions about yourself...and one of those questions is always, 'What part of town do you live in?' which is creepy. Otherwise you get to hear about their modeling gigs and improv classes and screenplays, and if you're lucky maybe they'll hand you their phone and you get to flip through their pictures of a blurry Jessica Alba running to her car. In short, it's a total picnic."

Kate is a good audience through this routine, giggling and accenting the funniest bits with table-taps. The Dutch website guys gawk. One runs inside to fetch a pitcher of beer. "So nobody special?" says Kate.

Amanda carefully, effortlessly makes a funny face and flutters her eyes in *I wish* fashion. "Nope, nobody."

"Did you know butterflies taste with their feet?" Kate says.

The website guys text more friends, they arrive, the group splinters and regenerates, and eventually Amanda and Kate are sitting with complete strangers, looking out over a random dark square whose ghostly playground equipment coalesces and evaporates via passing headlights. They've guzzled much free beer, and share disbelief at how pleasant and easygoing the whole scene is. Amanda goes inside to pee.

Kate remembers she stashed the day's mail in her bag. It's mostly old gig handbills and Chapsticks and tuning keys in there, but she finds the envelopes. Among Hoop's credit card statement and junk solicitations, she finds a letter for her.

First she sees "Binghamton" in the return address and it's an unwelcome slap.

The thought is: it would be easy to just throw this away.

Inside, there's one folded sheet of typewriter paper. The texture alone—rough, sharp-edged—is enough to drain two decades from Kate, so again she's a child fumbling through a hidden box of this paper, unable to imagine her parents having even a few sheets' worth of things to say. In its thickness it doesn't want to unfold. A postcard slides from within, and glides to the table.

The typing paper bears four handwritten words from her father: "This came for you."

The postcard depicts a night sky and the Eiffel Tower in front of the Monte Carlo hotel, and is stamped with the phrase *Greetings From Las Vegas*. She flips it over and reads loopy cursive:

Kate dear,

My girl is in LA so I am writing this while I think of it instead of calling & she will send it. An old lady never tells her age but I will say I am now a year older & the gift you want is more years but a sweet friend offered another. He asked me to play in the fall show of Shania. I told him I cannot. My legs! They are still pretty but weak. He said do I know someone & I know you. The pay is good. Come to Vegas & meet him & he will love you.

–Billie

Amanda returns and sits. Her beautiful features are flushed with travel and alcohol. Kate watches her survey the boys around them, feels the air change for her reappearance. As diverse as Amsterdam can be, tonight Amanda stands apart from these sallow people, with her coiled hair and cinnamon skin. She has a speck of black pepper on her cheek, and how that reinforces her lack of vanity: she didn't even check her reflection in the bathroom! Kate swells with love, also wondering if she could really tolerate becoming a drummer-in-residence playing country music in Las Vegas. She withholds the news of this possibility, at least for a little while.

That night Amanda sleeps in her hotel bed again. Her return ticket to the States is in the bedside Bible drawer: it's for Saturday, the day after the Melkweg show. She has Caleb's credit card for any Buggy Whips who choose to accompany her.

STARK RAVING CLEAN

Sebastian has Anissa in the T-square position: she's on her back, knees-up, he's on his side beneath her legs. He's thrusting conscientiously.

She's quiet, eyes closed, absorbed in effort. He feels her fingertips on his wrist, tapping with concentration. He tries to interpret the touches as strikes on a piano keyboard, wonders what the composition would sound like. But of course, she's no musician, she's a model: the rooftop presenter from yesterday.

He snake shimmies, pushing a rhythm, locked on her face for signs of discomfort. Anissa is a natural beauty, curvy and wild, exhaling now like a hissing cat. He tries to remember the teachings he's read. He must toss aside his attachment for his body and realize he's everywhere. He must truly enter his senses and the shaking that sex engenders. He must be uninterruptedly aware and feel the consciousness of these women as his own consciousness. He must *become* them.

Anissa grimaces and moans. Her back arches.

The way to be present is to know the space between two breaths. The self vanishes in the instant between inhale and exhale.

She says, "*Oui*. Fuck me."

His next thrusts push deeper. He will have peace because he'll recognize the unreality around him. The constructs. Whatever happens will happen. There's no figuring anything out. She went down on him in a taxi.

Anissa's face constricts and her hips come off the bed. He finds his thrusts more difficult to finish as she squeezes him. She says, "Ohhhhhhhhhhhhhhhhhhhhhh!"

Her hips leave him. His cock flops out and he feels uncoordinated and bad, but she's growling and her taps on his wrist become a gouge. He looks up at her pelvis and sees a mist issuing from her, and she goes, *"Awwwwwwwwwwwwwww!"* and the mist becomes a stream arcing over their bodies. She thrashes, squirting everywhere, and this makes him feel superhuman, it makes him so happy, until he realizes this is lust for achievement— what he's just *done to* her, a race he's just won—and he isn't actually generous at all but instead just wants to be perceived as the world's best lover.

Later he leaves her apartment. He feels alone, and becomes swarmed by the urge to find amphetamines. He walks a mile to Nassaukade where the Dutch-language Back to Basics meeting is letting out, and the English-language Just For Today meeting is starting up its weekly commitment-speaker session. Right across the Singelgracht, literally maybe five hundred feet away, is the Melkweg. Sebastian realizes how grubby he must look, what he must smell like. He sits between Bertrand and Sonja, older veterans whose eyes get big as jewels when the commitment-speakers talk, and he watches the newcomer addicts trying to steady themselves enough to pour creamer into their coffee. He prepares himself to identify with whatever will be said, all for the purpose of this one night, he won't use *tonight*, and no promises beyond that. He tries to make his eyes big as jewels.

A guy in a blue sports coat steps to the podium and speaks in a British accent. "My name is Roger and I'm an addict. My story isn't so different. I got blasted on vodka and Statteras. I hit my wife and daughter until they split. I did a two at Winchester and it was just as easy to find pills in the bin. I was lucky: my parole officer was NA and he turned into my sponsor. But I still punched and I still got punched. I still beat up my girlfriend. I got sorry for myself and used bags and bags of Zonegrams and Geodons, got more sorry for myself. I could've been arrested so many more times."

Sebastian is listening, but is also thinking about Anissa. Why did she agree to sleep with him? Why do any of the women agree? By now he'll see himself mid-seduction—brushing his fingers on a face, breathing into an ear, placing his palm against a tummy—and it's impossible for him to mean it. Do they want him because they think he's a young rock star? Maybe. Also he's a robot: shy/aggressive, reserved/blunt, brooding/passionate.

"I won't waste your time with 'Mommy didn't love me' and 'Daddy drank and hit me.' If that's the story you tell yourself, I don't judge you. But I was just a prick. I was afraid of life without drugs. The popular speakers are the ones who make it a bit funny, but bugger that. I shat blood for years. I broke both hands and all my original teeth. I killed somebody's cat 'cause I lost my stash. I was ugly."

Sebastian's pose lured Anissa. His pose tricked her into believing he was worth her attention. He tricks them. There is no actual self there. And they aren't selves to him. They are small noses and undrawn mouths, the transaction is as false as false can be. But of course that's his problem, too, because they *are* selves, he just doesn't care enough to know them. Why does he do it? And why do they fall for it? Once he has them naked, their judgment is impaired. He sees the strands of his personality—seduction techniques, affability, torment over writing music, fear of death— working to cover something....

"I was sure there were things I couldn't make it through if I was clean. I don't know what they were. But something might happen that'd be so painful, I'd have to use to survive. And if those painful things were out there, waiting for me, what difference did it make? I might as well just use now. But even if you could take a drug that didn't make you act like a prick or fill your shit up with blood or cost you every penny you ever made...even if there weren't any consequences? You still shouldn't. *I* still shouldn't, anyway."

It's not that Sebastian sleeps with these women—Hoop calls it *being a swordsman*—to make himself feel better. He doesn't feel all that great. Sometimes it's a one-time thing, there's no further communication, and sometimes they text him and ask for another encounter, but he's on to the next, not so much because he thinks the next will lead anywhere. If he's honest, often he catches himself being embarrassed: for the presumption of connection. It's maybe a little humiliating being a hookup. It'd be all right if he could do it not *wanting* something from them. If he could really be the cold bastard they later claim he is. But there he is every time trying so hard to make it mean something in the philosophical sweep of his life, and then it doesn't, and an orgasm only lasts so long no matter how pretty the woman who induces it. So why *not* on to the next? It's…reassurance? If these girls in bars and cafés evaluate his face and his music and his repartee and find him worthy, well shit. It's another way to keep checking in on what the world thinks of him. But he doesn't want to care what the world thinks of him. If only he could stop!

"The first year sober, I ran around like a bloody fool. Anyone drank a beer I had to sprint out of the room. I got addicted to reality TV, and football, and gourmet bloody coffee. I was still a prick. They have that expression, 'stark raving clean.' That was me. You sit there every night staring down at the floor looking to fill the hole with something else instead of wondering why there's a hole in the first place. Of course I used again. Of course I did. I nabbed a dozen Percocets from an old girlfriend—anyway, they were supposed to be Percocets—and I had a seizure. And that seizure. Let me tell you. You want something to get your mind and your will and your soul all lined up. There's nothing like a seizure to bring out the inner fascist."

Sebastian is so low. The floor threatens to swallow him up. But he's really listening.

"The thing I never got through my bloody skull was I could keep coming back to NA, even if I was using. That's what I hope you take away tonight. If you go out and use tonight, it doesn't mean you can't come back tomorrow. It's part of the process: getting so bad you give up every illusion you have about control. You can't fucking control it, you just can't. I hope you can at least hear these words. Don't be ashamed to come back. You *have* to come back."

It gets better later. He and Scott bring guitars to their local and sit out front in the evening sun. This place is a Thai restaurant but Scott just drinks lager, for which he's occasionally charged by a waitress who has extra smiles for Sebastian. Scott knows a million progressions and Sebastian usually has no idea what they're playing, but a passer-by will stop and say, "I love that song!"

When they noodle out here, Sebastian can tolerate the guitar. Scott knows to back off when a divertissement takes hold of Sebastian—something that may morph into a song idea—and Sebastian has grown to appreciate Scott's unshakable guardianship of the groove. He's always bouncing *right there*, a bass player on guitar (though Sebastian doesn't say this), making a path anyone could follow.

"I saw a little sign at Winston," says Scott. "Not a sign, just a photocopy, but nice. Hoop made them?"

"Probably, yeah."

Of course, musical partnerships end. All partnerships, maybe. Scott can't play everything that's in Sebastian's head and they get into arguments that are ostensibly about this incapacity. Scott feels his task is to impress the kid. He censors half his ideas imagining Sebastian's labored smile.

"What about like this," Scott says, and he plays a little chromatic twiddle: F-F#-G. Sebastian picks it up, takes the barre chords apart and fingers variants, his hands are on autopilot and meaning is gone again. What a damn relief. This, he knows how to do.

"And you come in up here," says Sebastian, leaving the first twiddle and playing another higher up on the Top Grand's neck.

"Oh, right."

"So it's one, two, three, four...and just wait on me, right?"

"I like it. It's ballsy."

"But so then there's room for a little piece on the downbeat, okay, so go ahead and play that one from the start...and then right here...."

"..."

"Right *here*."

"Ah, that's awesome, okay. And so then I play this...."

"Maybe that's keyboard, though."

"Ha, don't be coy with me, you can play both."

"..."

"So meanwhile, I go here, and it's a natural lead-in to a chorus."

"..."

"Yeah, great. Cool, go again."

"You like it better when I...?"

"I guess it depends on how big we make the chorus."

"Pretty big, right?"

"That's what I was thinking, so then it's just...."

"Yeah!"

"Yea-heh-heh!"

The Whips songs came in this kind of rush, are still coming.

And as the musical sophistication grows, Scott feels pressure to make better lyrics. He used to imagine his words coming out of Amanda, but personally he doesn't want to sing about love games anymore. If someone asked him whether he'd rather be successful or important, well, he hasn't matured *that* much. But what about both? His notebook is on the table, and as they keep figuring out this weird new tune, he sing/reads a chorus:

Be cruel, do what you do
I remember a time
When the world saw through
Don't do me no favors
Somehow I'll subdue
Vanity is forever
L.A. is for you
Be cruel, just do what you do

Sebastian's brow crinkles at this taste of bitterness but he doesn't say anything: he wonders if Scott has written these words for his benefit. He plays a fun off-the-cuff solo and laughs when Scott shouts, "Make sure you remember that!" which is funny because Sebastian always remembers.

Scott knows he shouldn't care about a deal. Deals are a token from bygone days. Of course. But Hoop says Vechter Records will be there Friday; even after the mess with Jacob, having a label on their side still feels so much easier than do-it-yourself. He still wants to be immortal and it makes him feel old.

Bigger, though. He tears up these lyrics. Be big.

They play for an hour and the waitress brings food. Sebastian puts his guitar down like he'd be fine never picking it up again. Scott has to keep the Ovation in his lap for a few minutes. They're eating spring rolls. Then a song comes over the p.a.: the singer is lost in half-hiccupped Auto-Tune, the beat is spastic. It's fucking awful.

Scott can tell from just a few seconds: it's a new Honeystuck song.

"Man," he says. "Uh, I better go drop the guitar at home. Want me to take yours?"

" . . . "

"We're about done, right?"

"I guess. No thanks. I'm good, I'll hang onto it."

"Later, dude."

Sebastian thinks he must've said or done something wrong. He rewinds the conversation. But Jesus, Scott takes offense so easily, a dynamic that's been grinding Sebastian down for years. He sighs. Caroming back and forth between euphoria and isolation is terrible for him. Why does Scott have to be oversensitive? Sebastian chews another gratis spring roll.

And Scott trudges away from the song's radius. If he can't hear it, it doesn't exist, and Honeystuck can't have another hit.

It's a couple blocks to the apartment and Scott is shielding himself from his inadequacies; as he approaches home two figures materialize, sitting beside their front door. One is Amanda, talking, more animated than he's seen her all week when she isn't playing Ginger. The other is a young girl with green hair.

At least actual physical events happening in the world can send his self-loathing, if not into the background, at least into a slightly ignoble middle ground.

"Here he is," says Amanda, getting up from the sidewalk.

"Hey," he says. "Hi?"

The girl doesn't move. She's cross legged on the ground, chin-in-hands.

"We were just waiting for you," Amanda says. "You guys know each other. You know Sofie, right?" She makes a concerned private face for Scott. "She came by looking for you. I asked if she wanted to come inside."

"Hey, Sofie," says Scott. "Sure, what's going on? Looking for Hoop?"

Amanda pantomimes a needle against her own arm, and Scott nods.

"Sofie?" The girl's shoulders shake. She covers her eyes. Scott squats beside her and smells unwashed hair. "Do you feel bad?" He looks up at Amanda. "That's a stupid question. Sofie, are you overdosing?"

"No."

"But you're...?"

The girl nods.

"That's all right," says Amanda.

"You want me to call Hoop?" Scott says.

"No."

Scott sits on the cooling sidewalk, places his guitar between them. "You want to come inside? Maybe get something to eat or drink? Or you can just tell us. Why are you…sad?"

"Not sad," Sofie says.

"…"

"Yesterday I watch you come home." She's slurring a little. "I think: maybe I talk with you."

"That's cool," says Scott. "We can talk."

"No! I am not a baby."

"All I said is we can talk."

Sofie lowers her hands and he can see her pixie features, smooth and still forming. She's crying and grimy and her chin is scraped. She looks at him with love in her dark eyes.

"You tell us," Scott says.

The girl looks up at Amanda, and says, "We can go to Levy."

"What's the levy?"

"…"

"Okay, sure. Let's do it. Let's get up and go to the levy."

"But not her," Sofie says.

"Not her. That's rude, Sofie. Amanda was taking care of you."

Amanda picks up the Ovation. "It's fine. It's no problem."

Sofie begins to stand. "She is too pretty."

"I'll just be inside, Scott. Kate's coming back and we're going to dinner and some…drinks."

"…"

"Text if you need anything."

"…"

"…"

"*Dank je wel,*" says Sofie, too late.

A Citroën putters down Wilhelminastraat and its sideview mirror bangs against a parked SUV. Scott helps Sophie all the way up, watching the door through which Amanda just walked. Eternally, everything: stuff he cannot have. He realizes that he's remembering driving in Los Angeles, a hundred years ago.

Sofie is tiny and clad in an oversized black sweatshirt and torn black-lace leggings. He can see sections of tattoos on her calves. "She is your girlfriend?"

"No," he says.

"…"

"How did you know we live here, Sofie?"

"..."

Scott wonders if he's old enough to be this girl's father. He guesses it's close. And what a notion! The idea that he could be anybody's father!

"I am very weak," she says.

"..."

"I am very shame to be high."

He doesn't indulge the instinct to be avuncular. He takes her seriously, and nods.

They walk. She leads him north. Amsterdam rolls away, a merciless sprawl. The sky is still light.

He doesn't ask questions. He lets her speak when she wants. For some reason, suddenly, there's no question of leaving her alone.

She tells him about her eyebrow piercings, how they became infected in the spring and how ill she got. She talks in the language of an everlasting present he identifies with extreme youth, or maybe it's extreme poverty. Anyway, his lack of judgment doesn't feel like a strategy. He's really not judging. She's this spirited person living within her life's confines as we all live within confines, and this is only the second time he's met her, but that's all right.

She chose him, stalked him, whatever. He has to respect that. She's in bad shape and wherever she's going, he discovers he'll follow her all the way.

She pines before a clothing store's shuttered window and regularly examines her heavy-lidded reflection in passing glass. And she talks and talks—she doesn't miss school, her friend Sabine is a great runner and could easily win a gold medal at the Olympics, the birds near the IJ are magic but some are evil—while Scott walks and listens. She touches his arm and wordlessly asks if it's okay to hold his hand.

Her palm is freezing. She says, "Can a human be happy always?" Her pupils are unnaturally tiny.

He thinks about this.

"Ah," she says. "Do not say an answer!"

He can't know her, not all at once. He won't presume to try.

They walk a long time before he really wonders where they're going, and if she has an actual destination in mind. They're in a neighborhood with an elevated highway rushing somewhere nearby. They could be anyplace, any of the American urban underbellies where motels are cheap. Scott doesn't feel unsafe, but he can't pretend to possess Sofie's citizenship. She moves with the ease of the ruined.

"It is Levy," she says. They turn up the walk of a new brick structure that's the last thing before a complicated-looking highway onramp. The glass doors say: *Voedselbank Levy*. Sofie says, "You are hungry?"

They step inside. Dozens of people are holding paper plates, standing on a line that weaves through many indoor picnic tables. The big room ends in a kitchen and smells like roast beef. Sofie detours down a short corridor and puts her sweatshirt in a locker. Scott can also see a washer/dryer. He says, "This is where you sleep?"

"No!" says Sofie. She leads him back to the front room; her t-shirt is too big and bears the word *GEZELLIGHEID* and a Netherlands flag. "It is for food and TV and bread and a doctor!"

Three passing staffers greet her by name. The mix here skews toward older disheveled folks, cognitively disabled people and Asian immigrants. A few young kids are watching television in a conference room. A fat man is shrieking in the corner as an administrative-looking lady tries to calm him down. There's another line: it snakes to a different room where people wait holding clear plastic bags and receive pieces of fresh produce. Despite its outward chaos, this place is a series of systems and the veterans understand where to queue, sit, eat, talk. Someone is calling out "now serving" numbers in Dutch. The administration lady walks this way, saying many hellos, and shakes Scott's hand.

"Welcome," she says. "I am Tess. You are American. And you are new?"

"I guess so."

"You are Sofie's friend. Hello, Sofie. Did you eat your apple? Sofie and I talked about the apples, we had lovely ones this afternoon. You are welcome anytime for lunch and dinner. We do not ask questions. If you need a doctor, make an appointment. I am glad to see you."

Tess leaves them, and Scott says to Sofie, "I can tell you did *not* eat your apple."

She sticks out her tongue.

"You look a little better," he says. "You sound better."

"No! You will stay with me to eat!"

"Okay. Yes. I'll stay."

They have a vegetarian option. Sweaty kitchen volunteers are proud to snatch away his plate and ladle beans and rice from a private stash. If their smiles are a bit forced, Scott pardons them. When they sit and Sofie introduces him to other diners, he plays it too cool, trying to show how normal this is for him, how enlightened and humanistic he is.

"Where do most of these people live?" he privately asks Sofie.

She squints at him. Her pupils have expanded and she's shivering a little. "Maybe...inside their house?"

"Oh, right, so you don't have to be homeless...."

"And maybe they take care of you also," says Sofie. "Maybe we eat together tomorrow also."

"Maybe," he says.

Several of the diners smell like boiled cabbage and eat with their mouths open. When they laugh, food particles fly. A boy Sofie's age holds court across the table, spouting cool judgments in Dutch and working his gum like a stunt driver; Scott wants to ask where he got his pricy bomber jacket. It's the forced togetherness of high school homeroom. He finds himself calculating how long good form requires him to stay.

He goes to the restroom and on the way back Tess buttonholes him. She says, "We do not have many rules here. But no drugs. It is very strict."

"Great. I agree. No drugs."

"You see, I know Sofie is not your daughter."

Scott feels his face lift sideways. "Yes. True."

"..."

"Jesus, you think I'm her dealer?" Tess spreads her fingers. "What, you think I'm her *pimp*?"

"Everyone is welcome here. You are welcome here. Please ask if you need help, but no drugs."

"Lady, she literally just showed up stoned on my doorstep. I asked if I could take her anywhere, and she said here."

"Very well," Tess says.

"..."

"Did you eat enough? I hope you enjoyed."

"..."

"At nine we close. No exception."

He walks back to the table and becomes charming.

He tells Sofie about a musician who rather than letting one set of fingernails grow long, instead grew one set of toenails and became the world-famous foot-guitarist, and this delights her. He tells the kid in the bomber jacket he has a face for radio. He says, "Here's a puzzle for everyone. You can only ask yes-or-no questions. A man lies dead on the ground, a piece of straw in his hand. What happened?" Sofie and other teens—bomber-jacket boy included—gather around, ask a hundred questions. Scott keeps looking around for Tess, so she can see how beloved he's instantly become. The kids all slap him five and laugh and guess at the puzzle, which is a nights-on-the-road special: the man was in a hot-air balloon that was going down and drew the short straw. He leads them in a rousing version of "Call Me Maybe" (whose lyrics they all know), they eat stale donuts for dessert and as they walk out into the night together, he feels relief knowing he'll never return. Sofie hugs him and runs off into the dark.

SEVERED BOUNCING FINGERS

Kate and Amanda eat a quick dinner then walk to a tourist bar off the Rembrandtplein. Kate isn't paying attention, Amanda just kind of angles her inside, and Kate has done *so* much evaluating of random ambient music in her bandmates' presence she feels herself wanting to just switch off her ears entering this chintzy place. Which is why it takes her a few minutes to realize this is a karaoke bar.

It seems the only Dutch people in here are the bartender and the DJ; there are Germans and French Canadians and Japanese and a big family of Nigerians including children kicking a soccer ball against the walls. One of the Nigerians chooses to sing "Yellow Submarine" and this emboldens the Germans to do "I Love Rock And Roll," which initiates a steady stream of cheese like "Rock And Roll All Nite" and "Hit Me With Your Best Shot." Amanda tries to get Kate onstage for a duet.

Kate says, "Oh, they don't have nearly enough alcohol." So Amanda sings "Party In The U.S.A." solo. Well, some part of Kate would like to be unshameable.

She watches the performance. Amanda is no ham, which is what makes her so seductive. The really good actors in high school—there were a couple, though they fended off teachers' entreaties to go pro—had that thing of being understated and overstated, the way you somehow instantly know a "man-on-the-street" interview subject is a professional: they're *too* natural. Wow, and isn't that a miniature revelation about Amanda. She's too natural! Just walking around in life! She's up there bubbly but not overly bubbly, making the right notes seem like a challenge but not a struggle, pretending she's overcoming shyness as though she's mimicking tiny hip wiggles she's seen pop stars make, as though she didn't invent them herself.

Kate realizes it's microscopically obnoxious Amanda picked this place. Maybe more than microscopically.

Brave stage-goers follow Amanda, with different ambitions. They all clap and laugh and drink. Kate thinks about how long they have to stay here, and whether Amanda is deriving morale from superiority. Amanda thinks this is so much more comfortable than anything she experiences with Caleb's "friends," and she'd do anything to get more of it.

The DJ goes on break.

"What's next?" Kate says.

"Well," says Amanda. "I thought maybe dancing. But I'm delaying us, because we have an admirer in our midst." Her eyes go to the bar—its nauseating pink neon, the Grolsch sign and dangling beer steins and televised soccer matches—and they see the DJ spying on them. Discovered, he turns and laughs at something the bartender hasn't said.

"Ah."

"Not me," Amanda says. "I'm serious. When I was up there, his eyes never left you."

Kate cringes. She feels the cringe spring from her organs, from her cells, a twitch borne of life as she's lived it. It's foolish, she's foolish, every mother's daughter has heard that a boy would be lucky to have her. Jack Dooley's tongue is once again in her mouth and it tastes so stupid.

"I told you, you look *good*."

"..."

"I'll talk to him."

"You do," says Kate, "and I shave your head in your sleep."

"Empty threat. We don't live together anymore."

"I'll hire head-shaving ninjas to sneak into your hotel."

"I'm sure this happens all the time and you just don't notice. One more set. Let's just see."

Kate swigs the rest of her Malibu-and-Diet. She's living in Vegas. She's touring Europe as a Whip. She's rooming with

Amanda in L.A. She's hitchhiking with strangers. The next thing obviates the trials of now. Amanda puts another round on Caleb's card.

They flip through the laminated pages and Amanda picks "Against All Odds," one she remembers her parents singing as a duet at Christmas. The picture zones her out: close bodies and ornaments, a scratchy sweater, Lacey's thickening neck in profile and the bun in her hair, how old was Amanda, maybe 5? The presumption of an intact family has long since ceased to be painful or controlling, it's an excuse, it's a pair of shoes that happen not to fit any longer. The whole time she's giving the DJ a side-eye, reckoning.

He goes back on duty, and on a slip of paper, beneath the song title, Amanda writes, "She's a sweetheart! Go talk to her!"

He does.

While Amanda hits the high notes, here he comes. His name is Max and he tells Kate she's pretty, and scurries away.

What the fuck, Kate thinks. *What the fucking fuck.*

Max cuts short this next set and for a while they drink as a trio, and Kate keeps expecting him to take her aside and ask if Amanda is single.

"Last night," he says, "I went roller skating with friends. Not the kind of roller skating with, *pft*, one row on the bottom, not rollerblading. It's two rows of wheels, the old-fashioned kind of skates that smell very bad. For nostalgia, maybe. Except none of us actually had skates like these when we were children."

"Okay," says Kate.

"They play old disco music and go in a circle, then blow the whistle, time to go around the other way. One woman, she wanted to skate with me and so I did, she was a friend of my friend but I didn't know her. I thought she was being...aggressive, and I wasn't interested in her, but she was also nice and smiling. So okay, I skate with her and she skates *around* me, spinning around me, and it's all fun. But then the next time I go around she's gone. Okay. No problem. I'm relieved. She's gotten the message, right? Better not to have to talk about it. Better to part politely. The Dutch, we don't want an uncomfortable conversation: my parents stay married because to be divorced requires an uncomfortable conversation. I skate around again, feeling cool, but now it seems none of my friends are skating. Where'd they go? Where are they? They're all gathered around the woman who wanted to skate with me, who's crying, and telling them that I…caressed her in the.…" He points at his own breast.

"…!"

"It wasn't funny!"

"Oh," Amanda says, "we're only laughing because we believe you."

But Max is breezy and laughs, too. "Oh, well. Tch. Eventually the woman admitted she was drunk and I hadn't touched her. But it was a scary few moments! Too much drama for your mama. I don't know why I'm telling this story! But I'll say this: most of my stories are embarrassing, and end with me *not* touching a lady."

They all laugh together.

Kate says, "I think this is a setup. You know Gertie Bakker, don't you?"

"Who's that?" he says.

Amanda puts her arm around the drummer. "Kate has nothing keeping her in Amsterdam," she says. "In fact, I'm trying to convince her to move back to the States so we can be in a band together again."

"I've never been to America," says Max. "My job is too dumb."

"It *is* pretty dumb," Kate says.

"But fun!" says Amanda.

Max says, "Being a musician: that's fun. Going bar to bar carrying around this machine, uf. So to keep you here, I must…marry you quickly?"

"Well," says Kate. "Pretty much."

Max is a blushing, short, natty dude in a corduroy jacket and granny glasses, spiky and handsome with a whiff of insanity about him, like, eyes a little too big, laugh a little crazed. Plus why isn't he trying for Amanda? He's flirting but it's impossible to tell what he really means. She can't tell how drunk he's getting. She can't tell how drunk *she's* getting.

"Why don't we all go to a movie?" Amanda says.

Max says, "Yes!"

"Will you get in trouble for leaving?" says Kate.

Max says, "Probably, yes!"

There's a movie house around the corner, a crazy three-story Art Deco structure bearing the words Theater Tuschinski. While

Max is buying tickets, Amanda says, "This is where I say good evening."

"No. Don't."

Amanda arches one eyebrow.

"This is fast," says Kate. "And why are you even doing this? You really do want me to ditch Amsterdam. You want me to come home."

"True."

"So why are you trying so hard to be a good wingman?"

It's nighttime but still bright, a time of day that reminds Kate of that one walk through a Vegas casino: permanent twilight. And that same kind of casino swarm is here on Reguliersbreestraat, tourists wandering around trying to find seams in an impossible place's majesty. But Kate sees an old lady dressed in black, with long legs and arms that end in an unfortunately Marfan-style stunted torso, and this woman is sucking her teeth and laughing and talking to herself, well kempt wearing pricy eyeglasses but mad. She flaps one elbow conversationally and barks at a passing schnauzer. Kate wonders why her eyes find this one lady. There are hundreds of people here.

"Think about it this way," Amanda says. "It's probably all part of my scheme."

Kate watches the old woman spit on the window of a sandwich shop.

"I encourage a love affair? How could I *not* have your best interests at heart? But deep down I know: he's just some random guy. How likely is it that we just stumbled onto your soulmate in a karaoke bar? I'm pretty clever here. I look like the good guy, I win your trust, things don't work out. Boom. You're on a plane."

Kate laughs, stops laughing.

"No," says Amanda. "C'mon. This place has been good for you. An outpost that still brings out the best in a good person."

"I don't know if I even like him. The first thing he said was about touching some girl's boob. And you're leaving me alone."

"Yup."

"I mean, I know he's not dangerous."

"Yup."

"You want things from me, Amanda. You want me to convince the guys. It feels really tough to take things you say at face value right now. We're doing pretty well here. Things could change pretty soon." The old lady snakes through the tourist hordes, down this brick lane, arms a good yard ahead of the rest of her.

"Kiss him, don't kiss him."

"Don't judge us," Kate says. "You just got here."

"Okay."

"I'm tipsy."

"Me, too."

But Kate doesn't believe that. Has she ever even seen Amanda drunk? "That thing you said, about a place bringing out the best. That was a pretty nice thing to say."

"Yeah," says Amanda. "Let me get out of here before one of us barfs."

And she leaves Kate, thinking nobody could ever fault her for spreading around so much truth.

Max returns one of the tickets and they watch *Grand Budapest Hotel* as a twosome. Kate loves it so much her stomach hurts. After, they walk around the block and sit in a café, and she can't get the image of Jeff Goldblum's severed bouncing fingers out of her mind.

"What does it feel like," Max says, "to have a big show coming up so close?"

"Hm. There've been *so* many. Madison Square Garden. Wembley. I'm so jaded, can I even tell anymore?"

"…"

"I don't think I'll get nervous until right before. Somehow I think I convince myself it isn't real. And then maybe I'm surprised it is." She looks at her hands, hates them.

"Well, I'm impressed by the ambition of…. *A big show!* I have so many plans but I never do them. Sometimes I bring music to a party and put on a little DJ show. But that's all. Easier to see fame with her arms out, standing in every tomorrow just waiting for me. Easier to make a YouTube video every day that nobody will ever see."

"…"

"I will come see you play Friday."

"Well," she says, "now I really do feel pressure. Yeah, I'm always so sure I've finally gotten rid of all my…whatever, delusions. Like, *now* I'm finally seeing things. *Now* I'm finally seeing the truth. And then a little while later I look back and see, nope, that was a delusion, too."

Max really seems to think about this. "Yes," he says. "But worse to keep the same delusion forever."

Kate tells him about Binghamton. She feels like they're young children inhabiting an adult conversation, but it's a good feeling, they're confederates.

Max sips an espresso. "And the brilliant fellows in the band. Are any of them...your boyfriend?"

"Ah. That would be a definite negatory."

He seems very cool filing away this information, and for a moment it's possible to believe he asked for the purpose of census taking.

"Tell me about where you grew up," she says.

"Mijdrecht? Ugh. More boring than you can imagine. People in the city don't need stories about the country."

"Well, come on. What's it like?"

"It was on a farm. But it was...a tourist farm? 'Come see the men dance in funny clogs, come eat some cheese.' I milked cows and I planned my escape, ha ha." She likes his chin, the way it puckers toward a cleft when he smiles.

"You don't have to tell me the real story," says Kate.

"Really. Sleepwalking people and tall grass. I went to university in London."

"Okay."

He tells her fish-out-of-water stories, bumpkin stories, quite polished. The first time he rode the tube. The first time he ate Indian food. He's really quite compact and handsome; his fingers are small and his storytelling gestures large. They're formal together, knees occasionally striking each other and recoiling. He's not really so frivolous. He's not really this slacking rudderless DJ, or not just. There's too much effort in his self-sabotage.

"For a time I went to a coffee bar in London every day," he says. "I often sat next to the same lady. Girl. A student, like me. She saw my books and said she already took that class, it was a business class, very boring. She had a posh accent and her clothes were very nice. I didn't have experience with a girl like this. She tells me she broke up with her boyfriend recently but maybe they weren't even broken up, she wasn't sure. One day she says, 'We should meet for dinner.' So probably I think we'll go as friends, though this girl...she was posh, and I wasn't sure. I could hope. The day of our dinner, I went to the same restaurant for lunch first, so I'd be sure to understand the menu and the food types. She was...enigmatic? Quiet and bored with me, or maybe she was merely sad over the wonderful boyfriend. The only sign of happiness from her was a song playing in the restaurant. She asked do I love this song? And I said oh my goodness, yes, love's an understatement, it's my favorite. But of course I'd never heard it before. And now she grows interested and asks all my favorite music and before I can answer—because I can't answer, I don't know any popular music—she tells me all *her* favorite music and I agree with all of it, what a coincidence! The night is ending and maybe it's been very good, maybe I've shown her how perfect I can be for her to replace the boyfriend. And she says, 'The very very best is Mint Royale.' And unfortunately I don't realize this is another popular music act. So I decide to finally be bold, and I will disagree and finally have my own opinion! So I say, 'No, I'm afraid I don't like Mint Royale, I prefer chocolate.' And she laughs at me but I don't understand the laughter, and she sees this, and she understands I really did mean ice cream. And finally I can see her pitying me, what a foolish Dutch...*boerenpummel?* My chance is over with the posh girl, but this was the day! This was the day I decided to learn everything about music! And look where it's gotten me! Ha ha."

"Let me ask you something," Kate says. "Do these stories of you being a loser work on most lady tourists?"

He blinks and smiles, but the smile warps a little.

"I mean, you're very funny."

"..."

"But it's okay: we can talk about real things."

Max seems to contemplate getting up from this table, walking out of this café. Then he winks at her, says softly, "I don't look for tourists. I really don't. I just liked you."

Kate feels momentum gather between them: the intimate, illogical flash that insists, *Confess to a stranger.* She says, "I had to go back to Binghamton for my mother's funeral. It was awful."

Max isn't smiling now. He's thinking, maybe resisting that same confessional urge, but then he says, "I will never go back, even when they die."

"..."

He's still charming, but seems older. He pulls his wrists off the table in small surrender. He says, "We could go to a place and drink something stronger."

So they get out of the lovely obnoxious tourist district, south to a side street of museums and artist studios. A perfect bar presents itself: candlelit and almost empty. They sit at a small table, quite close to each other, and Max says, "What do you want to know about me?"

"..."

"I have no girlfriend. I don't hustle tourists."

Kate says, "Every band needs a Mussolini." She looks at him, knows him, doesn't know him at all. She doesn't know what she's doing here. They're drinking whiskey. "I was in a religious cult," she says. "I think I was brainwashed."

He asks the story. She tells it, the first time ever. Well, she's appropriated vignettes and dialogue before, but with invented contexts; she wrote "Dancing With The Women" but never told them how. Here she is, she's known Max five hours. Sun, Maizie, Inch, Charlene, James Randolph…not funny, not ironic. Partway through, she feels herself adding urgency to the tale, not only trying to make it make sense but also trying to justify why this is all coming out now, here, with this impish goof. *Maybe just say it once, a person I'll know for one night, send it away sealed with a person who'll forget it.* Listening, his face becomes an animal's: little movements, trying to see her from every possible angle. "Charlene is the only one I ever saw again," she says. "But I guess there's still time." She's not crying.

He looks crazed again. He gets up to use the restroom and orders them another round. He's a strange person who tries hard not to be strange.

What does it feel like to have said all this, to have told the story of the mass murder, the van, the Piggly Wiggly, Dax and *Divine Love*, the condoms, the deprogramming? It feels like nothing. It didn't happen. It didn't happen. Wow, is she pretty messed up.

Max brings two new highball glasses, uses them to slide aside their old ones. He says, "I lived for the football team in Mijdrecht: it's a team called Argon. We're in a very low division. When I was young, all I wanted to do was play for Argon. Everybody told me I was too small and too skinny, but I was very obsessed. In secret I dribbled on my knees for an hour, two hours. I didn't realize what a small team it was, just amateurs dreaming of the big time. To me it *was* the big time. I walked three kilometers to go to the matches. I can't get excited about the World Cup, but even now I still love my stupid little home team. In '07, I listened on the radio and we won the *Hoofdklasse* and I cried." Max's half-grin complicates itself in a memory he's fighting off. He says, "Playing for them was a hard dream to kill but my family did it."

"..."

"It was worse than I usually tell my friends. Do you really want to hear?"

"Yes."

He bites his lips. The jazz saxophone coming from the ceiling improvs into a few bars of "Jailhouse Rock."

"My father says he is a descendant of Justus Velsius, the original Dutch born-again madman. Our farm was clogs and cheese, and also faith healing."

"Oh."

"Yes. People came from all over Europe and also America, and we traveled sometimes, too. Praying or driving someplace to pray, many many sick people with tumors bulging out of their bodies begging my parents to heal them."

"Wow."

"So. It was fine when I was very small. My sister and I were his weapons. He'd say, 'You must look clean and holy and always keep your mouth small and your eyes closed when we pray around the people.' At first it didn't seem so bad, when the world is all the same people, the family and the flock. Mischief, oh, mischief for us was finding a movie magazine and hiding it to read in the night. I believed. I saw my father heal people. They fell down. Or they moved their arthritic hands, suddenly able to play the trumpet again. We didn't take much money. My father was true to his cause. So any temptation you have to disobey, any time other children make noise or eat a whole box of communion wafers, it's easy to believe that God has better things in mind for me, that being good for my father is what God wants. My father couldn't sing well but he led the many hundreds clapping and sweating, and if my posh London girl had asked me about Christian hymns I would've known them all. I saw men throw away their crutches. I saw sick babies stop coughing. It was a family proverb that my father could pray over burns and heal them. He told everyone I was his pride.

"But of course things changed. Probably I knew what football was, but there was a revival somewhere in Bavaria and the tent was set up next to a mountain. A boy asked me to kick a football with him, so I slipped out. It was so fun! But he hit and starved me for leaving the tent."

Her parents never spanked Kate, and they didn't deny her musical pursuits. This is where her mind goes: the ways it wasn't so bad for her.

"They took football away because it was a distraction from God. But if you take a thing away.... At first we had no school. Just read your scripture and copy the words onto blank paper. But I wanted to go. There was a school he agreed to in Demmerik, five kilometers from home but I could ride my bike. Even in winter! It was a terrible place: one hour of silent prayer on your knees, and the priest hit you with a paddle if you moved. But my father didn't know what time the school let out. Somehow he never checked, so I could sneak away to the *weide* there and kick with my friends. It was a narrow strip, and the ball fell in...but I always made it home and he never imagined.

"Then my friends said, 'Argon, Argon, Argon.' Soon my heroes were Lokken and Van Kuyvenhoven and Oosterling. I wasn't allowed to carry money but I was a good beggar; I came to a match with a friend's parents or found an extra ticket from somebody pulling up in a car. Maybe I was a team mascot. I looked forward to the weekends and he watched me lie to my mother about where I was going.

"One little grandstand with a ceiling but no walls, the players just below us close enough to touch. In cold, in heat, the announcer voice calling out substitutions, and otherwise fans just standing around leaning their elbows on the fence just a few feet from the action. I lived and died. It was the only thing I cared about, Argon's clumsy attack and clumsier defense, my friends and I would run along the opposite side of the field trying to stay level with the ball and wish it forward. Someone knew that the big clubs always had kids asking them for autographs, so we asked, and the players—who were probably plumbers and insurance men—laughed and signed our notebooks. And how *we* played: never at the sportpark, of course, but wherever we could, there's no shortage of open space in Mijdrecht. Hours and hours, and the children knew I had to keep out of sight in case my father left the farm. This was a good childhood and it happened for a long time, and then...."

Max reaches below the table and lifts his jacket and shirt. The first thing Kate notices is his incongruous white paunch, but she doesn't care, he's still adorable. He turns away and shows a foot-long scar down his right side that looks like a section of folded cardboard.

"He hit me with a manure fork."

"Jesus."

Max puts his shirt down and laughs. "The name was mentioned yes."

"You were a little kid," says Kate.

"I was occupied by the devil and he needed an exit hole." Out of nowhere Max kisses her. She feels him gulp for air, doesn't know whether it's a sob.

After, they don't look at each other. There's a bartender and a couple holding hands on a bench in the corner and two suited men speaking quietly two tables over, and the candle between Kate and Max has a long wick and a puddle of wax like butterscotch. It's what Kate asked for. She's on that reverse-bungee.

"It has a happy ending," she says. "You got out."

"It's only a half-hour drive from here. I pretended I was not afraid of the city. I believed he must be right about some things, and the sins of Amsterdam must be one. Gomorrah! So even as I got older, I never came here. It was many more years of praying and healing. Now I discovered some of his healed were actors. They were convincing, the way they were surprised when they fell. He never took much money, though, and this is something I told myself as a teen: he is good…even if he lies sometimes, he does it for good. In Budapest, in Vienna, in Sofia, we were in mansions, the people who engaged us had so much money and they *must* have offered him, but he never accepted. He wasn't corrupt, not in that way. He believed. The flock would ask if I had the touch, did he pass it down. And he'd look at me and say, 'Yes, but he is too wicked.'"

She works her thumb over the back of his hand.

"A teacher told me about a scholarship and I applied in secret. I don't remember deciding. I really don't. I was still carrying his pulpit, still wiring his microphone. I was a roadie for him! But at the same time, I was applying. One fall day I vanished, no goodbye. I hitchhiked. My sister still lives on the farm, I think."

He's speaking to no one, to empty air filled by bullshit.

"That feeling," he says, "was strong. He could tell me about every sinner boiling in hell. He could describe the disbeliever's liver torn from the body. But the scariest thing was thinking about what else there was. Everything I didn't know. What could happen. But I had to. I had to."

Something inside her chest flutters. She wants to cry and laugh.

NEVER SINGING PROBABLY

She's still asleep in the early evening when Caleb calls.
"Thank God," he says.
"..."
"Did I wake you up?"
"No," she says. "No."
"I don't know why I let myself get so freaked out, it's obvious you're okay."
"What's...? Hey, sorry. What time is it there?"
"I finally got through."
She looks around the room. She hasn't let them clean it for days.
"Don't take it as neediness," says Caleb. "What a cliché: I just wanted to hear your voice. But please accept the, ah, extenuating circumstances."
"Actually, hey, I lied. I did just wake up. Sorry."
"Oh." Like an unimpressed audience, some satellite's algorithmic hiss increases during his long pause. "Oh. Do you have CNN?"
Amanda turns on the TV. A commercial airplane originating in Amsterdam has gone down over Ukraine. Everyone is presumed dead. There are pictures of children's shoes in trees.
She watches the coverage. Families have gathered at Schiphol to ask airport officials for answers, and the public has also begun a vigil there. There are maps of flight plans, file footage of soldiers

dickying with rocket launchers, ID badge photos of the pilot (who, it's pointed out again and again, was Muslim), and many talking heads. She phones Scott.

"Will you come over?" she says.

"We're watching it here."

"..."

"Come over here so we're all together."

"Scott. Please."

He taxis to Keizersgracht. The city is astir per usual. Foot traffic spills onto crosswalks; street acrobats juggle sticks with other sticks; underage boys shout and shove; a male/female couple strays from its herd to argue; a crashed bicyclist accepts help from strangers; a painter drinks wine under a tree. But flags are at half-mast. The cab crosses a busy road near the Singelgracht and Scott sees a nest of wrapped flowers and lit votives surrounding a travel agency's door. He arrives and finds Amanda red-eyed and still watching. It emerges that pro-Russian separatists in Ukraine probably shot the plane down by mistake.

"But they keep talking about 9/11," says Amanda.

"I heard."

She's spent this week twisting herself into such awful shapes. She sinks to the floor and watches more reporting. Her hand is over her mouth.

They find it difficult to judge the event's size. The American news anchors are stern and breathless, but they also get stern and breathless when a cheerleader's mom goes missing or nude celebrity photos leak. It becomes a hyperbole contest, as a parade of experts explains how Europe's time of slumber is over, how air travel will never be the same anywhere, how a land war in Crimea is now imminent. Amanda and Scott take it all in, hating it, unable to switch it off. The cycle goes around for hours: the same footage, the same headshots, the same interviews. But changing the channel feels like disrespect.

She says, "I remember they made us change out of our gym clothes and wait on the curb for our parents."

"Yeah," he says. "I tried calling my brother and parents from English class and the phones were busy, but the wrong kind of busy, that weird busy signal. I couldn't even get voicemail. To me that meant they were on one of the planes."

"..."

"I wrote a poem."

"I just cried at home and watched TV," she says. "If I could cry for hours, y'know? It wouldn't be true, if I could make myself upset enough. If I could act as crushed as when a character died on a show I liked."

"It's normal. When it's something that big."

"Do you remember it was something you asked a new person about, when you wanted to be their friend? 'Where were you? What did you do?'"

"…"

"It was a way to signal: 'I am taking you seriously. I really mean it.'"

"I do remember," he says. "I remember people having that conversation in high school all the time. But then it stopped. I can't really remember when it stopped. Maybe it was a few years after? Maybe more?"

"…"

"I don't even know what replaced it. 'Who do you think is funniest on *Family Guy*?'"

"…"

"…"

They take calls from the States: Amanda's mom and sister, Scott's parents and brother. Eventually the hotel windows grow dim and the broadcast starts to include interviews with families of presumed victims. Official manifests haven't been made public, but these family members are at the airport, volunteering to talk. One shows pictures of little boys on their way to visit their grandmother. Another describes soccer fans flying to Asia for an exhibition tour. Amanda begins to weep; Scott sits on the bed, puts his hand on her shoulder.

She looks up at him. His eyes are CGI-blue and on her.

This isn't how it was supposed to go. It was supposed to be tomorrow night, after the Melkweg show, amid the fever of accomplishment and just hours in advance of her departure. A wonderful memory and a carrot on a stick. Not this.

She tries to make herself wait by sitting on the toilet for a while. It's a tiny w.c. sealed off from the rest of the hotel room, and she doesn't turn on the light. She wonders if this is what the final moments in the fuselage were like.

She thinks about the Lermontov novel she just finished, the

cliff-side duel where Grushnitsky has the first shot at Pechorin but loses his nerve and intentionally only grazes his knee. And Pechorin, the man of intellect, kills Grushnitsky without hesitation and says, "*Finita la commedia.*" Yes, Pechorin, the heartless bastard Amanda wants to meet in the flesh, the one who said, "I often wonder why I'm trying so hard to win the love of a girl I have no desire to seduce and whom I'd never marry."

She leaves the w.c. and reassumes her spot on the floor, before the television. Scott says, "The first time I went to New York I was visiting my brother before he dropped out. I remember sitting in his dorm and he was like, 'Hey, let's get pizza and a movie.' So I got my coat and he was like, 'No, there's a website.' It was this thing where they'd deliver literally *anything* in one hour. I was probably...12 maybe. And even then I remember thinking, 'How hard would it be for someone to take us over? Just threaten to stop our supply of Doritos.'" He rubs his eyes and points to the TV. "How are we not supposed to feel small and give up?"

Amanda looks at his stocking foot. "It's okay to feel small," she says. "Maybe just don't give up."

Now CNN is cycling through the family interviews over and over. The parents of a student flying to Australia to start an internship. The son of recently retired parents heading for a Mediterranean holiday.

Yes, she's able to wait until tomorrow. But she's doing calculations: what if the Melkweg show is canceled? There may not be time.

"Now it just feels like we're watching just to punish ourselves," says Scott.

"Maybe we should be punished," Amanda says.

" . . . "

"Or maybe it's the least we can do."

They know the day's true meaning is inaccessible to them. They aren't *of* this place and that means their horror is half-an-inch deep. But they're still both so sad.

Scott has a Death Cab For Cutie song in his head, and he says the words:

There's no comfort
In the waiting room
Just nervous pacers

Bracing for bad news

Amanda wants him to stop talking.

She thinks, *I tried to be good.*

She reaches up and feels for his gone toe through its sock. His leg slides away but she catches his ankle and rolls down the sock, feeling him watching. She goes slowly, an inch of fabric per second, and finally the sock is off and here it is: the scar-tissue button where his big toe should be. She advances a forefinger. What will it feel like?

She touches it.

He yelps and jumps off the bed. She puts up her hands.

But he exhales smiling unhappily, the furthest thing from a laugh there is in the world, and he says, "I'm sorry. I'm only kidding. It doesn't hurt."

"Dickhead! Not funny!"

And even now, there's a precipice to be backed away from.

But no.

She stands and turns off the TV and she's quite a bit shorter than he is, and she kisses his neck.

Right here. Pressed right against him. That weight against his ribs, those are her actual breasts. She's touching his sides to keep him in place. Her nose manipulates his earlobe.

"You're confused," he says.

"You're probably right," she says.

"What about Bazzy?"

"..."

"I know how we got the Melkweg."

"That's what you think?" She's breathing into his scruff.

"Of course."

"You've been running around tormented, haven't you?"

"..."

"I didn't," she says.

He pushes away. "It doesn't make sense," he says. "Why get us a show here? You want us back in the States."

She's wearing the same gray t-shirt she slept in all morning. She pulls it halfway up.

And he sees how stupid he is. She didn't need to actually fuck Bazzy. The implication was enough. She wanted Scott half-blind, stumbling-around jealous.

"I really didn't sleep with him," she says.

He kisses her.

It's a ripsnorter. They each feel overrun by the cavern of mouth, so strange how when it's done right this negative space can be a force, and barely touching another person's inner lip and tongue and teeth can feel like falling forward into darkness.

She says, "Hoo," and maybe a twist of smoke comes out of her mouth.

"Meh," he says, trying to fake a grin.

She walks away, up the granite step into the bathroom, and throws the t-shirt at him. She drops her pajama bottoms, opens the shower stall door and turns on the water.

He knows. She tortured him to get him to this point. And now she wants to give him a reason to leave that's stronger than anything the Whips can offer to make him stay. He knows, but he's past the point of resisting. He clambers up into the bathroom, removes his clothes.

Against her tautness he feels coarse and unprocessed. He hugs her from behind, fits his chest against her shoulders...and pushes her face into the shower spray. She coughs and kicks backward at him, elbows him laughing, feels his cock pressing against her butt. He clasps those breasts, the ones in his dreams. He kisses her neck, feels her kiss his ear. She leans back against him so her chin tilts up and her head rests on his shoulder. The water is hot. She reaches behind and grips his cock and tells herself this doesn't have to mean anything more than either of them wants it to. He groans and coaxes apart her legs, reaches two fingers inside.

Their hands move like this for a long time. Their sighs are as loud as the shower.

He steps from her, positions himself. She bends forward and here's the cold tile against her palms and the hot water against her shoulders. He's in, it's impossible, he looks down between his grasping hands and sees that infinity tattoo, and it's bouncing against him. She's the most beautiful person he's ever seen. She's smart and funny and very mean. He goes slowly. She wants to be neutral about this much-anticipated moment: he feels pretty great—he's the perfect height, at the perfect angle, the right force and just the right depth—but she can observe these things dispassionately knowing the game's final stages. He speeds up and feels her back arch, feels the motley mechanisms inside her pull and press. Maybe this isn't wrong.

She sees this picture of herself, finally doing this, and remarks to herself how cool she is. Then she looks down between her own brown feet and sees his white ones pointing the same way, sees the missing toe.

Suddenly there's no cool observation. She feels her body begin to buck. Her arms are out, her palms are on the wall, and her head is down, staring at the reality of his foot. The rest of her shudders, but her eyes stay locked on the part of him that isn't there.

And she orgasms harder than she's ever done, shouting.

They go again in the bed, and she makes him go a third time, standing by the windows.

Finally she puts on a shirt and Scott sits naked on an empire chair in the corner.

He says, "This is something we do now?"

"Do you want it to be something we do now?"

"Come on. You can't be so blatant about it."

"We just needed to think about something else for a little while."

"..."

"It happened, Scott."

It did. He has a pillow across his groin. Does he really think she's so cold, so beyond redemption? Does he really think she'd sink this low without loving him at least a little? He wants to say no, but after so much time in orbit around her.... "You're leaving," he says. "I get it. Maybe...can't we just fall asleep together one time? Nobody would have to know. Wouldn't that be nice?"

Her body is still humming a high D.

Is it because Scott is secretly what she always wanted? Or is it because she's a fitful schemer whose emotional defenses have momentarily caved? It's been enough to think about Kid Centrifuge done right, backed by Flood money and no pop-star marketing plan, but what if an actual truth has just collapsed on her? Something about the boy next door, or something about an affinity for standing still. Out loud, she laughs at herself.

"Sorry you find the notion so ridiculous," says Scott. He sees the anfractuous curve of her bare leg.

"Get dressed," she says, putting on jeans.

He looks wounded. But he's actually downshifted into

thinking: *I won. We finally did it, and now it's out of my system.*

And maybe it isn't really out of his system, probably it isn't, but the alternative—and he knows this, too—is yet another acknowledgment that the things he wants most are so totally outside his control as to be fucking *celestial* or something. It's been difficult to live these twenty-eight years with molten feathers where his heart's supposed to be. He says, "Hey, can you help me out? I have a cramp right here," and points to his lips.

They text the others. Nobody wants to sleep.

Hoop suggests they convene in Jordaan: a neighborhood with the usual streets of crosshatched brick too narrow for significant car traffic, but with a suburban adult feel compared to the messy tourist districts just east. Even this late, there will be people out and about, to tell them what's really happening, what it really means.

And it's so strange to be walking around inside somebody else's heartbreak.

They meet and eat and drink and wander around Jordaan. People tell them Holland is very small, and everyone knows someone who knows someone who was on that flight. Maybe ten different people tell them this. Hoop seems to know many people who hang out around here, and tonight these folks all ask the bandmates if the U.S. will invade Russia.

"The Hague will never call out Putin by name," says one guy. "Shell puts billions into the Siberian oil fields."

"That is just the beginning!" says someone else. "We flatter ourselves that it is still *Dominee* and *Koopman*. But we are the place where the world makes a company headquarters. 'You do not like taxes? Come in, come in!' The Russian mafia puts money in our hands, and we get on our knees at the river and clean it."

Anyway, the city isn't shut down. It's Thursday night and except for a few shouting matches the good times promised by youth roll on. Welcoming hugs and inquiries are shadowed by an acknowledgement of tragedy, but people still smile and indulge. Tomorrow, maybe, will come enormity.

"The show," Sebastian says. "What do we do? Does it get rescheduled?"

"Yeah, of course," says Kate. "Right?" They watch Hoop for a reaction. Sanne and Arthur, the wiry burnouts who double as their unofficial crew, arrive and become a momentary focus: what do they know, are their families okay. Sanne has brought a bag of sandwiches. They chew. The right reaction is overreaction; it's impossible to be too sympathetic. Nearby bottles clank together like church bells. Arthur says his mother's neighbor was on MH17.

Do they write a song? Do their roots here grow deeper in sick counterbalance?

This neighborhood bar is packed. They're in a cocoon of light and sweat and willful amnesia within this moonlit tomb of a city. Sebastian reads the young faces around him. Nobody knows how to act. He keeps smiling but is less and less interested in catching his reflection in the windows that surround them. Everybody he follows on Twitter—every celebrity, every obscure singer and sound guy he's met along the way—is still sending out sympathy tweets from thousands of miles away.

He feels legitimately shaken. He can't remember a time when his musical gifts felt less consequential. There actually are people in the world who don't care about craft or nuance, who just machine-gun people out of the sky. First and foremost—in a way that has never previously quite clicked—he knows he's a boy.

He remembers the memory stick in his back pocket and hands it to Scott. "It came today. The new Spoon."

"Man. Thank you."

"I know. But I had it with me."

Scott closes his fist around it. He says, "The, ah, Anne Frank House is like two blocks that way. I feel like I should finally go."

Sebastian heard this kind of thing from Scott on the road: they should make time to visit this civil rights memorial or that Native American heritage center. And if Scott's tone hadn't been so resigned to his bandmates' lack of curiosity, maybe the suggestions wouldn't have rankled Sebastian. (Scott didn't really want to perform those dusty historic ministrations; he just liked making everyone feel bad.) Tonight, though, there's real pain in the declaration, and Sebastian nods emptily.

Hoop tells him, "If they tell us to play tomorrow, we play tomorrow. If they tell us it's rescheduled, we play when they say." Sebastian doesn't ask what happens if it's never rescheduled.

He watches Scott watching Amanda, same as it ever was. Kate has been texting with her workout pal Gertie all afternoon, and now Gertie is here, too, along with another Dutch kid. They're all such fast friends. Sebastian thinks how laughable it would be to call Anissa and ask her to hang out for comfort's sake.

He realizes he hasn't meditated today. And did he yesterday? He's guilty, knows Hoop meditates at least twice per day, but for Sebastian it's complicated: hearing his chant, slowing his thoughts. It rouses panicky feelings from early childhood. The very young Sebastian would lie in bed trying to sleep, certain that unless he paid attention to his breathing, it would stop: the moment he relaxed, his chest no longer seemed to rise or fall on its own. Now meditation has brought that old panic to the surface. Maybe that's a good thing. But as so often seems to be the case, what others find simple Sebastian overcomplicates. He sips club soda and cranberry…and sees Kate steal a kiss from the Dutch kid.

It's one of those things: *Huh!* Like anticipating a car accident moments before it happens.

Stolen Dutch kiss.

Song title alert.

He looks around the room and sees dozens of people in profile with lights shining through hairdos, making ghosts of them, or album covers.

For a little while people talk to him seriously about air travel, and he contemplates the deliciousness of their adult beverages.

Everything is fine. He sits in a booth in a corner. The drone in here is complete and he closes his eyes.

Everything is not fine. Sweat smoke essence of rose Amanda and airplane. Dbm6 Gadd9 C♯♯6/9 A7b5 Bb13th. Coddled and untouched the boy peeks up from privilege who doesn't know what he doesn't know. One says we aren't famous enough one says follow me both say relinquish the illusion of the control I control. Imagine not smiling. The only honest way to live with the certainty of death is walk outside every morning and blankly follow the wind without a thought any plan or routine is a denial of dying. The fun they all fun is playacting. A smile is a trick a plea a pacifier a surrender. Whatever you do is enough because what do I deserve whatever I do is never enough because I can always please you more. Clothes hair belt control socks shoes. But. There is music you always forget the feeling. Refuge escape release. Chordkeyboardbarreguitarbeatrepeat. The opposite of death and also the same. Well, listen. Death doesn't think of itself. Airplane home Amanda alongside going down.

"Hey? Hey!"

He shakes out. Four rows of teeth are above him, attached to two women holding pint glasses.

"Is dese stoel vrij?"

He's making progress. He doesn't bend over backwards and he disagrees when he disagrees and his stubble is unattractively long. He can walk the line. And these girls aren't even all that pretty, and he invites them to sit. Sanne and Arthur also join.

Amanda feels the room heat up and there's something to be said for inciting via absence, so she leaves the Whips alone for a while. She ditches the bar and walks, exhausted and tipsy and jittery, internationally inexperienced and perhaps entering a dangerous neighborhood. There's no way of knowing: Amsterdam all looks the same. She steps across a side canal breathing deep and trying not to imagine what it was like inside that incinerating plane. Things are quiet here. A row of darkened gables fans away. She stops near an array of parked bicycles whose front wheels are locked off the ground, giving an impression of synchronous stunts.

So: back to Manhattan Beach and the contestants and waking up wondering who, if anyone, is next to her. Never singing probably.

She remembers this morning's dream, the dream Caleb's call interrupted. She was wandering across a college campus with her father. They were smiling and easy on a grassy quad. The buildings were old and dripping with ivy and the sky was lovely. But the ground shook. Amanda told her father it must be an earthquake and they should stay in the open away from falling debris. But he shouted, "It's happening again!" and in the dream she remembered that aliens had previously attacked Earth and were now in the process of hunting down humanity. She saw spaceships collapse out of the blue sky and bombard the ground with laser fire. Her father sprinted away with a crowd of students and more ships greeted them, blasted them. Clotted earth rose like a tsunami and crushed them. Amanda ran in a different direction, down an alley. An explosion discharged an avalanche of falling bricks and she saw people smashed and decapitated. She loped breathless, avoiding death again and again as so many others were killed. She saw a concrete sewer pipe big enough to hide in. A nearby man also made a break for this pipe and she saw him carved open by a blue flash. But Amanda made it, stooped over, not looking back.

The pipe led to a subterranean lair where a human resistance had gathered. Amanda caught her breath and looked up through a grate. Silver ships streaked by the hundreds, each pilot executing a tiny part of the overall blitzkrieg. She thought about her unlikely escape, how every time she zigged the alien fire zagged killing dozens who weren't her. Someone in this cavern offered her body armor. She handed it down the line, to a weeping teenage boy. Her new group made a plan to rally with the army's vestiges inside a parking garage. Someone barked orders. But Amanda began to suspect she was dreaming, and in the logic of the dream couldn't die. The group made a break for it, passing into daylight and through a narrow library passage. She saw the crying boy take a bloom of fire in the face. He collapsed flipping over, skull charred and melted. Amanda stopped and turned around. An alien attacker swerved to avoid shooting her, and slammed its ship into a clock tower.

In the garage they pressed their heaving backs against sandbags. Camo-dressed soldiers fingered outdated automatic weapons. Someone wondered whether the ships might just target the garage's topmost level and bring the structure crashing down on them. The old woman beside Amanda was weeping and shaking and bleeding, and to calm her down Amanda shared her suspicion that she was dreaming this scenario and couldn't die. The woman made a mistrustful expression, but when they all moved again, she stayed super-close. Blue streaks showered the group as they ran and howled and were killed, but Amanda and the old woman remained untouched. Again, Amanda halted and looked up. Alien ships magically parted.

And soon the survivors were coming back this way. They gathered around her, clawing at her, battering each other to stand in Amanda's proximity. They wanted to live, and in this desire began tearing her apart. Caleb called just in time.

An American male voice says, "Don't freak. I'm not sneaking up on you."

She's standing on a nondescript bridge. Canal boats are tied up below and she churns this railing in her fists. Hoop is in the street behind her.

"There should be a formal discussion," he says.

" . . . "

"And I don't mean to sound possessive, but I should be there when it happens."

"It's possible," says Amanda, "that you started this conversation without me."

He steps up to the sidewalk, beside her. "Tell me about the

buyer. Maybe I've crossed paths with him."

Amanda points to ten-and-two. "Buyer? I'm not sure what you...."

"It's pretty shitty trying this right under my nose. And even shittier pretending not to know what I'm talking about. Why wouldn't you come right to me?" Hoop is pudgy and hairy and wears a t-shirt that's too tight and reads *Alpha-Bits*.

"..."

"I admit we don't know each other," Hoop says. "This is my first time managing, but I've been around management my whole adult life, and I'm *old*. I like *Vampire* a lot."

"Sebastian tattled."

"It doesn't matter who. They all know."

She smiles at a particular wattage men have been known to enjoy. "I guess I'm impressed," she says. "Our old manager would definitely have already shoved me into the water."

"..."

"It's their decision. You're right, I don't know where that leaves you, Hoop."

"I know the kind of impression you're used to making. In some ways you have it really easy, and I'm sure in other ways it can be hard to get taken seriously. I've met a *lot* of performers, Amanda. I mean we're talking hundreds. I've been in those rooms. I've watched the ones with charisma coming out of their pores. I'm immune. So instead, what I see is: everything about you screams, 'I want to be the biggest thing ever.' I knew it the first ten seconds I saw you."

"..."

"But Jesus, *why* do you want it? Do you know what it's like to be really big? Your life gets turned over to these guys...how can I explain them? They're not bad guys, not really, but they're dead-eyed and they walk really fast and they whisper in your ear and tell you to sign up for a VH1 reality show because it's good for ticket sales. They're slaves to coke and they're the first person you see coming offstage. They're proud of the limos they get you: you wouldn't fucking *believe* how much limo envy there is, people get fired because some competing act had a better limo. But it's not even all that, it's not really their fault everything is so sanitized and undistinguished from everything else, they probably really are usually acting in your bottom-line interests even if it means appearing with T.I. and pretending you love it when he yells unintelligibly into the mic. The problem with getting really big, I mean *really* big, is now you're a slave to The Market, you're a slave to What The Kids Want, and I don't mean to disparage America's current youth culture but *fuck* what the kids want. Or what I really mean is: they don't know *what* the fuck they want. They never do. They never have. But now these guys have built a delivery mechanism to keep shoveling the exact same shit in a shiny new package every single day—they call it *content*—and these guys' job when they're with you is to hold the shovel. But you know all this. You literally went through all this with Sidelong. Why would you want to do it again? Why wouldn't you want to do your own thing, make the noises you want to make, and have a certain subset of people like you for you?"

"What a speech," says Amanda. "Reasonable and insulting all at once."

"There's a way to do right by everyone," he says. "Come over permanently. Apply for reinstatement."

"Yeah, how did you end up deciding on Amsterdam, anyway? Pretty random. However many months stuck here, and I have to come over and close a deal so they finally get to play a big venue."

Hoop's civil façade wanes. "Maybe they're trying to make it the right way this time. Let the music do the talking, not relying on T&A."

"This is 'making it?'" she says. "Look around, man. You're setting up camp in a rest stop. All those great bands played here, yeah, then they *moved on*."

"That's cute. You think geography still matters. Christ, you can record shit on the moon, nobody cares. Can't you see they're waking up? They're world citizens now. It's a matter of perspective."

"So why Amsterdam? Why not New York or L.A. or a million places in between?" She thinks of him staggering around that after-hours club. "Oh, I know what you told *them*, somewhere new to find their authentic sound. Such bullshit. To me it looks like running away to the furthest corner where nobody's gotten the word yet. No, this is about you, Hoop. You had other things in mind. A place where it's easy to find shit to put in your veins and up your nose."

Hoop says, "Why do *I* find your ho*tel* a little suspicious?

Who's paying that bill? The same mystery investor buying your record out of limbo? If you already signed something, Amanda, you have an obligation to tell them. *Vampire* is theirs, too, and I'll make goddamn sure they sue."

"Jesus, I have a job," she says. "I make my own money."

"…"

"Are you a hobbyist, Hoop? Because it seems to me like this is your new hobby."

"Nobody's going back with you," he says.

"Maybe not right away," she says. "But we'll see."

Hoop is good at flinging shit, but doesn't seem to like it. He breathes deep like he's all Zen, and says, "But so hey, the rooftop show. You were great."

"Well. Thanks."

"It's obvious what they see in you."

She releases her grip on the railing. "Scott once told me he wished he could hear every song he was ever going to write all at once, like on his deathbed, only without actually dying. He meant it like: hearing the progress he'll make as a songwriter. I wish I could hear those songs, too, just to prove to you how many of them I'm singing on."

He smiles. "Stay in Amsterdam. Personally, I'd welcome you back." He thinks he's being charming, and maybe he is. Anyway, he's inconsequential.

They walk back toward the bar, and pass lighted posters for a movie Caleb executive-produced last year. They're about to rejoin the Buggy Whips when Hoop taps her hand and salutes, disappearing across one of these countless canals which in the semi-dark seem more like trapdoors.

When she reenters the bar, they tell her Scott went home to get some sleep.

I DREAM ABOUT AN ISLAND

Sebastian has also left.

He's crammed into Sanne's ancient Polo hatchback, weaving across both lanes of a freeway that leads far out of town. Sanne is drunk and probably high, but driving. Arthur is asleep in the passenger seat. The amateur roadies told Sebastian they have a friend he should meet tonight; he didn't ask them why, assumed it would be a jaunt across town. They've been driving for more than thirty minutes.

What the hell is he doing?

I am untethered. As untethered as I've been since Bed-Stuy, except now I get in cars driven by asshole stoners. Why don't I know more people? Wasn't that what was always missing, isn't that the thing that could've kept me sane? I was sending out all those online personal ads; I should've just gone driving with crackheads. Would've saved a lot of time and travel.

It's just hard not to be shaken by the world today.

Sanne is singing along with the radio: British dance pop. His falsetto seems impossible to sleep through, but there Arthur is.

A sign indicates "Haarlem – Centrum" and they turn off, into an endless winding suburb of unremarkable two-story flats gone aphasic in the tiny hours. Sanne drives on the wrong side of the street but knows where he's going: a half-mile strip of identical pink apartments, maybe a hundred of them, scoured in sodium light. Sebastian and Sanne get out; Arthur stays unconscious in the car.

Sanne chooses one of these apartment doors and unlocks it.

He's a cipher to Sebastian: a guy who gets bombed at Whips shows and hits on fans who want to talk to the band, and then bangs the Yamaha into various doorframes and light posts. Nobody *doesn't* have an internal life, Sebastian knows, nobody *doesn't* imagine himself spinning wildly at his own story's center, but what could Sanne and Arthur's story be? They materialize at gigs.

This apartment is small and bears the reggae-club stink of infinite bong hits. Sanne thumps upstairs. Sebastian looks around, and realizes this trek is certainly about drugs. And it makes sense: the roadies aren't aware enough of their surroundings to know Sebastian is sober. He's annoyed, so annoyed, probably some dealer lives here and maybe this is some stupid gesture of Sanne's, some effort to get to know Sebastian better via annihilation. He sits on a tartan couch and looks out a window at a sky the color of crabmeat. Wasn't it fully dark as they were driving? Will he have to sleep here, on this stained, garbage-strewn furniture? What does a Dutch crack den look like?

How close is Sebastian to a nervous breakdown?

He thinks about calling his parents again, tries calculating the time difference. Then he decides not to be happy-go-lucky. He doesn't want to stay here. He should stick up for himself.

He climbs the stairs. There's one bedroom up here: a guy who isn't Sanne sits at a desk, typing on a laptop.

Sanne is just coming out of the bathroom. He says to the man at the desk: "Hi, Dino? *Ik ben er.*"

"All right," says Dino, without looking up. "Cut it close why don't you?" He's a skinny black kid in a HUF snapback and a Last Kings tanktop, and he types faster than a speeding bullet. "You don't have to do much. But I need you guys in the *room*."

"…"

Dino types and types. Sebastian can see his screen. It mostly looks like numbers and backslashes and hash signs and exclamation points.

"18:30 hours on the west coast," Dino says. "Hurry the fuck up. Time to do this."

Sanne leaves Sebastian in the hallway. There's another computer on the bed, and Sanne opens it, clicks on things, gives a sigh of hard work about to commence. Sebastian just stands here invisible.

Then Sanne pukes. The first splash surprises him and hits his laptop and the bed, whereupon he multitasks: filling a trashcan with the rest of his stomach's contents while also wiping the computer with a pillow. Sebastian watches Dino, who keeps typing.

"Clown," he says. "Go get some paper towels and a damn breath mint. And where's the other one of you?" He finally lays eyes on Sebastian. "You're Hoop's boy?"

Sebastian's scalp prickles. "What?"

"Are you Hoop's boy? Sanne, I'm serious, get that smell out of here." Sanne runs to the bathroom carrying the laptop and trashcan.

"Wait," says Sebastian. "You're American?"

" . . . "

"Uh, yeah. I don't know if I'm his boy. But I know Hoop, yeah."

"Sebastian, right?" Dino says. "Sufferin' Saint Sebastian." With one foot, he drags a second rolling chair out of the corner. "Hell yeah, I'm American. You're New Jersey, right? I'm Seattle."

" . . . "

Dino returns to his typing; Sebastian feels high. This is the friend? Sebastian tries to place him as the owner of this apartment, the occupant of this bedroom. The walls have racecars on them. Key-clicking is muffled in blue shag. Rows of matchbox cars on the window ledge. Baseboard disfigured by chair marks, like the shadows of fat chipmunks cast by a small nuclear detonation. It does smell like puke in here.

"Well," never breaking stride with the typing, "Hoop said you'd want to be here for this."

Sebastian sits. "How'd you know I'm from Jersey?"

His fingers are inexhaustible. "Oradell Class of 2010, no college, FICO score pretty well nonexistent. Yeah, I mean, Hoop's a good dude, but if he wants someone in the room with me, I'm not just taking his word."

" . . . "

"But you're really just a musician. I heard some of your songs. Mostly hip-hop for me: you like Tyga?"

Sebastian almost says, *Oh, he's the best.* "Don't know him."

Dino clicks a song and it's got a solid bassline but mostly consists of a couple guys bragging about all their possessions, along with the line:

You kiss her on the mouth
Ask her how my dick tastes

"How do you do that?" says Sebastian. "Type like that, and play music and talk?"

"Hey! Sanne! Get in here, and get Arthur up here, too!" Dino reaches into a desk drawer and comes out with a thumb drive whose plastic case is purple camouflage. "Those dudes are a mess," he tells Sebastian. "People say they helped with the Spamhaus thing last year? I have doubts. All I know is they can't control it around the kush. I think they contract for IBM, but I would not want to see that code."

"…"

Sanne and Arthur come in bleary-eyed and sulky. They sit on the bed, avoiding the barf stain. Each has a laptop.

"Follow instructions," Dino tells them. "Don't try and grow a brain. And hey. Hey!" The sleepy Dutch guys perk up. "Don't go thinking you know me. I'm leaving your charming home this morning, and you're never seeing me again. But I know you. Right?"

"*Ja.*"

"I've got your BSNs. Do you have a full appreciation of the shit I can bring down on your lives in all of about three minutes?"

"*Ja,* Dinosaur."

Dino knuckle-taps Sebastian's knee and pulls a funny little face, then he plugs the purple-camo thumb drive into his laptop. "'Many Bothans died to bring us these tokens.'"

Sebastian just goggles. The words…he can't make them stiffen into meaning. The levels of misapprehension here…just…won't…who is this scrawny kid, why do Arthur and Sanne know him—Arthur and Sanne are *hackers?*—what possible reason could they have for believing Sebastian would want to be here, how is Hoop involved?

"All right, guys. So the point here isn't havoc on their network. I'll get the server names, I'll fry the algorithms. All you're doing, *all* you're doing, is running those protocols."

"…"

"Say it."

"*Ja,* Dinosaur."

Dino puts on headphones.

Sebastian's sudden fear is that this has something to do with the plane crash.

But that's crazy, right? This Dino. He knows Hoop, now Hoop is some kind of terror mastermind?

Sebastian checks his phone, but has no signal; Dino taps a small black box on the desk and says, overloud: "Jammer."

Jammer.

Jammer?

What the what?

This longest day, the objective truth of mass murder, the shock on Wilhelminastraat watching TV and answering the phone, Hoop making call after call nominally to check on Dutch friends but so insistent and determined it seemed to Sebastian that Hoop was petitioning to disprove the news, and Sebastian found himself believing Hoop could do it, so he could hope it was all a hoax...and now the maze has led all the way out here? Dino will confirm the hoax, reveal its purpose? Sebastian forces himself to recall yesterday's NA meeting. And lyrics from the old days:

I dream about an island
I dream about an island
I dream about an island

But wait. What does Sebastian really know?

He touches Dino's shoulder. "So you said Hoop's name. So what? So you know his name. That doesn't mean you actually know *him.*"

Dino takes off the headphones.

"These guys could've told you his name. They're our roadies."

"So...I guess it wasn't made clear to you," Dino says. "This takes a while, and I need to, like, concentrate."

"What I'm saying is: how can I be sure you really know Hoop?"

Dino draws off a can of bitter-lemon soda. He scratches his elbow, which bears a black tattoo of a bar code. "Dude," he says. "How can I be sure you're not undercover Interpol?"

"..."

The kid sighs the complex sigh of a chess player made to partially reveal intent. He pinches his nose's bridge and brings up a

Most Wanted page bearing a sketch artist's rendition of his own face.

It reads: The Dinosaur (True Identity Unknown): Reward = €100,000.

Dino says, "I had a friend, his solution was you walk up to the guy you think might be setting you up, and you say, 'Ask me to commit a crime.'"

" . . . "

"And if the guy does it, he can't be undercover, because it'd be entrapment. Not sure that works. My friend is doing twenty in Big Spring."

Sebastian reads a list of misdeeds below Dino's picture: Operation Payback. Pirate's Lagoon. PlayStation Network Attack. Operation Megaupload. "I don't understand why I'm here," Sebastian says. "I don't understand what you're doing."

Dino grabs his headphones again, but delays putting them over his ears. "Hoop really didn't tell you?"

"Tell me what? How do you know him?"

"That's classified." He laughs, a stuttering high-pitched fake laugh, and it's so nerdy Sebastian feels sad and worried for him. "Well, gotta give it up to his discretion."

" . . . "

"Yeah, we're hacking iTunes?"

You're...?

" . . . "

"Maybe you've heard of it?"

You're...?

" . . . "

Sebastian realizes: he's so tired.

The click-clacking swarms him under. Six hands.

He sits back and watches these guys who seem small and powerless and self-contained, motionless except for their fingers, and yet from this bleak apartment deep in the rectum of nowhere, keystrokes register as cannon fire.

Hacking iTunes...?

Well, is it Hoop again, the trickster, throwing in with people who want to do *something*, battle the unbattlable?

Dino sips from his bitter-lemon can every five minutes. Sebastian watches him slashing into faraway servers, opening code and finding filenames, digging deep into networks Sebastian can't imagine. The world is really out there connected like this.

All he can do is sit here and puzzle over why Hoop is even involved. And why tell Sanne and Arthur to bring Sebastian here, to see this?

Their faces. Blue with monitor light, thick-lidded, bored by havoc.

What?

Maybe to someone smarter or more experienced, sitting here would be exciting. Maybe this is something that happens in college: one meets computer geniuses, one marvels at their dexterity and the walls that fall.

Sebastian falls asleep.

He dreams he's home, and his mom is driving him to the Buddhist temple in Englewood, a place she would never go. Her car cassette player burps out a song he doesn't like, but he doesn't want to say anything. They're going to meditate as a tandem, because someone told Sebastian that people meditating together can create a powerful field state. But Tina loses control on Route 4, and they crash, tumbling in the car like a never-ending cement mixer. As they trace some complex geometric pattern down a country road and gather sand and road salt into the cabin, his mother becomes Amanda and he realizes the annoying song—which is still playing—is "Density of Joy." He can see Amanda's forehead gashed, her teeth knocked loose. He reaches for her but can't tell down from up.

"The key is digging into Hadoop," Dino is saying. Sebastian lifts his head and it's fully light outside. "Anyway, what the clowns have been doing," he points to Arthur and Sanne, sweaty and still typing, "is supplying our fake numbers realistically, across many clusters, over time. So even though everybody will know the charts are bullshit, the data itself will look legit. And I'm breaking the algorithms, so they won't be able to rebuild right away."

Sebastian remembers it's the morning of the Melkweg. What is any of this, compared to that?

He falls back asleep. He tries to get back into the rolling car, to recapture the accident, just so he can be beside her again. The best he can do is an amusement park. He's beneath a roller coaster track, and the roller coaster is frequently zooming overhead, and he wants to peer up and see if Amanda is riding, but he keeps having to duck down just in time, to avoid being decapitated. He doesn't understand why he's looking for her in the dream, but he is.

"Okay," says Dino, "I guess now comes your part."

He shakes up out of the amusement park.

"Saint Sebastian. Hey. You're up."

"..."

"Hoop really didn't tell you this? Songs, brother. I need songs. And Hoop thought you should be the one to pick them."

"..."

"We're making the new Top 40. C'mon, man, what do you want on there?"

MINOR IN MINOR TIMES

By Friday there's a pyramid of flowers at the airport, and also at the Netherlands embassy in Kiev. The king and queen are shown signing a condolence book. A Ukrainian woman describes how a falling piece of metal killed her cat.

The Melkweg is its own industrial complex bordered by canals. Like many great institutions, its diffidence is what terrifies new disciples. The Whips pretend to appreciate the redbrick exterior of one of the world's greatest rock venues; they look around but they don't see much.

"We should go in," Scott says, leaning his guitar case against the holy brick. The afternoon is perfect and warm. Hoop texted them to come down and talk with Bazzy's brother-in-law Hugo.

He didn't say the show was on, but he did say bring gear.

But they aren't going in, not yet.

They haven't slept. The others think Sebastian spent the night with one of his hussies; Kate and Scott were separately insomniac at home, with mid-20th-century glass no match for the sounds of sidewalk grief. They don't know where Hoop slept. The morning's cab driver switched off the news when they climbed in, became good-humored when he saw they were Americans, but Sebastian's knee accidentally bumped the radio knob back on. It's hard for Scott and Sebastian not to look down at themselves—dark suits lately cleaned—and think funereal thoughts.

"What do we...?" says Sebastian.

"..."

"What do we even want?"

The Leidsegracht sends a shaving of itself under the venue, and boats are parked here, covered by drum-tight canvases. The water is brown and choppy—as if the Melkweg is sending out a submerged disturbance—and it simply ends where a newer part of the building begins, slopping up against poured concrete with a weird and inconsistent inflection. It goes *slap-TAP, slap-slap-TAP, SLAP-tap-tap*. All three of them watch and listen.

"What do we want," says Kate. "A good question on a few levels."

Scott says, "I think a good question on exactly zero levels. We want to get signed again. We want someone to pay for us to make a new record and set up a tour again. We want everything we've always wanted because otherwise what's any of this been for?"

"We want what we had," Sebastian says. "We want what we almost had."

"Sure. Definitely. Yes."

"Maybe they're rescheduling," says Sebastian. He still feels out of body. "Maybe they just want to meet us and, like, understand our vibe better."

"And play just for them?" Kate says. "In our Sunday best?"

"Sure. Maybe."

Scott says, "Why turn ourselves in knots before we even know what they're thinking? Let's go in."

"Would you play a day after 9/11?" says Kate. "And please don't tell me 9/11 was bigger, because if we're judging this by how many people died, I'll scream."

"I'm just saying we don't have all the information. We came all the way down here."

And yet Kate got ready this afternoon expecting to play! Because that's what you do. She hears Billie's voice telling her so. *Do not be dramatic. Do not pretend to understand. You do one thing, so do the thing.* She and Scott looked at each other raccoon-eyed this morning and believed they were in unspoken agreement. And maybe they were! It's probably the correct advice. *Do what you do.* (Of course, Billie might also call her Claudia.)

"It's only more if you make it."

"I think too late," Kate says.

"Jesus, you're going back and forth. Make up your mind."

"What does Sebastian want? Sebastian, what do you want?"

Sebastian wants to leave it up to fate. But he can't say that, because in his recent experience *fate* is actually a bandmate making a decision on his behalf.

"I'll tell you what I really want," says Kate. "I want us to make up our minds before we go in there. I don't want them telling us what to do."

"We didn't make up our minds?" Scott says. "We didn't make up our minds just by coming down here?"

She shakes her head. "I don't know." And she sees it: this conversation is itself a pantomime of a show, as they march around gyrating, inhaling deeply, looking for cues, soloing.

Scott does his Scott thing, literally kicks the ground. "Seriously? It's this kind of shit," he says.

"What kind of shit?"

"…"

"Really, what kind of shit?"

"Surprise, I'm the bad guy," says Scott. "Man, I'm fucking tired of being the one keeping us on point."

"Scott."

"I'll say it. I don't want to be anybody's daddy, telling you to…eat your vegetables. Just once what would happen if *you* guys schmoozed, if *you* guys told the club owner to go fuck himself, or sent out emails, or made phone calls, or worried about money, or worried about Hoop." He sees their eyes on him. "'Oh, here he goes again, Mr. Control Freak making our cool lives miserable.' You feel bad we have to play, like for once you *actually* have to do something you don't want to do? Well, Jesus, welcome to my goddamn life!"

"Calm down, man," Sebastian says.

Scott whirls on him. *"Don't fucking tell me to fucking calm down!"*

"…"

Everything goes from blood to ice.

Atom bombs and blunt razors.

Scott understands Kate's point, while not wanting to. Probably he's trying on certainty, as a pose. But he didn't spend the night awake wondering whether they'd play. No, he busied his mind crafting the comforting words he'd say to the crowd as the frontman, the heartfelt and peaceful ways he'd make them feel connected and better. *We can't really know what you're going through, but we want to be here with you so you can be here with each other, and that way you'll understand your numbers and realize no small group of evil people can ever win.* Or: *This is what those evil men can't stand the idea of: all of you getting together with love in your heart...look around and see how different you all are, but you're all here for the same reason.* Or: *We're here for you, and we'll be whatever you want us to be.* And turning his speech over and over, he clearly heard the potential self-congratulatory fraudulence, and checked if he really meant his words, so often that he became unable to tell.

He says, "I'm sorry. Just.... Listen to me."

Kate can see Sebastian is ready to hit Scott.

She steps between them, a hand on each.

They are, of course, not really even talking about what they're talking about. They've done what they were supposed to do: roll with bad fortune, build anew, learn fresh goals and prize their presumptive freedom. But they are far from home and now again maybe it doesn't matter what they think. The constraints of this life feel, in this moment, the same as their old constraints. And maybe what it boils down to is: they are minor in minor times. To fret and struggle and be inside one's head 24/7 making plans and trying to do brilliant work requires something resembling ego. In fact, it is to presume one's essentialness. So it's the truest insult imaginable to devote all that time and excavate one's soul, and then realize the results only aspire to footnote status. Yes, art should be for its own sake, but it turns out the delusion necessary to create the thing also tends to build expectations that the world will understand how indispensible the thing is. When that doesn't happen? That is a truly special kind of punishment.

"Stop," Kate says. "We know what you do, Scott. We also know you're a good person."

"..."

"But no matter what we decide, right now you're out of line."

Scott looks around to gauge whether strangers have seen his embarrassing display. There's a movie theater across the street and a closed-circuit camera above them, but somehow nobody has stopped to take note of the raving lunatic. That's comforting for a moment, and then feels typical.

Sebastian says, "It's funny you think you've really been holding something back. As if this is the first time you ever made that speech. It's like: 'Scott's mad again.' 'Oh yeah? Why?' 'Well, we're making him run our *lives*.'"

Scott is in New York. He's in Minneapolis, Austin, Massachusetts, Port-au-Prince. He's the asshole running around knocking over furniture telling everyone how to be. But dammit, how else will anything ever get done? In a small voice he says, "I don't ever feel any different. I guess either I'm never stressed-out or I always am."

Sebastian's fists slacken. He says, "Christ, the second one."

"..."

In the course of airing discontents, they've moved between two massive nautical-looking chains that rise into the sky, and Sebastian actually sees them for the first time: they're attached to checkered-steel beams that give this building its steampunk aspect, and the whole thing is a drawbridge that presumably lifts this ground away to reveal what's beneath. Probably a loading dock. The blue-neon Melkweg sign above them chooses this moment to flicker on. Sebastian fits his hand inside one of the chain links and imagines someone throwing a switch just then, raising the drawbridge, mangling him and putting an end to his musical turmoil. He says, "Am I the only one, something like yesterday happens, I just want to go home. Like, actual home. See my parents."

Kate and Scott look at each other, and Kate says, "Yeah, you probably are."

"Not just parents. You know what I mean."

Kate says, "You mean Amanda."

"No," Sebastian says, drawing his hand out of the steel link. "Maybe. We're up in the air."

Scott manages to feel a sweet silver edge of pleasure hearing this.

"But I believe she really has some kind of deal waiting for us," says Sebastian. "She wouldn't just lie."

They do go inside.

Hoop meets them near the box office. He's standing with Bazzy and Hugo, the brother-in-law booker. Nobody is smiling. Posters advertise upcoming weekly shows: Tuesdays are DJ Riptide with Kendrick Jones, Wednesdays feature six-hour Dirty Dutch raves, Saturdays are Encore club nights that last 'til 5 a.m. Here at the end is a big poster for tonight:

JULY 18
QUEEN MOTHER DILEMMA
THE BUGY WHIPPS
SACRED KITTEN

"Yeah, I know," Hoop says. "But it's on. We're playing."

Scott nods quick, four or five times. Inside, this place is like a subway terminal. The legendary Old Hall is over there, just through those doors.

"Just so you know," says Hoop. "The others are already here. Dutch bands, ready to go."

A ponytailed dude on a stool waves hello. There are stairs up, stairs down, catacombs that lead to a newer venue. Recessed lighting, expensive carpet, the hush of permanent intermission. They are rock stars shuttled in off the street, ducking their heads despite high ceilings, a fizzy Midas touch landing on anyone lucky enough to witness. Scott and Sebastian shake hands with Bazzy and Hugo, who is a slouched, ugly character in a too-big blue shirt and a tie depicting pyramids of cartoon cheerleaders. His beard is neglected and his mustache lifts to the left, to account for a natural snarl.

They begin a route past a huge metal information desk, right turn, toward the wall marked *Oude Zaal*.

But Kate isn't walking with them.

She says, "Wait."

They do.

"We can't do this."

Hugo looks at Scott.

"Kate," says Hoop.

"I'm serious," she says.

"..."

"What you are not going to do," says Hugo, "is tell the Dutch how the Dutch should respond."

She doesn't care that these five men are staring at her in varying states of impatience and incredulity. She doesn't care that some of the men are about to tell her she's overreacting. Enough.

Hugo says, "If we say a thing is not canceled, it is not canceled." His bearing is a lifer's. Bazzy is at his elbow in a lemon-colored suit, fuming.

"After everything we've been through," Kate says, "if we think it's tasteless, we're not doing it."

"What do you think you do?" Hugo says. "Do you think you cure disease? You think you will take the time you save tonight and personally hunt down the soldiers who did this? You entertain. You help them forget. When else do they need you but now?"

"Oh, you're going on," Hoop says.

"We're not," Kate says. "Or I'm not."

"A funny way to cut your throat," says Hugo. "Telling people how to feel."

Sebastian says, "Hang on. Cut our throat. That's a little much."

"You think so? I will make you a promise. Play this show tonight or you never play here, ever. And the Paradiso. And," he snaps his fingers, "where else, Bazzy?"

Bazzy says, "Ah, many other places. I will make calls."

"Hoop," she says, "that's why we're even here. You said so we don't have to compromise."

"Hang on," says Hoop. "Emotions are running understandably high."

"I wasn't sure until we walked in here," Kate says. "But I'm sick to my stomach. I know we're not Dutch. But what's happening matters."

Sebastian sees Hoop glaring. He also observes Kate's trimmer waist and hips and wonders when she started looking so good.

"When did I say you don't have to compromise?" says Hoop. "You have to compromise!"

Scott also looks at Kate. She doesn't seem angry, or vindictive, or unreasonable. Her spine is straight, yes, and her shoulders are pulled back with an umbrage that reads like pride, but mostly she just seems sad. And it's really stupid to have this thought, but he thinks, *Oh, you can just be sad.*

She says, "You aren't the ones up there."

"It's muscle memory," says Hoop. "If it were just another show, of course. But Kate."

"A funny way to cut your throat," Hugo says.

This is happening way too fast. If everything has been leading to this night, how can it be going away so fast? Scott watches it go. He's thinking, *But we didn't decide this together!* and also, *Is this what I meant by doing the dirty work?* Already Kate can't believe what she's saying, keeps checking Sebastian's eyes but he won't look at her. It's wrong! She's probably wrong! A part of her wants someone to make a convincing case for playing; she can see she's suddenly built it up into something so big. Where *was* this decisiveness before? All because her stomach is queasy?

"I want us to stop," Hoop says. "I want us to realize the favor these kind gentleman have done us. I am one hundred percent sure playing is the right thing. Kate. An acoustic set. Something low-key and thoughtful. You can express yourself. You can say whatever you want."

"I don't think so, Hoop. I'm really sorry."

They all turn to Scott.

It's a moment of power they give him. Eyes like an audience's eyes. On the one hand it shouldn't be such a big deal, on the other hand of course it should. Meaning is where you make it and it's all semiotics. But this is the singing he can do, straight from the Grand Mal: a song to convince Kate or alternately to convince Hoop, puff out your chest and decide for everyone. The frantic scurrying sound of his voice, all the talk, these months and years, they are in a vehicle propelled by his words.

Somehow, right now, Scott finds he's able to keep his trap shut. Maybe Kate gives him the strength.

Hugo walks away with that sniffy European discourtesy that can scan as sophistication. Bazzy gives a departing *"Neek hallak"* and follows his brother-in-law through a door marked *VERBODEN TOEGANG* trying hard not to look like he's groveling.

"How does this help anyone?" Hoop says. "The show goes on without you, and you get blackballed in the process? Jesus. Take a minute. I get it, but he's not kidding. I can't get you a gig like this again."

Scott feels calm. He says, "Hold on. Who got us the gig?" Kate and Sebastian watch him.

"What's that supposed to mean?" says Hoop.

"I don't know whether we should play," Scott says. "I was pretty sure we should. But I mean, let's be honest how this happened in the first place. I was there that night."

"What?"

"..."

"What, that bet?"

"..."

"C'mon. I was on Bazzy for weeks."

"And then suddenly he changes his mind?"

"Bet?" Kate says.

"Oh, Bazzy was wasted," says Hoop. "We had this joke bet. If I won, he had to get you guys booked. But I *lost*."

"Yeah. Then Bazzy takes Amanda home and suddenly we've got a show three spots above our weight class."

"Hold on," Sebastian says. "What?"

Hoop claps his palms together. "That's just not.... I worked him for *weeks*. What did she tell you?"

"You mean she didn't drive off with him," says Scott. "You mean she didn't come back hours later and take a shower first thing."

"Either way," Hoop says. "Whatever. That just makes it more essential to take advantage of tonight. I'm an incompetent manager, and you fell ass-backwards into the show of a lifetime. Fine. I admit everything. Even more reason you can't back out."

"I can't," says Kate. She looks at Sebastian, who shakes his head. She says to Scott, "Play solo. It's fine."

Scott's eyes squinch. In the span of half-a-second, he thinks: *What set list would I play by myself would I call myself the Buggy Whips wouldn't that be confusing would it mean the end of the band how could I spin it and not have them hate me how could I spin it and not have me hate myself isn't this a chance to show them I care what they think but do I really care what they think is there an objectively right thing to do is there ever an objectively right thing and if there isn't doesn't it matter what my best friends think they really are my best friends but I doubt they'd say I'm one of their best friends I'd be too afraid to ask and either way I'm way too afraid to break up after all this time so if this is a choice between sticking together and not disappointing a powerful booker it shouldn't be any choice at all.* Well, but he does have a choice, and he sees it's nothing to do with the actual plane crash.

But how crazy is that! This thing that actually happened in the world, this tragedy. He supposes maybe what Kate's talking about is sensitivity to actual suffering outside the spacesuit. What Scott's talking about is...what people think of him? The thing to do—the thing he never does—is trust. "Of course not," he says. "It matters what everyone wants. I'm with Kate."

Hoop looks at Sebastian, using all his charismatic powers.

They both seem to understand how inappropriate this is. Sebastian makes a bee-stung upper lip and stays silent.

"Crazy," Hoop says. "Just crazy."

But now that it's decided, angels polish their halos.

At the hotel, Amanda slips on a black Herve Leger number with a sweetheart neckline and sleeves to her elbows, the only expensive thing she packed, held in reserve in case of emergency. It's unclear if they'll ask her onstage. Hair up, face unpainted, she's the opposite of her strumpet *Price Is Right* persona and the embodiment of a certain kind of safe bohemian fantasy. She dons Dolce & Gabbana glasses with prescription-free lenses, and heads out to the show.

ALL OUR AIMING

They leave Hoop behind at the Melkweg. Exiting the complex feels final. Sebastian says, "I guess this means we're going back to the States," and underneath the day's dread Scott feels marginally heartened, hearing the word *we*. They stand outside a Burgermeester realizing they don't have enough money to eat.

"We know everyone at the smaller clubs that they know," Kate says. "They can't get us banned. It was hot air."

Cars and vans and bikes are parked three-deep all around them, but there are no people. A postcard rack wobbles in the wind. A fruit stand is unattended. Sebastian peeks in the burger shop window and does see a few diners, is how he knows this isn't an apocalyptic dream, or the apocalypse.

He says, "What did we do?"

But he's a little proud, and he looks at his bandmates and they seem proud, too.

"Yeah," says Kate. "Pretty stupid." She says this immodestly, not as if this is another mistake in a long history of them, but rather because events conspired and as creatures of belief, they had no choice.

Scott remembers a *Simpsons* rerun from one of a hundred empty motel afternoons—a guy waiting on line for the Itchy & Scratchy movie plummets to his death—and he says, "I regret nothiiiiiiiiiing!"

Kate pulls out her sticks and taps Swiss army triplets on a light post.

They stand here together. Traffic and pedestrians do filter past now, the city crashing elastic.

Eventually Sebastian says, "So what the hell. *Amanda* got us that gig?" He and Kate inspect Scott. "What did she tell you?"

"Nothing." The Burgermeester is playing a Pink Floyd song that makes him think of his dad. "I was connecting dots."

"..."

"I was there when she went off with Bazzy. I was there when she came back to the apartment. That's all." And he doesn't know what he believes. He knows he can't trust what Amanda said, that she didn't sleep with that little troll. He watches Sebastian working something out behind those pretty eyes. Kate drums on the light post again.

"What if she really can get us a deal for *Vampire?*" says Sebastian. "Why can't it turn out like we thought it would?"

"Because it doesn't make sense," Kate says.

"..."

"Scott called around for months. We were radioactive. I'm not making that up, right?"

Scott has the Tele with him, in its case. By rote, he looks around to see if any women notice him, being cool, carrying a guitar. "You're not making that up," he says.

"So she's throwing around money, staying in a $250-a-night hotel, are we stupid? What changed?"

"..."

"I'll tell you what changed. She's got a boyfriend. Like: in the business. And if he actually agreed to anything *Vampire*-wise, which I'm sorry Sebastian, I'm still not sure I totally buy. But if he did, it's only to keep her happy."

Sebastian sags and breathes out hot fire.

"And here's another thing," says Kate. "There's something *you're* not telling us, Tungsten. I know you. You weren't just guessing about Bazzy and Amanda. I mean, believe me. Nobody's less surprised than me."

"..."

Kate presses a stick hard against his biceps. "Seriously. What did she really tell you? And when?"

"Nothing," he says. "Why would she tell me anything?"

"That," and Kate lets herself appear comically suspicious, "is a good question."

He stares her down, shrugs, she mirrors him sarcastically, he gives nothing away. Except she's pretty sure he's giving something away.

So now they've done this. Each of them entertains the idea of sprinting back to the Melkweg and apologizing, but nobody moves. Scott and Sebastian feel sweaty in their getups. Kate wants to go running but knows she'd last about five minutes. Sebastian gets the idea that they should play a little show right here in front of this burger joint, it's one of those cheesy rock scenarios, they should sit out here on the stoop and he can play guitar and Kate can tap the light post and Scott can sing, and people will gather around and clap and tell them they're wonderful, and of course a label exec will stroll past—or maybe the exec will be in a limo driving with the windows down—and the resolution they expected tonight will be realized in this roundabout way, as a reward for their moral fiber. He actually fires mind-bullets at Kate and Scott, trying to get them to start playing something.

Scott says, "I think I need to walk."

"It's too far," says Kate.

"Not home," he says. "Just somewhere."

"Okay. Do you have cab fare for us?"

He hands them all he has.

"Recharge, regroup," Kate says, not sure what the hell she actually believes.

"..."

"There's nothing so big we can't deal with it. A few breaths. Time makes it better."

"..."

"Scott."

He leaves them, carrying the guitar. It's summer when he moves down Elandsgracht, fall by the time he rounds onto Nassaukade, his head full of dashed hopes and Amanda.

Of course Kate's conclusion must be true: Amanda isn't paying for this vacation with *Price Is Right* money. He's known this without wanting to consider it.

His selective blindness is something else.

Well, there's one pleasure he can indulge. He fuddles around with his phone, pretending he doesn't notice that he has no new texts, clicking to the latest song files on here. He puts in his earbuds, and plays the new Spoon record.

And it's one more blasphemy.

It has so much synth.

He listens through once: thirty-eight minutes. Yes, it has a couple fun buzzy guitar rockers, but also many computer-generated beats and orchestral electronic vistas and robot noises. He forces himself to make it through every song but layers of ore expand in his stomach. He hears something else in the music, too: the crackle and splinter of a toppling stronghold.

When the album is finished, he finds he's far north into an unfamiliar part of Amsterdam's ramble: oaks on either side of a busy two-lane artery and endless four-story apartments that could be tenements. Apparently he's been moving parallel to the canals because he hasn't crossed one for like a mile. Once you live here for any significant duration, he realizes, *not* crossing over canals becomes unnerving.

He keeps walking for a long time. The sky gets darker in its interminable fashion.

He's all the way to the Westerpark. That's how he knows where he's headed.

A path runs beneath railroad tracks and lands in an outgrowth of office parks that, Dutch signage aside, could be anywhere. Smoked glass and octagonal atria, inscrutable corporate emblems and ample executive parking. He crosses a street called Accumulatorweg. The sidewalk ends and he sees the neighborhood he wants, across a minor freeway. He climbs up the road's shoulder slipping on grass, calibrates the traffic, sprints across the eastbound then the west. He puts on an old Spoon song and Britt Daniel sings:

Sometimes I think that I'll find a love
One that's gonna change my heart

He halts at the darkened glass doors marked *Voedselbank Levy* and plunks down his guitar. He can see all those picnic tables in the dining room, empty, scrubbed after the fashion of an army at rest. Nobody visible inside, nobody standing around outside. He knocks once, then again. He never wants to see Amanda again.

Except maybe one more time before she leaves.

Tess answers. She recognizes him straight away and allows the kind of smile that's actually a frown. But she unlocks the doors. It's still dusk out here but it's after ten, so he knows what's coming.

"Hello again, it is good to see you but we are closed."

"I know. I'm sorry to bother you."

"I cannot make exceptions. If you are very hungry I am sorry."

"Do you...?" He backs down one of the front steps, putting himself at her eye level, lower: submissive. "Do you need any help in there cleaning up?"

He wants his generosity to bust through her frost. But she says, "No, the volunteers have already done this."

"Oh. Is there...anything else I can do?"

"No."

He goes into charm overdrive. "I don't know what I did to irritate you, but is it too late for me to apologize? I didn't know this place even existed but I think it's so great."

"We have a coordinator for volunteering," Tess says. "I can give you her email."

"Uh, sure. Yes. That would be great." Holding the door open with one leg, she leans out of sight and returns with a business card. Scott says, "I wonder if you saw Sofie today?"

"I am not allowed to discuss who."

"Fine. No problem. I'm sorry to bother you. It's, ah, been a," voice cracking a little, "pretty tough couple days...."

He can't lay himself barer than this. In the movie of this moment Tess sighs and commiserates: the city and country are in shock, the world's violent currency is out from its hiding place. Surely everyone feels vulnerable. Yes, and the sources of his personal wounds are mixed, but just now anyone with a wound will do. But Tess closes and locks the door. She's gone without giving him another look.

Whatever you want, it's not my job to make it easy for you.

He backs away from the food bank grinning. He doesn't want what he wants.

So he keeps on north, wearing his suit, carrying his guitar. There's an incredibly loud superhighway, but it rises so high from the ground he can't see the cars. Nobody seems to be hanging out in these underpasses, though the graffiti is spectacular. Masked children sailing in a giant wooden clog, making a hole in the clog with an old-fashioned eggbeater drill. Vincent Van Gogh reaching a disproportionately huge hand toward the viewer and saying the word *PRATEN*. A giant, gas-masked octopus destroying a city skyline. A windmill being birthed from a celestial vagina. As darkness finally arrives, his phone's flash is insufficient for decent pictures, but he tries anyway.

He keeps going, thinking at some point the land must end in water. Finally he reaches a massive power station, and the IJ is just beyond. A dozen figures sit on a pier, wearing more clothing than the weather demands. Their shadows are fidgety and wild-haired. Scott steps out among them and says, "Do you guys know a green-haired girl named Sofie?"

They don't, but they invite him to sit.

Kate and Sebastian are back in the Wilhelminastraat apartment, avoiding the TV. They can't take any more. Sebastian sits slumped at the end of the couch; Kate is lengthwise with her feet resting on his chest. They're too broke to go out solo and probably don't feel like it anyway. Each has options: Max or the triathlon crew, Anissa or one of the others. Maybe they're mourning, but it feels like general gloom. Kate has Speedy Ortiz blasting from her phone, no earbuds. Their ankles joggle in unison.

"Great song," says Sebastian.

"It's called 'American Horror.'"

"…"

Kate says, "How many people in the history of the world will get to hear this song?"

"Ugh," he says. "Don't."

"Which is bigger: the number of people who'll ever hear this song, or the number of people who'll go to the next Skrillex show?"

"I really don't blame you," he says. "I wasn't kidding: I'm glad you stood up."

But Kate doesn't really believe this. Her second thoughts are having second thoughts. By now their set would probably be over; would they already be signed? Hoop seemed damn sure. Amsterdam is dead, only a few months after the States.

"Gertie made fun of me for still having MP3s on my phone," she says. "Apparently it's all Spotify now."

"…"

"I just want to sleep."

"You want me to get up?" says Sebastian.

"What am I doing? What kind of life is this?"

"..."

"You were doing it," Kate says. "Do you ever think what would've happened if you never met us? You had great songs. You might be a huge star by now."

"Why does everybody do that?" says Sebastian. "Everybody thinks I was—"

"I know, I'm sorry I—"

"Listen to it sometime, Kate. You think I was getting played in clubs? You think people were *dancing?*"

"No, I know. You're right. You know what? Someone was telling me they've got this thing called a genius grant. The U.S. government just gives you money for being a genius. You'd have that by now."

He settles down, blushing. "Well, thanks." He hasn't said anything about his adventures with Dino last night, not even to Hoop. He checked iTunes this afternoon and didn't see anything weird.

"Instead we had to drag you down. Into the muck of being a rock god."

They play songs and more songs. Summer Fiction. Alvvays. Cloud Nothings. Apex Manor. Telekinesis. All these close friends they've never met.

A beep interrupts the music. It's a text.

"The new boyfriend?" Sebastian says, and his stomach flutters uselessly.

"No!" says Kate. "What? No."

"C'mon tell me. You met him training?"

"It's not even.... It's Gertie. Checking if we're okay."

"..."

"I know the guy you *mean*. But.... No, not training. God, the guys we train with, they're a walking dumb-blond joke. Louis and Marcel are pretty sure paramedics come from Paraguay. Hey, you know what? There's a race in August they want me to try, a sprint relay and they want me to do the run. At least I have to stick around for that, right?"

"..."

"His name's Max."

He looks at her bare calves. When Kid Centrifuge first hit the road she didn't shave often, but now her legs are smooth and brown, not what you'd call slim but definitely thinner and powerful in a mama-lion way. "I saw you with him last night. I was trying not to spy."

"I wanted him to meet everyone," she says. "He's a good guy, really. You don't have to worry."

"Good." He drums his palms on her feet.

"It's…." She snorts. "He's a little…aimless. Maybe just what I need after all our aiming."

"Nothing's any different," he says. "Hoop'll get us something else at Winston or one of the other places."

This thought, the picture of staying just where they are: Kate feels panicked then calm, knowing she can't do it anymore.

A Moonbabies song starts: "War On Sound." Dream-pop with tempo changes and strange vocal intonations:

Hey, it'll be all right
I just found myself in ways I couldn't help

Kate thinks how easy it is when you're on the edge to make every song you listen to the soundtrack of your life.

Sebastian likes this song, loves it, knows he'd never have heard it without Kate. He puts his hands around one of her knees and says, "Food?"

"Sebastian, you're the only one who's got any balance. I know you still go to meetings and everything, but you're also the closest to happy. And that's the thing that makes people like you, that makes people, whatever…calm around you."

She looks at him tenderly, and he has a feeling that among everyone he knows, Kate understands him best.

She flips around on her phone, scanning through a long list, and plays "Density of Joy."

"Oh," he says. "Hooray."

"Ha, I never understood why they had to hire that dope in the vest for the video," Kate says. "We had our own little stud muffin already right there in the band."

His hands are still on her legs. She's flirting, he's pretty sure she's flirting. Basically she's the person he feels closest to, and this has been true for years. But he didn't want her then.

Now he looks down at her t-shirt that's draped just right—the outline of a surprisingly hard abdomen and surprisingly big breasts—and she doesn't often tease him like this, which he reads as Kate feeling vulnerable, and he feels pretty vulnerable, too. His shoulders fall forward and his eyes narrow.

He hopes it isn't too late.

He's tired of worrying about consequences. He's sure other people don't worry as much as he does. Don't things usually work out all right? Don't women usually like him? *Turn off your mind*, seems to be a good summary of everything he reads these days.

He sweeps her legs off him, down to the floor.

He leans over: she's the one he's never let himself really see. Face so much prettier. Skin clearer. Shit, he doesn't need some world-altering beauty launching a thousand ships, he loves Kate from the inside-out. This is right, this is what they always say a man should look for. He wants this moment to mean something. It's vital and cardiac-worthy and life-altering. He leans way in.

His lips fall across hers.

She shoves him away.

Hard.

"What are you doing?"

His retreat is swifter than his approach. "Sorry! Oh...!" Adrenaline saturates his organs.

"..."

"I'm so.... Shit!" He stands and walks to the kitchen. "It's really not because.... It's not because you're working out now."

On hearing this, on knowing he's lying, she has to admit: she wants to hurt him. She puts her legs back up on the couch. "Jesus. Maybe I would've said yes, like, last year or whatever."

"I know. I get it. Now you have Max. Please rewind. Just forget this. Please."

"'I have Max?'" She actually sneers. "I just met the guy. He's nice. It has nothing to do with some other.... But of course that's what you think. The only way I could ever turn you down is if I'm blind in love with somebody else."

"No-no," he says.

"Then what, Sebastian? What the hell?"

But she's the kind of person who lets this slide, isn't she? What's ever been the point of indulging anger? She sees herself, knows she's going to get up and hug him reassuringly, the same way if her mother or Inch were here explaining themselves, Kate would wave her hand and pretend the past didn't matter. What good does discussing old wounds do?

"My wires," says Sebastian. "My wires got crossed for just...two seconds. You're right, we're friends." He's running water over dirty dishes, no soap, just absently wetting them down.

She's hurt, is why she's angry. She says, "You and Amanda: was there ever a worse goddamn couple?"

"..."

"You played sweet boy genius, she played man-eater. What bullshit. You weren't innocent. You were either stupid or willfully ignorant. Imagine what it was like for us, with that going on. What it was like for me. And meanwhile you and I...." Her voice is softer, clotted with feeling. "We could talk, right? We told each other things. But.... I never even let myself dream it. I knew how you saw me, it was all over your face. You were handsome, I was fat."

"..."

"Not fun. Not fun to be looked at like that. And now I'm supposed to, what? Be the one who makes you feel like a grownup? Suddenly, because you think I'm not available?"

"No," Sebastian says, and it tastes like ashes.

"You don't need me," says Kate. She sits up and starts tapping her phone again. "Just go find another stupid pretty girl."

He can't look at her, can't respond. With his fingernails, he tries scrubbing gray mash from a plate, but it's dried-on and won't relent. He digs, digs, digs, until it starts to hurt, and he keeps digging.

Kate leaves the apartment. He tries to say something else, to get her to stay. But he's too humiliated. She clomps out, slams the door, takes the future with her.

Pain, yes.

What has he done?

What has he done?

Does he...? Does he really want her like that?

This, finally, is the very end of it. His bottom.

Helplessness, yes, he's been on board with that for a while. This is hopelessness. This is not knowing which way is up, and betraying your best friend. He is thoroughly abject, thoroughly out of control. And so ashamed.

It comes clear he could kill himself.

Easily.

Jump into traffic, leap off a building, take a cleansing dose of heroin. There's no God, there's no point. Rather than running around hurting everyone he knows, he could stop.

His death won't even ripple the pool. Scott will drive ever forward, Kate will raise a brood with Max, Amanda will sleep with every powerful person she meets. An explosion. Something fiery, gas in an industrial kitchen, a single lit match and an end to all his self-doubt, no more spluttering—musical or otherwise—to hurdle his fears.

And wow, do these suicidal thoughts ever calm him. He knows they're right; their rightness fills him with love.

He releases the plate and looks down the kitchen counter, at knives in their butcher-block sheath. He withdraws the longest knife, a nasty carver with a saw-toothed blade.

He thinks he really might do it.

The long dance with death began when he was...six? His father was with him in his bedroom, they were playing Incredible Hulk, where his dad would lie on the bed, calm, and Sebastian would hug him, and then his dad would pretend to transform into the Hulk: begin writhing around, become insanely strong, and Sebastian would laugh breathlessly and keep hugging, trying to contain the Hulk, but he was so strong, his dad would go, *"RAWWWR!"* and it was just so funny to be holding on, knowing he wouldn't be hurt but feeling ungovernable strength like this, being tossed around...and the phone rang and his mom called upstairs and his dad picked up the phone in the office and then his dad was crying, he'd never seen his dad cry, it was so frightening Sebastian wet his pants: his dad raced into the upstairs bathroom and slammed shut the door and howled: his own father— Sebastian's grandfather—had passed away. They didn't make Sebastian walk near the casket but from a distance he remembers his grandfather staring up in profile, a patrician nose surrounded by white silk.

He looks at the carving knife in his hand.

Then something cold floods down his spine.

Stark raving clean.

And he is. That's what this is. He's stark raving clean.

Kate is outside in the warm night, feeling an east wind, heartbeat flamming. Now she feels horrible for him. She can see how embarrassed he must be; she doesn't want the power of being the wanted one. Well, and now it's not so different from the question of what happened to her when she was a little girl. The thing she never wanted to know, the yellow paper she tore up in her father's dining room. As though tearing that paper closed the matter forever. We don't get to decide. We don't get to decide what the world outside ourselves will afflict us with. She's in the bike lane beside those two always-humming metal boxes and she kicks one so hard maybe her toe breaks.

She gets another text; this one's from Amanda. It reads:

>show cx? wayn?

Kate sighs. She texts back:

>Just couldn't. I know. Shot our own foot big time.

She waits for the inevitable rebuke.

>??? they z whole show cx???

Amanda's textese is legendary, but this is pretty unambiguous. Still, it doesn't necessarily mean what it means. Amanda is all politics now, an arm-twister. So the calculation becomes: why might she lie about tonight's whole bill being canceled? Again, Amanda texts >wayn? and Kate texts back >Where are YOU now? and they pick a meeting place.

It's a fifteen-minute walk to the glass-box Grand Hotel; on the way she calls the Melkweg and gets a Dutch-language recording. She texts Hoop, doesn't hear back.

The hotel lounge features giant photorealist butterflies on its walls. Amanda is sitting in front of a martini, overdressed in an expensive frock designed not to look expensive, clavicle bare and tits pushed north. Kate sits across from her, back in the land of frump-by-comparison.

"Last we heard," Kate says. "They were going ahead without us."

"The place is dark," says Amanda. "Big sign: 'God bless the Netherlands.'"

"..."

"Oh and gee, thanks for letting me know you weren't

playing."

"Well gee," says Kate, "right back at you. Thanks for having sex with Scott."

Amanda puckers and sips the top inch off her martini. "He told you that?"

"Basically."

"..."

"Not talking about one of the world's great poker faces," Kate says.

"Um, that's.... Listen."

"And there's this," Kate says. She shakes through her bag's contents, finds the postcard. "You did this, too?"

Amanda looks at the Eiffel Tower, flips the card over, reads Billie's proposition. "Whoa, this is amazing."

"..."

"Did I what? Did I...? There's a postmark."

"My dad forwarded it. I don't know what her handwriting.... You're crafty, how hard would it be? Quick trip and mail it from there. Or even better: have someone else do it."

Amanda's brow scrunches adorably. She deals the postcard back to Kate like it's the ace of diamonds. "You're saying I sent this. Because what a great plan, entice you to the States with a fake job offer that could be disproven with a single transatlantic phone call."

"I thought about that, it's like driving a—"

"What are you even talking about?"

"Dirty tricks," Kate says. "My God, Amanda. What happens when Scott follows you home like a lost dog and has to meet the guy who's buying *Vampire* for you? And what, Sebastian and I are so weak we have no choice? Or are you fucking Sebastian again, too?"

"This isn't...." Amanda sees Kate throb with something like rage. "What did I do? You've...built this case against me."

"Manipulating us. Maybe always."

"Have I lied? Have I lied about what I want? I want you guys to come back."

"I mean, you were born with nice bone structure. Major accomplishment by you. Congratu-fucking-lations."

"..."

"You did it, right? You've been fucking Scott."

"…"

"…"

"One time. Yesterday."

"Which wouldn't be so bad," says Kate, "but I know why you did it. This is *Scott* we're talking about. You know what it'll do to him. He'll start cutting off his ears and mailing them to you."

Amanda says, "He's tougher than you think." She drinks another sip. "I've thought about it a bunch of times before: what would he be like? Believe me, Kate, he's just as suspicious. More."

"…"

"Maybe I don't always know why I do things."

"Bullshit!" Kate says. Her voice reverberates around this place. "You know exactly why. You always do. I've only known one other person who's…. And she was a fucking sociopath!"

"…"

"You always knew how Scott felt. Seriously, how could you do that to him?"

"…"

"…"

"I guess probably I'm not as nice as you thought."

The foot traffic in here is light. Their waitress is standing against a heavy-looking door, playing the customer eye-contact game: how much is enough to warrant a check on their table. This wears Kate out, and not just because she can't pay for her own drink. Enough damn code and subtext. Come over or don't.

"I'm done," says Kate. "This is it."

"What are you done with?" Amanda says. "You know what? I'm tired of dancing around this, so I'll just say it. You guys are making fools of yourselves here. You're not making any money at all, Hoop doesn't know what he's doing, and that's not even the worst part. What, you hated our song, so now you're taking lessons in how to be serious? 'Yeah, let's bend over backwards and do it like they did it in 1960!' You think because there's a couple words in there about business and injustice or whatever, now you matter? I dunno, Kate, it's still pretty fucking oblique. 'Capital letter made of suede.'"

"…"

"I mean, congratulations. You're such heroes for *not* playing a rock show tonight."

Kate feels shabbiness fold over her heart. Amanda knows

how to hurt her. "Then why are you even here? If we're so fucked up."

"Because you don't have to be. You're a million miles from home and at least that far away from breaking through. You can see that, right? You can see how the guys are drifting, trying to be so serious and authentic and it's landed you in a foreign country with an inexperienced manager, poorer than we ever were in New York, begging people totally outside the heart of the industry to pay attention? What's the absolute best thing that could happen to you in Amsterdam? I can't even come up with a scenario. There's no money here. There's no rock scene. It's just a fun town where people get fucked up and then go home. Think about everything that needed to go wrong for you to wind up slaving away out here. What good does it do, mixing into things that are so far outside? I've got us a way back in. Come back. We're friends and we're great together." Amanda smiles painfully. She'd had a notion to secretly gather all their passports before tomorrow morning, have them drop her at Schiphol and "spontaneously" offer up Caleb's credit card for a preposterously expensive impulse trip home.

"Jesus. What does being someone's friend even mean to you?"

"Then take the Vegas job," says Amanda. "Go play for Shania. Just get out of here. Seriously. I don't think you understand what it looks like from the outside. Sure, it sounds fine. But it looks so super sad and desperate."

Kate stands and stomps out of the lounge. Amanda drinks her drink. She has a wish to be kinder and simpler, but at the same time she knows there are still angles to play with Scott and Sebastian, hell, maybe even with Kate, after they both cool off. She's upset over this fight, and the things she just said. But this isn't the end: she sees all these Amandas wandering off into the multiverse, setting snares of self-discovery. No, even though she'll be leaving them behind for now, it's not the end.

And Scott spends the night on the streets. The pier-people aren't all homeless; some are addicts and a couple may be undercover cops. Nobody is particularly funny or delightful: people laugh at stupid shit, like somebody knocking someone else's cigarettes into the IJ. When a few weathered guys detach from the group and walk inland, Scott tags along. He has this dumb hope that they'll lead him to wherever Sofie sleeps.

Streetlights here are off or busted and these warehouses have no lit windows or signboards; the half-attendant moon is a solo act. Scott's new pals aren't aimlessly searching: they make for the last building on the left and slide particleboard away from a first-floor window. It's blue out here, it's black in there. The others climb in, so Scott does, too. He thinks: *Boy, I guess I'm having some kind of crisis, huh?*

But even as his eyes adjust it's obvious he won't be able to identify the sleepers without unwrapping them. It's a curled-up colony in here, snoring or whispering, and hell maybe there are also folks sleeping upstairs. He finds an open spot and sits on the crunchy floor, still wearing his suit. But he can't stop his mind from racing to that concrete slab in Croix-Deprez: those rough boys reveling in The Sinister's wake. How long would he have lasted sleeping among them, with his nice shoes and wallet? His nobler molecules try to convince him to stay the night, but the rest of him wonders what's to be gained by taking that chance.

He knows he's soft, as if knowing makes it okay.

So he gets out and walks more, all night. Never straying too far from this neighborhood, wondering if he'll run into Sofie, also wondering why that should matter. He remembers her puking at the NA meeting.

But who is he to be anyone's guardian? He listens to the new Spoon record again.

Kate finds the apartment dark. Maybe the boys are all tucked away in their rooms. She can't handle much more catastrophe, arranges herself face down on the couch and slides her palms deep into the cool, crumby cushions. Does she have a song in her head? No, and how weird. Maybe it means something: no melody, no beat.

Everything she's made, she now relinquishes into the kingdom of this couch. Go. Go to Vegas and fade into the wallpaper. She'll be a made woman. She'll be a pro. She swoops above herself seeing agony's needlework in her bare shoulders' twitch.

She dreams she hears one of them crying.

He listens to the synth-heavy Spoon songs again. And again. Walking across jungly sidewalks, sitting on an unpainted bench, leaning against a fence that protects a parking lot. "Outlier" is practically disco. "Inside Out" is pure Lana Del Ray. "New York

Kiss" is, what, LCD Soundsystem?

And this isn't some fashion-slave, Pitchfork-approved band he can dismiss. This is Spoon!

If Drake Tungsten has embraced these plastic beats and overproduced echoes, Scott Tungsten may just be helpless.

By sunrise he's a zombie, and knows these songs by heart.

He stakes out the food bank. It's not even eight o'clock and the place doesn't open until noon, but several men loiter in front. Are they hungry guests, already forming a line? He considers joining them, maybe questioning them, but someone unlocks the front door and they tranquilly file in.

Sleep deficiency and hunger make him feel altered. There's a lack of consequence as he lopes across the street, bounds up the stairs, pulls at the door. It's locked again. Were the men even really here? He knocks and nobody comes.

He wanders around the building. There's a service driveway, and he follows it through a narrow opening. He checks his left hand and yes, he's still holding the guitar case. Around the corner is an empty loading area, with vertical plastic strips protecting open double-doors.

He steps inside.

It's a pantry, connected to the kitchen and a walk-in freezer. The men from outside are here: scurrying, carrying boxes of vegetables, crates of milk and bread, organizing, sorting, silent. Something about their lack of eye contact and artless posture makes Scott think the men are mostly cognitively disabled. Pans clatter in the kitchen, Radio 2 is playing, someone issues a veteran guffaw.

"And you are?" This is an American woman, waddling in carrying a platter of day-old pastry, a smeary peacock-feather tattoo on her biceps.

"I'm new. Scott."

"Hi, New Scott. You're a little overdressed. Tess didn't mention, did you do orientation?"

"Not yet."

"Know what? We're shorthanded, put on gloves from that box, just listen to Kirsten. She must be downstairs. She'll be back in a minute, stay here." So he stands to one side. A couple beefy college kids enter through the back door and hoist boxes over their heads. A diesel truck thunders outside and delivers another pallet of donations and everyone jokingly groans, the shy cognitively disabled guys included. A middle-aged Dutch lady emerges from a service elevator and starts flinging around produce. Kirsten.

He follows her lead. He evaluates ears of corn, composts rotten mushroom packages, runs milk and juice into a back room, adheres to the complicated equations that dictate where stray donated potatoes and onions are stored. Non-moldy vegetables go on one set of shelves, fruit on another, more plentiful items on the bottom, liberal criteria for what constitutes "spoiled." He's not exactly sure what the end game is here, but Kirsten says they have to be finished sorting all these donations by noon, and yet another delivery from outlying farms will arrive any moment.

Kate and Sebastian text separately, wondering where he is.

They didn't offer to accompany Amanda to the airport, and she didn't ask.

She takes a last look around her hotel room, in theory to be sure she hasn't left anything behind.

A battered Škoda brings her ten miles west to the airport. Security doesn't seem significantly altered, but the flower-mountain in front of the terminal has grown by several layers. She walks to international check-in, sits on a weird cubist couch, realizes she's posted up beneath a sign that says: *Departures 4*.

She tastes her lips. They don't taste like Scott.

Back to California, and there are Pushkin books she hasn't read: she knows it's pure vanity, but she'll bring *Eugene Onegin* to the *Price Is Right* until someone makes a comment. Then she'll exchange a generous explanation of the book for a dazzled nod.

And try again! This trip was a frivolity. There's so much time, so many producers and managers before whom she can place herself, while at the same time living comfortably like a damn adult. A man in a pilot's uniform walks by rolling a suitcase behind him, and he gives Amanda a professional nod. She wonders where he's headed.

Things are still so good.

She drags through her contact list, first with the intention of deleting Kate, Sebastian and Scott. Instead, she bypasses Mom, and presses Dad.

It rings. She almost hangs up. What the hell is she doing?

"Hello, Pish?"

"…"

"Pish, you there?"

"I'm here."

"Let me.... We're at a restaurant. Just...hang on."

She can't breathe.

"All right," he says. "Are you still there?"

"Of course I'm still here."

"You're calling me! I'm so glad."

"..."

"How are you? Is everything okay?"

How is she supposed to answer that? "I'm about to get on a plane."

"I'm so proud of you, Pish. First a music star, and now we see you on TV. Would you believe it was Shirley who picked you out on TV? One day she just goes, 'I think I saw your daughter.' I'm at work in the afternoon, and Shirley hasn't seen a picture of you in a long time, but she recognized you, she.... Anyway, isn't that something else? I tape it every day now."

"..."

"The point is I'm proud of you, honey."

She catches herself about to laugh, as life's stupid pageant fills her heart. She says, "It's giving you too much credit to say you had one single thing to do with the way I turned out."

"I guess.... I guess you calling doesn't mean you're not mad."

"*You* could've called. You could've been persistent."

"I tried. You know I tried. You never returned.... I figured the graceful thing was leave you alone."

"Mm-hm. The way you left Lacey alone, when she had your grandson."

"That's different. You know how she feels. But Lacey was older. You and I had a different relationship, Pish. That's why we stayed close. You followed me everywhere when you were little."

She pinches her thigh through denim, hard. "I didn't know any better."

"But you did call today," he says. "Even if it was to tell me how mad you are."

"I called to tell you you're an asshole."

"..."

"..."

"And you," he says, "are a smart, witty, beautiful young lady."

"Who deserved a better father."

"Who deserved a better father."

"When I'm unhappy, I blame you. When I'm happy, I thank Mom."

"Okay."

"I called because.... I wanted to prove you wouldn't say some magic words that would.... I wanted to prove you're just some guy. You're just a guy who's always been selfish."

"I agree with you," he says. "I'm sorry."

"..."

"I don't care why you called. I'm just glad you did."

"..."

"Now you won't be able to get rid of me. I'm serious. Get ready for some calls, kiddo."

"I don't do whatever because of you."

"Yes," he says.

Amanda watches a family zigzag past, two very small children reaching up clutching a parent's hand. She closes her eyes.

Her father says, "You're going on tour? Is that why you're getting on a plane?"

"No."

"Kid Centrifuge, right?"

"Uh, not anymore, no."

"Oh," he says. "I thought maybe that's why you called. There's all that news today about iTunes."

She traps her lips with her teeth, lets them go. "News."

"I was reading the paper and there's a list of music, and there it was: 'Density of Joy' by Kid Centrifuge. Computer hackers did whatever they do, and made all these random songs look like the biggest hits in the world."

"..."

"A lot of songs were on the list. 'Gimme Shelter' and 'Piece of My Heart' and 'I Will Dare' were on there: some of my all-time favorites, and it reminded me to download them on my phone. Anyway, they couldn't figure it out at first. But it's a computer hack, and there's your song again, first on a TV commercial and now this. I told Shirley, 'Getting this kind of publicity, so many people will see that name.' The paper said these songs could all get like a million downloads out of the blue."

Her father has been tracking her career and knows her band's name. Is this consolation? She doesn't know how to feel. She doesn't want to talk with him any longer. She wants to be alone, but she also wants to be aware that people are watching her, being alone.

A semi-coherent thought whistles by, easy to dismiss: what accident could she engineer that would keep Caleb vital and prosperous and available, but cost him a big toe?

Sebastian finally gets a return text from Scott: an unfamiliar address and an invitation to join him for lunch. He steps into the living room and shows it to Kate, who received the same thing. Scott doesn't respond to further inquiries, and so bears the aura of a deposed king still issuing mystified orders. They assume it's something to do with last night. Kate says she needs a break, and goes back to her earbuds. It's Sebastian who decides he should get out of the apartment this afternoon.

"But you really don't have to come along," he says. "I'll be fine."

"Yeah, I know," says Kate, putting on shoes.

"Cool."

They walk out to Overtoom and get a westbound tram, then change to a northbound train: the first time either of them has been on Amsterdam's metro.

"But nothing from Hoop?" Kate says.

"No," says Sebastian.

Otherwise they're wordless for eight stops.

She thinks he seems all right. She doesn't really regret her harshness. He's a boy. She does love him and maybe even romantically, because otherwise how could his kiss have caused such a rampage? But he needs to grow up. She's taken the pureness of his heart on faith and oversimplified him. Maybe the thing that helps him dig up songs is a thing that, beneath his general kindness, knows only plunder.

His eyes are closed and he's focused on his breathing, trying to hear his heartbeat over the train's noise. There's an 8:15 meeting tonight at the Alano. To him, it's progress that he momentarily forgets she's even there.

Here comes the end of the line, and they get off. They find the address, but it's not a restaurant. There are rows of indoor picnic tables and dozens of people queued up. Somebody hands Kate a numbered slip of paper.

It's some kind of shelter. Many folks are in line for lunch;

others are waiting to step into a pantry to be given fresh food. They see Scott behind a counter, helping distribute produce. He's sweaty and gray, still in his dark suit. A white-haired woman with gold incisors stands before him, touching vegetables and then insisting she can still exchange them. Someone in line smells like sauerkraut brine, and a cognitively disabled kid stacking chairs out in the dining room is singing tunelessly. Kate recognizes the girl calling out numbers near Scott by her green hair.

"Why are we here?" Sebastian mumbles to Kate.

"He doesn't look so good," she says.

They call hello and he gestures them over. Someone hoists a crate of arugula and begins restocking a shelf, and water droplets spritz everyone.

"You can have one vegetable from the top shelf," Scott says to the next person in line. "One from the middle. Two from the bottom." This tiny limping Asian woman smiles, pointing gracelessly at a row of green peppers, grunting and shaking her head as Scott offers the first, then the second, then the third, only happy when he's selected the fourth and puts it in her plastic bag. She waves the bag to encourage him to give her more peppers. "Only one. Sorry. One. Only one. No, sorry. I can only give you one. One. Only one."

"Saint Tungsten?" Sebastian says.

Still bagging and instructing, stooping to find the least-dented yams, he considers Kate. "She's gone?"

"Assume so."

"You guys didn't take her? What happened?"

They both look at Sofie, who's looking at Scott.

"Same reason you didn't take her?" Kate says. "Or maybe not."

The next tiny Asian person holds out his bag, deeply nodding and repeating unfamiliar names for the leafy greens. Kirsten shuffles past carrying a broom and clears her throat.

"I guess we'll see her soon enough," says Sebastian.

Over a crackling p.a. Sofie says, *"Drieënveertig en vierenveertig. Dames en heren.* Number forty-three and forty-four."

Scott plops tomatoes too soft to sell into the next bag. "Maybe eat some lunch is why I texted," he says. "It's free. No sorry, only one. One. One. Anything from over here? No, only one. Sorry. Only one."

Kate looks around. Over in the dining room, people are ladling out meals. For a moment it feels humiliating to consider accepting charity. But she sees all these folks in lines and at tables, and of course she's no different. And God, hasn't she been taking Hoop's handouts for months? She and Sebastian wander away from Scott and the fresh-food distribution. At the picnic tables and back in the kitchen everyone is smiling. Kate assumes Amanda made it to the airport, wonders what she's having for lunch.

They get a couple plates of chicken bestrewn with unfamiliar veggies, some of which turn out to be Sichuan peppers. There's a lemony aftertaste, and a few bites in Kate says, "Hey, do you feel funny?"

Sebastian wonders if this is a taunt about last night.

But he can't trust his impulses, not when all he feels about everyone is *please love me please love me please love me.* He's stark raving clean, sitting across from Kate, completely without a game plan. All that's left is: make it through today. And isn't that what Hoop's been telling him for a year? He says, "I don't know if funny, exactly?"

"I mean my tongue is numb. It doesn't taste spicy, but I kind of...can't feel my mouth?"

"Yeah, you're right." Sebastian licks his lips. "Totally bizarre."

"Everything in my mouth feels like it's...falling athleep?"

Sebastian says, "I thee what you're thaying."

"Ith ith the chicken doing thathhh to uthhh?"

"Thithhh theemth like thomething they thould've thold uthhh."

"Thuth thuth thuth."

"Thhhhhhhhhhhhhh."

"Thuthuthuthuthuthu."

"Thhhhhhhhhhhhhhhhhhhhhh."

"Ha," Kate says. "I think we should write a song like this. You know, like, four minutes of just us making noises with our numb mouths."

Sebastian says, "Isn't that already what we do?"

Someone in the kitchen has music on. It's something Scott once played for Sebastian: "Double Trouble" by Otis Rush, twelve-bar blues in D-minor with legitimately difficult fills. Sebastian takes another bite of the anesthetizing chicken and looks at Kate's wrists because he can't look at her face. "You know what? This guy playing. He's left-handed, but he grew up not having a left-handed guitar. So he learned to play upside-down on a regular guitar, with low E on the bottom." Still not making eye contact: "Scott told me."

"Huh." Smiling at him, power fluxing between them all backwards.

Food distribution ends, and Scott and Sofie join them for lunch. It's a noisy scene: mostly the oblivious multilingual squawking of families who've long since made eating here a routine, but also Kirsten laughing too loudly at a young child's joke and someone spilling a lunch on the floor so his dish spins to a protracted halt like a dropped coin and the sarcastic adolescent cheers that result and a baby crying and a guy who looks like a goateed consumptive cowboy telling his table a story in several characters' voices. In this chaos, the Whips are silent. They eat multiple servings, pat their tummies, and assume the pose of a regiment whose yarns have all been shared.

Many folks leave after eating, but some families stay. Small kids watch TV, old ladies play Rummikub, a new shift of volunteers scrubs the kitchen. Sofie sits with them, maybe clean today. A table of teens starts up a dance party of malnourished American hip-hop and R&B, and the Whips look at one another and laugh.

"Maybe you will play for me," Sofie says. She fetches Scott's guitar. "Please play!"

"I can do that," he says.

And while Scott sets up his phone as an amp, Sebastian finally gets a text from Hoop:

>Hugo will reschedule.

Tingling with the fresh skin of the forgiven, Sebastian thinks: *Here we go again.* He looks down and realizes he accidentally put on a pair of Scott's shitty tennis sneakers this morning. His phone bloops, Hoop again:

>Need bail. Police station on Beursstraat. Please don't judge.

But for the moment, Sebastian stays. He changes to the seat next to Kate, while Sofie darts around the room telling everyone to be quiet. Scott plugs in the old Tele and thinks about what to play. Someone had on some beautiful blues during lunch, and that gives Scott the idea that maybe these kids need to know all they've missed. So he thinks back to the opening licks of a B.B. King song he learned in high school. He sees this makeshift crowd wake up, hearing a dumb skinny white boy actually tearing it up a little. He growls:

When I first got the blues
They brought me over on a ship
Men were standing over me
And a lot more with a whip—

"Scott!" says Kate. She drapes a platonic arm around Sebastian, thinking at the very least she needs to call Billie, maybe make a trip to Vegas, just to investigate. "Come on, Saint Tungsten! Little bit of a downer! Kids want something fun!"

Scott sees Sofie's enormous eyes. She doesn't mind, she's happy just to see him play. He tries to laugh and finds himself almost blubbering. He strums the relentlessly upbeat chords that begin "Sliding Around In Socks" and sings words he knows so well:

Bom-bom-bom...
Dee-daw, deebadee-daw
Let's slide around all day
Bee-baw, beebadee-baw
With you I'll always stay!

ARTIST REGISTER

ABOUT THE AUTHOR

Christopher Harris is the author of two previous novels, *Slotback Rhapsody* and *The Big Clear*. He lives in Amherst, MA, USA.

That's not his guitar, but he wishes it were.

(Thanks to the Gibson Guitar Showroom in Austin, TX.)